# CANTOS DEL PUEBLO

# CANTOS DEL PUEBLO

The United Methodist Publishing House
Nashville, Tennessee

CANTOS DEL PUEBLO



ISBN 0-687-00998-7

*Este libro ha sido impreso en papel libre de ácido.*

IMPRESO EN LOS ESTADOS UNIDOS DE AMÉRICA

# INDICE GENERAL

# PREFACIO

«Bueno es alabar a Jehová y cantar salmos a tu nombre, oh Altísimo; anunciar por la mañana tu misericordia, y tu verdad en las noches.»
Salmo 92:1-2

Una parte integral de la adoración del pueblo hispano ecuménico ha sido la música. La riqueza y diversidad de la himnología contemporánea ecuménica que surge del pueblo hispano promete renovar la vida y misión de la iglesia. *CANTOS DEL PUEBLO* es una pequeña contribución hacia este fin.

Durante una encuestra que se llevó a cabo entre en pueblo hispano metodista para determinar las necesidades de las congregaciones en cuanto a la música en su adoración, varias congregaciones indicaron el deseo de tener un himnario con letra solamente. Con esta petición en mente, La Casa Metodista Unida de Publicaciones ofrece este himnario, el cual es una compilación de doscientos himnos que han sido escogidos del himnario metodista *MIL VOCES PARA CELEBRAR*. Para tratar de ser fiel a las diferentes tradiciones y estilos de música, se han escogido himnos de diferentes paises, tradiciones, y ritmos. Hay un número de himnos apropiados para el Año Cristiano, así como himnos que ayudan a la persona en su jornada espiritual.

La música de los himnos se encuentra en el himnario *MIL VOCES PARA CELEBRAR*.

Cuando se combinan las diferentes tradiciones hispanas, los diferentes ritmos de los pueblos y el gozo y gratitud que causa al pueblo a alabra a Dios con sus voces, con palmadas de manos y con instrumentos musicales, verdaderamente se «está de fiesta con Jesús.» Esperamos que *CANTOS DEL PUEBLO* sea de bendición para el pueblo ecuménico hispano dondequiera que el pueblo se reúna.

Se agradece la contribución de La Casa Metodista Unida de Publicaciones en el apoyo y publicación de este recurso.

# LA TRINIDAD

## 1. A Dios el Padre celestial

A Dios el Padre celestial,
al Hijo nuestro Redentor
y al eternal Consolador
unidos todos alabad. Amén.

LETRA: Thomas Ken, 1674; trad. desconocido

## 2. A nuestro Padre Dios

1. A nuestro Padre Dios alcemos nuestra voz,
¡Gloria a El! Tal fue su amor que dio
al Hijo que murió, en quien confío yo.
¡Gloria a El!

2. A nuestro Salvador demos con fe loor,
¡Gloria a El! Su sangre derramó;
con ella me lavó y el cielo me abrió.
¡Gloria a El!

3. Al fiel Consolador celebre nuestra voz,
¡Gloria a El! Con celestial fulgor
nos muestra el amor de Cristo, el Señor.
¡Gloria a El!

4. Con gozo y amor, cantemos con fervor
al Trino Dios. En la eternidad
mora la Trinidad; por siempre alabad
al Trino Dios.

LETRA: Anónimo

## 3. Gloria Patri

Gloria demos al Padre,
al Hijo y al Santo Espíritu;
como era al principio,
es hoy y habrá de ser
eternamente. Amén.

LETRA: Doxología menor, siglo III-IV; trad. desconocido

### 4. Te loamos, oh Dios

1. Te loamos, oh Dios, con unánime voz,
que en Cristo tu Hijo, nos diste perdón.

*Coro*
¡Aleluya! te alabamos. ¡Cuán grande es tu amor!
¡Aleluya! te adoramos, bendito Señor.

2. Te loamos, Jesús, quien tu trono de luz
has dejado, por darnos salud en la cruz.
*(Coro)*

3. Te damos loor, santo Consolador,
que nos llenas de gozo y santo valor.
*(Coro)*

4. Unidos load a la gran Trinidad,
que es la fuente de gracia, virtud y verdad.
*(Coro)*

LETRA: William P. Mackay, 1863; trad. de H. W. Cragin

# DIOS CREADOR

## Alabanza y Gratitud

### 5. A Dios supremo creador

1. A Dios, supremo creador,
cantamos gloria, prez, honor.
¡Alabadle, aleluya!
Pues con su sabio y gran poder
nos dio la vida y todo el ser.

*Coro*
¡Alabadle, alabadle, aleluya,
aleluya, aleluya!

LETRA: Leopoldo Gros, 1925

2. A Cristo, amado Redentor
loamos con ferviente amor.
¡Alabadle, aleluya!
Su santa sangre derramó;
de culpa y mal nos redimió.
*(Coro)*

3. Al Santo Espíritu de paz,
al buen Consolador veraz,
¡Alabadle, aleluya!
Cantamos con sagrada unción
loores mil de corazón.
*(Coro)*

4. Al uno, trino y santo Dios
alzamos con fervor la voz.
¡Alabadle, aleluya!
Pues digno es El de adoración,
de gratitud y bendición.
*(Coro)*

## 6. Mil voces para celebrar

1. Mil voces para celebrar
a mi Libertador,
las glorias de su majestad,
los triunfos de su amor.

2. Mi buen Señor, Maestro y Dios,
que pueda divulgar
tu grato nombre y su honor,
en cielo, tierra y mar.

3. El dulce nombre de Jesús
nos libra del temor;
en las tristezas trae luz,
perdón al pecador.

4. Destruye el poder del mal
y brinda libertad;
al más impuro puede dar
pureza y santidad.

LETRA: Charles Wesley, 1739; trad. de Federico J. Pagura

5. El habla y al oír su voz
el muerto vivirá;
se alegra el triste corazón,
los pobres hallan paz.

6. Escuchen, sordos, al Señor;
alabe el mudo a Dios,
los cojos salten, vean hoy
los ciegos al Señor.

7. En Cristo, pues, conocerán
la gracia del perdón
y aquí del cielo gozarán,
pues cielo es su amor.

## 7. Señor, mi Dios

1. Señor, mi Dios, al contemplar los cielos,
el firmamento y las estrellas mil,
al oír tu voz en los potentes truenos
y ver brillar el sol en su cenit,

*Coro*
Mi corazón se llena de emoción.
¡Cuán grande eres, oh Señor!
Mi corazón se llena de emoción.
¡Cuán grande eres, oh Señor!

*Coro alterno*
*Mi corazón se llena de emoción:*
*¡Cuán grande es El! ¡Cuán grande es El!*
*Mi corazón se llena de emoción:*
*¡Cuán grande es El! ¡Cuán grande es El!*

2. Al recorrer los montes y los valles
y ver las bellas flores al pasar,
al escuchar el canto de las aves
y el murmurar del claro manantial,
*(Coro)*

3. Cuando recuerdo del amor divino
que desde el cielo al Salvador envió,
aquel Jesús que por salvarme vino
y en una cruz por mí sufrió y murió,
*(Coro)*

LETRA: Stuart K. Hine, 1953; trad. de A. W. Hotton

4. Cuando me llames, Dios, a tu presencia,
al dulce hogar, al cielo de esplendor,
te adoraré, cantando la grandeza
de tu poder y tu infinito amor.
*(Coro)*

## 8. ¡Santo! ¡Santo! ¡Santo!

1. ¡Santo! ¡Santo! ¡Santo! Señor omnipotente,
siempre el labio mío loores te dará.
¡Santo! ¡Santo! ¡Santo! Te adoro reverente,
Dios en tres personas, bendita Trinidad.

2. ¡Santo! ¡Santo! ¡Santo! En numeroso coro,
santos escogidos te adoran con fervor;
de alegría llenos, con sus coronas de oro,
rinden alabanza a ti, oh Creador.

3. ¡Santo! ¡Santo! ¡Santo! La inmensa muchedumbre
de ángeles que cumplen tu santa voluntad,
ante ti se postra, bañada de tu lumbre,
ante ti que has sido, que eres y serás.

4. ¡Santo! ¡Santo! ¡Santo! Por más que estés velado
e imposible sea tu gloria contemplar;
santo tú eres sólo y nada hay a tu lado
en poder perfecto, pureza y caridad.

5. ¡Santo! ¡Santo! ¡Santo! La gloria de tu nombre
vemos en tus obras en cielo, tierra y mar.
¡Santo! ¡Santo! ¡Santo! La humanidad te honre,
Dios en tres personas, bendita Trinidad.

LETRA: Reginald Heber, 1862; trad. de Juan Bautista Cabrera

## 9. Jubilosos, te adoramos

1. Jubilosos, te adoramos, Dios de gloria, Dios de amor;
ante ti las almas se abren como flores ante el sol.
Desvanece toda nube de pecado, de dolor.
Oh Dador de gozo eterno, cúbrenos con tu esplendor.

LETRA: Henry Van Dyke, 1907; trad. de Federico J. Pagura

2. Jubilosa, en cielo y tierra, te circunde tu creación;
astros y ángeles te canten en perpetua adoración.
Campo y selva, monte y valle, la pradera, el vasto mar,
fuentes y aves, en tu nombre, nos invitan a cantar.

3. Tú, que siempre nos perdonas, danos hoy tu bendición;
tú, que todo proporcionas, da tu paz al corazón.
Eres Padre; Cristo, hermano; quienes se aman, tuyos son.
Llévanos al gozo eterno, por la senda de tu amor.

4. Oh mortales, vuestras voces al celeste coro unid;
el amor de Dios impera, lo creado va a reunir.
Marcharemos entonando nuestro cántico triunfal;
a través de la contienda, vida y gozo vencerán.

## 10. Al despuntar en la loma el día

1. Al despuntar en la loma el día,
al ver tu gloria nacer,
se llena el campo de tu alegría,
se ve la yerba crecer;
y yo, Señor, que temía
que no fuera como ayer
te veo aquí como siempre
en mi vida y en mi ser.
Te veo aquí como siempre
en mi vida y en mi ser.

2. Se mezcla el sol en el horizonte
con un verde cafetal,
en la espesura canta el sinsonte,*
vuelve la vida al corral;
y siento el aire fragante,
mezcla de aroma y sudor,
y tú me pides que cante,
y te canto, mi Señor.
Y tú me pides que cante,
y te canto, mi Señor.

* *ave, pájaro*

LETRA: Heber Romero de la liturgia criolla, 1980

3. Quisiera ser como aquel arroyo,
grato para refrescar,
o el arrullar de tu pensamiento
que se escucha en el palmar.
Como el cantío de un gallo,
como el trinar del zorzal,*
mi voz se alza en el viento,
oh mi Dios, para cantar.
Mi voz se alza en el viento,
oh mi Dios, para cantar.

## 11. Te alabaré, Señor

1. Te alabaré, Señor, con todo mi corazón,
con todo mi corazón; te alabaré, Señor.
Contaré todas tus maravillas, todas tus maravillas;
te alabaré, Señor.

2. Me alegraré en ti y me regocijaré,
y me regocijaré; te alabaré, Señor.
Cantaré a tu nombre, oh Altísimo, oh Altísimo,
te alabaré, Señor. te alabaré, Señor,
Te alabaré, Señor.

LETRA: Basada en Salmo 9:1-2

## 12. Alzo mis manos

1. Cuando pienso en lo que has hecho en mi vida;
las grandezas que tú haces cada día,
yo me postro humillado ante ti
mi Salvador.
Te alabo Dios, te adoro Dios.

2. Cuando pienso en lo que has hecho en mi vida;
las grandezas que tú haces cada día,
yo me postro humillado ante ti
mi Salvador.
Te alabo con todo el corazón.

3. Alzo mis manos para darte la gloria
y ofrecerte mi vida, Señor, en sacrificio a ti.
Alzo mis manos para darte la gloria
y ofrecerte mi vida, Señor, en sacrificio a ti.

LETRA: Roberto Rodríguez, 1993


# Su Naturaleza Divina

## 13. El amor de Dios

1. Como la playa, como el pasto verde,
viento y refugio es el amor de Dios.
Libres nos hizo sobre el vasto mundo
para aceptarle o responderle, «no».

*Coro*
Como la playa, como el pasto verde,
viento y refugio es el amor de Dios.

2. La libertad de ser nosotros mismos
para vivir, soñar, crear, servir;
la libertad como una tierra fértil
que se convierte en pródigo jardín.
*(Coro)*

LETRA: Anders Frostenson, 1968; trad. inglés, Fred Kaan; trad. español Federico J. Pagura

3. Aún así, murallas nos separan
y tras las rejas nos podemos ver.
Nuestras prisiones son nuestros temores,
fuertes cadenas atan nuestro ser.
*(Coro)*

4. Júzganos, Padre y al juzgar perdona,
que en tu perdón hallamos libertad;
y no hay fronteras que tu amor no cruce
por liberar a nuestra humanidad.
*(Coro)*

## 14. Grande es tu fidelidad

1. Oh, Dios eterno, tu misericordia
ni una sombra de duda tendrá;
tu compasión y bondad nunca fallan
y por los siglos el mismo serás.

*Coro*
¡Oh, tu fidelidad! ¡Oh, tu fidelidad!
Cada momento la veo en mí.
Nada me falta, pues todo provees.
¡Grande, Señor, es tu fidelidad!

2. La noche oscura, el sol y la luna,
las estaciones del año también,
unen su canto cual fieles criaturas,
porque eres bueno, por siempre eres fiel.
*(Coro)*

3. Tú me perdonas, me impartes el gozo,
tierno me guías por sendas de paz;
eres mi fuerza, mi fe, mi reposo
y por los siglos mi todo* serás.
*(Coro)*

* *Padre*

LETRA: Thomas O. Chisolm, 1923; trad. de Honorato Reza, alt.

## 15. La palabra del Señor es recta

*Coro*
La palabra del Señor es recta
y sus obras son maravillosas.
La justicia y el derecho
tienen tronos a su diestra
y de su misericordia
llena está toda la tierra.
Y de su misericordia
llena está toda la tierra.

1. Con su divina palabra
fueron creados los cielos;
del aliento de su boca
se formaron los luceros.
El como en odre recoge
del inquieto mar las aguas,
del abismo hace un estanque,
de los ríos las cañadas.
*(Coro)*

2. Témale toda la tierra,
póstrense todos los pueblos;
obras tan grandes y excelsas
a su mandato surgieron.
Frustra el Señor los designios
de los que en el mal se embriagan.
Sólo sus planes y juicios
se confirman y proclaman.
*(Coro)*

LETRA: Juan Luis García, 1979 (Sal. 33:4-11)

## 16. Santo (Holy)

Santo, santo, santo, santo,
santo, santo es nuestro Dios,
Señor de toda la tierra,
santo, santo es nuestro Dios.
Santo, santo, santo, santo,
santo, santo es nuestro Dios,
Señor de toda la historia,
santo, santo es nuestro Dios.

Que acompaña a nuestro pueblo,
que vive en nuestras luchas,
del universo entero el único Señor.
Benditos los que en su nombre
el evangelio anuncian,
la buena y gran noticia
de la liberación.

*Holy, holy, holy, holy*
*holy, holy is our God,*
*God of all the earth and heaven,*
*holy, holy is our God.*
*Holy, holy, holy, holy,*
*holy, holy is our God,*
*God, the Lord of all our hist'ry*
*Holy, holy is our God.*

*Who accompanies our people*
*who lives within our struggles*
*of all the earth and heaven,*
*the one and only Lord.*
*Blessed those who in the Lord's name*
*announce the Holy Gospel,*
*proclaiming forth the good news*
*of liberating power.*

LETRA: Guillermo Cuéllar, de La Misa Popular Salvadoreña, c. 1986; trad. de Linda McCrae (Isa. 6:3)

## 17. Dios de las aves

1. Dios de las aves, Dios del gran pez,
de las estrellas, Dios;
¡cómo lo creado te teme, cómo lo creado te adora!

2. Dios de los sismos, del temporal,
de la trompeta, Dios;
cómo lo creado te invoca, cómo lo creado te implora.

3. Del arco iris, de la cruz
y del sepulcro, Dios;
¡cómo hablar de tu gracia, cómo expresarte las gracias!

4. Dios del que enfermo o hambriento está
y del derrochador;
¡cómo los seres se cuidan, y cómo sienten la vida!

5. Dios del que es prójimo o rival,
del garfio de poder;
¡cómo de amor platicamos y cómo de paz hablamos!

6. Dios de los tiempos, cercano Dios,
de amante corazón;
¡qué es en tus hijos el gozo, cómo decimos hogar!

LETRA: Jaroslav J. Vajda, 1983; trad. de Federico J. Pagura


## 18. Heleluyan (Aleluya)

Heleluyan, heleluyan; hele, heleluyan.
Heleluyan, heleluyan; hele, heleluyan.

Aleluya, aleluya; ale, aleluya.
Aleluya, aleluya; ale, aleluya.

LETRA: Tradicional Muscogee (Creek) nativo americana

## 19. El amor de mi Señor

1. No hay amor como el de Dios
   que me llena el corazón;
   que penetra en mí, que me inspira más,
   el amor de mi Señor.

   *Coro*
   El amor de mi Señor
   me renueva el corazón,
   dulce amor de Dios tierno y puro es,
   el amor de mi Señor.

2. Borrará mi rebelión
   el amor de mi Señor.
   La bondad de El es consuelo en mí,
   pone paz en mi aflicción.
   *(Coro)*

3. No hay amor como el de Dios
   que me imparte protección;
   me redimirá y me sostendrá
   el amor de mi Señor.
   *(Coro)*

LETRA: Rafael Cuna, 1940


## 20. Te alabarán, oh Jehová

Te alabarán, oh Jehová, todos los reyes,
todos los reyes de la tierra,
porque han oído los dichos de tu boca
y cantarán de los caminos de Jehová.
*(Se repite)*

Porque la gloria de Jehová es grande,
porque Jehová es perfecto en sus caminos,
porque Jehová atiende al humilde,
mas mira de lejos al altivo.
*(Se repite)*

LETRA: Basada en Salmo 138:4-6

# La Creación

## 21. El mundo entero es

1. El mundo entero es del Padre celestial;
su alabanza en la creación escucho resonar.
¡De Dios el mundo es! ¡Qué grato es recordar
que en el autor de tanto bien podemos descansar!

2. El mundo entero es del Padre Celestial;
el pájaro, la luz, la flor proclaman su bondad.
¡De Dios el mundo es! El fruto de su acción
se muestra con esplendidez en toda la expansión.

3. El mundo entero es del Padre Celestial
y nada habrá de detener su triunfo sobre el mal.
¡De Dios el mundo es! Confiada mi alma está,
pues Dios en Cristo, nuestro Rey, por siempre reinará.

LETRA: Maltbie D. Babcock, 1901; trad. de Federico J. Pagura


## 22. Cantemos al Señor

1. Cantemos al Señor un himno de alegría,
un cántico de amor al nacer el nuevo día.
El hizo el cielo, el mar, el sol y las estrellas,
y en ellos vio bondad, pues sus obras eran bellas.

*Coro*
¡Aleluya! ¡Aleluya! Cantemos al Señor.
¡Aleluya!

LETRA: Carlos Rosas, 1976

2. Cantemos al Señor un himno de alabanza
que exprese nuestro amor nuestra fe, nuestra esperanza.
En toda la creación abunda su grandeza;
así nuestro cantar va anunciando su belleza.
*(Coro)*

## 23. Muchas y grandes tus obras, Dios

1. Muchas y grandes tus obras, Dios,
en cielo y tierra son.
Tu mano las estrellas forjó,
montes y llanos, tu creación.
A tu mandato el agua brotó,
acata el mar tu voz.

2. Haznos gozar en tu comunión,
Dios de la eternidad.
Ven a morar en nuestro ser;
dones de gracia se hallan en ti.
Danos, Señor, tu vida sin fin:
vida eterna en ti.

LETRA: Joseph R. Renville, © 1846; pará. de Philip Frazier; trad. de Alberto Merubia
(Sal. 104:24-30; Jer. 10:12,13)

## 24. Alabanza

1. Al caer la lluvia resurge con verdor
toda la floresta. ¡Renueva la creación!
Mira el rojo lirio; el duende* ya brotó.
¡Bella primavera que anuncia su fulgor!

*Coro*
Toda flor silvestre, la maya*, el cundeamor* . . .
¡Todo manifiesta la gloria del Señor!
¡Cómo se te alaba en toda la creación!
Yo quisiera hacerlo en forma igual, Señor.

2. El coquí* se alegra, se siente muy feliz,
¡canta en su alabanza: «coquí, coquí, coquí!»
El pitirre* canta y trina el ruiseñor.
¡Cuán alegremente alaban al Creador!
*(Coro)*

* *duende = flor*
* *maya = planta*
* *cundeamor = arbusto*
* *coquí = ranita*
* *pitirre = avecilla*

LETRA: Pablo Fernández Badillo, 1977

# JESUCRISTO REDENTOR

## Alabanza y Gratitud

### 25. Cuánto nos ama

¡Cuánto nos ama Jesús! ¡Cuánto nos ama Jesús!
Su vida dio por ti y por mí.
¡Oh, cuánto me ama, oh, cuánto te ama,
cuánto nos ama Jesús!

LETRA: Kurt Kaiser, 1975; trad. de Salomón Mussiett, alt.


### 26. Jesús es mi Rey soberano

1. Jesús es mi Rey soberano,
mi gozo es cantar su loor;
es Rey, y me ve cual hermano,
es Rey y me imparte su amor.
Dejando su trono de gloria,
me vino a sacar de la escoria
y yo soy feliz, y yo soy feliz por El.

2. Jesús es mi amigo anhelado
y en sombras o en luz siempre va,
paciente y humilde a mi lado,
ayuda y consuelo me da.
Por eso constante lo sigo,
porque El es mi Rey y mi amigo
y yo soy feliz, y yo soy feliz por El.

LETRA: Vicente Mendoza, 1920

3. Señor, ¿qué pudiera yo darte
por tanta bondad para mí?
¿Me basta servirte y amarte?
¿Es todo entregarme yo a ti?
Entonces acepta mi vida,
que a ti sólo queda rendida,
pues yo soy feliz, pues yo soy feliz por ti.

## 27. Grato es contar la historia

1. Grato es contar la historia del celestial favor;
de Cristo y de su gloria, de Cristo y de su amor;
me agrada referirla, pues sé que es la verdad;
y nada satisface cual ella, mi ansiedad.

*Coro*
¡Qué bella es esa historia!
Mi tema allá en la gloria
será la antigua historia
de Cristo y de su amor.

2. Grato es decir la historia que antigua, sin vejez,
parece al repetirla más dulce cada vez;
me agrada referirla, pues hay quien nunca oyó
que para hacerle salvo el buen Jesús murió.
*(Coro)*

3. Grato es contar la historia; el que la sabe ya,
parece que de oírla sediento aún está.
Y cuando el nuevo canto en gloria entonaré,
será la antigua historia que en vida tanto amé.
*(Coro)*

LETRA: Katherine Hankey, © 1868; trad.
de Juan Bautista Cabrera, alt.

## 28. Jesu tawa pano (Heme aquí, Jesús)

Jesu, tawa pano,
Jesu, tawa pano,
Jesu, tawa pano,
tawa pano, mu zita renyu.

Heme aquí, Jesús,
heme aquí, Jesús,
heme aquí, Jesús,
heme aquí, por tu gracia, Jesús.

LETRA: Patrick Matsikenyiri, 1990; trad. de Pedro P. Pirón


## 29. Del santo amor de Cristo

1. Del santo amor de Cristo que no tendrá su igual,
de su divina gracia, sublime y eternal;
de su misericordia, inmensa como el mar
y cual los cielos alta, con gozo he de cantar.

*Coro*
El amor de mi Señor
grande y dulce es más y más;
rico, inefable, nada es comparable
al amor de mi Jesús.

2. Cuando El vivió en el mundo la gente lo siguió
y todas sus angustias en El depositó;
entonces bondadoso, su amor brotó en raudal
incontenible, inmenso, sanando todo mal.
*(Coro)*

3. El puso en las pupilas del ciego nueva luz,
la eterna luz de vida que brilla en la cruz
y dio a las almas todas la gloria de su ser,
al impartir su gracia, su Espíritu y poder.
*(Coro)*

4. Su amor ha sido el faro que no se apagará,
es luz resplandeciente que siempre alumbrará;
y el paso de los años habrá de confirmar
lo eterno y majestuoso de aquel amor sin par.
*(Coro)*

LETRA: Lelia N. Morris, 1912; trad. de Vicente Mendoza, alt.; Carlos Pastor López, estr. 4

## 30. En momentos así

En momentos así levanto mi voz,
levanto mi canto a Cristo;
en momentos así levanto mi ser,
levanto mis manos a El.
Cuánto te amo, Dios, cuánto te amo, Dios;
cuánto te amo, mi Dios, te amo, Dios.

LETRA: David Graham, 1980; trad. desconocido, alt.


## 31. Hay momentos

Hay momentos que las palabras no me alcanzan
para decirte lo que siento por ti, mi buen Jesús.
Hay momentos que las palabras no me alcanzan
para decirte lo que siento por ti, mi buen Jesús.
Yo te agradezco por todo lo que has hecho,
por todo lo que haces y todo lo que harás.
Yo te agradezco por todo lo que has hecho,
por todo lo que haces y todo lo que harás.

LETRA: Autor desconocido

## 32. En Jesucristo, mártir de paz

1. En Jesucristo, mártir de paz,
en horas tristes de tempestad,
hallan las almas dulce solaz,
grato consuelo, felicidad.

*Coro*
Gloria cantemos al Redentor,
que por nosotros vino a morir;
y que la gracia del Salvador
siempre dirija nuestro vivir.

LETRA: Fanny J. Crosby, 1873; trad. de E. A. Monfort Díaz, alt.

2. En nuestras luchas, en el dolor,
en tristes horas de tentación,
Cristo nos llena de su vigor
y da aliento al corazón
*(Coro)*

3. Cuando en la lucha falta la fe
y siente el alma desfallecer,
Cristo nos dice: «Siempre os daré
gracia divina, santo poder».
*(Coro)*

## 33. Grande gozo hay en mi alma

1. Grande gozo hay en mi alma hoy,
pues Jesús conmigo está;
y su paz, que ya gozando estoy
por siempre durará.

*Coro*
¡Grande gozo! ¡Cuán hermoso!
Paso todo el tiempo bien feliz,
porque veo de Cristo la sonriente faz.
Grande gozo siento en mí.

2. Hay un canto en mi alma hoy,
melodías a mi Rey;
en su amor feliz y libre soy
y salvo por la fe.
*(Coro)*

3. Paz divina hay en mi alma hoy,
porque Cristo me salvó;
las cadenas rotas ya están,
Jesús me libertó.
*(Coro)*

4. Gratitud hay en mi alma hoy
y alabanzas a Jesús;
por su gracia a la gloria voy,
gozándome en la luz.
*(Coro)*

LETRA: Eliza E. Hewitt, 1887; trad. anónimo

## 34. Junto a la cruz

1. Junto a la cruz do Jesús murió,
junto a la cruz do salud pedí,
ya mis pecados El perdonó.
¡A su nombre gloria!

*Coro*
¡A su nombre gloria!
¡A su nombre gloria!
Ya mis pecados El perdonó.
¡A su nombre gloria!

2. Junto a la cruz donde le busqué,
¡cuán admirable perdón me dió!
Ya con Jesús siempre viviré.
¡A su nombre gloria!
*(Coro)*

3. Fuente preciosa de salvación,
qué grande gozo yo pude hallar,
al encontrar en Jesús perdón.
¡A su nombre gloria!
*(Coro)*

4. Tú, pecador, que perdido estás,
hoy esta fuente ven a buscar;
paz y perdón encontrar podrás.
¡A su nombre gloria!
*(Coro)*

LETRA: Elisha A. Hoffman, 1878; trad. de Vicente Mendoza

## 35. ¿Con qué pagaremos?

1. ¿Con qué pagaremos amor tan inmenso,
que diste tu vida por el pecador?
En cambio recibes la ofrenda humilde,
la ofrenda humilde, Señor Jesucristo, de mi corazón.

LETRA: Autor desconocido

2. Y cuando la noche extiende su manto,
mis ojos en llanto en ti fijaré;
alzando mis ojos veré las estrellas,
yo sé que tras ellas, cual Padre amoroso, tú velas por mí.

3. No puedo pagarte con oro ni plata
el gran sacrificio que hiciste por mí;
no tengo que darte por tanto amarme.
Recibe este canto mezclado con llanto y mi corazón.

## 36. Sólo tú eres santo

1. Sólo tú eres santo, sólo tú eres digno,
tú eres hermoso y maravilloso.
En la cruz moriste y resucitaste;
tú me diste vida y muy pronto volverás.

2. Sólo tú eres santo, sólo tú eres digno,
tú eres hermoso y maravilloso.
Derrama tu Espíritu y que tu luz brille;
que tu gloria llene ahora mismo este lugar.

LETRA: Autor desconocido; adap. de Kenneth R. Hanna; estr. 2 de Jorge Lockward, 1994


## 37. Es Jesús nombre sin par

Cristo, Jesucristo es un nombre sin igual.
Verbo, Dios es Cristo, como olor a lluvia es El.
Cristo, Jesucristo, cielo y tierra gloria den.
Reyes, reinos al fin pasarán,
mas su nombre es eternal.

LETRA: Gloria Gaither y William J. Gaither, 1970; trad. de Pedro P. Pirón

# Adviento

## 38. Toda la tierra

1. Toda la tierra espera al Salvador
y el surco abierto, la obra del Creador;
es el mundo que lucha por la libertad,
reclama justicia y busca la verdad.

2. Dice el profeta al pueblo de Israel:
«De madre virgen ya viene Emanuel».
Será «Dios con nosotros», hermano será;
con El, la esperanza al mundo volverá.

3. Montes y valles habrá que preparar;
nuevos caminos tenemos que trazar.
Dios está ya muy cerca, venidlo a encontrar
y todas las puertas abrid de par en par.

4. En un pesebre Jesús apareció,
pero en el mundo está presente hoy.
Vive en nuestra gente, con ellos está;
y vuelve de nuevo a darnos libertad.

LETRA: Alberto Taulé, 1972


## 39. El Dios de paz

1. El Dios de paz, el Verbo eterno,
en nuestras almas va a morar.
El es la luz, camino y vida,
gracia y perdón para el mortal.

*Coro*
Ven, Salvador, ven sin tardar,
tu pueblo santo esperando está.

2. Viene a enseñarnos el sendero,
viene a traernos el perdón.
Viene a morir en un madero,
precio de nuestra redención.
*(Coro)*

LETRA: Anónimo; adap. por la Comisión del Himnario *Albricias*

3. Por una senda oscurecida
vamos en busca de la luz;
luz y alegría sin medida
encontraremos en Jesús.
*(Coro)*

4. Brilla en la noche nueva Aurora,
Sol de Justicia, Sol de Paz;
toda la humanidad añora
al que la viene a salvar.
*(Coro)*

5. Nuestro Señor vendrá un día
lleno de gracia y majestad
para llevar al pueblo suyo
hacia su reino celestial.
*(Coro)*

## 40. Oh ven, Emanuel

1. Oh ven, oh ven Emanuel,
rescata ya a Israel,
que llora en su desolación
y espera su liberación.

*Coro*
Vendrá, vendrá Emanuel,
¡alégrate, oh Israel!

2. Sabiduría celestial,
al mundo hoy ven a morar.
Enséñanos y haznos saber
en ti lo que podemos ser.
*(Coro)*

3. Anhelo de los pueblos, ven,
en ti podremos paz tener;
de crueles guerras líbranos
y reine soberano Dios.
*(Coro)*

4. Ven tú, oh Hijo de David,
tu trono establece aquí;
destruye el poder del mal.
¡Visítanos, Rey celestial!
*(Coro)*

LETRA: Antífonas latinas, siglo IX; trad. de Federico J. Pagura

## 41. Dad gloria al Ungido

1. Dad gloria al Ungido, al Hijo de David;
su reino ha venido, su nombre bendecid.
De todo ser cautivo, El es la libertad;
es gracia que nos limpia de toda iniquidad.

2. Vendrá cual fresca lluvia la tierra a saturar,
a su glorioso paso las flores se abrirán.
Será sobre altos montes heraldo de la paz;
y en valles y collados justicia brotará.

3. Los que de Arabia lleguen ante El se humillarán;
quien venga de Etiopía, su gloria admirará.
De todo el mundo naves vendrán a ofrecer,
con devoción, tesoros y ofrendas a sus pies.

LETRA: James Montgomery, 1821; trad. de Juan Burghi

## 42. Junto al Jordán

1. Junto al Jordán se oye el clamor
de Juan Bautista, el precursor.
Anuncia que ya viene aquél
que habrá de ser nuestro Emanuel.

2. Recto ha de ser el proceder del pueblo
que ahora aspira a ser
el templo de su habitación
y objeto de su redención.

3. Cual nuestra sola redención
te acoje nuestro corazón,
pues sin tu gracia, Salvador,
fallece cual marchita flor.

4. Rescátanos ya del sufrir;
no nos permitas sucumbir.
Y que tu esplendorosa faz
al mundo alumbre y traiga paz.

5. Jesús, que viene con virtud
y cuyo adviento trae salud,
el Padre y el Consolador
reciban gloria, prez y honor.

LETRA: Charles Coffin, 1736; trad. de Dimas Planas-Belfort

## 43. La puerta abrid de par en par

1. La puerta abrid de par en par
al Rey de gloria que ha de entrar.
El Rey de reyes, el Señor,
del mundo entero el Salvador,
que a tierra trae salvación.
Con júbilo entonad canción
al Hijo, al Creador
y al gran Consolador.

2. La roca de la fe load,
que es tono de eternal bondad.
Ceñido está de puro honor;
su cetro celestial es amor.
A nuestra angustia fin pondrá.
Al Rey y amigo ensalzará
la gran congregación
que halló su redención.

3. ¡Feliz el pueblo que del Rey
acate la doctrina y ley!
¡Bendito el corazón y hogar
en que este Rey consiga entrar!
Es sol de honor y de virtud
que alumbra al mundo y da salud,
del mundo el hacedor
y nuestro defensor.

4. Ven, Jesucristo Salvador,
de nuestras vidas el Señor.
Otórganos tu santa paz
y enseña tu bendita faz.
Y el Paracleto mostrará
la senda que a ti guiará.
¡Loor a ti, Jesús,
oh sol de eterna luz!

LETRA: Georg Weissel, siglo XVII; trad. de Dimas Planas-Belfort

## 44. ¡Hosanna en el cielo!

Santo, santo, santo es el Señor;
Dios del universo, santo es el Señor.
¡Hosanna en el cielo! ¡Hosanna en la tierra!
¡Bendito el que viene en el nombre del Señor!
¡Hosanna en el cielo! ¡Hosanna en la tierra!
¡Bendito el que viene en el nombre del Señor!

LETRA: Basada en Apocalipsis 4:8; Juan 12:13

# Navidad/Epifanía

## 45. La primera Navidad

1. La primera Navidad anunciada fue
a unos pobres pastores cuidando su grey;
una noche silenciosa de frío invernal,
un coro celeste la vino a anunciar.

*Coro*
Noel,* Noel, Noel, Noel,
hoy ha nacido el Rey de Israel.

2. Una estrella luminosa en oriente brilló
y su luz desde lejos la tierra inundó;
ni de noche ni de día dejó de alumbrar
el astro del cielo, con luz sin igual.
*(Coro)*

3. Por la luz de la estrella se echaron a andar
tres magos y sabios de tierra oriental;
su intento era sólo un rey encontrar,
siguiendo la estrella por todo lugar.
*(Coro)*

4. La estrella que hacia el norte su rumbo tomó
en Belén de Judea al fin reposó;
y el pesebre en que yacía el niño Jesús,
se halló de repente bañado de luz.
*(Coro)*

* *Navidad*

LETRA: Tradicional de Inglaterra; trad. de Federico J. Pagura

5. Cuando entraron los tres sabios al rústico hogar,
con gran reverencia quisieron honrar
con ricos dones, ofrendas de amor:
incienso, oro y mirra, a Cristo el Señor.
*(Coro)*

## 46. Venid, pastores

*Coro*
Venid, pastores, venid,
oh venid a Belén, oh venid al portal.
Yo no me voy de Belén sin al niño Jesús
un momento adorar.

1. Y la estrella de Belén nos guiará con su luz,
hasta el humilde portal, donde nació Jesús.
*(Coro)*

2. De la montaña el pastor a Belén presto va
para adorar a Jesús que nació en el portal.
*(Coro)*

3. No oyes el gallo cantar con su potente voz,
anuncia al mundo que ya Jesucristo nació.
*(Coro)*

LETRA: Villancico de Puerto Rico

## 47. Oh, pueblecito de Belén

1. Oh, pueblecito de Belén,
afortunado tú,
pues en tus campos brilla hoy
la perdurable luz.
El Hijo, el Deseado
con santa expectación,
por toda gente y toda edad
en ti, Belén, nació.

LETRA: Phillips Brooks, © 1868; trad. de T. M. Westrup, alt.

2. Allá do el Redentor nació
los ángeles están
velando todos con amor
al niño sin igual.
¡Estrellas muy brillantes,
a Dios la gloria dad,
pues hoy el cielo nos mostró
su buena voluntad!

3. ¡Cuán silencioso allí bajó
preciado y puro don!
Así también aquí dará,
sus bendiciones, Dios.
Ningún oído acaso
perciba su venir,
mas el de humilde corazón
le habrá de recibir.

4. Oh Santo Niño de Belén!
Desciende con tu amor
y echando fuera todo mal,
nace en nosotros hoy.
Angélicas criaturas
le anuncian al nacer;
ven con nosotros a morar,
Jesús, Emanuel.

## 48. Oh, santísimo, felicísimo

1. ¡Oh santísimo, felicísimo,
grato tiempo de Navidad!
Al mundo perdido Cristo le ha nacido.
¡Alegría, alegría, cristiandad!

2. ¡Oh santísimo, felicísimo,
grato tiempo de Navidad!
Coros celestiales oyen los mortales.
¡Alegría, alegría, cristiandad!

LETRA: Johannes Falk, 1816; trad. de Federico Fliedner

3. ¡Oh santísimo, felicísimo
grato tiempo de Navidad!
Príncipe del cielo,
danos tu consuelo.
¡Alegría, alegría, cristiandad!

## 49. Ve, di en la montaña

*Coro*
Ve, di en la montaña,
sobre los montes por doquier;
ve, di en la montaña
que Cristo ya nació.

1. Pastores, sus rebaños
de noche al cuidar,
con gran sorpresa vieron
gloriosa luz brillar.
*(Coro)*

2. Y luego, asombrados,
oyeron el cantar
de ángeles en coro
las nuevas proclamar.
*(Coro)*

3. En un pesebre humilde
el Cristo ya nació.
De Dios amor sublime
al mundo descendió.
*(Coro)*

LETRA: Espiritual afro-americana; adap. por John W. Work; trad. de Anita González

## 50. Angeles cantando están

1. Angeles cantando están
tan dulcísima canción;
las montañas su eco dan
como fiel contestación.

*Coro*
Gloria, en lo alto gloria,
gloria, en lo alto gloria a Dios.

*Coro alterno*
Gloria in excelsis Deo,
gloria in excelsis Deo.

2. Los pastores sin cesar
sus loores dan a Dios;
cuán glorioso es el cantar
de su melodiosa voz.
*(Coro)*

3. Hoy anuncian con fervor
que ha nacido el Salvador;
los mortales gozarán
paz y buena voluntad.
*(Coro)*

4. Oh, venid pronto a Belén
para contemplar con fe
a Jesús, autor del bien,
al recién nacido Rey.
*(Coro)*

LETRA: Villancico de Francia, siglo XVIII; trad. de George P. Simmonds, estrs. 1, 2, 4; anónimo, estr. 3

## 51. Entre pajas ha nacido

1. A subir al monte voy a decirle al jibarito
que Jesús el Salvador entre pajas ha nacido;
entre pajas ha nacido.

LETRA: Pablo Fernánez Badillo, 1975

2. El que viene a libertar de miseria al campesino
y la sed a mitigar entre pajas ha nacido;
entre pajas ha nacido.

3. Del bohío* en el batey** declaremos que ya vino;
en pesebre el niño Rey entre pajas ha nacido;
entre pajas ha nacido.

4. El que trae amor y paz para el pobre en su destino,
el que viene a consolar entre pajas ha nacido;
entre pajas ha nacido.

* *bohío—casa de paja*
** *batey—patio*

## 52. ¡Dichosa tierra, proclamad!

1. ¡Dichosa tierra, proclamad
que vino ya el Señor!
En vuestras almas preparad
un sitio al Redentor,
un sitio al Redentor, un sitio a nuestro Redentor.

2. ¡Dichosa tierra, el Salvador
triunfante ha de reinar!
Resuenen coros, coros de loor
en cielo, tierra y mar, en cielo, tierra y mar,
en cielo, tierra y vasto mar.

3. Cese en el mundo la aflicción,
y ahuyéntese el dolor;
que brote en cada corazón
paz, gozo y santo amor, paz, gozo y santo amor,
paz, pleno gozo y santo amor.

LETRA: Isaac Watts, 1719; trad. de S. D. Athans

4. El rige al mundo con verdad
y gracia sin igual.
Su amor sublime y gran bondad
jamás tendrá su igual,
jamás tendrá su igual,
jamás, jamás tendrá su igual.

## 53. Oíd un son en alta esfera

1. Oíd un son en alta esfera:
«¡En los cielos, gloria a Dios,
al mortal paz en la tierra!»,
canta la celeste voz.
Con los cielos alabemos,
al eterno Dios cantemos,
a Jesús, que es nuestro bien,
con el coro de Belén.

*Coro*
Canta la celeste voz:
«¡En los cielos, gloria a Dios!».

2. El Señor de los señores,
el Ungido celestial,
por salvar los pecadores
vino al seno virginal.
Gloria al Verbo encarnado,
en humanidad velado;
gloria al Santo de Israel,
cuyo nombre Emanuel.
*(Coro)*

3. Eres Rey de paz eterna,
gloria a ti, a ti Jesús;
entregando el alma tierna,
tú nos traes vida y luz.
Has tu majestad dejado
y buscarnos te has dignado;
para darnos el vivir,
a la muerte quieres ir.
*(Coro)*

LETRA: Charles Wesley, 1739; adap. por George Whitefield; trad. de Federico Fliedner

## 54. Noche de paz

1. ¡Noche de paz, noche de amor!
Todo duerme en derredor.
Entre los astros que esparcen su luz,
bella, anunciando al niñito Jesús,
brilla la estrella de paz,
brilla la estrella de paz.

2. ¡Noche de paz, noche de amor!
Oye humilde el fiel pastor
coros celestes que anuncian salud;
gracias y glorias en gran plenitud,
por nuestro buen Redentor,
por nuestro buen Redentor.

3. ¡Noche de paz, noche de amor!
Ved qué bello resplandor
luce en el rostro del niño Jesús,
en el pesebre, del mundo la luz.
Astro de eterno fulgor,
astro de eterno fulgor.

LETRA: Joseph Mohr, 1818; trad. Federico Fliedner

## 55. Llegó la nochebuena

1. Ya llegó la nochebuena,
ya llegó la navidad,
cantaremos alabanzas
para el niño que vendrá.

*Coro*
¡Vamos todos a esperarlo,
vamos todos a Belén,
que Jesús en un pesebre
para todos va a nacer.

2. Llevaremos para el niño
lo mejor del corazón,
el deseo de encontrarlo,
la esperanza del perdón.
*(Coro)*

LETRA: Tradicional de Argentina

3. Recibamos la enseñanza
que este niño hoy nos da:
siendo rico se hizo pobre
por amor a los demás.
*(Coro)*

## 56. Venid, fieles todos

1. Venid, fieles todos, a Belén marchemos,
de gozo triunfantes y llenos de amor,
y al Rey de los cielos humilde veremos.

*Coro*
Venid, adoremos, venid adoremos,
venid, adoremos a Cristo el Señor.

2. El que es Hijo eterno, del eterno Padre
y Dios verdadero que al mundo creó,
del seno virgíneo nació de una madre.
*(Coro)*

3. En pobre pesebre yace reclinado,
al mundo ofreciendo eternal salvación,
el santo Mesías, el Verbo humanado.
*(Coro)*

4. Cantad jubilosas, celestes criaturas;
resuenen los cielos con vuestra canción.
¡Al Dios bondadoso gloria en las alturas!
*(Coro)*

5. Jesús, celebramos tu bendito nombre
con himnos alegres de grato loor.
Por siglos eternos la humanidad te honre.
*(Coro)*

LETRA: John F. Wade, c. 1743; trad. de Juan Bautista Cabrera, alt.

## 57. Tras hermoso lucero

1. Tras hermoso lucero, los magos viajaban
pensando al palacio llegar.
Y llevaban regalos preciosos
al Rey que deseaban venir a adorar.
Al llegar a Belén, ¡ved qué bella!
al llegar a Belén, ved la estrella.
Con su luz alumbraba un establo y allí,
en el heno, dormía el gran Rey.

2. En el campo pastores cuidaban ovejas
y vieron un gran resplandor.
Luego el ángel del cielo les dijo:
«Os doy nuevas que hoy nació el Salvador».
Muchos ángeles bellos cantaron
al Señor, al Eterno alabaron.
Los pastores buscaron al niño y allí,
en el heno, dormía el gran Rey.

3. Ofrecieron los magos al niño Jesús
ricos dones con gran devoción.
Los pastores humildes le dieron
cariño de tierno y de fiel corazón.
Yo también, oh Jesús, hoy me acerco;
yo también, oh Jesús, hoy te adoro
y te ofrezco mi vida, regalo de amor.
¡Haz en ella tu trono, mi Rey!

LETRA: Catalina Bardwell de Noble, 1950

## 58. Niño lindo

*Coro*
Niño lindo, ante ti me rindo,
niño lindo, eres tú mi Dios.
Niño lindo, ante ti me rindo;
niño lindo, eres tú mi Dios.

1. Esa tu hermosura; ese tu candor,
el alma me roba, el alma me roba,
me roba el amor.
*(Coro)*

LETRA: Tradicional de Venezuela

2. La vida, bien mío y el alma también
te ofrezco gustoso, te ofrezco gustoso,
rendido a tus pies.
*(Coro)*

3. Adiós, tierno infante, adiós niño, adiós.
Adiós, dulce amante, adiós, dulce amante,
adiós, niño, adiós.
*(Coro)*

## Ministerio

### 59. Todos los días, nace el Señor

1. Para esta tierra sin luz, nace el Señor;
para vencer las tinieblas, nace el Señor;
para cambiar nuestro mundo,
todos los días nace el Señor.
Todos los días nace el Señor.

2. Para traer libertad, nace el Señor;
rompiendo nuestras cadenas, nace el Señor;
en la persona que es libre,
todos los días nace el Señor.
Todos los días nace el Señor.

3. Para quitar la opresión, nace el Señor;
para borrar la injusticia, nace el Señor;
en cada pueblo que gime
todos los días nace el Señor.
Todos los días nace el Señor.

4. Para vencer la pobreza, nace el Señor;
para los pobres que sufren, nace el Señor;
por la igualdad de las gentes,
todos los días nace el Señor.
Todos los días nace el Señor.

5. Para traernos la paz, nace el Señor;
para esta tierra que sangra, nace el Señor;
en cada uno que lucha,
todos los días nace el Señor.
Todos los días nace el Señor.

LETRA: Juan Antonio Espinosa, 1976

6. Para traernos amor, nace el Señor;
para vencer egoísmos, nace el Señor;
al estrechar nuestras manos,
todos los días nace el Señor.
Todos los días nace el Señor.

7. Para este mundo dormido, nace el Señor;
para inquietar nuestras vidas, nace el Señor;
en cada nueva esperanza
todos los días nace el Señor.
Todos los días nace el Señor.

## 60. Dancé en la mañana

1. Dancé en la mañana
cuando el mundo nació
y dancé en las estrellas,
la luna y el sol;
descendí de los cielos
y en la tierra dancé
y fue mi cuna allá en Belén.

*Coro*
Ven, pues, conmigo a danzar,
que el Señor de la danza soy;
y doquier estén
allí también yo estoy
y en la danza a todos
les puedo guiar.

2. Para el fariseo
y el escriba dancé,
no quisieron danzar
cuando yo les invité;
y llamé pescadores:
a Jacobo y a Juan;
la danza pudo continuar.
*(Coro)*

LETRA: Sydney Carter, 1963; trad. de Federico Pagura

3. Dancé en un sábado
   y un cojo sané
   y la gente piadosa
   me dijo que era infiel;
   me azotaron, me hirieron,
   me colgaron al fin
   en una cruz para morir.
   *(Coro)*

4. Dancé en un viernes
   de tinieblas sin par,
   con el diablo a cuestas
   no es fácil danzar;
   enterraron mi cuerpo
   como un último adiós,
   mas soy la danza y aquí estoy.
   *(Coro)*

5. Postrado en la tierra,
   a los cielos salté,
   pues la danza yo soy
   y yo nunca moriré;
   viviré en ustedes,
   si es que viven en mí,
   en la danza que no tiene fin.
   *(Coro)*

## 61. Tenemos esperanza

1. Porque El entró en el mundo y en la historia;
   porque quebró el silencio y la agonía;
   porque llenó la tierra de su gloria;
   porque fue luz en nuestra noche fría;
   porque El nació en un pesebre oscuro;
   porque vivió sembrando amor y vida;
   porque partió los corazones duros
   y levantó las almas abatidas.

   *Coro*
   Por eso es que hoy tenemos esperanza,
   por eso es que hoy luchamos con porfía,
   por eso es que hoy miramos con confianza
   el porvenir en esta tierra mía.
   Por eso es que hoy miramos con confianza,
   por eso es que hoy luchamos con porfía;
   por eso es que hoy miramos con confianza,
   el porvenir.

LETRA: Federico J. Pagura, 1979, adap.

2. Porque atacó a ambiciosos mercaderes
y denunció maldad e hipocresía;
porque exaltó a los niños, las mujeres
y rechazó a los que de orgullo ardían;
porque El cargó la cruz de nuestras penas
y saboreó la hiel de nuestros males;
porque aceptó sufrir nuestra condena
y así morir por todos los mortales.
*(Coro)*

3. Porque una aurora vio su gran victoria
sobre la muerte, el miedo, las mentiras,
ya nada puede detener su historia
ni de su reino eterno la venida.
Porque ilumina cada senda en gloria
y las tinieblas derrotó con lumbre;
porque su luz es siempre nuestra historia
y ha de llevar a todos a la cumbre.
*(Coro)*

## 62. Jesús

1. En un pueblito lejano un niño alegre crecía,
junto a José y María, en la humildad de su hogar.
Nadie sabía que llegaría a ser del mundo el Salvador.
Cuando jugaba nadie pensaba que era el Mesías que Dios
envió.

2. Entre aserrín y maderas su adolescencia pasaba;
las manos se maltrataba al trabajar sin cesar.
Manos pequeñas, aún tan tiernas, ya conocían lo que es
luchar.
Nadie sabía que al fin un día en una cruz le iban a clavar.

3. Pequeño niño de aldea, que en humildad te formaste;
el mundo no supo darte un lugar donde nacer.
Yo no sabía que por mi culpa viniste al mundo para sufrir.
Tanto en la tierra como en el cielo quiero cantar de tu amor
por mí.

LETRA: Noris Sambrano, © 1987

## 63. Cuando al Jordán fue Cristo

1. Cuando al Jordán fue Cristo y Juan le bautizo,
no fué perdón pidiendo, pues El jamás pecó.
Con los arrepentidos se identificó
y trajo buenas nuevas, el reino se inició.

2. El vino a ser tentado, que es nuestra condición;
sobre una cruz clavado, nos trajo salvación.
Y cuando la paloma del cielo descendió,
ocultos años cesan, la gracia comenzó.

3. Los votos que te hacemos, permítenos cumplir.
Los yugos que tenemos, ven tú a destruir.
¡Desciende y danos vida, que nuestro anhelo es,
tras la Resurrección gozar Pentecostés!

LETRA: Fred Pratt Green, 1973; trad. de Alberto Merubia


# Cuaresma

## 64. Salmo 51

1. Ten piedad de mí, oh Dios, conforme a tu bondad,
tu misericordia borre mi maldad.
Lávame del mal y límpiame de iniquidad;
contra ti no quiero pecar.

*Coro*
Vuélveme, Señor, a gozarme en ti,
a sentir la paz de tu perdón;
me sustente la nobleza de tu amor.

2. Reconozco que yo fui rebelde sin razón,
mis pecados pongo delante de ti.
Contra ti pequé y sólo a ti yo defraudé;
a tus ojos culpable soy.
*(Coro)*

3. Lávame, Señor y hazme más puro* que una flor,
crea un nuevo corazón dentro de mí.
Cantará mi lengua tu justicia y tu perdón;
alabanza te ofreceré.
*(Coro)*

* *pura*

LETRA: Rafael D. Grullón, 1970

## 65. Mantos y palmas

1. Mantos y palmas esparciendo va
el pueblo alegre de Jerusalén.
y a lo lejos se vislumbra ya
en un pollino al Señor Jesús

*Coro*
Mientras mil voces resuenan por doquier,
hosanna al que viene en el nombre del Señor.
Con un aliento de gran exclamación
prorrumpen con voz triunfal:
«¡Hosanna! ¡Hosanna al Rey!
¡Hosanna! ¡Hosanna al Rey!»

2. Como en la entrada de Jerusalén,
todos cantamos a Jesús el Rey,
al Cristo vivo que nos llama hoy
para seguirle con amor y fe.
*(Coro)*

LETRA: Rubén Ruiz Avila, 1972 (basada en Mt. 21:8-9; Mc. 11:8-10; Lc. 19:36-38; Jn. 12:12-13)


## 66. ¿Presenciaste la muerte del Señor?

1. ¿Presenciaste la muerte del Señor?
¿Presenciaste la muerte del Señor?
Oh, al recordarlo a veces tiemblo, tiemblo, tiemblo.
¿Presenciaste la muerte del Señor?

2. ¿Viste cuando clavàronle en la cruz?
¿Viste cuando clavàronle en la cruz?
Oh, al recordarlo a veces tiemblo, tiemblo, tiemblo.
¿Viste cuando clavàronle en la cruz?

3. ¿Viste tú cuando el sol se oscureció?
¿Viste tú cuando el sol se oscureció?
Oh, al recordarlo a veces tiemblo, tiemblo, tiemblo.
¿Viste tú cuando el sol se oscureció?

4. ¿Viste cuando su espíritu entregó?
¿Viste cuando su espíritu entregó?
Oh, al recordarlo a veces tiemblo, tiemblo, tiemblo.
¿Viste cuando su espíritu entregó?

LETRA: Espiritual afro-americana; trad. de Federico J. Pagura, estrs. 1-3, 5; Lois C. Kroehler, estr. 4

5. ¿Viste cuando la tumba le encerró?
¿Viste cuando la tumba le encerró?
Oh, al recordarlo a veces tiemblo, tiemblo, tiemblo.
¿Viste cuando la tumba le encerró?

## 67. La cruz excelsa al contemplar

1. La cruz excelsa al contemplar,
do Cristo allí por mí murió,
nada se puede comparar
a las riquezas de su amor.

2. Ved en su rostro, manos, pies,
las marcas vivas del dolor;
es imposible comprender
tal sufrimiento y tanto amor.

3. El mundo entero no será
dádiva digna de ofrecer;
amor tan grande y sin igual,
en cambio exige todo el ser.

LETRA: Isaac Watts, 1707 (Gl. 6:14); trad. de *El Abogado Cristiano Ilustrado*

## 68. En el monte Calvario

1. En el monte Calvario estaba una cruz,
emblema de afrenta y dolor;
y yo amo esa cruz do murió mi Jesús,
por salvar al más vil pecador.

*Coro*
¡Oh yo siempre amaré esa cruz,
en sus triunfos mi gloria será;
y algún día, en vez de una cruz,
mi corona Jesús me dará!

2. Aunque el mundo desprecie la cruz de Jesús,
para mí tiene suma atracción;
pues en ella llevó el Cordero de Dios
de mi alma la condenación.
*(Coro)*

LETRA: George Bennard, 1913; trad. de S. D. Athans

3. En la cruz de Jesús, do su sangre vertió,
hermosura contemplo sin par;
pues en ella triunfante a la muerte venció
y mi ser puede santificar.
*(Coro)*

4. Yo seré siempre fiel a la cruz de Jesús,
sus desprecios con El llevaré;
y algún día feliz con los santos en luz,
para siempre su gloria veré.
*(Coro)*

## 69. Cristo por nosotros

1. Cristo por nosotros, 2. Cristo por nosotros,

3. Cristo se humilló; 4. y se hizo obediente

5. incluso a la muerte 6. y muerte de cruz.

7. Y Dios le exaltó 8. y le dio un gran nombre

9. sobre todo nombre, 10. sobre todo nombre.

LETRA: William Loperena, basada en Filipenses 2:8-9


## 70. La semilla

1. La semilla en tierra descansando está,
pero tiene vida y despertará.
Tu Palabra es vida, ¡oh Señor!
que renueva al mundo por tu gran amor.

2. Fuiste tú colgado en la cruenta cruz,
puesto en un sepulcro, lejos de la luz.
Solo descansas en la oscuridad,
pronto viene el día y la claridad.

3. Como la semilla, te levantarás;
a la vida plena pronto volverás.
¡Día glorioso de esplendente luz
brilla ya, venciendo la tumba y la cruz!

LETRA: J. M. C. Crum, 1928; trad. de Samuel Acedo, alt.

4. La semilla espera lluvia y calor;
mi alma así espera del Señor su amor,
dándome fuerza, alegría y paz,
viviendo triunfante delante de su faz.

# Resurrección/Exaltación

## 71. La tumba le encerró

1. La tumba le encerró, Cristo, mi Cristo;
El alba allí esperó Cristo el Señor.

*Coro*
Cristo la tumba venció y con gran poder resucitó;
de sepulcro y muerte Cristo es vencedor;
vive para siempre nuestro Salvador.
¡Gloria a Dios! ¡Gloria a Dios! El Señor resucitó.

2. De guardas escapó Cristo, mi Cristo;
el sello destruyó Cristo el Señor.
*(Coro)*

3. La muerte dominó Cristo, mi Cristo;
y su poder venció Cristo el Señor.
*(Coro)*

LETRA: Robert Lowry, 1874; trad. de George P. Simmonds


## 72. Al Cristo vivo sirvo

1. Al Cristo vivo sirvo, El en el mundo está;
aunque otros lo negaren, yo sé que El vive ya.
Su mano tierna veo, su voz consuelo da
y cuando yo le llamo, muy cerca está.

*Coro*
El vive, El vive, hoy vive el Salvador;
conmigo está y me guardará mi amante Redentor.
El vive, El vive, me imparte salvación.
Sé que viviendo está porque vive en mi corazón.

LETRA: Alfred H. Ackley, 1933; trad. de George P. Simmonds

2. En todo el mundo entero contemplo yo su amor;
y al sentirme triste consuélame el Señor.
Seguro estoy que Cristo mi vida guiará
y que otra vez al mundo regresará.
*(Coro)*

3. Gozaos, oh cristianos, hoy himnos entonad;
eternas aleluyas a Cristo el Rey cantad.
Ayuda y esperanza es del mundo pecador,
no hay otro tan amante como el Señor.
*(Coro)*

## 73. Hoy celebramos con gozo

1. Hoy celebramos con gozo al Dios todopoderoso,
al creador de la tierra y dador de todo bien;
al que vino hasta nosotros y murió en una cruz,
que ha vencido a las tinieblas y a la muerte destruyó.

*Coro*
¡Cristo vive!
Celebremos y esperemos su gran don;
Santo Espíritu divino, ven a nuestro corazón.

2. Celebremos jubilosos
al Dios de la salvación
que nos da esperanza y vida
y se goza en el perdón.
Con panderos y con palmas
entonemos la canción,
celebrando al Dios viviente,
dance nuestro corazón.
*(Coro)*

3. Acudamos hoy, hermanos,
a esta fiesta del amor;
hemos sido convocados
por el Padre Celestial.
Celebremos hoy unidos
este día del Señor,
estrechándonos las manos,
somos el pueblo de Dios.
*(Coro)*

*(Coro alterno al final de la última estrofa)*
*Alabanzas den al Padre*
*y a su Hijo Redentor;*
*a su Espíritu alabemos*
*quien nos une en su amor.*

LETRA: Mortimer Arias, 1971

## 74. Camina, pueblo de Dios (Nueva creación)

*Coro*
Camina, pueblo de Dios, camina, pueblo de Dios.
Nueva ley, nueva alianza en la nueva creación.
Camina, pueblo de Dios, camina, pueblo de Dios.

1. Mira allá en el calvario, en la roca hay una cruz;
muerte que engendra la vida, esperanza, nueva luz.
Cristo nos ha salvado con su muerte y resurrección.
Todas las cosas renacen en la nueva creación.
*(Coro)*

2. Cristo toma en su cuerpo el pecado, la esclavitud.
Al destruirlos, nos trae una nueva plenitud.
Pone en paz a los pueblos, a las cosas y al Creador.
Todo renace a la vida en la nueva creación.
*(Coro)*

3. Cielo y tierra se abrazan, nuestra alma halla el perdón.
Vuelven a abrirse los cielos para el mundo pecador.
Israel peregrino, vive y canta tu redención.
Hay nuevos mundos abiertos en la nueva creación.
*(Coro)*

LETRA: Cesareo Gabaráin, 1979


## 75. Cristo ya resucitó, ¡Aleluya!

1. Cristo ya resucitó, ¡Aleluya!
y la muerte El venció, ¡Aleluya!
Su poder y su virtud ¡Aleluya!
cautivó la esclavitud. ¡Aleluya!

2. El que al polvo se humilló, ¡Aleluya!
vencedor se levantó; ¡Aleluya!
Y cantamos en verdad ¡Aleluya!
su gloriosa majestad. ¡Aleluya!

LETRA: Michael Weisse, estrs. 1-3, siglo XVI; Charles Wesley, estr. 4, 1745;
trad. de Juan Bautista Cabrera

3. El que a muerte se entregó, ¡Aleluya!
El que así nos redimió, ¡Aleluya!
hoy en gloria celestial ¡Aleluya!
reina en vida triunfal. ¡Aleluya!

4. Cristo nuestro Salvador ¡Aleluya!
de la muerte vencedor. ¡Aleluya!
Pronto vamos sin cesar ¡Aleluya!
tus loores a cantar. ¡Aleluya!

## 76. ¡Vive el Señor!

1. Dios nos envió su Hijo Cristo,
vino a salvar, sanar y amar.
Vivió y murió por rescatarnos;
vacía está la tumba. ¡Vive el Señor!

*Coro*
¡Vive el Señor! Triunfaré mañana.
¡Vive el Señor! Ya no hay temor.
Porque yo sé que el futuro es suyo,
digno es vivir la vida. ¡Vive el Señor!

2. Encantos mil da una criatura,
tomada en brazos al nacer;
aún mayor es la certeza
que triunfará mañana, pues ¡Vive el Señor!
*(Coro)*

3. Y cruzaré un día el río,
hasta el final batallaré;
y tras la muerte, la victoria:
veré su luz de gloria. ¡Vive el Señor!
*(Coro)*

LETRA: Gloria y William J. Gaither, 1971; trad. de Pedro P. Pirón

## 77. A Cristo coronad

1. A Cristo coronad divino Salvador,
sentado en alta majestad, es digno de loor;
al Rey de gloria y paz loores tributad,
y bendecid al Inmortal por la eternidad.

2. A Cristo coronad Señor de nuestro amor,
al Rey triunfante celebrad, glorioso Vencedor.
Potente Rey de paz el triunfo consumó
y por su muerte de dolor, su gran amor mostró.

3. A Cristo coronad Señor de vida y luz;
con alabanzas proclamad los triunfos de Jesús.
A El sólo adorad, Señor de salvación;
loor eterno tributad de todo corazón.

LETRA: Matthew Bridges, estrs. 1-2, 1851; Godfrey Thring, estr. 3, 1874; trad. de E. A. Strange, alt.

# Pentecostés

## 78. En un aposento alto

1. En un aposento alto, con unánime fervor,
ciento veinte esperaban la promesa del Señor.
Con estruendo de los cielos descendió la gran virtud;
todos fueron inspirados por el fiel Consolador.

2. Este gran poder antiguo es del fiel celeste don;
prometido a los creyentes de humilde corazón.
Dios está restituyendo este gran Pentecostés
y el Espíritu sus dones nos reparte otra vez.

*Coda*
En un aposento alto, con unánime fervor,
ciento veinte esperaban la promesa del Señor.

LETRA: H. W. Cragin, 1895

## 79. Santo Espíritu, excelsa paloma (Holy Spirit, from Heaven Descended)

1. Santo Espíritu, excelsa paloma,
inmutable ser del Trino Dios;
mensajero de paz, que procedes del Padre,
hoy consuélanos con suave voz.
Tu fragancia y llenura anhelamos;
embalsama tu templo, tu altar;
y la sombra feliz
de tus alas de gracia nos cobije,
¡oh amigo sin par!

2. Santo Espíritu, fuego celeste,
en el día de Pentecostés,
cual la nube de gloria, bajaste a la iglesia
como al templo de Sión otra vez.
Para el nuevo cristiano eres sello;
cada uno de ti tiene un don.
Todo* hijo* de Dios
elegido es y goza ya las arras
de tu salvación.

3. Santo Espíritu, aceite bendito,
cual producto del verde olivar;
luminaria y calor en la tienda sagrada
donde Aarón se acercaba a adorar.
Agua viva y regeneradora,
santifícanos contra el mal;
somos uno en Jesús,
los creyentes del mundo, por tu santa
labor bautismal.

4. Santo Espíritu, viento potente,
fuente y fuerza de paz y de amor;
paracleto veraz que consuelo nos brindas
y abogas a nuestro favor.
Sénos luz que ilumine la Biblia,
nuestros pies dirigiendo al andar.
Hoy rendimos a ti
nuestras almas ansiosas; sólo ungidos
podremos triunfar.
**toda *hija*

LETRA: Felipe Blycker J., 1977; trad. inglés Felipe Blycker J.

1. Holy Spirit, from heaven descended,
in the form of a dove you were seen;
with a message of love from the Father above
giving comfort to all who believe.
How we long for your fragrance to fill us;
we confess our deep need for your grace;
shelter us with your wings, tune our heart as it sings,
lift our eyes to behold Jesus' face.

2. Holy Spirit, with flame you anointed
the believers on that Pentecost,
bringing heavenly light and imparting great might
to believers as sign to the lost.
As the tower of fire was for Israel,
fill our lives now with light from on high;
you have sealed everyone who is bought by the Son.
May our works his great name glorify.

3. Holy Spirit, flow freely among us,
sacred oil giving sight where sin blinds;
just as Aaron of old lit the lamps in the cold,
warm our hearts and illumine our minds.
You have baptized us into one body;
Living Water, now cleanse and renew.
Sanctify us we pray, that God's Word we obey,
and to Christ may we ever be true.

4. Holy Spirit of God, breathe upon us;
fill our hearts with your love, joy, and peace;
Paraclete, you are nigh, interceding on high,
grant that our meager faith would increase.
Be our lamp to interpret the Scriptures,
be our guide to instruct in the way.
We surrender our will as our cup you refill
to victoriously live every day.

## 80. Espíritu de Dios

1. Espíritu de Dios, llena mi vida,
Espíritu de Dios, llena mi ser.
Espíritu de Dios, nunca me dejes,
yo quiero más y más de tu poder.

2. Espíritu de Dios, que bautizaste
a Pedro, a María, Andrés y Juan,
derrama tu poder como aquel día,
bautiza con tu fuego celestial.

3. Espíritu de Dios, que descendiste
allá en Jerusalén, ven otra vez.
Tu fuego alentador sature mi alma,
en mí, quiero sentir Pentecostés.

LETRA: Francisco A. Feliciano, 1985


# Reinado

## 81. Eres digno

Eres digno, eres digno, eres digno de adoración.
Eres digno, eres digno, eres digno de adoración.
Rey glorioso, majestuoso, eres digno de adoración.
Rey glorioso, majestuoso, eres digno de adoración.

LETRA: Legado oral de la iglesia latinoamericana

## 82. ¡Majestad!

¡Majestad! ¡Gloria a Su Majestad!
Dad a Cristo toda gloria, honra y loor.
¡Majestad! Autoridad real
sale de El, con gran poder.
¡Viva el gran Rey!
Alabad, glorificad su santo nombre;
exaltad, magnificad a aquél que es Señor.
¡Majestad! ¡Gloria a Su Majestad!
El que murió, resucitó, hoy es el Rey.

LETRA: Jack Hayford, 1981; trad. de J. Alfonso Lockward

## 83. El es Rey

El es Rey, es Señor.
Cristo ya resucitó y es Señor.
De rodillas todos hoy confesemos:
¡El es el Señor!

LETRA: Basada en Filipenses 2:9-11; trad. de Felicia Fina


## 84. Ved al Cristo, Rey de gloria

1. Ved al Cristo, Rey de gloria, es del mundo el vencedor;
de la muerte surge invicto, todos démosle loor.

*Coro*
Coronadle, santos todos,
coronadle Rey de reyes.
Coronadle, santos todos,
coronad al Salvador.

2. Exaltadle, exaltadle, ricos triunfos trae Jesús;
en los cielos coronadle, en la refulgente luz.
*(Coro)*

3. Pecadores se burlaron, coronando al Salvador,
hoy los ángeles y santos lo proclaman su Señor.
*(Coro)*

4. Escuchad las alabanzas que se elevan hacia El.
Victorioso reina Cristo, adorad a Emanuel.
*(Coro)*

LETRA: Thomas Kelley, 1806; trad. anónimo

## 85. Alabad al gran Rey

1. Solemnes resuenen las voces de amor,
con gran regocijo tributen loor
al Rey soberano, el buen Salvador;
dignísimo es El del más alto honor.

*Coro*
Alabad, alabad, alabad al gran Rey.
Adorad, adorad, adoradle su grey.
Es nuestro escudo, baluarte y sostén
el Omnipotente, por siglos. Amén.

2. Su amor infinito, ¿qué lengua dirá?
y ¿quién sus bondades jamás sondeará?
Su misericordia no puede faltar,
mil himnos alaben su nombre sin par.
*(Coro)*

3. Inmensa la obra de Cristo en la cruz,
enorme la culpa se ve por su luz.
Al mundo El vino, nos iluminó
y por nuestras culpas el Justo murió.
*(Coro)*

4. Velad, fieles todos, velad con fervor,
que viene muy pronto Jesús, el Señor.
Con notas alegres vendrá a reinar;
a su eterna gloria os ha de llevar.
*(Coro)*

LETRA: Fanny J. Crosby, 1875; trad. de Roberto C. Savage, alt.

# ESPÍRITU SANTO CONSOLADOR

## 86. Dios nos ha dado promesa

1. Dios nos ha dado promesa:
lluvias de gracia enviaré,
dones que os den fortaleza;
gran bendición os daré.

*Coro*
Lluvias de gracia,
lluvias pedimos, Señor.
Mándanos lluvias copiosas,
lluvias del Consolador.

2. Cristo nos dió la promesa
del Santo Consolador,
dándonos paz y pureza
para su gloria y honor.
*(Coro)*

3. Muestra, oh Dios, al creyente
todo tu amor y poder,
eres de gracia la fuente,
llena de paz nuestro ser.
*(Coro)*

4. Obra en tus siervos piadosos
celo, virtud y valor,
dándonos dones preciosos,
dones del Consolador.
*(Coro)*

LETRA: Daniel W. Whittle, 1883; trad. anónimo, alt.

## 87. Santo Espíritu, desciende

1. Santo Espíritu, desciende
a mi pobre corazón;
llénalo de tu presencia,
haz en mí tu habitación.

*Coro*
¡Llena hoy, llena hoy,
llena hoy mi corazón!
¡Santo Espíritu, desciende
y haz en mí tu habitación!

2. De tu gracia puedes darme,
inundando el corazón;
ven, que mucho necesito,
dame hoy tu bendición.
*(Coro)*

3. Débil soy, oh sí, muy débil,
y a tus pies postrado estoy,
esperando que tu gracia
con poder me llene hoy.
*(Coro)*

4. Dame paz, consuelo y gozo,
cúbreme en tu perdón;
tú confortas y redimes,
tú me das la salvación.
*(Coro)*

LETRA: E. H. Stokes, 1879; trad. de Vicente Mendoza

## 88. Envía, Señor, tu Espíritu

*Coro*
Envía, Señor, tu Espíritu,
que renueve nuestros corazones.

1. Envíanos, Señor, tu luz y tu calor;
alumbre nuestros pasos, encienda nuestro amor.
Envíanos tu Espíritu y un rayo de tu luz
encienda nuestras vidas en llamas de virtud.
*(Coro)*

LETRA: Joaquín Madurga, 1979

2. Envíanos, Señor, tu fuerza y tu valor;
que libre nuestros miedos, que anime nuestro ardor.
Envíanos tu Espíritu, impulso creador,
infunda en nuestras vidas la fuerza de tu amor.
*(Coro)*

3. Envíanos, Señor, la luz de tu verdad;
alumbre tantas sombras de nuestro caminar.
Envíanos tu Espíritu, su don renovador
transforme nuevas vidas y nuestro corazón.
*(Coro)*

## 89. Satúrame, Señor

1. Satúrame,* Señor, con tu Espíritu;
satúrame, Señor, con tu Espíritu,
y déjame* sentir el fuego de tu amor
aquí en mi corazón,** oh Dios.
y déjame* sentir el fuego de tu amor
aquí en mi corazón,** oh Dios.

2. Bendíceme,* Señor, con tu Espíritu;
bendíceme, Señor, con tu Espíritu,
y déjame sentir el gozo de tu amor
momento tras momento, oh Dios.
y déjame sentir el gozo de tu amor
momento tras momento, oh Dios.

3. Envíame,* Señor, con tu Espíritu;
envíame, Señor, con tu Espíritu,
y déjame sentir tu corazón de amor
y al mundo proclamarlo, oh Dios.
y déjame sentir tu corazón de amor
y al mundo proclamarlo, oh Dios.

* *satúranos, déjanos, bendícenos, envíanos*
** *en nuestro corazón*

LETRA: Autor desconocido, estr. 1; Comité de *Celebremos*, estrs. 2-3, 1991

## 90. Abre mis ojos a la luz

1. Abre mis ojos a la luz,
tu rostro quiero ver, Jesús;
pon en mi corazón tu bondad
y dame paz y santidad.
Humildemente acudo a ti,
porque tu tierna voz oí;
mi guía sé, Espíritu Consolador.

2. Abre mi oído a tu verdad,
yo quiero oír con claridad
bellas palabras de dulce amor,
¡oh, mi bendito Salvador!
Consagro a ti mi frágil ser,
tu voluntad yo quiero hacer,
llena mi ser, Espíritu Consolador.

3. Abre mis labios para hablar
y a todo el mundo proclamar
que tú viniste a rescatar
al más perdido pecador.
La mies es mucha, ¡oh Señor!
obreros faltan, de valor;
heme aquí, Espíritu Consolador.

4. Abre mi mente para ver
más de tu amor y gran poder;
dame tu gracia para triunfar,
hazme en la lucha vencedor.
Sé tú mi escondedero fiel,
aumenta mi valor y fe;
mi mano ten, Espíritu Consolador.

5. Abre las puertas que al entrar
en el palacio celestial,
pueda tu dulce faz contemplar
por toda la eternidad.
Y cuando en tu presencia esté,
tu santo nombre alabaré;
mora en mí, Espíritu Consolador.

LETRA: Clara H. Scott, 1895; trad. de S. D. Athans

## 91. Dulce espíritu

Hay un dulce espíritu aquí
y yo sé que es el Espíritu del Señor.
La expresión en los rostros es señal,
pues se siente la presencia del Señor.

*Coro*
Tierna paloma, fiel Consolador,
mora en nosotros, llénanos de tu amor.
Por tus bondades te hemos de alabar;
sabremos, sin dudar, que aquí en este lugar
nos renovó el Señor.

LETRA: Doris Akers, 1962; trad. de Pedro P. Pirón

# EXPERIENCIA CON CRISTO

## Invitación

### 92. A Jesucristo ven sin tardar

1. A Jesucristo ven sin tardar,
que entre nosotros hoy El está
y te convida con dulce afán,
tierno diciendo: «Ven».

*Coro*
¡Oh, cuán grata nuestra reunión,
cuando allá, Señor, en tu mansión,
contigo estemos en comunión,
gozando eterno bien!

2. Piensa que El sólo puede colmar
tu triste pecho, de gozo y paz;
y porque anhela tu bienestar,
vuelve a decirte: «Ven».
*(Coro)*

3. Su voz atiende sin vacilar,
con gozo acepta lo que hoy te da;
tal vez mañana tarde será,
no te detengas: «Ven».
*(Coro)*

LETRA: George Frederick Root, siglo XIX; trad. de Juan Bautista Cabrera

### 93. Con voz benigna

1. Con voz benigna te llama Jesús,
invitación de puro amor.
¿Por qué le dejas en vano llamar?
¿No escucharás, pecador?

*Coro*
Hoy te convida; hoy te convida,
voz bendecida, benigna convídate hoy.

2. A los cansados convida Jesús,
con compasión mira el dolor;
tráele tu carga, te bendecirá,
te ayudará el Señor.
*(Coro)*

LETRA: Fanny J. Crosby, 1883; trad. de T. M. Westrup

3. Siempre aguardando contempla a Jesús,
¡tanto esperar, con tanto amor!
Hasta sus plantas ven, mísero y trae,
tu tentación, tu dolor.
*(Coro)*

## 94. Cristo es la peña de Horeb (Christ Is the Mountain of Horeb)

1. Cristo es la peña de Horeb, que está brotando
agua de vida saludable para ti.
Cristo es la peña de Horeb, que está brotando
agua de vida saludable para ti.
Ven a tomarla que es más dulce que la miel;
refresca el alma, refresca todo tu ser.
Cristo es la peña de Horeb, que está brotando
agua de vida saludable para ti.

2. Cristo es el lirio del valle de las flores,
El es la rosa hermosa y pura de Sarón.
Cristo es la vida y amor de los amores,
El es la eterna fuente de la salvación.
Ven a buscarla en tu triste condición;
refresca el alma, refresca todo tu ser.
Cristo es el lirio del valle de las flores,
El es la rosa hermosa y pura de Sarón.

1. Christ is the Mountain of Horeb overflowing,
the source of water giving everlasting life.
Christ is the Mountain of Horeb overflowing,
the source of water giving everlasting life.
Come now and taste this fountain flowing ever sweet,
refresh your spirit, refresh your body and soul.
Christ is the Mountain of Horeb overflowing,
the source of water giving everlasting life.

2. Christ is the flower of the Lily of the Valley,
He is the Rose of Sharon, beautiful and pure.
Christ is the life and the love of truest loving,
He is the source of our salvation evermore.
Come now and find the cure for all your grief and pain,
Refresh your spirit, refresh your body and soul.
Christ is the flower of the Lily of the Valley,
He is the Rose of Sharon, beautiful and pure.

LETRA: Autor desconocido, alt.; trad. inglés de Alice Parker

## 95. Oh, deja que el Señor

1. Oh, deja que el Señor te envuelva
con su Espíritu de amor,
satisfaga hoy tu alma y corazón.
Entrégale lo que te impide
y su Espíritu vendrá sobre ti
y vida nueva te dará.

*Coro*
Cristo, oh Cristo,
ven y llénanos;
Cristo, oh Cristo,
llénanos de ti.

2. Alzamos nuestra voz con gozo,
alabando al Señor,
con dulzura le entregamos nuestro ser.
Entrega toda tu tristeza
en el nombre de Jesús
y abundante vida hoy tendrás en El.
*(Coro)*

LETRA: John Wimber, 1979; trad. desconocido


## 96. ¿Quieres ser salvo?

1. ¿Quieres ser salvo de toda maldad?
Tan sólo hay poder en mi Jesús.
¿Quieres vivir y gozar santidad?
Tan sólo hay poder en Jesús.

*Coro*
Hay poder, poder, sin igual poder
en Jesús quien murió.
hay poder, poder, sin igual poder
en la sangre que El vertió.

2. ¿Quieres ser libre de orgullo y pasión?
Tan sólo hay poder en mi Jesús.
¿Quieres vencer toda cruel tentación?
Tan sólo hay poder en Jesús.
*(Coro)*

3. ¿Quieres servir a tu Rey y Señor?
Tan sólo hay poder en mi Jesús.
Ven y ser salvo podrás en su amor.
Tan sólo hay poder en Jesús.
*(Coro)*

LETRA: Lewis E. Jones, 1899; trad. de D. A. Mata

## 97. Cuán tiernamente Jesús hoy nos llama

1. Cuán tiernamente Jesús hoy nos llama
con insistente bondad;
toca a las puertas del alma y espera
con amorosa ansiedad.

*Coro*
«Venid a mí, venid
los que cansados estéis».
Cuán tiernamente Jesús hoy nos llama.
¡Oh pecadores, venid!

2. ¿Cómo podemos oír que nos llama
y no atender a su voz?
¿Cómo escuchar que nos llama a seguirle
y nunca de El ir en pos?
*(Coro)*

3. Con fiel paciencia, su amor admirable
El sin medida nos da.
A todo pueblo y a toda persona
siempre llamando El está.
*(Coro)*

LETRA: Will L. Thompson, 1880; trad. de Vicente Mendoza

## 98. Tú has venido a la orilla (Pescador de hombres) (Lord, You Have Come to the Lakeshore)

1. Tú has venido a la orilla,
no has buscado ni a sabios ni a ricos,
tan sólo quieres que yo te siga.

*Coro*
Señor, me has mirado a los ojos
y sonriendo has dicho mi nombre;
en la arena he dejado mi barca;
junto a ti buscaré otro mar.

2. Tú sabes bien lo que tengo:
en mi barca no hay oro ni espadas,
tan sólo redes y mi trabajo.
*(Coro)*

LETRA: Cesáreo Gabaráin, 1979; trad. de Gertrude C. Suppe, George Lockwood, y Raquel Gutiérrez-Achón

3. Tú necesitas mis manos,
mi cansancio que a otros descanse,
amor que quiera seguir amando.
*(Coro)*

4. Tú, pescador de otros mares,
ansia eterna de almas que esperan,
amigo bueno, que así me llamas.
*(Coro)*

1. Lord, you have come to the lakeshore
looking neither for wealthy nor wise ones;
you only asked me to follow humbly.

*Refrain*
O Lord, with your eyes you have searched me,
and while smiling have spoken my name;
now my boat's left on the shoreline behind me;
by your side I will seek other seas.

2. You know so well my possessions;
my boat carries no gold and no weapons;
you will find there my nets and labor.
*(Refrain)*

3. You need my hands, full of caring
through my labors to give others rest,
and constant love that keeps on loving.
*(Refrain)*

4. You, who have fished other oceans,
ever longed for by souls who are waiting,
my loving friend, as thus you call me.
*(Refrain)*

# Arrepentimiento, Confesión, y Perdón

## 99. Tal como soy

1. Tal como soy de pecador,
sin más confianza que tu amor;
ya que me llamas, acudí.
Cordero de Dios, heme aquí.

2. Tal como soy, sin esperar
quitar la mancha del pecar.
Oh, pon tu sangre sobre mí.
Cordero de Dios, heme aquí.

3. Tal como soy, con mi aflicción,
mis dudas y mi tentación,
con los conflictos que hay en mí.
Cordero de Dios, heme aquí.

4. Tal como soy, sin paz, sin luz,
confiando sólo en tu virtud;
tu gracia quiero recibir.
Cordero de Dios, heme aquí.

5. Tal como soy, me recibirás;
perdón, consuelo, me darás,
pues tu promesa ya creí.
Cordero de Dios, heme aquí.

6. Tal como soy, tu inmenso amor
aleja todo mi temor.
Mi vida entera ofrezco a ti.
Cordero de Dios, heme aquí.

LETRA: Charlotte Elliott, 1834; trad. de J. Alfonso Lockward, estrs. 2-6; T.M. Westrup, estr. 1

## 100. Señor, apiádate de nosotros (Kyrie Eleison)

Señor, apiádate de nosotros,
Cristo, apiádate de nosotros.
O Cristo, danos la vida eterna.
Señor, apiádate de nosotros.
Cristo, apiádate de nosotros.

O Lord, have mercy upon your people,
O Christ, have mercy upon your people,
O Master, give us your life forever.
O Lord, have mercy upon your people,
O Christ, have mercy upon your people.

LETRA: Salmo 123:3

## 101. Compadécete de tu pueblo

Compadécete de nosotros, oh Señor.
Compadécete de nosotros, oh Señor.
Ten piedad de tu pueblo, Cristo, ten piedad.
Ten misericordia, ten piedad.
Compadécete de nosotros, oh Señor,
compadécete de nosotros, oh Señor.

LETRA: Clara Luz Ajo, 1983


# Fe y Justificación

## 102. Busca primero

1. Busca primero el reino de Dios
   y su perfecta justicia,
   que lo demás lo añadirá el Señor.
   Alelu, aleluya.

2. Sólo de pan, dice Dios, no vivirás,
   sino de toda palabra,
   que para ti el Señor pronunciará.
   Alelu, Aleluya.

LETRA: Karen Lafferty, estr. 1, 1972; estr. 2 anónimo; trad. desconocido

## 103. Herido, triste, fui a Jesús

1. Herido, triste, fui a Jesús,
mostréle mi dolor;
perdido, errante, vi su luz,
bendíjome en su amor.

*Coro*
En la cruz, en la cruz, do primero vi la luz
y las manchas de mi alma El lavó;
fue allí por fe do vi a Jesús
y siempre feliz con El seré.

2. Sobre una cruz, mi buen Señor
su sangre derramó
por este pobre pecador,
a quien así salvó.
*(Coro)*

3. Venció la muerte con poder
y el Padre le exaltó.
Confiar en El es mi placer,
morir no temo yo.
*(Coro)*

4. Aunque El se fue, solo no estoy;
mandó al Consolador;
divino Espíritu que hoy
me da perfecto amor.
*(Coro)*

LETRA: Isaac Watts, 1707; trad. de Pedro Grado, alt.

## 104. Sublime gracia

1. Sublime gracia del Señor,
que a un pecador salvó;
fui ciego mas hoy veo yo,
perdido y El me halló.

2. Su gracia me enseñó a temer,
mis dudas ahuyentó;
¡oh, cuán precioso fue a mi ser,
al dar mi corazón!

LETRA: John Newton, estrs. 1-3, 6, 1779; trad. de Cristóbal E. Morales, alt.;
Carlos Pastor López, estrs. 4-5, 1996

3. En los peligros o aflicción
que he tenido aquí,
su gracia siempre me libró
y me guiará feliz.

4. Jesús ha prometido el bien;
en El puedo yo confiar;
habrá de ser mi escudo fiel,
en mi peregrinar.

5. Veré mi cuerpo perecer,
cesando lo mortal;
mas nueva vida gozaré,
de eterno gozo y paz.

6. Y cuando en Sión, por siglos mil,
brillando esté cual sol,
yo cantaré por siempre allí
su amor que me salvó.

## 105. Inmensa gracia

1. Fue su gracia que ayer en la cruz El selló,
fue mayor, plena y fiel para mí.
Esa gracia fue tal que en el tiempo viajó
y mi ser dulcemente alcanzó.

*Coro*
Grande fue su amor, indecible amor,
que Jesucristo, por gracia me dio.
¡Gloria a El!
Concebirlo yo no podré jamás;
¡inmensa gracia de mi Salvador!

2. El amor de Jesús no se puede medir;
es mayor, pleno y fiel para ti.
El Señor quiere hoy que le entregues tu ser;
gozarás privilegio sin par.
*(Coro)*

3. Esa gracia eternal eficaz es aún
para aquél que abatido esté;
redención sin igual libremente obtendrá,
salvación y perenne salud.
*(Coro)*

LETRA: Rafael D. Grullón, 1979

## 106. Nuevos comienzos trae el día

1. Nuevos comienzos trae el día,
hay que evocar y proseguir;
ver del amor la gran regalía,
nuestro dolor no más sentir.

2. Pues por la muerte en el madero
y por la vida de Jesús,
Dios nos renueva por entero
y nos transmite vida y luz.

3. Quedan atrás ya los problemas,
con su angustia y dolor;
el Santo Espíritu nos consuela,
dando esperanza, fe y amor.

4. Otro principio y otra vida
de una nueva creación;
nuevos comienzos trae este día;
todo hace nuevo nuestro Dios.

*5. Hoy nos sentamos a su mesa
a compartir en comunión;
nuevos comienzos trae este día;
todo hace nuevo nuestro Dios.
** Se podrá usar para la Santa Comunión.*

LETRA: Brian Wren, 1978, alt. 1987; trad. de Alberto Merubia y J. Alfonso Lockward


## 107. Me ha tocado

1. En pecado yo vivía, en tinieblas y en error;
mas la mano de Jesucristo me tocó y ya salvo soy.

*Coro*
Me ha tocado, sí, me ha tocado y ahora sé que el Salvador
sana, salva y viene por mí; me ha tocado Cristo el Señor.

LETRA: William J. Gaither, 1963; trad. desconocido

2. Desde que encontré al Maestro, desde que salvó mi ser,
nunca dejaré de adorarle hasta que regrese otra vez.
*(Coro)*

## 108. Cuán glorioso es el cambio

1. Cuán glorioso es el cambio operado en mi ser,
viniendo a mi vida el Señor;
hay en mi alma una paz que yo ansiaba tener,
la paz que me trajo su amor.

*Coro*
El vino a mi corazón,
El vino a mi corazón,
Soy feliz con la vida que Cristo me dio,
cuando El vino a mi corazón.

2. Ya no voy por la senda que el mal me trazó,
do sólo encontré confusión;
mis errores pasados Jesús los borró,
cuando El vino a mi corazón.
*(Coro)*

3. Ni una sombra de duda oscurece su amor,
amor que me trajo el perdón;
la esperanza que aliento la debo al Señor,
cuando El vino a mi corazón.
*(Coro)*

LETRA: Rufus H. McDaniel, 1914; trad. de Vicente Mendoza

# Consagración y Santificación

## 109. Haz lo que quieras

1. Haz lo que quieras de mí, Señor;
tú el alfarero, yo el barro soy.
Dócil y humilde anhelo ser,
cúmplase siempre en mí tu querer.

2. Haz lo que quieras de mí, Señor;
mírame y prueba mi corazón.
Lávame y quita toda maldad
para que pueda contigo estar.

3. Haz lo que quieras de mí, Señor;
cura mis llagas y mi dolor.
Tuyo es, oh Cristo, todo poder;
tu mano extiende y sanaré.

4. Haz lo que quieras de mí, Señor;
de tu presencia dame la unción.
Dueño absoluto sé de mi ser
y el mundo a Cristo pueda en mí ver.

LETRA: Adelaide A. Pollard, 1902; trad. de Ernesto Barocio

## 110. Gracias, Señor

1. Gracias, Señor, por lo que me das,
gracias por bendecirme.
Gracias por tu fidelidad
y por tu provisión.

2. Te doy de lo que tú me das,
con gozo en mi corazón.
Recibe hoy mi ofrenda,
te la entrego a ti.

LETRA: Rafael Montalvo, 1993

3. Te amo, Dios, doy gloria a ti,
tú eres digno de loor.
Te adoro con mi vida
y con lo que me das.

4. Todo te pertenece a ti,
mi vida y todo mi ser.
Con gratitud te damos,
de lo que tú nos das.

## 111. Tuya soy, Jesús

1. Tuya* soy, Jesús, escuché la voz
de tu amor hablándome aquí;
mas anhelo en alas de fe subir
y más cerca estar de ti.

*Coro*
Aún más cerca, cerca de tu cruz
llévame, ¡oh, Salvador!
Aún más cerca, cerca,
cerca de tu cruz
llévame, ¡oh buen Pastor!

2. A seguirte a ti me consagro hoy,
impulsada** por tu amor,
y mi espíritu, alma y cuerpo doy
por servirte, mi Señor.
*(Coro)*

3. Oh, cuán pura y santa delicia es
de tu comunión gozar
y contigo hablar y tu dulce voz
cada día escuchar.
*(Coro)*

4. De tu grande amor no comprenderé
cuál es la profundidad,
hasta que contigo, Jesús, esté
en gloriosa eternidad.
*(Coro)*
* *Tuyo*
** *impulsado*

LETRA: Fanny J. Crosby, 1875; trad. de H. O. Costales, alt.

## 112. Acepta hoy esta ofrenda

1. Qué bello este momento; agradecido* me siento,
porque tu amor cada día llena mi vida.
¡Qué privilegio es darte y de esa forma alabarte!
Todo es tuyo, Señor, y lo compartes conmigo.

*Coro*
De tu bondad recibimos y de lo mismo te damos.
Con gratitud y amor, te adoramos Señor.

2. Acepta hoy esta ofrenda; mucho de mí representa.
Es mi trabajo y mi tiempo lo que te ofrendo.
Te entonamos canciones por todas tus bendiciones.
Todo lo das por amor; ¡toma, Señor, nuestros dones!
*(Coro)*

* *agradecida*

LETRA: Noris Sambrano, 1985


## 113. Salvador, a ti me rindo

1. Salvador, a ti me rindo y obedezco sólo a ti;
mi guiador, mi fortaleza, todo encuentra mi alma en ti.

*Coro*
Yo me rindo a ti, yo me rindo a ti;
mis flaquezas y pecados, todo traigo a ti.

2. Te confiesa sus delitos mi contrito corazón;
oye, Cristo, mi plegaria, quiero en ti tener perdón.
*(Coro)*

LETRA: Judson W. Van DeVenter, 1896; trad. de A. R. Salas

3. A tus pies yo deposito mi riqueza, mi placer;
que tu Espíritu me llene y de ti sienta el poder.
*(Coro)*

4. Tu bondad será la historia que predique por doquier;
y tu amor inagotable será siempre mi querer.
*(Coro)*

5. ¡Oh, qué gozo encuentro en Cristo! ¡Cuánta paz a mi alma da!
Yo a su causa me consagro y su amor, mi amor será.
*(Coro)*

## 114. Mi ofrenda

1. Por tu bondad, mi buen Señor,
salud y bien hallé.

*Coro*
La ofrenda que hoy traigo a tu altar,
recíbela Señor.

2. Me diste paz y por tu amor,
me diste libertad.
*(Coro)*

LETRA: Luis Angel Toro, 1943


## 115. Que mi vida entera esté

1. Que mi vida entera esté consagrada a ti, Señor;
que a mis manos pueda guiar el impulso de tu amor.

*Coro*
Lávame en tu sangre, Salvador, límpiame de toda mi maldad.
Traigo a ti mi vida, para ser, Señor, tuya por la eternidad.

LETRA: Frances R. Havergal, 1874; coro de William J. Kirkpatrick, 1903;
trad. de Vicente Mendoza, alt.

2. Que mis pies tan sólo en pos de lo santo puedan ir,
y que a ti, Señor, mi voz se complazca en bendecir.
*(Coro)*

3. Que mis labios puedan d testimonio de tu amor,
y mis bienes ofrendar sepa siempre a ti, Señor.
*(Coro)*

4. Que mi tiempo todo esté dedicado a tu loor,
y mi mente y su poder se consagren a tu honor.
*(Coro)*

5. Toma, Dios, mi voluntad, y hazla tuya nada más;
toma, sí, mi corazón y tu trono en él tendrás.
*(Coro)*

## 116. Amarte sólo a ti, Señor

1. Amarte sólo a ti, Señor, amarte sólo a ti, Señor,
amarte sólo a ti, Señor, y no mirar atrás.
Seguir tu caminar, Señor, seguir sin desmayar, Señor,
seguir hasta el final, Señor, y no mirar atrás.
Seguir tu caminar, Señor, seguir sin desmayar, Señor,
seguir hasta el final, Señor, y no mirar atrás.

2. Confiar tan sólo en ti, Señor, confiar tan sólo en ti, Señor,
confiar tan sólo en ti, Señor, y no mirar atrás.
Seguir tu caminar, Señor, seguir sin desmayar, Señor,
seguir hasta el final, Señor, y no mirar atrás.
Seguir tu caminar, Señor, seguir sin desmayar, Señor,
seguir hasta el final, Señor, y no mirar atrás.

LETRA: Basada en Juan 14:21; autor desconocido

## 117. Hazme un instrumento de tu paz (Oración de San Francisco)

1. Hazme un instrumento de tu paz;
donde haya odio, ponga yo tu amor;
donde haya injuria, tu perdón, Señor;
donde haya duda fe segura en ti.

2. Hazme un instrumento de tu paz;
que lleve tu esperanza por doquier;
tu luz, doquiera haya oscuridad;
tu gozo, donde hay pena, oh Señor.

3. Maestro, enséñame a no buscar
querer ser consolado como consolar;
ser entendido como entender;
ser amado como amar.

4. Hazme un instrumento de tu paz.
Es perdonando que nos das perdón;
es cuando damos, que nos das, Señor;
muriendo es que volvemos a nacer.

LETRA: San Francisco de Asís, siglo XIII; trad. y adap. por Sebastian Temple, alt.


## 118. Dame un nuevo corazón

Dame un nuevo corazón, Señor;
un corazón para adorarte,
un corazón para alabarte.
Dame un nuevo corazón, Señor.

Dame un nuevo corazón, Señor;
un corazón para adorarte,
un corazón para alabarte.
Dame un nuevo corazón.

LETRA: Eleazar Inciarte, 1984

# Confianza y Seguridad

## 119. Jehová te guiará

Jehová te guiará por siempre, en las sequías saciará tu alma;
y dará vigor a tus huesos, Jehová te guiará por siempre.
Y serás como huerto de riego, como manantial de aguas
cuyas aguas nunca faltan. Jehová te guiará por siempre.

LETRA: Basada en Isaías 58:11, alt.

## 120. Me guía El

1. Me guía El, con cuánto amor
me guía siempre mi Señor;
al ver mi esfuerzo en serle fiel,
con cuánto amor me guía El.

*Coro*
Me guía El, me guía El,
con cuánto amor me guía El;
no abrigo dudas ni temor,
pues me conduce el buen Pastor.

2. En el abismo del dolor
o en donde brille el sol mejor;
en dulce paz o en lucha cruel,
con gran bondad me guía El.
*(Coro)*

3. Tu mano quiero yo tomar
ya que me das seguridad,
pues sólo a quien te sigue fiel,
se oyó decir: «Me guía El».
*(Coro)*

4. Y mi carrera al terminar
y así mi triunfo realizar,
no habrá ni dudas ni temor,
pues me guiará mi buen Pastor.
*(Coro)*

LETRA: Joseph H. Gilmore, 1862 (Sal. 23); trad. de Epigmenio Velasco, alt.

## 121. Oyenos, oh Dios

Oyenos, oh Dios,
óyenos, oh Dios.
Atiende a nuestra voz
y danos tu paz.

LETRA: Basada en Salmo 143:1, por George Whelpton, 1897; trad. George P. Simmonds


## 122. Oh Dios, sé mi visión

1. Oh Dios de mi alma, sé tú mi visión,
nada te aparte de mi corazón.
Día y noche pienso en ti
y tu presencia es luz para mí.

2. Sabiduría sé tú de mi ser,
quiero a tu lado mi senda correr.
Como tu hijo* tenme Señor,
siempre morando en un mismo amor.

3. Sé mi escudo, mi espada en la lid,
mi única gloria, mi dicha sin fin;
del alma amparo, mi torreón;
a las alturas condúceme, Dios.

4. Riquezas vanas no anhelo, Señor,
ni el hueco halago de la adulación;
tú eres mi herencia, tú mi porción,
Rey de los cielos, tesoro mejor.

5. Oh Rey de gloria, del triunfo al final,
déjame el gozo del cielo alcanzar;
alma de mi alma, dueño y Señor,
en vida o muerte sé tú mi visión.

* *hija*

LETRA: Antiguo de Irlanda; trad. inglés de Mary E. Byrne;
trad. español de Federico J. Pagura

## 123. ¿Cómo podré estar triste?

1. ¿Cómo podré estar triste, cómo entre sombras ir,
cómo sentirme solo y en el dolor vivir?
Si Cristo es mi consuelo, mi amigo siempre fiel,
si aun las aves tienen seguro asilo en El,
si aun las aves tienen seguro asilo en El.

*Coro*
¡Feliz cantando alegre, yo vivo siempre aquí;
si El cuida de las aves, cuidará también de mí!

2. «Nunca te desalientes», oigo al Señor decir
y en su palabra fiado, hago al dolor huir.
A Cristo, paso a paso, yo sigo sin cesar
y todas sus bondades me da sin limitar,
y todas sus bondades me da sin limitar.
*(Coro)*

3. Siempre que soy tentado o que en tinieblas voy,
cerca de El camino y protegido estoy.
Si en mí la fe desmaya y caigo en ansiedad,
tan sólo El me levanta, me da seguridad,
tan sólo El me levanta, me da seguridad.
*(Coro)*

LETRA: Civilla D. Martin, 1905; trad. de Vicente Mendoza


## 124. A solas al huerto

1. A solas al huerto yo voy,
cuando duerme aún la floresta;
y en quietud y paz con Jesús estoy,
oyendo allí su dulce voz.

*Coro*
El conmigo está, puedo oír su voz,
y que suyo, dice, seré;
y el encanto que hallo en El allí,
con nadie tener podré.

LETRA: C. Austin Miles, 1912; trad. de Vicente Mendoza, alt.

2. Tan dulce es la voz del Señor,
que las aves guardan silencio
y tan sólo se oye su voz de amor,
que inmensa paz al alma da.
*(Coro)*

3. Con El encantado yo estoy,
aunque en torno llegue la noche;
mas me ordena ir y a escuchar yo voy,
su voz, doquier la pena esté.
*(Coro)*

## 125. Dulce comunión

1. Dulce comunión la que gozo ya
en los brazos de mi Salvador.
¡Qué gran bendición en su paz me da!
¡Oh! yo siento en mí su tierno amor.

*Coro*
Libre, salvo,
del pecado y del temor.
Libre, salvo,
en los brazos de mi Salvador.

2. ¡Cuán dulce es vivir, cuán dulce es gozar
en los brazos de mi Salvador!
Allí quiero ir y con El morar,
siendo objeto de su tierno amor.
*(Coro)*

3. No hay que temer ni que desconfiar
en los brazos de mi Salvador;
por su gran poder El me guardará
de los lazos del engañador.
*(Coro)*

LETRA: Elisha A. Hoffman, 1887; trad. de Pedro Grado

## 126. El Señor es mi fuerza

*Coro*
El Señor es mi fuerza, mi roca y salvación.
El Señor es mi fuerza, mi roca y salvación.

1. El me guía por sendas de justicia,
me enseña la verdad.
El me da el valor para la lucha,
sin miedo avanzaré.
*(Coro)*

2. Ilumina las sombras de mi vida,
al mundo da la luz;
aunque pase por valles de tinieblas,
yo nunca temeré.
*(Coro)*

3. Yo confío el destino de mi vida
al Dios de mi salud;
a los pobres enseña el camino,
su escudo sólo es El.
*(Coro)*

4. El Señor es la fuerza de su pueblo,
su gran libertador;
El le hace vivir en la confianza,
seguro en su poder.
*(Coro)*

LETRA: Juan Antonio Espinosa, 1972


## 127. Dulce oración

1. Dulce oración, dulce oración, de toda influencia de maldad,
elevas tú mi corazón al tierno Padre celestial.
¡Oh! cuántas veces tuve en ti auxilio en ruda tentación;
y cuántos bienes recibí, mediante ti, dulce oración.

LETRA: William Walford, 1845; trad. de Juan Bautista Cabrera, alt.

2. Dulce oración, dulce oración, al trono excelso de bondad,
tú llevarás mi petición a Dios que escucha con piedad.
Por fe espero recibir la gran divina bendición;
y siempre a mi Señor servir, por tu virtud, dulce oración.

3. Dulce oración, dulce oración, que aliento y gozo al alma das,
en los momentos de aflicción consuelo siempre me serás.
Hasta el momento en que veré las puertas francas de Sión,
entonces me despediré, feliz, de ti, dulce oración.

## 128. Cristo, recuérdame

Cristo, recuérdame
cuando vengas en tu reino.
Cristo, recuérdame
cuando vengas en tu reino.

LETRA: Lucas 23:42; trad. de Felicia Fina

## 129. De paz inundada mi senda

1. De paz inundada mi senda ya esté
o cúbrala un mar de aflicción,
mi suerte cualquiera que sea, diré:
Tengo paz, tengo paz en mi ser.

*Coro*
Tengo paz en mi ser.
Tengo paz, tengo paz en mi ser.

2. Ya venga la prueba o me tiente Satán,
no amengua mi fe ni mi amor;
pues Cristo comprende mis luchas, mi afán
y su sangre obrará en mi favor.
*(Coro)*

3. Feliz yo me siento al saber que Jesús
libróme de yugo opresor;
quitó mi pecado, clavólo en la cruz.
¡Gloria demos al buen Salvador!
*(Coro)*

LETRA: Horatio Spafford, 1873; trad. de Pedro Grado, alt.

4. La fe tornaráse en gran realidad
al irse la niebla veloz;
desciende Jesús con su gran majestad.
Tengo paz, tengo paz en mi ser.
*(Coro)*

## 130. Todas las promesas

1. Todas las promesas del Señor Jesús
son apoyo poderoso de mi fe;
mientras luche aquí buscando yo su luz,
siempre en sus promesas confiaré.

*Coro*
Grandes, fieles,
las promesas que el Señor Jesús ha dado.
Grandes, fieles,
en ellas para siempre confiaré.

2. Todas las promesas para el pueblo fiel,
el Señor en sus bondades, cumplirá.
Y confiando todos para siempre en El,
paz eterna en su alma gozarán.
*(Coro)*

3. Todas las promesas del Señor serán
gozo y fuerza en nuestra vida terrenal;
ellas en la dura lid nos sostendrán
y triunfar podremos sobre el mal.
*(Coro)*

LETRA: R. Kelso Carter, 1886; trad. de Vicente Mendoza, alt.

## 131. El que habita al abrigo de Dios

1. El que habita al abrigo de Dios
morará bajo sombras de amor;
confiado y seguro estará
de los lazos del vil tentador.

*Coro*
Oh, yo quiero habitar al abrigo de Dios;
sólo allí encuentro paz y profundo amor.
Mi delicia es con El comunión disfrutar
y por siempre su nombre alabar.

2. El que habita al abrigo de Dios
para siempre seguro estará;
caerán miles en derredor,
mas a él no vendrá mortandad.
*(Coro)*

3. El que habita al abrigo de Dios
muy feliz ciertamente será;
ángeles guardarán su salud
y su pie nunca resbalará.
*(Coro)*

LETRA: Basada en Salmo 91, Luz Ester Ríos de Cuna, alt.


# Prueba y Consolación

## 132. ¡Oh, qué amigo nos es Cristo!

1. ¡Oh, qué amigo nos es Cristo! El llevó nuestro dolor
y nos manda que llevemos todo a Dios en oración.
Si vivimos desprovistos de paz, gozo y santo amor,
esto es porque no llevamos todo a Dios en oración.

LETRA: Joseph M. Scriven, 1855; trad. de Leandro Garza Mora, alt.

2. ¿Vives débil y cargado de cuidados y temor?
A Jesús, refugio eterno, dile todo en oración.
¿Te desprecian tus amigos? Cuéntaselo en oración;
en sus brazos de amor tierno paz tendrá tu corazón.

3. Jesucristo es nuestro amigo, de esto pruebas nos mostró
al sufrir el cruel castigo que el culpable mereció.
Y su pueblo redimido hallará seguridad,
fiando en este amigo eterno y esperando en su bondad.

## 133. Nada te turbe

Nada te turbe, nada te espante.
Quien a Dios tiene, nada le falta.
Nada te turbe, nada te espante.
Sólo Dios basta.

LETRA: Teresa de Jesús (Avila), siglo XVI

## 134. Nunca desmayes

1. Nunca desmayes en tu aflicción,
Dios cuidará de ti;
bajo sus alas de protección,
Dios cuidará de ti.

*Coro*
Dios cuidará de ti,
con tierno amor consolador;
El cuidará de ti,
Dios cuidará de ti.

2. En tus afanes y en tu dolor,
Dios cuidará de ti;
en lucha cruel con el tentador,
Dios cuidará de ti.
*(Coro)*

LETRA: Civilla D. Martin, 1904; trad. de S. D. Athans

3. Nada en la vida te faltará,
Dios cuidará de ti;
siempre su gracia te bastará,
Dios cuidará de ti.
*(Coro)*

4. En horas tristes de adversidad,
Dios cuidará de ti;
pon tu confianza en su gran bondad,
Dios cuidará de ti.
*(Coro)*

## 135. Bálsamo de amor en Galaad

*Coro*
Bálsamo de amor en Galaad, que alivia al que sufre.
Bálsamo de amor en Galaad, que sana al pecador.

1. Cuando siento que en mi vid es vana mi labor,
mi corazón renueva el buen Consolador.
*(Coro)*

2. Jamás te desalientes, Jesús tu amigo es.
Su apoyo te sostiene por esta y otra vez.
*(Coro)*

3. Si predicar no puedes, di que Jesús te amó,
y su preciosa vida por todos ofreció.
*(Coro)*

LETRA: Espiritual afro-americana; trad. de Oscar Rodríguez

## 136. Cristo, Cristo Jesús (Kyrie)

Cristo, Cristo Jesús, identifícate con nosotros.
Cristo, Señor y Dios, identifícate con nosotros.
Cristo, Cristo Jesús, solidarízate,
no con la gente opresora
que exprime y devora a la comunidad,
sino con el oprimido,
con el pueblo mío, sediento de paz.

LETRA: Carlos Mejía Godoy, 1968; basada en la Misa Campesina de Nicaragua


## 137. Sanidad integral

Sanidad yo anhelo, Señor,
sanidad integral en mi ser;
sanidad que hable de tu poder.
¡Manifiesta tu amor en mi ser!
¡Manifiesta tu amor en mi ser!

LETRA: Raúl E. Martínez, 1995

# LA IGLESIA

## Cuerpo de Cristo

### 138. Somos uno en espíritu

1. Somos uno en espíritu y en el Señor;
somos uno en espíritu y en el Señor
y rogamos que un día nuestra unión sea total.
Y que somos cristianos lo sabrán, lo sabrán,
porque unidos estamos en amor.

2. Trabajemos unidos, mano a mano en amor;
trabajemos unidos, mano a mano en amor,
ayudando al vecino como Cristo enseñó.
Y que somos cristianos lo sabrán, lo sabrán,
porque unidos estamos en amor.

3. Marcharemos tomados de la mano en unión;
marcharemos tomados de la mano en unión,
anunciando que en esta tierra vive y obra Dios.
Y que somos cristianos lo sabrán, lo sabrán,
porque unidos estamos en amor.

4. Gloria al Padre que es fuente de total bendición;
gloria a Cristo su Hijo que nos da salvación
y al Espíritu Santo que nos une en comunión.
Y que somos cristianos lo sabrán, lo sabrán,
porque unidos estamos en amor.

LETRA: Peter Scholtes, 1966; trad. de Federico J. Pagura, alt.


### 139. Iglesia de Cristo

1. Iglesia de Cristo, reanima tu amor
y espera, velando, a tu amado Señor.
Jesús, el esposo, vestido de honor,
viniendo se anuncia, con fuerte clamor.

LETRA: Mateo Cosidó, 1874, alt.

2. Si falta en algunos el santo fervor,
de todos la fe sea el despertador.
Velad, compañeros, velad sin temor,
que está con nosotros el Consolador.

3. Quien sigue la senda del vil pecador,
se entrega en los brazos de un sueño traidor;
mas para los siervos del buen Salvador,
velar, esperando, es su anhelo mejor.

## 140. ¡El cielo canta alegría!

1. ¡El cielo canta alegría! ¡Aleluya!
porque en tu vida y la mía
brilla la gloria de Dios.

*Coro*
¡Aleluya! ¡Aleluya!
¡Aleluya! ¡Aleluya!

2. ¡El cielo canta alegría! ¡Aleluya!
porque a tu vida y la mía
las une el amor de Dios.
*(Coro)*

3. ¡El cielo canta alegría! ¡Aleluya!
porque tu vida y la mía
proclamarán al Señor.
*(Coro)*

LETRA: Pablo Sosa, 1958


## 141. Juntos en armonía

Mirad cuán bueno es habitar los hermanos juntos,
juntos en armonía, juntos en armonía.
Porque allí envía Jehová bendición y vida eterna,
porque allí envía Jehová bendición y vida eterna.

LETRA: (Basada en Salmo 133:1, 3)

## 142. Somos uno en Cristo (We Are One in Christ Jesus)

Somos uno en Cristo, somos uno, somos uno, uno sólo.
*(Se repite.)*
Un solo Dios, un solo Señor, una sola fe, un solo amor,
un solo bautismo, un solo Espíritu y ese es el Consolador.

We are one in Christ Jesus, all one body, all one spirit, all together. *(Repeat.)*
We share one God, one mighty Lord, one abiding faith, one binding love,
one single baptism, one Holy Comforter, the Holy Spirit, uniting all.

LETRA: Autor desconocido; trad. al inglés de Alice Parker


## 143. Muchos resplandores

1. Muchos resplandores, sólo una luz:
es la luz de Cristo.
Muchos resplandores, sólo una luz
que nos hace uno.

2. Muchas son las ramas, un árbol hay
y su tronco es Cristo.
Muchas son las ramas, un tronco hay
y en El somos uno.

3. Muchas las tareas, uno el sentir:
el sentir de Cristo.
Muchas las tareas, uno el sentir
que nos hace uno.

4. Muchos son los miembros, un cuerpo hay:
ese cuerpo es Cristo.
Muchos son los miembros, un cuerpo hay
y en El somos uno.

LETRA: Anders Frostenson; trad. de Pablo Sosa

## 144. Firmes y adelante

1. Firmes y adelante, huestes de la fe,
sin temor alguno, que Jesús nos ve.
Jefe soberano, Cristo al frente va
y la regia enseña tremolando está.

*Coro*
Firmes y adelante, huestes de la fe,
sin temor alguno, que Jesús nos ve.

2. Al sagrado nombre de nuestro adalid,
tiembla el enemigo y huye de la lid.
Nuestra es la victoria, dad a Dios loor
y óigalo el infierno, lleno de terror.
*(Coro)*

3. Muévese potente la Iglesia de Dios;
de los ya gloriosos, marchamos en pos.
Somos solo un cuerpo y uno es el Señor,
una la esperanza, y uno nuestro amor.
*(Coro)*

4. Tronos y coronas pueden perecer;
de Jesús la Iglesia siempre habrá de ser.
Nada en contra suya prevalecerá,
porque la promesa nunca faltará.
*(Coro)*

LETRA: Sabine Baring-Gould, 1864; trad. de Juan Bautista Cabrera, alt.

## 145. En santa hermandad (United by God's Love)

1. En santa hermandad vamos a cantar,
en santa hermandad vamos a cantar.

*Coro*
Tú eres nuestro Redentor;
llénanos de amor.
Tú eres nuestro Salvador y Libertador.

2. Al Creador cantemos que nos dio su gracia.
Al Creador cantemos que nos dio su gracia.
*(Coro)*

LETRA: William Loperena, 1975; trad. al inglés de Carolyn Jennings

3. A Cristo ensalcemos por su santa alianza.
   A Cristo ensalcemos por su santa alianza.
   *(Coro)*

4. Al fiel Consolador demos alabanza.
   Al fiel Consolador demos alabanza.
   *(Coro)*

1. United by God's love let us sing together.
   United by God's love let us sing together.

   *Refrain*
   You, our Redeemer Jesus Christ
   fill us with your love,
   our Liberator Jesus Christ,
   Savior of the world.

2. Sing praise to our Creator, God of grace and mercy.
   Sing praise to our Creator, God of grace and mercy,
   *(Refrain)*

3. Sing praise to Christ the Savior, bringer of salvation.
   Sing praise to Christ the Savior, bringer of salvation.
   *(Refrain)*

4. And praise the Holy Spirit, Comforter most holy.
   And praise the Holy Spirit, Comforter most holy.
   *(Refrain)*

## 146. ¡Miren qué bueno!

*Coro*
¡Miren qué bueno, qué bueno es! *(se repite)*
Miren qué bueno es cuando los creyentes están juntos:

1. Es como aceite bueno, derramado sobre Aarón.
   *(Coro)*

2. Se parece al rocío sobre los montes de Sión.
   *(Coro)*

3. Porque el Señor nos manda vida eterna y bendición.
   *(Coro)*

LETRA: Pablo Sosa, 1972

## 147. Canto de esperanza

1. Cuando se va la esperanza,
   El nos habla y nos dice:
   Mira a tu hermano que vive y lucha,
   buscando un mundo mejor.
   Mira a tu hermana que vive y lucha,
   buscando un mundo mejor.

   *Coro*
   Cantemos a nuestro Dios,
   El es el Dios de la vida,
   porque El está con nosotros
   creando esperanza y libertad.
   *(Se repite el coro.)*

2. Cuando se va la esperanza,
   El nos habla y nos dice:
   Acércate a tu hermano y trabajen
   juntos buscando la paz.
   Acércate a tu hermana y trabajen
   juntos buscando la paz.
   *(Coro)*

3. Cuando se va la esperanza,
   El nos habla y nos dice:
   No se alejen de mi lado,
   permanezcan firmes, yo les sostendré.
   No se alejen de mi lado,
   permanezcan firmes, yo les sostendré.
   *(Coro)*

LETRA: Ester Cámac, 1987, alt.

## 148. Amaos los unos a los otros

1. ¡Amor! ¡Cuán hermosa es la palabra!
Dios es amor, Dios es amor.
Amor Cristo derramó por todos,
cuando en la cruz, con sangre, lo mostró.

*Coro*
Amaos los unos a los otros,
bello mandato que Cristo nos dejó.
A través del amor derramado,
en rescate por todos dio
una fuente sin par de amor.

Amaos los unos a los otros
en la desgracia, en el gozo y en la paz.
Cuando sientas que todos te dejan
y apurando mil penas vas,
como Cristo, derrama amor.

2. Jesús, en el aposento alto,
nos enseñó la gran lección
de aquel corazón dispuesto siempre
para servir a todos, por amor.
*(Coro)*

LETRA: Rafael D. Grullón, 1972


# Llamamiento a Misión

## 149. Amar

1. La gente de nuestros tiempos no sabe lo que es el amor;
se vive perdiendo el tiempo, buscando y sin encontrar.

*Coro*
Amar es entregarse
en alma y cuerpo a la humanidad;
vivir siempre sirviendo,
sin que se espere algo para sí.

LETRA: Jorge Clark Ramírez, c. 1974, alt.

2. En Cristo he encontrado un mensaje de paz y de amor;
   la muerte del crucificado es prueba de su gran amor.
   *(Coro)*

3. Debemos testificar que en Cristo hay redención,
   llevando este mensaje de muerte y resurrección.
   *(Coro)*

## 150. Jesús, Jesús

*Coro*
Jesús, Jesús, enséñame tú
a amar y a servir a toda tu creación.

1. Te arrodillaste a los pies de tus amigos, Señor;
   se los lavaste en señal de amor.
   *(Coro)*

2. Pobres y ricos serán, de toda raza y color,
   de todo pueblo y nación también.
   *(Coro)*

3. Hoy les queremos servir, hoy les queremos amar;
   iguales somos, Jesús, en ti.
   *(Coro)*

4. Nos capacita el amor, humildemente a servir;
   hemos así de vivir en ti.
   *(Coro)*

5. Nuestra rodilla doblar y así sus pies lavar,
   es el mandato que Dios nos da.
   *(Coro)*

LETRA: Tom Colvin, 1969; trad. de Felicia Fina, alt. (Jn. 13:1-17)

## 151. Heme aquí

1. Yo, el Dios del cielo y mar, oigo a mi pueblo clamar.
Del pecado y del mal, les salvaré.
Yo, Creador de luna y sol, Dios de vida y resplandor.
¿Quién mi antorcha llevará? Oh, ¿quién irá?

*Coro*
Heme aquí, Dios. ¿Tú me llamas?
En la noche escuché tu voz.
Con tu guía y tu apoyo, sostendré a tu pueblo con amor.

2. Yo, Creador de lluvia y flor, por mi pueblo en su aflicción
he llorado su amargor. Lejos están.
La dureza de su ser en amor convertiré.
Mi Palabra lo hará. Oh, ¿quién irá?
*(Coro)*

3. Dios del aire y del calor, tiernamente acogeré
al lisiado y al pobre. Les sanaré.
Pan y agua les daré y su hambre saciaré.
Vida en mí encontrarán. ¿Oh, ¿quién irá?
*(Coro)*

LETRA: Dan Schutte, 1981; trad. de Yolanda Pupo-Ortiz

## 152. Momento nuevo

1. Dios hoy nos llama a un momento nuevo,
   a caminar junto con su pueblo.
   Es hora de transformar lo que no da más
   y solo y aislado no hay nadie capaz.
   Por eso,

   *Coro*
   ¡Ven, entra a la rueda con todos, también!
   Tú eres muy importante. Por eso,
   ¡ven, entra a la rueda con todos, también!
   Tú eres muy importante. ¡Ven!

2. Ya no es posible creer que todo es fácil,
   hay muchas fuerzas que producen muerte;
   nos causan pena, tristeza y desolación.
   Es necesario afianzar nuestra unión.
   Por eso,
   *(Coro)*

3. La fuerza que hace hoy brotar la vida
   obra en nosotros dándonos su gracia.
   Es Dios quien hoy nos convida a trabajar,
   su amor repartir y las fuerzas juntar.
   Por eso,
   *(Coro)*

LETRA: Creación colectiva; trad. de Pablo Sosa, alt.


## 153. Sois la semilla (You Are the Seed)

1. Sois la semilla que ha de crecer,
   sois estrella que ha de brillar;
   sois levadura, sois grano de sal,
   antorcha que debe alumbrar.
   Sois la mañana que vuelve a nacer,
   sois espiga que empieza a granar;
   sois aguijón y caricia a la vez,
   testigos que voy a enviar.

LETRA: Cesáreo Gabaráin, 1979; trad. de Raquel Gutiérrez-Achón
y Skinner Chávez-Melo (Mt. 28:19-20)

*Coro*
Id, amigas, por el mundo, anunciando el amor,
mensajeras de la vida, de la paz y el perdón.
Sed, amigos, los testigos de mi resurrección.
Id, llevando mi presencia; con vosotros estoy.

2. Sois una llama que ha de encender
resplandores de fe y caridad;
Sois los pastores que han de llevar
al mundo por sendas de paz.
Sois los amigos que quise escoger,
sois palabra que intento esparcir.
Sois reino nuevo que empieza a engendrar
justicia, amor y verdad.
*(Coro)*

3. Sois fuego y savia que vine a traer,
sois la ola que agita la mar.
La levadura pequeña de ayer
fermenta la masa del pan.
Una ciudad no se puede esconder,
ni los montes se han de ocultar;
en vuestras obras que buscan el bien,
el mundo al Padre verá.
*(Coro)*

1. You are the seed that will grow a new sprout;
you're the star that will shine in the night;
you are the yeast and a small grain of salt,
a beacon to glow in the dark.
You are the dawn that will bring a new day;
you're the wheat that will bear golden grain;
you are a sting and a soft, gentle touch,
my witness wherever you go.

*Refrain*
Go, my friends, go to the world,
proclaiming love to all,
messengers of my forgiving peace,
eternal love.
Be, my friends, a loyal witness,
from the dead I arose;
"Lo, I'll be with you forever,
till the end of the world."

2. You are the flame that will lighten the dark,
sending sparkles of hope, faith, and love;
you are the shepherds to lead the whole world
through valleys and pastures of peace.
You are the friends that I chose for myself,
the word that I want to proclaim.
You are the new kingdom built on a rock
where justice and truth always reign.
*(Refrain)*

3. You are the life that will nurture the plant;
you're the waves in a turbulent sea;
yesterday's yeast is beginning to rise,
a new loaf of bread it will yield.
There is no place for a city to hide,
nor a mountain can cover its might;
may your good deeds show a world in despair
a path that will lead all to God.
*(Refrain)*

## 154. Vamos todos al banquete

*Coro*
Vamos todos al banquete, a la mesa de la creación;
cada cual, con su taburete, tiene un puesto y una misión.

1. Hoy me levanto muy temprano,
ya me espera la comunidad;
voy subiendo alegre la cuesta,
voy en busca de tu amistad.
*(Coro)*

2. Dios invita a todos los pobres
a esta mesa común por la fe,
donde no hay acaparadores
y a nadie le falta el conqué.*
*(Coro)*

LETRA: De la misa popular de México, en «*Cantemos en Comunidad*», c. 1980, alt.
Usado con permiso de Lutheran Human Relations Assn.

3. Dios nos manda hacer de este mundo
una mesa donde haya igualdad;
trabajando y luchando juntos,
por el bien de la humanidad.
*(Coro)*

* *conqué: expresión regional de Centro América. Denota la comida básica que acompaña al pan o tortilla. La última frase se puede sustituir por «donde todos puedan comer».*

## 155. Usa mi vida

1. Muchos que viven en tu derredor,
tristes, hambrientos están;
tú, por tu vida, les puedes llevar
gozo, luz y bendición.

*Coro*
Usa mi vida, usa mi vida
para tu gloria, oh Jesús.
Todos los días y hoy quiero ser
testigo tuyo, Señor, por doquier.

2. Di a los tristes que Dios es amor,
El quiere dar su perdón
a los que vienen a Cristo Jesús,
buscando paz, salvación.
*(Coro)*

3. Toda tu vida hoy rinde al Señor;
cada momento sé fiel,
otros que vean en ti su amor,
pronto se rindan a El.
*(Coro)*

LETRA: Ira B. Wilson, c. 1909; trad. de J. F. Swanson

## 156. Sal a sembrar

1. Sal a sembrar, sembrador de paz,
sigue las huellas del buen Jesús;
muy ricos frutos tendrás, si fiel
sigues la senda de paz y luz.

LETRA: Autor desconocido, alt.

*Coro 1-3*
Ve, ve, ve, sembrador; ve, ve, siembra la paz.
Habla doquiera del Señor y de su santa paz.

2. Vasto es el campo, sal a sembrar,
labra el terreno que Dios te da;
si siembras siempre confiando en Dios,
El tus esfuerzos coronará.
*(Coro)*

3. No desperdicies el tiempo, ve,
siembra palabras de vida y paz;
semilla eterna que dé su mies,
rica semilla que no es fugaz.
*(Coro)*

4. Dios lo ha mandado, sal a sembrar
nuevas de vida, de amor y paz;
tal vez te cueste dolores mil,
mas en los cielos tendrás solaz.
*(Coro)*

*Coro 4*
Voy, voy, voy Salvador;
voy, voy, siembro la paz,
hablando siempre del Señor
y de su santa paz.

## 157. Entre el vaivén de la ciudad

1. Entre el vaivén de la ciudad,
más fuerte aún que su rumor;
en lid de raza y sociedad,
tu voz oímos, Salvador.
2. Doquiera exista explotación,
falte trabajo, no haya pan;
en los umbrales del terror,
oh Cristo, vémoste llorar.

3. Un vaso de agua puede ser,
hoy, de tu gracia la señal;
mas ya las gentes quieren ver
tu compasiva y santa faz.

LETRA: Frank Mason North, 1903; trad. anónimo, alt.

4. Hasta que triunfe tu amor
   y el mundo pueda oír tu voz
   y de los cielos, oh Señor,
   descienda la Ciudad de Dios.

## 158. Sembraré la simiente preciosa

1. Sembraré la simiente preciosa
   del glorioso evangelio de amor.
   Sembraré, sembraré mientras viva,
   dejaré el resultado al Señor.

   *Coro*
   Sembraré, sembraré
   mientras viva, simiente de amor;
   Segaré, segaré,
   al hallarme en la casa de Dios.

2. Sembraré en corazones sensibles
   la doctrina del Dios del perdón.
   Sembraré, sembraré mientras viva,
   dejaré el resultado al Señor.
   *(Coro)*

3. Sembraré en corazones de mármol
   la bendita palabra de Dios.
   Sembraré, sembraré mientras viva,
   dejaré el resultado al Señor.
   *(Coro)*

LETRA: Autor desconocido; trad. de Abraham Fernández, alt.

## 159. Cuando el pobre

1. Cuando el pobre nada tiene y aun reparte,
   cuando alguien pasa sed y agua nos da,
   cuando el débil a su hermano fortalece,

   *Coro*
   va Dios mismo en nuestro mismo caminar,
   va Dios mismo en nuestro mismo caminar.

LETRA: J. A. Olivar, 1971, (Mt. 25:31-46)

2. Cuando alguien sufre y logra su consuelo,
cuando espera y no se cansa de esperar,
cuando ama, aunque el odio le rodee,
*(Coro)*

3. Cuando crece la alegría y nos inunda,
cuando dicen nuestros labios la verdad,
cuando amamos el sentir de los sencillos,
*(Coro)*

4. Cuando abunda el bien y llena los hogares,
cuando alguien donde hay guerra pone paz,
cuando «hermano» le llamamos al extraño,
*(Coro)*

## 160. Enviado soy de Dios (Sent Out in Jesus' Name)

Enviado soy de Dios, mi mano lista está
para construir con El un mundo fraternal.
Los ángeles no son enviados a cambiar
un mundo de dolor por un mundo de paz.
Me ha tocado a mí hacerlo realidad;
ayúdame, Señor, a hacer tu voluntad.

Sent out in Jesus' name, our hands are ready now
to make the earth the place in which the kingdom comes.
The angels cannot change a world of hurt and pain
into a world of love, of justice and of peace.
The task is ours to do, to set it really free.
O, help us to obey, and carry out your will.

LETRA: Anónimo centroamericano, siglo XX; adap. y trad. al inglés de Jorge E. Maldonado, alt.


## 161. Tocad trompeta ya

1. Tocad trompeta ya, alegres en Sión;
al mundo proclamad la eterna redención.

*Coro*
¡El «Jubileo» celebrad!
¡El «Jubileo» celebrad,
que es año pleno de bondad!

LETRA: Charles Wesley, 1750; trad. de G. H. Rule, estr. 1-3, alt.; Alberto Merubia, estr. 4 (Lv. 25:8-17)

2. A Cristo predicad; decid que ya murió
y con su potestad, la muerte destruyó.
*(Coro)*

3. Vosotros que el favor del cielo despreciáis,
ved que por el amor de Cristo lo alcanzáis.
*(Coro)*

4. Esclavos de maldad, tenéis liberación;
en Cristo hoy morad, gozando bendición.
*(Coro)*

## 162. De los cuatro rincones del mundo (From All Four of Earth's Faraway Corners)

1. De los cuatro rincones del mundo
se combina la sangre en las venas,
de este pueblo que canta sus penas,
de este pueblo que grita su fe;
recia sangre traída de España,
noble sangre del indio sufrido,
fuerte sangre de esclavo oprimido,
toda sangre comprada en la cruz.

2. De los cuatro rincones del mundo,
de florida campiña cubana,
desde Asia y la costa africana,
de Borinquen, Quisqueya y Aztlán,
a esta hora bendita nos trajo
el secreto designio divino,
que a todos ató en un destino
y de todos un reino creará.

3. Por los cuatro rincones del mundo
el pecado construye barreras;
mas la fe no respeta fronteras,
la justicia y la paz triunfarán.
A los cuatro rincones del mundo
somos pueblo que anuncia el mañana,
cuando a todos en paz soberana
Dios en lazos de amor unirá.

LETRA: Justo L. González, 1987; trad. de George Lockwood

1. From all four of earth's faraway corners
flows together the blood of all races
in this people who sing of their trials,
in this people who cry of their faith;
hardy blood that was brought by the Spanish,
noble blood of the suffering Indian,
blood of slaves who stood heavy oppression,
all the blood that was bought on the cross.

2. From all four of earth's faraway corners,
from the flowering meadows of Cuba,
from the African coast and all Asia,
from Borinquen, Quisqueya, Aztlán,
God in secret has long been designing
to this moment so blessed to bring us,
bind us all to the same destination
and a Kingdom create of us all.

3. In all four of earth's faraway corners
sin is building embittering barriers;
but our faith has no fear of such borders,
we know justice and peace will prevail.
To all four of earth's faraway corners
we're a people who point to tomorrow,
when the world, living sov'reign and peaceful,
is united in bonds of God's love.

# LAS SAGRADAS ESCRITURAS

## 163. Padre, tu palabra es

1. Padre, tu palabra es mi delicia y mi solaz;
guíe siempre aquí mis pies y a mi pecho traiga paz.

*Coro*
Es tu ley, Señor, faro celestial,
que en continuo resplandor,
norte y guía da al mortal.

2. Si obediente oí tu voz, en tu gracia fuerza hallé
y con firme pie y veloz, por tus sendas caminé.
*(Coro)*

3. Tu verdad es mi sostén contra duda y tentación
y destila calma y bien cuando asalta la aflicción.
*(Coro)*

4. Son tus dichos para mí, prendas fieles de salud;
dame pues, que te oiga a ti, con filial solicitud.
*(Coro)*

LETRA: Juan Bautista Cabrera, 1914, alt.

## 164. Tu palabra es, oh Señor

1. Tu palabra es, oh Señor, don precioso de tu amor,
que contiene, con verdad, tu divina voluntad;
que me dice lo que soy, de quién vine y a quién voy.

2. Me reprende al dudar y me exhorta sin cesar;
es cual faro que a mi pie va guiando por la fe
a las fuentes del amor de mi dulce Salvador.

3. Oigo en ella clara voz del Espíritu de Dios,
que vigor al alma da, cuando en aflicción está;
ayudándome a triunfar de la muerte y del pecar.

4. Por su fiel promesa sé que con Cristo reinaré;
que su juicio llegará y el pecado destruirá.
Tu palabra es siempre aquí un tesoro para mí.

LETRA: John Burton, 1805; trad. de Pedro Castro

## 165. ¡Oh! Cantádmelas otra vez

1. ¡Oh! Cantádmelas otra vez, bellas palabras de vida;
hallo en ellas mi gozo y luz, bellas palabras de vida.
Sí, de luz y vida son sostén y guía.

*Coro*
¡Qué bellas son, qué bellas son,
bellas palabras de vida!
(Se repite.)

2. Jesucristo a todos da bellas palabras de vida;
oye su dulce voz, mortal, bellas palabras de vida.
Bondadoso, te salva y al cielo te llama.
*(Coro)*

3. Grato el cántico sonará, bellas palabras de vida;
tus pecados perdonará, bellas palabras de vida.
Sí, de luz y vida son sostén y guía.
*(Coro)*

LETRA: Philip P. Bliss, 1874; trad. de Julia A. Butler

## 166. Cristo me ama

1. Cristo me ama, bien lo sé,
su palabra me hace ver
que los niños son de aquél,
quien es nuestro amigo fiel.

*Coro*
Cristo me ama, Cristo me ama,
Cristo me ama, la Biblia dice así.

2. Cristo me ama, bien lo sé,
en la cruz por mí murió,
pues su amor tan grande fue
y por eso lo amo yo.
*(Coro)*

3. Cristo me ama, bien lo sé,
El jamás me dejará;
obediente le seré,
pues su ayuda me dará.
*(Coro)*

LETRA: Anna B. Warner, 1860; trad. anónimo

# LOS SACRAMENTOS

## Bautismo

### 167. Señor, tú me llamas

1. Señor, tú me llamas por mi nombre, desde lejos;
   por mi nombre cada día tú me llamas.
   Señor, tú me ofreces una vida
   santa y limpia; una vida sin pecado, sin maldad.

   *Coro*
   Señor, nada tengo para darte;
   solamente te ofrezco mi vida
   para que la uses tú.
   Señor, hazme hoy un siervo útil
   que anuncie el mensaje,
   el mensaje de la cruz.

2. Señor, tú me llamas por mi nombre, desde lejos;
   por mi nombre, cada día tú me llamas.
   Señor, yo acudo a tu llamado cada instante,
   pues mi gozo es servirte más y más.
   *(Coro)*

   *Coda*
   Señor, tú me llamas por mi nombre desde lejos;
   por mi nombre cada día tú me llamas.

LETRA: Rubén Giménez, c. 1977


### 168. Bautizados, renovados

1. Somos bautizados, somos renovados,
   somos revestidos del Señor.
   Pueblo suyo somos, a Dios confesamos.
   Démosle la gloria y todo honor.

2. Pueblo redimido, pueblo consagrado
   para hacer la obra del Señor.
   Pueblo suyo somos, a Dios confesamos.
   Démosle la gloria y todo honor.

LETRA: Raquel Mora Martínez, 1992

# Santa Comunión

## 169. De rodillas partamos

1. De rodillas partamos hoy el pan,
de rodillas partamos hoy el pan;

*Coro*
De rodillas estoy,
con el rostro al naciente sol.
¡Oh Dios, apiádate de mí!

2. Compartamos la copa en gratitud,
compartamos la copa en gratitud.
*(Coro)*

3. De rodillas loemos al Señor,
de rodillas loemos al Señor.
*(Coro)*

LÈTRA: Espiritual afro-americana (Hch. 2:42); trad. de Federico J. Pagura


## 170. El Señor nos ama hoy

1. El Señor nos ama hoy como nadie nos amó.
El nos guía como un faro en un mar de oscuridad.
Al comer juntos el pan, El nos brinda su amistad;
es el pan de Dios, el pan de la unidad.

*Coro*
«Es mi cuerpo: tomad y comed,
es mi sangre: tomad y bebed;
pues yo soy la vida, yo soy el amor».
¡Oh Señor, condúcenos hasta tu amor!

2. El Señor nos ama hoy como nadie nos amó.
«Donde dos o tres, unidos, impulsados por mi amor,
os juntéis para cantar, estaré presente yo»,
ésta fue la fiel promesa del Señor.
*(Coro)*

3. El Señor nos ama hoy como nadie nos amó.
«El mayor entre vosotros hágase como el menor;
he lavado vuestros pies, aunque soy vuestro Señor;
repetid entre vosotros mi lección».
*(Coro)*

LETRA: Anónimo

4. El Señor nos ama hoy como nadie nos amó.
«Los que tengan hambre y sed vengan a mí y los saciaré
pues yo soy el pan vital y agua que no da más sed
y por siempre en vuestras vidas moraré».
*(Coro)*

## 171. Una espiga (Sheaves of Summer)

1. Una espiga dorada por el sol,
el racimo que corta el viñador,
compartimos ahora en pan y vino de amor,
recordando el cuerpo y sangre del Señor.

2. Compartimos la misma comunión,
somos trigo del mismo sembrador.
Un molino la vida nos tritura con dolor;
Dios nos hace pueblo nuevo en el amor.

3. Como granos que han hecho el mismo pan,
como notas que tejen un cantar,
como gotas de agua que se funden en el mar,
los cristianos un cuerpo formarán.

4. A la mesa de Dios se sentarán;
todos juntos su pan compartirán.
Una misma esperanza caminando cantarán;
en la vida como hermanos se amarán.

1. Sheaves of summer turned golden by the sun,
grapes in bunches cut down when ripe and red,
are converted into the bread and wine of God's love
in the body and blood of our dear Lord.

2. We are sharing the same communion meal,
we are wheat by the same great Sower sown;
like a millstone, life grinds us down with sorrow and pain,
but God makes us new people bound by love.

3. Like the grains which become one same whole loaf,
like the notes that are woven into song,
like the droplets of water that are blended in the sea,
we, as Christians, one body shall become.

4. At God's table together we shall sit.
As God's children, Christ's body we will share.
One same hope we will sing together as we walk along;
brothers, sisters, in life, in love, we'll be.

LETRA: Cesáreo Gabaráin, 1973; trad. al inglés de George Lockwood

## 172. Te ofrecemos, Padre nuestro (Let Us Offer to the Father)

*Coro*
Te ofrecemos, Padre nuestro,
con el vino y con el pan,
nuestras penas y alegrías,
el trabajo y nuestro afán.

1. Como el trigo de los campos
en un pan se convirtió,
así haz de nuestras vidas
hoy el cuerpo del Señor.
*(Coro)*

2. A los pobres de la tierra,
a los que sufriendo están,
cambia su dolor en vino,
como uva en el lagar.
*(Coro)*

3. Estos dones son el signo
del esfuerzo de unidad
que la humanidad realiza
en el campo y la ciudad.
*(Coro)*

4. Es tu pueblo quien te ofrece,
con los dones del altar,
la naturaleza entera,
anhelando libertad.
*(Coro)*

5. Gloria sea dada al Padre
y a su Hijo Redentor
y al Espíritu Divino
que nos llena de su amor.
*(Coro)*

LETRA: De la Misa Popular Nicaragüense, 1968; trad. al inglés de Alice Parker

*Refrain*
Let us offer to the Father,
with the bread and with the wine,
all our joys and all our sorrows;
all our cares, Lord, all are thine.

1. As the growing wheat will ripen
let us show to all the world
we can grow and ripen also
in the living of the Word.
*(Refrain)*

2. Let the poor and heavy laden
gather at the Savior's sign,
where their grief will turn to gladness
as the grapes are pressed to wine.
*(Refrain)*

3. From the country, from the city,
from the riches of the land,
we bring back to our Creator
many gifts of heart and hand.
*(Refrain)*

4. All your people here together
bring you offerings of love,
joining with your whole creation,
seeking liberty and peace.
*(Refrain)*

5. Glory be to God, the Father
and to Christ, the living Son,
who together with the Spirit
make the Holy Three in One.
*(Refrain)*

# CONGREGADOS PARA ADORAR

## Apertura del Culto

### 173. Entra en la presencia del Señor

Entra en la presencia del Señor con gratitud
para adorar de corazón.
Entra en la presencia del Señor con gratitud
y alza con júbilo tu voz.

Da gloria y honra y alabanza al Señor.
Oh, ¡Cristo! nombre sin igual.

LETRA: Lynn Baird, c. 1988


### 174. Para la gloria de Dios

Para la gloria de Dios es que vengo a cantar, ¡oh gloria!
Para la gloria de Dios canto esta canción, ¡oh gloria!
Para la gloria de Dios quiero yo vivir sirviendo aquí. ¡Sí!
Para la gloria de Dios es que vengo a cantar.

¡Gloria! Este es mi canto; Cristo la razón de mi cantar.
¡Gloria a mi Rey y Señor! Hoy le alabo con el corazón.
¡Gloria! Así mis manos hoy levanto al cielo en comunión.
¡Gloria a mi Rey y Señor! Hoy le alabo con el corazón.

LETRA: Rafael Grullón, 1986


### 175. Señor, llévame a tus atrios

Señor, llévame a tus atrios,
al lugar santo, al altar de bronce;
Señor, tu rostro quiero ver.
Pasaré la muchedumbre
donde el sacerdote canta;
tengo hambre y sed de justicia
y sólo encuentro un lugar.
Llévame al lugar santísimo,
por la sangre del cordero redentor.
Llévame al lugar santísimo,
tócame, límpiame, heme aquí.

LETRA: Dave Browning, 1986; trad. de Marcos Witt

## 176. Señor, ¿quién entrará?

1. Señor, ¿quién entrará en tu santuario para adorar?
Señor, ¿quién entrará en tu santuario para adorar?
El de manos limpias y un corazón puro
y sin vanidades, que sepa amar.
El de manos limpias y un corazón puro
y sin vanidades, que sepa amar.

2. Señor, yo quiero entrar en tu santuario para adorar.
Señor, yo quiero entrar en tu santuario para adorar.
Dame manos limpias y un corazón puro
y sin vanidades, enséñame a amar.
Dame manos limpias y un corazón puro
y sin vanidades, enséñame a amar.

LETRA: Anónimo; basada en Salmo 15

## 177. Dios está aquí

Dios está aquí,
tan cierto como el aire que respiro,
tan cierto como la mañana se levanta,
tan cierto como que le canto y me puede oír.

LETRA: Autor desconocido

# Clausura del Culto

## 178. El culto terminó

1. El culto terminó, vamos ya de este lugar;
Señor, hoy tu bendición nos venga a acompañar.
¡Aleluya, Aleluya!
Tu presencia nos venga a acompañar.
¡Aleluya, Aleluya, Aleluya!

2. Señor, que nuestras vidas reflejen tu amor,
alentando al afligido con himnos de loor.
¡Aleluya, Aleluya!
Nuestras vidas reflejen tu amor.
¡Aleluya, Aleluya, Aleluya!

LETRA: Irene Gómez, 1971; trad. del portugués de David Achón, Raquel Gutiérrez-Achón y Gertrude Suppe

3. Luchemos con valor y de todo corazón,
ya que el culto terminó, continuemos la misión.
¡Aleluya, Aleluya!
Lucharemos de todo corazón.
¡Aleluya, Aleluya, Aleluya!

## 179. Unidos

Unidos, unidos, en tu nombre unidos.
Unidos, unidos, en tu nombre unidos
pues en este mundo paz y amor queremos,
pues en este mundo paz y amor queremos.
Unidos, siempre unidos, tomados de las manos,
iremos por el mundo cantando al amor.
La gloria de Jesús, al fin resplandecerá
y al mundo llenará de amor y de paz,
de amor y de paz.

LETRA: Benjamín Villanueva, 1973


## 180. La paz esté con nosotros (Hevenu Shalom Aleichem)

La paz esté con nosotros,
la paz esté con nosotros,
la paz esté con nosotros.
Que con nosotros siempre,
siempre esté la paz.

Hevenu shalom aleichem.
Hevenu shalom aleichem.
Hevenu shalom aleichem.
Hevenu shalom, shalom,
shalom aleichem.

LETRA: Cesáreo Gabaráin

## 181. Sagrado es el amor

1. Sagrado es el amor
que nos ha unido aquí,
a los que creemos del Señor
la voz que llama a sí.

2. A nuestro Padre Dios
rogamos con fervor,
alúmbrenos la misma luz,
nos una el mismo amor.

3. Nos vamos a ausentar,
mas nuestra firme unión
jamás podráse quebrantar
por la separación.

4. Allá en la eternidad
nos hemos de reunir
y en dulce comunión y paz,
por siempre convivir.

LETRA: John Fawcett, 1782; trad. anónimo, alt.

# OCASIONES ESPECIALES

## Matrimonio

### 182. El amor

1. El amor, el amor
   es sufrido y es sacrificial.
   Quien ama es capaz de morir,
   quien ama siempre debe
   tratar de no herir.
   El amor es benigno
   y es así porque Dios es amor.

2. El amor, el amor
   nunca piensa solo para sí;
   se goza siempre de la verdad,
   perdona y nunca guarda rencor;
   todo lo cree.
   El amor verdadero
   es así porque Dios es amor.

LETRA: Rafael D. Grullón, 1987; basada en 1 Corintios 13


### 183. Escucha, ¡oh Dios! la oración

1. Escucha, ¡oh Dios! la oración que se dirige a ti,
   por los que en perdurable unión, se unen hoy aquí.

2. Que tu mirada de bondad disfruten, buen Jesús;
   infunde en ellos la piedad, concédeles tu luz.

3. Su hogar bendice, Dios de paz; que tengan tu sostén
   y que, confiados en tu amor, unidos siempre estén.

4. Haz sobre ellos descender tu santa bendición,
   en ti, que puedan obtener eterna salvación.

LETRA: Del Latín, siglo XVII; trad. desconocido, alt.

# Funerales/Conmemoración

## 184. Pues si vivimos

1. Pues si vivimos, para El vivimos
   y si morimos para El morimos.
   Sea que vivamos o que muramos,
   somos del Señor, somos del Señor.

2. En esta vida frutos hay que dar
   y buenas obras hemos de ofrendar.
   Sea que demos o recibamos,
   somos del Señor, somos del Señor.

3. En la tristeza y en el dolor,
   en la belleza y en el amor,
   sea que suframos o que gocemos,
   somos del Señor, somos del Señor.

4. En este mundo por doquier habrá
   gente que llora y sin consolar.
   Sea que ayudemos o alimentemos,
   somos del Señor, somos del Señor.

LETRA: Estr. 1 basada en Romanos 14:8; Roberto Escamilla, estrs. 2, 3, 4


## 185. Himno de promesa

1. Bellas flores guarda el bulbo,
   la semilla, un manzanal;
   el capullo nos promete
   mariposas a volar.
   En el frío y crudo invierno,
   primavera oculta está.
   ¿Cuándo y dónde? No sabemos;
   sólo Dios nos lo dirá.

LETRA: Natalie Sleeth, 1986; trad. de Alberto Merubia

2. Hay un canto en el silencio,
melodía por brotar;
nuevo día nos anuncia
la más densa oscuridad.
Del ayer viene el mañana;
su misterio ¿cuál será?
¿Cuándo y dónde? No sabemos;
sólo Dios nos lo dirá.

3. Nuestro fin es el comienzo,
nuestro tiempo, infinidad.
En la duda hay fe latente;
en vivir, eternidad.
Al morir, resucitamos;
victoriosos al final.
¿Cuándo y dónde? No sabemos;
sólo Dios nos lo dirá.

## Acción de Gracias

### 186. Nos hemos reunido

1. Nos hemos reunido en tu nombre, oh Cristo,
te damos las gracias por tu gran bondad.
Con muchos cuidados nos has socorrido;
¡bendito sea tu nombre por la eternidad!

2. Oh sé con nosotros, Señor admirable
que «venga tu reino», cantamos aquí.
Contando contigo se vence al enemigo;
la gloria y el honor rendiremos a ti.

3. Aquí te exaltamos, oh líder triunfante,
orando que siempre nos libres del mal;
y tus redimidos, seguros, protegidos,
daremos a tu nombre loor eternal.

LETRA: *Nederlandtsch Gedenckclanck,* 1626; trad. al inglés de Theodore Baker; trad. al español de J. Alfonso Lockward

## 187. Dad gracias

Dad gracias de corazón, dad gracias al santo Dios,
dad gracias porque el Padre a su Hijo dio.
Dad gracias de corazón, dad gracias al santo Dios,
dad gracias porque el Padre a su Hijo dio.

Que hoy diga el débil, «fuerte soy»,
diga el pobre, «rico soy»,
por lo que hizo el Señor por mí.

Que hoy diga el débil, «fuerte soy»,
diga el pobre, «rico soy»,
por lo que hizo el Señor por mí.

¡Gracias dad! ¡Gracias dad!

LETRA: Henry Smith, 1978; trad. de Alberto Merubia (Cl. 3:13)


# Año Nuevo

## 188. Principia un año nuevo

1. Principia un año nuevo; que sea, oh Señor,
un año en que nos muestres de nuevo tu amor;
un año de progreso y de prosperidad,
un año en que gocemos tu gran fidelidad.

2. Principia un año nuevo; en ti hemos de confiar;
seguros en tu mano podemos descansar.
Tu gran misericordia, tu gracia y bondad,
en este nuevo año queremos disfrutar.

3. Principia un año nuevo; ayúdanos, oh Dios,
a ser más consagrados, más prestos a tu voz;
y sea allá contigo, o en la tierra aquí,
que en todo siempre demos la gloria sólo a ti.

LETRA: Frances R. Havergal, 1874; trad. de Esteban Sywulka B.

## 189. Oh nuestro Padre, nuestro Dios

1. Oh nuestro Padre, nuestro Dios,
que guías al mortal:
el año nuevo a ti, Señor,
queremos consagrar.

2. El cielo, el orbe, el mundo están
diciendo tu bondad;
la vida, el tiempo pasarán
según tu voluntad.

3. Haznos sentir la vanidad
de cuanto existe aquí;
grandezas, bienes, potestad
perecerán al fin.

4. Oh Dios, pedimos que nos des
en tu servicio ardor;
firme esperanza, viva fe
y más ardiente amor.

LETRA: Autor desconocido

# Dedicaciones/Aniversarios

## 190. Hoy queremos presentarte

1. Hoy queremos presentarte nuestros niños, oh Señor;
te pedimos que les seas un amigo protector,
que les cuides y les guardes con tu espíritu de amor
y que cada niño tenga tu perfecta bendición.

2. Como padres y amigos, congregados en tu altar,
suplicamos que nos muestres tu poder y tu bondad.
Estas tiernas criaturas reconocerán tu voz;
puedes encauzar sus pasos, ser su guía y su Dios.

3. En sus brazos, Jesucristo, a los niños los tomó;
demostrándoles cariño, con sus manos los tocó.
Hoy también, igual que Cristo, deseamos dedicar
estos niños que traemos, a tu reino celestial.

LETRA: Vernon L. Peterson, 1932

## 191. Los niños son de Cristo

1. Los niños son de Cristo, El es su Salvador;
son joyas muy preciosas, comprólas con su amor.

*Coro*
Joyas, joyas, joyas, joyas del Salvador,
están en esta tierra, cual luz y dulce amor.

2. Los niños son tesoros, pues que del cielo son;
luz refulgente esparcen en horas de aflicción.
*(Coro)*

3. Los niños son estrellas de grata claridad;
quiere Jesús que anuncien al mundo su verdad.
*(Coro)*

4. Los niños son de Cristo, por ellos El vendrá;
y con El, para siempre, dichosos vivirán.
*(Coro)*

LETRA: H. Pearson, 1902; trad. de H. C. Ball

## 192. ¡Señor! ¿Qué es nuestro templo?

1. ¡Señor! ¿Qué es nuestro templo si tú no estás presente?
¿Qué tienen sus paredes, sus bancos y su altar?
¿Qué el coro melodioso o el órgano potente,
si acaso tu presencia no habita en el lugar?

2. ¿Qué valen nuestras voces unidas en un canto,
palabras o silencios, discursos, oración,
si tu hálito divino no cubre como un manto
el íntimo aposento de cada corazón?

3. ¿Qué valen ceremonias, los credos, simbolismos,
los salmos de alabanzas, la bíblica lección,
si en medio de tu pueblo hay un profundo abismo
que priva a nuestras almas de franca comunión?

4. ¡Señor, llena este templo con tu presencia pura;
que en el silencio grato de tu feliz mansión,
unidos como hermanos se eleven a la altura
las fervorosas notas de nuestra adoración!

LETRA: Federico J. Pagura, 1942

# El Hogar Cristiano

## 193. Cuando las bases de este mundo

1. Cuando las bases de este mundo tiemblan
y el mal corrompe nuestra sociedad,
nuestras plegarias hacia ti se elevan
por la familia, por la humanidad.

2. Haz que los lazos que en amor estrechan
la recta y santa vida conyugal,
suaves y tiernos, pero firmes sean;
nada los pueda nunca quebrantar.

3. Los padres críen con temor sus hijos,
sin irritarlos, en amor y fe;
sean los hijos siempre agradecidos,
nunca se aparten de tu santa ley.

4. Que ni el dinero ni el placer se tornen
en falsa meta del moderno hogar.
Busquen servirte y ofrecer sus dones
a un mundo lleno de necesidad.

LETRA: Federico J. Pagura, 1957


## 194. En medio de la vida

1. En medio de la vida estás presente, oh Dios,
más cerca que mi aliento, sustento de mi ser.
Impulsas en mis venas mi sangre al palpitar
y el ritmo de la vida vas dando al corazón.

*Coro*
O Dios de cielo y tierra, te sirvo desde aquí;
te amo en mis hermanos, te adoro en la creación.

2. Estás en el trabajo del campo o la ciudad,
y es himno de la vida el diario trajinar.
El golpe del martillo, la tecla al escribir
entonan su alabanza al Dios de la creación.
*(Coro)*

LETRA: Mortimer Arias, 1971

3. Estás en la alegría y estás en el dolor,
compartes con tu pueblo la lucha por el bien.
En Cristo tú has venido la vida a redimir
y en prenda de tu reino, el mundo a convertir.
*(Coro)*

4. Estás en la familia, huésped de cada hogar,
oyente invisible de nuestro conversar.
Bendices nuestra mesa y no nos falta el pan,
Cuidas de nuestros hijos, frutos de nuestro amor.
*(Coro)*

## 195. Danos un bello hogar

1. Danos un bello hogar:
donde la Biblia nos guíe fiel,
donde tu amor bienestar nos dé,
donde en ti todos tengan fe.
¡Danos un bello hogar!
¡Danos un bello hogar!

2. Danos un bello hogar:
donde la madre es fuerte y fiel
y su ejemplo se puede ver,
donde tu amor reine por doquier.
¡Danos un bello hogar!
¡Danos un bello hogar!

3. Danos un bello hogar:
donde el padre, con devoción,
sepa mostrarnos tu compasión,
do todos vivan en comunión.
¡Danos un bello hogar!
¡Danos un bello hogar!

4. Danos un bello hogar:
donde los hijos, con decisión,
sigan a Cristo de corazón,
do se respire tu bendición.
¡Danos un bello hogar!
¡Danos un bello hogar!

LETRA: B. B. McKinney, 1949; trad. de Guillermo Blair, alt.

# MUERTE Y VIDA ETERNA

## 196. Cuando la trompeta suene

1. Cuando la trompeta suene en aquel día final
y que el alba eterna rompa en claridad;
cuando las naciones salvas a su patria lleguen ya
y que sea pasada lista, allí he de estar.

*Coro*
Cuando allá se pase lista, cuando allá se pase lista,
cuando allá se pase lista, a mi nombre yo feliz responderé.

2. En aquel día sin nieblas en que muerte ya no habrá
y su gloria el Salvador impartirá;
cuando los llamados entren a su celestial hogar,
y que sea pasada lista, allí he de estar.
*(Coro)*

3. Trabajemos para Cristo desde el alba al vislumbrar;
siempre hablemos de su amor y fiel bondad.
Cuando todo aquí termine y nuestra obra cese ya
y que sea pasada lista, allí he de estar.
*(Coro)*

LETRA: J. M. Black, 1893; trad. de J. J. Mercado, alt.

## 197. Cantad del amor de Cristo

1. Cantad del amor de Cristo,
ensalzad al Redentor;
tributadle, santos todos,
grande gloria y loor.

*Coro*
Cuando estemos en gloria,
en presencia de nuestro Redentor,
a una voz la historia
diremos del gran vencedor.

LETRA: Eliza E. Hewitt, 1898; trad. de H. C. Ball

2. La victoria es segura
   a las huestes del Señor;
   ¡oh, luchad con la mirada
   puesta en vuestro protector!
   *(Coro)*

3. El pendón alzad, cristianos,
   de la cruz y caminad;
   de victoria en victoria,
   siempre firmes avanzad.
   *(Coro)*

# LA IGLESIA TRIUNFANTE

## Comunión de los Santos

### 198. Fe de los santos

1. Fe de los santos, ejemplo tan fiel
frente a espada, fuego y terror.
Nos regocija saber que su fe
estuvo puesta en el Señor.

*Coro*
Fe de los santos, viva fe,
también será nuestro sostén.

2. Fe de los santos, que nos inspiró
a serle fieles hasta morir.
Por la verdad que viene de Dios,
hay libertad en nuestro vivir.
*(Coro)*

3. Fe de los santos, que inspira amor
hacia los nuestros y a los demás.
La predicamos confiados en El,
viviendo con fidelidad.
*(Coro)*

LETRA: Frederick W. Faber, 1849; trad. de Salomón Mussiett


### 199. Gracias, Dios vivo

1. Gracias, Dios vivo, por los que anunciaron
en tiempos idos tu merced y gloria;
y los caminos con valor trazaron,
de nuestra historia.

2. En noche oscura fue tu cruz su guía;
tu cruz su sombra bajo el sol candente.
En luz y sombras, en su pecho ardía
tu luz fulgente.

3. Muy rudos golpes en la lid sufrieron,
empero al débil tú tornaste fuerte;
y, sin desmayo, ellos te sirvieron
hasta la muerte.

4. Hoy que nos toca continuar su historia,
no te pedimos que nos des reposo
hasta, con ellos, compartir en gloria
tu eterno gozo.

LETRA: Justo L. González, 1988

# SEGUNDA VENIDA Y REINADO DE JESUCRISTO

## 200. Jesucristo, esperanza del mundo (Jesus Christ, Hope of the World)

1. Un poco después del presente alegre el futuro proclama
   la fuga total de la noche, la luz que ya el día derrama.

   *Coro*
   Venga tu reino, Señor; la fiesta del mundo recrea
   y nuestra espera y dolor transforma en plena alegría.
   Aie, eia, ae, ae, ae.

2. Capullo de amor y esperanza, anuncio de flor que será,
   promesa de hallar tu presencia que vida abundante traerá.
   *(Coro)*

3. Anhelo de un mundo sin guerras, nostalgia de paz e inocencia,
   de cuerpos y manos que se unen, sin armas, sin muerte o
   violencia.
   *(Coro)*

4. Nos diste, Señor, la simiente, señal de que el reino es ahora;
   futuro que alumbra el presente, viniendo ya estás sin demora.
   *(Coro)*

1. A little beyond this our time the future announces with gladness
   no war, no disaster, no crime, no more desolation, no sadness.

   *Refrain*
   Lord, thy kingdom come; the joy of our world recreate
   and all our hope and our longings transform in the fullness of life.
   Aie, eia, ae, ae, ae.

2. A bud of your hope is sprouting the token of flowers in spring:
   a world to arrive, no doubting, with justice and joy that you
   bring.
   *(Refrain)*

LETRA: Silvio Meincke, 1982; trad. del portugués de Pablo Sosa

3. We hope to cast out all our hate, we long for a world of pure beauty,
in which peace will never abate and justice will be, then, our duty.
*(Refrain)*

4. The seeds of your kingdom we bear, your future is drawing so near:
the earth with your help we prepare until you, in fullness, appear.
*(Refrain)*

## 201. Cantan los ángeles con dulce voz

1. Cantan los ángeles con dulce voz,
cantan los pueblos con sonora voz;
Cristo vendrá, nuestro Rey vencedor.
Cristo vendrá otra vez.

*Coro*
Viene otra vez, viene otra vez,
en gloria viene al mundo otra vez.
Viene otra vez, viene otra vez,
en gloria viene a reinar.

2. Ved en la tierra, los aires y el mar
grandes señales cumpliéndose ya;
todo indicando que pronto vendrá
nuestro glorioso Señor.
*(Coro)*

3. Todos los muertos en Cristo saldrán
de sus sepulcros; gozosos irán
para encontrar a su Rey vencedor.
Cristo vendrá otra vez.
*(Coro)*

4. Ven en las nubes, ¡oh buen Salvador!
¡Ven a la tierra, glorioso a reinar!
¡Ven, que tu Iglesia te espera, Jesús!
Cristo vendrá otra vez.
*(Coro)*

LETRA: Thoro Harris, 1914; trad. de H. C. Ball, alt.

# RECONOCIMIENTOS

5 Letra, Editorial Concordia; 3558 S. Jefferson Ave., St. Louis MO 63118-3968.

6 Trad., The United Methodist Publishing House.

7 Trad., Manna Music, Inc.; 35225 Brooten Rd., Pacific City, CA 97135.

8 Trad. de Juan Bautista Cabrera.

9 Trad. Abingdon Press.

10 Letra, Heber Romero; Bellavista 28, Reparte Escambray, Santa Clara, V.C., Cuba.

11 Letra, basada en Salmo 9:1-2.

12 Letra, Roberto Rodriguez; P.O. Box 607, Throggs Neck Station, Bronx, NY 10465.

13 Letra, Anders Frostenson; trad. inglés de Fred Kaan; trad. español Hope Publishing Company; 380 S. Main Pl., Carol Stream, IL 60188.

14 Trad., Honorato Reza, alt.; Hope Publishing Co., 380 S. Main Pl., Carol Stream, IL 60188.

15 Letra, Juan Luis García; 423 SW Beacon Blvd., Miami FL 33135.

16 Letra, Guillermo Cuéllar, Trad. de Linda McCrae (Is. 6:3) Parroquia San Francisco, CA. Delicias del Norte, Guatemala.

17 Letra, Trad., Jaroslav J. Vajda; 3534 Brookstone S. Dr., St. Louis, MO 63129.

18 Transcripción, The United Methodist Publishing House.

19 Letra, Abingdon Press.

20 Letra basada en Salmo 138:4-6.

21 Trad. Federico J. Pagura; Entre Ríos 5020, 2000 Rosario (Santa Fe), Argentina.

22 Letra, Resource Publications; 160 E. Virginia St. #290, San José CA 95112.

23 Trad. Abingdon Press.

24 Letra, Pablo Fernández Badillo; Apartado 744, San Antonio, Puerto Rico 00690.

25 Letra, trad., Word, Inc.; 3319 West End Ave. Suite 200, Nashville, TN 37203.

28 Letra, Patrick Matsikenyiri; P.O. Box 1320, Mutare, Zimbabwe; trad. Abingdon Press.

29 Letra, estr. 4 Abingdon Press

30 Letra, C.A. Music (div. de Christian Artists Group); 209 Chapelwood Dr., Franklin, TN 37069.

36 Letra, estr. 2: Abingdon Press.

37 Letra, Gaither Music Company; P.O. Box 737, Alexandria, IN 46001.

38 Letra, OCP Publications; 5536 NE Hassalo, Portland OR 97213.

40 Trad., Federico J. Pagura; Entre Ríos 5020, 2000 Rosario (Santa Fe), Argentina.

42 Trad., Editorial Avance Luterano; 2053 Woodland Hgts. Glen, Escondido, CA 92026.

43 Trad., Editorial Avance Luterano; 2053 Woodland Hgts. Glen, Escondido, CA 92026.

45 Trad., Abingdon Press.

49 Adap., The United Methodist Publishing House.

51 Letra, Pablo Fernández Badillo; Apartado 744, San Antonio, Puerto Rico 00690.

52 Trad., Word, Inc.; 3319 West End Ave. Suite 200, Nashville, TN 37203.

59 Letra, Juan Antonio Espinosa; OCP Publications; 5536 NE Hassalo, Portland OR 97213.

60 Letra, Hope Publishing Co.; 380 S. Main Pl., Carol Stream, IL 60188.

61 Letra, Federico J. Pagura; Entre Ríos 5020, 2000 Rosario (Santa Fe), Argentina.

62 Letra, Casa Bautista de Publicaciones; Apartado 4255, El Paso, TX 79914.

63 Letra, Trad., Hope Publishing Co.; 380 S. Main Pl., Carol Stream, IL 60188.

64 Letra, Abingdon Press.

65 Letra, The United Methodist Publishing House.

66 Trad.: estrs. 1-3, 5; Federico J. Pagura; Entre Ríos, 5020, 2000 Rosario (Santa Fe), Argentina; estr. 4, Lois Kroehler; 1739 Rainier Ave., Bremerton, WA 98312.

68 Trad., Word, Inc.; 3319 West End Ave. Suite 200, Nashville, TN 37203.

69 Letra, Abingdon Press.

70 Letra, trad., Oxford University Press; Walton Street, Oxford 0X2 6DP England.

71 Trad., Elizabeth R. Donaldson; P.O. Box 80554, San Marino, CA 91118-8554.

72 Letra, trad., Word, Inc.; 3319 West End Ave. Suite 200, Nashville, TN 37203.

73 Letra, Mortimer Arias; "Mi Amor" Colón y Nandú, 15100 Salinas, Uruguay.
74 Letra, Cesareo Gabaráin, OCP Publications; 5536 NE Hassalo, Portland OR 97213.
76 Letra, trad., Gaither Music Company; P.O. Box 737, Alexandria, IN 46001.
79 Letra, trad., Philip W. Blycker; 8625 La Prada, Dallas, TX 75228.
80 Letra, Abingdon Press.
82 Letra, Trust Music Management, Inc.; P.O. Box 9256, Calabasas, CA 91372.
83 Letra, trad., Abingdon Press.
85 Trad., Benson Music Group; 365 Great Circle Rd., Nashville, TN 37228.
88 Letra, OCP Publications; 5536 NE Hassalo, Portland OR 97213.
89 Letra, estrs. 2-3, Celebremos/Libros Alianza; A. A. 100, Cúcuta, Colombia.
90 Trad., Word, Inc.; 3319 West End Ave. Suite 200, Nashville, TN 37203.
91 Trad., Manna Music, Inc.; 35255 Brooten Rd., Pacific City, OR 97135.
94 Trad. inglés, Abingdon Press.
95 Letra, Music Services (div. de Christian Artists Corp.); 209 Chapelwood Dr., Franklin, TN 37069.
98 Letra, Cesareo Gabaráin, OCP Publications; 5536 NE Hassalo, Portland OR 97213.
99 Trad., estrs. 2-6: Abingdon Press.
101 Letra, Clara Luz Ajo; Rua Russia #621, Apt. 17 Taboao, Sao Bernado do Campo, Brasil.
102 Letra, The Copyright Company; 40 Music Square E., Nashville, TN 37203.
104 Letra, estrs. 4-5: Abingdon Press.
105 Letra, Abingdon Press.
106 Letra, trad., Hope Publishing Co.; 380 S. Main Pl., Carol Stream, IL 60188.
107 Letra, Gaither Music Company; P.O. Box 737, Alexandria, IN 46001.
108 Letra, Word, Inc.; 3319 West End Ave., Suite 200, Nashville, TN 37203.
110 Letra, Rafael Montalvo; Calle Pina #258, (casi esq. Independencia), Ciudad Nueva Apt. 98-2, Santo Domingo, Rep. Dominicana.
112 Letra, Casa Bautista de Publicaciones; Apdo. 4255, El Paso, TX 79914.
114 Letra, Luis Angel Toro; L 10 Pascua St., Arecibo, PR 00612.
117 Trad. y adap., OCP Publications; 5536 NE Hassalo, Portland OR 97213.
118 Letra, Eleazar Inciarte; 4423 Louisburg Rd. Raleigh, NC 27604.
121 Trad. Elizabeth R. Donaldson; P.O. Box 80554, San Marino, CA 91118-8554.
122 Trad., Federico J. Pagura; Entre Ríos 5020, 2000 Rosario (Santa Fe), Argentina.
123 Trad. Word, Inc.; 3319 West End Ave., Suite 200, Nashville, TN 37203.
126 Letra, Juan Antonio Espinosa; OCP Publications; 5536 NE Hassalo, Portland OR 97213.
128 Trad., Abingdon Press.
131 Letra, Luz Ester Ríos de Cuna, alt.; Benson Music Group; 365 Great Circle Rd., Nashville, TN 37228.
135 Trad., Comité Ecuménico del Himnario en Español; 12029 Gurley Ave., Downey, CA 90242.
136 Letra, Carlos Mejía Godoy; Bosques de Altamira, Farmacia 5, Avenida 250 metros al oriente, Managua, Nicaragua.
137 Letra, Abingdon Press.
138 Letra, trad. The Lorenz Corporation; 501 E. 3rd St., P.O. Box 802, Dayton, OH 45401-0802.
140 Letra, Pablo Sosa; Espartaco 634, 1406 Buenos Aires, Argentina.
141 Letra, Ministerio Musical Panamericano; Apartado 82 Bulevares, Edo de México, 53140 México.
142 Trad. Abingdon Press.
143 Trad. Pablo Sosa; Espartaco 634, 1406 Buenos Aires, Argentina.
145 Letra, Abingdon Press; trad., The Pilgrim Press; 700 Prospect Ave., Cleveland, OH 44115.
146 Letra, Pablo Sosa; Espartaco 634, 1406 Buenos Aires, Argentina.
147 Letra, Abingdon Press.
148 Letra, Abingdon Press.
149 Letra, Casa Bautista de Publicaciones; Apdo. 4255, El Paso, TX 79914.
150 Letra, trad., Hope Publishing Co.; 380 S. Main Pl., Carol Stream, IL 60188.
151 Letra, trad., OCP Publications; 5536 NE Hassalo, Portland OR 97213.
152 Letra, Creación colectiva; Caixa Postal 49012, 23021-970 Rio de Janeiro, Brasil.
153 Letra, trad., OCP Publications; 5536 NE Hassalo, Portland OR 97213.

154 Letra, Lutheran Human Relations Assn.; 2703 N. Sherman Blvd., Milwaukee, WI 53210.
159 Letra, OCP Publications; 5536 NE Hassalo, Portland OR 97213.
160 Adap., trad. Abingdon Press.
161 Trad., estr. 4: Abingdon Press.
162 Letra, trad., Abingdon Press.
167 Letra, Casa Bautista de Publicaciones; Apdo. 4255, El Paso, TX 79914.
168 Letra, Raquel Mora Martínez; 2501 S. 78th St., Lincoln, NE 68506.
169 Trad., Federico J. Pagura; Entre Ríos 5020, 2000 Rosario (Santa Fe), Argentina.
171 Letra, OCP Publications; 5536 NE Hassalo, Portland OR 97213; trad. The United Methodist Publishing House.
172 Trad. inglés, Abingdon Press.
173 Letra, Integrity Music, Inc.; P.O. Box 851622, Mobile, AL 36685.
174 Letra, Abingdon Press.
175 Letra, trad., Tempo Music Publications, Inc.; 3773 W. 95th St., Leawood, KS 66206.
178 Letra, Norah Buyers; P.O. Box 2259, El Granada, CA 94018.
179 Letra, Benjamín Villanueva; 7114 Richwood, Houston, TX 77087.
180 Letra, OCP Publications; 5536 NE Hassalo, Portland OR 97213.
182 Letra, Abingdon Press.
184 Letra, estrs. 2, 3, 4: Abingdon Press.
185 Letra, Hope Publishing Co.; 380 S. Main Pl., Carol Stream, IL 60188.
186 Trad. Abingdon Press.
187 Letra, Integrity Music, Inc.; P.O. Box 851622, Mobile, AL 36685-1622.
188 Trad., Celebremos/Libros Alianza; A.A. 100, Cúcuta, Colombia.
190 Letra, Herald Publishing House; P.O. Box 1770, Independence, MO 64055.
192 Letra, Federico J. Pagura; Entre Ríos 5020, 2000 Rosario (Santa Fe), Argentina.
193 Letra, Federico J. Pagura; Entre Ríos 5020, 2000 Rosario (Santa Fe), Argentina.
194 Letra, Mortimer Arias; "Mi Amor" Colón y Nandú, 15100 Salinas, Uruguay.
195 Letra, trad. Broadman Press.
198 Trad., Abingdon Press.
199 Letra, Abingdon Press.
200 Letra, Silvio Meincke; Canabarro, 95890-000 Tuetonia-R5, Brasil; trad., Pablo Sosa; Espartaco 634, 1406 Buenos Aires, Argentina.

# INDICE POR TEMAS

## INDICE POR TEMAS

INDICE POR TEMAS

# INDICE DE PRIMERAS LÍNEAS Y TÍTULOS

# INDICE DE PRIMERAS LÍNEAS Y TÍTULOS

## STUDIES IN COMPARATIVE PHILOSOPHY AND RELIGION

**Series Editor: Douglas Allen, University of Maine**

This series explores important intersections within and between the disciplines of religious studies and philosophy. These original studies will emphasize, in particular, aspects of contemporary and classical Asian philosophy and its relationship to Western thought. The editor welcomes a wide variety of manuscript submissions, especially works exhibiting highly focused research and theoretical innovation.

*Varieties of Ethical Reflection: New Directions for Ethics in a Global Context,* by Michael Barnhart

# Varieties of Ethical Reflection

## *New Directions for Ethics in a Global Context*

Edited by Michael Barnhart

*Studies in Comparative Philosophy and Religion, No. 1*

LEXINGTON BOOKS
*Lanham • Boulder • New York • Oxford*

LEXINGTON BOOKS

Published in the United States of America
by Lexington Books
A Member of the Rowman & Littlefield Publishing Group
4720 Boston Way, Lanham, Maryland 20706

PO Box 317
Oxford
OX2 9RU, UK



British Library Cataloguing in Publication Information Available

**Library of Congress Cataloging-in-Publication Data**

Varieties of ethical reflection: new directions for ethics in a global context / edited by Michael Barnhart.
p. cm.
Includes bibliographical references and index.
ISBN 0-7391-0443-8 (alk. paper)
1. Ethics. 2. Globalization—Moral and ethical aspects. I. Barnhart, Michael, 1956–. II. Series.

BJ1031 .V37 2002
170'.9—dc21 2002010430

Printed in the United States of America

The paper used in this publication meets the minimum requirements of American National Standard for Information Sciences—Permanence of Paper for Printed Library Materials, ANSI/NISO Z39.48–1992.

# Contents

# Acknowledgments

The editor wishes to thank and acknowledge the following periodicals and journals for permission to reprint David R. Loy's, Damien Keown's, and Carl B. Becker's contributions.

David R. Loy's chapter originally appeared in *International Studies in Philosophy* 26, no. 4 (1994): 47-67, edited by Stephen David Ross.

Damien Keown's chapter originally appeared in *Journal of Law and Religion* 13, no. 2 (1998-99): 385-405, edited by Marie A. Failinger.

Carl B. Becker's chapter originally appeared in *Drug Information Journal* 31, no. 4 (1997): 1089-96, edited by Tom Teal.

The editor also wishes to thank The City University of New York's support for this project through a PSC-CUNY research grant for 1997-98 and the National Endowment for the Humanities for grant support over the summer of 1997.

# Introduction

## Michael Barnhart

### I

This collection represents an attempt to sample the impact on philosophical ethics achieved by extending the circle of customary textual sources and widening the range of problems considered. Because this seems to be the direction ethics is in fact moving in, we believe that our collection represents a contemporary and vital change percolating through contemporary intellectual life. It is now commonplace to call for the inclusion of the world's variety of cultural and religious perspectives in confronting longstanding ethical and political issues. The treatment of women, sharing of wealth and income, respect for the environment, the spread of democracy and human rights, economic globalization, the pervasive influence of information technologies such as the Internet, and the onward march of biotechnological progress represent just a few of the bewildering array of issues that confront humanity as a whole. It seems ill-advised—if not impossible—to attempt to deal with these issues relying only on Western philosophical resources. In a multicultural world, world problems must be confronted multiculturally; that is, from a variety of cultural perspectives. In fact, meaningful participation in larger dialogues regarding world issues must require a kind of global consciousness, an awareness of the limits of one's own voice, and perspective in a sense of where the divergences lie. One can only hope to foster such awareness by thinking through the range and limits of the different philosophical and religious traditions inspiriting the world's variegated cultures.

Each one of our collected papers attempts at least one of the following necessary tasks in expanding philosophical ethics. First, the range of available theoretical perspectives must be broadened. Of course in so doing, the question of what constitutes an ethical theory must also be confronted. Each of the chapters in Part One directly confront this issue through a comparative evaluation of the strengths and weaknesses of the principal Asian traditions against the background of Western ethical theory. Though no uniform consensus regarding a "best" ethical theory emerges, one does develop a certain strategic sense of both the shortcomings and possibilities within such theories generally. Before closing this introduction, I will attempt to say something more substantive about this sense.

Secondly, broad issues of relativism, universalism, and the commensurability of ethical "vocabularies" need to be directly confronted in considering the significance and merits of any such comparative investigations. The attempt to qualitatively reflect on distant vocabularies always entails such questions, but particularly an endeavor that recognizes real and profound differences of this sort already and implicitly proposes a response to the universalism-relativism debate. Later I will comment on what that might be.

Thirdly, the practical and policy oriented aspects of such a broadened perspective need to be addressed. Ethics has always had practical ramifications, and in fact, much contemporary thinking has suggested that practical affairs can have theoretical ramifications, forcing a rethinking of the theoretical basics. A distinct group of chapters reflect on both of these issues weighing up how such "real world" concerns as gender and technology, biomedical technology in particular, are influenced by and in turn influence varieties of ethical reflection.

Lastly, some readers may wonder at the confinement of this discussion to principally South and East Asian traditions, particularly Buddhism, Hinduism, Confucianism, and Taoism. This is not meant to suggest that Judaism, Islam, or traditional African perspectives, for example, do not have something to say on these matters. They most assuredly do. Rather, the traditions represented here demonstrate, I believe, the most systematic philosophical challenge to those theories that have reigned dominant in Western ethical discourse. Though I regard the terms "East" and "West" as hackneyed and misleading, I do think there is a kernel of truth in the idea of an "Eastern" way of thinking, or as I would prefer to put it, that there is a family resemblance between the above-mentioned Asian traditions that is philosophically significant and that emphasizes elements of ethical discourse that are quite different from those within the Judaeo-Christian and Islamic traditions. Alternatively, there are family resemblances within the Judaeo-Christian, Islamic, and even African traditions which feature prominently in contemporary Western ethical theory but which only weakly correlate with those in the Buddhist, Hindu, Confucian, and Taoist traditions.[1] I will not attempt to directly argue for this schematization, although I believe a careful reading of those chapters in the first or "theory" section of the book will bear this rough generalization out.

Let me begin though, by touching on a basic background issue that motivates our collection of essays and the issues it raises—why traditional ethical theories associated with the Western philosophical tradition are not sufficient resources in dealing with the sorts of issues touched on above and in the collection. I will then elaborate further, as promised, on the general philosophical problems that accompany such a globalization of ethical reflection. Finally, I will comment specifically on the role of each of our contributed essays in light of these general problems.

## II

Two major challenges push ethics beyond the Western tradition. The first is internal and is, in a word, relativism. The second is more external and concerns the context in which issues such as human rights or environmental degradation are addressed, that is the globalization of human problems. With regard to the first of these challenges, whatever one may think of relativism as a "doctrine," its underlying critique of philosophical certainty is devastating. A common thread in all our chapters is that ethics cannot be fully grounded in apodeictic intuitions, the authority of "pure reason," or in some general cluster of cultural universals such as a general abhorrence of murder or theft. The problem with all such philosophical strategies is, as Joseph Margolis has pointed out, their lack of any decisive legitimating argument.[2] In regard to intuitions, if *x* is an intuition, then there seems little one can say in regard to its necessity. How can *x* be necessary or how can one show that *x* is necessary if *x* simply "comes" to one? There seems no perspective on which to sort out what necessarily occurs to one from what contingently does so. If *x* is "just there" in one's consciousness, one is in no position to examine its provenance. Yes, it may just appear to me that torturing others is abhorrent and I can't imagine it being otherwise. But the same may be said of many circumstances. For example, I can't really imagine what would be the case had life not evolved on earth. It hardly follows from that fact that life necessarily evolved as it did. Nor does the presence of some moral fact in my conscience allow me to draw any larger conclusions regarding the constitution of human moral consciousness generally. The same can be said with regard to such collective intuitions that a society, for example, may harbor and that constitute a culture. The important question is not whether we have them, nor even whether they are widely or universally shared. The question of legitimacy is why we have them, whether they are necessary in some sense, and whether they are deservedly authoritative. Answering this challenge usually involves some appeal to rationality as the ground of moral authority.

In regard to the authority of reason, though, the relevant question is reason as opposed to what? For Kant and others in the tradition of moral rationalism (Alan Donagan for example) the answer is reason as opposed to inclination.[3] But even accepting the terms in which Kant frames the issue—reason versus inclination—it is very hard to defend against the Humean observation that reason is just one more inclination human beings follow.[4] And just as other inclinations hardly command us absolutely, it is very difficult to see why reason should do so also. Of course, Kant argues that reason is opposed to inclination insofar as reason is the recognition of unconditional necessity in the form of general and invariant rules, whether of those that govern nature or those that govern our actions. But while reason itself is not an inclination, the tendency towards reasonableness is, and the challenge regarding reason's authority is not whether reason is based on necessity but whether necessity, moral necessity, is based in reason, a challenge that is reflected in the persistence of the question, why be reasonable? Why should moral goodness always be a matter of acting reasonably?

In fact, Kant himself seems to realize that this is a relevant question. At the beginning of *Metaphysics of Morals* he offers what is in effect an argument about why we must link moral goodness with adherence to law in the pursuit of duty for duty's sake. Kant's discussion would be entirely unintelligible if these links were, as he says, analytic. They are rather *a priori* synthetic and so require an argument, one that should also serve to demonstrate the practical necessity of duty within a moral life. Remember that Kant ties these various concepts together by reference to the notion of a will that is good in itself. A good will is the only thing that is good in itself, that is not in need of any supplementary accomplishment in order to guarantee its goodness. Further, the major practical purpose of reason is to control the will, so a will regulated according to its natural governing principle, namely reason, is a good will. Thus, reason is the guarantor of the will's goodness insofar as it serves to effectively regulate the will. As he remarks, "reason is given to us as a practical faculty, i.e., one which is meant to have an influence on the will."[5]

But as Kant also remarks, "there is something so strange in this idea of the absolute worth of the will alone, in which no account is taken of any use, that . . . the suspicion must arise that perhaps only high-flown fancy is its hidden basis." Of course, after making this remark Kant goes on to argue why nature must have designed reason to give us the capacity to control our will, not that a good will is incontestably good in itself. But in fact, he offers no argument to back up the absolute goodness of a purely good will. Yes, on its own terms, such a will is, by definition, good. But is it really so? Even if it gives rise to no good "effects"? It may be true, as Kant has earlier pointed out, that other human qualities and inclinations—self-control for example—are diminished by the absence of good will. But it doesn't follow from this observation that good will unaccompanied by good effects is not itself diminished in some sense. Commonly, good will does not count for much unless it is matched with action and the vigorous inclination to see its effects in deeds. Furthermore, good will practiced in ignorance of the needs and feelings of others is generally less esteemed than good will informed by a knowledge of those factors. Consequently, the proposition that the will is the measure of its own goodness doesn't even match our ordinary moral intuitions, the beginning of Kant's moral philosophy. Rather, the goodness of a good will is a problem for us and one that we typically address by considering factors other than those internal to the will itself. Consequently, when Kant attempts to erect the authority of reason on its sovereignty over the good will and hence, over all questions of moral goodness, he is addressing only the question of what makes the will good, not why exhibiting good will alone automatically qualifies us as morally good.

This is all a long-winded way of saying that the authority of reason requires a decision on our part; that is, we must ask whether it is worth submitting to principle and duty for the sake of law and reason. If this is a real decision, then its basis remains open, which in turn suggests that "reason," however understood, is not necessarily authoritative. As with reason and intuition, so with the tendency to ground our moral sensibilities and judgments in some more local considerations, such as culture, history, tradition, or as Rorty has proposed, our sense of solidarity with others. While all of these are important elements in defining our personal and public conscience, none of them are decisive and, because they vary with time and circumstance, they invite the very kind of relativism that moral theories were meant to exclude. Thus, we still lack much in the way of a comprehensive account connecting moral evaluation and local values. Furthermore, the contemporary swing toward grounding morality in the local remains focused on the question of legitimacy while often neglecting any "thick" description of moral phenomena. For all their shortcomings, the great moral philosophers, Aristotle, Kant, and Mill all dealt with a very rich set of issues, foremost among them being some sort of account of exactly what it is to value something whether it be a good, an end, or another moral agent. Many contemporary moral philosophers either ignore these issues altogether or rehash much of what has already been said within the tradition.

Consider, only briefly, two examples: Alasdair MacIntyre and Richard Rorty.[6] MacIntyre's celebrated revival of Aristotelian moral theory rests on two obvious pivots. The first is Aristotle's account of the virtues, updated to explain not so much what dispositions are internal to the best kind of life but rather what sort are internal to successful participation in human "practices." While this represents an interesting application of Aristotle's approach, it offers a decidedly conservative perspective on human conduct, serving up little in the way of innovative moral description. The second pivot consists in a rejection of what MacIntyre calls Aristotle's "metaphysical biology," his assumption of a distinctive human essence. Conceptions of the good life and nobility of purpose are just too various in the flow of history and the range of culture to permit the kind of generalizations that Aristotle makes. Rorty, on the other hand, goes one step further and combines antiessentialism with a pronounced reluctance to connect an understanding of the good life with *any* particular set of dispositions, no matter how beholden they may be to the specifics of one's time and place. Rorty's account of what makes a life worth living is, to put it mildly, thin. He calls it liberal and ties it to the human aspiration to invent or reinvent oneself in the face of one's society and its traditions, what he calls one's "inherited vocabulary." The liberal life is one haunted by a version of the "anxiety of influence," and it is no wonder that commentators familiar with the aspirations and ideals of non-Western cultures and ways of thinking note that this sort of anti-traditionalism is exactly what gives liberalism such a bad name in illiberal or "traditional" cultures.[7] Of course, to be fair to Rorty, he draws a rather decisive private/public distinction and insists that such reinvention, liberal ironism, is a private project, part of leading a liberal life, and is not necessary to a liberal political commitment—this only requires a desire to avoid cruelty. But Rorty's concession doesn't change the essential and calculated emptiness of what he believes counts, in general terms, as a good life.

In both cases, we get little sense as to exactly what constitutes moral deliberation and reflection, either because all the essential stuff has already been said long before or because there really isn't very much to say at a general level.[8] However, given the lack of philosophical attention paid to non-Western material, neither conclusion seems particularly warranted. If the above survey of contemporary moral theory is at all correct, it appears a remarkably propitious time to seriously critique the moral or ethical resources of very different ways of thinking, and even if one doesn't believe that human thinking can vary "incommensurably," we have hardly plumbed all the resources on offer. Relativistic thinking, and I don't mean anything terribly precise by that, has opened the door to the possibility of a wide divergence in our conceptions of the good life and human nature, even if such differences are mostly lexical or sentential following Rorty and Davidson. The continual recycling of old philosophical paradigms within the Western European tradition ought to awaken hunger for genuinely different, if not new, descriptions of human nature and its aspirations.

And if the search for novelty in moral reflection is not enough, another "external" motivation should prompt us to reach out to other traditions. This consideration has to do with the nature of the challenges facing human beings generally and the context of their resolution, if that is not too hopeful a word. It is at this point a cliché to point out the global dimensions of humanity's problems. Environmental degradation or the protection of human rights both involve the whole world and must be addressed with cultural difference firmly in mind. One cannot hope, for example, to successfully defend human rights, such as the right not to be tortured, without tailoring both the definition and the defense of those rights to the different ways in which the world's traditions have understood the role of the individual in society and the relative balance of power between these two entities. Similarly, the loss of plant and animal species due to poaching and so on cannot be successfully handled without involving the interests of those who poach as a means of subsistence and influencing their understanding of the resources they exploit. This, of course, requires addressing how different human societies traditionally have understood the natural world and their entire conception of themselves. Hence, moral discussions that hinge on a limited conception of the goals, values, and context of a good life will have correspondingly less leverage in the increasingly global context of human disputation and conflict resolution.

## III

Western moral philosophy clearly leans toward universalism because of the particular process of abstraction out of which it is built, involving at least three basic distinctions: nature versus nurture, reason versus inclination, and theory versus practice. The first of these gives rise to the idea of something distinctive in regard to human beings that sets them aside from the rest of creation. If nature and natural endowment are not destiny, then there is some special element in *human* nature that is dependent upon human practices for its expression. This special element makes human nature different from natural nature, and since ethics covers the rules of human conduct and therefore nurture, nature and nature's laws whatever they might be underdetermine ethics. Nurture, among other things, socializes human beings, instructs them in the rules of mutual association, provides a sense of identity and purpose in life, and transmits the store of acquired knowledge. If this process is conceived as distinct from nature and the instruction nature provides, it serves then to locate moral knowledge, which covers the rules nurture conveys, outside the purview and scope of nature. Hence the origin of the so-called naturalistic fallacy.

The second and third distinctions suggest the direction in which ethical theorizing itself must move. On the one hand, if reason can be distinguished from inclination, then to the degree that ethical reflection is a rational enterprise, it too must be purified of any influences that stem from inclination. Hence, emotion, prejudice, instinct, and gut feeling, to name just a few, find little or no place in serious moral deliberation. Because the dictates of the heart are very much a part of one's inherited tradition and culture, the reason/inclination distinction gives rise to an equally firm morality versus culture distinction. On the other hand, the theory/practice distinction suggests that rules are fundamentally different from their application and hence also that theoretical speculation is a unique and distinctive activity, autonomous in regard to human conduct, and appropriately positioned to render judgments from on-high.

As our reflections on the question of "legitimation" make clear, all three of these distinctions and their corollary by-products are open to serious challenge. Once the assumption of a distinctive human nature is given up, the basis on which one can identify a pivotal difference between human nurturing and the practices of animal nature dissolves as well, leaving the door open to an evolutionary perspective that explains human nurturing practices as fully adaptive responses to the external "natural" environment. A fully naturalized explanation that requires no assumption of either inter- or intraspecies human uniqueness or difference becomes possible. Similarly, maintaining the distinction between reason and emotion or inclination becomes increasingly difficult when relativist challenges to the legitimacy of duty for duty's sake and other apodeictic rationalist principles are pushed home to their logical conclusion. If reason reflects a particular body of ossified inclinations, then ethical theory itself may vary in direct proportion to the variety of human practices the world over. Stated in terms of the theory/practice distinction, the practical determinations people make in everyday life, as influenced by the wealth of factors a social science might in fact discover, are as much or more a part of ethical theory as any abstruse speculations regarding such universal yet "thin" terms as "good," "right," "just," and so on.

I might add that already contemporary 'applied' philosophical ethics has witnessed challenges to these distinctions and their bias towards universalistic ethical theorizing and reflection. In environmental ethics, for example, the suspicion that animal nature and human nature and animal nurture and human nurture may not stand on opposite sides of an ontological chasm has inspired an attempt to recast ethics so that it accounts for our conduct in and towards the natural world as well as the human.[9] The anthropocentrism of traditional Western ethics has admittedly constituted something of an obstacle to this endeavor, but this has in turn inspired calls for a complete review of ethical theory itself and the possibilities for re-imagining man's place in nature. Obviously, non-Western sources provide much that may prove useful to such a project.[10]

But it is particularly in regard to the reason versus inclination and reason versus practice distinctions that contemporary ethical reflection has encountered profound challenges. For example, much current debate over the usefulness and applicability of the notion of "universal" human rights stems from the perceived embeddedness of 'rights' in the Western-European traditon. Westerners, so the challenge goes, have a peculiar and historically instilled inclination to insist on certain individual rights, an inclination not universally present in other peoples. Absent *a priori* arguments based on the authority of autonomous reason, it is very difficult without turning to the conceptual resources of these other traditions themselves to make out any sort of case on behalf of such rights.[11] Consider also, how biomedical ethics in particular has seen challenges to the reason/application distinction. As new technologies such as gene therapy have increased our capacity to affect the nature of disease and health, unresolved problems regarding the permissibility of such interventions have multiplied wildly. Many of these dilemmas do not yield to conventional ethical reflection, and furthermore, for many bioethicists, no one ethical theory appears sufficiently powerful to provide answers to all questions and conflicts. Hence, some philosophers who focus on these problems have come to invert the theory over practice hierarchy, seeing practice as the source of principles and ethical reflection as a unique kind of speculative enterprise utterly unlike theory building in, for example, the natural sciences.[12] In other words, many have concluded that we cannot start with theory first, resolving all conceptual questions, and then seek to apply our rules to cases. Rather, we must constantly adapt theory to cases and perhaps even jettison theory altogether at times as unique cases arise. Ethical reflection is a process of achieving "reflective equilibrium" rather than a deductive application of rules to circumstances. Obviously, as biomedical issues crop up in other cultures, according to this way of thinking, they will have to be dealt with using normative resources potentially quite different from those which Americans or Europeans are at all familiar with, and, of course, the results of such developments will be difficult, at best, to anticipate from where we presently stand.

Adding such trends together (and this represents one of the "external" challenges to ethical reflection), it appears that the kinds of problems that consume political and legal discourse and permeate contemporary society have stimulated ethical reflection to reconsider its traditional parameters and universalistic assumptions. However, we have only begun to embark on a re-examination of the basic operating assumptions and only begun to re-imagine basic distinctions such as the nature/nurture distinction. All of this requires cross-border thinking, and all of this should prod ethical reflection into a more global consciousness. However, in doing so we must confront a basic theoretical issue: what happens when the constitutive distinctions within Western ethical theory are systematically recast in a very different philosophical context? What can we learn by thinking through the rudiments of our philosophical vocabulary along systematically different lines?

This last problem constitutes much of the subtext for the chapters in the first and second parts of the book. Each author confronts and wrestles with the ways in which various thinkers have attempted to reconceive ethics outside the traditional Western dichotomies. So, turning to basic texts, we begin with Russell Kirkland's discussion of the *Daode Jing* and its basic moral teachings. Noting that the issue of what the text's fundamental moral position is has never been fully addressed, Kirkland outlines how the text casts ethical problems outside the traditional nature/nurture distinction. According to Kirkland, how we can achieve a kind of "bio-spiritual self-cultivation" becomes the fundamental moral problem. In this sense, human nurture, the nurture necessary for moral self-cultivation, must become more natural, more attuned to the inner forces driving our individual human nature. In a similar vein, Kirill Thompson's paper asks how we can reconceive ethical judgment following Chu Hsi's model of "investigating things to extend knowledge." This is not a matter of impartial scientific examination but an attempt to conceive ethical judgment as both self-critical reason and sensitivity to context—"a working knowledge of the constitutive patterns/principles of reality and society in the light of which the norms and ritual actions prescribed for upright interpersonal relationships and intercourse are devised." Turning to the thought of the Daoist philosopher Zhuangzi, Alan Fox, in his chapter, sketches a "concrete ethics" which compares favorably to the pragmatism of William James. Drawing on such examples as the master chef, Cook Ding, who develops such mastery at slicing up meat that he never dulls his blade by hitting the bones, Fox attempts to discern a model of true mastery or skill in practical affairs, what some writers have called a "social virtuosity."[13] Such an ideal has little to do with "formulas" or principles but rather model an understanding of judgment as contextually determined. Ethics is about sensitivity to context as opposed to rule following, and as sensitivity grounds judgment our "practical" reason can no longer be opposed to our inclinations.

Lastly, Section One looks at the reason/application distinction in normative ethics through David R. Loy's discussion of Buddhist ethical judgment particularly in regard to the role of instrumental rationality and the relation of means to ends. Noting that Western ethics has treated practical reason as almost entirely preoccupied with questions regarding means, Loy offers a Buddhist alternative that can also address issues of ends without falling into the Platonic trap of supposing a determinate answer to questions regarding what is the good for human beings or what is the specific nature of the human. In other words, Loy offers a Buddhist-inspired description of a kind of practical reasoning that is beyond the means/ends or reason/application distinctions.

Thus, each of the chapters in Section One challenges the universalizing distinctions in Western ethical theory in one way or another. Whether it is nature/nurture, reason/inclination, or reason/application, the point is that other traditions of philosophical ethics have found one way or another to provide normative guidance that do not hinge on these distinctions or, in fact, require their equivalence. Furthermore, a close reading of these chapters suggests, I believe, some sense of both the shortcomings and the possibilities for ethical theory. Specifically, it is that the study of ethical theory and dialogue across a variety of ethical theories does not so much identify what are the best normative principles as serve to outline those considerations that define the path of moral cultivation and judgment. Of course, in different cultures and at different times, different considerations have been specially relevant to such self-cultivation. For example, in enlightenment Europe, autonomy and personal freedom emerged as dominant considerations in the cultivation of a moral sense, one that can prescribe duties to oneself. Or, in pre-Ch'in China, deference to and respect for elders and society represented important elements of the capacity for moral judgment. But all of these approaches single out specific factors that direct and condition the use of moral judgment without it being the case that any one factor, or combination of factors, offers a definitive account of the nature of such judgment.

However, in reaching beyond the Western philosophical tradition in this manner, invariably we face questions regarding the basis on which we can compare such disparate "vocabularies" between, say, the Aristotelian terminology of virtue and the Chinese Taoist or Confucian terminology of *ren*. Neither universalism nor relativism seem particularly helpful in framing a response to such questions. Universalism seems unhelpful because it suggests the possibility of a uniquely correct solution to the problem of multiple vocabularies; that is, it regards such pluralism as a problem to be solved. Relativism appears unhelpful because incommensurability and hence, mutual unintelligibility, invariably threaten any attempts at comparison and dialogue, thus undermining the meaningfulness of any kind of ethical pluralism, any alternative to one's local ethical context.[14] Both chapters in Section Two address this problem and each proposes a different kind of approach to navigating the Scylla and Charybdis of universalism and relativism. On the one hand, Stephen Angle attempts to show how the context of use that governs a particular set of ethical norms can set it apart from another without at the same time making the two absolutely incommensurable. That is, one need not insist that users of different ethical systems speak different languages in effect or use languages that can never be translated. Rather, the expressive capacity of different languages, and hence different ethical systems, as well as the purposes to which various discourses may be put, impose certain practical limitations to the achievement of a single all-embracing ethical system. Taking a somewhat different tack, Samuel Fleischacker argues the novel thesis that cultural difference is not so much a fact that philosophy must explain, but a goal at which we must aim. That is, we have a moral obligation to preserve cultural variety in order to preserve constructive competition between different and available ways of conducting not just an individual life, but a life in a socio-cultural context. In a sense, Fleischacker's proposal is to generalize Mill's idea of individual experiments in living to the idea of different cultural experiments in forms of life. Thus, the question isn't whether cultural variety is possible. The question is: is it desirable?

At this point in philosophy, the relativism/universalism debate may seem so intractable that little remains to be added. But in the reflections of Angle and Fleischacker as well as in the discussion of various challenges to Western ethical theory, a variety of novel responses begin to emerge. On the one hand, the variety of ethical theories suggests that there may be more to moral cultivation than any single theory can encompass. This accords both with the universalist view that all such theories converge in significant ways in that they all seem to be talking about moral phenomena in ways that can be made intelligible in each other's terms. It also accords with the relativist insight that one cannot definitively say which among these various theories or moral vocabularies is the right one. No one sort of moral language seems adequately comprehensive and responsive to every single moral problem or issue. There are obviously many conceptions of what is moral or ethical. On the other hand, Angle and Fleischacker show us not only how we can conceptually entertain ethical and cultural pluralism, but also that such pluralism itself enjoys a moral priority over its opposite. That is, the salient issue is not whether ethical variety is conceptually intelligible, but whether it is desirable, whether it is worth fostering. Both chapters suggest that it is.

Finally, we must ask how such variety impacts on the attempt to apply ethics to real world problems and issues. Though the inclusion of non-Western perspectives in the discussion of issues in law, medicine, politics, and so on has been long in coming, such contributions are now burgeoning at a steady rate. Furthermore, philosophers who take a comparative perspective have increasingly turned their attention to practical and applied issues.[15] However, certain characteristic themes have emerged in such discussions, and it is such themes that the contributions to this volume highlight. The first has to do with the question of whether issues of gender and gender discrimination transcend the boundaries of culture and tradition. Especially, if we must leave the issue as to ethical universalism versus relativism significantly unresolved, then the questions of gender must be addressed in very specific terms. Both contributions to this area make very specific claims in regard to gender but from two different directions and drawing two rather different conclusions.

In "Ethics in the Female Voice: Murasaki Shikibu and the Framing of Ethics for Japan," Mara Miller argues for the possibility of a critical and to some extent autonomous moral voice emerging within the confines of a patriarchal culture such as that of medieval Japan. Tracing the evolving and distinctive moral thinking of the author of Japan's famous literary work, *The Tale of Genji*, Miller shows how Murasaki adopted and improvised on a basic Buddhist framework in order to develop a strikingly contemporary-sounding feminist ethic of care. Incidentally, Murasaki saw her efforts as directed toward developing a sensitivity that applied to men as well as women and hence transcended a rather rigid gender role differentiation. Taking a rather different tack and arriving at a rather different view of the relations between gender, culture, and ethics, Lucinda Joy Peach argues that there are certain basic incompatibilities between support for women's rights as universal human rights and support for rights of cultural self-determination. Noting a contradiction inherent in international human rights law between these two sorts of rights, Peach concludes by urging that we may have to choose between cultural rights and women's rights with an argument as to why the priority must be given to women's rights.

One interesting element in this discussion of gender is the potential incompatibility between an ethical perspective and that of a culture. While with Fleischacker we may view the maintenance of a cultural tradition as a moral obligation and essential to our moral health, both Peach and Miller point out ways in which even culturally situated modes of ethical reflection tend to develop independence from their cultural horizon. Miller's discussion of Murasaki clearly reveals her as a moral critic with an independent voice that had a socially transformative impact on Japanese culture, and Peach considers the possibility of issues on which no compromise between the advocates of cultural rights and women's rights is possible. Reconciling the irreconciliable, of course, requires appeal to a higher authority and suggests the independence from culture of such legal and moral authority.

Echoing this theme of the potential conflict between the demands of culture and the requirements of justice, Purushottama Bilimoria examines the emergence of a concept of "native right" within the Kantian-Utilitarian liberal tradition as applied to the British colonization of India. Interestingly, Bilimoria heads in quite the opposite direction of Miller and Peach by documenting the ways in which, in the Indian experience, a universalist ethics, namely Western liberalism, failed to morally preempt the issue of social justice, itself falling back on "native" tradition in the form of personal law. Philosophically, Bilimoria's case hangs less on the overdetermining character of culture in regard to one's personal identity and standards of moral judgment than on various self-contradictions which lie at the heart of liberal thinking particularly on the issue of a native right to the possession of one's lands and wealth. Bilimoria's is an interesting corrective to any naive faith in the power of universalism to transcend the bewildering complexities of cultural difference when dealing with the real world.

Lastly, the book turns to the problems of bioethics in a non-Western setting. Two directly contrasting chapters, those of Damien Keown and Michael Barnhart, examine the general Buddhist attitude toward such standard bioethical conundrums as assisted suicide, euthanasia, and even abortion. Obviously, one feature of shifting philosophical paradigms is the displacement of the parameters of birth and death, and thus of human nature in general. Buddhism, in contrast to the Judaeo-Christian context, tends to view human life as capable of mundane rebirth and, perhaps most importantly, without any identifiable essence such as a soul or personal ego. The relevant question debated by Keown and Barnhart concerns what the bioethical implications of such constitutive beliefs in fact are. For Keown, Buddhist bioethics involves a generalized respect for life that forbids such acts as euthanasia and, though he doesn't explicitly discuss the matter in his chapter, abortion as well. Buddhists defer to nature in settling questions of birth and death; it is human arrogance for us to so drastically intervene. By contrast, Barnhart argues for, what he terms, a more "liberal" view, one that accepts certain kinds of action, including perhaps some kinds of suicide, that are performed in the service of such Buddhist values as are attached to enlightenment (nirvana) and compassionate action. The section concludes on Carl B. Becker's somewhat hopeful suggestions as to just what sort of clinical practices East Asian values, especially Buddhist values, might entail.

Taking all three of the essays addressing bioethical issues together, a number of new themes emerge. First, it is apparent that speaking in the name of one ethical tradition, in this case Buddhism, is hardly enough to resolve practical issues, such as that of assisted suicide. Different ways of applying Buddhist values may actually point to very different ways of interpreting Buddhist values, and it may even be the case that one's preferred manner of interpretation is not solely based on textual or philosophical concerns but also on how the interpretation cashes out practically. In fact, as one reads these three essays, the suspicion grows that the divergences may have a great deal to do with the authors' own moral preferences. How one interprets an ethical theory may depend as much on one's ethical sentiments as it does on achieving a consistent account of moral judgment.[16] Or, as many bioethicists have noticed, practice drives theory as much as the other way around. One possible lesson, then, is that the problem of ethical convergence should be looked upon not so much as a theoretical problem—as the problem of finding the correct universal theory—but a practical problem of finding a rule or compromise we can all live with. The theory, then, will take care of itself.[17] Second, while looking at the Buddhist context focuses our attention on the differences of different ethical universalisms, because Buddhist ethics are in fact universalistic insofar as they are taken to be binding on all, we shouldn't miss the possible similarities either. Most of these consist in the similarities of application between two ethical systems. For Keown, it is the similarity between a Catholic natural law approach and a Buddhist account of the virtues, while for Barnhart it is the similarity between Buddhist values and a liberal emphasis on responsible autonomy. Does, therefore, ethical convergence consist more in a strategy of reflection on the practical problems of applying various principles than a brute and largely abstract comparison of contrasting theoretical perspectives? Of course, the answer to this question hinges partly on whether we see ethics as a largely abstract theoretical enterprise and applied ethics as a "top down" application of principle, or whether we see ethics as a kind of "bottom up" devising of principles to clarify and extend our intuitions regarding particular cases. If the latter is the case, we must also concede the possibility that no lasting theoretical superstructure may ever emerge out of such a process, nor may any internally consistent and coherent ethical theory either. That is, convergence may be at the cost of coherence.

That said however, we must also acknowledge another more universalist tendency in these chapters. All three authors endeavor to shape a moral approach to a variety of bioethical issues on the inspiration of a reading, not only of Buddhist values, but of Buddhist values that exhibit wide acceptance generally. Keown and Barnhart, especially, go to some length to illustrate connections between Buddhist moral sensibility and that of other traditions. So, while working within the hypothesis of moral pluralism, they both take steps in another direction, that of consensus building. And while consensus is not moral universalism per se, the dialogical nature of the enterprise cannot preemptively limit the degree of consensus that may be achievable in time.

All of which brings us back to the sort of problems raised by the earlier chapters in Section Three of the book. One salient theme is the issue about the autonomy of moral consciousness. To what extent is our moral consciousness in regard to gender discrimination or rights to self-determination beholden to culture and tradition? To what degree can a moral voice preempt those of one's particular society? However one tends to answer this question in the abstract, the urgency of the various issues confronted in this section tends to push us toward a form of moral reflection that leaves open the possibility of some sort of emergent consensus, if not outright moral universalism. That is, we tend to look for linkages between the respective moral traditions, linkages that are philosophical and guide our reflections toward reasonable consensus. Thus, just as the first section of the book strikes a balance between the relativist sensibility, that there are indeed different ethical systems which must be understood primarily in their own terms, and the universalist sensibility that these different systems are still ethical in some shared and meaningful sense, so the end of the book, while respecting the variety of perspectives that influence our responses to practical problems, also tends to endorse the autonomy of the moral voice, despite the fact that we lack the theoretical vocabulary to fully define and legitimate its sphere of authority.

All of which leads me to suggest a final lesson that might be drawn from such a juxtaposition of different projects as is evidenced in this book. I said before that perhaps some overall substantive conclusions respecting universalism might be forthcoming. If anything, the collective weight of these essays, to my mind, suggests the following kind of universalism. Traditionally, universalism is looked on as the model of a formal theory as found in mathematics and science. There, universalism amounts to a set of consistent theorems within an axiomatic structure where connections between propositions are primarily logico-deductive. But perhaps ethics, being practical and oriented toward human concerns, enjoys more the structure of the human or social sciences. That is, it aims for rough generalizations that depend on empirical evidence regarding individually held beliefs. Obviously, this is not the place to develop the case for such a view, nor can I adequately explain it, although a number of philosophers have moved in this direction.[18] However, if so, then the kind of universalism that might prevail within philosophical ethics would be an emergent sort, based on a developing congruence of basic attitudes and beliefs among human beings. It would not be a universalism that could be divined as a principle of pure reason, nor from considerations regarding human happiness generally. Thus, such an ethical universalism would not exhibit Kantian or Aristotelian foundational strategies, nor would it be Utilitarian. Because it would rest on dialogical consensus, it wouldn't insist on any universal calculation based on what was to everyone's advantage and imposed hegemonically from above. That is, it wouldn't be a "top-down" universalism but more the "bottom-up" kind; call it "emergent" universalism. But rather than just representing strategic compromise, or mere agreement in regard to particular cases, agreement would extend to the level of values, in other words, in regard to principles and virtues. That is, it might also be called a "constructivist universalism." I see no argument ruling out such a possibility *a priori*. Certainly, it satisfies the relativist requirement that values reflect commitments within a form of life because such dialogical participation and its maintenance would, at least to a certain degree be a form of life. Or, perhaps we should say, the process of dialogue and consensus seeking would be part of many different forms of life.[19] Perhaps, hopefully, the sometimes competing voices in the book represent just such a move in this direction.

## Notes

1. One of these family resemblances might well consist of belief in the soul, a concept vital to the Judaeo-Christian tradition as well as the Islamic and almost entirely foreign to Hinduism, Buddhism, Taoism, or Confucianism. See, for example, Peter D. Hershock, *Reinventing the Wheel: A Buddhist Response to the Information Age* (Albany: State University of New York Press, 1999), Chapter One.

2. See Joseph Margolis, *Pragmatism Without Foundations* (Oxford, U.K.: Basil Blackwell, 1986) and *Life Without Principles* (Cambridge, Mass.: Blackwell Publishers, 1996).

3. See Alan Donagan, *A Theory of Morality* (Oxford, U.K.: Oxford University Press, 1977).

4. Hume makes the celebrated claim that reason alone cannot motivate the will. Obviously, since reason cannot supply its own form of motivation, then we need to discover an inclination to be reasonable. Being reasonable doesn't mean just using reason, it means having some inclination to do so. Thus, being reasonable is a form of inclination. See *A Treatise of Human Nature*, Book Two, Part Three, Section Three.

5. See Kant's *Metaphysics of Morals*, translated by Lewis White Beck, (New York: Macmillan, 1959), 12.

6. See particularly Alasdair MacIntyre's *After Virtue: A Study in Moral Theory* (Notre Dame, Ind.: University of Notre Dame Press, 1984) and Richard Rorty's *Contingency, Irony, and Solidarity* (Cambridge, U.K.: Cambridge University Press, 1989).

7. See Randall Peerenboom, "The Limits of Irony: Rorty and the China Challenge," *Philosophy East and West* 50 (April 2000), 56-90.

8. Left out are thick descriptions of moral decision making and moral phenomenolo-

gies, but these do not often seek to give a general account of the moral but a moral account of select emotions or dispositions. I am thinking primarily of such works as Felicia Ackerman's bioethical fiction. See for example "Buddies," *The APA Newsletter on Philosophy and Medicine* 99, no. 1 (1999), 101-7 or "Break, Break, Break," *The APA Newsletter on Philosophy and Medicine* 99, no. 2 (1999), 258-62.

9. Specifically, Aldo Leopold's celebrated "land ethic" which involves an expansion of our traditional regard for human beings to a general regard for the natural environment which ultimately sustains us. See Aldo Leopold, "The Land Ethic," in *A Sand County Almanac* (New York: Ballantine, 1970).

10. For a discussion of the challenge environmental ethics poses for ethics in general and the advantages or disadvantages in turning to non-Western sources, see Roger T. Ames and J. Baird Callicott eds. *Nature in Asian Traditions of Thought (*Albany: State University of New York Press, 1989).

11. For an in-depth discussion of the bearing of other intellectual traditions on the entire human rights issue, see *Negotiating Culture and Human Rights*, edited by Lynda S. Bell, Andrew J. Nathan, and Ilan Peleg (New York: Columbia University Press, 2001).

12. For a discussion of this alternative, its contrast with what is known as "principlism," and the arguments in its favor, see John D. Arras, "Getting Down to Cases: The Revival of Casuistry in Bioethics," *Journal of Medicine and Philosophy* 16 (1991): 29-51.

13. A number of writers have developed this theme in regard to Buddhism. See Peter D. Hershock, *Liberating Intimacy: Enlightenment and Social Virtuosity in Ch'an Buddhism* (Albany: State University of New York Press, 1996) and Christopher Ives, *Zen Awakening and Society* (Honolulu: University of Hawaii Press, 1992).

14. Of course, not all those who espouse a relativist approach would agree. See, for example, Joseph Margolis, *Life Without Principles.* Margolis at many points argues that incommensurability and intelligibility are very different issues, as does Alasdair MacIntyre. However, while the incommensurable other may not be unintelligible to me, he or she may well be incomparable.

15. As, for example, is evidenced by the topics of the last three East-West Philosophers' Conferences in Hawaii: Culture and Modernity, Justice and Democracy, and Technology and Human Values.

16. Joseph Margolis, *Life Without Principles*, makes this point over and over again though in respect to moral theorists generally. They are usually attempting a self-justification of their own moral preferences rather than a straightforward account of morality itself.

17. To some extent this echoes the sort of strategy that Rawls has endorsed in *Political Liberalism* (New York: Columbia University Press, 1993) and Charles Taylor as well. See his essay "Conditions of an Unforced Consensus on Human Rights," in *The East Asian Challenge for Human Rights*, Joanne R. Bauer and Daniel A. Bell, eds. (Cambridge, U.K.: Cambridge University Press, 1999).

18. Rorty, Bernstein, Margolis, and even Habermas and Rawls have tended in this direction. Also, Charles Taylor, "Conditions of an Unforced Consensus on Human Rights." Especially in regard to Habermas and Rawls, the moral issue is not to identify specific ethical principles but the constructive framework whereby such rules may be determined. Margolis and John Mackie argue for a more open-ended constructive arrangement that stipulates those conditions and rules that curb or redirect our more selfish tendencies. My point is that all of these approaches to ethics represent a movement away from the *a priori*, Kantian strategy toward a more contextualized one, although certainly Rawls and Habermas reserve a role for *a priori* reasoning in regard to the framework in which agreement or consensus is to be

achieved. For Bernstein's approach see Richard Bernstein, *Beyond Objectivism and Relativism* (Philadelphia: University of Pennsylvania Press, 1985).

19. This, I believe, is the kind of "overlapping consensus" of the political sort that Rawls favors in *Political Liberalism.*

# Part One:

# Ethics in Comparative Context

*Chapter One*

# Self-Fulfillment Through Selflessness: The Moral Teachings of the *Daode Jing*

**Russell Kirkland**

"What are the moral teachings of the *Daode jing*?"[1] Since the *Daode jing* is one of the most well known works of any civilization, it may seem surprising that such a simple question has not already been satisfactorily addressed. But in fact there has been little effort to address directly this clear and basic question. The reasons for this state of affairs are too complex to pursue fully here, for they involve the unexamined biases, misconceptions, and conceptual omissions heretofore inherent not only in the thought of Western interpreters but also in that of modern Chinese interpreters.[2] It does, however, seem proper to sketch the current state of Western thought on the issue, and to consider the most immediate and significant reasons for the deficiencies that afflict the field. Then, through textual exegesis, I shall seek to demonstrate that the *Daode jing* displays a distinct and comprehensible moral perspective.

## Preliminary Considerations

As I will elaborate below, there was really no such thing as "Taoism" in classical China. The concept of "philosophical Taoism" is essentially a fiction, embraced by people of different ages and cultures for specific and identifiable social, intellectual, and historical reasons.[3] I shall attempt to put "philosophical Taoism" aside, and examine the thought-content of a single specific text—the *Daode jing*. In doing so, I shall attempt to write as though the text existed in a vacuum. As far as possible, I shall ignore other texts, like the *Zhuangzi*, for while such texts may share with ours certain themes and perspectives; there is no logical basis for assuming that the writers of any part of the *Daode jing* would necessarily share any given perspective in the *Zhuangzi*. The same is true for the entire commentarial literature. My purpose here is not to find a common "Taoist morality," but merely to extract from a single text such moral ideas as might be present. I shall, for the most part, assume that the effort to do so is hampered rather than aided by common concepts concerning the supposed "general framework of Taoist thought."

Of course, I am also writing here as though we may legitimately discuss "the *Daode jing*" as though it were a coherent text. Such an assumption sets aside several important issues, including that of textual history. At present, there is actually no way to identity the "real"or "original" text of the *Daode jing*, so there is essentially no such thing as "the *Daode jing*" except in some socially agreed upon sense.[4] In what follows, I do not necessarily claim to discern "the original meaning" of the text, in whole or in part. I shall merely attempt to read the text as we currently have it in order to identify such moral ideas as it might contain. Secondly, I shall beware the common fallacy of assuming a general consistency within the text. Since it is apparently *not* the work of a single person, it would be illogical to assume that an idea found in one passage necessarily bears implications for any other particular passage. Failure to beware such fallacious assumptions has often led interpreters to construct vast and sometimes impressive thought-systems for the *Daode jing*, though whether such systems were actually present in the minds of the actual writer(s) of any given passage remains dubious. There has been a very common tendency to "import ideas" from *Zhuangzi*, from the commentator Wang Bi, even from Neo-Confucian sources. My assumption shall be that some passages of the *Daode jing* are probably more closely related than others, and that we will find abundant "inconsistencies" unless we acknowledge the plurality of layers and voices embodied in the text. So while I shall attempt to remain alert to the fact that passage A and passage B may share a given idea incompletely, if at all, I shall seek meaningful patterns of thought among such passages by noting pertinent philological data.

## "Morality"and the *Daode jing*: The State of the Field

A decade ago, I noted that it had long been supposed that Taoist values were inherently egocentric, and that, between both Chinese and Western interpreters, Taoists "have been censured for fostering a selfish disregard of the legitimate needs and concerns of human society."[5] Sadly, such remains the general state of affairs. Blinded by the late-imperial Confucian conceit that Taoists are characteristically apathetic if not antipathetic toward social concerns, Western interpreters have found little to say about Taoist moral teachings. Considering the near-prehistoric nature of his efforts, we may excuse Max Weber for finding little to say on the issue.[6] But my attempt to assess current thought regarding the issue among sinologists and philosophers led to a finding that was both surprising and distressing: with few exceptions, such writers have continued to find little to say.[7]

In this connection, I must note that I was particularly interested in the analyses of people knowledgeable in the Western field of philosophy: I assumed that the most likely place to find coherent assessments of the moral teachings of the *Daode jing* would be among those who have endeavored to write as systematic thinkers, particularly since "ethics" is a principal concern among those who practice "philosophy" in the Western academy. Of course, thoughtful consideration of Chinese texts and traditions is still fairly rare in Western philosophy. Among the few who combine sinological expertise with philosophical competence, fewer still have addressed the issue in question. Occasionally, a non-sinologist will enter the fray, as Herbert Fingarette did in his stimulating treatment of Confucius.[8] The most prominent non-sinologist to address the issue of morality in a Taoist context seems to be Arthur C. Danto.[9] Since Danto's views have been somewhat influential, it is with them that I shall begin. In the 1988 edition of his work, Danto presents the following assertions:

> Taoism seems to dissolve any relations we may have to one another and to replace them with the relationship we have to the universe at large. The question it poses is . . . how to close the gap between the world and ourselves, how to 'lose' the self. Whereas it is just that gap that is presupposed by the moral questions of classical China and perhaps by the concept of morality itself. They suppose the gaps that need closing are those that separate us from one another. However, these are not relevant in closing the gap between the Way and ourselves, which is the source of the only kind of infelicitude thinkers like Lao Tzu regard as worth healing. . . . Exactly the space that Taoism intends to collapse is what makes morality possible at all. By this, I mean the possibility of morality as such, not this or that moral system.[10]

Danto concludes his book with the allegation that "Taoism's" failure to provide a space for morality

> does . . . entail a kind of censure of the philosophies of Lao Tzu and the others we have discussed, Confucius being an exception, because in enjoining the collapse of the conditions that made morality possible, they fall under a moral violation by our criterion. And so they merit blame of a kind.[11]

There are doubtless those who would be more charitable, and would refrain from assigning "censure" or "blame" for such a supposed failure. But the question remains whether Danto is correct in his fundamental assessment.

For the moment, I shall pass over the common, but dubious, assumption that there was a person named "Lao Tzu" whose "philosophy" is enshrined in the *Daode jing*.[12] My real concern is Danto's contention that such "philosophies" as we find in the *Daode jing* preclude the very possibility of "morality as such." I shall not, in this connection, object to his fundamental assumptions concerning the nature of "morality." Rather, I wish to question his assertion that "Taoism" per *se* renders "morality" *per se* conceptually impossible.

In his chapter on Confucianism and Taoism, Danto writes as follows:

> With Confucius one begins to get a glimpse of something that has been lacking in the philosophies we have touched upon in this book [i.e., philosophies of India and China], namely a genuine moral idea. Taoism pictures the person as a wanderer in the void, and perceives his happiness to lie in drifting with the stream, unanchored by the network of demands and responsibilities. The Confucian, by contrast, has endorsed and internalized these responsibilities and yields to them, sacrificing or postponing his own happiness if need be, or merely identifying it with moral submission. . . . [In Taoism, the] happiness one is concerned with is one's own, logically independent of the happiness of others. . . . Moral education, to which Confucius devoted immense attention, consists less in the inculcation of rules, which is only moral training and can be given to dogs, but in getting men to assume attitudes towards themselves that are logically connected with the attitudes others take toward themselves. . . .[In Taoism, however, the] follower of the Way is necessarily a loner.[13]

Within these remarks are some observations that are true and important, and others that are highly debatable. Is it actually true that for "Taoists," "the happiness one is concerned with is one's own, logically independent of the happiness of others"? As we shall see, the answer is decidedly negative.

One of the reasons for Danto's confusion—which is, to be fair, a common confusion indeed—is that he has fallaciously conflated the thought of the *Daode jing* with that of the *Zhuangzi*, succumbing to the common but historically false reification of a philosophical "school" of "Taoism." Such was not well appreciated when Danto first wrote. But any philosopher should beware the facile conflation of two entirely different thinkers or texts: Plotinus was not Plato, Luther was not Paul, and Shankara did not write the *Upanisads*. By neglecting the real possibility (in fact, the near certainty) of significant distinctions between the thoughts found in the *Daode jing* and those found in the *Zhuangzi*, Danto, like so many others, has falsely accused the writers of the former as having accepted the assumptions and conclusions of the latter. To argue, for instance, that "Taoism pictures the person as a wanderer in the void, and perceives his happiness to lie in drifting with the stream" is clearly to ignore all the social and political teachings of the *Daode jing*, and to assume, quite falsely, as it turns out, that the *Zhuangzi* is not merely *representative* of "Taoism," but actually *normative*.[14]

Recent research by A.C. Graham and others has made it abundantly clear that the term "Taoism" refers to nothing that really existed in pre-Han intellectual history. Neither Chuang Chou nor the composers of the *Daode jing* seem to have been aware of each other's writings, and the term *daojia* did not exist until early Han times. It remained no more than a bibliographic classification until about the 3rd century C.E., i.e., several hundred years after the *Daode jing* took its present form. As Harold Roth has put it, "the 'Lao-Zhuang' tradition to which [most twentieth-century Chinese and Western scholarship] refers is actually a Wei-Jin literati reconstruction, albeit a powerful and enduring one."[15] Roth's present work suggests that certain localized groups in pre-Han China may have shared certain meditative practices, and in that sense it might seem legitimate to refer to such groups as having practiced "Taoism" in some meaningful *social* sense.[16] There are even some little-known texts that seem to preserve some of their teachings.[17] But there is so far no evidence that the writer(s) of the *Daode jing* (or of the *Zhuangzi*) were members of such a group, much less of any "philosophical school."[18] So it is fallacious to argue that "Taoism pictures the person as a wanderer in the void": even if such a statement is an accurate expression of some of the ideals found in the *Zhuangzi*, it is certainly *not* an accurate expression of the ideals embodied in the *Daode jing*, as I shall demonstrate.[19]

Most importantly, I shall argue that, in terms of the teachings of the *Daode jing*, Danto is incorrect when he maintains that within such teachings "[the] happiness one is concerned with is one's own, logically independent of the happiness of others." In fact, I shall argue that Danto, like many other interpreters, Western and Chinese alike, has issued his assessment (and in this case, his "censure") of "Taoism" without having given the *Daode jing* a full and fair reading.[20] I shall demonstrate that the *Daode jing* does *not* in fact enjoin "the collapse of the conditions that make morality possible."

## The Presence of Moral Values in the *Daode Jing*

In the past, interpreters have often ignored or misconstrued the moral ideas present in the *Daode jing*, for at least three reasons. First, as noted above, interpreters have often fallaciously conflated it with other texts, such as the *Zhuangzi*, in which such ideas are far less apparent. Secondly, they have often been hoodwinked by the tendentious claims of non-Taoists (particularly post-T'ang Confucians) that "Taoists have no morality." Confucians easily drew the inference that "Taoists have no morality" simply because "Taoists," by definition, do not share *Confucian* moral beliefs. Just as "mainstream Confucians" long ignored or censured Xunzi's teachings because his beliefs were no longer "mainstream," so Confucians may have recognized elements of interest in the *Daode jing*, but would never read it sympathetically: to them, it was unthinkable that a coherent and respectable moral philosophy could exist in a non-Confucian text.

Thirdly, the moral teachings of the *Daode jing* have often been overlooked because interpreters have given improper weight to certain passages. For instance, *Daode jing* 2 opens with lines that read something like the following: "When everyone in the world knows the pleasantness of the pleasant, there is unpleasantness;

When everyone knows the goodness of the good (*shan*), there is not-goodness."[21] Some interpreters have read these lines as showing that a fundamental principle of the *Daode jing* is "the relativity of value judgments."[22] But such is not the case. Note that in this passage the quality of "goodness" is contrasted not with a separate quality of "badness," but rather with "not-goodness," which apparently just means a relative lack of "goodness."

Chapter twenty-seven bears out that interpretation. Its opening lines use the term *shan* as an indicator of skill or excellence at a given activity, such as speaking or counting. Then the following lines expand the meaning of *shan* into what seems to be a *moral* context: "The sage is constantly good at saving people, so that there is no one who is abandoned; [He] is constantly good at saving things, so that there is nothing that is abandoned."[23] The precise meaning of these lines may be open to question, but they certainly suggest that *the ideal person takes steps to include others, in some meaningful and beneficial sense*. They also suggest that such inclusion is not only *impartial*, but also *universal*, and that such universality is a significant ideal. *Shan*, "goodness," here, is thus not a quality in itself (contrasting, for instance, with "badness"), but rather a type of *ideal involvement with others*. The subsequent lines (Henricks lines 9-12) explain that both the *shan* person and the non-*shan* person have value, and that each has, ideally at least, a meaningful relationship to the other: the *shan* person should be the teacher or leader of the non-*shan* person. The *shan* person is therefore not a person who is morally "good" in the sense that he/she fulfills general social norms, nor one who is good in the sense that he/she practices such Confucian virtues as "benevolence," but rather in some other sense (to be discussed below).[24] And as such, the *shan* person warrants the reader's approval and emulation, for, as chapter 79 indicates, even the "Way of Heaven" itself approves of and supports such a person: "The Way of Heaven has no favorites, It's always with the good man (Henricks translation)." But the full meaning of the term *shan-ren* ("good person") in this passage remains to be seen. The preceding lines concern the value of not exacting payment for debt, whether financial or moral, and the "good" person is said to be one who creates harmony in such situations by forgiving others' debts.[25] Such ideas may also be pertinent for understanding chapter 49, where the ideal person appears to "be good (*shan*)" toward all others impartially, both those who are *shan* and those who are not.[26]

Thus, the *Daode jing* commends "goodness," which an ideal person practices. Furthermore, that practice involves *extending oneself toward others impartially so as to benefit them*, and possibly even to engender "goodness" in them as well. It seems to me that such ideas closely approximate moral values, at least in Arthur Danto's terms. Furthermore, if traditional readings of *Daode jing* 27 are correct, a duty of the person of "goodness" is to serve as instructor to persons who lack such "goodness." Thus we see brief but suggestive indications of a concept of *moral education*.

## Implicit Moral Reasoning in the *Daode Jing*

I can endorse Danto's contention that "moral education" does *not* consist in "the inculcation of rules, which is only moral training and can be given to dogs."[27] But Danto argued that Confucians display "a genuine moral idea" because they recognize themselves as part of a human "network of demands and responsibilities." It is this characteristic of "Confucianism" that Danto opposes to the characteristics of "Taoism." Is that characterization accurate? Or is it possible that a "Taoist" could actually have *a sense of responsibility toward others*, analogous to, albeit distinct from, that which Confucius expected of his followers? If so, why have interpreters of the *Daode jing* failed to notice it?

Both traditional Confucians and modern interpreters cite several passages in the *Daode jing* as revealing antipathy toward moral values. One is the notorious opening of chapter 5:

> Heaven and Earth are not "benevolent" (*ren*):
> They take all things (lit., "the myriad things") to be [like] hay or dogs.
> The Sage is not "benevolent":
> He takes all people (lit., "the hundred clans") to be [like] hay or dogs.[28]

Interpretations of this passage vary, but it is hard to miss the implication that one ought, in some sense, to live without regard for others, just as, for instance, nature's rains come regardless of whether any given living thing is thereby given more abundant life or drowned. However, it is necessary to take into account here the intellectual history of ancient China, for "benevolence" is not just a term of ordinary discourse, but a technical term in the vocabulary of the classical Confucians, particularly that of Mengzi (Mencius). One can in fact read this passage as a direct argument *against* Mengzi's teachings that one ought to cultivate a set of moral feelings (compassion, respect, shame, etc.) that he alleges to be intrinsic to human nature.[29] The argument here, as I read it, is that while such feelings may be visible in some humans' lives, they are not evident in the broader world, beyond human society: Heaven-and-Earth shows no compassion, respect, or shame when it sends a typhoon toward human habitations. Thus, the lesson is that *one should emulate Heaven-and-Earth, not those human individuals who have cultivated Mengzi's ideal feelings*. One could even ask: how could compassion, respect, or shame be intrinsic to the human constitution (as Mengzi claims) when they are clearly extrinsic to the constitution of the world as a whole? *If one judges human activity by how well it correlates to activity seen in "nature,"* then the Mencian "moral feelings," which are absent in "nature," actually appear quite unnatural.

Here we see a fundamental element of what one *could* call "Taoist moral reasoning."[30] Confucians based their moral reasoning on specific assumptions, such as that humans are the world's principal (if not only) agents of goodness: "Nature," they reason, may indeed be amoral, but humans at times display goodness, and ought to become more conscientious in practicing such goodness. But a critic might retort: "If what you call 'moral goodness' is seen nowhere in the world except in humans, then it is a logical possibility (if not, indeed, an inevitability) that 'moral goodness' *does not belong in the world*—that humans have been engaging in practices that are *contrary to life itself.* So we are logically required to examine critically the alleged benefits of such actions." Whether such reasoning was actually conducted by the person(s) who penned the lines on "straw-dogs" in *Daode jing* 5, it is quite conceivable. Such reasoning could be considered an example of "Laoist moral reasoning."[31] A person who lives in accord with such reasoning would seem to qualify as "a conscientious moral agent," as defined by James Rachels:

> The conscientious moral agent is someone who is concerned impartially with the interests of everyone affected by what he or she does; who carefully sifts facts and examines their implications; who accepts principles of conduct only after scrutinizing them to make sure they are sound; who is willing to 'listen to reason' even when it means that his or her earlier convictions may have to be revised; and who, finally, is willing to act on the results of this deliberation.[32]

In what follows, I shall attempt to demonstrate that the *Daode jing* includes numerous passages that contain readily discernible moral teachings—*teachings that are based upon moral reasoning, expect moral reasoning of the reader, and enjoin moral action* (or, more accurately, "moral nonaction") based upon the true implications of the facts of life.

## A Non-Humanistic Morality?

In certain regards, the assumptions of the *Daode jing* overlap (but do not entirely coincide) with those of the *Zhuangzi*. Both deny the validity of certain common Confucian assumptions. Most classical Confucians (including Xunzi and Dong Zhongshu) held that humans play a crucial role in bringing order to the world: though the ultimate source of life's proper order may be "Heaven" (*Tian*), "Heaven" cannot of itself guarantee the fulfillment of its own designs, so it is ultimately within the human sphere that life is given its true meaning and direction. Further, both the ruler and the properly cultivated individual have crucial roles to play in that process: bringing order to life is thus a process that simultaneously comes down from the top of society, the worthy ruler, and works upward from the basis of society, the moral individual. This perspective might be styled a religious humanism, in that Confucians assume that human society is the primary focus of life's meaning and value, though such goods are ultimately grounded in "Heaven."[33]

Certainly by Han times, similar assumptions had come to dominate "Taoism," as seen most clearly in the *Huainanzi*, where the primal "Tao" holds a position comparable in some ways to the Confucians' "Heaven." Such concepts actually go back to the *Daode jing*, which even refers in several chapters to "the Tao of Heaven."[34] But though the *Daode jing* is here, as in other regards, closer to the Confucian position than is the *Zhuangzi*, it nonetheless rejects the common Confucian assumption that the world inherently tends toward chaos and requires the redemptive activity of human society.[35] The *Daode jing* asserts that the natural reality it calls the Tao is a perfect and ineluctable force for the fulfillment of life. Far from needing humans to complete its activity, the "Tao" is, despite appearances, the most powerful force that exists, and it *inevitably* leads all situations (even human government) to a healthy fulfillment—*provided* human beings *not interfere* with it.[36] It is this assumption of a benign and largely trustworthy natural order—seldom perceptible in the *Zhuangzi*—that provides a potential basis for a non-humanistic religious morality.[37] From this perspective, Confucians *wrongly* fear that life will end in chaos without the redemptive activity of humanity: in truth, because of the beneficent activity of the natural force called the Tao, we can rest assured that life will proceed harmoniously, except for the deleterious effects of misguided human activity. *Human activity* (*wei*) is thus *not redemptive at all*, but precisely the opposite. And the moral responsibility of the individual is thus to *refrain* from such activity, to desist from misguided interference in the inherent tendencies of the world.

Whereas a humanistic perspective assigns a generally positive value to what humans "contribute" to life, the perspective of the *Daode jing* is non-humanistic (or even "anti-humanistic"), for it assigns a generally negative value to what humans add to the life process. So whereas Mengzi insists that one has a moral responsibility to cultivate "benevolence," chapter 5 of the *Daode jing* argues that one has a moral responsibility *not* to do so. According to such "Laoist moral reasoning," cultivating qualities that are generally absent in other domains of life is introducing an unnatural and unhealthy element into the world. In this light, a "Taoist" can quite certainly be "someone who is concerned impartially with the interests of everyone affected by what he or she does," and is thus "a conscientious moral agent."

In fact, according to the moral reasoning perceptible in the *Daode jing*, such a person is eminently *more moral* than a Confucian. The Mohists accused the Confucians of "partiality," because a Confucian, as a devotee of "filial piety," is concerned with the interests of his parents, above—and in extreme cases, possibly to the exclusion of—the interests of other persons to whom he is unrelated.[38] But "Laoists" could accuse the Confucians of partiality on another level: Confucians are concerned with the interests of human beings, above—and in extreme cases, to the exclusion of—the interests of other beings. For instance, *Analects* 10:17 relates the following: "The stables caught fire. The Master (i.e., Confucius), on returning from court, asked, 'Was anyone hurt?' He did not ask about the horses."[39] To be fair, Confucius is *not* recorded as having said, "Only humans deserve life, and if a stable catches fire, let it burn as long as no one dies but the horses."[40] But the lesson of the passage is clear: the horses' lives were, to Confucius, of no moral concern. That "moral people" could hold such a view is entirely credible, for it is still a common view among many modern people, who will, for instance, readily sacrifice test-animals in seeking a cure for a human malady: the facts that such a cure may never be applied to save the lives of non-humans, or that the happiness of the test-animals is disregarded, are to many people not compelling moral concerns. The Laoist (like some modern animal-rights advocates) might ask: If "the conscientious moral agent" is "someone who is concerned impartially with the interests of everyone affected by what he or she does," does that "everyone" really mean *everyone*, or just certain someones? Laoists, I propose, articulated an ethic that remains largely unrecognized because it was a *non-humanistic ethic*, because their "impartial concern" reached beyond human society, and asked about "respect for others" in a broader sense.[41]

But would it be correct to conclude that such a "non-humanistic ethic" was actually an *anti-humanistic* ethic? Such would seem to be Danto's assumption, when he asserts:

> the moral questions of classical China and perhaps . . . the concept of morality . . . suppose the gaps that need closing are those that separate us from one another. However, these are not relevant in closing the gap between the Way and ourselves, which is the source of the only kind of infelicitude thinkers like Lao Tzu regard as worth healing . . .

Is that assertion true?

Let us consider the opening lines of *Daode jing* 75: "The people are hungry: It is because those in authority eat up too much in taxes / That the people are hungry."[42] Here we see a concern with excessive taxation as an issue of social justice, which could be quoted by politicians of our own day. Clearly here, and in several other passages, like *Daode jing* 72, we see a moral condemnation of governmental oppression, and it is quite evident that "Lao Tzu" regards such oppression as an "infelicitude" that is indeed "worth healing."

The only remaining question would seem to be whether "the Taoist" is "a conscientious moral agent" in the sense of someone "who, finally, is willing to act on the results of [moral] deliberation." Does the *Daode jing* enjoin action to restore harmony to the world? The answer seems to be a qualified yes, but the Laoist view would once again challenge the propriety of the question. *Why need morality involve the willingness to "act"?* Once again, "Laoist moral reasoning" argues (e.g., in chapter 29) that because the world is inherently "good" to begin with, any extraneous action on the part of humans can logically only cause disturbance. So *the "conscientious moral agent" is someone who is ultimately willing not to act on the results of moral deliberation.* It is not that one should act *without* moral deliberation, but rather that one should deliberate appropriately, and then should bring one's behavior into accord with reality by *refraining from action.* Most specifically, one should refrain from acting on the basis of specious moral reasoning, such as that of Confucians, who, from a Laoist perspective, could be said to be busy trying to teach young men to develop *un*-natural feelings like "benevolence" while ignoring the horses dying in the burning stables. So instead of advocating "benevolence" (or "impartial solicitude," *jian'ai,* like the Mohists), some passages of the *Daode jing* advocate "compassion" (*ci*), which seems to mean something like "caring enough for others to refrain from interfering with them."

## *Wuwei*

Some might wonder that I have so far not mentioned the world-famous concept of *wuwei.* It is that concept, more than any other, that has become associated with the *Daode jing.* A surprising number of interpreters (including many who have never read the text itself) find the concept easy to explain. Some of these explanations make sense. But the assumption that the term *wuwei* is a limpid term, the meaning of which is easily explainable, is quite false. Indeed, a careful reading of the text shows that the term has a variety of meanings, which are at times fairly difficult to reconcile.

The question here is whether the term *wuwei* has moral implications. For instance, while many believe that it denotes a condition of "naturalness" or "spontaneity," a careful reading of the text indicates that it does not, on the whole, promote such qualities.[43] Indeed, many passages give advice for ruling a state, or even for waging war, and no "natural" creature ever "spontaneously" engineered a government or armed for formal combat! The *Daode jing* is not a text that instructs the reader to withdraw from society, or even to "rise above" it in some ineffable mystical state: to the contrary, it conveys concepts of healthy and effective methods for *engaging* in social activity.

In the *Daode jing* the term *wuwei* is one element in an intricate, sometimes inconsistent, complex of ideals and images. That complex includes analogies to the natural qualities of water as well as analogies to "feminine" behaviors, such as those of a selfless mother. But it also includes shrewd propositions (including a dissonant image of "feminine wiles") to be used in seeking success in a variety of activities, including both statecraft and war.[44] While one or two chapters exhort the reader to *wei wuwei* (i.e., to "act without acting"), several others acknowledge that "acting" (*wei*) is fully justified in certain terms.[45] And one chapter (43) praises the "advantages" (*yi*) of practicing *wuwei.* Entranced by Wei-Jin images of Taoist "spontaneity," some interpreters have been uncomfortable with the idea that *wuwei* could ever have been a practice intended to lead to beneficial results, and have argued (at least before the discovery of the Mawangdui texts) that the text of chapter 43 was defective.[46] But the idea that proper behavior leads to "benefits" (*li*) is actually quite common in the text.[47] And indeed, much of it is written as though its lessons are primarily principles for seeking and gaining personal, political, and military success.

Some people are displeased by such facts, perhaps because they have succumbed to the modern notion that the ideas in the *Daode jing* are an expression of a sublime "wordless wisdom" (such as Zen is often naively supposed to be). They construe such "wisdom"—for reasons that involve historical issues within their own tradition—to be "other" than rational thought. To such readers, it is objectionable to suggest that *the Daode jing teaches the reader how to figure out how to live his life in such a way that he attains worthy and sensible goals.*[48] Here, again, interpreters have too often read the *Daode jing* in terms of the *Zhuangzi*. The *Zhuangzi* often seems to reject the idea that life is comprehensible or predictable. But the *Daode jing*, like virtually all of the later Taoist tradition, holds firmly to the belief that *life is indeed comprehensible, and in fact superlatively predictable, so long as one has learned the key lessons.* It describes and explains behaviors that the reader *ought* to embrace and practice; suggests *reasons* why these behaviors are *preferable* to others; and gives examples of persons (and other forces, like "water" and "the female") who have modeled a correct conduct of life. It further makes clear that such behaviors are continuous with the subtle operation of the primal force of life ("the Tao"), and that failure to adjust one's life to accord with that force is both unwise and improper.

In so far as *wuwei* is key for the *Daode jing*, it thus constitutes an element in a rational program to convert the reader into a "conscientious moral agent," into someone who, in Rachels' words, "carefully sifts facts and examines their implications; who accepts principles of conduct only after scrutinizing them to make sure they are sound." The *Daode jing* admonishes the reader to emulate "the Way of Heaven," which is "good (*shan*) at *planning*" (chapter 73), and if one's life is "planned" in accordance with wise principles, one will *benefit*, and *others will benefit as well* (chapters 8, 81).

## A "Golden Rule" in the *Daode Jing*? Self-Fulfillment vs. Self-Interest

As Danto illustrates, Taoism has traditionally been read in *Confucian* terms, i.e., in terms of a supposed antagonism between laudable "concern for others" and contemptible "concern for self." His charge that "Taoism seems to dissolve any relations we may have to one another and to replace them with the relationship we have to the universe at large" is essentially the same charge leveled against Buddhists, Taoists, and "heterodox" Confucians by Neo-Confucians since Zhu Xi (1130-1200).

And Danto's charge that the issue in Taoism is "how to 'lose' the self" is an extension of the same charges.

If we now shed that tendentious stance, and simply read the *Daode jing* itself, the issue of "self" takes on a very different cast. It is true that it asks the reader to understand life in terms of primordial realities of which the writer of chapter 25 "does not yet know the name."[49] And some chapters do suggest a process of bio-spiritual cultivation, i.e., a type of "meditation." Nonetheless, the text is clearly not designed to be a manual for "Taoist meditation." In fact, we know just what such a manual would look like, for we have it—the *Neiye*.[50] The *Daode jing*, though doubtless influenced by the *Neiye* in a variety of ways, has a different set of concerns: rather than focusing upon a pursuit of spiritual states, the *Daode jing* teaches *practical* lessons about the living of human life, and commends certain specific behavioral patterns. Such patterns, it argues, will conduce to a long and natural life, a life in which *one achieves self-fulfillment as one is selflessly benefiting the lives of others.*

The *Daode jing's* paradoxical blend of "self-fulfillment" with "selflessness" has befuddled traditional Confucian readers and modern interpreters alike. Some modern efforts to interpret "Taoist thought" have further muddled the issue by asserting an affiliation of the thought of the *Daode jing* (and brother *Zhuangzi*) to the "egoism" of Yang Chu. Some have even labelled Yang's principles "proto-Daoism."[51] But such characterizations make sense only within a Confucian frame of reference, and do not withstand critical analysis.

The view that the *Daode jing* has a Yangist substratum is based on a common misreading of the closing lines of chapter 13. According to the received text, those lines are usually read as follows: "Hence he who values his body more than dominion over the empire can be entrusted with the empire. He who loves his body more than dominion over the empire can be given the custody of the empire (Lau translation)." But there are several problems here. First of all, the parallelism in the received text is absent from the Mawangdui texts: there, the first line is not *gui i shen wei tian-xia*, but rather *gui wei shen yu tian-xia*, which Henricks renders as "one who values acting for himself over acting on behalf of the world."[52] Interpreters commonly assume that the issue here is an antagonism of interest: "acting for the world" is assumed to stand in opposition to "acting for oneself." I question that assumption. The argument that the passage commends acting to preserve one's own physical well-being is quite clearly refuted by the preceding lines: there, one's "body/person/self" (*shen*) is valued *negatively*: not only is it a source of peril, but it is the only conceivable source of peril. One's *shen* is not in any sense presented as a locus of positive value. Indeed, far from arguing for valuing the "body/person/self," the chapter asks the reader to ponder whether one would not be better off *without* it. Read in that context, the chapter's concluding lines would logically suggest that *the ruler ought to subordinate self-interest to the public interest,* just as does *Daode jing* 78 (Henricks lines 9-10).

This is not the place for a full discussion of the political ideals of the *Daode jing*, but there is abundant evidence that the text exhibits a coherent set of values relating to "self" and "other," and that it commends *a personal morality as well as a political theory*. That morality is not the Christian Golden Rule of "love others as you love yourself," nor is it the Confucian Golden Rule of "do not do unto others what you yourself do not desire" (*Analects* 12:2, 15:24). Rather, it is, if you will, a "Laoist" Golden Rule: "proper behavior will bring benefit to oneself *as* it brings benefit to others." The core issue here is not that of facing a dilemma (do I love myself more, or do I love others more?) and making a choice. Perhaps Yang Chu posed such a dilemma, but Yang did not write the *Daode jing*.[53]

I believe that Arthur Waley and Michael LaFargue are on the right track when they read chapter 13 as consisting of *quotations* from a "Yangist" source, with which the present writer is *taking issue*.[54] Hence, it would actually mean something like the following:

> [You have heard it said that]
> "To one whose value (*gui*) is acting for self over acting for the world,
> One may hand over the world";
> [But verily, verily *I* say unto you]
> To one whose (social) concern (*ai*) is *using himself* (in acting or non-acting) *for the world*,
> One may entrust the world.[55]

This reading accords with the point of the rest of the chapter—that thinking primarily of oneself is a disastrous and foolish course—and with much of the rest of the text. For instance, chapter 72, employing the same verbs found in the present lines, states that the Sage *zi ai er bu zi gui*, "is concerned about himself but does not value himself."

One of the clearest, but most neglected, teachings of the *Daode jing* is that the reader should behave like "the Sage" and like "the Dao," each of which acts (or non-acts) to *benefit others with no thought of self-benefit*. The opening of chapter 8, for instance, reads: "Superior goodness (*shan*) is like water: Water is good (*shan*) at benefitting (*li*) the myriad things, and yet retains (its) tranquility."[56] The reason that water is an apt image here is that it suggests a behavior that provides *benefits for others with no loss to oneself*. The same connotation seems to be present in passages that liken "the Sage" or "the Tao" to *a selfless parent* who "gives birth to [the myriad things], nourishes them, matures them, completes them, rests them, rears them, supports them, and protects them" (ch. 51, Henricks translation). In such passages, it seems impossible to find Yangist sentiments. Rather, what we see here is a moral idea, or rather a complex of moral ideas, at the core of which is the premise that *living so as to benefit others is in no way incompatible with one's own true fulfillment*.

Here the idea of *wuwei* becomes pertinent, for the *Daode jing* is replete with passages that argue along the following lines:

> *People constantly assume that they ought to act in their own self-interest, putting themselves first, taking instead of giving, living or ruling or fighting with deliberate self-interest. Such assumptions are disastrously wrong. Fighters with such assumptions are killed (and kill others needlessly); rulers with such assumptions fall from power (and impoverish and oppress the people); and anyone with such assumptions will actually undermine his own real interests, not only by having his plans fail, but ultimately by dying a premature death* (cf. chap. 50).

In regard to the *Daode jing*, at least, Arthur Danto is one-hundred-eighty degrees from the truth when he says that in "Taoism . . . [the] happiness one is concerned with is one's own, logically independent of the happiness of others." The *Daode jing* actually teaches *the exact opposite*: one who believes that he may act as though his own self-interest matters and others' do not will suffer and fail. Paradoxically, *true self-fulfillment rests in overcoming the assumption that it is in one's best interest to act with self-interest; in fact, it is in one's best interest to act without regard to self-interest.*

Danto argued that "the Confucian," in contrast to "the Taoist," endorses and internalizes a "network of demands and responsibilities . . . and yields to them, sacrificing or postponing his own happiness if need be." He is partly correct, for the *Daode jing* never teaches that moral action means acting to benefit others in such a way that one's own happiness is compromised. Rather, it insists that *only by acting to benefit others can one expect to achieve happiness.* In fact, in the *Daode jing, the two goals are logically intertwined.* "The Dao" and the "Sage" *never* think of *themselves*, they think only of *others*. And yet, by so doing, they place themselves beyond the context in which others resent or compete with them, and thereby win respect and honor (e.g., chap. 51). One's real fulfillment thus lies *not* in *sacrificing* one's own happiness, any more than in blindly pursuing such happiness. Rather, one should act (or non-act) selflessly for the sake of others, and the results will include those rewards that are truly meaningful for oneself.

The editor of the received text may have sensed the importance of this lesson when he took the present chapters 80-81 out from between chapters 66 and 67 (in the earlier Mawangdui edition), and made the concluding lines of the *Daode jing* to read as follows:

> The sage does not hoard.
> Having bestowed all he has on others, he has yet more;
> Having given all he has to others, he is richer still.

The Way of Heaven benefits and does not harm;
The Way of the Sage is bountiful and does not contend.[57]

## An Apophatic Morality? Self-Restraint on Behalf of the World

Clearly, the reader of the *Daode jing* is expected to recognize, and learn from, a key paradox:

To yield is to be preserved whole.
To be bent is to become straight. To be empty is to be full.
To be worn out is to be renewed.
To have little is to possess (chap. 22; Chan translation).

In sum, *to forego one's apparent self-interest leads to true self-fulfillment.*

Some may ask how such an ideal may have evolved among those who composed the *Daode jing*. The answer depends on one's idea of who those people were. One view (Confucio-centric to the core) holds that "the Taoists" were simply people who found reason to criticize the Confucians: they were merely individuals who, like Mozi, heard the Confucian gospel and found fault with it. At present, however, the most serious research notes the profound correlations between the *Daode jing* and earlier texts like the *Neiye*, which seem to have originated in a community that shared specific practices of biospiritual cultivation.[58] To read the *Daode jing* as "a philosophical text" in the sense of an exposition of speculative ideas divorced from the living of one's actual life is to misunderstand it (as, indeed, it would be to read Confucius or Mozi or Mengzi in that manner). So if the *Daode jing* is to be read as a product of parties who emerged from a community like that which produced the *Neiye*, one must ask whether and how its moral ideals correlate with the cultivational practices characteristic of such a community.

I contend that the moral teachings of the *Daode jing* can indeed be explained, to some extent, in terms of the cultivational practices outlined in texts like the *Neiye*. However, I shall not contend that such an explanation is either necessary or sufficient for making sense of the *Daode jing*. In other words, I believe that the morality of the *Daode jing* can be meaningfully understood as "an apophatic morality," but that it must ultimately be understood in a different context as well.

The thematic continuities linking apophatic cultivation and the ideals of the *Daode jing* are fairly clear. The general teaching of the apophatic tradition is that the practitioner should empty her/himself of excessive internal activity: it "involves the progressive emptying out of the usual contents of consciousness—thoughts, feelings, desires—through an inner contemplative process."[59] The composer of the *Daode jing*, I propose, considered its moral teachings to be harmonious with such practices, and may even have considered them a natural extension of those practices, though the evidence to support the latter conclusion is scanty.

The common link between apophatic self-cultivation and proper moral behavior would seem to be the ideal of learning to practice what we might call "enlightened self-restraint." In apophatic meditation, one learns to quiet the heart/mind, because its "usual contents" hamper one's efforts to attract and assimilate the forces that conduce to a full and healthy life. Thus, *the wise practitioner pursues his true fulfillment by exercising enlightened restraint regarding the "thoughts, feelings, desires" that people generally mistake to be indicators of what they should have or do (i.e, as indicators of how to achieve their self-interest).*

The moral teachings—and indeed the political teachings—of the *Daode jing* can readily be interpreted as an extension of such a pursuit. For instance, the concluding lines of chapter 64 read: "Therefore the sage desires not to desire, and does not value products that are hard to obtain; He learns not to learn, and returns to what the multitudes have passed by; He is able to enhance the myriad things' being as they are (*ziran*), and does not dare to act."[60] Here, "the sage" can be read as an ideal for the wise individual. But a passage in chapter 3, similar in both thought and construction, indicates that these ideals are appropriate for a person who governs:

> Therefore the governing of the sage is to empty his/her/their heart/mind, fill his/her/their belly, weaken his/her/their will, and strengthen his/her/their bones. He is constant in causing the people to be without thought and without desire. He causes those who have thought not to dare to act, and that is all. In this manner, there is nothing not governed.[61]

Here, the political ideal is a ruler who figuratively *extends* the processes involved in apophatic cultivation. This is clearly not self-cultivation, but rather "other-cultivation." And yet, the contents of the process are strikingly similar, beginning with the goal of "emptying the heart/mind" (*xu xin*) and continuing through the goals of minimizing thought and desire.[62]

*Much* of the *Daode jing* commends *self-restraint* as the *key* behavioral ideal (as in the final lines of chapter 64, discussed above). Numerous chapters suggest that one should practice self-restraint, in seeking satisfaction of personal desires as well as in seeking credit or praise from others. Various terms, from different sections of the text, all seem to suggest "self-restraint." One is the phrase *zhizu*, "knowing when things are sufficient," found in chapter 44 as well as in chapter 46, where we read something like the following:

> Among misdeeds, there is none greater than having things that one desires (to have *or* do);
> Among excesses, there is none greater than not knowing when things are sufficient;
> Among misfortunes, there is none greater than desiring to obtain.

> So the sufficiency of knowing when things are sufficient (*zhizu*) is a lasting sufficiency.[63]

Chapter 33 adds, "one who knows when things are sufficient (*zhizu*) is rich." A related phrase is *zhizhi*, "knowing when to stop," which seems to connote not just knowing when things are truly well as they are, but knowing when not to go forward with a personal desire or intention (chapters 32 and 44).

An even clearer expression of these ideas is the phrase *bugan*, "not daring *or* venturing (to do X)." It appears in two passages (chapters 30 and 69) that explain how to conduct warfare with proper restraint.[64] But it is more generally used in a broader context, as seen above in relation to chapter 64 (in which the sage "does not dare to act") and chapter 3 (in which he "causes those who have thought not to dare to act"). A somewhat ambiguous usage appears in chapter 73: "If one is courageous in daring/venturing, there will be killing; If one is courageous in not daring/venturing, there will be life."[65] But the clearest indication of the meaning of *bugan* may be seen in chapter 67:

> I constantly have three treasures:
> Hold onto them and treasure them.
> The first is called "compassion" (*zi*).
> The second is called "restraint."[66]
> The third is "not daring to be at the forefront of the world."
> Now being compassionate, one can be courageous.
> Being restrained, one can be expansive.
> Not daring to be at the forefront of the world, one can be the leader of the things that are completed.[67]

Each of the "three treasures" is a behavioral ideal. It is noteworthy that the second and third both enjoin the person to hold himself back, to practice *self-restraint*. But it is also noteworthy that the first is an attitude of *positive concern for others*.[68] While the precise sense of the passage is open to argument, one plausible interpretation would be as follows: *"having the courage to hold back in regard to one's ideas/feelings concerning one's own self-interest makes it possible for one to be courageous in expanding oneself in compassionate regard for others."* Such a reading would be consistent with the sense of most of the passages discussed above.

It should also be noted that the ideal of "enlightened self-restraint" in the *Daode jing* is far from any notion of "losing the self": it is not a teaching of self-abasement or self-sacrifice. In Taoism generally, there is seldom any notion that it is proper to relinquish what is good or necessary for one's own well-being.[69] In the *Daode jing*, there is no ascetic ideal, and no implication that one's personal reality is in any sense unreal or unworthy. Rather, the *Daode jing* seeks to alert the reader to the *benefits* that *both self and others* will enjoy if one is perceptive enough and humble enough to forego shortsighted pursuit of self-interest. It urges one to neglect *neither* self *nor* others, to pursue an enlightened life-orientation wherein

> Having bestowed all he has on others, he has yet more;
> Having given all he has to others, he is richer still.
> The Way of Heaven benefits and does not harm;
> The Way of the Sage is bountiful and does not contend (ch. 81).

## Notes

1. A version of this paper was presented at a meeting of the Society for Asian and Comparative Philosophy, held in conjunction with the 1996 annual meeting of the American Philosophical Association, Eastern Division.

2. A preliminary exploration of these matters may be found in my article, "Person and Culture in the Taoist Tradition," *Journal of Chinese Religions* 20 (1992), 77-90. A different perspective stressing philosophical issues is Chad Hansen, *A Daoist Theory of Chinese Thought: A Philosophical Interpretation* (New York: Oxford University Press, 1992), 1-29. More generally, the inherited interpretive problems that have resulted from orientalist approaches are explored in J. J. Clarke, *Oriental Enlightenment: The Encounter between Asian and Western Thought* (London: Routledge, 1997).

3. See, e.g., "Person and Culture in the Taoist Tradition"; and Steve Bradbury, "The American Conquest of Philosophical Taoism," in *Translation East and West: A Cross-Cultural Approach*, ed. by Cornelia N. Moore and Lucy Lower (Honolulu: University of Hawaii College of Languages, Linguistics and Literature and the East-West Center, 1992), 29-41. The social and intellectual history of the Western concept of "Taoism" has yet to be written.

4. Specialists will be aware that archeological finds in the late twentieth century have given us two "new" editions of the text: the Mawangdui manuscripts, which apparently date to ca. 200 BCE; and the recently discovered Guodian manuscript, which seem about a century older. The Guodian text, which has not yet been translated, lacks much of what appears in the other, later editions. Since scholars have just begun to analyze it, I shall not attempt to explore it fully here. Also, I have found too few differences between the received text and the Mawangdui editions to justify separating them for the purpose of this study. I shall therefore note textual variations only where circumstances warrant. For the received text, I follow the *Zhuzi jicheng* edition of the Wang Bi text, as printed in *Kondordanz zum Lao-tzu* (München: Seminar für Ostasiatische Sprach- und Kulturwissenschaft der Universität München, 1968). For the Mawangdui text, I use the versions published by Robert G. Henricks in his translation, *Lao-tzu Te-tao ching* (New York: Ballantine Books, 1989). For convenience, I shall refer to sections of the text according to the numbering in the received text. The Mawangdui editions have the sections in a different sequence; Henricks, however, continues to number them as in the received text, so that his translation begins with "chapter 38" and concludes with "chapter 37." On the assumption that most readers will still think

of the chapters in the traditional numbering, and will find that numbering in most editions and translations, I shall continue to employ it here. The Guodian materials can be found in *Guodian Chumu zhujian* [The Bamboo Writing-Slips from the Chu Tomb at Guodian] (Beijing: Wenwu chubanshe, 1998).

5. Russell Kirkland, "The Roots of Altruism in the Taoist Tradition," *Journal of the American Academy of Religion* 54 (1986), 60.

6. Max Weber, *The Religion of China: Confucianism and Taoism*, translated by Hans H. Gerth (New York: The Free Press, 1951), devotes one incoherent page (204-5) to the topic, "The Ethic of Taoism."

7. It is notable that a recent collection of fine studies on Zhuangzi refers explicitly to ethics in its title: *Essays on Skepticism, Relativism, and Ethics in the Zhuangzi*, edited by Paul Kjellberg and Philip J. Ivanhoe (Albany: State University of New York Press, 1996). Yet none of the contributors seem to find in *Zhuangzi* anything worth discussing as "ethics."

8. Herbert Fingarette, *Confucius: The Secular as Sacred* (New York: Harper and Row, 1972).

9. Arthur C. Danto, *Mysticism and Morality: Oriental Thought and Moral Philosophy*, originally published in 1972 (New York: Basic Books). The most recent edition (1988) is from Columbia University Press.

10. Danto, 118-19. This argument by Danto has found its way into the broader literature, as seen, e.g., in a publication by two British philosophers, Diané Collinson and Robert Wilkinson, *Thirty-Five Oriental Philosophers* (London and New York: Routledge, 1994), 138.

11. Danto, 119-20.

12. On the subject of the "authorship" of the *Daode jing*, see my entry, "The Book of the Way," in Ian McGreal, *Great Literature of the Eastern World* (New York: HarperCollins, 1996), 24-29. On the figure of "Lao-tzu," an ever-changing cultural construct, see Judith M. Boltz, "Lao-tzu," in *The Encyclopedia of Religion* (New York: Macmillan, 1987), 8:454-59; A. C. Graham, "The Origins of the Legend of Lao Tan," in his *Studies in Chinese Philosophy and Philosophical Literature* (Albany: State University of New York Press, 1990), 111-24; and Livia Kohn, *God of the Dao: Laozi in History and Myth* (Ann Arbor: University of Michigan, Center for Chinese Studies, 1999).

13. Danto, 114-17.

14. The Taoist tradition of China—generally still ignored by modern philosophers and intellectual historians—actually gives the *Zhuangzi* very limited importance. Though some Taoist intellectuals continued to draw upon it for terms and ideas, the majority of Taoists gave it little attention, and were seldom discernibly influenced by it. The *idea* that the *Zhuangzi* is a primary Taoist text is actually a *non-Taoist idea*, specifically a Confucian and Western construct. On the historical origins of such constructs, see Kirkland, "Hermeneutics and Pedagogy: Methodological Issues in Teaching the *Tao te ching*," in Warren Frisina and Gary DeAngelis, ed., *Essays in Teaching the Tao te ching* (Atlanta: American Academy of Religion / Scholars Press, in press); and Norman J. Girardot, *"The Whole Duty of Man": James Legge (1815-1897) and the Victorian Translation of China* (Berkeley: University of California Press, forthcoming).

These facts have not prevented many modern interpreters from maintaining the fallacious category of "Lao-Zhuang thought," and reifying it as "Taoism." This problem has afflicted works by otherwise competent and thoughtful interpreters: see, e.g., Donald Munro, *The Concept of Man in Early China* (Stanford, Calif.: Stanford University Press, 1969). Increasingly, as Western thinkers become more familiar with (and admiring of) the *Zhuangzi*, they have virtually reversed the traditional Chinese reification to create a new beast that seems to need the name "Zhuang-Lao thought." We see it, e.g., in Hansen's stimulating book *A Daoist Theory of Chinese Thought.* In his chapter on *Laozi,* Hansen goes so far as to write as follows: "Laozi's position . . . remains a way station in Daoist development. . . .We still have no final answer to the question, 'What should we do?' Can we coherently see this book as giving the answer? . . . If there is some advice, some point, Laozi could not state it. And so neither can I. But Zhuangzi can! Daoism must still mature more" (202, 230). So not only was there such a thing as "Daoism" in ancient China, but it must be defined in terms of "Zhuangzi," for "Laozi" was too inarticulate to be able to express it! The Hegelian implication that "Daoism" inevitably marched upward to its shining peak in "Zhuangzi" (and then, of course, "degenerated" into "superstition") is egregious enough without relegating the *Daode jing* to the back porch as "immature Daoism."

15. Harold Roth, "Some Issues in the Study of Chinese Mysticism: A Review Essay," *China Review International* 2 no. 1 (Spring 1995), 157. The origins of the bibliographic concept of a *daojia* in Han historiography is discussed in A.C. Graham, *Disputers of the Tao: Philosophical Argument in Ancient China* (LaSalle, Illinois: Open Court Publishing Co., 1989), 170-71.

16. See Harold D. Roth, "Redaction Criticism and the Early History of Taoism," *Early China* 19 (1994), 1-46; and *Original Tao: Inward Training (Nei-yeh) and the Foundations of Taoist Mysticism*, in progress.

17. I refer primarily to a highly important 4th-century-BCE text called the *Neiye* (preserved in *Kuanzi*, ch. 49). See especially Roth, "The Inner Cultivation Tradition of Early Daoism," in Donald S. Lopez, Jr., ed., *Religions of China in Practice* (Princeton, N. J.: Princeton University Press, 1996), 123-34; and Kirkland, "Varieties of 'Taoism' in Ancient China: A Preliminary Comparison of Themes in the *Nei yeh* and Other 'Taoist Classics'," *Taoist Resources* 7.2 (1997), 73-86. Other ancient texts that preserve similar teachings include passages of the *Lüshi chunqiu*; the "Jie-Lao" and "Yü-Lao" chapters of the *Hanfei* (ch. 20-21); and the "Xinshu" sections of the *Kuanzi* (ch. 36-37).

18. E. Bruce Brooks and Taeko Brooks have recently argued that—(t)he Dauists do not form a *philosophical* group in this period; the root insight of many who later came to be included in that rubric is the technique of meditation, which was apparently known in (the state of) Lu by the 05c (i.e., the fifth-century BCE)—Brooks, *The Original Analects* (New York: Columbia University Press, 1998), 7. The geography and dating of such matters remain the subject of debate.

19. In "Varieties of 'Taoism' in Ancient China," I show that the *Neiye* lacks the moral or political teachings found in the *Daode jing*. Yet its ideals are quite distinct from those of Zhuang Zhou, and do not fit Danto's model. If one wished to find the overlap among *Zhuangzi*, the *Neiye*, and the *Daode jing* and reify it as "Taoist thought," one is likely to find so little meaningful overlap that little of any specificity could be said about it.

20. Naturally, it goes without saying that he censures "Taoism" without having given any of the *hundreds* of texts of *later* Taoism a fair reading. For a survey of the ethical dimensions of the Taoist tradition as a whole, see my entry, "Taoism," in *The Encyclopedia of Bioethics*, 2nd edition (New York: Macmillan, 1995), 5: 2463-2469. For suggestions as to incorporating texts and thinkers of Later Taoism into our coverage of Taoism, see my article, "Teaching Taoism in the 1990s," *Teaching Theology and Religion* 1.2 (1998), 121-29.

21. Because of textual variations, the precise sense of these lines remain in question. The term *mei* is generally translated "beauty," and the term *e* as "ugliness"; but considering the use of the latter term elsewhere (e.g., in Xunzi, where it means the general "foulness" of "human nature"), I take it to connote a more general unpleasantness than what literally meets the eye. It should also be noted that common interpretations of usage in Xunzi might lead one to expect *e* to be contrasted here with *shan* ("goodness"), but such is not the case.

22. E.g., Chen Guying, *Laozi jinzhu jinyi* (Taibei: Taiwan Shangwu yinshuguan, 1970), translated as Ch'en Ku-ying, *Lao Tzu: Text, Notes, and Comments*, translated by Rhett Y. W. Young and Roger T. Ames (San Francisco: Chinese Materials Center, 1977), 59.

23. Such is the reading in the received text. In the Mawangdui texts, the first line is the same but the second line differs slightly. The passage does not appear in the Guodian materials.

24. In *Law and Morality in Ancient China: The Silk Manuscripts of Huang-Lao* (Albany: State University of New York Press, 1993), R. Peerenboom agrees that "Lao Zi, like Confucius, rejects rule ethics," but he contends that the *Daode jing* contains a situational ethics and regards social consensus as the highest ideal (187-89). Such an interpretation seems to project a late-twentieth-century Western morality upon a text from ancient China. Such interpretations may persuade modern (or postmodern) people that "Daoism" is a wise philosophy for today, but I will contend that no one in ancient China was constructing philosophies to be applied in an alien culture, and we must beware interpreting the *Daode jing* as a tract for our time.

25. Graham shows how easy it is to overinterpret a passage. In discussing this line, he states, "The good man is the one who by adapting himself to the Way has learned both to survive and (a theme however of Chuang-tzu rather than *Lao-tzu*) reconcile himself to misfortune and death; it is because alone among men he is on the side of the Way that the Way works in his favour." Graham, 231. But in point of fact, there is nothing in chapter 79 of the *Daode jing* about "survival"; nothing about reconciling oneself to misfortune; nothing about "adapting oneself to the Way"; and nothing to suggest that the "good man" is "on the side of the Way."

26. Henricks lines 3-5. The Guodian materials lack this passage, and the Mawangdui texts here are too fragmentary to be very reliable.

27. It seems wrong to say that dogs can receive "moral training": one can train a dog to act "properly" (e.g., not to relieve itself in certain places), but behavioral conditioning seems logically distinct from "moral" training: we can also train a child not to relieve itself in certain places, but whether such training is "moral" in quality seems quite dubious. Confucius (*Analects* 2:7) argues that filial piety is a sham if it consists of just providing for parents' physical needs, for one does that even for animals. "Without reverence," he asks, "what is the difference?" One might object that "reverence" is merely an emotion, but the true position of Confucius, I think, is that one ought to feel the feelings that come from a full recognition of one's debt to one's parents, and ought to behave so as to express (to parents, family members, and others) a sincere willingness to make payment on that debt (whether or not it is ever fully payable). It is debatable whether "filial piety" in this sense fits Danto's definition of moral education as "getting men to assume attitudes towards themselves that are logically connected with the attitudes others take toward themselves." Confucius, I believe, would maintain that the practice of filial piety is right in itself, irrespective of the attitudes that parent or child might harbor: acting as a true human being involves a wholehearted commitment to following the transcendentally authoritative patterns of social interaction (*li*) that are ordained by Heaven (*Tian*) and modelled by our exemplars (the "sage-kings"). One

might argue that Confucius is suggesting a "religious ethic," which we could distinguish from a "social ethic" (which would involve only issues of whether people seek to contribute to others' happiness, without reference to any other value). But such was not Danto's position.

28. This passage is another example of how interpreters, Asian and Western alike, have, almost uniformly, fallen victim to unthinking eisegesis. A *Zhuangzi* passage mentions "straw-dogs" that were used in ancient sacrifices, and virtually all interpreters have, without any other justification, proclaimed that the present lines "refer" to such a phenomenon. But there is actually no good reason to assume any such reference, any more than any mention of people wearing red coats in colonial America should automatically be assumed to "refer" to British soldiers. And certainly, the writer of this passage had never read *Zhuangzi*. The easier, and more sensible, reading of this passage is that of the commentator Wang Bi, who explained: "Heaven and Earth do not make the grass grow for the sake of beasts, yet beasts eat grass. They do not produce dogs for the sake of men, yet men eat dogs" (Richard John Lynn, *The Classic of the Way and Virtue: A New Translation of the Tao-te ching of Laozi as Interpreted by Wang Bi* (New York: Columbia University Press, 1999, 60; oddly, Lynn's translation of the passage ignores Wang's explanation).

29. It is intriguing, and perhaps historically revealing, that the Guodian texts lack these four lines, though lines 5-7 do appear there. A reasonable conjecture is that the "anti-Mencian" sentiments of lines 1-4 were added after the "text" was transmitted from Chu to Lu, and revised to respond to various Confucian doctrines. For the teachings of Mengzi, see especially the pertinent sections of Philip J. Ivanhoe, *Confucian Moral Self Cultivation* (New York: Peter Lang, 1993) and *Ethics in the Confucian Tradition* (Atlanta: Scholars Press, 1990); and Lee H. Yearley, *Mencius and Aquinas* (Albany: State University of New York Press, 1990).

30. Note the quotation marks here, indicating that it would be unwarranted to reify any particular element of the *Daode jing* as representing a "Taoist" idea. Such ideas may or may not appear in any of the other texts that one may label "Taoist."

31. Elsewhere, I have used the term "Laoist" for the traditions of the oral community from which the earliest layers of the *Daode jing* seem to have emerged. Here, however, I am expanding the term to serve as a descriptor of the teachings of the extant *Daode jing* as a whole.

32. James Rachels, *The Elements of Moral Philosophy* (New York: Random House, 1986), 11.

33. The religious dimension of classical Confucianism has often been overlooked, both in China and in the West, because with the conspicuous exception of Dong Zhongshu, Confucian theorists rarely attempted to provide an explicit analysis of the nature or activities of "Heaven," or of its relationship to humanity. The humanistic thrust of Confucianism in its *practice* seems to have minimized theoretical interest in the non-humanistic implications of what one might well call Confucian theology. See further Edward J. Machle, *Nature and Heaven in the Xunzi: A Study of the Tian Lun* (Albany: State University of New York Press, 1993), and my entry, "Tung Chung-shu," in Ian McGreal, ed., *Great Thinkers of the Eastern World* (New York: HarperCollins, 1995), 67-70.

34. See chapters 47, 73, 77, 79, and 81. None of those chapters appear in the Guodian manuscripts, a fact that suggests that the phrase *Tian-zhi Dao* was added in Lu to help those who saw *Tian* as a source of life's goodness—such as the Confucians and the Mohists —to

accept *Dao* as playing an analogous role. It is also interesting that such a meaningful phrase seldom appears in the much longer text of *Zhuangzi*, and there is little trace of such ideas in the *Neiye*.

35. Such is clearly Xunzi's position. Mengzi famously insisted that "human nature" tends inherently toward moral behavior, but he admitted the frailty of that tendency: in all but the "gentleman," social pressures lead the individual astray, and constant attention and effort are necessary for one to maintain a moral course. Xunzi argued that "human nature" cannot be trusted, and that humanity is redeemed by the "artificial activity" (*wei*) of the ancient sage-kings, who created and bequeathed to us the proper values and patterns of behavior. Mengzi seems unable to explain why individuals are so susceptible to bad influences, or how such influences first originated. As usual, it is difficult to discern how Confucius might have addressed such issues: his concern was that society *had* derogated from the proper path, and that exceptional individuals must work to restore society by means of moral activity.

36. See further my entry, "Taoism," in *Philosophy of Education: An Encyclopedia*, edited by J.J. Chambliss (New York and London: Garland Publishing, 1996), 633-36.

37. Benjamin Schwartz writes of "the Lao-tzu's continuing overwhelming concern with human life and hence the presence of a somewhat inconsistent 'moralism' and even 'humanism' which he seems to share with his predecessors [i.e., Confucius, etc.]." Benjamin I. Schwartz, *The World of Thought in Ancient China* (Cambridge, Mass.: Harvard University Press, 1985), 204. But the rest of the passage is given over to discussions of "mysticism" (a major theme for Schwartz) and "naturalism," and one searches in vain for an elaboration upon the *Daode jing's* "moralism" or "humanism." In fact, his only other reference to the text's "moralistic torque" seems to appear as an assertion of "a basic inconsistency [in] the entire vision of the Lao-tzu" ( 213). Apparently, Schwartz saw or felt something vaguely "humanistic" in the *Daode jing*, but was never able to make sufficient sense of it to overcome the Confucian assumption that the teachings of the *Daode jing* are antipathetic to moral and social concerns.

38. For example, if one see two burning houses, one of which contains his own parents and the other of which contains the parents of someone else, the Mohist would say that both sets of people are equally deserving of being saved. The Confucian would disagree, arguing that one has an extra moral obligation to one's parents, because without them he would not have come into existence or lived to maturity.

39. Translation from D.C. Lau, *Confucius: The Analects*, 2nd ed. (Hong Kong: The Chinese University Press, 1992), 93.

40. To Mengzi, at least, compassion for non-human life is within the realm of Confucian values, as seen in *Mengzi* 1A.7.

41. Peerenboom, stretching the sense of *Daode jing* 27, argues that "Lao Zi's expansion of the sage's domain of concern to nonhuman elements in one's environment differentiates his position from the anthropocentric concerns of Confucius" (189). But one must once again be careful not to confuse the non-anthropocentrism of the *Daode jing* with late-twentieth-century attitudes. I see no justification for Peerenboom's assertion that in the *Daode jing*, "Each person and each thing possess an inviolability, an integrity, that must be accounted for in the resulting sociopolitical and cosmic order" (ibid.). To the contrary, as I have argued elsewhere, "Taoists lacked the notion that the individual—or even the human species—is an independent locus of moral value. In fact, Lao-Chuang Taoism can easily be read as a concerted effort to disabuse us of the absurd notions of self-importance that most people tacitly embrace as natural and normal. Hence, the very concept of 'rights'—for indi-

viduals or groups, humans, or animals—makes no sense whatever in Taoist terms." "Taoism," *Encyclopedia of Bioethics*, 2466.

42. Translation from D.C. Lau, *Lao-tzu Tao te ching* (Harmondsworth: Penguin, 1963), 137. Later, Lau translated the Ma-wang-tui texts, but the fact that it was published in Hong Kong (Hong Kong: Chinese University of Hong Kong, 1989) meant that it received little attention in the West. It has now been re-published in North America (New York: Alfred A. Knopf, 1994), with a new introduction by Sarah Allen. Readers who compare Lau's translations, however, will find some changes that owe nothing to differences in the Chinese edition being translated.

43. Here, again, we must be careful not to read alien ideas into our text. While *ziran* ("spontaneity") is a conspicuous ideal in Wei-Jin thought (e.g., in the Xiang/Guo commentary to the *Zhuangzi*), it is a minor element in the *Daode jing*. The term appears only four times (chs. 17, 23, 25, and 64), and it is by no means clear that it ever connotes "spontaneity." E.g., the end of ch. 64, translated below, says that the Sage can "enhance the *ziran* of the myriad things," and it is hard to understand how a ruler or exemplary person could cause others to be more "spontaneous."

44. It seems certain that the term *wuwei* originated in circles outside those from which the *Daode jing* itself emerged. The term was not only used by Confucius, but was a component of the political philosophy of the "Legalist" Shen Buhai (d. 337 BCE). See, e.g., H.G. Creel, *Shen Pu-hai: A Chinese Political Philosopher of the Fourth Century B.C.* (Chicago: University of Chicago Press, 1974), es 176-79.

45. Chapters 2, 51, and 77 (and chapter 10 in the received text) seem to endorse "acting" in relation to others, provided one's actions are not possessive or controlling. The phrase *wei wuwei* appears in Guodian A, and in two chapters of the received text (3 and 63), but it is absent from the Mawangdui text of chapter 3.

46. See Lau, 1963 translation, 189n.

47. The term *li* appears in nine chapters of the received text, and in the opening lines of Guodian A, which are becoming famous for lacking the attack on Confucian values seen in the corresponding lines of the received text (chapter 19). In the received version, the Confucian virtues are excoriated along with "sageliness" (elsewhere the human ideal of the *Daode jing*), and "benefit" is disparaged, in a context that suggests "selfish struggle for personal profit" (in just the way Mengzi criticized the term). However, other chapters (e.g., 8, 73, and 81) clearly use the term *li* positively. And the Guodian text which has "benefitting the people" valued positively, and no attack on "sageliness" now shows that a late redactor mangled the text in an effort to discredit the Confucians of northerly states like Lu.

48. I use the masculine pronoun here simply because as a matter of fact, if not intention, the ancient reader of the *Daode jing* was male.

49. Whereas the received text reads, *wu bu zhi qi ming* ("I do not know its name"), the Mawangdui texts both read, *wu wei zhi qi ming* ("I have *not yet* come to know its name"); the same is true of Guodian A, save for the absence of the pronoun. The implication is that "it" is not ultimately ineffable after all.

50. One should note that when compared to the teachings of the *Neiye*, the suggestions for "meditation" in the *Daode jing* are so vague as to seem unpracticeable.

51. Hansen, 195.

52. The corresponding passage of Guodian B is too fragmentary to permit sound comparisons.

53. Henricks ( 212-13) interprets the passage in a Yangist sense, since it is quoted in a late chapter of the *Zhuangzi* where the sense seems to be Yangist. But the fact remains that the person who wrote the *Zhuangzi* passage is other than the person who wrote the *Daode jing* passage, and there is no reason to assume that what one person thought is the same as what the other person thought.

54. See Michael LaFargue, *The Tao of the Tao Te Ching* (Albany: State University of New York Press, 1992), 40, 182; and Arthur Waley, *The Way and its Power* (London: George Allen & Unwin, 1934), 157. Waley and LaFargue are apparently correct that the term *ruo* was originally a second-person pronoun, for the Mawangdui B-text uses the pronoun *ru* in the second line. That fact, and the completely different grammatical structure of the two lines in the Mawangdui edition, lead one to believe that the first line is not an expression of the writer's own thought, but rather a quotation ("Yangist," if you like) which the writer is attempting to use to re-direct the reader's perspective in a completely different direction.

55. The *yi/wei* construction in the second line denotes "to use X in doing Y, or to use X for Y," and the verb *ai* is used in the general sense of "concern or solicitude," as in Mohist discourse (though the overall lesson here is decidedly non-Mohist).

56. The received text reads, *er bu-zheng*, "and does not compete." The Mawangdui A-text reads *er you jing*, "and has tranquility," while the B-text read *er you zheng*, "and has competition." Henricks suggests (272 n. 117) that the *you* in the B-text "is copy error for *fu* ('*does not* compete *with them*')." His suggestion is plausible, but leaves other questions unanswered, such as whether the *you* in the A-text is also a copy error (in which case its *jing* must also be an error). I shall assume that both texts are correct because *zheng* is the phonetic element in *jing*, and can simply be read as the base character, the proper denotation of which was more clearly indicated by the addition of a radical in text A. The Guodian materials lack this passage.

57. Lau translation, capitalizations added. Peerenboom seems to arrive at a similar insight when he states that the sage "seeks his own fulfillment in and through that of others . . . [because] in interpersonal transactions the gain of one need not entail the loss of another" (186-87). But much of the rest of his interpretation seems excessively idealized and communitarian.

58. See above, note 16.

59. Harold D. Roth, "Evidence for Meditative Stages in Early Taoism," *Bulletin of the School of Oriental and African Studies* 60 (1997), 295-314.

60. The texts (including Guodian A and C) hardly differ at all here. Henricks argues ( 150) that in the final line of the Mawangdui text the negative *fu* ("not X it"), instead of *pu* ("not X"), means that it should read, "He could help all things to be natural, yet he dare not do it." Even if we accept the Mawangdui reading (which I am inclined to do), I am not convinced that Henricks' interpretation is correct. For one thing, it requires the conjunctive *er* to carry a reversive sense in the last line (he . . . *and yet* . . . ) that it clearly does *not* carry in the first two lines, even as Henricks reads them. Secondly, I am unconvinced that *wei* should be read as shorthand for the action (or non-action) indicated in the first clause. Since many passages explain how the sage "acts without action," it seems quite possible to infer precisely such non-active behavior on the part of the sage in the first clause. Hence both the grammar and the general teachings of the text seem to suggest that the final words should be read as meaning the same as the words *bugan wei* found in the received text. Indeed, Henricks himself reads *fugan wei* in precisely this sense in a parallel construction in chapter 3 ( 192).

61. In the first line, the pronominal *qi* is generally read as meaning "the people's . . . ,"

as in the following lines, but such an assumption may not be justified. The line can also be logically read as meaning that the sage "empties *his* heart/mind . . . ," and that such apophatic therapy provides appropriate preparation for achieving the goals laid out in the following lines. The chapter's opening lines, however, do not seem to support such an interpretation. As one would expect, this passage is lacking from the Guodian materials.

62. If we read *zhi* as "thought," not "knowledge," the entire passage loses its notorious "Legalist overtones." But it remains unclear how one could cause other people to "be without thought and without desire." Prima facie, such an extension of apophatic ideals into the political sphere seems out of accord with the assumptions behind the *Neiye's* practice of self-cultivation, i.e., that each person must cultivate him/herself, in an "inner" process. Clearly, there were different concepts of self-cultivation among its proponents in ancient China. Even Mencius began with many of the same assumptions, and added others (e.g., the importance of acts of moral rightness), so that the cultivation of one's personal *ch'i* made sense (at least to him) in terms of the inherited Confucian moral scheme (see *Mengzi* 2A.2).

63. The text here is slightly uncertain, because the first line is not present in the received text, and significant portions of the the subsequent lines are missing in the fragmentary Mawangdui texts. But all four are present in the Guodian A text (though the second and third lines are inverted).

64. The Guodian materials lack chapter 69, but Guodian A does include most of chapter 30 (= Henricks' lines 1-2, 6-13). It thus seems that the earliest version of the *Daode jing* did not criticize Confucian values, but did criticize warfare.

65. Interpreters since Wang Bi have read the final verbs as passive: "one who is brave in daring will be killed; one who is brave in not daring will stay alive." But there is nothing in the passage that leads logically to such a reading, and several facts suggest otherwise. First of all, reading the verbs in the active voice is the most natural reading. Secondly, if the first verb really meant suffering death (rather than inflicting it), one would expect the verb *si*, "to die," not *sha*, "to kill." Thirdly, there is nothing else in the present chapter (or, for that matter, in the chapters preceding or following it) suggesting a goal of "staying alive." But the subsequent chapter *does* warn against inflicting death upon others. I have therefore rendered the lines as grammar and context suggest, and left the meaning ambiguous. The passage does not appear in the Guodian materials.

66. Apparently based on Wang Bi's comment, virtually all translators render *jian* here as "frugality," which makes little sense: it is hard to think of other passages that commend any behavior in economic terms, or of a sensible explanation of such a commendation. According to Karlgren (*Grammata Serica Recensa* no. 613e), *jian* carried the original meaning of "restrict" or "restricted," and in this passage such a usage can be readily explained. It seems intriguing that the term appears nowhere else in the text.

67. This passage is not in the Guodian materials. For the final line, I follow the Mawangdui texts, which have a *wei* before *cheng*, indicating that *cheng* is not a verb ("to become"), but rather a modifier of *qi*. Most translators insist on reading a political reference into this line, for no good reason that I can surmise, save that traditional commentators liked to find such references. We must remember that such commentators were from a tradition that could not read early Zhou folk songs without interpreting them as advice for the ruler.

68. On this teaching, and its endurance in later Taoism, see further my "The Roots of Altruism in the Taoist Tradition."

69. Readers of the late-imperial "Taoist novel," *Qizhen zhuan*, translated by Eva Wong

as *Seven Taoist Masters* (Boston: Shambhala, 1991), might retort that self-sacrifice is a theme of that novel: in one episode a character even sacrifices her beauty by disfiguring her face. But readers must bear in mind that the novel is *fiction*: there is actually *no* good reason to believe that any Taoist woman ever really maimed herself for religious purposes. That idea evidently arose in the mind of the anonymous novelist, and cannot be shown to reflect the beliefs or values of anyone other than himself. For the realities of women in Taoism, see my entry in *Encyclopedia of Women and World Religion* (New York: Macmillan, 1999) II: 959-64. In real life, Taoism, in all its forms, characteristically commends *self-cultivation*, not self-sacrifice. What could be said is that many forms require *self-discipline* as a *prerequisite* to self-fulfillment. See, e.g, the materials analyzed in Kirkland, "The Making of an Immortal: The Exaltation of Ho Chih-chang," *Numen* 38 (1991-92), 201-214. And such expectations of self-discipline were quite consistent with what we find here in the *Daode jing*.

## *Chapter Two*

# Ethical Insights from Chu Hsi


## Kirill Ole Thompson


During the past several decades, Anglo-American ethics has turned from the metaethical analysis of basic ethical terms to the reflective application of ethical theories to pressing moral issues of the day. Forces from several directions have contributed to this shift. Significantly, during the 1960s and 70s a range of social-moral issues came to the fore that philosophers no longer could choose to ignore. Students wanted more relevance in what they were learning. Concurrently, applied ethics began to show promise.

Despite this practical turn, ethical discussion has remained at a high level theoretically, which has resulted in an ever-increasing sophistication in practical ethical discourse. Yet, this in itself has at times yielded problems of other sorts. For example, the rational analytic process can lead the arguments away from the original motivating concerns regarding the issues. It can also sanitize and trim away the meat and texture of the issues. Moreover, even academic philosophers are wont to spin analyses of ethical issues in ways that support their commitments, predilections, and biases, rather than attempt to achieve the most perspicacious view.

There is another respect in which the increased theoretical sophistication might incline ethical discussion to go astray, in much the way that traditional philosophy often did. I am thinking of attempts to understand the paradigmatic logical operation of ethical concepts, such as, for example, the concepts of honesty and truth-telling. An established body of psychological and linguistic research shows that a significant gap exists between the way in which we think and talk about these concepts in the abstract and our actual speech performances. Even though a high premium is placed on honesty and truth-telling in our society, various studies reveal remarkably high incidences of lying in everyday life. For the sake of discussion, let us say that people "lie" (i.e., purposely misconstrue the facts) in nearly 50% of their verbal exchanges. While this figure might seem to be hasty or based on faulty sampling, researchers find significant levels of lying in society from top to bottom in a wide variety of communication contexts. It is noteworthy that exceptions tend to occur in communities whose religions stress individual conscience and those in which individuals take truth-telling as a matter of personal integrity. The figures cover, not merely the accepted falsities of polite social intercourse, but lies told about important matters between closely related people, such as best friends, significant others, and even spouses.

Fortunately, only a relatively small portion of lies told are purely self-serving or otherwise ill-intended, the majority of lies fall in a broad range of altruistically motivated white lies. That is, it seems people are raised to have the attitude that it is sometimes better to speak a varnished truth than the unvarnished truth. (This learning seems to occur at the subconscious level, since people generally are not fully aware that they are varnishing the facts quite so much; of course, many people do this quite consciously.) In daily life, many people are thus in the habit of crafting lies that they believe will achieve certain good ends, such as lies to make people feel better, or to avoid distressing them, or even to protect others from judgmental or vindictive people. Poorly crafted or otherwise ineffective lies will be criticized, less for being lies *per se* than for being inept or insensitive or blatant lies. By the same token, truth-tellers can be similarly criticized for being inept or insensitive in telling the truth. Clearly, the unvarnished truth is not the bottom line in commonplace acceptable social intercourse; efforts are made to give and save face, to protect feelings and to maintain interpersonal harmony. Ironically, it seems that it is the people who tend to demand truth from others and be judgmental that are the ones most often lied to, and who themselves must lie when suddenly caught in questionable circumstances. This is not to suggest that truth is not a value and not an essential part of common parlance, just that human beings are prone to modify the truth for the sake of certain interpersonal needs.

Could it be that other moral concepts are similarly modified and qualified in daily life as well, and largely so that people can achieve more goodness than would be achieved by straight applications of the moral concept? Does our way of thinking as philosophers blind us to the actual intricacies of ethical discourse in the stream of life? In this sense, was Camus setting up a humanly impossible standard of directness and truth-telling with his character Meursault in *The Stranger*? To what extent can we maintain character and integrity in our social intercourse without causing hurt and harm, like Gregors Werle in Ibsen's *The Wild Duck*?

The ethical thought of Chu Hsi (1130-1220), an astute observer of human relationships and behavior, contains some insights of relevance to problems of these sorts.[1] This study fleshes out these insights in the context of Chu's practical philosophy and uses them to reexamine several familiar ethical problems. At the outset, I want to offer the disclaimer that I am pushing the implications of Chu's position somewhat farther than he himself would have done. All the same, the discussion is based squarely on his ethical insights and suggestions. The key area of Chu's ethical thought focused on in this study includes his notion of "appropriateness" (*yi*), and his epistemic/ practical methodology, summed up in the call to: investigate things to extend knowledge (*ke-wu chih-chih*).[2] Chu advocated this methodology in part to stress the need for people, as viable moral agents, to notice the fine details, the distinguishing features—of particular situations— and to have on that basis a sense of how to tailor the most discerning, appropriate responses.

Now, let us review Chu's overall system in order to grasp the context for understanding his epistemic/practical methodology. While displaying a remarkable development in his ethical thought, throughout his career Chu Hsi focused on the twin problems of: (1) determining the conditions of moral agency, and (2) setting forth a viable program of moral self-cultivation on that basis. Chu saw moral agency as the expression of a moral will, which he understood to be the achievement of an inner self-mastery (*chu-tsai* ) that forms the core of a person's character, moral cognizance, and responsiveness. On this view, self-cultivation aimed at nurturing self-mastery thus must include forming a concentrated, reverent mind-set (*ching*) and a discerning sense of appropriateness(*yi*).[3] Early on, Chu had emphasized the need to attain a working knowledge of the constitutive patterns/principles (*li*) of reality and society in the light of which the norms and ritual actions (*li*) prescribed for upright interpersonal relationships and intercourse are devised. [Hereafter, the term "norm(s)" will stand for "norm(s) and ritual action(s)".] He later found that establishing the determination (*li-chih* ) to seek self-realization and conduct oneself appropriately counted for as much as the long-term cultivation process itself, during which one can lose sight of one's purpose and be side-tracked.[4] Moreover, while still maintaining the importance of the norms for character-building and for social order, Chu began to emphasize the need to build up a sympathetic but realistic grasp of the warp and woof of real human life—viewed, of course, in the perspective of such broad Confucian ethical ideals as human-heartedness (*jen*) and fairness (*kung*). He understood that, although the norms are broadly applicable and reliable, many situations call for specially tailored responses.[5]

Consequently, against the moral intuitionism prevalent at the time in Neo-Confucianism, as espoused by his teacher *Li* T'ung (1093-1163), his contemporary Lu Chiu-yuan (1139-1193), and others, Chu argued intuitionism is inadequate for dealing with the complex human affairs people are apt to encounter in their lives.[6] Thus, he advocated dedicating oneself to the study of the patterns/ principles (*li*) of relationship, interaction, and change among all things, among human beings in particular. He regarded "investigating things to extend knowledge" as the surest way to deepen and broaden our discernment of the patterns that constitute our lived-world. Such knowledge, importantly, sharpens our sense of appropriateness by attuning us to the subtle distinguishing features of particular situations.

We may pause to note that Greek and Roman Stoicism presented a similar array of positions. Early on, Philo and others argued that moral virtue involved grasping the moral rules and applying them skillfully in appropriate situations. In fact, these Stoics conceived the exercise of virtue on the model of a deductive inference in which an act or a situation was judged to fall under a general rule that prescribed a due response. A later Stoic, Ariston, however, denied that rule-following was an essential element in moral realization and the exercise of virtue.[7] He offered a variety of arguments to show that what is morally essential about rules is obvious to the well-disposed, virtuous person. Details concerning rules often turn out to be rather *ad hoc*, akin to old wives' tales, and if misapplied may be counter to the animating spirit of the rule. Mastery of specific rules does not necessarily add up to a comprehensive realization of virtue, and most importantly, making rules detailed enough to fit the complexity of human affairs requires an absurd amount of qualification and detail. So much detail that one could never resolve what to do in a complex situation. On the other hand, a well-disposed person often does see through complexities to the ethical crux of a situation and knows what to do. He or she doesn't need to perform elaborate casuistry and mental acrobatics to reach that point. However, if pressed to offer a justification or some rationalization, he or she should be able to offer an account of the intuitive response that captures the key concerns, and shows why they override competing concerns.

On his part, Chu Hsi conceived the world as a patterned (*li*) totality made up of a dynamic vapor (*ch'i*), that under various conditions condenses and solidifies into countless permutations, from the purest transparent *yuan-ch'i* (primordial *ch'i*), to the Yin-Yang poles modulated by the primal *t'ai-chi* (supreme polarity) pattern, to the *wu-hsing* (five phases), each of which bears an identifying inner pattern (*hsing*) that involves interconvertability and recombination with the other four, and finally to the phenomenal world: Heaven, Earth, and the myriad things (*t'ien-ti wan-wu*).[8]

The term *li* (pattern) is roughly a functional parallel of the Western term "principle", as applied in natural as well as normative contexts. But, as A.C. Graham has usefully pointed out, the term "*li*" is better rendered "pattern", because "*li*" refers ultimately to the immanental, constitutive formations of things, relations, processes, and events.[9] In Chu's system, "*li*" does not refer to abstract principles, or to propositions that would fit into abstract theories and logical inferences. *Li* turns out to form an ecological array involving the inner patternings of both individual things and their nests and networks of relative intercourse. Accordingly, as Ames and Hall have shown with regard to Confucius' thought, Chu's system manifests a system of *aesthetic order* rather than *logical order*.[10]

The world presents a vital tapestry of relationships, processes, events, and things spontaneously arrayed in aesthetic order. For Chu, *li* are manifested three-dimensionally and present different faces from different angles.[11] Thus, *li* are manifested as inherently perspectival. Chu adopts metaphors of the grains in wood, the lines in jade, the "veins" in a leaf, and even the texture of beef, to stress that *li* are manifested immanently rather than abstractly and thus are to be sought concretely by observing phenomena in the world, not by abstract ratiocination.[12] Moreover, the *li* are never presented in their putative optimal pure forms. They always appear conditioned by the purity of the *ch'i* through which they are manifested and of the environing conditions.

*Li* also structure the human mind, thought and language, such that human beings are predisposed to grasp and attempt to respond appropriately to, the things and situations they encounter. Objective learning on this view can be understood as a facet of self-learning: indeed, by the principle of continuity, objective understanding enhances self-understanding, for by comprehending the warp and woof of the outer *li* of things, one gains insight into the inner *li* constituting one's mind and character.[13] Moreover, it is important to stress that, for Chu, while *li* structure the mind, thought and language, this is not just at the cognitive level: *li* also structure the inner patterning (*hsing*) that predisposes us to have our characteristically human emotions (*ch'ing*) and responses (*kan-ying*) under various sets of conditions.[14] Simply put, in Chu's Confucian view, *li* and *hsing* predispose us to be sensitive and responsive; metaphorically, they provide the hardware of human nature. Self-cultivation and moral reflection, on the other hand, are the means by which we actively condition and fine-tune these predispositions of sensitivity and response; they thus function as the software for cultivating personhood.

For Confucianism, education is primarily ethical and cultural in nature. It aims to inculcate standard upright patterns of individual and interpersonal conduct—in part to overcome the dissonance caused by individual and familial variations by attuning each person to the harmonic resonance of the society. This learning is to take place initially in the family, in the clan, and then to be extended outward into society, as outlined in the *Hsiao-hsüeh* (Elementary learning) and the *Ta-hsüeh* (Great learning; advanced learning).[15] At the initial stage, the learner masters the basics of individual and interpersonal conduct in the family, which ideally reflect actual feelings and express sincere intentions. Chu speaks of the importance of performing ethical action in the right spirit: being filial out of actual filial love, being fraternal out of genuine fraternal love. In this respect, Chu understands learning the norms to be a two-fold process of developing one's feelings for and appreciation of others, that is, one's altruistic impulses, while overcoming one's tendencies toward selfcenteredness.[16] What was of fundamental ethical consequence in all this for Chu was the idea that, as one learns to identify self and other in terms of specified interpersonal relationships, one begins to feel a balanced reciprocity and sense of oneness with others.[17]

Chu's ideas of patterns and norms are more immanental and practical than the Stoic ideas of principles and rules. Moreover, taken together, they are understood to constitute the order and ambiance, the warp and woof of a way of life, whereas the Stoic rules are more like limiting conditions that proscribe certain spectra of unwanted behavior. Understandably, therefore, the traditional Chinese books of rites and rituals that defined life in Confucian society—some of which Chu revised, edited, and commented upon—were more comprehensive and detailed than anything Ariston might have fearfully imagined about rules.

These then are the contours of Chu's well-considered approach to moral self-cultivation and social ethics. Now, standard ethical norms work well in standard situations, in normal families, in good communities, and in ordinary social circumstances. But, Chu also understood that people are awfully complex and that human affairs often become complicated, get out of hand, and go awry. In a word, life is just not that ideal, not that simple; we are sometimes apt to encounter ethically anomalous situations to which the standard sets of feelings and responses prescribed by the received norms just do not fit. Indeed, there are many situations when standing on the norm and being moralistic would make matters worse (an insight animating utilitarianism and pragmatism vis-a-vis deontologism). Chu himself said that one must have ample experience and self-cultivation so that "if by chance an anomalous affair comes up, one can grasp it. One wants to be in a position to grasp such affairs thoroughly in order to understand their unfamiliar aspects."[18]

At the same time, Chu considered how to tailor responses appropriate in problematic situations under the rubric of *ch'üan* (expedient means, discretion).[19] He noted several types of situations in which recourse to discretion and expedient means might be advisable: (1) extraordinary situations that cannot be covered by standard norms (in principle), (2) urgent situations that require a direct violation of the received norm to be resolved, and (3) situations in which it is prudent not to observe the relevant norms.[20] Situations of the first kind include those that call for a disruption of a given human order, for example the removal of an evil authority figure, such as a cruel despot. For situations of the second type, Chu had in mind emergencies in which one must violate a received norm in order to perform an emergency action, such as grasping the hand of a drowning sister-in-law, or shoving an old lady out of the path of a runaway oxcart. Finally, the third type of situation includes those in which it would be more compassionate to overlook the ritual requirements, such as in cases of condoning the remarriage of a widow.

We might observe that cases of the first type can be condoned only as a means of last resort, taken under extensive advisement. Some such cases, such as the plots to assassinate Adolf Hitler, are unquestionably morally justified and commendable. (On the other hand, the failure of Western intelligence forces to assassinate Pol Pot decades ago reflects a deep moral depravity, especially as it was their installation of a military government in Cambodia that led to Pol Pot's rise to power.) Other cases, however, have proven to be deeply problematic, as illustrated in Shakespeare's *Julius Caesar*.[21] The principals must be circumspect, have impeccable motives, and consider the long-range consequences of their plan. The authority figure must be someone recognized to be evil by all people who know what he is about, his true colors, conditions not necessarily met in Caesar's case. Chu brought up cases of the second type mainly to remind his straight-laced students that in daily life they should act as much on instinct and common sense as on the norms. For example, norms governing personal relationships, such as those between brother and sister-in-law, are intended to uphold mutual propriety and respect and thus to facilitate social harmony. Hence, it is not necessary to observe such norms in an emergency, or even at times when the touch of a comforting hand would be appreciated.

Cases of the third sort are interesting because they involve sidestepping a norm for the sake of the happiness and/or welfare of a person or persons. Some norms, some traditions, are valued and upheld precisely for the sacrifices they entail, for example in the name of interpersonal fidelity—a widow's continuing loyalty for her departed husband. (Oddly, no such norm governed widowers in old China.) Cases of this sort involve weighing one's sense of compassion over against traditional requirements. In cases such as these, while we recognize the purpose of the ritual requirement, our discretion tells us that a nontraditional resolution, even one in clear violation of the norm, would be more compassionate and in a deeper sense ethical than would observance of the norm.

Clearly, these considerations lead us into unmapped ethical terrain. How far can one justifiably take such sidestepping of the applicable norms? What qualifications and restrictions apply? For his part, Chu Hsi mentioned at least two qualifications: a weak qualification that the expedient adopted not be otherwise ethically objectionable,[22] and a stronger qualification stipulating that the expedient adopted comply with the Way—that it satisfy some basic moral value, at least as basic as the values expressed in the relevant standard norm.[23] Thus, any exercise of discretion undertaken in light of one's sense of appropriateness (*yi*), if exercised with sufficient probity and care, should satisfy the moral values embodied in the Way more adequately than would a routine application of the standard norm.

Nonetheless, ever cognizant of moral weakness, Chu insisted on the established probity and integrity of anyone who would venture to use discretion and exercise expedient means.[24] He stated, for example:

> Intending to weigh a situation carefully [in order to exercise expedient means], one must have cultivated the inner root daily, so that one's mind is sensitive, perspicacious, pure, and integrated; [in that case,] one still must naturally weigh such situations carefully. As Ch'eng Yi (1033-1107) has said, "Be reverent in order to straighten oneself within; practice appropriateness in order to square situations without. One's sense of appropriateness comprises the moral fiber which one expresses through ritual action." (*Yü-lei* 37:6a, par. 36)

Only those who have extensively "investigated things to extend knowledge" and who are conversant with the subtle patternings of the human heart and human affairs would be qualified to consider exercising expedient means over simply following the norms. (Chu told his occasionally priggish students that well-disposed people, even if morally untutored, can be more discerning and have more discretion than some academicians.)

The Stoic Seneca argued in parallel fashion that it is more important to understand the reasons we follow the rules than simply to make them more complicated to better fit human affairs. Knowing why we follow the relevant rules under certain circumstances provides the master key for understanding the rationale of the rules and thus for being able to make due responses to situations to which no rules properly apply or even to those for which conflicting rules apply. Interestingly, some Stoics also noted that constellations of specific rules correspond to specific family and social roles, as did Confucians.[25]

At this point, we should note some tensions due to cross-purposes in Chu's position. As noted, Chu stressed making careful observations of situations in order to tailor the most fitting responses in context. At the same time, however, he held the philosophical conception of a cultivation process whereby one comprehends ever more fundamental, ever more far-reaching patterns (*li*) that shape nature and moral value. That is, Chu sometimes construed the project of "investigating things to extend knowledge" as an ascendant movement in moral self-cultivation, whereby the learner finally arrives at the pinnacle—*t'ai-chi* (supreme polarity—that embraces and subsumes all derived "patterns". To Chu, grasping the *t'ai-chi* was tantamount to grasping the master key: it represented for him the apex of being and value and thus bestowed self-realization and sagehood on those who could comprehend and embrace it.[26] While this conception charts an ideal path to the pure, compassionate mind-set characteristic of sagehood, it obscures Chu's usual emphasis on fine-tuning and sharpening moral discernment and responsiveness in the middle of things—in full view of the complex makeup of situations and with an understanding of people as they really are. This conception also neglects Chu's equal emphasis on the claim that "patterns" and corresponding inborn dispositions (*hsing*) are manifested only in concrete, specific *ch'i*-formations; and, thus, that (1) "patterns" are to be discerned in their fine particularity, that (2) the moral impulses one feels are to be nurtured in the stream of human life, and that (3) the emotions, when not obscured by desires or other obsessions, are immediate expressions of our fundamental inborn dispositions.

How, too, to square this broad vision of probing inquiry with the constrictive Confucian moral psychology constructed round the virtues of human-heartedness, appropriateness, ritual propriety, and wisdom, and their attendant emotions? I would argue that these virtues functioned ultimately as thematic foci for self-cultivation as one establishes moral bearings and a balanced interpersonal stance. One needs to go through an initial stage of mastering these basic virtues in order, to (1) reinforce one's altruistic impulses and curtail the egoistic ones, (2) be inclined to seek principled rapport and harmony in interpersonal affairs, and (3) be moved by a sense of oneness with others and with all things. I would argue that, subsequently the more human phenomena that one observes and considers in advanced level learning and cultivation, the more one feels a broad sympathy for others that transcends the narrowly graded-love, the so-called love with distinctions that is denoted by the term "*jen*" (human-heartedness) in Confucianism.[27] The more one observes of the nuances of human affairs and the springs of human action, the more that one will exercise a personally cultivated sense of appropriateness. The more one fine-tunes one's style of interpersonal conduct, the more one will express deference and respect in ways that do not necessarily coincide with the ritual norms. In this way, one will build up a repertoire of conduct that reflects one's personal discernment and discretion, that expresses one's personal attainment and style.

It is noteworthy in this connection that Chu, on occasion, modeled his ethical conception of observing situations and fashioning the most appropriate response on the butcher character, Cook Ting, portrayed in the *Chuang Tzu* as a skilled artisan: just as the sure blade of Cook Ting's cleaver goes straight to the cartilage between the bones, the cultivated sense of appropriateness (*yi*) of Chu's moral adept strikes straight at the heart of interpersonal situations.[28]

A.C. Graham once contrasted Chu's perception/response model (*kan-ying*) of ethical action to that of Chuang Tzu by suggesting that Chu's notion of appropriate response is informed by rigorous adherence to rules and principles, whereas Chuang Tzu's is relatively intuitive and spontaneous.[29] Yet, this apparent contrast can be resolved by separating the stages of cultivation and mastery: Chuang Tzu's skilled artisans, such as Butcher Ting, all had to undergo prolonged periods of rigorously controlled apprenticeship before they could forget the "knowing that" in an integrated, spontaneous process of "knowing how." And, for his part, Chu Hsi knew that the years of learning and practice—one's ethical apprenticeship—culminate in a responsive moral agent who can operate as intuitively and spontaneously in his sphere as Chuang Tzu's skilled artisans do in theirs. Chu's moral adept is, in effect, an artisan of interpersonal intercourse. Chu could rightfully claim Confucius as a prime model for this view. After years, decades of self-cultivation, Confucius could say: "At sixty, my ear was attuned. At seventy, I could give my heart free rein and without overstepping the mark." (*Analects* 2/4)

Let us now review some basic features of Chu Hsi's "appropriateness" approach to ethics and then attempt some applications to contemporary ethical problems: First, one is to become well-versed in the received norms and rituals that circumscribe interpersonal relationships and prescribe upright behavior in general society. Second, one is to have made ample observations and responses in life situations. Third, one is to have observed and reflected upon ways in which others act and respond in situations, for reference. Fourth, through extensive observation and experience, one is to be cognizant of the range of considerations that come into play in life situations: moral principle, utility, fairness, sympathy, compassion, and so forth.[30] Fifth, one is to remain flexible and open-minded, as well as to avoid making surmises, being insistent, stubborn, or self-centered. (See Confucius, *Analects* 9/4).

According to this view, while observing the ethical norms and rules of thumb in his or her community, the moral adept possesses a store of personal ethical sensitivity, responsiveness, and resourcefulness, by which to fashion the most fitting responses to situations.

Now let us attempt to apply Chu's broad ethical approach to several moral issues in contemporary Western ethics, proceeding from general to more specific problems. Indeed, our treatment of the two general cases might seem to be rather routine, but it seems useful to start by rehearsing relatively routine issues before proceeding.

First, then, let us consider the problem of the moral acceptability of abortion. Granted that, as a Confucian, Chu emphasized the preciousness of the "life-impulse" (*sheng-chi; sheng-yi*) and would tend to dislike the prospect of aborting a human fetus, let us see how his methodology might cut across some of the standard arguments for and against abortion.[31] Arguments against abortion tend to stem from attestations to the "personhood" of the fetus and the "sanctity" of human life, and attempt on that basis to construe abortion as a form of murder. Arguments in favor of abortion must first attempt to deny the personhood of the fetus, particularly during the first and sometimes into the second trimester of gestation, and stress the "right" of the pregnant woman to decide whether or not to terminate the pregnancy.

Applying Chu's method, there is no way to observe or otherwise discern the metaphysical principle of soul that underlies the personhood argument. No trace of soul in the Christian sense is open to observation, or shown as an ontological requirement in traditional Chinese logic.[32] Moreover, personhood itself is a cultural achievement, not a metaphysical given in Confucian thought. People achieve personhood through cultural learning and practice.[33] Second, viewing human life as essentially continuous with nature, Chu will not *a priori* be able to assign a sanctity to the fetus *qua* human that would not apply to the fetuses of other life forms. The most he might argue is that human fetuses are distinguished by their pedigree. Yet, the logic of his system would require him to assert this as a difference of degree rather than kind; whatever a fetus' pedigree, one has to achieve personhood through cultural learning and practice.

Consequently, this simple application of Chu's premises and methodology to the problem of abortion would seem to warrant a pro-choice position, with the usual provisions and qualifications. At the same time, Chu would want to encourage people to regard conception, gestation, and birth as serious matters and to conduct their intimate lives with caution and a sense of responsibility. Moreover, as a philosopher deeply interested in the spark of incipient life, Chu would be inclined to encourage people to avoid aborting a fetus in the absence of independently compelling reasons to do so.[34]

The second ethical issue is a somewhat broader one: how to establish the legitimacy of environmental ethics. Chu's philosophy already presents the world as a textured, multi-layered, ecological system in terms of putative immanental patternings (*li*) of structures and relationships. He has a keen sense of polarity, interdependence, environing conditions, environment, and so forth. Value itself is seen to derive from the creative "patterns" (*li*) intrinsic to formative reality that underwrite change, process, order, development, harmony, and bounty in the world. Value thus is construed as resident in the world and not solely a matter of human assignations. (There is an assumption at work here that human values are genuine and effective to the extent that they reflect, express, and foster in the human realm features of the natural order that give rise to order, development, harmony, and bounty.) Chu did not articulate his view of the natural order in what to us would be a definitive way, mostly because his categories are aesthetic and traditional rather than logical and analytic. Moreover, to past Confucian thinkers, the natural realm appeared to be relatively unproblematic and able to take care of itself. They were content to sketch out its features as a backdrop for viewing more pressing issues in the human realm.[35]

We recall that Chu grounded his ethics of appropriate response on the methodology of "investigating things to extend knowledge." Working from his initial sense of the integrity and value discernible in the natural order and given our current knowledge of ecological systems as well as the environmental impact of human activities, Chu would definitely have to envision and accept the expansion of ethics. Ethical values, discourse and judgment must recognize the obligation to protect endangered species, notably by preserving their natural habitats. Concerning the opposition between our obligations to ecological systems comprising the natural environment and the right to exploit natural resources for monetary gain, Chu would inevitably recognize the value of ecological systems, especially those most at risk, and would argue that commercial interests must adapt themselves to the ecological setting. That is, their environmental impact must be minimal. In addition, they must not be granted a free hand to develop, and indeed should in fact utilize a portion of their profits to enhance the area in which they operate.[36] Humankind is to operate in harmony with nature, rather than treat nature merely as a repository of raw materials (provided by a putative divinity for humankind) up for grabs for commercial exploitation. Chu recognized that we ourselves are products of nature, that we reflect and ultimately depend on nature. Thus, we ought to strive to conduct our lives in unison with nature—in terms of her constituent patterns of order, her constituent ecological systems—such that nature and humanity will flourish together in perpetuity.

Interestingly, the ethical issues of abortion and ecology will inevitably come together at certain points in human development. Because human survival is dependent, ultimately, on natural resources provided by the natural environment, when human populations and consumption (and disposal) levels increase toward levels beyond what the natural environment can sustain, radical conservation and population control measures will have to be adopted. Natural resources must be replenished and human populations forced to recede. Such measures, including family planning, birth control and, inevitably, abortion, will have to be employed, not just to ensure the quality of human life and the survival of endangered species and their habitats, but to ensure the very survival of humankind. It is ironical that opponents of family planning, birth control, and abortion decry these measures as "unnatural" interventions in the divine process of procreation, when in fact they are destined to be measures essential for the resurrection and salvation of nature itself. Ironically, too, it is "artificial" advances in nutrition and food production, medicine and child care, that have engendered the on-going population explosion.

Finally, let us consider a specific ethical problem that challenges our ethical assumptions more sharply. This case, presented by Anton Chekhov in his classic tale, "The Lady with the Dog," involves marital infidelity.[37] For various reasons, this case lies outside the domain of interpersonal relations considered by Chu Hsi in his serious ethical discourses. Simply, differences in social milieu and the constitution of marriage between traditional China and bourgeoisie Europe at the turn of the century preclude us from speculating on Chu's possible attitude toward cases of this sort. Bear in mind, therefore, that we are entertaining this ethical problem as a thought-experiment, as a test application of Chu's methodology of "investigating things to extend knowledge" for our own purposes.

The story's plot unfolds out of the chance encounter between a middle-aged man, Gomov, and a young woman, Anna, both of whom are married and occupy enviable positions in Russian bourgeoisie society. The young, unattended lady he observes at the seaside resort of Yalta intrigues Gomov. Eventually, he chances to have a word with her while they are seated at adjacent tables in a restaurant. Although shy and uncertain at first, they manage to hit it off and gradually grow close. It transpires that she is married to a dull, inattentive husband, a lackey careerist who thinks only of his bosses and official duties, while he is married to an impersonal society lady who fancies herself clever but who lacks sensitivity and honest human feelings. Gradually, Anna and Gomov find in each other everything they had wanted to find in marriage but hadn't. Finally, after a prolonged period of soul-searching and emotional encounters,[38]

> Anna... and he loved each other, as people who are very close, intimate, as husband and wife, as dear friends, love one another. It seemed to them that fate had intended them for one another.

This story has a unique quality: that is, for a century attentive readers, including eminent literary critics, by and large have accepted Anna and Gomov's love as legitimate and haven't tended to pass moral judgment on this aspect of the story. A remarkable fact, given the emphasis placed on marital fidelity in society and the negative assessments that circulate concerning common garden variety cases of infidelity, cases that may or may not share the distinguishing features of Anna and Gomov's affair.[39]

Our interest in the story stems from the fact that there appear to be few if any ethical grounds forthcoming from the standard ethical theories—deontologism, utilitarianism, virtue ethics—on the basis of which to accept the affair. (So far, I can envision only an act-utilitarian approach, but even that would require some finessing.[40]) In spite of this, virtually every reader comes away from the story sympathizing with Anna and Gomov and accepting their affair, most considering it "well and good," even if not unambiguously "right".

Perhaps we can find a solution to this puzzle in Chu's notion of exercising one's cultivated sense of appropriateness, as informed by considerations of salient facts about the principals, about their respective family situations, about their sincerity and sense of responsibility, and so forth. As noted, such observations and considerations can include empathetic self-reflection, such as by imagining oneself in the shoes of the two principals as well as those of their respective spouses.[41] At any rate, most readers appear to take the view that to understand is to sympathize and accept regarding Anna and Gomov.

Let us review some main features of Anna and Gomov's affair, as presented by Chekhov. First off, the respective spouses are two self-centered, unfeeling, somewhat caddish individuals who regard marriage as a social convention in which the preciousness of the mate lies more in the face and social advantages he or she affords than in love and understanding. Second, the two principals have settled into the affair inadvertently, as it were, more out of a gradually growing sense of need and love than out of any active intention to be unfaithful. Indeed, it is their spouses' lack of feeling that makes it psychologically possible for them to become involved with each other. Third, the affair does wrack Anna's conscience, for she had sincerely hoped and imagined that love and happiness would be found in marriage; for his part, Gomov, "only now when he was gray-haired, had... fallen in love, properly, thoroughly in love for the first time in his life."[42] Anna has transformed him into a new, feeling man. Fourth, all the basic feelings of kindness, tenderness, and love that make life meaningful, gradually appear for Anna and Gomov, yet they still endeavor to avoid harming their respective families as they seek a way to establish a viable life together.

In sum, in his realistic narrative, Chekhov underscores the emptiness of the respective marriages and the self-centeredness and lack of feelings displayed by the respective spouses, on the one hand; and, the richness of the affair and the sincere love that Anna and Gomov experience together, on the other. It is this arrangement of the facts that inclines readers to accept the protagonists in their love and quest to start life anew.

Chekhov adds luster to the affair by stressing the sense of self-realization that Anna and Gomov experience as a direct result—this love of their's had changed them both."[43] This qualified success enjoyed by Anna and Gomov in this story contrasts sharply with the failures experienced by most Chekhov characters who seek self-realization in other ways.[44] For example, in "About Love," a male character, Alekhin, tells the story of his having loved a married woman, Anna Alekseevna, while being unable to express his feelings for her or liberate her from the spiritual squalor of her marriage due to his lack of tenacity and courage.[45] Failing to effect their mutual self-realization, he appears weak and mediocre: a moral failure. His ineptitude condemns them both to lead empty, unfulfilled lives—he as an isolated bachelor maintaining an unprofitable country estate and she as a neglected wife on the eastern frontier, far from human society. In "Gooseberries," a character seeks redemption by becoming the owner of a modest country estate. Unfortunately, he knows nothing about actual country life and ends up just loafing about, relishing his pond and the gooseberries grown on his bit of land. Meanwhile, the estate turns decrepit, as he fails to press his workers to repair the buildings and maintain the equipment, to look after the livestock or to tend the crops. Having been a petty government functionary, he knows only to consume and enjoy. So, finally, he looks remarkably like one of his hogs to his visiting brother, who laments the tendency of men to hanker after an illusory idyllic life in the country rather than seeking ways to parlay their talents and resources to alleviate the pervasive suffering in the world.

Turning back to "The Lady," one important feature that distinguishes Anna and Gomov's affair from garden-variety cases is that Chekhov has given us the salient details, the relevant facts. Thus, Chu Hsi's method of observation and reflection can be brought into play. Affairs are usually clandestine and kept secret. Thus, casual observers register only that two people appear to be unfaithful to their respective spouses, but they lack access to the salient facts necessary for sympathetic understanding. Casual observers only note the generally blameworthy feature of infidelity, but can't discern whether or not there are mitigating circumstances, as most readers are willing to see in the case of Anna and Gomov. Gossip further beclouds people's discernment, but that often doesn't prevent them from passing judgment. From the epistemic viewpoint that Chu sought to stress, Chekhov's narrative functions to expand the readers' sympathy and moral consciousness by revealing the conditions and emotional dynamics of the case.

A final disclaimer: admittedly, we cannot presume to know how Chu Hsi himself would view Anna and Gomov's affair because he lived in a different social milieu. Marriage in traditional China, especially in the elite classes, was basically a social institution, an agreement between two families. Indeed, the tensions in Chekhov's story reflect tensions implicit in the shift from traditional marriage, as a social, interfamily agreement, to modern bourgeoisie marriage putatively based on love. Ironically, the institution of love-based marriage was intended to provide the conditions for a sort of perfect mutual self-realization between lovers, through which they might fulfill themselves by building a complete life and family together. If this is the agreed upon function of marriage in modern society, then it is natural that people like Gomov and Anna whose spouses did not understand or seek to fulfill this essential aspect of marriage should find themselves searching for more meaningful relationships.

In closing, we note that Chu's method of "investigating things to extend knowledge" (so as to sharpen one's sense of how to fashion the most appropriate responses to situations) brings to light and clarifies a standard human ethical procedure. That is, when we confront a new complex situation, rather than immediately view it through the blinkers of certain pre-assumed principles or under a certain ethical theory *per se*, we typically first attempt to determine the particular facts and features of the case, and then bring a variety of considerations—ethical and non-ethical, rational and conative, analytical and intuitive—to bear. As we become more fully aware that this is our most versatile mode of apprehending and responding to complex situations, we can become more systematic and circumspect in fashioning judgments and responses in this way. In his own tradition, Chu made a very significant contribution to the understanding of ethical judgment and response by revealing the practical limitations of responsive intuitionism and by discussing in detail a self-conscious critical approach to life situations. Indeed, a number of his related insights can help us to sharpen our ethical insight today as well.

## Notes

1. For information on Chu Hsi and his thought, see Wing-tsit Chan, *Chu Hsi: Life and Thought* (Hong Kong: Hong Kong University Press, 1987); Chan, *Chu Hsi: New Studies* (Honolulu: University of Hawaii Press, 1989); and, Chan, ed., *Chu Hsi and Neo-Confucianism* (Honolulu: University of Hawaii Press, 1986).

2. This expression comes from the *Ta-hsüeh* (*The Great Learning*), one of the essential early Confucian documents selected and compiled by Chu Hsi to form the *Ssu-shu* (Four Books), which has since been recognized as the canonical compendium of classical Confucian thought. See Daniel Gardner, *Chu Hsi and the Ta-hsüeh*: *Reflections on the Confucian Canon* (Cambridge, Mass.: Council of Asian Studies Harvard University, 1986), esp. 53-59. Chu Hsi's extensive discussions on the meaning and implications of "investigate things to extend knowledge" are recorded in *Chu tzu yü-lei* (Classified dialogues of Master Chu), ch. 15. [*Chu tzu yü-lei* hereafter cited as YL.]

3. For discussion, see the author's "*Li* and Yi as Immanent: Chu Hsi's Thought in Practical Perspective," *Philosophy East and West* 38/1 (January 1986): 30-46.

4. See Ch'ien Mu, *Chu tzu hsüeh t'i-kang* (Overview of Chu Hsi's Learning) (Taipei: Tung-ta, 1986), ch. 20, 123-27.

5. Chu said, for example, "The norm just preserves the general, upright *li*. But, in subtle, complicated situations, the norm is not directly applicable. Thus, one needs to exercise expedient means (discretion) to do what is most fitting and fulfill the intended function of the norm. (YL 37:10a, par. 49.)

6. For discussion, see Ch'ien Mu, ch. 17, 105-109, and ch. 22, 138-146.

7. Julia Annas, *The Morality of Happiness* (Oxford, U.K.: Oxford University Press, 1995), 99.

8. Chou Tun-I (1017-1073) articulated this conception in *Diagram of the Supreme Polarity Explained* (*T'ai-chi t'u shuo*). For discussion, see Joseph Needham, *Science and Civilisation in China v. 2*: *History of Scientific Thought* (Cambridge, U.K.: Cambridge University Press, 1956), 455-472, and A.C. Graham, "What Was New in the Ch'eng-Chu Theory of Human Nature, in Chan ed., *Chu Hsi and Neo-Confucianism*, 147-149.

9. Graham, 155, n. 5.

10. See Roger Ames and David Hall, *Thinking Through Confucius* (Albany: State University of New York Press, 1987), 16 and 131-38.

11. Graham, 148, Ch'ien Mu, 133.

12. Needham, 473, Thompson, 32-33.

13. See Ch'ien Mu, "Chu Hsi on mind and *li*," *Chu tzu hsin-hsüeh-an,* vol. 2 (New critical anthology of Chu His's works) (Taipei: San-min, 1976), 31-38.

14. See Graham, pp. 152-54, Ch'ien Mu, *ibid.*, "Chu Hsi on the emotions," pp. 25-30, and "Chu Hsi on mind, *hsing*, and the emotions," 31-38.

15. Chu Hsi edited both texts. See Gardner regarding the *Ta-hsüeh.*

16. Confucius' *Analects* reads 12/1 reads: "Mastering the self and practicing ritual action comprise being human-hearted." Chu Hsi adopted "mastering the self" as an element of self-cultivation and self-realization. See Ch'ien, *Overview*, ch. 19, 113-23.

17. Graham, 142-43 and 150-51.

18. YL, ch. 19.

19. Confucius mentions *ch'üan* in *Analects* 9/30, 18/8, and 20/1. Chu discusses *ch'üan* in YL, ch. 37, and in his commentary on the *Analects of Confucius.*

20. See Wei Chung-t'ing, "Chu Hsi on the Standard and the Expedient," in Chan ed., *Chu Hsi and Neo-Confucianism*, 255-72.

21. Oliver Stone's film *JFK* explores the problem of deluded, violent but self-righteous patriots.

22. Wei, 260. Effecting the removal of a despot would require undertaking many ethically undesirable actions.

23. Wei, 259. Permitting the remarriage of a widow for example would express deeper humanitarian principles than would observing the ritual ban on remarriage.

24. See Jiang, Xinyan, "What Kind of Knowledge Does a Weak-Willed Person Have?—A comparative study of Aristotle and the Ch'eng-Chu school," *Philosophy East and West* 50/2 (April 1998).

25. Annas, 107.

26. See Chu's supplement to the *Ta-hsüeh*, ch. 5, in Gardner, 104-5.

27. See *Mencius* 1A/7, 3A/5, and 7A/45.

28. See Thompson, 39-40.

29. Graham, 143-45.

30. For a meaningful discussion about the role that such 'considerations' play in determining ethical responses to situations, see Edmund Pincoffs, *Quandaries and Virtues: Against Reduction in Ethics* (Lawrence: University Press of Kansas, 1986), 53-70.

31. Ch'ien Mu, *Overview*, ch. 9, 55-60.

32. At birth, refined *ch'i* gathers to constitute souls to animate the body and the mind. At death, this *ch'i* disperses and returns to the natural environment.

33. See Ames and Hall, *Thinking Through Confucius*, 73, 89-110, and 118-24.

34. Consider Chu's reflections on the *Fu* hexagram in the *I Ching* and on a related poem by Shao Yung (1011-1077). See Ch'ien Mu, *Overview*, 56-8.

35. He noted that men of wisdom and high ethical attainment spontaneously extended their sympathy and compassion to nature. For instance, he gave the examples of Chou Tun-I refusing to cut the grass outside his window and Chang Tsai (1020-1077) feeling sympathy for a donkey whose sharp brays he heard. (Chu Hsi ed., W.T. Chan trans., *Reflections on Things at Hand* (New York: Columbia University Press, 1967, 302-3.

36. The notion of *yi* (appropriateness) is ethically more fundamental than the notion of *li* (utility). Moreover, the goal of balanced, equable utility is part and parcel of *yi* considerations. See Fung Yu-lan, D. Bodde, trans., *A History of Chinese Philosophy*, vol. 1 (Princeton, N.J.: Princeton University Press, 1952), 127-31.

37. Citations are from Ralph E. Matlaw ed., *Anton Chekhov's Short Stories* (New York: Norton, 1979), 221-35. This edition of Chekhov's stories also contains Virginia Llewellyn Smith's insightful critical discussion, selected from her *The Lady with the Dog*, 351-7.

38. Chekhov, 234.

39. We are reminded of the sensationalist articles, "Adultery: A New Debate about the Oldest Sin," that appeared in *Newsweek*, 9/20/96, in the wake of the Dick Morris scandal. The Morris case didn't display any of the mitigating features discernible in Anna and Gomov's affair.

40. A physician and sensitive observer of human life, Chekhov himself held the view that, given the inherently tragic character of human life, individuals have the right to seek self-fulfillment and happiness, provided they do so with sensitivity and discretion.

41. Graham, 150-51.

42. *Chekhov*, "The Lady," 234.

43. *Chekhov*, 235.

44. For example, in the tales, "Gooseberries" (185-94), "About Love" (194-201), "A Doctor's Visit" (202-11), and "The Betrothed" (247-63), also in *Anton Chekhov's Short Stories.*

45. *Chekhov*, 194-201.

*Chapter Three*

# Concrete Ethics in a Comparative Perspective: Zhuangzi Meets William James

**Alan Fox**

## Introduction

This essay has several objectives. One is to articulate the notions of "abstract" and "concrete" as descriptions of relative categories of ethical reflection. Hopefully this will lead to a broader sense of the range of ethical alternatives, that is, from the completely concrete to the utterly abstract. Another is to locate examples of these categories in various traditions, both "Eastern" and "Western." Finally, I will conclude that the more "concrete" alternatives offer deeper and richer nuances, which more thoroughly clarify moral situations and more effectively suggest sufficiently subtle approaches and responses. Even though concrete approaches are often undervalued, they will be shown to represent a thoroughly viable alternative, and occasionally in fact a reaction, to the historical dominance of the abstract in academic philosophy.

I will proceed by first defining concrete versus abstract approaches to philosophical or metaphysical discourse. Then I will specify what is meant by an abstract ethics as opposed to a concrete one. Once these categories have been clearly established, I will identify prominent proponents of primarily concrete philosophies in both the Classical Chinese (Zhuangzi) and the modern American (William James) philosophical traditions, in order to emphasize the broad applicability of the categories. Since the concrete thinkers we will be discussing can both be seen as reacting to the abstract traditions that precede them, this trajectory will give us a chance to explore the dialectical character of the controversies and dichotomies, as well as the controversy over dichotomy, at stake. Along the way, brief mention will be made of other examples from the historical archive, as suggestions for further development.

Although the idea of a "concrete philosophy" cannot be easily reduced to any simple correspondence with other categories or systems, there can be found in it elements of pragmatism, relativism, skepticism, nominalism, functionalism, and existentialism, which do not yet conflict with a basically analytic approach. I will recommend a kind of concrete analytic pragmatism as exemplified, arguably, in Zhuangzi and James. It is important to emphasize that I am not reducing Zhuangzi's and James's positions to any simple common denominator. What I am saying is that despite their differences on other points, they have this interesting feature in common, and that finding other, diverse examples of this feature further demonstrates its validity as a category of ethical reflection.

## Concrete versus Abstract Metaphysics

The terms "abstract" and "concrete" initially refer here to two alternative approaches to, or kinds of, metaphysics. Specifically, "abstract" means what is considered apart from specific instances whereas "concrete" always refers to a specific instance. For example, "red" is an abstraction, since it can be theoretically considered without reference to any particular red thing. "That red apple" is a more concrete reference, referring to a specific instance of apple. But it still depends on the abstractions "red" and "apple" for its meaning. We see then that all words refer to abstractions, since a word like "horse" generalizes all horses without referring to any particular one of them.

What I am calling an abstract metaphysics is one which prioritizes (logically, ontologically, epistemologically, etc.) the abstract over the concrete, and vice versa. That is to say, abstractions are more real and true than particulars. A classic example of an abstract metaphysics would be found in the work of Plato. Not only does Plato often suggest that abstract essences or "forms" (*eidos*) exist independently, apart from the particular instances which reflect them, but he further considers these abstract essences to be more real than their concrete particulars. In other words, not only does Beauty exist independently from beautiful things, but furthermore Beauty is more real than beautiful things, for a number of reasons.[1]

We can thus imagine a billiard ball, whose mass can be hypothetically represented as a single point, the point at its center of gravity. If we understand the principles and have acquired the skill, we can treat the ball as if it were nothing but this point at its center of gravity, ignoring its color and texture and so on, and accurately predict how the momentum of another point coming in with a certain trajectory will affect the first point. Thus we can predict the movements of the balls with reference only to the points. But we must also keep in mind that geometric points have no dimensions, no extension in space, they exist only as abstractions. We don't seem to be able to actually take away the color and texture and hardness and find pure "ball." This abstraction is a useful one, and has its heuristic value, but the abstract metaphysical view is one that further claims that the abstract point is more real than the actual ball, even though the actual ball falling into the actual pocket is what actually constitutes scoring an actual point.

The concrete metaphysical stance, on the other hand, prioritizes the concrete over the abstract. This will be articulated in more detail below, but it is initially worth pointing out that the concrete stance is comparable, though not reducible, to a number of common Western models of inquiry. For instance, it is somewhat pragmatic, but cannot be identified with pragmatism since there are also abstract forms of pragmatism. This will be illustrated below through a comparison of two of the most influential and formative of the so-called pragmatists, William James and C.S. Peirce. We will later distinguish James's and Peirce's definitions of pragmatism and pragmatic philosophy, and in so doing we will clarify the essential differences between an abstract and a concrete pragmatism.

It is important also to emphasize that pragmatism need not be seen as being at odds with analytic philosophy. That is, some forms of concrete pragmatism can be described as thoroughly analytic, in some senses. The modern scholarly analytic philosophical paradigm, as instigated by Russell and Wittgenstein, involves a careful examination of thought and language with the goal of breaking claims down into basic, elementary, fundamental propositions which then are understood to directly represent actual states of affairs. This project can, however, take off in two different directions, perhaps illustrated best by the difference between Russell and the early Wittgenstein on exactly this point. Whereas Wittgenstein argued that properly analyzed propositions reveal the structure of reality, Russell more reservedly concluded only that experiential events could really be said to exist. Furthermore, Russell claimed that the results of philosophical analysis would be a series of elementary propositions which themselves would be an accurate representation of immediate, more or less sensory experience.

My point is that the analytical method need not serve the purpose of reducing reality to a series of universal propositions or descriptions, thus prioritizing the abstract above the concrete. In other words, analytic philosophy is not necessarily committed to the abstract paradigm, though historically it has been thoroughly embedded in it. Rather than using analysis to arrive at some abstract truth, which is obscured through the ordinary use of language, a concrete analytic would seek to carefully analyze the use of the words and language with which we describe the properties or nature of our experience of ostensible things, seeking to uncover assumptions and abstractions which cause us to misinterpret our experience.

For example, to the extent that someone has formed some abstract, universal conception of Blacks or Jews or Arabs, to that same extent it is likely that their experience of any such individual will be interpreted in a certain way precisely because of the abstraction. That is, they won't see individuals "as they are." On the other hand, concrete pragmatists will also find careful analysis of language and concepts useful, but only within certain limits and for certain purposes, for instance, in describing and predicting events, not in reducing reality to a simple formula.

The concrete, pragmatic question then shifts from "What is the case?" to "What claims can be justifiably made?" or, better yet, "To what extent is such and such a claim valid?" This is the analytic element in the model, and therefore, there can be concrete as well as abstract forms of analytic philosophy. This project parallels other modes of thinking, including the Buddhist notion of *pratityasamutpada* or "inter-dependent origination," and the findings of modern "Fuzzy Logic" theorists.[2]

The idea of *pratityasamutpada* emphasizes that though things are not completely identical to each other, neither are they completely different. Though things, such as you and I, or apples and oranges, are identifiably distinct, still, when we try to draw a line between you and I, it becomes impossible to do since I am defined by you to such a large extent. So the proper jurisdiction for the disputations of philosophy is limited to arguments over criteria—given a certain criteria, does it or does it not make sense to make a given claim? Similarly, "Fuzzy Logic" argues that it makes as much if not more sense to describe situations in ways which are not logically dichotomous than to describe them dichotomously. What is called "fuzzy" logic is perhaps more accurately described as "multivalent," since it is not dependent on an abstract, bipolar logic of true/false. Things can actually be more or less the case, not simply be or not be the case.

The dichotomous logic of traditional scholastic philosophy is itself an abstraction, since logical operators can be used without reference to any particular claims. Such abstractions are indeed pragmatically justified in cases where the criteria are carefully enough specified. This is the sense in which even a concrete theorist might make use of them. In this case, the analysis consists of carefully establishing criteria and then applying them. Clarifying the sense or senses in which true statements are in fact "true" would be the goal of a concrete, pragmatic analytic philosophy. That is, things are said to be what they are to the extent that they satisfy the criteria for being what they are. So in fact, things can be more or less what they are, and the simplistic abstraction of dichotomy is abandoned. So concrete philosophy is somewhat pragmatic, though not completely, and somewhat analytic, though only in some senses.

A concrete ethics will also be seen to be somewhat relativistic, though it cannot be reduced to relativism and thus be easily dismissed, since it does privilege certain modes of conduct and attitude. To be precise, there is a prioritization of concrete success or pragmatic validity, and there is a clear recognition of real constraints and inevitabilities present in the world. The usual objection to a thoroughgoing relativism is that it places equal value on all views, which implies that any moral claim is equally valid, including contrary claims. But this is not what is being proposed here. For the concrete pragmatist, there are priorities, namely, efficacy and applicability. Not every approach is as good as any other. Given a range of approaches to a situation, some better suit the situation than others. Although it might sometimes be difficult to determine the absolute best approach, sometimes it is also easy to eliminate the worst ones. There is an acknowledgment that the world presents real constraints, and that the best approach is therefore always going to be the one which best accommodates these constraints. The overriding concern is that it works, even though there might be different notions of what it is supposed to work for, what end it is seeking to serve.

Similarly, if there is any kind of skepticism at stake, it can only be a Pyrhonnic one, since it does not, nor can it responsibly, deny the possibility of absolute reality or knowledge. What the concrete pragmatist does is to ask the question, "how can you be sure you actually do know?" Or, "to what extent is it meaningful to say you know?" This places the concrete facts and criteria in a position of greater importance than the abstract theories used to explain or coordinate these facts, and places the burden of proof on those who claim certainty or self-evidence. It thus resists the temptation to retreat into generalities in order to deal with the unique or novel, and emphasizes remaining situated in the present moment, experiencing directly the novelty and variety of phenomena.

Our emphasis on the proper use of language seems somewhat nominalistic. However, there is no denial of real existents, universal or otherwise, since such claims would imply that the criteria are absolutely fixed. Things and events aren't reduced to their names or descriptions. The concern with analyzing terms and propositions, moral or otherwise, is heuristically justified because of the carelessness with which such claims are ordinarily declared. Certainly, one of the important concrete questions will be, "to what extent is it justified to call a thing by a certain name," that is, to what extent does it fulfill the criteria for us calling it what it is.

This model is also somewhat "functionalistic," but not entirely. Certainly, from the concrete, pragmatic point of view, it makes sense to relate what an experience is to what it does. But, consistent with its Pyrhonnian element, the concrete approach avoids reducing what something is to what it does. Rather, it would be better to represent it by saying that the responsible goal of properly analyzing experience is to carefully analyze the criteria for including a certain experience into a certain category, and thus carefully scrutinizing the validity of our various inductive conclusions from experience. That is, the concrete approach does not entail the claim that things are nothing but their functions, but that function is one of the criteria for including a certain thing in a certain category.

Since the objects of the analytic approach are the statements or propositions we posit about the world, it is consistent at this point to emphasize that, when concretely analyzed, statements will turn out to be about what happens, and not about what is the case. As Russell suggests, analytically elementary propositions that describe phenomenological, experiential events, and conclusions about the ontological status of the experience (i.e., that something exists, something is independently real, etc.) are inductively inferred from the empirical facts of an event. Therefore, again, the skepticism inherent in this position is limited to epistemological and linguistic events, and does not, nor can it, represent a claim about reality. Rather, we might say that it reflects the limitations inherent in all claims, and is therefore more a claim about claims than a claim about reality, since claims about reality are seen as requiring further analysis to arrive at their elemental, phenomenological ground.

This position can also be described as basically existentialist, in the sense that the existentialists were more concerned historically with the real problems of lived experience than with the philosophical and theological abstractions of their scholastic counterparts. When Sartre pronounces that "existence precedes essence," he comes very close to the claims of concrete pragmatism. Still, the wide variety of philosophical attitudes among the so-called existentialists makes it very difficult to pin down a particular position that corresponds to the description.

It should be clear at this point that the concrete pragmatic analytic, as described here, cannot be reduced to either pragmatism, relativism, skepticism, functionalism, or existentialism, though it bears traces of all of them, while remaining basically analytic at heart.

We find examples of abstract metaphysics all over the philosophical map, from India to China to Greece. In most such cases, it seems that the abstract universals are distinguished from and prioritized over the concrete particulars. However, certain *Dao*ist texts such as the *Laozi* and the *Zhuangzi*, and also some modern thinkers such as the American pragmatist William James, seem to challenge if not reverse that priority, regarding instead the particular, the immanent, and the concrete as of equal or greater value than the universal, transcendent, or abstract. It seems clear that most of the dominant trends in the history of scholastic philosophy have consistently prioritized abstraction, as is illustrated by the fidelity offered to abstract, dichotomous logic as the analytic method of choice. The movements that react to this by championing the concrete, on the other hand, have consistently defined themselves in terms of their particular dialectical relationship with their rivals.

Certainly it could be argued that Buddhism begins as a concrete response to the abstract metaphysics of the Hindu philosophers. The Hindu notion of *atman* or "true self" is an abstraction of the first order. One of the formulae to express the fundamental reality of *atman/Brahman* in Hindu metaphysics is the phrase *neti neti*, which means "not this, not that." It is not difficult to imagine someone pointing at things and dismissing them, saying "not this, not that," and arriving at the ultimate conclusion that "it" is nothing that can be pointed to. If there is no concrete instance of it to which we can point, than the idea in question is thoroughly abstract. The Buddhist response to this is to consider the lineage of priests as a line of blind men, each holding onto the coat tails of the man in front of him.

Other examples of the concrete/abstract controversy include the existentialists, who were reacting to the overly abstract metaphysics of the scholastics. See for instance the work of Sartre, who tells us that:

> we will be able to find still more general and barren rubrics if we classify the taste for sports as one aspect of the love of chance, which will itself be given as a specific instance of the fundamental fondness for play. It is obvious that this so-called explanatory classification has no more value or interest than the classifications in ancient botany; like the latter it amounts to assuming the priority of the abstract over the concrete - as if the fondness for play existed first in general to be subsequently made specific by the action of these circumstances.[3]

Clearly, the problems caused by prioritizing the abstract over the concrete are familiar problems to existentialists in all traditions.

I suggest that the concrete approaches have been inappropriately undervalued, and that they represent viable alternatives to the abstract metaphysical view. But more importantly, since metaphysical views seem to entail ethical implications, I will also articulate some differences between concrete and abstract ethical stances, and to show that the concrete metaphysical view entails coherent and practical ethical implications.

## James and Peirce: Concrete and Abstract Pragmatism

William James and his ostensible mentor Charles Peirce are best known for their contributions to the development and popularization of pragmatism. Despite their apparent similarity in this regard, their positions came to vary greatly over issues directly relevant to the current discussion.

Specifically, it is important to remember that the idea of a concrete philosophy, though entailing a certain amount of pragmatism, cannot be reduced to pragmatism. Peirce's form of pragmatism, for instance, can be described as an abstract pragmatism. If there are abstract and concrete forms of pragmatism, then "concrete" and "pragmatic" cannot be reduced one to the other.

Charles Peirce is often considered the father of modern American pragmatism. In 1878 he published a seminal paper entitled "How to Make Our Ideas Clear," in which he established the basic principle of pragmatism as a theory of criteria for meaning. In it he wrote:

> Consider what effects, which might conceivably have practical bearings, we conceive the object of our conception to have. Then, our conception of these effects is the whole of our conception of the object.[4]

The goal of Peirce's pragmatic maxim is to carefully analyze our ideas by tracing out the practical consequences of using them. In other words, the only way to find out if an idea is meaningful is by observing its practical or conceivably practical effects in experience. Peirce's principle, therefore, became a method of obtaining clarity in our ideas so we could communicate more effectively with one another about what actually is or would be, in truth, the case. The meaning of any given proposition depends on its practical consequences and Peirce believed that if we applied this pragmatic tool, we could eliminate frivolous and unnecessary linguistic and semantic disputes.

But the important point to note here is that Peirce's pragmatic approach was only meant to offer criteria for meaning that could help clarify our ideas. It was not intended to be a theory about the nature of truth as we see later in the work of James. That is, for Peirce, truth is not determined by what is useful or practical. What is real is actually or potentially objectively real. This is made clear when Peirce says:

> The real is that which is not whatever we happen to think it, but is unaffected by what we think of it. . . . That is real which has such and such characters, whether anybody thinks it to have those characters or not.[5]

Or, as Irving Copi characterizes it, "it will still be the real essences of things that are destined to be known by Peirce's ultimate community of knowers."[6] Peirce's disagreement with James leads him to carefully distance himself from the latter by emphasizing that the truth is not dependent on the perspective that we take. Peirce is interested in carefully analyzing the use of words, but this is done in the interest of better describing the nature and properties of real things, and in the anticipation of arriving at better expressions of a very singular, and essentially abstract, truth. For Peirce, the purpose of philosophical analysis is to clarify the practical validity and universality of our ideas about things, but he remains convinced that there in fact exist, independent of our ideas about them, real things with real natures and properties.

This leads Peirce to a very optimistic appraisal of science and the scientific method, which relies at least to a certain extent on induction, which is a form of abstraction. Peirce says:

> To satisfy our doubts, therefore, it is necessary that a method should be found by which our beliefs may be caused by nothing human, but by some external permanency - by something on which our thinking has no effect. . . . Such is the method of science. Its fundamental hypothesis, restated in more familiar language, is this: there are real things, whose characters are entirely independent of our opinions about them; those realities affect our senses according to regular laws, and, though our sensations are as different as our relations to the objects, yet by taking advantage of the laws of perception, we can ascertain by reasoning

> how things really are; and any man, if he has sufficient experience and reason about it, will be led to the one true conclusion.[7]

In this light, Peirce considered himself a "scholastic realist," with respect to his theory of reality, while James was more of a nominalist. As John Dewey pointed out, Peirce's pragmatism stressed the importance attached "to the greatest possible application of the rule, or the habit of conduct—its extension to universality."[8] Keep in mind that James, and in general, concrete philosophers, are not anti-inductive.[9] Induction has its place in a successful and practical approach to daily life. But simply because inductively derived abstractions have heuristic value, does not necessarily entail that they be granted ontological and epistemological priority.

Even though Peirce never formulated a complete systematic ethical theory, it seems likely from the above that he would have sought to have grounded it in a normative, formulaic approach. Peirce often criticized James for being too relativistic, an epithet commonly directed at pragmatists. However, if James's pragmatism is to be regarded as relativistic at all it is only because, like Zhuangzi's, it is completely concrete and situational, in fact, anti-formulaic. That is, James's pragmatism takes into account that every situation has to be taken on its own terms, while Peirce envisioned reality as a place where man was not the measure of things because the world acts according to general rules and laws. It is in this sense primarily that Peirce's pragmatism is abstract.

William James took his place in history as one of the most popular, yet misunderstood, philosophers of the twentieth century with the publication of his book, *Pragmatism,* in 1907. In this book, James formulated his own version of pragmatism, in which he was led to view the approach as not only a theory of meaning, of value to the clarification of ideas, but also as a sort of theory of truth, suggesting that "truth" be understood in terms of "validity," specifically, the validity of particular claims. For this reason among others, Peirce renamed his approach "pragmaticism," to further distance himself from James.

James's model was deeply indebted to Peirce's, but they were clearly not the same. James agreed with Peirce that the pragmatic approach to meaning could help us avoid unnecessary verbal and semantic disputes by tracing the practical consequences of our ideas, but he disagreed on the role of science. James argued that science does not offer the only support for truth and meaning, and so besides empirical evidence he also takes into account the hopes and beliefs of human beings. James formulates his theory of meaning as follows:

> The pragmatic method is primarily a method of settling metaphysical disputes that otherwise might be interminable. Is the world one or many? - fated or free? - material or spiritual? - here are notions either of which may or may not hold good of the world; and disputes over such notions are unending. The pragmatic method in such cases is to try to interpret each notion by tracing its respective practical consequences. What difference would it practically make to any one if this notion

> rather than that notion were true? If no practical difference whatever can be traced, then all dispute is idle.[10]

Thus for James a statement is valid and in that sense meaningful if it makes a practical difference in one's life to believe it. This illustrates the humanistic element in James's thought. Furthermore, James's conception of meaning has a variable and situational feature in that the world is not some completely fixed and absolutely ready-made structure into which we are born, but rather it is a place that is always evolving and changing, in fundamental ways. It is a place that we help, existentially, to create. Since our perspective in the world is finite and subject to error, therefore, we must always be re-evaluating our theories and conclusions about reality.

But James goes further. He also suggests that the idea of truth itself should be treated pragmatically. For James, truth is not some property inherent in things, but is instead inextricably tied to our beliefs and ideas about things. According to James, the truth or falsity of a claim depends on whether or not we can verify it in our experience. In this sense, a belief is true insofar as the expectations it fosters can be verified and corroborated. James believed that the question we should be asking ourselves is not "what is real?" but rather "to what extent are the claims we are making about the world valid?" It would be arrogant for us to dogmatically claim that truth is absolute and unchanging, when our experience of the world is situated in a relative time and place. As James says:

> True ideas are those that we can assimilate, validate, corroborate, and verify. False ideas are those that we can not. That is the practical difference it makes to us to have true ideas; that, therefore, is the meaning of truth, for it is all that truth is known as. . . . The truth of an idea is not a stagnant property inherent in it. Truth happens to an idea. It becomes true, is made true by events.[11]

That is, the only claims that can be said to be true are those which have been tested in our experience and found to work. We might extend this in a multivalently logical way to say that these claims are true to the extent that they are tested in experience and found to work. James further says about truth that

> ideas (which themselves are but part of our experience) become true just in so far as they help us to get into satisfactory relation with other parts of our experience.[12]

He also says that "The true, to put it very briefly, is only the expedient in our way of thinking . . . and expedient in the long run and on the whole course."[13] Therefore to call an idea true is to have it run the gauntlet of all our other beliefs over time. This is perhaps one of the biggest misconceptions about William James, since he is not saying that we can just choose any idea we like and call it true. An idea must be ruled expedient over the long run, and must not clash with other vital beliefs whose expectations have been corroborated in our experience and woven into our general pattern of expectation which constitutes our everyday attitude. As one scholar puts it, "In James's view, then, we are left in a world where truth means verification. Truth, as we know it, is not something absolute and fixed, and if we think of it in these terms, we move to the level of an unwarranted abstraction."[14] Or, as another pragmatist, John Dewey, says: "Anything is 'essential' which is indispensable in a given inquiry and anything is 'accidental' which is superfluous."[15]

It is important to emphasize that we are describing James as a concrete pragmatist because he is, as he says, concerned with "the distinctively concrete, the individual, the particular, and effective as opposed to the abstract, general, and inert."[16] He says, in *Pragmatism*, that:

> It is astonishing to see how many philosophical disputes collapse into insignificance the moment you subject them to this simple test of tracing a concrete consequence. There can be no difference anywhere that doesn't make a difference elsewhere—no difference in abstract truth that doesn't express itself in a difference in concrete fact and in conduct consequent upon that fact, imposed on somebody, somehow, somewhere, and somewhen. The whole function of philosophy ought to be to find out what definite difference it will make to you or me, at definite instants of our life, if this world formula or that world formula be the true one. . . .A pragmatist turns his back resolutely and once for all upon a lot of inveterate habits dear to professional philosophers. He turns away from abstraction and insufficiency, from verbal solutions, from bad *a priori* reasons, from fixed principles, closed systems and pretended absolutes and origins. He turns toward concreteness and adequacy, toward facts, towards action and towards power. That means the empiricist temper regnant and the rationalist temper sincerely given up. It means the open air of possibilities of nature, as against dogma, artificiality, and the pretense of finality in truth.[17]

## Concrete versus Abstract Ethics

To begin with, a key distinction between an abstract and a concrete ethics would be the respective presence or absence of an ethical formula. To be sure, formulae themselves are abstractions, since they represent attempts to address all or large categories of events, novel or otherwise, in a more or less universal manner, without necessary reference to any particular instance.

Much as the formula "2+2=4" can be considered without necessary reference to any particular objects (since two and two of anything equal four of anything), an abstract ethics would seek to generate and apply ethical rules to cover more or less all situations of a more or less general kind, governed by a principle which is not seen as completely identical with any particular instance of itself. Even though some formulae have complex sub-mechanisms constructed in order to deal with unusual situations, such contingency plans are themselves somewhat rule-driven, and usually, only minimally customize a basic formula, which is still taken as universally valid. The so-called "Ten Commandments," for instance, don't indicate any exclusions, and though such criteria are later introduced by the rabbinical tradition, even these exclusions are frequently established in formulaic and universal terms.

This kind of abstract, normative ethics is the standard mode of ethical inquiry in contemporary and also in classical philosophy, for the most part, and is frequently the ground against which the concrete theorists, such as the ones discussed in this chapter, distinguish themselves. Being based on immanence and particularity, a concrete ethical stance does not lend itself to expression in formulaic terms. In the *Zhuangzi*, for example, we see a clear resistance to formulaic or forced behavior, which the text refers to as "*jixin*," anachronistically translatable as a "mechanical" or "robotic" mind or attitude. Thus, rather than discovering a new or better formula for behavior, the *Zhuangzi* emphasizes developing sensitivity to the infinitely diverse and variable demands and constraints of unique situations, and responding to each different situation in such a way that respects the subtle nuances of novelty and individual, concrete differences.

Yet another example of the paradigm is Aristotle's response to Plato's metaphysics. Although Aristotle was an abstract thinker in many ways himself, in at least certain ways he was more concrete than Plato. For instance, for Plato, as indicated earlier, the abstract forms such as "Beauty" and "the Good" exist independently of any concrete instance of them. Aristotle argues, on the other hand, that abstract universals, though different from their concrete instances, are never found anywhere but in the concrete instances. Furthermore, Aristotle's ethics is sometimes described as a "virtue ethics," implying that ethical excellence entails the development of certain character virtues. For Aristotle, what the good man does is good because he is good, whereas for Plato, the good man is good because he does what is good. The difference has been described this way:

> Throughout the subsequent history of Western civilization, ethical views that looked to a supernatural source, such as God or pure reason, for standards of evaluation stemmed from the metaphysics of Plato, while naturalistic philosophers who found standards of value in the basic needs, tendencies, and capacities of man were guided by Aristotle. . . . Thus Plato's goal for philosophical ethics was to make human nature conform to an ideal blueprint while Aristotle tailored his ethical principles to the demands of human nature. . . . Aristotle begins his study by searching for the common feature of all things said to be good and, in contrast with Plato, who held that there is a Form of Good in which all good things 'participate,' Aristotle concludes that there are many different senses of 'good' each of which must be defined separately for the limited area in which it applies. Each such 'good' is pursued by a specific practical art of science."[18]

It is useful here to emphasize again that I am not claiming that Aristotle is an exclusively or thoroughly concrete thinker. Rather, that the concrete/abstract paradigm is useful in placing them along a continuum, such that Aristotle, at least on certain issues, is a more concrete thinker than Plato. Irving Copi says:

> For Aristotle, the distinction [between the essential properties and other properties of a thing] is twofold: first, the essential properties of an object are those which are retained by it during any change through which the object remains identifiably the same object; and second, the essential proprieties of an object are most important in our scientific knowledge of it.[19]

And when he further says, "Since Locke's nominal essences are abstract ideas, they are immediately subjective in a way that Aristotle's essences are not,"[20] he is clearly identifying Aristotle as more concrete than Locke.

Behavioral formulae are often useful, as guides or rules of thumb, but they remain approximations, and therefore the obstinate commitment to and application of them under all circumstances disregards the fact that the world is constantly fluxing and changing. This process is described by the literary Daoists in terms of ideas like *Dao*, the natural course of events, and *taiji*, the principle according to which all processes revert to their opposites. Therefore, no matter how generalizable a formula might be, there are bound to be circumstances whose given conditions, constraints, and concerns don't fit the pattern exactly, and so require a different approach.

From the concrete perspective, what is problematic is the obstinate commitment to a principle, not the merely heuristic, provisional adoption of it. This also reminds us of Buddhism, where the Buddha ostensibly found it possible to speak using a pronoun equivalent to "I" while not thereby committing himself to a belief in a permanent self. Because things are not entirely the same, it is meaningful to distinguish between you and I. But because things are also not entirely different, the meaningfulness of the reference does not require a commitment to its absolute, autonomous, dichotomous reality. This makes it important to ask about an ethical theory, to what extent it can be concrete while still remaining normative enough to be of value to us, pragmatically.

## Concrete Ethics in the *Zhuangzi*: Finding the Fit

When we consider the situation of the classical *Dao*ist text, the *Zhuangzi*, it becomes clear that the author of the Inner Chapters[21] is at least occasionally targeting and lampooning the various "theoreticians" of his time, such as the Mohists, the so-called "Sophists," and the Confucians, among others. Frequently, Zhuangzi refers to the difficulties faced in attempting to reconcile the various philosophical reflections in which these scholarly types were prone to indulge. He seems clearly skeptical of reaching certainty through argument, since language is so mercurial. So we turn to Zhuangzi for our primary example of the concrete, pragmatic approach to ethics. Keep in mind that I am not attempting to reduce Zhuangzi to this viewpoint, nor am I assuming that he was consciously intending to advance this paradigm. I am using the text as an example of what I am talking about, without claiming that Zhuangzi would be in complete agreement with me on how to best interpret his own writing.

Preliminarily, in terms of ethics, Zhuangzi claims that "the genuine person precedes genuine knowing" (*qie you zhen ren er hou you zhen zhi*).[22] This suggests a kind of "virtue ethics" (or at least a "virtue epistemology") which demands, not adherence to an ethical formula, but rather development of one's character. The truth, according to Zhuangzi, is what the true person knows. Similarly, we could say that good is what the good person does. As a specific paradigm for efficacious behavior, the *Zhuangzi* endorses what it (and other *Dao*ist texts) calls *wuwei* or *weiwuwei*, literally "non-making," "non-contrivance," or "non-doing;" or "doing without doing," "acting without acting," and so on. This seems to be the primary practical principle revealed in and privileged by the text. Although the phrase is rarely used in the first seven chapters, its presence can be felt throughout the text. According to the *Zhuangzi*, this mode of action is made available to us in a certain way, namely by finding the "fit" (*shi*).

One who has found this fit remains, for the most part, invisible or at least inconspicuous by virtue of his or her perfect integration into their surroundings. In the Outer Chapters the idea of the fit is explained in this way:

> If the feet are forgotten [*wang*], then the shoes fit. If the waist is forgotten, the belt fits. If awareness of right and wrong is forgotten, the mind fits. If there is no internal change nor external following, one's acumen fits. When one fits from the start, and there is never lack of fit, then there is the fit of forgetting all about the fit.[23]

The perfect fit, then, is transparent. For most of us, this fit needs to be found because we have lost our knack for natural conduct and so our conduct is "ill-at-ease" or "dys-functional." Zhuangzi describes this condition in chapter 2:

> When most people sleep, their souls are confused; when they awake, their bodies feel all out of joint. Their contacts turn into conflicts, each day involves them in mental strife. They become indecisive, dissembling, secretive. Small fears disturb them; Great fears incapacitate them.
>
> Some there are who express themselves as swiftly as the release of a crossbow mechanism, which is to say that they arbitrate right and wrong. Others hold fast as though to a sworn covenant, which is to say they are waiting for victory. Some

> there are whose decline is like autumn and winter, which describes their dissolution day by day. Others are so immersed in activity that they cannot be revitalized. Some become so weary that they are as though sealed up in an envelope, which describes their senility. Their minds are so near death that they cannot be rejuvenated.[24]

The "dys-functional" attitude, then, is one in which response is impulsive, judgmental, stubborn, manic-depressive, and in conflict with the rest of the world. Contributing to our dis-ease is the fact that we blindly and obstinately insist on applying our values, outlooks, and perspectives without question in all situations, whether or not they are appropriate, and accepting them as beyond our control. This formulaic, rule based approach to experience will often confront situations for which the rule is not exactly appropriate, and consequently conflict or "friction" will result from trying to jam the square peg into the round hole. On the other hand, "finding the fit" or "fitting in" requires the ability to adapt to and change with the circumstances, rather than beating our heads against the wall of inevitability in a form of what psychologists call "obstinate progression."[25]

Finding this fit involves a kind of blending in with the circumstances, but it is crucially important to emphasize that this is not simply a matter of conforming to society and other forms of human contrivance (*wei*/doing *wei*/artifice). It is in fact accomplished by stripping away the artificial and arbitrary conventions of thought and behavior that are the result of social and cultural indoctrination. The *Zhuangzi* describes this eliminative and meditative process as "mind fasting" (*xinzhai*) and it culminates in the cognitive state which Zhuangzi describes as "*ming*" or "clarity." This fast of the mind seems to involve some sort of phenomenological epoché in which one loosens one's commitment to a particular sense of things, and allows things to reconfigure themselves in an infinite array of possibilities. In this sense, then, it in fact requires conforming to an extremely vast array of situational variables of which the culture of human contrivance is only one small part. Such an attitude might be described as "open-minded," and such action thus becomes non-contrived (*wuwei*), effortless, and unobtrusive.

We find expressions of this idea of "open-mindedness" in chapter two of the text. Watson's translation is as follows:

> Great Understanding is broad and unhurried; little understanding is cramped and busy. Great words are clear and limpid; little words are shrill and quarrelsome.[26]

What he translates as "great understanding" (*dazhi*) implies a sort of broad or vast comprehension, which suggests open-mindedness. The phrase reads "*dazhi xianxian*." If "*xian*" means, as many though not all commentators suggest, "broad" or "leisurely," then the doubling of the word suggests "expansive" or "broadly accommodating." This openness allows one to react more sensitively to subtle elements in experience. In terms of language, the willingness to surrender one's own perspective to the perspective of the other is in fact a prerequisite to effective communication. Zhuangzi laments, at the end of chapter 26:

> Words exist because of meaning; once you've gotten the meaning, you can forget the words. Where can I find a man who has forgotten words so I can have a word with him?[27]

Such a person is a desirable partner for conversation because he or she has no preferences at stake, and so will not insist on projecting any inappropriate meanings onto our statements. Such a person will come to terms with us, and understand us as we understand ourselves, by using language without being hampered by or fixated on any favorite or popular usage. This limits misunderstanding and, since clarity is a privileged cognitive mode, is thus of value.

Many interpreters have noted the *Zhuangzi's* concern with freedom. Since the idea of a "fit" implies a necessarily reciprocal relation between the various components of a situation, freedom in this sense must refer to a lack of constraints placed on natural response. Usually, these constraints take the form of the burden of convention and social artifice. Thus freedom does not imply the freedom to do whatever we want. This is because one cannot force the fit, one must rather find it, which involves meeting the world halfway. One must acknowledge the all too actual inevitabilities and limitations in one's situation. As a result, suggests Zhuangzi, the most effective mode of human experience is to blend or "fit" into any given situation in such a way as to allow ourselves to respond (*ying*) effortlessly and spontaneously, just like a well-balanced hinge. This mode of non-obtrusive experience is what is described as *wuwei*.

A good example of this is found in the story of Cook Ding, which is found early in chapter 3. According to Watson's translation, the story goes like this:

> Cook Ting was cutting up an ox for Lord Wen-hui. At every touch of his hand, every heave of his shoulder, every move of his feet, every thrust of his knee—zip! zoop! He slithered the knife along with a zing, and all was in perfect rhythm, as though he were performing the dance of the Mulberry Grove or keeping time to the Ching-shou music. . . .
>
> Cook Ting laid down his knife and [said], 'What I care about is the Way, which goes beyond all skill. When I first began cutting up oxen, all I could see was the ox itself. After three years I no longer saw the whole ox. And now—now I go at it by spirit and don't look with my eyes. Perception and understanding have come to a stop and spirit moves where it wants. I go along with the natural makeup, strike in the big hollows, guide the knife through the big openings, and follow things as they are. So I never touch the smallest ligament or tendon, much less a main joint.
>
> A good cook changes his knife once a year—because he cuts. A mediocre cook changes his knife once a month—because he hacks. I've had this knife of mine

> for nineteen years and I've cut up thousands of oxen with it, and yet the blade is as good as though it had just come from the grindstone. There are spaces between the joints, and the blade of the knife has really no thickness. If you insert what has no thickness into such spaces, then there's plenty of room—more than enough for the blade to play about it. That's why after nineteen years the blade of my knife is still as good as when it first came from the grindstone.[28]

Of course, the dignitary for whose benefit the good cook demonstrates his skill immediately sees the broader implications of "go[ing] along with the natural makeup," and concludes that "I have heard the words of Cook Ting and learned how to care for life!"[29] What Wenhui learns is that true mastery and skill involve a knack, not a formula. The ideal is to "follow things as they are" and thus never confront obstacles, just as water flows around a rock in the stream. The "spirit" or "daemonic" (*shen*) to which Cook Ding refers can be seen as the "autopilot" which guides us in the absence of conscious intention. A mundane example of this would be walking through a crowd of people without noticing the many various adjustments our bodies make to avoid hitting anyone. But this kind of response can hardly be planned. It must occur spontaneously and completely integrated into whatever situation is at hand. It also takes explicit account of actual inevitabilities. Cook Ding does not cut wherever he chooses to; this is not the kind of freedom he experiences. His freedom from constraint allows him to sensitively and accurately gauge the situation and then act unequivocally. He is effective to the extent that he avoids obstacles and conflicts.

Many commentators on the text seem to understand the *Zhuangzi* as advocating some form of abstract mysticism, which devalues the world of concrete realities. For example, Burton Watson, one of the foremost translators of the *Zhuangzi*, describes its attitude as one of "skepticism and mystical detachment."[30] He also claims that "Chuang Tzu's answer to the question [of how to live in a world dominated by chaos, suffering, and absurdity] is: free yourself from the world."[31] Watson does acknowledge that the sage does not "in any literal sense withdraw and hide from the world—to do so would show that he still passed judgment upon the world."[32] However, he still insists that in the state of *wuwei*, "Man becomes one with Nature, or Heaven, as Chuang Tzu calls it, and merges himself with Tao, or the Way, the underlying unity that embraces man, Nature, and all that is in the universe."[33]

I would say therefore that Watson seems to misunderstand on two counts. First of all, by representing *Dao* as some kind of abstract entity with which the sage merges, he seems to overlook the emphasis on immanence found throughout the text. Zhuangzi's outlook is not one that dismisses the natural world. Furthermore, Zhuangzi says specifically that *Dao* does not pre-exist the world. He says, "*Dao xing zhi er cheng*"[34] which can be rendered as "*Dao* is established as it is conducted," or "*Dao* operates and so is constituted," or something like that. That is, the operation of the world is *Dao*, *Dao* does not preexist the world in some abstract form waiting to come into manifest concrete existence.

Secondly, although Watson recognizes that Zhuangzi does not completely reject the world, I don't think he understands the extent of Zhuangzi's position. Watson suggests that this kind of rejection would imply judgmentalism, which he claims is inconsistent with Zhuangzi's characteristic attitudes towards judgmentalism. But we can go much further than that. Zhuangzi does not merely tolerate the world—he actually affirms it as wonderful and enjoyable, once one learns to fit in. The important thing is to find the fit.

> Watson's approach also allows him to dismiss some of what Zhuangzi says:
> Chuang Tzu invents a variety of mysterious and high-sounding pseudo-technical terms to refer to the Way or the man who has made himself one with it. . . . The reader need not puzzle over their precise meaning, since in the end they all refer to essentially the same thing—the inexpressible Absolute.[35]

As we have already suggested, Zhuangzi's so-called "Absolute," if he posits one at all, is not clearly transcendent. One of the "pseudo-technical terms" to which Watson refers is the "Great Clod," which is a very earthy, terrestrial expression. And it is not clear how the term "True Man" (*zhenren*) comes to be included in Watson's list of expressions for the "inexpressible ultimate," except to the extent that Watson insists that this genuine person is one who has reached a certain level of identification with the abstract entity he calls the "Absolute *Dao*."

But the *Zhuangzi* actually inspires us, not to remove or distance ourselves from the day to day world by identifying with some transcendental *Dao*, but rather to immerse ourselves in the world. Rather than understanding ourselves as apart from the world, we should understand ourselves as a part of it. Zhuangzi suggests that we seek to accurately perceive distinctions, not to allow them to become blurred in a condition of mystical transcendence. Clarity (*ming*), not obscurity, is the privileged state of mind.

To be fair, when Watson speaks of "freedom from the world," he might be referring to the world of society and convention. This would correctly imply that the condition of freedom requires that one must first discard the excess baggage of conventional values. But still, the problem is not that the values are conventional, nor is the problem necessarily the act of evaluating, itself. The problem is that we blindly and obstinately insist on applying our values, outlooks, and perspectives without question in all situations, whether or not they are appropriate, and accepting them as beyond our control. This formulaic, rule-based approach to experience will often confront situations that don't exactly correspond to the rule, and thus inappropriate responses will result. On the other hand, "fitting in" requires the ability to adapt and change with the circumstances, like Cook Ding does in the example cited below.

For Zhuangzi, freedom is the result of this "fit" (*shi*). But this kind of freedom is perhaps best understood as freedom from slavish, obstinate commitment to behavioral and evaluative formulae which cause us to act inappropriately, rather than freedom to act inappropriately if we so choose. For Zhuangzi "inappropriate action" is that which is contrary to natural trends, and so leads to conflict, friction, frustration, and "dis-ease," while appropriate, natural, or spontaneous (*ziran*) action leads to a condition of ease and contentment. Such "frictionless activity" (*wuwei*) leads to happiness.

Watson also describes the freedom of the genuine person (*zhenren)* as a "mindless, purposeless mode of life,"[36] but it is not at all clear that it is entirely purposeless. On the contrary, the prioritization of *ming* and *wuwei* indicates that life does in fact have meaning and purpose. On the basis of the story of Cook Ding, at least, it seems that Zhuangzi values the overcoming of conflict and friction. This is to say, we need to find our place (*shi*)—to reconcile ourselves to that which is outside of our control and operate within our parameters, instead of thinking of the limits as limitations and thus struggling obstinately and vainly against them. This image of the man in the middle serves nicely to describe the genuine person, who has become balanced and centered and is thus able to experience the pitch and roll of oppositions (*taiji*)[37] without being thrown off-balance by them. In a cognitive sense, the goal seems to be a kind of open-minded equanimity which is not flustered or disturbed by the unexpected. This is the example set by Cook Ding.

This kind of centering, by the way, is also emphasized in many forms of Asian Martial Arts, such as Chinese *taijiquan* or Japanese *Aikido*. In both of these, the goal is to become completely centered, so as to become rooted and immovable. Furthermore, someone who masters these techniques is also able to uproot others by entering into and thus appropriating their opponent's center. In fact, many aspects of Zhuangzi's concept of the "genuine person" (*zhenren*) correspond to the ideal of mastery in the martial arts. This is the case because traditionally the martial arts master is considered to have learned how to harmonize with his or her surroundings[38] and is therefore able to avoid friction or conflict. Traditionally, the highest form of mastery in the martial arts is modeled on the image of water, which overcomes by yielding, and thus avoids injury without causing harm to others.[39]

This sense of balance can be cultivated by becoming comfortable with shifting foundations. For example, one common training method in *taijiquan* is to train on the beach, so that the sand shifts underfoot and requires attention to balance. In this sense, it seems the *Zhuangzi* is endorsing the vertigo which results from shifting foundations, or at least attempting to make it familiar enough not to cause fear or forced response. We can, in fact, learn from our vertigo—we can use it to cultivate and develop a sense of balance that then allows us to adapt and conform to circumstances and conditions as they arise and change. To cling to our distinctions and their consequent evaluations, is a form of rigidity, which inevitably leads to dissonance, friction, and conflict. Vertigo teaches us fluidity and balance. So Zhuangzi constantly keeps us off-balance. As one recent commentator puts it, "He disorients us so he can reorient us,"[40] though it seems more likely, in terms of this current discussion, that he disorients us so that we can learn to orient ourselves in any novel situation, without relying on him.

Zhuangzi describes the *Daoshu* or "hinge of *Dao*" as a fulcrum that balances distinctions. Zhuangzi says:

> A state in which 'this' and 'that' no longer find their opposites is called the hinge of the Way. When the hinge is fitted into the socket, it can respond endlessly.[41]

This condition is one of open-mindedness, which does not obstinately insist on the world conforming to our pre-conceived preferences. The hinge serves as a standpoint or fulcrum according to which various distinctions are enabled. Seeing dichotomies in this way shows them to be complements, not opposites. To insist on preferring one alternative to another, is to establish evaluations, which we subsequently apply arbitrarily and indiscriminately.

So then the genuine person does not identify with his/her evaluations, but simply watches as all distinctions revolve around a central standpoint—a standpoint which is located at the *Daoshu* and serves as the pivot, the fulcrum. This permits effective and effortless adaptation to circumstances and conditions. As A.C. Graham points out in quoting from Chapter. 15: "Only when stirred will he respond, only when pressed will he move, only when it is inevitable will he rise up."[42] Graham says:

> The man who reacts with pure spontaneity can do so only at one moment and in one way; by attending to the situation until it moves him, he discovers the move which is 'inevitable' (*pu te yi*, the one in which he 'has no alternative') like a physical reflex. But he hits on it only if he perceives with perfect clarity, as though in a mirror.[43]

This kind of inevitability, furthermore, does not imply any kind of determinism. This is because the genuine person is not rigidly constrained to a single response, but rather inevitably slips into the most natural (comfortable: *shi*), most effortless groove. The "grooves" in this case are the limitations and inevitabilities one encounters in the world, and effortless activity follows the trajectory of the groove just as a surfer follows the motion of the wave, or Cook Ding finds the spaces between the bones.[44] This, of course, is why I emphasized earlier that Zhuangzi's understanding of freedom does not suggest the freedom to act inappropriately. The fact is that even though in any particular instance there may not be only one appropriate response, there is almost always, whether we recognize it or not, a most appropriate response. For Zhuangzi, this would seem to be the one which leads to the least conflict and the most efficient and effortless experience, as seen again in the story of Cook Ding. Besides, to describe the activity of the genuine person in terms of the free will/determinism paradigm would be to commit to one side of a polar dichotomy, and since the sage occupies the socket of the hinge, such descriptions are themselves inappropriate, simplistic, and unhelpful.

Zhuangzi describes the process by which the socket accommodates the hinge in this sense as self-forgetting (*xinzhai*: "mind-fasting").[45] Watson translates the relevant passages thus:

> May I ask what the fasting of the mind is?' Confucius said, 'Make your will one! Don't listen with your ears, listen with your mind. No, don't listen with your mind, but listen with your spirit. Listening stops with the ears, the mind stops with recognition, but spirit is empty and waits on all things. The Way gathers in emptiness alone. Emptiness is the fasting of the mind.'[46]

The word that Watson translates as "spirit" here is *qi* or "vital energy" which is described in the text as "vacuous" (*xu*) and yet "attendant upon things" (*er dai wu zhi ye*). That is, it is subtle, yet completely responsive. Mindfasting, then is the emptying of the mind to make room for the appropriate response to occur. It therefore involves the elimination of rigid, dogmatic, formulaic responses, and our self-identification with them, and this process enables frictionless (effortless: *wuwei*) and immediate response to circumstance. Graham suggests that "the Taoist is somewhere where this dichotomy [between rational detachment and decision making on the one hand, and romantic indulgence on the other] does not apply."[47] I would add that this "place" is in the socket of the hinge, at the fulcrum of all dichotomies. When we occupy that space, all things revolve around us, and we remain balanced and well-adjusted despite the unpredictability and inevitability presented by the world. We become at ease and comfortable (*shi*) with our surroundings, and thus seem invisible, or at least inconspicuous, to others.

## Conclusions

I have argued that the Daoist model for behavior and attitude as found in the *Zhuangzi* is based more on a concrete metaphysics than an abstract one. Such a stance considers and values the concrete, immanent, particular aspects of experience more than (or instead of) the abstract or general ones. There are ethical implications of this metaphysical stance. Any ethical theory based on a concrete metaphysics will be described as a concrete ethics, and these typically (?) reject formulaic approaches to behavior and morality. This means that any presentation of a concrete ethics must be descriptive or performative/transformative rather than prescriptive or normative. The behavior of exemplary individuals can be described through story telling, and such stories serve to shake the foundations of our narrow-mindedness, resulting in transformation. Therefore, at least in the

*Zhuangzi*, rather than attempting to articulate a theory, we find the attempt to provoke us out of our conditioned, habitual, formulaic, robotic responses to situations, and to goad us into acting more authentically, more responsively, more effortlessly. It must be emphasized, though, that the privileging of *ming* and *wuwei* clearly rules out any kind of ethical relativism, since, as we have seen, the Inner Chapters do seem to suggest that certain cognitive and behavioral conditions are better than others. Given that premise, the text seems to suggest that *ming* or clarity involves, not mystical obscurity, but more sensitivity to the subtle cues to be found in the environment which indicate the most natural or appropriate course (*Dao*). This sensitivity is acquired by clearing the mind of habitual or conventional responses and concerns. Similarly, *wuwei* in this sense implies acting flexibly, adaptively, and in a balanced or well-adjusted fashion.

Thus it can be said that the *Zhuangzi* describes the behavior and attitude of what we might call the "perfectly well-adjusted person," someone who is perfectly at ease in all situations. It is not clear, however, if Zhuangzi thinks that everyone should be like this, nor that everyone could be like this, or that anyone could be like this. To generalize in this fashion would itself be inconsistent with the non-formulaic personality of the text. Rather the text simply presents us with strange and unsettling, though ultimately fascinating and compelling, stories that disturb our balance and force us to adjust.

Clearly, we hear echoes of James here. It is this prioritization of the concrete over the abstract—where truth is not seen as abstract, absolute, and forever unchanging—that plays a significant role in James's ethical theory. James believed that every situation has its own unique novelties and inevitabilities. Therefore an ethical system that consists in the obstinate application of a general rule that must be obeyed at all times overlooks the subtle distinctions in the world. We need to become more sensitive and flexible in our approach to ethics because our value judgments may require alteration as our experience and knowledge of the world grows. James says:

> No particular results, then, so far, but only an attitude of orientation, is what the pragmatic method means. The attitude of looking away from first things, principles, categories, supposed necessities; and of looking towards last things, fruits, consequences, facts. . . . The pragmatist clings to facts and concreteness, observes truth as its works in particular cases, and generalizes. Truth, for him, becomes a class name for all sorts of definite working values in experience. For the rationalist it remains a pure abstraction, to the bare name of which we must defer. When the pragmatist undertakes to show in detail just why we must defer, the rationalist is unable to recognize the concretes from which his own abstraction is taken. He accuses us of denying truth; whereas we have only sought to follow it.[48]

In this way, James's concrete ethical model is recommended because it is more responsive to subtlety and therefore more efficacious.

As earlier indicated, there are many more examples we could offer of concrete philosophy. I am not planning to offer an exhaustive set of examples, but the ones I have offered support my claim that the concrete/abstract paradigm is useful in more cases than simply that of the *Zhuangzi*. The model illustrates certain controversies and offers some different ways of looking at old problems.

Of course, in proposing a paradigm of concrete versus abstract, I seem to be dichotomizing, which is itself an abstraction. But as William James says: "truth is an abstraction." I am not claiming truth. And I am emphasizing that particular philosophies can be described as more or less concrete and abstract, which mitigates the ostensible dichotomy. So the ironic dichotomy I propose is in some sense between those who are committed to dichotomies and those who aren't, or, as I once heard someone say, "There are two kinds of people in the world—those that think there are two kinds of people, and those that don't." As long as the dichotomy remains a useful one for heuristic purposes, then its use is justified, and to just that extent. Abstraction is not to be abandoned—a completely concrete person would never learn anything, never infer a future event from a present one. But neither is abstraction to be prioritized, and taken as more real than concrete events. As some semanticists say, "the map is not the territory," and "you can't eat the menu."

Furthermore, the concreteness of the models makes them more useful. Because they refer to the range of possibilities present in actual events, they are capable of much finer degrees of distinction than dichotomous, abstract, formulaic models. Their emphasis on subtle variations sidesteps simplistic abstractions, so that this dichotomy heuristically coordinates a number of other ostensible dichotomies, and in fact seems to resolve some of them in novel ways. For instance, it certainly transcends the simplistic, reductive, and completely misleading "East West" dichotomy, since we find both the abstract and concrete positions represented in Asian as well as Occidental thought. It also, as argued earlier, can be said to transcend the simplistic "analytic/pragmatic" dichotomy that plagues contemporary scholastic philosophy.

We tend to lose what Laozi calls *miao*, the sense of wonder which entails an enhanced appreciation of possibility, as we age because we learn to apply rules universally (as opposed to generally). This is the real meaning of the familiar adage "you can't teach an old dog new tricks." Certainly, our capacity for novelty decreases with age, arguably because of the sedimentation of our viewpoints, and the narrowing of our sense of possibility. We become more committed to a status quo, we come to have more at stake. This encourages us to adopt formulaic stances that then come in conflict with the constraints of the real world.

This is where the value of the concrete approach lay. We need to develop more subtle strategies for dealing with the infinite complexity of life. The universe does not always obey our rules. They don't always apply in the same way. Through the use of some concrete approach, such as *wuwei*, we can learn to be more sensitive to circumstance. The implications of this sensitivity are profound, since the lack of such sensitivity compels us to act inappropriately toward the environment, as well as toward our fellow human beings. We need to look at concrete situations and act accordingly, rather than adopt a rigid stance and defend it as though it was necessary.

## Notes

1. Among them: that Beauty will always be Beauty, but beautiful things will eventually decay and cease to be beautiful; that Beauty is purely Beauty, whereas beautiful things also participate in other essential realities; and that beautiful things depend on Beauty to be beautiful.

2. Fuzzy Logic is a term coined by Lotfi Zadeh, one-time chair of U.C. Berkeley's Electrical Engineering Department, to describe multivalued, rather than dichotomous, logic. The idea is that to describe things as being more or less what they are is more accurate than describing them as either being or not being what they are. The difference between this and probability is that according to probability theory, to say that something is nineth percent true is to say that, in the long run, it will be true ninety percent of the time. According to Fuzzy Logic, the same claim means that in any given case, the statement is ninety percent true. See, for instance, Bart Kosko, *Fuzzy Thinking* (New York: Hyperion, 1993).

3. Jean-Paul Sartre, *Existential Psychoanalysis*, trans. by Hazel Barnes (Washington: Henry Regnery Co., 1962), 30-31.

4. Quoted in H.S. Thayer, ed., *Pragmatism: the Classic Writings* (Indianapolis: Hackett Publishing Co., 1982), 45.

5. Quoted in Edward Moore, *American Pragmatism: Peirce, James, and Dewey* (New York: Columbia University Press, 1961), 59.

6. Irving Copi, "Essence and Accident," in *Aristotle: A Collection of Critical Essays*, J. Moravcsik, ed. (New York: Anchor Books, 1967), 166.

7. Quoted in Robert Almeder, *The Philosophy of Charles S. Peirce* (London: Basil Blackwell, 1980), 10.

8. Quoted in Thayer, 27.

9. In this sense, it is worth pointing out that science also takes abstract and concrete forms. Some scientists will claim "there are atoms" while others will simply acknowledge that "atoms" is a useful model for describing what happens in the lab.

10. William James, *Pragmatism*, Bruce Kuklick, ed. (Indianapolis: Hackett Publishing Co., 1981), 25-26.

11. *Pragmatism*, 92

12. *Pragmatism*, 30

13. *Pragmatism*, 100

14. John Roth, *Freedom and the Moral Life* (Philadelphia: Westminster Press, 1969), 98.

15. John Dewey, quoted in Irving Copi, "Essence and Accident," in Moravcsik, 154. See note 6.

16. Quoted in Thayer, 27.
17. *Pragmatism*, 27-28.
18. Raziel Abelson, "Ethics, History of," in *The Encyclopedia of Philosophy, Volume 3* (New York: MacMillan, Inc., 1967), 84.
19. Irving Copi "Essence and Accident," in Moravcsik, 157.
20. Copi, "Essence and Accident," 159.
21. The Inner Chapters are the first seven, most universally thought to be the work of a single author, and containing many of the most profound and artful expressions of the thought associated with the text. The other chapters are of controversial origins, and therefore it is precarious to use them in argumentation.
22. All textual references are to the Harvard Yenching Institute Sinological Index Series Supplement No. 20 (1956), *A Concordance to Chuang Tzu* (Cambridge, Mass.: Harvard University Press), hereafter described as the *Concordance*. This particular phrase occurs at Chapter 6, line 4, 15. Victor Mair translates it: "Only when there is a true man is there true knowledge." Mair, Victor, *Wandering on the Way: Early Taoist Tales and Parables of Chuang Tzu* (New York: Bantam Books, 1994), 52.
23. Concordance, chapter 19, p. 50, line 63 (my translation).
24. Victor Mair, *Wandering on the Way: Early Taoist Tales and Parables of Chuang Tzu* (New York: Bantam Books, 1994), 12-13.
25. This refers to a phenomenon observed, for instance, in the case of laboratory rats with certain kinds of brain lesion, who run into the walls of mazes and keep pushing against the wall, rather than turning in the direction of non-obstruction.
26. Burton Watson, *The Complete Works of Chuang Tzu* (New York: Columbia University Press, 1968), 37.
27. Watson, *Complete Works*, 302. Since this is from a chapter other than the "Inner" ones, its attribution is disputable, but I include it anyway since it expresses so well an idea found in the Inner Chapters. A more reliable example would be from Chapter 7: "The Perfect Man uses his mind like a mirror—going after nothing, welcoming nothing, responding but not storing." (Watson, *Complete Works*, 97.)
28. Watson, *Complete Works*, 50-51.
29. Watson, *Complete Works,* 50-51.
30. Watson, *Complete Works*, 2.
31. Watson, *Complete Works*, 3.
32. Watson, *Complete Works*, 5-6.
33. Watson, *Complete Works,* 6.
34. Concordance, Chapter 2, page 4, lines 33. Watson renders it "A road is made by people walking on it" (*Complete Works*, p. 40), but this is significantly one of the few times he translates *Dao* in this common sense rather than in its more technical sense.
35. Watson, *Complete Works*, 25.
36. Watson, *Complete Works*, 6.
37. Perhaps this is an idiosyncratic rendering, but *taiji* in general refers to the unity of yin and yang. As a principle, especially in the martial arts, it refers to the fact that everything which reaches its extreme turns into its opposite. Thus the world of *taiji* is the world of fluctuation and change, and the "perfectly adjusted person" is the one who most easily adapts and keeps his or her balance in the face of this "pitch and roll of oppositions."

38. The word *Aikido*, for example, translates as the "way of harmonizing energy," and suggests that success in the martial arts is a matter of overcoming by means of conforming to the movements of the opponent. Similarly, one sign of mastery in *taijiquan* is the ability to perform the exercises outdoors among the birds and animals without creating a disturbance among them. This requires that one's movements be perfectly natural and inconspicuous so as to blend in completely with one's environment.

39. As the Laozi suggests, "He who knows how to live can walk abroad without fear of rhinoceros or tiger. He will not be wounded in battle. For in him rhinoceroses can find no place to thrust their horn, Tigers no place to use their claws, and weapons no place to pierce. Why is this so? Because he has no place for death to enter." *Tao Te Ching*, tr. Gia-Fu Feng and Jane English (New York: Vintage Books, 1972), ch. 50, 52.

40. Bryan W. Van Norden, "Competing Interpretations of the Inner Chapters," unpublished paper presented to Columbia Seminar on Traditional China, January 16, 1994, 24.

41. Watson, *Complete Works*, 40.

42. A.C. Graham, "Taoist Spontaneity and the Dichotomy of 'Is' and 'Ought,'" in *Experimental Essays in Chuang Tzu*, 9. The phrase in Chinese reads, as translated by Watson (79): "reluctant, he could not help doing certain things," and Feng Youlan (93) as "he responded spontaneously, as if there were no choice." (*Concordance*, chapter 6, line 15).

43. Graham, "Taoist Spontaneity," 9.

44. This is also similar, by the way, to the way phonograph arms are designed in order to minimize friction of the stylus against the side of the groove in the record, and thus minimize wear and tear on both the record and the stylus.

45. Another relevant phrase that is even more ubiquitous is *wang* (*Íü*) or "forgetting," which shows up, among other places, in the story of Yen Hui and Confucius, found in chapter 6. The conversation ends in the following exchange: "Yen Hui said, 'I smash up my limbs and body, drive out perception and intellect, cast off form, do away with understanding, and make myself identical with the Great Thoroughfare. This is what I mean by sitting down and forgetting everything.' Confucius said, 'If you're identical with it, you must have no more likes! If you've been transformed, you must have no more constancy! So you really are a worthy man after all! With your permission, I'd like to become your follower.'" Watson, *Complete Works*, 90-91.

46. Watson, *Complete Works*, 57-58.

47. A.C. Graham, "Taoist Spontaneity," 10.

48. James, *Pragmatism*, 34.

*Chapter Four*

# Preparing for Something that Never Happens: The Means/Ends Problem in Modern Culture

**David R. Loy**

> When I think of all the books I have read, wise words heard, anxieties given to parents . . . of hopes I have had, all life weighed in the balance of my own life seems to me a preparation for something that never happens.
>
> — William Butler Yeats

Yeats died in 1939. Today in Japan, where I write this, toddlers take entrance exams to get into the best kindergartens, because the best kindergartens help you to be accepted into the best primary schools, which help you get into the best middle schools, which help you get into the best high schools, which help you get into the best universities, which help you get hired by the best corporations, where assuredly your difficulties are far from over. . . . Some of the obvious problems with this have been publicized—e.g., teenage suicides due to academic pressure, many others so traumatized they refuse to attend school—but the greater tragedy is whole generations of students so burnt out preparing for "examination hell" that they are brain-dead by the ripe age of nineteen. Since the sole reason for studying is to pass university entrance exams (your university, not your academic performance while there, determines your employment prospects), there is little incentive to study once you are in—and, of course, any personal motivation for an education has been eliminated in the process.

Needless to say, this is only one example of a more widespread problem with education today. Those of us who teach philosophy soon realize that our role is not Socratic: among other problems, the structure of higher education makes that almost impossible. The system of grading, credits, and degrees is a prime example of what I will call *means-ends reversal*: inevitably one learns to study in order to pass exams, get credit, earn degrees, win fellowships, and so forth, rather than understanding that process as encouraging an *e-ducere* imperfectly (if at all) measurable in those terms. We readily acknowledge the intrinsic value of lifelong learning, yet this inversion is now so deeply rooted that it is taken for granted and one mentions it at the risk of being dismissed as naive. Bertrand Russell already noticed the problem many decades ago: education today has become one of the main obstacles to intelligence and freedom of thought.

This chapter, however, is not another polemic on what is wrong with our educational systems. I want to reflect more generally on the duality between means and ends—not the usual problem of omelette and eggs, but their divergence in the modern world. I am concerned about the way contemporary culture has become so preoccupied with means that it loses ends—or, more precisely, they become inverted, in that means, because they never culminate in an ends, in effect have come to constitute our ends.

Heidegger does not use the same vocabulary but this way of formulating our problem is consistent with his later thinking about technology, which for him too is a means that has become more than a means: *Technik* is the particular "way of revealing" whereby Being manifests itself today. "Everywhere everything is ordered to stand by, to be immediately at hand, indeed to stand there just so that it may be on call for a further ordering." He calls this *Bestand* "the standing reserve."[1] *Technik* discloses all beings as raw material to be exploited by the human subject; and the subject also becomes raw material for exploitation, as we too become objectified by our own objectifications. The point of *Bestand* is not so much that our activities require such a "standing-reserve" as that, for reasons we do not fully understand, we want to have such a standing-reserve always available. That is, we desire limitless convertible means which may be directed to any ends, even as—or all the more because—we no longer know what goals to seek, what values to value. In this way *Bestand* too loses ends, for *Technik,* because unable to provide an answer to our ultimate questions about what is valuable and meaningful, has itself become our answer.

If it is true that today "end-less means" have become our common goal, the taken-for-granted value, how important is that? What are its causes; and insofar as it is problematic, are there alternatives? We shall begin by considering what Max Weber (1864-1920) wrote about the rationalization and disenchantment of the modern world. Weber himself noted that the "formal rationality" pre-eminent today deals only with means and cannot answer our ultimate questions about goals and values. This aspect of his thought is familiar, yet just as important is another, lesser-known side of his social theory: his analysis of our reactive flights into subjectivity—inner-worldly responses to the rationalization of the world which do not escape the problem but aggravate it. Weber's study of the origins of capitalism suggests not only that it had religious roots but that it may still retain a religious character. Then must any "solution" to the rationalization and disenchantment of the world also have something of a religious character?

Part two turns to Weber's colleague Georg Simmel (1858-1918) in order to contemplate the example *par excellence* of means-ends inversion: money as it functions today. Simmel's magnum opus *The Philosophy of Money* contains, appropriately, the most profound reflections on the means-ends split in modern culture. It also challenges our understanding of their bifurcation by arguing that the distinction between them, including our quest for the ultimate meaning of life, is quite a recent cultural development. Our yearning for an ultimate is a product of our dissatisfaction with the possibilities contemporary life provides, due to its sacrifice of substantial values for instrumental rationality. But is there any way out of this "iron cage"?

We conclude with some Buddhist-related reflections on how one might respond to this problem. For Mahayana Buddhism our contemporary bifurcation between means and ends is another version of dualistic (and delusive) thinking which should be related to the more fundamental duality between subject and object. That will enable us to appreciate how the Buddhist deconstruction of subject-object duality points toward a way to resolve the means/ends split.

## Weber

> Precisely the ultimate and most sublime values have retreated from public life either into the transcendental realm of mystic life or into the brotherliness of direct and personal human relations. It is not accidental that our greatest art is intimate and not monumental, nor is it accidental that today only within the smallest and most intimate circles, in personal human situations, in pianissimo, that something is pulsating that corresponds to the prophetic pneuma, which in former times swept through the great communities like a firebrand, welding them together.[2]

Today the distinction between public and private has become so absolute that we have difficulty comprehending how anything could weld whole civilizations together. What has taken the place of prophetic *pneuma* for us? "The fate of our times is characterized by rationalization and intellectualization and, above all, by the 'disenchantment of the world.'"[3] *Zweckrationalitat* is better translated as a purposive-rational or instrumental-rational orientation; its complement is *Entzauberung,* the "de-magic-ing" of the world. *Zweckrationalitat* is a good example of what Wittgenstein called family resemblances: no single characteristic is common to all the types Weber analyzed. Instrumental rationalization is a family of separable although interrelated processes which have different historical roots, develop in different ways and occur at different rates, and tend to promote different interests and groups. Examples include an increasing emphasis on calculability in various institutions; a rule-determined bureaucratic administration; the specialization and compartmentalization of knowledge; and, more generally, more impersonal control over the ways we live and the decisions we make.[4]

Weber distinguished such formal rationality from what he called substantive rationality. Our problem today may be described in terms of the conflict between them: "Formal rationality refers primarily to the *calculability of means and procedures,* substantive rationality to the *value* (from some explicitly defined standpoint) *of ends or results.*"[5] From the perspective of a substantive rationality whose concern is to actualize particular goals and values, instrumental rationality can be profoundly *irrational.* This irreducible antagonism between the formal rationality of our modern social and economic order and its irrationality from the value perspectives of equality, fraternity, love, etc., is for Weber "one of the most important sources of all 'social' problems."[6] Weber explicitly describes capitalism, his most famous example of rationalization, as involving the "domination of the end (supply meeting demand) by the means."[7] The purely formal nature of instrumental rationality, its indifference to all substantive ends and values, defines what is unique about our modern world and demonstrates what is morally and politically problematic about it.[8]

What allows instrumental rationality to become so problematic is the obvious fact that today we do not agree about what goals and pursuits most deserve to be valued; and in this matter—which is, of course, the most important matter—instrumental rationality, no matter how sophisticated, cannot help us. Weber knew his Nietzsche: the fate of our culture, which has "tasted the fruit of the tree of knowledge", is "to have to know that we cannot read the meaning of the world in the results of its investigation, no matter how perfect, but must instead be in a position to create that meaning ourselves." Yet such creation tends to be frustrated by the increasingly incomprehensible complexity of the modern world, whose organization escapes questions about value and morality by objectifying human activities into more impersonal processes. The "disenchantment of the world" means not so much the debunking of magic and superstition as the tendency to devalue all mysterious and incalculable forces in favor of the knowledge "that one can, in principle, master all things by *calculation.*" Yet this proven calculability conceals what Lawrence Scaff calls a Simmelian paradox, for

> its extension throughout culture as a possibility to be applied only "in principle" is accompanied by the *individual's* diminishing knowledge and control over all the conditions of life. We can interpret this to mean that each of us comes to be surrounded by and dependent on myriad complex "processes," from economic transactions to nuclear fission, affecting the immediate experienced world and the prospects for continuation and transformation of that world, which we individually cannot possibly comprehend, much less control.[9]

Consider, for example, that complex of rationalized economic forces known as the stock market. If we ignore such ineliminable abuses as insider trading, its functioning is governed by an impersonal rationality that bypasses all the ethical dimensions to the issues of how people earn their livelihood. The leveraged-buyouts popular in the 1980s were often justified as beneficial to the economy, but those decisions were made according to equations that determined how much debt could be borne, not its effect on people and their communities. Economics is a moral science because the problem of who gets what is inevitably a moral issue, yet economists and their clients strive to quantify economic processes into mathematical formulae that can be calculated and manipulated as if they were as impersonally valid as Euclidean geometry. The belief that an "invisible hand" will beneficently regulate the economy, if only government intervention were removed, is an almost perfect example of formal-instrumental rationality swallowing substantive rationality; and the never-ending controversy this belief generates demonstrates Weber's point about the irresolvable antagonism between such rationality and the more substantive rationality for which such a belief is deeply irrational.

The economic example is appropriate because Weber is best known for his controversial theory which locates the origins of capitalism in the "this-worldly asceticism" of Calvinist, especially Puritan, ethics. Qualifying rather than rejecting materialistic determinism, *The Protestant Ethic and the Spirit of Capitalism* argues that "idealist" factors sometimes affect the direction of historical development. Calvinism believed in the predestination of only a select number for heaven, which encouraged what became an irresistible need to determine whether one was among the chosen; such predestination made sacraments unnecessary and led to a devaluation of the sacred; in its place, economic success in this world came to be accepted as the demonstration of God's favor; this created the psychological and sociological conditions for importing ascetic values from the monastery, where they had been the prerogative of religious orders, into one's worldly vocation, as one labored to prove oneself by reinvesting any surplus rather than consuming it. The crux of Weber's essay reflects on how, in this complex interweaving of materialist and idealist factors, the original intention behind an activity may eventually be transformed into something quite different:

> The Puritan *wanted* to work in a vocation; we *must* do so. For when asceticism was carried out of monastic cells into vocational life and began to dominate inner-worldly morality, it helped to build the tremendous cosmos of the modern economic order. This order is now bound to the technical and economic presuppositions of mechanical, machinelike production, which today determines with irresistible force the life-style of all individuals born into this mechanism, *not* only those directly engaged in economic enterprise, and perhaps will determine it until the last ton of fossil fuel is burned. In Baxter's view the care for external goods should only lie on the shoulders of the saint like "a light

> cloak, which can be thrown aside at any moment." But fate decreed that the cloak should become an iron cage.[10]

We are a long way from Adam Smith's invisible hand. Weber's metaphor is less sanguine: the original Calvinist vocational ethos now "prowls about in our lives like the ghost of dead religious beliefs", conquered by a rationalized civilization of large-scale production and ravenous consumption that today rests on merely mechanical foundations.[11]

An important implication of this has not been much noticed and perhaps was not fully understood by Weber himself. His sociology of religion distinguishes more ritualistic and legalistic religions, which adapt themselves to the world, from salvation religions more hostile to it, which obey sacred conviction rather than sacred law. The latter are often revolutionary due to the prophecy and charisma that motivate them, missionary because they seek to inject a new message or promise into everyday life. Their efforts to ensure the perpetuation of grace in the world ultimately require a reordering of the economic system. Weber noticed that adherents of this type of religion usually "do not enjoy inner repose because they are in the grip of inner tensions."

All this serves just as well to describe the Puritans discussed in *The Protestant Ethic,* which leads to the supposition that capitalism began as, and may still be understood as, a type of salvation religion: dissatisfied with the world as it is and compelled to inject a new promise into it, motivated (or justifying itself) by faith in the grace of profit and concerned to perpetuate that grace, with a missionary zeal to expand and reorder (rationalize) the economic system.

This suggestion challenges our usual distinction between secular and sacred, between the economic sphere and the religious one—a distinction which as many anthropologists have noticed is a late development, the exception rather than the rule. Weber's argument suggests that although we think of the modern world as secularized, its values (e.g., economic rationalization) are not only derived from religious ones (salvation from injecting a revolutionary new promise into daily life), they are largely the same values, albeit transformed by the loss of reference to an other-worldly dimension. Or, more precisely, these values have been distorted by the fact that our no longer other-worldly yet still future-oriented motivation has become unconscious, which implies, according to psychoanalytic theory, that those values will be projected and objectified. This sheds light on Weber's enigmatic claim that "Today the routines of 'everyday life' challenge religion" because *heute aber ist es religioser 'Alltag',* the religious has become everyday/ordinary.[12] The routinization of our lives challenges religion because our new values constitute an alternative to its older forms. But then the rationalization and disenchantment of the world is not so much an alternative to religion as a particularly heretical—and perhaps demonic?—form of it.

I shall not attempt to evaluate the lengthy scholarly debate that Weber's thesis has provoked,[13] but if true it is a paradigm case of means swallowing ends: Puritanism initially bifurcated the means (capital accumulation) from the goal (assurance of salvation); in its preoccupation with this means the original goal became attenuated, yet inner-worldly asceticism did not disappear as God became more distant and heaven less relevant; in our modern world the original motivation has evaporated but our preoccupation with capital and profit has not disappeared with it; on the contrary, it has become our main obsession. As Weber emphasizes, the ascetic vocational ethos may have lost its original meaning yet that does not make it any the less powerful. Our type of salvation still requires a future-orientation. As Norman Brown puts it, "We no longer give our surplus to God; the process of producing an ever-expanding surplus is in itself our God."[14] In contrast to the cyclic time of pre-modern man, which is maintained by seasonal rituals of atonement, capitalist time is linear and future-directed, because it reaches for an atonement (originally, to be one of the elect who will be saved) that can no longer be achieved because it has disappeared as a conscious motivation. But as an unconscious motivation it still functions, for we continually reach for an end that is perpetually postponed—which in effect makes the means into our ends. So our collective reaction has become the need for growth: the never-satisfied desire for an ever-higher "standard of living" (because those who now understand themselves as consumers can never have too much) and the gospel of sustained economic "development" (because corporations and the GNP are never big enough).[15]

The psychic toll of such a perpetual future-orientation, of this means which never reaches fulfilment in an ends, is not difficult to imagine. So it is no surprise that modernity is also characterized by compensations for the increasing rationalization of the world. In reaction to its objectivity and impersonality, there has developed what Weber called a "subjectivist culture" which attempts to redeem us by cultivating an *Innerlichkeit* inwardness. Traditionally religion has offered whatever salvation has been necessary, but the loss of belief in a "higher" world has removed that avenue of escape without eliminating our psychological need for a redemption from this world. The nineteenth century found a temporary alternative in the Hegelian and Spenglerian creeds of social evolution, yet by Weber's day liberal historicist belief in progress was being discredited and replaced by "value spheres" that sought an inner-worldly redemption. A new place of refuge was discovered or invented: hypertrophied subjectivity. In various essays Weber focussed on three such spheres whose "irrationality" (or non-rationality) we seize upon as a relief from the seemingly inexorable rationalization of the world: an absolute ethics of "brotherliness" which for many of his contemporaries would be embodied in socialism; aestheticism; and eroticism.

The problem with brotherliness as an absolutist ethics is that, unless still rooted in religious, other-worldly imperatives, it is plagued by a dilemma. One must choose between idealistically hoping to end all forms of domination or accepting the expediencies necessary for effective political action. "If the former, then one must be prepared to live with the maddening incongruities between ideal and real. If the latter, then one must be prepared to live with the diabolic uncertainties of responsibility for consequences of action."[16] Concern for results entails the loss of redemptive purity, but purity can be preserved only by withdrawing into a subjectivity which will become that much more inner-worldly as it becomes more alienated from a world increasingly preoccupied with results and efficiency.

Originally the other two value spheres, art and eros, were like ethics closely associated with religion, but today they too have become autonomous. The more we self-consciously elevate them into absolutes, and the more we understand them to preserve "the most irrational and thereby real kernel of life," the more aesthetic and erotic pursuits have taken over "the function of a this-worldly salvation from the routines of everyday life and, above all, from the increasing pressures of theoretical and practical rationalism."[17] Weber, like Simmel, had some contact with the aesthetic circle of Stefan George and he observed with disapproval how George developed into a "prophet" of aestheticism. Simmel, himself somewhat of an aestheticist, noticed that one who lives in more direct contact with nature may enjoy its charms yet "lacks that distance from nature that is the basis for aesthetic contemplation and the root of that quiet sorrow, that feeling of yearning estrangement and of a lost paradise that characterizes the romantic response to nature."[18]

This insight becomes even more important when extrapolated: then it asks us to consider not only whether our valuation of aesthetic experience but whether our very notion of aesthetic experience might be modernist: that is, historically-conditioned by the same social forces that have disenchanted the world. The implication is that *our aesthetic sensitivity to music, poetry, painting, etc., has developed in response to (and reciprocally encouraged) the de-aestheticization of the routine everyday world.* In other words, certain types of "bracketed" sensory experience have been privileged, and our responsiveness to them has become much more sensitive, as the rest have been devalued. Kant's famous definition characterizes aesthetic experience as non-intentional and disinterested, in sharp contrast with the utilitarian, means-ends preoccupations of daily life; yet perhaps this is less a definition than our modern construction of aesthetic experience. This suggests a similarly disturbing question about brotherliness: has preoccupation with a purist personal ethics also developed in reaction to (and in its turn encouraged) the "de-ethicization" of our more objectified and bureaucratized social world—e.g., the loss of community that has accompanied modernity?

Our third escape from the disenchanted everyday is eroticism, which we now experience as closest of all to the real and natural because we understand it as the ultimate font of life; for only in the secret, inward sphere of the irrational, far beyond the banalities of routine existence in the everyday, can one directly sense life's pulsating forces. To assume its fullest meaning, "life" in this world, the only world there is, must be lived "beyond good and evil." Only under such conditions can its irrational core—eroticism—ever be imagined to offer an avenue of eternal renewal and escape.[19]

Yet to express the dualism this way, by dialectically opposing "life" to the rational, makes us wonder whether such eroticism too might be another historically-conditioned conception. Insofar as the parallel with aestheticism and brotherliness continues to hold, we may also ask whether *sexuality in the modern world has been hyper-eroticized in reaction to the de-eroticization of the rest of everyday life.* The question is awkward because it is difficult to gain a sense of what other alternatives there might be to the banalities of the more public everyday world today. Does our contemporary preoccupation with sex as that which frees us from the routinized utilitarian world reflect a commensurate lack of sensitivity to a larger "erotic" dimension—for example, a playfulness now almost completely lacking in the more "serious" economic and political spheres? To try to evaluate this (and our other two suppositions) is not easy and would take us beyond the bounds of this chapter, yet some psychologists have reached similar conclusions about *eros*.[20]

With all three-value spheres the flight into subjectivity appears to be a dialectical reaction to the rationalization of the objective world. *Rather than providing an inner-worldly salvation, however, each seems to aggravate the problem it flees.* An absolute ethic of brotherliness can maintain its purity only by becoming irresponsible (in the literal sense: unable to respond) and therefore more alienated from more rationalized social forces. By developing an acute sensitivity to art, music, literature, etc., we may have acceded to the de-aestheticization—part of the disenchantment—of everyday life. And by becoming preoccupied with the erotic as the "most real kernel of life", have we become desensitized to the routinization of the "less real"? If so, what we understand to be the solution is actually part of the problem. In this way modern culture has ended up deeply divided against itself, with the impersonal *objectivist* tendency towards rationalization at war with the *subjectivist* value-spheres that develop in hostility to it—yet each dialectically reinforcing the other. The deceptive possibility of a private escape encourages us to yield to the degradation of the public realm, which in turn encourages the development of subjectivist culture.

For Weber "the spheres of the irrational, the only spheres that intellectualism has not yet touched, are now raised into consciousness and put under its lens. This modern intellectualist form of romantic irrationalism . . . may well bring about the very opposite of its intended goal." How might that happen? Scaff points to a paradox that emerges from the dependence of subjectivist culture on its objectivist enemy: "the blossoming of an inwardness of cultural redemption was scarcely imaginable without the new technologies of publication and communication, the cultural hothouse of the modern city, new possibilities for economically independent urban existence—or, in short, the complete intellectualization of even the most sacred value-sphere of subjectivity."[22]

Weber wrote in the earliest decades of the last century. Since then, the subjective value spheres that were supposed to be refuges from the instrumentalized public sphere have themselves been colonized by the forces they were supposed to protect us from. The aesthetic world, in all its various forms, is increasingly at the mercy of markets; what popular music is available, for example, is increasingly controlled by corporate bean-counters, not by musicians themselves. American teenage culture was created in the 1950s when it was realized that teenagers' disposable income had become large enough to target. Rock music has always been mostly about sex and rebellion, and today entertainment corporations have become more sophisticated in using those themes to sell not only music but clothes, etc. The result is generations whose values have been commercially manipulated and molded during their vulnerable years, whose main relief from instrumental "production values" is consumption values. The other side of this is that we find collective escapes from our hypertrophied subjectivity and utilitarian everyday lives in the ec-stasies of mass concerts and sports events. Hardly the refuges Weber had in mind!

To understand both Weber's insights and these more recent developments, I think that Scaff's sociological explanation needs to be supplemented by a more Buddhist perspective, for which the basic problem may be more simply understood as the unfortunate bifurcation between an increasing sense of self-consciousness that by definition feels alienated from an increasingly-objectified rationalized world. Since for Buddhism such a Cartesian-like subject is a delusion—an incorrect understanding of ourselves which is in fact the very source of our *duhkha* "suffering"—any salvation from modern *Zweckrationalitat* which involves a subjectivist withdrawal from it, thus granting it free reign within the objectified world, will only increase the anxiety and instability of such a groundless sense-of-self.

From his Weberian perspective, Scaff agrees that the sense "of an increasingly radical tension between this world and the thought-to-be-inviolable self seems to be at the basis of our most serious and austere responses to a disenchanted fate." He concludes that "[w]hat we now need is not so much seductive 'grand narratives' and enticing routes of escape, but rather temporally bounded, self-restrained, and specific inquiries that bring our history back into view and retrieve the concrete and particular, the locally expressed, the individually experienced, the detailed."[23] He does not elaborate on what these might be. Weber was pessimistic about our escaping the iron cage while finding his own personal solution in an "ethic of responsibility." That seems to have been his attempt to integrate substantial rationality with instrumental rationality by combining a passionate comittment to ultimate values with a dispassionate analysis of the best ways to pursue them.[24] As a modernist ethics this is admirable and perhaps necessary, yet it cannot be a sufficient response to the problem of modernity, insofar as its dilemma is rooted in our subjectivist alienation from a disenchanted world. If even capitalism has religious origins, as Weber argued, and still retains a religious character, as I have suggested, perhaps the solution must also have a religious character—religious in the sense that it addresses directly the fundamental and increasingly radical tension between an objectified world and the subjectified self.

## Simmel

Modern times, particularly the most recent, are permeated by a feeling of tension, expectation, and unreleased intense desires—as if in anticipation of what is essential, of the definitive meaning and central point of life and things. This is obviously connected with the overemphasis that the means often gain over the ends of life in mature cultures—the growing significance of the means goes hand in hand with a corresponding increase in the rejection and negation of the end.[25]

Simmel's most sustained meditations on the problem of means and ends are found in what he considered his magnum opus, *The Philosophy of Money* (henceforth PhM). Perhaps only the chapter on "Filthy Lucre" in Brown's *Life Against Death* equals its wealth of insight into the role of money in our lives—a role which, it hardly needs to be pointed out, continues to increase in modern life along with instrumental rationalization and subjectification generally.

Higher concepts in philosophy are able to embrace an increasing number of details only by a corresponding loss of content. Money for Simmel is an exact sociological counterpart, "a form of being whose qualities are generality and lack of content." For Norman Brown too, money can be the purest symbol of all "because there is nothing in reality that corresponds to it."[26] Hence its unparalleled usefulness as a measure of everything else, and the inevitability by which such a perfect means becomes the end:

> Never has an object that owes its value exclusively to its quality as a means, to its convertibility into more definite values, so thoroughly and unreservedly developed into a psychological value absolute, into a completely engrossing final purpose governing our practical consciousness. This ultimate craving for money must increase to the extent that money takes on the quality of a pure means.... Money's value as a *means* increases with its *value* as a means right up to the point at which it is valid as an absolute value and the consciousness of purpose in it comes to an end. (PhM 232)

Money has become most important in those times when other value-pursuits such as religion, which encourage satisfaction with more modest circumstances, lose their attraction. Simmel compares our present situation with the decline of Greece and Rome, when all of life came to be colored by monetary interests. He calls it an irony of history that, as the intrinsically satisfying purposes of life become atrophied, precisely that value which is nothing but a means assumes their place. (PhM 236) Later Brown would use psychoanalytic theory to relate money's hypertrophy with unconscious guilt and fear of death.

However, its increasing importance for us is only part of a more general transformation of all the elements of life into means, as sequences that had previously terminated in autonomous purposes have become mutually connected into more complex teleological structures. Today, in place of earlier, relatively self-satisfying ends Simmel like Weber sees "objectively and subjectively calculable rational relationships" that "progressively eliminate the emotional reactions and decisions which only attach themselves to the turning points of life, to the final purposes." Among the many examples he discusses is the English landed gentry, whose transformation into a class based on more portable wealth has been held responsible for a decline in their communal social responsibilities. Rural self-governance had been based on the personal participation of this class, which has now yielded its paternalistic role to the more impersonal State. (PhM 431, 343)

Yet money has also enabled people to join groups without needing to sacrifice any personal freedom. This is an exemplary difference from medieval types of association, which tended not to distinguish between people as individuals and people as members of a group. Medieval associations encompassed all one's interests—economic, political, familial, and religious alike. This is consistent with Weber's point about the modern development of subjectivist value-spheres, but Simmel's response is more positive. Money should be given its due:

> Thus money, as an intermediate link between man and thing, enables man to have, as it were, an abstract existence, a freedom from direct concern with things and from a direct relationship with them, without which our inner nature would not have the same chances of development. If modern man can, under favourable circumstances, secure an island of subjectivity, a secret, closed-off sphere of privacy—not in the social but in a deeper metaphysical sense—for his most personal existence, which to some extent compensates for the religious style of life of former times, then this is due to the fact that money relieves us to an ever-increasing extent of direct contact with things, while at the same time making it infinitely easier for us to dominate them and select from them what we require. (PhM 469)

Simmel had stronger ties with *fin-de-siecle* aestheticist culture than Weber did and was less inclined to dismiss it as the reactive pole of a dialectical problem. On the other side, however, this quotation suggests that he was also less sensitive to the intrinsic connection between the modern "feeling of tension, expectation and unreleased intense desires" he noticed and our modernist subjectivity alienated from an increasingly disenchanted objectivity.

Yet their differences are less important than what they have in common. Just as Weber traces capitalism back, in part, to a vocational ethos imported from Puritanism into the economic sphere, Simmel also reflects on the religious significance of money. He notices that all Greek money was originally sacred, for it emanated from the priesthood, along with other standard concepts of measure (weight, size, time, etc.); money bore the symbol of the common god because the priesthood at that time represented the unity of the various regions. Brown's *Life Against Death* supplements this sociological explanation with a psychoanalytic one that accounts for why money continues to be sacred for us: "the money complex, archaic or modern, is inseparable from symbolism; and symbolism is not, as Simmel thought, the mark of rationality but the mark of the sacred." As Ernest Becker explains it, the first coins were minted and distributed by temples because they were medallions inscribed with the god's image and embodying his protective power. Containing such *mana,* they were naturally in demand, not because you could buy things with them but vice-versa: since they were popular you could exchange them for other things. The consequence was that "now the cosmic powers could be the property of everyman, without even the need to visit temples: you could now traffic in immortality in the marketplace." This eventually led to the emergence of a new kind of person "who based the value of his life—and so of his immortality—on a new cosmology centered on coins."[27]

Simmel is not unaware of the relation of symbolism with the sacred, for he notices a profound parallel between money and God:

> In reality, money in its psychological form, as the absolute means and thus as a unifying point of innumerable sequences of purposes, possesses a significant relationship to the notion of God. . . . The essence of the notion of God is that all diversities and contradictions in the world achieve a unity in him, that he is the *coincidentia oppositorum.* Out of this idea, that in him all estrangements and all irreconcilables of existence find their unity and equalization, there arises the peace, the security, the all-embracing wealth of feeling that reverberate with the notion of God which we hold.
>
> There is no doubt that, in their realm, the feelings that money excite possess a psychological similarity with this. In so far as money becomes the absolutely commensurate expression and equivalence of all values, it rises to abstract heights way above the whole broad diversity of objects; it becomes the centre in which the most opposed, the most estranged and the most distant things find their common denominator and come into contact with one another.[28]

So it is no coincidence that money exhibits the same duality in function as religion: it is one in the series of human concerns, yet also transcends the others as an integrative force which supports and infuses all other concerns. (PhM 485)

Then perhaps God and money suffer from similar problems. The difficulty with God, as usually conceived, is that in order to encompass all things he becomes so attenuated that his being is difficult to distinguish from nonbeing—which has made it easy for him to disappear altogether for us, or (as Simmel's analogy suggests) for his role to be assumed by money. We have noticed that money too is a perfect symbol because it has no content of its own; yet that is also what allows its means to become the end, what encourages us to take its no-thing-ness as more real than anything else. Preoccupation with either type of nonbeing devalues, and encourages a withdrawal from, the sensory world of more transitory beings. We attain a sterilized Being apparently immune to its impermanence but, like Midas, we have become unable to appreciate its charms.

*The Philosophy of Money* concludes by relating the domination of monetary relationships today with the way that the relativistic character of existence finds increasing expression in our lives, for "money is nothing other than a special form of the embodied relativity of economic goods that signifies their value." (PhM 512) To a Buddhist this suggests a rather different analogy between money and *shunyata,* the concept of "emptiness" in Mahayana Buddhism. *Shunyata* has often been reified into an Absolute or a Buddha-nature taken to constitute the essential nature of all things, but for Nagarjuna (whose *Mulamadhyamikakarika* is the most important text of Mahayana philosophy) *shunyata* is a heuristic term used to describe the relativity, and therefore the lack of self-existence (in Derridean terms, lack of self-presence) of all phenomena. Nagarjuna took pains to emphasize that there is no such thing as *shunyata*: "*Shunyata* is a guiding, not a cognitive, notion" employed to "exhaust all theories and views; those for whom *shunyata* is itself a theory they [Buddhas] declared to be incurable" (*Mulamadhyamikakarika* 24:18, 12:8). If we misunderstand this the cure becomes more dangerous than the disease, for "the feeble-minded are destroyed by the misunderstood doctrine of *shunyata,* as by a snake ineptly seized by the tail rather than by the neck" (24:12). Money—also nothing in itself, merely a symbol—is equally indispensable because of its relativism, its unique ability to convert something into anything else. But woe to those who grab this snake wrongly: who mistake the symbol for reality, this means for the end.

Simmel's concern with means-ends teleology derives from a fundamental paradox or irresolvable conflict that he believed to characterize all developing cultures. Life always produces cultural forms in which it expresses and realizes itself: these include sciences, technologies, and systems of law as well as religions and works of art. Such forms provide the flow of life with content and order. Yet, although arising out of the life process, once objectified such forms no longer participate so directly in life's ceaseless rhythm of decay and renewal. They become cages (we are reminded of Weber's iron cage) for the life-force that creates them but then transcends them; they remain fixated into identities whose own law and logic inevitably distance them from the creative process that produced them in the first place.[29]

As a culture evolves more such forms are produced and take on a life of their own, which entails a developing relationship between them and the creative impulse that produces them. Teleological series lengthen and ramify. A very rudimentary example is basic tools. A knife is very useful but it already complicates things. As well as learning how to use it efficiently and safely we must learn how to make it, which requires further teleological chains to locate and work the right kind of bone or stone. So a developing culture constructs increasingly complex mechanisms of interlocking preconditions that become necessary to fulfil each step of the means.

A more intellectual example is the difference between Socrates and academic philosophy professors today. Socrates wrote nothing, and as far as I know he may have read nothing. In fact, he didn't "do philosophy" at all; he talked with people in the marketplace and at dinner-parties. How far would he get in a modern philosophy department? In order to become a professional philosopher today, aspirants must read hundreds of books and scholarly papers, write scores of essays, pass dozens of tests, obtain three degrees, publish in reputable journals . . . by which time one has been thoroughly socialized into focusing on certain types of questions according to peer-approved methodologies.

Simmel was so impressed by this tendency that he considered it the tragedy of culture: once cultural forms exist, they become the unavoidable objects by whose assimilation we become acculturated—and with whose acculturation we necessarily become preoccupied, at the cost of a more direct relationship with the creative impulse. For prehistoric societies the *terminus a quo* as well as the *terminus ad quem* of cultural forms usually remained within the lifetime of their creator; the invention of writing systems constituted evidently the greatest quantum leap outside that boundedness. Today we are all technicians of teleologies whose *termini* are not only unknown but unimaginable. The incalculable abundance of modern artifacts and the continual ramification of modern teleologies means that in order to play whatever role we may within our own culture, we must subordinate ourselves more and more to them. Scholars need only reflect on the changes within their own disciplines during the past generation or two. The flood of noteworthy books and papers threatens to become a tidal wave that will submerge those who try to keep up with all the developments in their fields. A theoretical physicist once told me that specialists whose researches are interrupted for a year may never be able to catch up afterwards.

A consequence of this heightened teleological consciousness, and of our own diminishing role within it, is the peculiar frustration of a life impelled to seek beyond itself for what it suspects will never be found and never be fulfilling.

> A developing culture not only increases the demands and tasks of men, but also leads the construction of means for each of these individual ends even higher, and already often demands merely for the means a manifold mechanism of interlocking preconditions. Because of this relationship, *the abstract notion of ends and means develops only at a higher cultural level.* Only at that level, and because of the numerous purposive sequences striving for some kind of unification, because of the continuous removal of the specific purpose by a larger and larger chain of means—only then does the question of ultimate purpose, that lends reason and dignity to the whole effort, and the question of why emerge. The idea of an ultimate purpose in which everything is again reconciled, but which is dispensable to undifferentiated conditions and men, stands as peace and salvation in the disunited and fragmentary character of our culture. (PhM 360, my italics)

This is one of those compelling insights which forces us to redefine our problematic. Lengthening teleological chains are what lead us to ask about the end, the ultimate purpose of life. What is distinctive about our situation today is not so much means-ends inversion as our more basic sense that they are divorced. Modernity is better defined as the aggravated awareness of a split between them. Then our need for absolute ends and goals reflects our tendency to make everything into a means to something else. A yearning for meaning and ultimate purpose is the other side of our inability to be satisfied with the possibilities our culture offers us, a dissatisfaction which, ironically, can be traced back to its sacrifice of substantial values for instrumental rationality.

When the problem is viewed from this perspective, what "solution" is possible? The answer would seem to be none whatsoever so long as we understand any alternative as a particular goal to be gained *by means of* instrumental rationality. For that approach is itself the problem. Then no seductive grand narrative or enticing mode of escape, as Scaff puts it, and no political or metaphysical end of history can be expected to fulfil us. What other alternative can there be? Wittgenstein points us in the right direction: if the abstract notion of ends and means develops only at a higher cultural level, "the solution to the problem of life is seen in the vanishing of the problem."[30] But now that the problem of life weighs so heavily upon us, modernists and postmodernists alike, how can it ever disappear?

## The Nonduality of Means and Ends

> The perplexity of utilitarianism is that it gets caught in the unending chain of means and ends without ever arriving at some principle which could justify the category of means and end, that is, of utility itself. The "in order to" has become the content of the "for the sake of"; in other

words, utility established as meaning generates meaninglessness. (Arendt)[31]

It is by no means an objective truth that nothing is important unless it goes on forever or eventually leads to something else that persists forever. *Certainly there are ends that are complete unto themselves without requiring an endless series of justifications outside themselves. . .* If no means were complete unto themselves, if everything had to be justified by something else outside of itself which must in its turn also be justified, then there is infinite regress: the chain of justification can never end. (Yalom)[32]

We, at the present day, can hardly understand the keenness with which a fur coat, a good fire on the hearth, a soft bed, a glass of wine, were formerly enjoyed. (Johann Huizinga, *The Waning of the Middle Ages*)[33]

We have seen that Weber's modern world is characterized not only by instrumental rationality and disenchantment but also by compensations that emphasize an inner-worldly salvation for the self. Increasing objectification correlates with increasing subjectification; and although one could argue about which preceded which, the more important point is that each aggravates the other. Extrapolating a hint of Simmel's, I have suggested that Weber's subjectivist refuges themselves contribute to the world's disenchantment. Circumscribing our aesthetic sensibilities within narrowly-defined limits may help to de-aestheticize the everyday world; the hypertrophy of sexuality today perhaps contributes to de-eroticizing the rest of our routinized existence; and preoccupation with living a morally-pure life within our own circle encourages us to reject the rest of the world as irredeemably corrupt—which can become a classic case of self-fulfilling prophecy. The increasing commodification of these value-spheres since Weber has not stopped this dialectic.

I mentioned that this way of formulating our situation is especially meaningful for Buddhism, since the sense of dualism between subjectified self and objectified world is understood as the crucial delusion that causes us to suffer, as we try to secure a sense-of-self which because it is illusory can never ground itself. Contrary to the other-worldly salvations sought by most religions, Nagarjuna makes it clear that the goal of Buddhist practice is another way of experiencing this world: "The ontic range of nirvana is the ontic range of the everyday world; there is not even the subtlest difference between the two" (*Mulamadhyamikakarika* 25:20). In Weber's terms, Buddhism may be understood to promote the re-enchantment of our everyday world—re-aestheticizing, re-eroticizing, and re-ethicizing the whole of it—by reducing our dualistic sense of alienation from it until we realize that we are nothing other than it. In this concluding section we need to see what such a re-enchantment has to do with teleology and the split between means and ends.

For Simmel, modern culture is characterized by a widening divergence between means and ends. Lengthening and ramifying teleological chains lead to means drowning out goals, a process best exemplified in the role of money today. As money becomes the absolute value, in which our consciousness of purpose reaches its end, the other activities of life become demoted into our methods to attain it. Schopenhauer said that money is human happiness *in abstracto*, sought by those no longer capable of human happiness *in concreto*; our preoccupation with this "purest" symbol refutes the common belief that the modern world is materialistic. Rather, we are obsessed with the symbolic meaning of money and the commodities it buys.[34]

Simmel observes that only in more ramified cultures does the question of ultimate purpose emerge. As teleological chains multiply, we begin to wonder *why?* and yearn for some reconciliation that can unify our fragmented lives. For Buddhism, however, this modern sense of a growing bifurcation between means and ends is another example of our more general problem with dualistic thinking. Usually we dualize (e.g., good vs. evil, success vs. failure) in order to affirm one term at the price of its opposite. In this case we use the means to get some ends, yet the same paradox bedevils us: the opposites are so dependent upon each other that each gains its meaning only by negating the other. A life self-consciously "good" is preoccupied with avoiding evil, my desire for success is equalled by my fear of failure, and when ends disappear into the future they reappear the only place they can. The further our goals and purposes are projected into an indefinite future, the more inexorably our means take over their role. Weber characterized modernity as emphasizing instrumental rationality at the price of more substantive rationality, yet the better way to express it is that instrumental rationality has become our substantive rationality: in reaction to our confusion about what to value, we have come to value *Zweckrationalitat* itself. Unfortunately, such instrumental rationality grants us no peace. Being a means, *Zweckrationalitat* is always going somewhere, but, being a means, it can never rest anywhere. Hence the peculiarly modern feeling of tension, expectation, and unreleased desires that Simmel notices: our perpetual anticipation of something essential yet to occur, Yeats' sense of a whole lifetime preparing for something that never happens. No wonder, then, that we cannot understand the keenness with which a fur coat, a good fire on the hearth, and a glass of wine were enjoyed in medieval times; for today they do not satisfy us.

This inability to be satisfied is a good Buddhist definition of our *duhkha,* whose usual translation "suffering" leaves much to be desired. *Duhkha,* the first of Shakyamuni Buddha's four noble truths, is characteristic of life generally, which makes the restlessness of modern culture an aggravated version of the more general problem with being human. Buddhism traces this most fundamental *duhkha* back to the delusion of self: the sense of a self that is other than the world is something which, by definition, can never be satisfied. Lacking any being or ground of its own, the self is best characterized as an ongoing process which seeks perpetually, because in vain, for some way to feel secure, to make itself real.[35] The intensified psychological *duhkha* of modern life corresponds to our intensified individualistic subjectivity. This enables us to relate Simmel's increasingly ramified and increasingly frustrating teleological chains with Weber's dualism between the rationalized objectification of a disenchanted world and the subjectification necessary for an inner-worldly escape from it. *If the modern, more subjectified ego-self is a delusion that is never satisfied, it will understand its dissatisfaction as due to not having attained its goals; and as attaining the more modest goals of the past (e.g., a glass of wine before the fire) brings no satisfaction, the need will develop to project more ambitious goals at the end of a lengthening teleological chain.*

If so, the only solution is to deconstruct the sense of a bifurcation between such an alienated self and its objectified, disenchanted world. In this context, we need to see how Buddhism relates this deconstruction of self to the deconstruction of causality, insofar as the problem of means and ends relies upon our more basic notion of cause and effect.[36] Then what will happen to the self when the causal relation it elaborates to make itself real turns out to be problematical? Nietzsche (whom Weber and Simmel read) traced the fiction of self back to the fiction of intentionality, the supposed need for an agent to cause the action. His critique of the self follows from his critique of causality, which led him to conclude that "everything of which we become conscious is a terminal phenomenon, an end—and causes nothing."[37] Mahayana Buddhism reached similar conclusions by a different route, which offers a more practical path to overcome our subject-object, means-ends dualities. For this our point of reference is again Nagarjuna's *Mulamadhyamikakarika.*

The relationship between cause and effect was one of the main issues of classical Indian philosophy. Nagarjuna's own approach, however, seems paradoxical. On the one hand, causality is the main weapon he uses to demonstrate the interdependent relativity of phenomena and therefore their lack of self-existence. On the other hand, probably the most important verse in the *Mulamadhyamikakarika* seems to deny causality and interdependence from what is evidently a "higher" point of view: "That which, taken as causal or dependent, is the process of being born and passing on, is, taken non-causally and beyond all dependence, declared to be nirvana" (25:9). This climactic chapter of the *Mulamadhyamikakarika* argues that, if there is no self-existence, then the enlightenment of nirvana, the Buddhist goal, must also be *shunya*—that is, even nirvana cannot be said to exist. Nagarjuna turns traditional Buddhism upside-down by asserting there is no specifiable difference between *samsara* (our everyday world of *duhkha*, in which are the things that are born, change, and pass away) and nirvana. There is, however, a change in perspective, or a difference in the way things are "taken"—a difference that may be important if we want to avoid always preparing for something that never happens.

The irony of Nagarjuna's approach to the interdependent relativity of things is that his use of causation also denies causation. Having deconstructed the self-existence of things (including us) into interdependent conditions, causality itself disappears, because without *any-thing* to cause or be effected, the world will not be experienced in terms of cause and effect. Once causality has been used to refute the apparent self-existence of objective things, the lack of things to relate-together also refutes causality. If things originate (and change, cease to exist, etc.) there are no self-existing things; but if there are no such things then there is nothing to originate and therefore no origination. It is because we see the world as a collection of discrete things that we need to superimpose causal relationships, to glue them together.

This transforms the Buddhist doctrine of dependent origination into an account of non-dependent non-origination. It describes not the interaction of things but the sequence and juxtaposition of appearances—or what could be called appearances if there were some non-appearance to be contrasted with them. Without any self or essential "thing-ness" *behind* appearances, however, no such contrast is possible. Origination, duration, and cessation become "like an illusion, a dream, or an imaginary city in the sky" (*Mulamadhyamikakarika* 7:34). It is not self-causation, for the category of causality is eliminated altogether. This is *tathata,* the thusness or just *this*!-ness which describes the way an enlightened being lives, according to Buddhism.[38]

This, of course, does not eliminate causality experienced "as if" in everyday life (Nagarjuna ends up with a two-tiered concept of truth), but it does enable us to experience the everyday world in a fresh, non-causal way. The crucial difference from our usual understanding becomes clear if we translate Nagarjuna's dialectic into our problematic: *if there are only means, then there are no means, for every event becomes an end in itself.* Ultimately, events are not to be justified by their reference to some other events, for example, by their effectiveness in producing some other event. To live only in a causal, means-ends world is constantly to overlook the most obvious thing about this world and ourselves we are "in." The challenge, for a Buddhist, is to realize this and then to live it—a task that soon exposes our inability to dwell in the present, the sense-of-self's need to flee its own sense-of-lack now by projecting itself into the future and identifying itself with its goals, which we hope will make us feel more secure, more *real.* In this way the deconstruction of the cause/effect duality also leads to deconstructing the duality between the objectified world and subjectified self.

Here there is not the space to describe how meditation practices can lead to "forgetting the self,"[39] but the result of that conflation is less the sense of an alienated self which needs to use instrumental rationality to try to get something from the world. This breaks the vicious circle between the increasing objectification of the world and the increasing subjectification of an internalized self. It would also transform our utilitarian, bureaucratized world, for we would become less tolerant of many of the "means" we accept today once we realized that they are also ends. For example, we would work less, and change the quality of our work, if we stopped thinking of work as merely a means to buying all those commodities that are supposed to satisfy us. We would not tolerate the ugly, functionalist architecture that now plagues most urban environments, but demand that buildings be beautiful to look at as well as practical to work in.

Needless to say, meditation practices and experiences are not confined to Buddhism, yet the Buddhist understanding of this process, which emphasizes deconstructing both causality and subject-object duality, presents our problem and its solution in a manner easily related to what Weber and Simmel have noticed about modern culture. In place of end-less means, this gives us something that might be described as meaning-ful ends or end-full means; that is, life becomes play.

Something is play when its meaning is self-contained, because nothing needs to be gained from it. From the broadest perspective, then, we are always playing; the question is not whether we are playing but how. Do we suffer our games as if they were life-or-death struggles, because they are the means by which the self hopes to ground itself sometime in the future (by qualifying for heaven, becoming rich, famous, etc.), or do we dance with the light feet that Nietzsche called the first attribute of divinity? In Derrida's terms, it is the difference between dreaming of deciphering a truth which will end play by restoring self-presence, and affirming a play which no longer seeks to ground itself. For Buddhism the latter is possible only insofar as the self is not alienated from its world, for the alienated ego-self is that which, due to its intrinsic instability, seeks to ground itself, and therefore needs to objectify its world as its place to do so.

"So our grand destiny is . . . to *play*?" Does our incredulity reflect the absurdity of the proposal, or do the negative connotations of the word reveal less about play than about us: our self-importance, our need to stand out from the rest of creation (and from the rest of our fellows) by pursuing lengthening teleological chains. The loss of such self-preoccupation makes true play possible:

> To be playful is not to be trivial or frivolous, or to act as though nothing of consequence will happen. On the contrary, when we are playful with each other we relate as free persons, and the relationship is open to surprise; everything that happens is of consequence. It is, in fact, seriousness that closes itself to consequence, for seriousness is a dread of the unpredictable outcome of open possibility. To be serious is to press for a specified conclusion. To be playful is to allow for possibility whatever the cost to oneself.[40]

The problem with instrumental rationality is, finally, its seriousness, which presses for specified conclusions and is not open to the unpredictable. When everything that happens is of consequence—not because of its utilitarian consequences, but because we are open to it—the world becomes re-enchanted. If Buddhism is right, however, the cost of this is nothing less than one's self.

*End and Goal.*—Not every end is a goal. The end of a melody is not its goal; but nonetheless, if the melody had not reached its end it would not have reached its goal either. A parable. (Nietzsche)

## Notes

1. Martin Heidegger, "The Question Concerning Technology" in *The Question Concerning Technology and Other Essays*, William Lovitt trans. (New York: Harper Colophon, 1977), 5, 12, 17.

2. "Science as Vocation," in *From Max Weber: Essays in Sociology*, Hans Gerth and C. Wright Mills eds. and trans. (New York: Oxford University Press, 1946), 155.

3. *From Max Weber: Essays in Sociology*, 155.

4. See Rogers Brubaker, *The Limits of Rationality: An Essay on the Social and Moral thought of Max Weber* (London: Routledge, 1991), 9.

5. *The Limits of Rationality*, 36 [Brubaker's italics].

6. Max Weber, *Economy and Society*, 2 vol., Geenther Roth and Claus Wittich eds., (Berkeley: University of California Press, 1978), 111. See *The Limits of Rationality*, 4.

7. Max Weber, "Socialism," trans. D. Hytch, in *Max Weber: The Interpretation of Social Reality*, J.E.T. Eldridge, ed. (New York: Shocken, 1980), 202.

8. *The Limits of Rationality*, 10.

9. Lawrence A. Scaff, *Fleeing the Iron Cage: Culture, Politics, and Modernity in the thought of Max Weber* (Berkeley: University of California Press, 1989), 227.

10. Scaff's translation in *Fleeing the Iron Cage,* 88.

11. Quoted in *Fleeing the Iron Cage*, 89.

12. "Science as Vocation" in *From Max Weber*, 149.

13. For an early overview, see S.N. Eisenstadt ed., *The Protestant Ethic and Modernization: A Comparative View* (New York: Basic Books, 1968), especially 67-86.

14. Norman O. Brown, *Life Against Death: The Psychoanalytic Meaning of History* (New York: Vintage, 1961), 261.

15. In Brown's psychoanalytic terms, the result is "an economy driven by a pure sense of guilt, unmitigated by any sense of redemption," which is "the more uncontrollably driven by the sense of guilt because the problem of guilt is repressed by denial in to the unconscious." (*Life Against Death*, 272).

16. *Fleeing the Iron Cage*, 98-9.

17. *From Max Weber,* 345; cf. *The Limits of Rationality*, 78-9.

18. Georg Simmel, *The Philosophy of Money*, David Frisby ed., Tom Bottomore and David Frisby trans., from the 2 ed. of 1907 (London: Routledge and Kegan Paul, 1978), 478.

19. *Fleeing the Iron Cage*, 109.

20. This is one of Norman Brown's main points in *Life Against Death* and *Love's Body*.

21. *From Max Weber*, 143.

22. *Fleeing the Iron Cage*, 112.

23. *Fleeing the Iron Cage*, 240-1.

24. See *The Limits of Rationality*, 108.

25. *The Philosophy of Money*, 481, altered. Weber was a friend of Simmel's and benefited from his writings, including *The Philosophy of Money*, yet this influence, although no doubt considerable, is not well understood. See, e.g., *Fleeing the Iron Cage*, chapter 4, "The Sociology of Culture and Simmel."

26. *The Philosophy of Money*, 221; *Life Against Death*, 271.

27. *The Philosophy of Money*, 187; *Life Against Death*, 246; Ernest Becker, *Escape from Evil* (New York: The Free Press, 1975), 76, 79.

28. *The Philosophy of Money*, 236. Simmel also notices a very different parallel: "The indifference as to its use, the lack of attachment to any individual because it is unrelated to any of them, the objectivity inherent in money as a mere means which excludes any emotional relationship—all this produces an ominous analogy between money and prostitution." (77)

29. See Simmel's *Conflict in Modern Culture and other Essays*, K. Peter Etzkom trans. (New York: New York Teachers College Press, 1968), 11.

30. *Tractatus Logico—Philosophicus* 6.521.

31. Hannah Arendt, *The Human Condition* (Chicago: The University of Chicago Press, 1958), 154. The same point can be made about pragmatism.

32. Irvin D. Yalom, *Existential Psychotherapy* (New York: Basic Books, 1980), 466 [Yalom's italics].

33. Johann Huizinga, *The Waning of the Middle Ages*, F. Hopman trans. (New York: Penguin, 1987), 9.

34. *In The Hour of Our Death* (New York: Penguin, 1981) Philippe Aries turns our usual critique upside-down. "It is difficult for us today to understand the intensity of the [late medieval] relationship between people and things." The modern world is not really materialistic, for "things have become means of production, or objects to be consumed of devoured. They no longer constitute a 'treasure'. . . . Scientists and philosophers may lay claim to an understanding of matter, but the ordinary man in his daily life no more believes in matter than he believes in God. The man of the Middle Ages believed in matter and in God, in life and in death, in the enjoyment of things and their renunciation." (136-7).

35. For more on this, see my *Lack and Transcendence: Death and Life in Psychotherapy, Existentialism, and Buddhism* (Atlantic Highlands, N.J.: Humanities Press, 1996).

36. Simmel notes that "the whole structure of means is one of causal connection viewed from the front" (*The Philosophy of Money*, 431).

37. Friedrich Nietzsche, *The Will to Power*, Walter Kauffmann and R.J. Hollingdale trans. (New York: Random House, 1968), 265, no. 478. See also no. 666 on 352.

38. The aporias of causality are well known in Western philosophy, mainly due to Hume's critique. Nagarjuna's version points to the contradiction necessary for a cause-and-effect relationship: the effect can be neither the same as the cause nor different from it. If the effect is the same as the cause, nothing has been caused; if it is different, then any cause should be able to cause any effect (*Mulamadhyamikakarika* 10:19, 22). Weber too abandoned the one-dimensional causal model, ordered from the foundation upward (e.g. Marxist materialism) in favour of what may be understood as a network model of causality. (For more on this, see *Fleeing the Iron Cage*, 48-9, and my *Nonduality: A Study in Comparative Philosophy* (New Haven: Yale University Press, 1988), chapter six).

39. James P. Carse, *Finite and Infinite Games* (New York: Free Press, 1986), 15.

40. Friedrich Nietzsche, *The Wanderer and His Shadow*, no. 204, in *Human, All Too Human*, R.J. Hollingdale trans. (Cambridge: Cambridge University Press, 1986), 360.

41. Nietzsche, *Human, All Too Human*, 360.

# Part Two:

# Ethics in Cultural Context—

# Variety or Relativism?

*Chapter Five*

# Pluralism in Practice: Incommensurability and Constraints on Change in Ethical Discourses

**Stephen C. Angle**

Imagine an Aristotelian giving money away to a poor person. He judges his own action to be magnanimous. If a Confucian were to observe this action, though, he might conclude that the Aristotelian had violated socio-ethical norms, or *li.*[1] Assuming that other Confucians agreed, the Aristotelian's conduct could be held up as a negative example to be used in teaching young Confucians. In and of itself, however, the Confucian's judgment would give the Aristotelian no reason to change his conduct, since "lacking in *li*" is not a category in the language by which he judges conduct. This begins to suggest that Aristotelians and Confucians may assess behavior, intentions, and character traits in different terms. I will summarize this type of difference by saying that different cultures can have different ethical systems.[2]

Western ethical philosophers have tended to downplay or ignore these differences by basing their theorizing almost exclusively on Western ethics (which I call morality). Twentieth-century critics, cognizant of the depth and persistence of differences between ethical systems, have challenged the idea that our understanding of ethics should be based only on morality. Morality seems clearly to be just one ethical schema among many, one instance of a more general phenomenon. While the critics have not denied that it is worthwhile to try to better understand morality, they have insisted that any theory seeking to explain the nature of ethical value itself must be more broadly based. Many of these same critics have gone on to argue that differences between ethical systems can be irreducible. They reject Kant's vision of one and only one set of ethical norms applicable to all rational beings in favor of a plurality of ethical systems. I label this position ethical pluralism.

One early theorist who supported ethical pluralism was Ruth Benedict. In her pioneering *Patterns of Culture*, she wrote that different cultures travel along "different roads in pursuit of different ends, and these ends and these means in one society cannot be judged in terms of those of another society, because they are incommensurable."[3] Benedict's invocation of incommensurability to justify ethical pluralism has been followed by many subsequent writers and criticized by many others. Despite the attention that it has received, though, incommensurability remains an obscure concept. It holds out the promise of explaining why ethical systems appear to be persistently, even irreducibly plural, but it is beset with problems of all kinds. In this essay, I begin by considering two particularly vexing problems and the solutions to them that one advocate of incommensurability, Alasdair MacIntyre, has proposed. In each case, I argue that MacIntyre's solutions are inadequate. In the balance of the essay, I develop an alternative approach to incommensurability that avoids the difficulties that plagued MacIntyre and yet delivers on the idea's promise to ground ethical pluralism.

## Problems with Incommensurability: Translation and Davidson's Challenge

It is natural for incommensurability to be understood in terms of an inability to translate between two languages. In "Incommensurability, Truth, and the Conversation between Confucians and Aristotelians about the Virtues,"[4] MacIntyre stresses numerous difficulties with translation, among them the fact that Aristotle's Greek has no word for the Chinese term *li*. *Li*'s original meaning was something like holy rite, and was extended by Confucian thinkers into a quite general norm for proper action. Neither Greek words that were used for religious rituals, nor those used for customs, come close to matching the meaning of *li*. MacIntyre concludes that *li* cannot be translated into Greek, and this is one piece of evidence that the two languages are incommensurable.

As MacIntyre realizes, though, two different problems can arise for theorists who link their notions of incommensurability too closely to translation. One is that it would seem to rule out the possibility that two speakers of the same language might nonetheless adhere to two different, incommensurable conceptual schemes. The other problem is that according to an argument widely attributed to Donald Davidson, the idea that two languages can fail to be inter-translatable—and are thus incommensurable—is actually unintelligible.

MacIntyre seeks to avoid these pitfalls by putting some distance between incommensurability and translation. He insists, for instance, that although Galileo and his Aristotelian contemporaries spoke the same language, the conceptual schemes expressed by their different physical theories were incommensurable. He is never very clear, though, just what conceptual schemes are, and we are left wondering why translation between incommensurable schemes is sometimes possible and sometimes not. I'll propose a precise and consistent relation between schemes and languages in Part II, and argue that there is actually a sense in which Galileo's language cannot be translated into the Aristotelians'.

MacIntyre has a more sustained and novel response to the Davidsonian argument.[5] MacIntyre believes that the argument has two premises: (1) all we have to do to assure understanding of another culture's point of view is to translate their language, and (2) nothing that we can identify as a language could resist translation. MacIntyre contends that these premises rest upon:

> a way of translating texts from alien and different cultures, and of responding to them, which is central to the cosmopolitan cultures of those modern internationalized languages-in-use, such as contemporary Trans-Atlantic and Trans-Pacific English, one of whose central features is that utterance in them presupposes only the most minimal of shared beliefs. These are languages, so far as is possible, for anyone at all to use, for those who are equally at home everywhere and therefore nowhere.[6]

MacIntyre's idea, which he develops more fully elsewhere, is that certain modern languages that are spoken around the world have been, in a sense, neutered: in order to be usable by people from widely-different cultural backgrounds, these languages have lost some important characteristics that all local languages once had.[7] The chief features that he says internationalized languages have lost are: first, naming systems that presuppose certain beliefs on the part of the language's speakers, and second, a tight relationship between canonical texts expressing "strong, substantive criteria of truth and rationality" and acceptable utterances.[8] What we are left with are languages in which "the relationship of a name to what is named will have to be specifiable . . . independently of any particular scheme of identification embodying the beliefs of some particular community," and in which formerly canonical texts now serve only as sources for literary allusions, not as standards of truth.[9]

How does MacIntyre think that the putative transition from local to internationalized languages might answer Davidson's challenge? Since the new languages have no tight connections to particular sets of beliefs, MacIntyre reasons, the sorts of obstacles that would stand in the way of translating from Aristotle's Greek to Confucius's Chinese, for example, are gone. The plausibility of Davidson's contention that we can translate anything that we can identify as a language into our own language, that is, rests on taking our own language to be one of these neutered modern languages. But once Aristotle and Confucius have been translated into English, they have lost their essential ties to particular beliefs that helped to define their standpoints. Once rendered into English, MacIntyre concludes, they are no longer genuine Confucianism nor genuine Aristotelianism, but merely new menu items for the "modern individualism of aestheticized personal choice."[10] Nothing has been done, in other words, to dissolve the incommensurability between the actual conceptual schemes of Confucianism and Aristotelianism.

I am dissatisfied with MacIntyre's response to Davidson for two reasons. First, MacIntyre has overstated the extent to which modern languages have been neutered. It seems true that the use of names may have changed somewhat along the lines he describes,[11] but the blanket claim that we no longer have canonical texts is surely false, especially in ethics. Many speakers of internationalized English, by no means limited to so-called fundamentalists, still look to the Bible, for instance, as expressing "strong, substantive criteria" of right and wrong. Many others look to more recent classics, like the Constitution. Admittedly, appeal to the Bible or the Constitution does not always settle disputes. For one thing, contemporary America is composed of many overlapping communities with commitments to different sets of canonical texts. It is also true that canonical texts must be interpreted, and that they therefore supply standards of right and wrong only together with the styles of reasoning and traditions of interpretation that have grown up around them. But in this we are no different from our predecessors of any age: texts are never self-interpreting.[12]

Second, MacIntyre's whole discussion of internationalized languages seems to me to misunderstand the nature of Davidson's argument. The essence of MacIntyre's response to Davidson, after all, is that although it appears that Confucian terms can be translated into English, this is in fact only a watered-down kind of quasi-translation. This response would only be harmful to Davidson, though, if Davidson's argument had used our apparent ability to translate Confucian Chinese into English as evidence for his conclusion. As we will see in more detail in Part II, Davidson's argument does not depend on any specific instances of successful translation, but instead relies on very general features of languages which apply equally to modern and to pre-modern languages. Davidson could easily accept MacIntyre's claim that current translations from Chinese into English are mere quasi-translations, in fact, because Davidson recognizes that it may be necessary to enrich or revise our language before true translation will be possible. I think we can conclude that MacIntyre has not succeeded in answering the questions revolving around the idea of translation that immediately confront a defender of incommensurability.

## Comparison and Commensuration

Historical encounters between cultures with very different ethical systems have not always ended with puzzled mutual incomprehension, as my discussion of incommensurability to this point might have suggested. Some early twentieth-century Chinese intellectuals, for instance, sought to incorporate Western insights into Chinese ethics, and some even turned away from their Confucian upbringings to advocate Western ideologies like anarchism, liberalism, or Marxism. Today some Americans have rejected the teachings of their own traditions to embrace the ethico-religious outlook of Buddhism or Daoism. If the different ethical systems in these examples are or were incommensurable, and if the move from one to another is at least upon occasion more than an "irrational" conversion, then an incommensurability theorist has another challenge to meet: how can two incommensurable systems come to be compared, and one chosen over the other?

MacIntyre's answer comes in several steps. He points out that even when two conceptual schemes are mutually incomprehensible, it still should be possible for an adherent of one to learn the other from the ground up. Having thus acquired a "second first language," both standpoints should now be intelligible to such a person. Each of the two standpoints, though, will only be intelligible in its own terms. A properly educated Greek-Chinese bilingual, for example, would be able to converse with Greek-speaking Aristotelians about whether some action was magnanimous, and also to discuss the fine points of *li* with Chinese-speaking Confucians. MacIntyre insists, however, that nothing has changed about the relationship between the two languages/conceptual schemes that would allow this bilingual to translate sentences from one to the other.[13]

MacIntyre adds, though, that such a bilingual "will be able to understand what would have to be involved by way of an extension or enrichment of their own first language-in-use if it were to be able to accommodate a representation of the other."[14] On the face of it, this claim seems plausible; surely a bilingual would be in the best possible position to see where and how the two languages/conceptual schemes were incompatible, and how one would have to be changed in order to accommodate the other? I'll suggest in a moment that this picture is actually much too simple, but for the moment let's follow MacIntyre through to the end of his argument.

He next supposes that the needed enrichment has been carried out, and that each of the two "incompatible and incommensurable bodies of theory and practice has passed beyond the initial stage of partial incomprehension and partial misrepresentation of the other, by so enriching its linguistic and conceptual resources that it is able to provide an accurate representation of the other."[15] The final stage of the process occurs when adherents of one or the other of the rival traditions come to recognize the other tradition as superior, because (1) they see that their own tradition has failed by its own standards, and (2) the other tradition has the resources to explain the failure in considerable detail—"why it succeeded and why it failed at just the points and in just the ways" that it did.[16] Rational choice of one theory over the other is thus possible, even though the two theories have remained, MacIntyre insists, incommensurable throughout.

The key step in the process occurs when the bodies of theory are enriched in such a way that, despite the fact that they are still mutually incommensurable, each can accurately represent the other in its language. MacIntyre never explains just what it takes to be able to accurately represent something. Given his repeated mention of "enrichment," I gather that he is convinced that such a representation takes place by adding new words to the old language. His idea seems to be that the Aristotelians, having mastered Confucian Chinese as a second first language, could introduce a whole series of new terms into their Greek, each corresponding in meaning and reference to problematic (from the perspective of an Aristotelian moralist) Confucian notions.[17] The combination of existing Greek grammar and these new terms might be thought to enable accurate representation of Confucian discourse in Aristotelian Greek.[18]

Suppose it is possible, therefore, for a bilingual Greek-Chinese speaker to introduce all the specialized terms of Confucian ethics into Greek. This would be something like an English speaker's anglicizing foreign words, as when *déja vu* becomes deja vu, except that our bilingual could only communicate with other bilinguals or with Greek speakers who had learned the relevant concepts from the ground up, as a new part of Greek. Would such a process allow for comparison between the two theories despite the fact that they are still incommensurable?

Certain kinds of comparison were always possible. If an Aristotelian and a Confucian had observed someone performing an action, we could have asked them for their respective assessments.[19] We might learn that Confucians and Aristotelians don't always approve of the same actions. Each could give us reasons, furthermore, for their assessment, although these reasons would of course be couched in their own theoretical languages. The question is, does the fact that both theories can come to be "accurately represented" in one and the same language allow for some new type of comparison that makes rational choice between the theories possible?

I can't see how it would. If English and Chinese are incommensurable, why would removing the italics from Chinese words affect our ability to choose between a theory centered on li (instead of *li*) and a theory centered on virtue and the mean (or moral obligation or human rights)? Even though both theories are now expressed in the same language, they still are two separate and incommensurable theories, each with its own, distinctive concerns. If anyone is tempted to answer "now that they're part of the same language, we can try to find a new theory that contains versions of both sets of concepts—a theory that combines a respect for li with protection for individual human rights, for example," I would agree wholeheartedly but point out that you're not comparing the old theories at all. Rather you're constructing a new theory with new and somewhat different concepts (even if you still label them "*li*" and "human rights"). It also is true that if someone finds that an ethical theory has failed by its own standards, he or she might look for alternatives, and stick with one that didn't seem to have the same internal inconsistencies as the first one. This might be "rational choice," but it is not obviously "comparison" of the two theories. MacIntyre is right to see that internal criticism and language-enrichment are important parts of cross-cultural comparison, but his conception of the constraints on and the effects of linguistic change is much too simple. I'll explain what goes on in actual cross-cultural comparison near the end of Part II.

## A Different Picture: Translation, Languages, and Schemes

Ethical language, like all language, can be viewed from a number of different perspectives. We can consider the ends it can be made to serve, the norms that constrain its proper use, or the concepts it can express.[20] We can think of it as growing and changing through time, or as an abstract system of relationships at a particular point in time. The picture of incommensurability that I will sketch in this section draws on all these perspectives. In order to show how these different aspects of language relate to one another, I initially need to distinguish three concepts: *language-in-use*, *conceptual scheme*, and *discourse*.

*Language-in-use* is language viewed as a social practice engaged in by groups of people.[21] English, which has been spoken and written by certain groups for hundreds of years, is one example. Like many complex social practices, language-in-use is a difficult concept to define precisely. Languages-in-use are not individuated by particular sets of structural characteristics. It is evident that the vocabulary, grammar, and pronunciation of English, for example, have changed over time without the language ceasing to be English. Social perception is one useful criterion of identity: what do people count as instances of the same language? Different languages-in-use are not mutually intelligible, but only when applied in highly artificial conditions can we use mutual intelligibility to individuate languages-in-use. It is impossible, for instance, to put Confucius and Aristotle together in a room and test to see if they understand one another, since they have both been dead for more than two thousand years. Even when we are able to test two people, if they only partially understand one another, it remains ambiguous whether they speak the same language-in-use and we would have to fall back on social perception.

A very different perspective on language is that afforded by the *conceptual scheme*, or simply *scheme*. Schemes are abstractions: snapshots of all the things that can be said in a language at a given point in time. A scheme is expressed by a language-in-use, which means that the scheme gives an accounting of all the sentences that are "up for grabs as true or false"[22] in a particular language at a particular time. A scheme does not, in other words, primarily tell me what's true (for instance, that dogs bark); it tells me instead that my language contains the concepts *dog* and *bark*, and that I can say, among many other things, both "Dogs bark" and "Dogs don't bark."[23]

The conceptual scheme stresses the formal, systematic character of language. The *discourse*, in contrast, focuses our attention on the concrete purposes to which languages-in-use are put. A discourse is a particular arena of language use. Examples are political discourse, ethical or moral discourse, religious discourse, aesthetic discourse, scientific discourse, and biological discourse. Some discourses, as this list makes evident, are sub-sets of others. In each case, language use is combined with other activities in the pursuit of one or more goals. These goals, along with the goals of higher-level discourses and the standards recognized within the relevant discourses, constrain what is said and otherwise done within any given discourse.

I will elaborate on different facets of each of these three perspectives on language as I proceed through this section and the next. Before doing that, though, I need to introduce one final set of terms: *incommensurable* and *incommensurate*. Instead of making *incommensurable* into a vague, all-purpose term, applicable to languages, words, and conceptual scheme alike, I strive for more precision by separating out two notions. I will say that two languages-in-use are *incommensurate* if and only if concepts expressible in one cannot be expressed, at a particular point in time, in the other. Two conceptual schemes, in contrast, are *incommensurable* if and only if concepts expressible by one cannot be expressed in the other. The difference between the two notions turns on the fact that languages-in-use, being dynamic social practices, can change without losing their identity, while conceptual schemes, being momentary abstractions, cannot change without becoming new conceptual schemes. Two languages-in-use can be incommensurate at one time and not at another, but if two schemes are incommensurable they are always incommensurable. Whenever the conceptual schemes expressed by two different languages-in-use are incommensurable, the languages-in-use are incommensurate. Two incommensurate languages-in-use can become commensurate, therefore, only if the scheme expressed by one or both of the languages changes.

One final complication of my picture is prompted by situations like that faced, according to MacIntyre, by Galileo and his Aristotelian rivals: two incommensurable schemes within one and the same language-in-use. The same situation results, as I said above, from an attempt to add Confucian ethical terminology to Aristotelian Greek. The explanation of this possibility lies in seeing that a *fragment* of a given language-in-use corresponds to each discourse in which speakers of the language engage. Corresponding to culinary discourse, for instance, are all the terms—both common and specialized—that are used in the buying, selling, cooking, and consuming of food. It should be apparent that the contents of various language fragments can overlap, or even be subsets of larger fragments. As long as a particular discourse is fairly isolated, one language-in-use might contain two incommensurate fragments, each corresponding to that discourse. In such a situation there would be no single conceptual scheme expressed by the entire language-in-use; instead there would be two, largely overlapping schemes. The discourse in question must be isolated, in the sense that its terminology not permeate the language, because if the incommensurateness were more widespread, the mutual unintelligibility that would likely result between the two sets of speakers would suggest that what had been one language-in-use has now become two.

It should now be possible to clear up the relationship between translation and incommensurability. Confucian terms like "*li*" cannot be rendered in Aristotle's Greek because the concepts for which they stand are inexpressible in Aristotle's Greek as it stands: as MacIntyre points out, none of the terms that Aristotle would have had at his disposal, singly or in combination, can capture the same meaning.

How does MacIntyre know this? Ideally because he has learned both languages as what he calls second first languages, though in actuality MacIntyre is relying on the work of specialists for his information about Confucianism. Based on his understandings of the two languages/conceptual schemes, there is no way to express the content of a Chinese sentence containing "*li*," among other terms, with a corresponding Greek sentence.[24]

MacIntyre does say quite a lot in English, of course, about both the Confucian and the Aristotelian ethical systems. Does this mean that Confucian Chinese and Aristotelian Greek are at least commensurate with English, even if they are not commensurate with each other? If not, how could MacIntyre tell us so much about them in English? I believe, though I will not argue for it now, that neither Confucian Chinese nor Aristotelian Greek is commensurate with English. The answer to the apparent puzzle that results lies in seeing that MacIntyre is not, in fact, writing only in English. He uses numerous romanized terms like *ren* and *li*, *psyche* and *telos*. He uses these words not simply for effect, but because he believes he could not express the proper relation between the relevant Greek concepts or Chinese concepts any other way (short of writing entirely in Greek or Chinese). Although most of the words and the whole grammatical structure of the language in which he writes belong to English, that is, he is not writing any English familiar to his audience, but rather endeavoring to teach them the Confucian and Greek ethical systems in hybrid languages, English-Greek and English-Chinese.

I have already explained why simply dumping a whole set of new words into Greek, each corresponding to a problematic Chinese term, will not allow us to overcome the incommensurability between the two conceptual schemes, but merely shifts it to an incommensurateness between two competing fragments of Greek. This does not mean, however, that incommensurateness is a permanent relation. It can be overcome so long as speakers of one or the other of the incommensurate languages-in-use are willing to revise their languages. If we reinterpret one of Thomas Kuhn's famous examples of scientific incommensurability to mesh with the picture I am developing, we would conclude that the scientific fragment of Joseph Priestly's language was incommensurate with Lavoisier's. English sentences concerned with phlogiston and other related terms could not be expressed—were not candidates for truth or falsity—in Lavoisier's French. English natural philosophers who came to speak of oxygen and the like in lieu of phlogiston had revised their language-in-use, making it commensurate with Lavoisier's. If Aristotelians, Confucians, or both were willing to make revisions in a similar spirit, then their ethical languages might become commensurate.

What, then, of Davidson's argument that translation is always possible? Davidson essentially believes that a language's sentences can always be translated into sentences with the same propositional content in any other sufficiently rich language, and furthermore that there are no limits, at least *in principle*, on how languages can be enriched or revised. I will refer to this idea as the Accessibility of Content Principle, which can be summarized as:

> Any sentence in a language L is in principle translatable into a sentence with the same propositional content in any language L'.

The Principle says, in essence: yes, two languages can be incommensurate, but that has little theoretical significance, since this incommensurateness can always be overcome *in principle*.

We should first note that MacIntyre, like some others who have turned this argument to their own purposes, ignores the extent to which Davidson (often only implicitly, I admit) acknowledges that real change may be necessary for one language to be able to translate another.[25] Be that as it may, MacIntyre is right that Davidson has long been perceived as no friend of incommensurability.[26] Davidson has written that incommensurabilism "is a heady and exotic doctrine, or would be if we could make good sense of it. The trouble is, as so often in philosophy, it is hard to improve intelligibility while retaining the excitement."[27]

In approaching incommensurability, I have decided to strive for intelligibility at the risk of losing some of the excitement. By shifting my focus from incommensurable languages to incommensurate ones, I have removed any incompatibility between my theory and the Accessibility of Content Principle. As far as I can tell, the Principle will be true for at least the vast majority of cases, including every case that we humans have encountered so far. The Principle might have exceptions, for instance if we discover a species with which we can communicate about many topics, but which has a hard-wired inability to conceive of certain other things that we talk about.[28] At least for the time being, this sort of exception has no bearing on relations between the ethical languages with which we are concerned, and thus no current bearing on ethical pluralism. For the purposes of this essay, therefore, I will treat the Principle as true.

## Discourses and their Constraints

Davidson would say that by granting that two languages can never be incommensurable, I have drained the excitement out of the idea. I believe he would be wrong. The key to seeing that incommensurateness remains important despite the Principle lies in unpacking the Principle's *in principle* proviso. The most common explication of this proviso is that practical concerns like insufficient time, ingenuity, or contact with speakers of the target language are excluded from consideration. Incommensurateness would indeed be uninteresting if all it meant was that speakers of one language simply hadn't had enough time to figure out how to express another language's sentences. I will refer to this sort of practical consideration as a *fieldwork constraint*.

Fieldwork constraints are not the only type of practical limitations that the proviso idealizes away. The Principle relies on the proviso to ensure that a language-in-use can be changed in any way necessary. What would happen, though, if speakers of the language were uninterested in changing their language, or were positively opposed to the changes that would be needed to express some new content? Unlike an abstract conceptual scheme, recall, a language-in-use is a social practice that communities engage in for concrete purposes. Suppose these purposes are not served by the linguistic changes required to overcome incommensurateness?

I will call this second kind of practical limitation a *discourse constraint*, since the individual or communal goals, which could hinder change, are parts of the various discourses in which we use language. Discourse constraints cannot be dismissed quite as rapidly as fieldwork constraints, for the sources of discourse constraints can be deeply rooted in a culture. Wilhelm von Humboldt, a pioneering student of non-Western languages, wrote more than 150 years ago that "[e]very language would be able to indicate everything, if the people it belongs to were to traverse every stage of their culture."[29] I reject the teleology built into Humboldt's picture, but the remark is perceptive nonetheless. The expressive capacity of a language-in-use is constrained by the culture of the language's speakers, and changing a culture is often no simple matter. Despite the truth of the Principle, the importance of discourse constraints makes incommensurateness important. In the remainder of this section, I will examine two types of discourse constraints: *discourse-governing norms* and *purposes*.

## Discourse-Governing Norms

Some discourses, like the moral or the aesthetic, have as their subject matter certain types of norms. "Do not inflict unnecessary pain" is an example from moral discourse. I will call such an injunction a *simple norm*. A norm becomes *discourse-governing* when it functions to regulate additional discourses. Epistemic norms, for instance, concern the standards to which we ought to adhere when deciding what to believe: do we accept something because it is asserted in a newspaper, or do we need more evidence? How do we judge scientific theories? What makes for a good judge of character? These questions are part of epistemic discourse, and relative to that discourse, their answers are first-order norms. Many other discourses, though, take the deliverances of epistemic discourse more-or-less for granted. A practicing scientist, for instance, rarely steps back to ask herself whether the fact that her theory accounts for all known data and is supported by repeatable experiments should give her confidence that the theory is true; rather, she accepts these norms as guiding her scientific practice and discourse. Many cultures' ethical discourses are also regulated by discourse-governing epistemic norms. It is a commonplace in our culture, for instance, that for one to make a fair moral judgment, one must take care to weigh competing interests carefully. If I were to object to a proposed tax plan as unjust because it increased my burden more than it did others', for instance, I could be judged to have violated relevant epistemic norms if I failed to take into account that others had previously borne a disproportionate burden.

A recent analysis of the roles that discourse-governing norms can play in both intra- and inter-cultural ethical disputes is Allan Gibbard's discussion of normative objectivity in *Wise Choices, Apt Feelings*. In one example, he imagines himself arguing with an "ideally coherent anorexic" who believes that it "makes sense to starve herself to death for the sake of a trim figure."[30] Now suppose the anorexic were to challenge the epistemic basis for Gibbard's conviction that her course of action is irrational. Gibbard writes that:

> I of course can issue the same challenge to her, and the mutual challenges may do nothing to advance the conversation. They may be met with mutual dogmatism. Or instead they may undermine the confidence of both of us, leaving us normative skeptics. They may, on the other hand, allow for some further assessment of our opposing normative claims. She, after all, can lay claim to one special source of normative authority: it is she who is living her life; it is she who experiences what it is really like to be in her circumstance. I must answer this epistemological argument with one that favors my own normative authority, or else I must give up the claim I have been asserting. This may in the end not resolve our fundamental disagreement, but then again it might.[31]

How might the disagreement be resolved? If Gibbard comes to realize that the anorexic has a convincing story she can tell explaining how she knows that she's being rational, and he has no such story for himself, he might give in. He might grant, in other words, that the discourse-governing norms that he accepts as regulating his discussion of rationality do not give him grounds for rejecting this particular anorexic's claim to be rational. Not to give in would be dogmatic, since it would mean refusing to grant the anorexic epistemic legitimacy, despite the fact that she meets all the requirements of his own epistemic norms.

This is not to imply that dogma has no place in debates between discourses. As Gibbard points out, "[d]ogma has a price. Ordinarily it ends discussion. One can be baldly dogmatic toward someone only if one is willing to dispense with him as a discussant."[32] Sometimes groups may be willing to pay these prices. Or they may find different ways to exclude others, short of mere dogmatism. They may be able to explain to their own satisfaction why members of the different group are poor normative judges, even if they fail to convince those others. This can happen, for instance, when two groups' epistemic norms differ. Consider what might happen if MacIntyre's Aristotelians tried to convince the Confucians to abandon judging things in terms of what the Aristotelians might term "your so-called *li*." Supposing that enough of the non-ethical fragments of their languages were not incommensurate, they might be able to debate this idea without the Aristotelians being able to "accurately represent"—recall that MacIntyre thought this necessary— *li* in their language.

The epistemic norms to which the Confucians might appeal in order to justify or explain the importance of *li* would include belief in the words of the sages, both as recorded in the various Classics and as confirmed by the spontaneous reactions of properly-trained contemporary Confucians. Aristotelians might insist on reasoning from certain first principles which are necessary for objectivity, an objectivity which, MacIntyre says, "is already itself understood in a specifically Aristotelian way as both presupposing and employing formal and teleological principles alien to many rival modes of thought."[33] Whether or not these differing epistemic notions would be incommensurate themselves, the result of this debate is almost sure to be inconclusive.

Had the discussion led the two groups to discover that they shared epistemic norms, the result might have been to put pressure on one or both to revise their ethical languages, or else perhaps to recognize that under their different social and physical environments, the same epistemic norms lead to different ethical norms.[34] Either outcome might have been enough to allow them to engage in further trade, debate, or whatever it was that brought them together in the first place. An inconclusive result, though, would tend to lessen or even sever mutual interaction, just like a thoroughly dogmatic response. I noted above that Gibbard has suggested that we might be unwilling to settle for such results due to the costs or prices that would have to be paid. I now want to look at the issue of costs more carefully. We will see that not only can costs sometimes drive us together, but they can also serve to keep us apart.

## Purposes

Discourses are carried on within particular *institutional contexts*, and these contexts make available a variety of *purposes* for which one might engage in a given discourse. In its narrowest sense, for instance, scientific discourse is carried on in labs and conferences among professional researchers; if we speak more broadly, we will see scientific discourse in newspaper articles and in discussions between non-specialists (like philosophers), in children's television shows and in high school biology classes. In similar fashion, the contexts in which we find ethical or moral discussion in our society also vary widely. Moral considerations are debated in courts, and so become intertwined with legal discourse. Morality is taught in churches, in homes, and in schools. It is invoked in political discussions, and it is dissected in philosophical journals.

With different settings come different purposes that participation in a discourse might promote. A recent *Los Angeles Times* article on the challenges atheists faced when raising children quoted several members of the clergy insisting that the only justification for morality was God's will: without religious faith to back it up, they said, morality would degenerate into a terrible subjectivism. What purposes might be served by such an assertion? Decreasing the number of children that turn into moral degenerates, advancing the debate over "why be moral?" and bringing more people back to the church are a few of the possibilities. This last purpose might well further a clergyperson's ability to make a living, as well as to save souls; the first would improve social harmony. The second, which involves an academic debate, might be sought out of curiosity, desire for the truth, or desire to win professional esteem, among other reasons.

My point is not that hidden behind seemingly disinterested discussions of morality we find selfish motives, though that will sometimes be the case. My goal is rather to flesh out abstract talk of "costs": every discourse, including ethical discourse, involves concrete purposes that can be furthered or frustrated if the people engaging in the discourses choose to revise their language or the norms by which the discourse is constrained. How might the costs that can be associated with language revision work to keep Confucian ethical talk incommensurate with Aristotelian? The early Confucians were masters of the intricate rituals that had been tightly linked to the exercise of authority on all levels of the Shang and Zhou states. As the Zhou Kingdom disintegrated into several warring states, the central practical goal of Confucius and his followers came to be reuniting and re-harmonizing the land under a humane, ritually-proper leader. They developed an extensive philosophic explanation of the need of society for proper ritual (*li*). Their theorizing about *li* was no simple rationalization of their own importance to society, but profound philosophy—arguably of relevance even to the contemporary West.[35] At the same time, though, a revision of their ethical language such as to downplay the importance of *li* would have deprived them of much of their livelihood. Their concrete purposes, the discourse-governing norms to which their ethical discourse was subject, and their first-order ethical beliefs all tended to reinforce one another. It is thus no coincidence that they vigorously opposed the attempts of rivals like the Mohists and Legalists to remove *li* from the center of attention.

In order for two incommensurate ethical systems to reach the point that they actually can be compared, and one assessed in terms of the other, a very different process from the one MacIntyre envisions will have to take place. MacIntyre is correct to see that criticism internal to one system—often accompanied, to be sure, by various sorts of external stimuli—can induce people to look to other cultures' systems in search of answers. Incommensurateness must be overcome via linguistic revision, however, before real comparison can begin. I have discussed the case of Liang Qichao, an early twentieth-century Chinese intellectual, in considerable detail in other writings. Liang was driven to criticize the Chinese ethical tradition in part because of a strongly felt goal of saving his nationality from extinction. I have found that on the way to comparing the Confucian ethical tradition with various Western ethical theories, he reinterprets both so as to arrive at a hybrid system that is neither his original Chinese conceptual scheme, nor a completely Western one, in which both quasi-Confucian and quasi-Western concepts can be expressed. Although I cannot go into the details here, I show elsewhere that the sum of Liang's purposes and discourse-governing norms, many of which remain distinctly Confucian, have the result that the hybrid at which he arrives is much closer to the Chinese system with which he began than to the Western systems he studied.[36] In Liang's case, linguistic revision allowed him to overcome incommensurateness, but the discourse constraints of Confucian ethical discourse continued to make their presence felt nonetheless.

As far as MacIntyre's Confucians and Aristotelians are concerned, though, both very different discourse-governing norms and different purposes for engaging in ethical discourse make it likely that neither group would be willing to revise its ethical languages in such a way as to overcome the initial incommensurateness. Without some significant stimulus that changes this equation, the two languages are likely to remain incommensurate, with neither side able to express concepts central to the other's ethical thought, indefinitely. Even after acknowledging the truth of the Accessibility of Content Principle, that is, we are left with a version of incommensurability that, while not perhaps the exciting (and unintelligible) thesis that Davidson and others have taken themselves to be opposing, is nonetheless important to a fuller understanding of the role of language in our lives and cultures—and is quite possibly all that proponents of incommensurability have ever really wanted. In the final section of the essay, I will consider to what extent ethical pluralism can be said to follow from my understanding of incommensurability.

## The Tie to Pluralism

At the very beginning of this chapter, I defined ethical pluralism as the view that ethical systems were irreducibly plural. The terms of this definition need some clarification. Saying that ethical systems are plural, to begin with, is not the same as saying that adherents of one system cannot assess the conduct of adherents of another system. Recall the magnanimous Aristotelian who was criticized by a Confucian, despite the mutual incommensurateness of their ethical languages. We can agree that ethical systems are plural, in other words, without insisting on judging people only in their own terms.

Our next question is how to interpret the requirement that ethical systems be not just plural, but *irreducibly* plural. The irreducibility in question can be interpreted in more than one way. Are the systems in question to be thought of as abstractions, akin to my notion of conceptual scheme, or as embodied practices, more like my languages-in-use? Are they irreducible, in other words, in practice or in principle?

Since I have maintained that conceptual schemes can be mutually incommensurable, it follows that if ethical systems are modeled on such schemes, then they can be irreducible in principle. This is all the more true since abstractions of ethical systems would have to be considerably more narrowly-defined than the corresponding conceptual scheme, for the following reason: schemes, you may recall, are essentially lists of sentences that are potentially true or false. They tell us what words and sentences a given language has at its disposal. They don't tell us what is true and what is false. An ethical system, in contrast, will tell us that lying is wrong, not that it is either wrong or not wrong. Countless sentences and combinations of concepts that are countenanced by a given conceptual scheme, that is, will be ruled out by the ethical system to which it corresponds. If schemes can be incommensurable, therefore, then surely ethical systems can be as well. Since two incommensurable systems can never be completely compared to one another, we seem to have arrived at one version of irreducible pluralism.

It is not, however, a particularly interesting pluralism. Far more important and interesting are real ethical systems: not some abstraction from Confucianism at a particular moment, but Confucianism as it historically lived and breathed (and perhaps continues to live and breathe). Are the ethical systems of actual cultures, with their capacity to grow and change, irreducibly plural? With the move from static abstraction to dynamic reality, we move from potentially incommensurable relations to potentially incommensurate ones. It immediately follows that any pluralism that results must be practical rather than principled. If actual ethical systems are persistently plural, it is only because of contingent factors that could, at least in our imagination, be removed. Among the cultures that have interacted with one another and yet have incommensurate ethical languages, we can expect that discourse constraints have hindered commensuration. These cultures, we might say, demonstrate a modest kind of ethical pluralism: their ethical systems have proved to be irreducibly plural in practice.

Pluralism-in-practice seems particularly appropriate for ethics, which after all is concerned above all with practice—how we should act, what sorts of people we should become—much more than with theory. What are the practical implications of recognizing that we may well face pluralism-in-practice in today's world? The lesson of pluralism-in-practice is that ethical languages are tied together with other aspects of groups' cultures so as to be resistant to change. We can thus expect that the differences we now perceive between our own ethical system and other systems, and even those among the ethical systems of different sub-cultures within our country, will continue well into the future. Whether this diverse future will be a peaceful one depends on whether the norms of different groups' ethical systems include injunctions to be tolerant of peoples whose ethical systems persistently differ from their own.[37]

## Notes

1. See below for further discussion of *li*.

2. By ethical system, I mean any set of norms governing individual and inter-personal behavior that both (1) involves some notion of well-being or good life, and (2) is contrasted

by its users with selfishness or mere prudence. I discuss this definition in Stephen C. Angle, *Concepts in Context: A Study of Ethical Incommensurability*. Ann Arbor: University Microfilms; 1994, 3-5.

3. Ruth Benedict, *Patterns of Culture* (Boston: Houghton Mifflin, 1934), 223.

4. Alasdair MacIntyre, "Incommensurability, Truth, and the Conversation between Confucians and Aristotelians about the Virtues," in *Culture and Modernity*, ed. Eliot Deutsch (Honolulu: University of Hawaii Press, 1991), 104-122.

5. As I explain in Part II, the argument MacIntyre discusses here is quite different from Davidson's actual argument in Donald Davidson, "On The Very Idea of a Conceptual Scheme," in Donald Davidson, *Inquiries Into Truth and Interpretation* (Oxford, U.K.: Clarendon Press, 1984), 183-198.

6. MacIntyre 1991, 114.

7. See Alasdair MacIntyre, *Whose Justice? Which Rationality?* (Notre Dame: University of Notre Dame Press, 1988), ch. 19 and "Relativism, Power, and Philosophy." in *Relativism: Interpretation and Confrontation*, ed. Michael Krausz (Notre Dame: University of Notre Dame Press, 1989), 182-204, especially section 4.

8. MacIntyre 1988, 377, 384.

9. MacIntyre 1989, 193-4.

10. MacIntyre 1991, 115.

11. For those familiar with Saul Kripke's argument that the meanings of proper names cannot contain descriptive content, MacIntyre makes the following response: "What this argument shows is, not that the names of persons do not or cannot have informational content, but that either they lack such content or it is true of them that their use presupposes commitment to a belief, such that were this belief discovered to be false, the name would not continue to be used in the same way." MacIntyre 1988, 377. For Kripke, see Saul Kripke, *Naming and Necessity* (Cambridge, Mass.: Harvard University Press, 1980), Lecture One, 61-2 and passim.

12. On "styles of reasoning," see Ian Hacking, "Language, Truth, and Reason." in *Rationality and Relativism*, Martin Hollis and Steven Lukes, eds. (Cambridge, Mass: MIT Press, 1982), 48-66; that texts do not interpret themselves is of course one of Wittgenstein's most important lessons.

13. MacIntyre 1991, 111.

14. MacIntyre 1991, 111.

15. MacIntyre 1991, 117.

16. MacIntyre 1991, 117.

17. Davidson would reject this approach out of hand, since his holistic approach to the theory of meaning will not countenance terms' having atomistic references and meanings. I will discuss a different kind of enrichment, more congenial to Davidson, in Part II.

18. One important assumption that this picture requires is that the grammar of Chinese is not one of the sources of incommensurability. Some discussions of linguistic relativity tend toward the opposite position, for instance, by suggesting that Chinese has difficulty expressing counterfactuals—Alfred Bloom, *The Linguistic Shaping of Thought: A Study in the Impact of Language on Thinking in China and the West* (Hillsdale, N.J.: Lawrence Erlbaum Associates, 1981). Even if this is true—and Bloom's evidence is spotty at best—though, it does not by itself have the consequence that Chinese is incommensurable with English or with Greek. At most, Bloom shows that some things are easier to express in English than in Chinese, but these things are nonetheless expressible in Chinese without any linguistic innovation. Incommensurability thus is not at issue.

19. This is not to suggest that "actions" are pure, empirical data, nor that "observation" is somehow language neutral. Confucians might not see an action where Aristotelians do, but I presume that most of the time they will, even if they disagree vehemently about what action it was.

20. Some philosophers have argued that ethical language differs considerably from other types of language, even to the extent of not expressing propositional content. In Angle 1994, ch. 2, I argue that while ethics might have an unusual metaphysics and epistemology, its semantics is quite ordinary.

21. MacIntyre employs the term "language-in-use" in a somewhat similar way; see MacIntyre 1988, ch. XIX.

22. The phrase, though not the understanding of conceptual scheme, is Ian Hacking's; see Hacking 1982.

23. Conceptual schemes will, of course, tell us what is conceptually true, although according to my definition of conceptual scheme, this may be limited to (1) facts about logic and (2) trivial facts about the language to which the conceptual scheme is related, such as "it is conceptually true that: 'snow is white' is true in English if and only if snow is white."

24. This assertion deserves much more discussion than either MacIntyre gives it or I have time for. While it is easy to demonstrate with simple, artificial languages that one such language can be unable to express concepts contained in another, proving that natural languages can exhibit similar failures is far more complex, and depends on which semantic theory one accepts as the best for modeling the conceptual contents of natural languages. For an extended discussion based on Davidsonian semantics, see Angle 1994, ch. 4.

25. Steven Lukes and Martin Hollis, for instance, persistently interpret Davidson as believing that we must attribute some particular "core of beliefs" to others if we are to find them explicable. This (as they also point out) is actually their own argument, which they incorrectly read into Davidson. See, e.g., Steven Lukes, "Relativism in its Place." in *Rationality and Relativism*, eds. Martin Hollis and Steven Lukes (Cambridge, Mass.: MIT Press, 1982), 261-305.

26. An earlier effort to make sense of incommensurability in Davidsonian terms is Chapter 9 of Ramberg, 1989. Ramberg's account is insightful and I have learned much from him. We part company, though, when it comes to elucidating how incommensurability can explain breakdowns of communication: Ramberg believes this is a matter of the disruption of our "linguistic conventions" (130) while I resist appeal to conventions and instead turn to discourse constraints—like Davidson; see "A Nice Derangement of Epitaphs." in *Truth and Interpretation: Perspectives on the Philosophy of Donald Davidson.* Ernest LePore, ed. (Oxford, U.K.: Basil Blackwell, 1986), 433-446. For an excellent argument, very much in the Davidsonian spirit, against relying on "linguistic conventions" in our analyses, see also Robert Brandom, *Making It Explicit: Reasoning, Representing, and Discursive Commitment* (Cambridge, MA: Harvard University Press, 1994).

27. Donald Davidson, *Inquiries Into Truth and Interpretation* (Oxford, U.K.: Clarendon Press, 1984), 283.

28. This type of exception was suggested to me by Brian Loar.

29. Wilhelm von Humboldt, *On Language: The Diversity of Human Language-Structure and Its Influences on the Mental Development of Mankind*, trans. Peter Heath (Cambridge: Cambridge University Press, 1988), 157.

30. Allan Gibbard, *Wise Choices, Apt Feelings* (Cambridge, Mass.: Harvard University Press, 1990), 192.

31. Gibbard 1990, 193.

32. Gibbard 1990, 197.

33. MacIntyre 1991, 108-9.

34. Although he doesn't discuss the possibility that the first-order norms in question might be incommensurable, Gibbard does point out the possibility that the same epistemic norms might, in different environments, yield different first-order norms; he terms it "relativism." See 1990, 208-211.

35. See, e.g., Herbert Fingarette, *Confucius—The Secular as Sacred* (New York: Harper & Row, 1972) and Roger T. Ames and David L Hall, *Thinking Through Confucius* (Albany, N.Y.: State University of New York Press, 1987).

36. See Angle 1994, chs. 3 and 5.

37. My thanks to Michael Barnhart and Samuel Fleischacker for their astute and generous comments on an earlier draft of this essay, and to Manyul Im for first suggesting that I distinguish between "incommensurable" and "incommensurate."

## *Chapter Six*

# The Moral Interpretation of Culture


## Samuel Fleischacker


I have argued in a number of places that "culture" should be regarded as a moral posit.[1] I mean by this to agree with hermeneutical social scientists like Clifford Geertz that the existence of "cultures" should be regarded as an interpretive assumption, a notion that precedes and shapes how we read sociological data rather than a "brute fact" to be read off from such data,[2] but to disagree with the reasons they offer for *why* we might make such an assumption. They tend to argue that the need leading us to posit "cultures" is an empirical one, that the notion is essential to doing proper descriptive work in the social sciences. But nothing like adequate evidence has yet shown that the hermeneutic, symbol-based approach to the social sciences they favor leads to better predictions of human behavior than carefully conducted research based on behavioral, sociobiological or other positivistic approaches.[3] Moreover, even if such hermeneutical programs should turn out, in general, to produce a successful kind of human science, it is doubtful whether the term "culture," in particular, will long remain a useful part of those programs. "Culture" is probably the most deeply contested term currently used in the social sciences, and the one most compromised by moral and political agendas; one may reasonably expect that even hermeneutically-oriented social scientists will one day want to do without it.[4] By contrast, positing the existence of "cultures" is essential to a variety of good moral projects, in my view. This is a controversial claim, but I am afraid my object in this chapter is not really to defend it—just to spell out more clearly what it means. What are the implications, especially for the debate between liberal individualists on the one hand, and communitarians on the other hand, of treating "culture" as a posit rather than an empirical fact, of treating cultures, not as something whose existence we can know but as something whose existence it is morally valuable to assume?

To say that the term "culture" is a moral one is to say that those who introduced it did so for moral purposes, and that it serves primarily moral purposes for those who have used it since. I don't mean to deny that the posit of a "culture" may on occasion be useful for purely descriptive purposes. Sometimes neither the interaction between general biological drives and an individual's environment, nor such super-individual entities as "religions," "states," or "societies," will provide as simple and successfully predictive an explanation of human behavior as an approach that makes use of "cultures." When we find Jews and Christians in India kissing icons or bringing a plate of nuts, sweets, and rose petals into their ceremonies, it makes the most sense to see this as a matter of Jews, Christians, and Hindus here sharing a "culture" rather than a "religion," let alone (merely) a political or social structure. And it seems very difficult to draw anything like an adequate account of the phenomenon out of a mode of explanation that stays at the level of atomic individualism. But it is far from clear that this is more than a matter of convenience, that cultural modes of explanation will necessarily resist reduction, in the further progress of the social sciences, to a more individualistic model, or at least to a simpler social model. It is on moral grounds, not empirical ones, that people are likely to be horrified at the idea of abandoning the notion of "culture."

Now this line of thinking may incline one toward supposing that *all* the basic terms of explanation in social science serve moral rather than empirical purposes, and while that position has a certain plausibility, and respected defenders, I don't quite want to commit myself to it—and don't think I need to. For "culture," rather more than other ways of characterizing human groups, is particularly vulnerable to Occam's Razor when taken empirically, and has rather stronger moral overtones than those alternative characterizations. To be a "culture," rather than merely a "society," a human group must pass down a distinctive symbolic system over time, and significantly influence the behavior of its members thereby. But the ideas a) that the meanings of symbols can be grouped together into cohesive and distinguishable systems, b) that a given system of meaning might be especially or solely accessible to one group of people rather than another, and c) that such a system can influence the behavior of individual human beings in ways irreducible to nonsymbolic forces, have all been under fierce attack throughout their entire history: first from behaviorists, then from Davidsonian philosophers of language, and most recently from deconstructionists. More deeply, the last assumption in particular, and perhaps the entire notion of integrated "symbol systems" running through all three assumptions, depends on a view of human beings as being able freely to create a symbolic universe for themselves—as, in Ernst Cassirer's terms, "symbol-making creatures."[5] It is hard to see how symbol systems can be understood as having an influence on us irreducible to material determination, let alone why that influence should be given so much importance, unless they are seen as some sort of expression of freedom. And if freedom is impossible to discern empirically, if it is something that appears real to us only as a presupposition of morality—as, following Kant, I presume—then "culture," if it is an expression of freedom, must similarly appear real to us only when our thinking is directed toward moral ends.

There is of course a bit of a paradox here. Surely we are *given*, we are *born into*, our cultures—that is precisely the feature of cultural belonging that most appeals to those who defend cultures. How then can they be seen as expressions of freedom in the Kantian sense? Do I want to say that individuals *choose* their cultures? Well, in part I do want to say precisely that. In the most straightforward sense, the choices of individuals have shaped cultures all through history: by way of the decision of some individuals to migrate, intermarry, or convert, or to join sects and rebellious movements within their culture; by way of the decision of other individuals, faced with similar opportunities, *not* to migrate, intermarry, join a sect, etc.; and by way of the decision of every individual to pursue the culture s religious, political, and other practices fervently or lackadaisacally, honestly or hypocritically, conservatively or with innovations, in accordance with this local authority or that one, in accordance with this local tradition or that one.[6] At the same time, however, I do not want to transform cultures into something fully a product of individual choices. A culture constitutes a *horizon for* choice, rather than a *result of* choices, but I will suggest that even the nonrational constraints imposed by cultural norms can be understood as a contribution to freedom, if and insofar as an individual endorses the existence of such constraints, endorses the very way in which they set limits to his or her autonomy. This latter claim is of course more than a little odd, especially in the context of a Kantian approach to morality. I will defend it later (section III); for the moment, I want merely to register that I recognize the important sense in which cultures are given to us rather than controlled by us, and that I will have something to say about how even that aspect of culture can enhance, not detract from, our freedom.

As my references to Kant suggest, I am treating "culture" as a posit of a broadly *liberal* approach to morality. This fits its entrance into moral and political thought surprisingly well. The notion was invented or discovered by late eighteenth and early nineteenth century thinkers (above all, Herder, Burke, and Hegel) who objected, from a position more or less within the Enlightenment project associated with Voltaire and Kant, to the thin notion of individual selves they saw around them, to the notion that results when one ignores the ways in which selves are enmeshed in social networks.[7] Culture is thus introduced by people who launched much the same critique of liberal individualism that is now being heard from the so-called "communitarians"—as one such figure, Charles Taylor, has often indicated.[8] The modern and the earlier communitarians, moreover, have similar moral reasons both for their critique of liberal individualism and for their residual attachment to liberal values. They believe that liberal individualism a) promotes a peculiarly human kind of misery that comes of isolation from other members of the species, and b) weakens the social framework providing the psychological underpinnings for individual responsibility. These are liberal reasons for opposing liberalism, and the critics who advance them usually also have liberal suspicions of traditional religious communities as oppressive and xenophobic, and traditional religious belief as based heavily on superstition. They promote "cultures," therefore, as a kind of naturalistic, flexible substitute for religions, as a species of community whose legitimacy is not contingent on the truth of a supernaturalist doctrine, is compatible with the equal legitimacy of other, similar communities, and is of a kind that can provide grounds for resisting, rather than going along with, oppressive authority structures.

That Herder has such a moral program behind his notion of culture is obvious. Herder is committed to the importance of cultures insofar as he wants the Enlightenment to recognize the rich emotional, social, and historical circumstances in the context of which individual capacities get developed, but at the same time he clearly recognizes the dangers of (a) xenophobic prejudices,[9] (b) clerical and other sacralized sources of authority,[10] and c) closed, static systems of belief.[11] Accordingly, he describes cultures as, and urges them to be, constantly striving, constantly "in progress" (Bunge, 45). He also urges his own particular community—the world of European Christianity, which he served in his capacity as a Lutheran pastor and an editor of hymnals and catechisms, as well as in his capacity as a philosopher—to reform itself in many ways: to educate its pastors better, to rethink its philosophical basis,[12] to place more emphasis on heartfelt commitment in its ceremonies, and to open itself more widely to toleration for Jews and other non-Christians (Bunge, 30-31). He is a defender of the separation of church and state, and an admirer of and participant in the program of Biblical criticism that had been opened up by Lessing.[13] In short, Herder looks for, and, perhaps over-optimistically, tries to discern in history, a world of progressive, self-critical, uncoercive, and tolerant cultures. He is not a conservative who endorses folkways simply *as is*, but a proponent of "enlightened" or "reformed" folkways—a prophet of Enlightenment to cultures as well as of cultures to the Enlightenment.

Similarly, by describing what used to be called "religions," first as "peoples" *(Völker),* and then as "cultures,"[14] many writers in the late eighteenth and early nineteenth century tried to distinguish what they liked about everyday modes of faith and practice from the oppressive, stodgy, and often corrupt institutions of organized religion, as well as from both the bad philosophy and the folk superstitions that they, like other Enlightenment thinkers, condemned in much of the Christianity they saw around them. The ideas out of which the notion of culture arose are products of the "Counter-Enlightenment," which constitutes a polemic against the Enlightenment's tendency to dismiss the sentiments, folkways, and informal beliefs by which ordinary people guide their lives,[15] but is also an offshoot of the Enlightenment itself. Jacobi, Hamann, Herder and the like *shared* the suspicion of Hume, Kant, and Voltaire toward standard philosophical defenses of religion.[16] And they did not share the unquestioned acquiescence in the beliefs of one's society, let alone the unquestioned trust in church authorities, characteristic of uneducated and unintellectual religious believers. Their anti-intellectual faith came *after* argument, was proffered to those who had already tried, and rejected, the route to religious commitment through argument. Jacobi and Hamann loved Hume because they thought Hume's arguments against religion made for a purer faith.[17] This is hardly the stance of the average churchgoer, who tends to think that his faith is underwritten by good arguments even if he does not quite grasp those arguments himself. Herder describes the inability of members of a *Volk* to think outside the "circle" of that *Volk*'s conceptions;[18] the members of the *Volk* themselves, however, do not normally see their conceptions as just "theirs." They tend to think instead that their "circle of conceptions" is a circle of the *right* conceptions. Indeed, they do not generally see the ways of their culture as "ways of a culture" at all, at least insofar as those ways comprise more than trivialities like cuisine. Rituals, attitudes toward the afterlife, ways of showing deference, and the like are generally seen as having some intrinsic importance, even as being the right, or the best, such rituals and attitudes for any human being to have. They are not seen as merely "folkways" except by those who try, from outside, to respect the insiders without themselves sharing the beliefs or practices in question.

So to see a culture *as* a culture at all involves a certain re-interpretation of what the culture is. "Cultures" are enlightened religions—religions that emphasize practice over doctrine, that view their doctrines as flexible and open to moral improvement, that have loosened the bonds of sacral hierarchies to make room for a more or less libertarian and egalitarian community of believers, and that try to work against their own tendencies toward xenophobia. To see all human communities as, essentially and ideally, cultures is to re-interpret those communities such that they are, in essence at least, compatible with liberalism.[19] On the cultural interpretation of communities, the beliefs and practices of those communities do not have to conflict, as at first sight they seem to do,[20] they can readily adapt themselves to modernity, and the ways of life they offer can be chosen freely by their individual members rather than imposed upon them. Cultures become a natural revelation of divinity—of a divinity that prizes human creativity and freedom—and they are seen to reveal the divine precisely in their variety, rather than in the truths that just one or a few of them might possess.[21]

This moral meaning of "culture" comes out especially clearly when we contrast the term with "race" and "nation," two words that track much the same groups. "Race" was originally used as almost an exact synonym for what we now call "culture"—Wynne writes of "the British race" (1600), Pope of "Troy's whole race" (1715)—or, when it was used biologically, referred to the whole of humankind: "the human race."[22] Over the past two centuries, however, it has increasingly become identified with supposed biological divisions within the human species.[23] Now, how useful these genetic markers are in distinguishing "Negroid," "Caucasian" and "Mongoloid" peoples is a question of some controversy among contemporary biologists, but even if there are, it is important that such groups are constituted by factors independent of people's choices. Choice will not make a person a "Caucasian," and choice cannot remove that status. It is difficult to conceive how something so entirely independent of choice can have any moral importance, at least within a liberal understanding of what morality is.[24]

"Nation" is a term for a kind of group identity that is more readily seen as a matter of choice, but the choices involved are by now generally understood as having specifically political implications.[25] Like "race", the term originally was used in much the way "culture" is now used—to designate the community into which one was born, whether or not that community had any claim to political autonomy[26]—but it has acquired specifically political connotations over the past two centuries.[27] To call a group a "nation" is standardly to say that it has a right to a state of its own. It neither follows from such a claim that the group has a way of life relevant to ordinary moral decisions, nor that anyone might be obligated by or drawn to such a way of life, if it does. And the claim to nationhood is addressed normally to other states, to political powers that currently either govern the people one believes should be included in one's nation or control the land in which one wants one's nation to be established. Insofar as the claim is addressed at all to one's fellow nationals, it is only meant to motivate them to participate in the struggle for statehood, not to affect any other aspects of their daily lives.

On the narrative I have been telling—and it is not a particularly controversial one—the term "culture" came to its present use during exactly the same period, and out of exactly the same nexus of historical factors, that gave rise to the modern meanings of "nation" and "race." Of the three, "culture" is clearly the one most relevant to individual moral decisions. Insofar as we distinguish "culture" from "nation," we are concerned with norms that influence more than the political decisions of their adherents, and that are maintained by more than political force, and insofar as we distinguish "culture" from "race," we show that we are concerned with norms at all, with something that is not merely part of an individual's biological inheritance. Finally, insofar as we distinguish "culture" from "religion," we are concerned with norms whose influence over individuals is not conceived to be underwritten by an unquestionable divine "Word," that is not, indeed, dependent on any set of explicit beliefs. What all four terms share is a concern for antiquity and unreason, for the survival of groups of human beings in more or less the same form over many generations, and for ways of maintaining that identity that for the most part bypass reason. But the four terms by now pick out sharply different forces as the basis for this identity. "Culture," "nation" and "race" have separated themselves out, and divorced themselves from "religion,"[28] in tandem with the growing spread of liberalism across the world, and in connection with the debate, largely provoked by liberalism, over the twin questions, (1) are human beings first and foremost individual choosers or first and foremost members of communities? and (2) if the latter, what kind of communities? A little-noticed irony is that the variety of kinds of groups available to answer the second question—nations, races, cultures, religions—has helped make the kind of group one belongs to, now, a matter of individual choice. Which group is central to one's identity is generally understood to be a matter of which group one *identifies oneself* with.

This enables us to put the issue at stake between liberal individualists and defenders of "culture" in sharp terms. The word "culture," we have seen, is not a synonym for "community" but a designation for one specific *kind* of community. Following Cassirer, I have described this kind of community as marked by the possession and enactment of a "symbol system." In the rest of this chapter I will use the term, more precisely, for communities (1) united around symbols and symbolic practices that are passed down over several generations, (2) that are passed down by way of the role-modeling and implicit, unargued teaching by which parents bring up their children, as opposed to the explicit teaching characteristic of a philosophical school, and (3) that are passed down in conjunction with some sort of story, perhaps only an implicit one, about how these practices conduce to a good human life.[29] This characterization captures the core of the way the term has actually been used over the last two centuries, and brings out the way that it tracks many of the uses of "religion" while avoiding the supernaturalist underwriting associated with the latter term. The job of a defender of culture is to show the liberal individualist why *this* kind of community is essential to human happiness or freedom. I shall argue in section II that contemporary communitarians, who often take themselves to be defending cultures, do not succeed in meeting that objective. In section III, I will sketch a defense of culture that I think does better. I will close, in section IV, by suggesting that the best response liberal individualists can make to such an argument is to develop, in practice, liberal kinds of community that compete with, and could perhaps substitute for, cultural communities. The argument between liberalism and its culture-vaunting competitors can I believe not be settled, even in theory, by theory alone.

## II

Herder's moral project is very much alive today among nationalists, cultural relativists, and multiculturalists. For most writers on the subject, cultures still represent (a) liberating and admirable human achievements, (b) more a set of practices or creative products than a set of beliefs, and (c) systems that at least in principle can be brought into harmony with one another. The problem is that some of these claims seem false: cultures are not necessarily liberating and do, often, conflict. One good reason for this is precisely that cultures usually do not see themselves *as* just cultures, that they do not see themselves in the noncognitivist light in which theorists of culture like to portray them. The beliefs of most cultures cannot be sloughed off as so much unnecessary superstitious baggage, to make room for a core of practices meant to express faith in some sort of "God of variety." Cultural practices and creative achievements tend to be informed by an entire network of beliefs: such that the discovery that a culture, in its creation or national-founding myths, has gotten the facts of astronomy or history wrong is often enough to severely shake up its adherents confidence in it.

Similarly, the notion that people are or ought to be "liberated" has tended in practice to threaten the very continued existence of many traditional cultures, not merely to lead them to reform themselves, and the suggestion that cultures should get along harmoniously, rather than try to impose themselves upon one another, has often not sat well with the views that members of a culture take it to represent. Herder envisioned a world in which enlightenment could be blended neatly into the ongoing ways of life of each people, so that aboriginal peoples, Muslims, Jews, and everyone else could develop their own indigenous "Enlightenment cultures." The problem of having an indigenous Enlightenment appeared to him as just the problem that German intellectuals faced in trying to borrow the enlightened ideas of the French without yielding to Francophilic affectations.

And the Germans eventually managed, through the work of people like Lessing and Herder himself, to develop their own, indigenous enlightenment. Surely, Herder presumably felt, others could do the same. We know now that he was here too optimistic, that the grafting of "enlightenment" onto folkways is not always so easy.

Pointing to these problems is one way of bringing out the fact that the claim to "culture" is not innocuous. Attempting to preserve cultures can have real costs. Trying to settle whether Israelis or Palestinians, or Pakistanis or Baluchis, or Bosnians or Eritreans or Kurds have a right to have their cultures preserved—settling whether they so much as *constitute* a culture with a right to preservation—has been the occasion for some of the angriest, and often bloodiest, political debates of the past century. We may not worry as much about such costs here in the United States, since "culture" tends to mean little more than ethnic cuisine in this nation of immigrants.[30] But consider the kinds of arguments that take place, even in the U.S., when a son or daughter of many a Jewish, Chinese, or Korean family wants to "marry out." I personally have heard, among my Jewish friends and relatives, many iterations of both the "love-is-the-most-important-thing" line of argument and the "don't-grant-Hitler-a-posthumous-victory" counterargument. Given that many of the people who engage in these arguments do not believe in God, let alone in any of the more specific tenets of the Jewish religion, this is generally a debate precisely over whether the value of preserving Jewish *culture* is great enough that it should trump even the great importance of sharing one's life with a person one loves (and of course the cultural issues are at least as much at the core of analogous arguments in Chinese and Korean households). It is very difficult to see why a culture's survival should merit such passionate defense, to see what could possibly be so important about a symbol system that its preservation merits the sacrifice of romantic love.

The most general issue at stake in both the political and the family arguments over the importance of culture is the fact that cultures necessarily divide people. Sometimes they do other, worse things—oppress their members, justify slavery or mass murder—but they don't *necessarily* do those things. They do necessarily divide people, and such divisions are both a fertile breeding ground for the demonization of outsiders, and turf struggles, that underlie many wars, and a barrier to romantic and other friendly ties that might otherwise spring up between individuals. A liberal, a person who thinks that people should get along as free equals and that international peace is ultimately possible thereby, should therefore maintain a presumption against placing emphasis on people's cultural ties; a liberal should not amiably abide claims to the importance of culture as compatible with liberal dreams.[31]

I think it is only against the background of this cost to claims for the importance of culture that an honest and adequately qualified defense of those claims can be launched. Given the costs, it should indeed be surprising that anyone with liberal sympathies in moral and political philosophy wants to preserve cultures. Often, those who claim to have sympathy for cultures in fact wind up defending *community* rather than culture. Let us consider some of the arguments around today in defense of community, with an eye out for the difference between community and culture. (1) One important line of argument to be found among contemporary communitarians is that cultures are constitutive of the self, and/or of the goods, the values, that any self pursues. Michael Sandel, Alasdair MacIntyre, and Charles Taylor have all put forward versions of this point. Sandel puts it this way:

> (2) [W]e cannot regard ourselves as independent [of our aims and attachments] . . . without great cost to those loyalties and convictions whose moral force consists partly in the fact that living by them is inseparable from understanding ourselves as the particular persons we are—as members of this family or community or nation or people, as bearers of this history, as sons and daughters of that revolution, as citizens of this republic. . . . To imagine a person incapable of constitutive attachments such as these is not to conceive an ideally free and rational agent, but to imagine a person wholly without character, without moral depth. For to have character is to know that I move in a history I neither summon nor command, which carries consequences none the less for my choices and conduct. . . . As a self-interpreting being, I am able to reflect on my history and in this sense to distance myself from it, but the distance is always precarious and provisional, the point of reflection never finally secured outside the history itself.[32]

Now this is unquestionably a deep and deeply fascinating view, and to my mind has a great deal of plausibility. Indeed, my own position in *The Ethics of Culture* can be characterized pretty well by saying that cultures constitute the goods we seek. But I urge there that such a view must ultimately depend on a kind of faith. Sandel and Taylor, especially, and to a lesser extent MacIntyre, all seem to think that a strong rational *argument* for the view can be made out—that reasons can be offered for the view that should in principle persuade anyone willing to accept the most basic, most uncontroversial, principles of moral reasoning. I don't see how. At best, the view depends on the premises that there are "real" or "objective" moral goods to be sought (in the case of Taylor and MacIntyre), or that there is a rich, substantive self to be constituted (in Sandel's case): both highly contentious metaphysical propositions. At worst, the view is bound to the very liberal voluntarism it claims to oppose, depending for its appeal on the fact that many individuals prefer to see their search for goods in such a culturally-mediated light. There is a hint of that in the quotation from Sandel above. Sandel grants that we are "self-interpreting beings," which means that we are free, as the liberals would have it, to evaluate and possibly reject any of our attachments and aims. But he says that unless we see ourselves, in this interpretive process, as constituted by our history and community, we will lack "character" and "moral depth" To which we are presumably expected to respond: "Who would want *that*?!"—But if the point is just that none of us *wants* to be characterless and shallow, then Sandel's argument itself turns in the end on our atomistic, individual preferences.

(3) For reasons like these, Will Kymlicka rejects Sandel's, MacIntyre's, and Taylor's defenses of culture and community.[33] His own defense of culture, which has been widely followed in recent years, depends on the psychological fact that individuals need interaction with small communities in order to gain confidence and self-respect, that such interaction buttresses every individual's ability to make free choices, and to take responsibility for those choices. Without cultural ties, he claims, the "choice" central to liberalism will not even be possible:

> [I]t's only through having a rich and secure cultural structure that people can become aware, in a vivid way, of the options available to them, and intelligently examine their value. Without such a cultural structure, children and adolescents lack adequate role-models, which leads to despondency and escapism. . . . [C]ultural structure [should be] recognized *as a context of choice*, . . . as a primary good within Rawls's scheme of justice[34]

Similarly, Yael Tamir argues (using "nation" for what Kymlicka calls a "culture") that

> [m]embership in a nation is a constitutive factor of personal identity. The self-image of individuals is highly affected by the status of their national community. The ability of individuals to lead a satisfying life and to attain the respect of others is contingent on, although not assured by, their ability to view themselves as active members of a worthy community.[35]

"Choice" is socially conditioned, these writers say, and will be incompatible with people's ordinary psychological needs unless it takes place in the context of a community supporting the projects that individuals choose. Without denying the truth of this empirical claim, I would simply point out that they are inadequate to defend *cultures* in particular.[36] The moral advantages here attributed to community can be outweighed by very significant disadvantages, and we need to ask whether cultural communities are the best or the only kinds of communities in which individuals can find support for their choices. Participation in a community of some kind may be essential to choice, but could such communities not be more open and fluid, less bound by tradition and authority, than are cultures? A healthy liberalism might want to underwrite untraditional, liberal individualist communities as an *alternative* to cultures, to provide the means by which cultures can gradually, peaceably disappear.

Is "liberal individualist community" an oxymoron? I don't think so.[37] The American "voluntary associations" that Tocqueville praised so highly, and many of the communities envisaged or developed by urban planners and non-Marxist socialists, have tried (a) to create communities *out* of the choices of the individuals who enter them, and (b) to achieve a governing structure that, to various degrees, strikes a balance between individual choice and communal activity. A community designed to foster individualism is not a logical impossibility; the question is whether it is psychologically possible. And the argument of those communitarians who look specifically to cultures as the context for freedom is that the kind of communities that liberal individualists form—rationally planned, ahistorical communities—will not do the psychological job needed to support individuals in their free choices. Cultural communitarians insist that a community needs to be bound together by tradition and fate, needs to be a product of historical circumstance rather than deliberate planning, in order to provide its constituents with adequately concrete role-models and options.

So the issue is ultimately joined between *rationally constructed* kinds of community and cultural or traditionally passed-down kinds of community. But, as far as I am aware, there is very little empirical evidence for the proposition that traditional communities are psychologically healthier for their members than deliberately constructed, ahistorical ones. Community centers, neighborhood groups, garden cities, kibbutzim, and communes all provide people with some kind of community—and often as rich a community, in terms of emotional bonds, role models, and the other psychological goods that communitarians emphasize as any traditional community. But the pursuit of *such* communities is fully compatible with an effort to eradicate *cultures*. Indeed that is precisely what the important liberal Joseph Raz implicitly recommends in political theory,[38] and the kibbutz movement in Israel has stood for in political practice. The question about whether cultures play a crucial role in morality then comes down to the question of whether traditional communities have something to offer that untraditional, rationally structured communities do not. Of course, in many cases a planned community will be badly planned, and will look terrible in comparison with most traditional communities. But is there any reason to suppose that rationally set up communities must *inevitably* or *essentially* fail to offer what cultures can offer, that there is something about cultures that rational planning *cannot* provide?

(4) Well, one reason to think that there might be some such advantage to cultures is the important conservative point, made by writers from Burke to Hayek, that human planning is always hubristic, that planners inevitably overlook small but crucial details about how people live, such that the ways of life they come up with turn out to be oppressive or miserable for those who actually live in them. Thus Le Corbusier designed the city of Chandigarh with the broad streets appropriate to a community of car users, completely ignoring the facts a) that the Indians who were to live there tend to use bicycles rather than cars, and b) that broad streets divide people up from one another in a way that destroys the possibility of a real neighborhood. Thus the "honest" and efficient office towers of Mies van der Rohe have made for alienating and unpleasant workspaces. And thus the child-care centers that kibbutzim set up to take the place of the family ran roughshod over the fact that parents, and especially mothers, have a strong, biologically-based desire to live more closely with their children than that (and

ultimately the centers have given way to models of child-rearing more like the traditional family).

Yet Chandigarh is regarded with considerable affection by the people who live there,[39] and in any case there are many examples of city planning that have worked well: Hausmann's Paris, the Ringstrasse in Vienna, Central Park in New York, the eighteenth century Rajasthani city of Jaipur, Radburn, New Jersey, and many others.[40] Miesian office buildings continue to be erected, and have made room for reasonably pleasant work spaces in some cases. Kibbutzim also survive, maintaining communal structures that are quite different from the norm in liberal, capitalist society, and they continue to attract enthusiastic new members. So it is hard to make out a general case against planned communities on the basis of the available empirical evidence.

Moreover, planned communities can build the Hayekian point into the way their planning works: can operate in a flexible enough way to make room for serendipity, and historical development, to alter the community over time. The Garden Cities worked by setting up associations to develop the cities over time, and leaving a fair number of decisions about the design of specific houses up to the individual inhabitants. Or take the American Constitution—an object of admiration for many conservatives, including Hayek. That was as rationally planned, as deliberately designed, a system of government as any country has ever had, but its generality and flexibility has enabled it to survive while long-entrenched, undesigned monarchies and empires crumbled all around it. Hayek himself acknowledges that law needs in part to be rationally designed—in part it grows up as what he calls a "spontaneous order"—and can be successfully so designed as long as the law-makers take into account the need for laws to constitute a general and easily understandable framework for daily life rather than a set of detailed intrusions into it.[41]

(5) One more argument for the value of cultures might see them as valuable "experiments in living." An empiricist about moral questions might welcome a variety of different ways of life as a means toward learning, in detail, what human happiness does and does not consist in. The variety of cultures provides a naturally occurring source of such alternative ways to live. Insofar as cultures represent human responses to a long accumulation of experience, and insofar as they differ, sometimes substantially, in those responses, they may be thought of as a vast scientific investigation into how human life is best led.

The most obvious philosopher on which to hang such a view is J.S. Mill. Mill's defense of liberty famously rests in large part on the advantages, for an empiricist about moral issues, of having many different ways of life going on at once, so that each of us can choose how to live with a rich, full awareness of what the alternatives to our choices look like. This seems to me both right and important. I learn most powerfully whether open marriages or institutional day-care centers are a good idea or not primarily by looking around at the results of such practices, not by considering theoretical arguments on the subject. On a larger scale, liberal individualists can test the value of their way(s) of life by assessing it against the background of more traditional ways of doing things, while members of traditional communities can, similarly, look at liberal ways of living either to encourage themselves in, or to rethink, their traditional norms. We do not like to think of human lives as "experiments," and that is perhaps why this way of presenting the relationship between liberalism and its alternatives is not much discussed, but as long as the adherents of both the traditional and the liberal ways of living are given the freedom to live as they wish, the participants in this "experiment" will be informed and active *choosers* of their participation.[42] The standard worries about treating people as objects of experiment therefore do not apply. The people here are not objects of anyone else's choices; rather the experiment comes about by way of each person's choices.

But, if we are casting about for reasons why we should approve of cultural commitments, there is once again no reason for the communal participants in this Millian moral experiment to be *cultures*, precisely, at all. All sorts of "life-styles" might be valuable sources of information about how humans best flourish; all sorts of communal ways of living might be particularly valuable sources for such information. It will probably not be possible to make sure that every imaginable life-style gets a chance to play itself out, however, and there is no reason, on Millian grounds alone, to give any special preference to the life-styles of traditional communities over those of planned, untraditional communities. Indeed, if the goal of the experiment is to determine the best way(s) of concretely embodying general liberal precepts, it would make sense for all the communities participating in the experiment to be explicitly liberal, untraditional ones. The value, for moral empiricists, of having a variety of communities around thus at best allows for, but does not require, the preservation of cultures.

## III

We are still missing a reason why guiding one's life in accordance with cultural norms might be morally better than guiding one's life by the norms of a liberal, untraditional community. Communitarians can show liberals why their own position might require a life in community, but stumble over why it should sanction life in *cultural* communities. To defend the latter, we need some reason for adhering to communal norms whose legitimation is traditional rather than legal-rational, in Max Weber's terms, to norms that in themselves may be without reason. What we need is thus a reason *for abjuring reason* in at least some of our decisions, for choosing *not* to run the maxims of choice, in those cases, through the test of our own reason—for choosing, quite precisely, to be *heteronomous* in those areas of our lives. Clearly, a hardline and thorough-going Kantian would have to regard the very possibility of justifying such a choice as absurd, as a contradiction in terms. And the hardline and thorough-going Kantian I am envisioning would and should regard only a life in liberal communities, not a life in cultures, as morally acceptable. But I think we can find a reasonable view of the moral value in adhering to cultures that will persuade even some—less "thorough-going"—Kantians. The kind of view I have in mind is one in which autonomy is required as a second-order norm for one's *overall* choices about how to choose—one's choice of a set of constraints on, and a general approach to, making choices—but is not necessarily required as a first-order norm governing the particular choices constituting one's ordinary, day-to-day life. Adherence to culture could then be justifiable if it is chosen on the second-order level, even though that choice would not only allow but require compromising one's autonomy in many, even most, of one's day-to-day decisions. How might one defend such a position?

In this section I propose one possible defense. If "culture" is a successor term to "religion," as I suggested in part I, then a defense of culture should perhaps be expected to resemble traditional defenses of religion. Take this as my excuse for arguing that a culture will function as a legitimate and healthy guide for a person's moral decisions only by way of a kind of *faith.* I will model this faith on the version of Christian faith defended by St. Augustine.

Augustine famously maintains that faith seeks understanding:[43] "By all means, once they have an unshakable belief in the truth of Holy Scripture's witness, let them go on by prayer and enquiry and right living to the pursuit of understanding—which means the seeing with the mind . . . of what is firmly held by faith."[44] One might wonder why faith is needed, however, if we can reach God through the understanding. Does "what is firmly held by faith" need to be firmly so held only for those incapable of seeing God with their minds directly? Sometimes that does seem to be Augustine's view:

> For the wise man imitates God to the extent of his endowment. But for the fool there is nothing closer for him to imitate sanely than a wise man. And since it is not easy to recognize him through reason . . . , it was necessary to present certain miracles to the very eyes (which fools use much more readily, than they do their minds), so that, moved by authority, men's lives and habits might first be purged, and thus become amenable to the acceptance of reason. . . . It is authority alone that moves fools to hasten on to wisdom.[45]

So only fools need faith? Of course not. Elsewhere Augustine explains why faith is essential to people of all intellectual levels. The teaching of God's suffering in Jesus, he says, is the best way to awaken the humility we all need:

> What is good for us to believe and to keep firm and unshaken in our hearts, is that the humility whereby God was born of a woman and brought by mortal men that shameful way to death, is the supreme medication for the healing of the cancer of our pride, and the profound mystery that can loose the fetters of sin.[46]

Exactly *what* about this teaching awakens humility is a bit unclear. Is it that we empathize with God and thereby ourselves are humiliated? Or are our minds drawn to the inference that if God could find something valuable in humility, *a fortiori* we should do so as well? Or is it simply that the mystery of such a strange teaching defeats our inclination to think we could grasp all truth by reason alone? It is probably something of all three. The last point, that the mere act of relying on faith rather than knowledge can be humbling, regardless of what the faith is in, comes out implicitly in the following passage:

> A sure faith is itself a beginning of knowledge; but sure knowledge will not be perfected till after this life when we shall see God face to face. Let us then be thus minded, convinced that the temper of the truth-seeker is safer than that of rashly taking the unknown for known.[47]

And elsewhere the point appears explicitly. In Book IV of *De Trinitate,* Augustine says that philosophers who suppose that their own reasoning can lead them to righteousness will be defeated by the very pride by which they maintain this:

> [Proud] persons promise themselves cleansing by their own righteousness for this reason, because some of them have been able to penetrate with the eye of the mind beyond the whole creature, and to touch, though it be in ever so small a part, the light of the unchangeable truth; a thing which they deride many Christians for being not yet able to do, who, in the meantime, live by faith alone. But of what use is it for the proud man, who on that account is ashamed to embark upon the ship of wood [i.e., the cross], to behold from afar his country beyond the sea? Or how can it hurt the humble man not to behold it from so great a distance, when he is actually coming to it by that wood upon which the other disdains to be borne?[48]

Here Augustine reverses the implication that only "fools" need faith, construing it as especially important to those whose intellectual virtues delude them into thinking they can find their own way to the moral virtues as well.

One more bit of Augustine before we proceed. The passage just cited ends with a beautiful comparison between progressing toward truth and coming home to one's "country." Similar journey and landscape metaphors appear throughout Augustine's writings, and in many of them what the landscape looks like changes considerably as we move closer to our goal:

> [M]uch will depend on whether I am shut off from the transparent heaven, beneath or within this fog of obscurity, or whether I stand as on a mountain top in the open air between, looking up to the unclouded light above me and down upon the thick mists below. Whence comes it that the warmth of brotherly love is kindled in me, when I hear of some man who has endured the sharpest torments in steady and undisfigured faith? Point out to me the man himself, and I am eager to meet him and know him, to be bound in friendship with him. . . . But suppose that as we talk he admits, or shows by some unconsidered remark, that even his faith is not

> what it should be, that he seeks in God for some material benefit and has borne his sufferings in that false hope. . . . At once the love which carried me toward him falls back rebuffed: it removes itself from the man's unworthiness, and remains in the unchanging pattern which had made me love him when I believed him worthy. If I do still love him, it is that he may become such as I have found him not to be. . . . But the pattern of truth, unshaken and steadfast, by which in the belief of his goodness I might have enjoyed his friendship, and by which I now seek his amendment—this pattern still sheds the constant and eternal light of pure and incorruptible reason, upon my mind's gaze, and upon that cloud of imaginings to which I look down from the mountain when I reflect upon the man I saw.[49]

We know, in this and similar cases, that we have misjudged someone because our friendships are guided by principles of virtue that are more reliable than the bits of information about people we evaluate in the light of those principles. We know also that we can at times be so immersed in the "mists" of personal relationships that we lose track of our reliable principles. And we know *that* because sometimes we get the chance to look back, retrospectively, at mistakes we have made in such circumstances from a position of clarity. For Augustine, there is presumably an analogy here with how our religious "country" appears before and after the journey of faith. From afar, before the journey, there are mists that make God look unreal, a product of our yearnings or at best something eternally unknowable. From near—once one has proceeded a ways along the journey—the mists appear to be the delusions of pride that keep even the wisest of arrogant men from being able to approach God. And the near perspective is the better, the more accurate one, revealing itself as such to one who comes to occupy it, just as the position on top of the mountain, above the clouds, is the better place from which to view those clouds, and is known to be such by one who attains it.

Finally, note that the faith-less philosopher in the "ship of wood" passage is able to "touch, though it be in ever so small a part, the light of the unchangeable truth." Augustine allows that non-Christian philosophers can arrive by reason alone at some of the central truths of Christianity—about the existence and general nature of God, especially—and indeed do so rather more adequately than many faithful Christians.[50] The point of the ship of wood passage is that the philosophers will not know God's nature or ways in *detail* without faith,[51] and that the faithful person will eventually do so regardless of how much they see at the outset. But the goal of the philosopher and the faithful person is the same—for both, it is *their* country that lies beyond the sea. Understanding will be inadequate without faith, but faith, in Christ on the cross, is a "ship of wood" that carries one ultimately to the land of full understanding.

What comparison can we draw between this notion of faith and the ethical faith a person might have in cultures? Well, let's start with the notion that a purely rational and a culturally faithful moral decision-maker have the same general telos, however that is to be played out in detail. Both seek freedom or excellence or well-being or whatever. Both acknowledge, moreover, *that* such a general characterization of their goal—of their country beyond the sea—can be laid out without faith. They agree also a) that "fools"—people incapable of reasoning well—may do best to rely on faith in the norms around them regardless of whether the goal can in principle be reached through reason alone, and b) that ultimately everyone should be able to recognize that the goal they have reached is indeed the one they were aiming at. That is, the "pure reasoner" readily grants the first of the Augustinian reasons for faith, while the "cultural fideist" grants that in the end understanding is indeed the relationship both want to have to their goals.[52] What they differ over is a crucial middle step: is there or is there not, between the initial rational sighting of a general goal for the moral life, and the more or less successful achievement of that goal, a need to put faith in a culture as the source of norms for one's everyday decisions? Is there something morally valuable about submitting one's daily decisions to old and socially-shared norms—about sexuality, decorum, treatment of animals, and the like—which have structured good lives in the past, but are not, in themselves, particularly reasonable? Or are nonrational norms and the communities they structure at best irrelevant to moral thinking?

An Augustinian faith in cultures would take the first line, on the grounds that only a humiliation of one's reason to the "mysteries" of nonrational norms can purge one of the pride by which the good life must remain ever a distant vision, an ideal land beyond the sea, rather than something one can actually attain. Once one undergoes this humiliation, moreover, one will begin literally to *see* the facts of one's moral landscape differently, and eventually see, in particular, why a path via culture-faith was the only way to achieve the kind of life one had earlier glimpsed philosophically. One also sees as "mists" or "fog" the kind of objections the pure reasoner tends to raise to this approach to ethics. After one has embarked upon culture-faith, such objections appear as products of the very pride that culture-faith is meant to overcome, as based on plausible but ultimately spurious and self-serving arguments.

To bring out the comparison between Christian faith and culture-faith more precisely, consider Augustine's need to make sense of a progression from understanding to faith to greater understanding. How can Augustine explain, to one who wants to rely on the understanding alone, the reasons for embracing faith while acknowledging at the same time that the faith thus embraced should be carried forth into a fuller understanding? One promising strategy is to suggest that there is a way of seeing things, a type of vision, that will not be possible until one has faith. And Augustine in fact repeatedly compares faith to vision: "May we say that we have known him by faith, but not as yet by sight? Surely, in faith we have both seen and known; for if faith does not yet see, why are the faithful called the enlightened ?"[53] The advantages of this comparison are a) that vision, both in its literal sense and in the metaphorical extensions of that sense that philosophers like to employ, is understood to be a way of grasping first principles, a way of picking up data or premises that will be crucial to further argument but are themselves prior to argument, and b) that we know of analogous cases in ordinary experience (in learning a craft, in appreciating the beauty of unfamiliar kinds of art, in coming to recognize what counts as polite behavior in a foreign country) in which a type of seeing can be impossible until one has gone through training, followed the lead of an authoritative guide, or undergone some other, nonrational process of transformation. Now a) and b) constitute something of an *argument* for the value to rationality of the nonrational transformation being urged. On Augustine's account, moreover, a promise is held out that understanding will continue to be the primary basis for accepting principles once the transformation is complete. We thus see how faith might be a step within the ongoing development of understanding, despite the way in which that step itself must defy understanding. If a case can now be made for how the specific faith being urged may offer a kind of vision that the pre-faithful understanding knows it needs, then a fairly complete argument has been given for the value, to understanding, of moving outside understanding. No more complete argument for faith can be given, because the full cognitive advantages of faith can by hypothesis appear only when one actually has faith (one can learn what is gained by seeing *that way* only once one is actually able to see that way), but the step of embracing faith has at least been made not antirational, which at first it may have seemed, and it will appear clearly rational, in retrospect, once one has adopted it.[54]

A case along these lines for the moral value of culture-faith can be laid out as follows:[55]

(1) A great hindrance to the pursuit of the ethical life is the self-centeredness by which each of us sees faults in, and responsibilities required of, others but is blind to our own faults and responsibilities. On Adam Smith's and Kant's (let alone St. Paul's, or Nietzche's, or Freud's) claims for the pervasiveness of self-deceit, even our seemingly most honest moments of moral self-scrutiny are usually but a masquerade for selfish purposes.[56] This strikes me as extremely plausible. One mark of a good novelist or playwright is the ability to show how even the worst of characters tends to provide himself with ingenious justifications for what he does, such that a murder or a lie turns out to be "not really" a murder or a lie at all, or to be a justifiable exception to such general laws of morality. And this is a mark of a good novelist because it is precisely how people act in real life, so as to maintain their self-respect even while behaving badly. And the most brilliant people, including the most brilliant of moral philosophers, often use their brilliance in their lives primarily as a tool for such casuistry. Who, in the philosophical community, has never witnessed an astute Kantian making use of Kant to explain how what seems a violation of Kantian principles in fact follows from those principles?[57]

From here it follows fairly readily (2) that any purely rational approach to ethics, any approach that construes ethics merely as a matter of grasping the right rules of conduct or the right outline of virtuous character, can all too easily play into our self-centeredness rather than work against it. The mere fact that we have found a good ethical theory—that we ourselves have discovered or understood it—enhances our arrogant sense of being able to rely entirely on our own resources, to grasp all ethically relevant facts by ourselves, and, inter alia, to recognize, by ourselves, our own bad actions, failures of judgment, and character blemishes. Our confidence in our understanding of ethical theory can thus take away from our willingness to listen to others, and add to our inclination to cover ethical blind spots with clever rationalizations.

These premises make it at least not unreasonable to consider (3) that a willingness to submit one's will, at least partially, to the norms and rituals of an authoritative tradition about how to live can be valuable for seeing certain things relevant to one's understanding of what the good life consists in. Humbling oneself to doing in practice what everyone else in one's culture thinks one should do can mitigate the arrogance—characteristic of professional philosophers especially but also of everyone who thinks they have worked out by themselves a good "philosophy" of life—by which people think they can figure out what to do in all circumstances by themselves. Such arrogance can blind one to the true value of settled practices, and to the character-limitations that are likely to prevent one from successfully carrying out anomalous life-styles. More positively, humbling oneself to doing what the unphilosophical "fools" around one do can lead one, in practice, to start experiencing the good effects of institutions and norms one would otherwise have dismissed. A utilitarian or situational ethicist who, against her theoretical views, submits to cultural norms urging extreme honesty may come to win certain kinds of respect from others, and develop a kind of self-respect, that she never had before. A Kantian may experience, on the contrary, the value to human relationships of cultural norms urging one to shade the truth, in the name of tact, on certain occasions. A person who has worked out a good argument for open marriage may find, on submitting nonetheless to cultural norms against adultery, that he experiences kinds of love he would otherwise never have come to know. Developing a habit of submitting in this way does not, of course, always lead people to become wonderful human beings. But it may so lead people, and some of us believe that it does so rather more often than do philosophical theories of morality. I have personally met few really brave, generous, honest, and kind academics, and considerably more people like that among those who guide their lives by a fairly unreflective faith in cultural or religious norms.

Of course the set of norms in which we put faith cannot help us morally at all if it is just any combination of nonrational norms and practices, but the norms of a culture will always have more going for them, ethically, than that. A culture, as opposed to a "cult" like the Aum Shinrikyo in Japan or David Koresh's followers in Waco, must by practically any definition exist over several generations. It must therefore contain within itself, at the very least, reasonably successful means of (a) settling disputes among people, (b) raising children, and (c) fostering stable and moderately happy marriages: otherwise it will not be able to maintain biological and cultural systems of reproduction.[58] Cultures also tend, over time, to differentiate themselves from other cultures, and thereby to define themselves, in moral terms: by emphasizing one set of virtues (e.g., military courage, discretion, a leisurely pace of life) over others (e.g., meekness and patience, sincerity, economic efficiency), or by interpreting virtues in terms of one set of daily practices and expectations rather than another, the members of a culture explain to themselves what is so valuable about remaining Scots, Sephardic, Kurdish, etc. rather than merging with the English, the Ashkenazim, the Turks, etc.

In addition, there is no reason why an individual should not, before submitting to a culture, select for herself what seems to her the *best*, morally speaking, of the cultures in which she feels she has a place. In saying this I presuppose, of course, that there is more than one culture to which each of us can submit. But surely this is true. As we saw earlier, whatever culture people are born into, they can switch cultural allegiances by way of migration, intermarriage, and conversion, and can remain within a culture while dissenting from its mainstream or allying themselves with groups bent on reforming or revolutionizing that mainstream. Today, moreover, as a result of cross-cultural marriages, and of childhood environments that combine several different cultures, people tend to be claimed by multiple cultures. In any case, the notion that choice goes into our adoption of a culture-faith is entailed by the defense of that faith we have been pursuing. On our Augustinian model, we need to evaluate our culture-faith against the backdrop of the ultimate land of ethical verities we have glimpsed from afar—considering, among other things, how likely it is that this particular ship of wood will take us there. Less metaphorically, the kind of moral argument I have offered for the value of submission to cultural norms cannot go through except against the background of some general principles of morality—by which self-centeredness, for instance, can be shown to be a moral flaw. So culture-faith must be conditioned by some degree of general moral understanding, and will be in contradiction with itself if it is directed toward a clearly *im*moral way of life.[59]

Precisely because culture-faith is conditioned in this way by moral understanding, it respects cultures much more in their own terms—as patterns of practice that express a *view* of the moral life—than does the standard Herderian interpretation of cultures. We submit in faith to a culture, indeed, but only once we have some reason to suppose that this culture will provide us with an adequate "ship of wood" to the morally good life. Since different ships may be able to provide different people with equally good passage to the same place, there is room here for pluralism. But the embarkation on one ship rather than another is also, to some degree, a judgment that that ship is better than its alternatives, and it is a judgment for which, in principle at least, there is a criterion for success or failure. No such criterion is available, however, at the *beginning* of the journey: on the hypothesis that faith is essential before one can so much as see the contours of the moral landscape adequately, the journey must actually be undertaken before one can know whether it is headed in the right direction or not. So whether one culture offers a given individual a better way of life than liberal individualism, or than another culture, must be worked out by that individual in practice, rather than through some theoretical proof that one of these alternatives is the best. I think this is the relationship most cultures actually do bear to one another—they view themselves as superior to others, but unprovably so, and are interested less in demonstrating the superiority of their practices to outsiders than in urging insiders to show, in their lives, how good the practices can be. Liberal individualists have on the contrary been more concerned to show in theory that their way of life is superior to the culturally-informed ways of life with which they compete than to demonstrate in practice that their approach in fact produces better people. That the issues between liberal individualism and culture-faiths of all kinds must be resolved in practice rather than in theory takes me to the position, and set of recommendations, with which I would like to close.

## IV

Is it really true that a faith in cultures improves people morally? If I could prove that it was, there would be no need for faith. That does not mean there is no evidence at all for the position: the reasoner and the fideist may agree, when looking from afar, that some committed adherents of cultures seem to lead rich and decent lives because of that commitment. That others do not, and that some people seem to live successfully without any deep cultural attachment, are facts the two will interpret differently. Over time, indeed, how they interpret those facts, and how important they take them to be, may lead them to switch places: the reasoner may be swayed by such facts into adopting a faith in a culture, while the believer may be led out of her faith by them. Facts are not irrelevant to culture-faith; they just underdetermine it.

I think this is a happy place to wind up. A less than fully rational faith is in many ways a better basis for a commitment to cultural norms than an argument that such commitment is the only or the best way to a rich and decent life. For one thing, acknowledging that one's commitment is based on faith is itself conducive to precisely the humility that I am claiming as the main advantage of cultural commitment. And the notion that argument is necessary to ground a moral view seems to me exactly what is opposed by one who says, "This is just the way we do things around here." For another thing, the one claim about the moral function of cultures that we can assert with some confidence is that whether cultures help or hurt people morally is, so far, quite unproven. That an adherence to cultures helps people lead decent and rich lives has certainly not been convincingly shown—which is one excellent reason why states should not coerce people into such commitments. That cultures are irrelevant, or even harmful, to the pursuit of the moral life seems to me equally undemonstrated—which is an excellent reason for governments, at the same time, not to try to eliminate cultural beliefs and practices.

One consequence of my defense of cultures via faith is that it offers cold comfort to nationalism and communitarianism, even in their liberal incarnations. If the moral value of cultures can be achieved only via faith, then the coercive mechanisms of the state should not be used to preserve those cultures. Faith is notoriously impervious, even resistant, to coercion, and what a liberal state, at least, can legitimately do must be justifiable to its citizens by reason alone. At the same time, as long as the claim that cultural ties are actually inimical to moral development remains unproven, it is just as inappropriate for a liberal state to promote that position. Moreover, the liberal individualist can easily allow that the ways of life based on culture-faith belong to the "experiments in living" worth pursuing, now that she has some independent reason for seeing the nonrational aspects of cultures as themselves a possible source of information about what kinds of practices best conduce to human well-being. So the liberal individualist need not want the state to oppose culture-faith.

But how might liberal individualists try themselves to refute cultural fideists? I propose that they will do best not to attempt a theoretical refutation of the fideist at all, but to try to demonstrate in *practice* that the fideist is wrong. As I have construed the debate between liberals and communitarians, the liberals claim that whatever an individual can gain from community may be found in liberal communities, and need not be sought for in cultural ones. If this is true, it needs to be demonstrated in experience. Good liberal communities need to be constructed, communities that foster individualism without anomie and survive for many generations.[60]

A problem of liberal individualism throughout its history, I think, is that it has not taken seriously enough the need to build communal practices around its values: it has either seen itself as value-neutral, or accepted the view of its critics on both the right and the left that community-building is not and cannot be a liberal project—that it must be a product of conservative values or socialist consciousness. Full blown, perfectionist liberals, from Madison and Mill through Joseph Raz and George Kateb, have not been value-neutral at all: they have stood for such concrete values as the dignity of working people, the importance of personal property but the greater importance of eliminating poverty, equality among races and between men and women, and the contribution to human excellence of broad-ranging experiments in artistic expression, scholarly research, and sexuality. Many such values can be fully realized only by way of communal forms, however, while requiring kinds of community quite different from those predominant in Western culture. It is a shame that experiments in alternative communal forms have almost always been carried out by people who saw themselves as opponents of liberalism—by Marxists, nationalists, religious reactionaries or followers of Marcuse. Liberals have generally been too moderate, and too worried about offending people, to attempt long-term experiments exploring the consequences of, say, atheistic education from childhood on, systems of property rights that abjure inheritance, or communal alternatives to the institution of marriage.

Let's pursue this last example. Conservatives and communitarians alike have warned us recently to beware of tampering with "family values." For the former, this means that we should discourage homosexuality, for the latter it does not, but both believe the government should encourage people to enter into, and remain in, a nuclear family. Why? Well, statistics show that children do much better when raised by two parents than by one. But is the only way to meet this need a return to the lifelong, monogamous nuclear family? Is there necessarily something wrong, for the children involved, about honest and mutually accepted polygynous or polyandrous arrangements? Such arrangements might well be better for children than the divorces, often bitter ones, that most people go through today. Perhaps we, as a society, ought to be actively exploring polygamous marriages more fully, at least as useful experiments—setting guidelines for them, providing financial incentives for them, and studying their effects.

More minimally, suppose we were to throw our energies whole-heartedly into helping single mothers to form supportive communities among themselves. Suppose public housing included units of a few apartments around a central courtyard, with some shared kitchen, dining, and living facilities for those who want to make use of them, and perhaps with a daycare and/or school in or next to the building. Only single mothers and their children would be eligible to live in the complex, and their occupancy would be contingent upon their taking a share of jointly-determined cooking, cleaning, and daycare responsibilities. Drugs and drunkenness would be forbidden, and sexual relationships might be expected to take place either off campus or in a set of rooms explicitly set aside for that purpose. In the event that a sexual relationship led to marriage, the mother and her children might be expected to leave the complex—but efforts would be taken to ensure that no-one felt any pressure to have their sexual life lead to marriage. Such an arrangement might shock traditional Christian, Jewish, and Muslim mores, but would surely provide the help for single mothers, the means of urging them to accept their responsibilities, and the provision of multiple role models in parenting, to which conservatives and communitarians have been pointing as advantages of the traditional family. And this arrangement would probably be far less prone than is the traditional family to breeding domestic violence and psychological abuse. On rational, secular grounds alone, it is hard to defend the traditional family in terms that would not also, and sometimes better, justify polygamous arrangements or communes of the kind I have described. Of course the fundamental reason why people in our society are likely to be horrified by these alternative arrangements is not a secular one at all—it will offend against their faith, or the remnants of it to which they still cling. And this faith is, for many people, above all a cultural rather than a religious faith, a faith in the way things have always gone on in Western communities rather than a faith in strict Christian, Jewish or Muslim views on nonmarital sex. A committed liberal individualist should combat that faith, where necessary, by showing what an alternative in practice looks like, and attempting to make that alternative work.

This way of settling the debate between liberal individualists and believers in cultures is one that can, in principle, be accepted by both sides. Culture-faith is directed to an empirical proposition, after all—that cultural communities can lead individuals to the human good, even as conceived in liberal terms, more competently than can any rationally structured, explicitly liberal community—and empirical propositions not only deserve but demand to be tested. An empirical faith ought not merely to tolerate, but actively to welcome, in Millian vein, attempts to show that its opposition is right. It strengthens the faith to have alternatives fail, of course, but that they will fail cannot be determined unless they are tried. In this light, it is in the interest of the very people who uphold the tried. In this light, it is in the interest of the very people who uphold the value of traditional communities to see untraditional communities established, and allowed to play themselves out as best they can.

On the other side of the coin, there is very little a liberal can simply *say* to refute a believer in culture. The fideist can always respond to philosophical arguments against relying on faith by pointing out that philosophical argument is precisely what her approach to morality is meant to combat, that the very stance that insists on such argument is what she considers to interfere with moral living. The liberal individualist's best response to such a position is to *show*, in practice, that a liberal individualist way of life can be superior to a faith-based way. When the fideist and the reasoner view their mutually shared country from afar, in the Augustinian scenario, they agree implicitly on what it will take to constitute a decent moral life. In principle they should eventually be able to demonstrate to one another, therefore, that they have succeeded, or failed, in approaching that distant country. But they cannot just make this point "from afar"—they must actually embark on their respective ships and sail. The liberal individualist is thereby challenged to put her actions where her mouth is, to cease merely making philosophical arguments against reliance on culture and demonstrate, in fact, that a liberal individualist community can flourish. In the terms of this debate, the terms set up by Augustine's journey metaphor, such practical success or failure will indeed count as the best *philosophical* argument that the participants can make.

All this means, of course, that the cultural fideist should also demonstrate in practice the moral advantages over liberalism of his or her submission to a culture. That demand should, however, be welcome to the fideist. For, in the first place, the fideist as I have construed him places great emphasis on the moral importance of humility. He should therefore have no objection to the humility imposed on him by dint of having to "compete" morally, as it were, with liberal alternatives; the challenge is likely to mitigate the cockiness or complacency with which he might otherwise pursue his culture's values. In the second place, the empiricism of culture-faith means that the fideist should be open to the possibility that his leap of faith was wrong, that the way of life to which he has committed himself may turn out to be morally inferior to that of another culture, or of liberal individualism. But liberal individualists, in their commitment to pluralism and freedom, are most likely to preserve ways of living other than their own. So the adherent of each culture-faith relies on liberal individualists to preserve his fallback options should his faith, at some point, appear to him misguided.

In this way, cultural fideists and liberal individualists can see themselves as helping each other, in a variety of pragmatic as well as philosophical ways. Believers in different cultures can, moreover, see themselves as helping each other, as providing informative rivalry and fallback options for each other, in much the same ways. This is perhaps the best accommodation they can all come to with one another, at least if, as I have presumed throughout, the fundamental philosophical issues between them cannot—yet—be resolved. Thus could something much like the vision of Herder still be realized:

> Do you see this flowing river? Look how it springs from a tiny source, swells, divides here, rejoins there, winds in and out, and cuts wider and deeper. Yet, regardless of its course, it still remains *water*! . . . Might it not be the same with the human race? . . . Human beings must pass through different periods of life! All periods are obviously in *progress!* . . . We never exist in our own period alone; we build on what has *gone before* . . . . The Egyptian could not have existed without the Hebrew; the Greek built on the work of the Egyptian; the Romans lifted themselves on the shoulders of the whole world. This is the genuine sense of "progress" and "continuous development" . . . (Bunge,45)

Not in spite of but by way of the differences among cultures, and between cultures and liberal individualist ways of living, will we learn from one another, and progress. But we can learn in this productive way from one another only if we remake our relationships to our cultures on the basis of faith, rather than either taking them for granted or trying to justify them by pure rational argument. Both the pre-Enlightenment view by which our cultures (religions) represent the obviously right way to live, and the post-Enlightenment attempts to construct good arguments for submitting to traditional communities, have justified theocratic and nationalist states that are oppressive to their own citizens and bloody to outsiders. Only if individuals who commit themselves to their cultures do so explicitly on the basis of faith, recognizing and accepting all the limitations that that entails, can cultures become the uncoercive, peaceful, and virtue-enhancing entities that Herder thought they already were.

## Notes

1. In, for instance, *The Ethics of Culture,* (Ithaca, N.Y.: Cornell University Press, 1994), ch. 5, or "From Cultural Norms to Universal Ethics: Three Models," *Cultural Dynamics* 11 (1), 1999.

2. See, for instance, Geertz, "Thick Description: Toward an Interpretive Theory of Culture," in *The Interpretation of Cultures*, (New York: Basic Books, 1973).

3. Charles Taylor provides perhaps the best explanation and defense of the hermeneutical conception of the social sciences in "Interpretation and the Sciences of Man," in *Philosophy and the Human Sciences*, (Cambridge, U.K.: Cambridge University Press, 1985). But Taylor has himself also shown as well as anyone why scientific explanation, properly understood, is something that aims at enabling us to predict and control what we explain— see "Rationality" in the same volume—and should be the first to concede that the hermeneutic approach he favors can be regarded as *scientifically* superior to its rivals if and only if it yields more successful predictions of and opportunities for control over human actions. Sometimes he does seem to imply that he has moral rather than scientific

reasons for favoring hermeneutic to positivistic social science, and, in any case, when he comes to discuss "culture" explicitly, he takes up a view very close to the one I will advocate here: "I would like to maintain that there is something valid in (the) presumption (that we owe equal respect to all cultures), but that the presumption ... *involves something like an act of faith.*" (Taylor/Gutmann, *Multiculturalism* (Princeton, N.J.: Princeton University Press, 1994), 66, my italics). For the importance of "faith" to an advocacy of cultures, see section III, below.

4. For doubts about the scientific usefulness of "culture," see Adam Kuper, *Culture: The Anthropologists Account*, (Cambridge, Mass: Harvard University Press, 1999).

5. Cassirer is the first and one of the only philosophers to lay out a view like this explicitly, although in recent years Taylor and Geertz have done so as well. See Cassirer, *An Essay on Man*, (New Haven: Yale University Press, 1944), chapters II and III, and the Taylor and Geertz works cited in notes 2 and 3 above.

6. Of course these are all located, limited choices, choices that are constrained by the opportunities to leave, or shape their tradition, open to each individual, but what choices are not so limited? Even proponents of the most extreme versions of Kantian autonomy do not expect individuals to hold all social and physical constraints in abeyance when they make their decisions; even a purely autonomous human being, should there be such a person, could not "choose" to live for 200 years, or to live in a social world utterly unlike all those around in his or her day.

7. "As ready as human beings are to imagine that they are self-made, they are nevertheless dependent on others for the development of their capacities. . . . Just as human beings do not spring from their own wombs at birth, they themselves do not give birth to the use of their own mental powers."—Johann Gottfried Herder, *Against Pure Reason: Writings on Religion, Language and History,* trans. and ed. Marcia Bunge, (Minneapolis: Fortress Press, 1993), 48-9. Quotations from this volume will henceforth be incorporated into the text as "Bunge, page number."

8. See, for instance, chapter 1, section 1 of *Hegel and Modern Society*, (Cambridge, U.K.: Cambridge University Press, 1979), "Language and Human Nature," and "Theories of Meaning," in Taylor, *Human Agency and Language: Philosophical Papers I*, (Cambridge, U.K.: Cambridge University Press, 1985), "The Politics of Recognition," in *Multiculturalism*, 30-32, or "The Importance of Herder," in Taylor, *Philosophical Arguments*, (Cambridge, Mass.: Harvard University Press, 1995).

9. His assessment of xenophobia is extremely astute and judicious:

> In (the) development of particular national tendencies toward particular forms of national happiness, the distance between one people and another can grow too great. Look how the Egyptian detests the nomadic shepherd and equally despises the frivolous Greek! Whenever the dispositions and spheres of happiness of two nations collide, there arises what we call prejudice, mob judgment, and narrow nationalism! But in its proper time and place prejudice is good, for happiness can spring from it. It thrusts peoples together toward their center, attaches them more firmly to their roots, causes them to flourish more fully in their own way, and makes them more ardent and therefore happier with their own tendencies and purposes. (from "Yet Another Philosophy of History," as excerpted in Bunge, 43-4).

10. He writes, for instance:

> *Christianity was to be a community governed by elders and teachers without any worldly authority.* These were to guide the flock as shepherds, decide their differences, correct their faults with zeal and affection, and lead them to Heaven by their counsel, their influence, their precepts, and their example. A noble office,

> when worthily executed . . . but how was it, when, in course of time, the shepherds treated their human flocks as actual sheep, or led them as beasts of burden to browse on thistles? how, when wolves, legally called, came among the flocks instead of shepherds? Childish obedience then soon became a Christian virtue: it became a Christian virtue, for a man to renounce the use of his reason, and to follow the authority of another's opinion instead of his own conviction. . . . Nothing now was prized so highly as faith, as quietly following the leader: the man, who ventured to have an opinion of his own, was an obstinate heretic, and excluded from the kingdom of God and the church. Bishops and their subalterns, in defiance of the doctrines of Christ, interfered in family disputes and civil affairs.

Herder, *Reflections on the Philosophy of the History of Mankind*, abridged and introduced by Frank E. Manuel (Chicago: University of Chicago Press, 1968), 275.

11. For his attack on dogma, consider the following passage:

> What does or can (religion) have to do with doctrines? Doctrines are propositions which we can argue for and against. In this sense, doctrines stand in opposition to religion. Religion does not require pro and con arguments. Rather, it requires the conscientious observance of an inviolable duty, or truth that is recognized in our innermost being. Religion is not the investigation of something that is called into question. Rather, it is the acting out of something that is unquestionable. (Bunge, 94. See also193-4.)

12. Herder was a fervent defender of Spinozism in the *Pantheismusstreit:* see Bunge, editor's introduction, 24-6, and the letters to Jacobi in Bunge, 120-5.

13. See Bunge, introduction, 24-6, 32, and the implicit references to Lessing in the excerpts on 50-51, 193-4 , 215, and 225.

14. The former was Herder's term, and was used by most other writers who followed in his train until Gustav Klemm coined the term *Kultur*, in its modern, anthropological sense.

15. Part of the polemic against pseudo-intellectual and Francophilic affectations summed up in Herder s outburst, " . . . if we have no *Volk*, we shall have no . . . literature of our own which shall live and work in us. . . . (W)e shall write eternally for closet sages and disgusting critics out of whose mouths and stomachs we shall get back what we have given." (Quoted in Gene Bluestein, "The Advantages of Barbarism: Herder and Whitman s Nationalism," *Journal of the History of Ideas* 24, (1963), 118).

16. Hamann was an important influence on Herder (see Bunge, editor's introduction, 6), and Jacobi was a close friend, if also an opponent in the *Pantheismusstreit*. Hamann writes, in a 1785 letter to Herder:

> Your theme of language, tradition and experience is my favourite idea, the egg I brood upon—my one and all—the idea of mankind and its history, the goal and jewel which is pinned to our common authorship and friendship.

More explicitly, he says in a slightly earlier letter that

> I am quite at one with Herder that all our reason and philosophy amount to tradition. . . . For me it is not a matter of physics or theology, but language, the mother of reason and revelation, their alpha and omega. (both excerpts in Ronald Gregor Smith, *JG Hamann,* (New York: Harper & Brothers, 1960), 246-7 and 252).

And Jacobi, according to Fred Beiser,

> recognizes the role of culture in the formation of interests, and . . . notes that cultural standards are frequently incommensurable with one another. In an early essay, for example, Jacobi writes that the philosophy and religion of one age are

often complete nonsense when they are judged by the standards of another. (Beiser, *The Fate of Reason*, (Cambridge, Mass.: Harvard University Press, 1987), 87).

17. For Jacobi's fondness for Hume, see Beiser, 3, 91. For Hamann's, see Beiser, 24 and Smith, *JG Hamann*, 50-52, 241-2, 244, 256-7.

18. "The ideas of every indigenous nation are . . . confined to its own region: if it profess to understand words expressing things utterly foreign to it, we have reason to remain long in doubt of this understanding . . . (One can) compose a catechism of (the Greenlanders ) theologico-natural philosophy, showing, that they can neither answer nor comprehend European questions, otherwise than according to the circle of their own conceptions." (*Reflections on the Philosophy* . . . ed. Manuel, 41).

19. The term "culture" itself connotes an expression of freedom. The word was originally used for what happens to land when it gets worked over, and its metaphorical application to products of the mind was always meant to capture the way in which such products are the end-result of a process of *activity*, a set of actions. "Culture" consisted in the broad education necessary to open ("enlighten") people's minds, so that they could think freely and humanely. Until the early nineteenth century, however, the word did not take a plural—one simply had "culture" or one did not. When Gustav Klemm coined the anthropological use of the word in 1834, it was crucial that it could take a plural, that different peoples had different "culture*s*." But otherwise the earlier meaning of the term carried over: such that, in its anthropological sense as well, "culture" was essentially something (a) acquired rather than inborn, (b) acquired through education rather than through force, manipulation, behavioral training, or the like: thus *freely* acquired, and (c) representative of, and a condition for, all that is best and most admirable in humanity.

Much of this view of culture, which has dominated anthropology from Klemm's day to our own, derives from Herder's notion of a *Volk*, which in turn was modeled on a Leibnizean monad: a *Volk*, for Herder, like an individual mind for Leibniz, was an irreducible and unique element of the universe, whose essence, and uniqueness, consisted in the way its view of the universe was arranged, in the composite whole that its various modes of thought and practice formed, rather than in any of those component modes themselves. Once again, emphasis is placed on how the culture *constructs* itself, on the activities it engages in by which it arranges a view of the world for itself, rather than on the content of the view at which it may arrive.

For more on the importance of "monadic" language to the history of nationalism and cultural anthropology, see chapter 5 of my *The Ethics of Culture*.

20. Herder made suggestions to help bring about, if not "ewigen Frieden," at least "a gradual lessening of war", in *Briefe zur Beforderung der Humanität*, §119 (*Herder Werke*, ed. Hans Dietrich Irmscher, (Frankfurt: Deutsche Klassiker Verlag, 1991), vol. 7, 719-26); his proposals comprised changes in consciousness about war, including the development of a nonmilitaristic patriotism. We see here how strongly the Counter-Enlightenment is an *heir* of the Enlightenment, not—merely—an opponent of it. For the Counter-Enlightenment, world peace must work *through* cultures rather than by the elimination of such divisions among people, but the goal of world peace continues to be regarded as possible and important. Similarly, I believe, the Counter-Enlightenment was generally committed to much the same view of the importance of individual liberty that the Enlightenment upheld. Herder, certainly, couched his defense of cultures and religions in terms that appealed throughout to the importance of these group phenomena *to* the individuals whose lives they informed (see Bunge, 50-51 for an explicit statement of this methodology).

21. For Herder and his followers, the variety of cultures complements, or even replaces, the Incarnation, as God's primary mark on human history. Herder modeled cultures on Leibnizean monads, which enabled him to maintain not only that each culture has a unique perspective on the world but that it is inherently good *because* it has a unique perspective—since goodness consists, in the Leibnizean view, in the flowering of as great a variety of things and perspectives as is compatible with order. So for Herder the uniqueness and the inherent value of any culture is guaranteed by the fact that it mirrors a benevolent God. It is not clear that full pluralism about cultures can survive the death of this theistic underpinning for its coherence.

22. See the Oxford English Dictionary, second edition, "race," second definition, 2b and 5.

23. The origins of a biological notion of "race", and the interrelationship of that notion with modern nationalism, is usefully discussed in Boyd Shafer, *Nationalism: Myth and Reality*, (New York: Harcourt Brace and Company, 1955), 33-9.

24. I say, "so entirely independent of choice" because cultural (and religious and national) status will also be something to some extent independent of choice but will at the same time not be impervious to choice: one is indeed normally born into a culture, but one can also leave that culture and join another one.

25. "Above all, the conception of a nation implies a common political sentiment. J. Holland Rose used nation as a political term, designating a people which has attained to state organization. Hans Kohn described the distinguishing characteristic of modern nations as the political doctrine of sovereignty. Carlton J.H. Hayes pointed out that the word nation has been used since the seventeenth century to designate the population of a sovereign political state, regardless of ethnic or linguistic unity. All agree on the essential *political* connotation of nation."—Louis L. Snyder, *Varieties of Nationalism: A Comparative Study*, (New York: Holt, Rinehart, and Winston, 1976), 18.

26. "There were varying applications of the term in the early Middle Ages, when *natio villae* was used to designate a kinship group in the village. In the later Middle Ages, students of the University of Paris were divided into nations according to their places of birth. In early modern times . . . the word began to take on confused meanings. In his *Faerie Queen*, Edmund Spenser spoke of a nation of birds, and Ben Jonson referred to physicians as a subtile nation. With the three partitions of Poland and the French Revolution in the eighteenth century, the word nation began to be used interchangeably with country." (Snyder, 17-18). On the meaning of "nation," see also Paul James, *Nation Formation*, (London: Sage Publications, 1996), 9-13, Elie Kedourie, *Nationalism*, third edition, (London: Hutchinson, 1985), 13-14, E.J. Hobsbawm, *Nations and Nationalism Since 1780*, second edition, (Cambridge, U.K.: Cambridge University Press, 1992), 14-24, and Walker Connor, *Ethnonationalism*, (Princeton, N.J.: Princeton University Press, 1994), 93-5. Connor notes the synonymity of "race" and "nation," even in the early twentieth century, at the top of 94.

27. Since 1780, according to Eric Hobsbawm; since the French Revolution, according to many other sources (including Snyder, in the passage cited above, Hans Kohn, and Elie Kedourie, see Kohn, *Nationalism: Its Meaning and History*, (Malabar, FL: Krieger Publishing Company, 1965), 22-9, and Kedourie, 12-19). Connor, on 221-2, brings some very interesting evidence to suggest that as late as 1910, many, many people even in Europe. did not yet see themselves in terms of what we would now consider their "national identity." (Thus what we would call "Croats" saw themselves as Dalmation, Istrian, Slavonian, etc., while "Italians" described themselves as Neapolitans, Calabrians, etc.) Hobsbawm's discussion (14-16) lends support to this suggestion.

28. That "nation" might have come to serve as a *replacement* for "religion" (and political duties and sacrifices as a replacement for religious ones) has been repeatedly suggested: see, for instance, Shafer, 141-3. I take "culture" to be a depoliticized version of "nation," with individualistic duties and means of expression—daily rituals, or the creation and appreciation of artworks—taking the place of political ones. The commitment to "culture," on the part of its avid advocates from Herder through Margaret Mead to contemporary "multiculturalists" in the educational and art worlds, much like the nationalists commitment to their nations, then stands in for religious faith just as nationalism does.

29. For an elaboration of this definition, see my *The Ethics of Culture*, chapters 3 to 5.

30. A well-known liberal, at a recent conference in which many participants worried about the threat globalization poses to the survival of traditional cultures, attested at the end to some bewilderment about what the fuss was about: "Here we are in New York," he said, "and right around the corner we can get Indian food, Chinese food, Thai food—whatever we want." He seemed quite sincerely to believe that such gustatory success was evidence enough for the flourishing of cultures.

31. Practically the only liberal I know who has honestly done this, in recent times, is George Kateb: see his attack on communitarianism and cultural pluralism in "Notes on Pluralism," *Social Research*, vol. 61, Fall 1994. My phrase "liberal individualism" is also indebted to Kateb: Kateb clarifies the differences among kinds of individualism, and vigorously defends "democratic individuality," as opposed to, for instance, "possessive individualism," in *The Inner Ocean: Individualism and Democratic Culture,* (Ithaca: Cornell University Press, 1992).

32. Sandel, "Justice and the Good," in Sandel (ed.), *Liberalism and Its Critics*, (New York: New York University Press, 1984), 172.

33. Kymlicka, *Liberalism, Community, and Culture*, (Oxford, U.K.: Clarendon Press, 1989), 50-58. Only the claim that a deliberating self always has some prior moral commitments can be made plausible, he shows, not the claim that the self is unable to revise each of those commitments. And the possibility of such revision is sufficient to yield the priority of the self to its specific commitments in the sense that liberals insist on such priority.

34. Kymlicka, 165-6.

35. Tamir, *Liberal Nationalism*, (Princeton, N.J.: Princeton University Press, 1993), 73. See also Daniel A. Bell, *Communitarianism and its Critics,* (Oxford U.K.: Clarendon Press, 1993), 95, 100-01, 107, and especially 110: "it would seem that (modern human beings have) evolved into sedentary creatures, into the kinds of beings with a deep need for identification with a community whose face can be recognized, and that fulfillment of this need is a condition of psychological stability."

36. Kymlicka is satisfied with the vague definition of "culture" as "a viable community of individuals with a shared heritage (language, history, etc.)" (168; see also 180n2 on why he thinks a more precise definition is impossible), and he is very dismissive of the notion that such communities need be concerned about maintaining any "sort of *character*," or any particular practices or religious beliefs, in order to survive. In the account of "culture" I lay out in section I of this chapter, concern about the hereditary "character" of a community—and that often means precisely its religious character—is just what is essential to calling a community a "culture" at all. Certainly it is hard to see otherwise why "shared heritage" should matter—and Kymlicka, I will argue, offers no good reason for prefering a community with a shared heritage to a community without one. But the political implications of dropping the concern for a shared heritage are tremendous: to use one of Kymlicka's own favorite examples, there is no reason at all, if a

liberal government needs to be concerned about the existence of communities but not about the existence of communities with a shared heritage, to prefer a policy preserving the Inuit people in Canada *as Inuit* over a humane and effective policy that disperses them into other, non- or multi-cultural communities, as long as those alternative communities provide their constituents with role-models and support structures. If it is at all possible to have healthy communities that foster liberal individualism—and the existence of psychologically healthy liberal individualists suggests that that is quite possible—then Kymlicka's arguments should give liberal governments no reason to preserve cultural communities instead.

37. Taylor notes that "There are not only atomist individualists (Nozick) and holist collectivists (Marx), but also holist individualists (Humboldt)—and even atomist collectivists, as in the nightmarish programmed utopia of B.F. Skinner," (in Taylor, *Philosophical Arguments,* (Cambridge Mass.: Harvard University Press, 1995), 185).

38. See Raz, *The Morality of Freedom* (Oxford, U.K.: Clarendon Press, 1986), 423-4.

39. I was told this over and over by people in Chandigarh when I visited in January, 1998, and the people I met from Chandigarh in other cities seemed to miss it a great deal. Moreover, the *Lonely Planet* guidebook to India regularly reports that "Indians are very proud of Chandigarh" and that its residents "feel that it is a good place to live" (Hawthorn, Australia: Lonely Planet Publications, 1997 edition, 245). See also Ian Buruma, "The Perils of Democracy," *New York Review of Books* 12/04/97, 14-15. For a very negative assessment of Chandigarh, see (in addition to most of the Buruma article) Joseph Giovanni, "Chandigarh Revisited," *Architecture* July, 1997, 41-45.

40. On Central Park, Radburn, and the whole issue of good and bad city planning, see Alexander Garvin, *The American City: What Works, What Doesn't,* (New York: McGraw-Hill, 1996), passim, but especially 40-45, 270-75.

41. See Friedrich Hayek, *Rules and Order* (vol. I of *Law, Legislation, and Liberty*), (Chicago: University of Chicago Press, 1973), especially 88 ff.

42. This is not true, of course, of the children in each community, but since that is as much a problem for the liberal individualist as for the traditionalist, I shall set it aside for the moment.

43. "Faith seeks, understanding finds." *The Trinity,* trans. John Burnaby, in *Augustine: Later Works,* vol. VIII of The Library of Christian Classics, (Philadelphia: The Westminster Press, 1955), 129.

44. *Augustine,* 177.

45. "The Advantage of Believing," trans. Luanne Meagher, in *The Fathers of the Church: Saint Augustine,* (Washington: Catholic University Press, 1947), ch. 15, 435-6.

46. *On the Holy Trinity,* trans. Rev. Arthur West Haddan, revised W.G.T. Shedd, in *The Nicene and Post-Nicene Fathers,* first series, vol. III, ed. Philip Schaff, (Buffalo: The Christian Literature Company, 1887), 44-5.

47. *Augustine,* 57 (IX.1).

48. Haddan translation, 79-80 (IV.15 (20)).

49. Burnaby translation, 64-5 (IX.11 (vi)).

50. He allows this in many other places as well: see for instance *City of God* VIII: 5-12.

51. See, especially, *De Trinitate* IV.16-17 (21-22), which immediately follows the penultimate quotation above.

52. The latter move differentiates an Augustinian believer from one who takes faith to be an end goal—from Kierkegaard, perhaps, and certainly from Hamann.

53. *Ten Homilies on I John*, in *Augustine: Later Works*, vol. VIII of The Library of Christian Classics, (Philadelphia: The Westminster Press, 1955), 292. See also the text to footnotes 43 and 45.

54. No more complete argument *should* be given, moreover, since what faith means, in the Christian context, is that the faithful one has submitted his or her desires, including his or her desire for knowledge, fully to the will of God, that she has humbled herself to the extent of being willing, if God so requires it, to renounce even her desire for knowledge, and that means that one who seeks faith merely in order to enhance his or her understanding will not, in fact, achieve faith. Augustine suggests that the faithful one who truly crucifies her will, including her will to understand, in this way, will ultimately "resurrect" to understanding after the crucifixion has been fully undergone.

55. There is a yet closer connection between Augustine's Christian faith and culture-faith than the one I am about to spell out. For Augustine, faith in Christ is a temporal means to, and shadow of, the eternal grasp of God at which we ultimately aim. As temporal beings ourselves, we need such a temporal "bridge" to eternal truths:

> faith concerning the things which in time the Eternal wrought for us and suffered, in the man whose humanity he wore in time and exalted to eternity . . . , temporal as it is, conducts us to the things eternal (*The Trinity*, Burnaby translation, 100. See also Haddan translation, 81-2 (IV.18 (24)).

We "die" to our own temporality by participating in Christ's passage from temporality to eternity. Less metaphorically: since the passage from temporal opinions to eternal truth is both essential and nonsensical on Platonic terms, Augustine is here arguing that a Platonic view of truth *needs* faith to be complete. Only faith could possibly carry us from the beliefs we begin with, in temporal shadows of eternal forms, to the eternal knowledge that grounds those beliefs.

Now a closely analogous passage is needed, in modern moral theory, from the non-temporal demands of utilitarian or Kantian theory to the way those demands can play themselves out within the temporal confines of an individual human life. Perhaps the most important moral function of cultures is that they provide temporal ways of instituting the eternal demands of morality: they split the moral life up into specific time-bound duties, indexed, communally, to the seasons of the year, and individually, to the various stages of life. Philosophical accounts of moral duties rarely have a good way of doing this, since any particular time-bound arrangement of duties is bound to be more or less arbitrary—it is hard to see how there could be good reasons why one such order might be better than any other. Cultures are also more alive to the contours of human time than are philosophical theories in that stories, the characteristic means by which cultures present their conceptions of the moral life, are intrinsically structured by time while theory is not. So a faith in the story and practices of a culture can serve as very much the same "passageway from temporality to eternity" that Augustine attributes to faith in Christ.

56. Adam Smith:

> When we are about to act, the eagerness of passion will seldom allow us to consider what we are doing, with the candour of an indifferent person. . . . When the action is over, . . . and the passions which prompted it have subsided, we can enter more coolly into the sentiments of the indifferent spectator. . . . It is seldom, however, that they are quite candid even in this case. . . . It is so disagreeable to think ill of ourselves, that we often purposely turn away our view from those circumstances which might render (our) judgment unfavourable. He is a bold surgeon, they say, whose hand does not tremble when he performs an operation upon his own person; and he is often equally bold who does not hesitate to pull off the mysterious veil of self-delusion, which covers from his view the

> deformities of his own conduct. Rather than see our own behaviour under so disagreeable an aspect, we too often, foolishly and weakly, endeavour to exasperate anew those unjust passions which had formerly misled us; we endeavour by artifice to awaken our old hatreds, and irritate afresh our almost forgotten resentments: we even exert ourselves for this miserable purpose, and thus persevere in injustice, merely because we once were unjust, and because we are ashamed and afraid to see that we were so. (*Theory of Moral Sentiments*, III.4.3-4).

And Kant:

> we cannot by any means conclude with certainty that a secret impulse of self-love, falsely appearing as the idea of duty, was not actually the true determining cause of the will. . . . Out of love for humanity I am willing to admit that most of our actions are in accordance with duty; but, if we look more closely at our thoughts and aspirations, we everywhere come upon the dear self, which is always there, and it is this instead of the stern command of duty (which would often require self-denial) which supports our plans.

Kant, *Foundations of the Metaphysics of Morals*, trans. L. W. Beck, (New York: Macmillan, 1959), 23-4 (Ak 407).

57. I think here of a recent conference on ethics at which practically all the famous attendees violated their own principles egregiously in the way they participated in the conference: a promoter of Habermasian "ideal speech conditions" asked for extra time for his own talk, two other promoters of fairness as a universal human ideal tried to re-write the agenda when it didn't meet their wishes, and a speaker in defense of listening to and learning from others attended only his own session.

I pick Kantians as my example because their principles seem least conducive to casuistry. Utilitarians are of course adept at explaining how anything they want to do is morally permissible. A more common tendency of Kantians, in particular, is to transform their personal whims into moral imperatives that everyone must follow.

58. Room remains here for oppressive practices like slavery and patriarchy—but I would suggest that at least the *means* of criticizing even these practices, in the name of a general principle that each human being deserves equal respect, will be built into practically every tradition. The fact that something like a notion of "natural law"—by which what a tradition has to say must be interpreted against the background of some more general conception of what is truly just and humane—exists so widely across traditions provides empirical evidence that this is in fact the case. From the uses of *li* in the Confucian tradition, to the Noahide laws in Judaism, to the notions of *dharma* in various Indic traditions and *adat* in various Malay traditions, to the "laws of humankind" among the Northern Barotse, it is striking how often one can find notions of (higher) law that transcend (ordinary human) law, notions by which the moral conventions of one's society must be interpreted in accordance with a higher moral standard. See, on this, Jeffrey Wattles, *The Golden Rule*, (New York: Oxford University Press, 1996), Clifford Geertz, *Local Knowledge*, (New York: Basic Books, 1983), 175-214, Max Gluckman, *The Judicial Process Among the Barotse of Northern Rhodesia*, (Manchester: Manchester University Press, 1967), and my *Ethics of Culture*, chapter 6.

59. To a considerable extent, this conditioning fits in with Augustine's understanding-to-faith-to-greater-understanding position, but to some extent the emphasis on prior understanding, in the cultural case, must be greater than in the Christian one. For Augustine, after all, the point is not merely faith but faith *in* one particular truth, which then turns out to be the source of all (particular) truths. The initial level of understanding is therefore only provisional, and is seen as such from the position of faith. In my account, the emphasis belongs on faith as such, and not on faith in any particular tradi-

tion—hence the pluralism I can allow for, as opposed to the very strict orthodoxy defended by Augustine—and the faith is needed only to change one's moral understanding, not to change one's grasp of truth in all areas. While one may, after embracing a culture-faith, come to regard one's prior grasp of moral principles as at best thin and naive, one need not come to regard one's prior scientific or philosophical beliefs as similarly inadequate. This means that the understanding that conditions faith in the cultural case is a real, not a provisional, understanding, and that the faith itself can therefore presumably fail, after being adopted, if the culture to which one has committed oneself does not in fact live up to the moral promise it seemed to hold out. Culture-faith is fallibilist; Augustinian faith is not.

60. I develop a detailed argument that this is the job liberals should take on in response to their communitarian critics in "Insignificant Communities," *Freedom of Association*, ed. Amy Gutmann, (Princeton, N.J.: Princeton University Press, 1998).

# Part Three:

# Ethics in a Diverse World of Conflict—

# Gender, Law, and Medicine

## *Chapter Seven*

# Ethics in the Female Voice: Murasaki Shikibu and the Framing of Ethics for Japan[1]

Mara Miller

A growing body of recent theory suggests that integrating women's voices into the canon of any given culture would result in the culture as a whole differing profoundly from the patriarchal patterns with which we are so familiar. The question has seemed largely hypothetical, however, since there are so few opportunities for study of the long-term effects of non-patriarchal voices or institutions on industrialized societies. Indeed, among industrialized/modernized nations, there is only one culture that has incorporated women's voices as an integral and highly significant part of its canon from earliest times. This is Japan, which, contrary to popular stereotype, has done so for close to a millennium and a half.

I have argued in an earlier article that the Japanese inclusion of the female voice has corresponded with fundamental differences from the patriarchal and phallocentric Symbolic Orders that are otherwise virtually universal.[2] In that chapter I focused on a set of connections that can be traced using Lacanian theory among writing, patriarchy as a system of gender-based domination and construction of "Subjects," the Oedipus complex within the individual psyche, and a set of legal, religious, and epistemological values.

Still unexplored from this point of view, yet particularly interesting, are the implications of women's voices in a number of areas closely related to ethics: notions of selfhood and personal identity, of agency and responsibility, of nature, humanity, and emotion; the structuring of "Subject/Object" relations; the construction of power, gender, and sex; the definition and recognition of the various virtues; and the sense of the ways in which aesthetics, ethics, social philosophy, and metaphysics are interrelated.[3] In spite of the vast Chinese and Korean legacies (Buddhism, Confucianism, and Taoism, law, and the ideographic writing system), in Japan these ethical concepts and constructs have repeatedly acquired distinctive forms, as have several of the specifically Confucianist ideas: filial piety, relational responsibilities, and self-cultivation.

The developments of Japan's distinctive forms of ethical thought and behavior have, of course, complex histories, shaped as they were by Shinto and other native institutions (everything from patterns of inheritance to the wet-rice form of agriculture).[4] But they are attributable as well to the roles played by women in the early formation of the canon of Japanese thought. As early as the Heian period (794-1186 C.E.) we find in women's writing versions of an ethics of care and situation ethics worked out in some detail. Indeed, women's writing—especially that by Murasaki Shikibu and Sei Shonagon—comprised virtually the only *sustained* pursuit outside of Japan's imported "axial-age" religions (Confucianism, Taoism, and Buddhism), of what Westerners consider ethical questions. (Women were prevented from contributing to the formal canon of Japanese religious thought by the fact that they were educated primarily in the Japanese vernacular writing system, while religious writing was all in Chinese characters.)

The relation between the gender of these Heian writers and the content and structure of the ethics they developed cannot be decided with certainty in this chapter. In this chapter, therefore, I would like merely to extend my earlier inquiry to ethics, with specific reference to the extraordinary yet recently neglected contribution of Murasaki Shikibu. The role Murasaki played in the construction, development, and dissemination of discursive practices that provided alternatives to the patriarchal and phallocentric Chinese ones is an ambitious project that has yet to be fully appreciated. (I am thinking here of such matters as the legitimation of non-religious art, and the proliferation of various modalities of Female Gaze.) And we are still farther from being able to assess Murasaki's extraordinary contribution to the integration (in what may well be the world's only example) of the "imaginary" into a Symbolic Order. (Those who are familiar with Japanese history are well aware of the many ways medieval warrior culture diminished both contemporary women's position and the influence of previous women's achievements. Nonetheless, from our current vantage point, the attempts to curtail Murasaki's influence in particular reveal themselves as manifestations of the "anxiety of influence"—particularly terrifying to warriors, no doubt, when that incontrovertible influence is that of a woman.)

This chapter is confined to two small parts of this grander project. After a brief introduction to Japanese women's voices and to Murasaki and her work in Part I, Part II outlines some of Murasaki's most important contributions to the history of ethics, indicating as we go the degree of originality in her work. (By "most important" I mean from the point of view of current Western ethics, philosophy and feminist theory; there is no room here for a consideration of which of these might have been the most influential on subsequent Japanese ethical thought or (still less) actual behavior, a more empirical and historical project than this one.) Part III examines in some depth one of the most intriguing, far-reaching and innovative aspects of this contribution, namely her recognition of the ways that an individual can make use of personal experience for the purpose of making a difficult decision, and her development of this recognition into a model for ethical decision-making.

## I: Women's Voices in Japan

The single most important female voice in the Japanese canon—arguably the single most important voice of either sex[5]—is that of novelist, poet, and diarist Murasaki Shikibu, who between 1000 and 1020 CE wrote the world's first psychological novel *The Tale of Genji* (*Genji Monogatari*).[6] The novel follows the lives of three generations: first the principal protagonist Prince Genji, his closest friend To no Chujo, and their lovers and wives, Komurasaki, Aoi, the Rokujo Lady, Sannomiya, and other ladies; and then Genji's son Yugiri, To no Chujo's son Kashiwagi, and their wives and lovers; and finally the generation of Kashiwagi's son (thought to be the son of Genji) Kaoru. The wide cast of characters permits the author to take up a wide range of ethical dilemmas within which certain themes are revisited with ethically significant variations in each case. The pattern of variation suggests an author who was philosophically-minded, working out the different combinations systematically, even if not abstractly.

Widely read during its own time, by everyone from young daughters of provincial governors to the powers-behind-the-throne and grandfathers of emperors,[7] *The Tale of Genji* has consistently garnered an extraordinary amount of interest over the past millennium. It became virtually "required reading" for poets and courtiers during Japan's Middle Ages,[8] attracting learned commentary from nobles, generals, and political advisors, and has served since at least the mid-twelfth century as a source of inspiration for writers and artists of all kinds—poets, dramatists, painters, print-makers, costume designers, and (today) novelists, video-makers, advertisers, and cartoonists.

Over the past three centuries it has become customary to read *Genji* for its aesthetics, its literary value, its poetics, its psychology, and its wealth of historical information—indisputably rich and productive veins, to be sure.[9] I would like, therefore, to propose here a "new" reading of *The Tale of Genji* as a work of ethics. This may seem radical, even preposterous, but such a reading is actually a return to earlier standards of interpretation, particularly those of the Middle Ages (the Kamakura (1186-1336) and the Ashikaga or Muromachi (1336-1573) periods), when commentators, readers, and writers alike were fascinated by the book's moral significance.[10]

At the same time, interpretations by Kamakura poets, literary critics, and anthologists were unstinting with their praise and established *The Tale of Genji* as essential to all subsequent poetry and poetic theory. Such work set the stage for early modern Japanese thinkers like Motoori Norinaga (1730-1801), a philologist, moralist, and social philosopher of far-ranging and disquieting import, regarded by many as "the greatest literary scholar the country has produced."[11] For Motoori, the aesthetic *becomes* a political category, and this is especially true of the aesthetic most fully developed by *Genji*, a form of indulgence in feeling called *mono no aware*, or simply *aware*. *Mono no aware* has been defined as "the deep feelings inherent in, or felt from the world and experience of it."[12] Both pleasant and unpleasant feelings (or occasions) are encompassed, both "exclamation[s] of joy or other intense feeling[s], [and] . . . sadder and even tragic feelings."[13] The term refers ambiguously "both to the source or the occasion of such feeling and the response to it."[14]

Long recognized as one of the most distinctive—and most loved—features of Murasaki's work, *mono no aware* has come to be considered one of the defining features of Japanese culture in general. In the modern period, under the influence of Kant, we became accustomed to thinking of art and aesthetics as essentially disinterested, that is, unrelated to categories of interest such as ethics and politics. By contrast, in the hands of Motoori, *mono no aware* became a means by which what was distinctive about Japanese culture could be recognized and, eventually, made to serve as the foundation for early forms of the Japanese state and Japanese national identity. It persists even to the present day; it can be seen, for instance, in movies, whose weeping samurai perplex American audiences unfamiliar with this value.

## II: Overview of Murasaki Shikibu's Thinking on Ethics

### The Basic Question: How Ought One to Live? The Ideal Life According to Murasaki

In *The Tale of Genji* Murasaki raises the question Bernard Williams identifies as not only the center of moral philosophy but the foundation for the forging of the discipline of philosophy itself: How ought one to live?

For the Euro-centric West, this question arose in ancient Greece when ethics began to distinguish itself as a branch of philosophy distinct from religion. In Japan, by contrast, until the modern period, there was virtually no separate discipline precisely analogous to philosophy, no study of philosophical questions that was distinctively philosophical—that is (by Western standards), at once secular, abstract, and systematic. Such philosophical exploration as there was took place within the larger spheres of either religion or literature. While both types of writers could be systematic, the religious were not secular, the literary not abstract. Both types of deviation from the Western philosophical norms have made it difficult to recognize the full value and implications of Japanese philosophical speculation. Some have even claimed that there is little or no (pre-modern) Japanese philosophy. Yet if one considers the nature and scope of the questions, and the systematic pursuit of the answers and conditions for answering, then some early Japanese literature is as fine philosophy as exists, and Murasaki's work must take its place as one of the most far-reaching and ground-breaking contributions ever made to the field of ethics anywhere.

Murasaki Shikibu raises—and answers—Williams's foundational question in a most systematic way by creating credible portraits of the ideal life, the ideal marriage (that between Genji and the character after whom the author has been given her nom de plume, Murasaki, whom I will call Komurasaki[15]), and the ideal education, and then goes on to recognize the importance of the distinctive forms these ideals take for men (in the eponymous character Genji) and women (in, for example, Komurasaki). In addition, she examines a number of specific ethical dilemmas that appear in many cultures and offers viable (often distinctively Japanese) ways of resolving them ethically.

Her focus on both men and women is both radical and deeply traditional. It is radical in that she advocates a broader education for women than was customary in her time,[16] and never ignores the social mores that place them at a disadvantage. At the same time, her confidence in the authority of poetry (written by both sexes and for both sexes, and celebrating the experience of both), and her assumptions that women are full moral agents and have access to sacred realities equal (or superior) to men's, are traditional Shinto. Her belief that women can aspire to full development was already a well-established tenet of Mahayana Buddhism, the form of Buddhism predominating in East Asia, and deeply pervaded the consciousness of the men and women of the Heian court. The Mahayana belief in the full Enlightenment of women is grounded in chapter twelve of the *Lotus Sutra*, in which the Dragon Kings daughter becomes instantaneously enlightened, but it is also found in a number of other sutras; Mimi Yiengpruksuwan has shown that one such sutra, which describes Paradise from a woman's point of view, provided the inspiration for the construction of the Byodo-in villa and its garden by the Fujiwara regent who was the father of the empress whom Murasaki Shikibu served (a garden that was widely imitated), and thus structured both the physical grounds and the mental reality of Murasaki and her associates.[17]

Murasaki's decision to present both male and female versions of "fully-realized" individuals (to use twentieth-century terms) has two interesting effects. It makes the work more easily relevant to post-/modern readers than ancient Greek philosophical models, which focused exclusively on men. And it allowed her work to influence (both directly, in terms of emulation, and indirectly, in terms of deliberate rebellion) Japanese models of development, both male and female, throughout subsequent Japanese history.

## Self-Reflection and the Ideal Life

Essential to Murasaki's conception of the ideal life are self-reflection and the deliberate adoption of ethical responsibility for one's actions. The plot establishes their importance; these traits (or virtues) are clearly discernible in all her main characters, even one so diffident and unheroic (even to the point of being Hamlet-esque) as Kashiwagi, whose story sets up the most radical of Murasaki's ethical innovations (discussed in the final section of this chapter).

At the opening of the chapter bearing his name ("The Oak Tree," Chapter 36 of the Seidensticker translation[18]), Kashiwagi has seduced Genji's wife Sannomiya (aka the Third Princess; whom Waley calls Nyohsan[19]). Sannomiya will soon bear his child, a situation with profound ramifications for Kashiwagi, his parents, his beloved Sannomiya, the child, and of course Genji. Genji has been especially fond of Kashiwagi, the son of Genji's closest friend, To no Chujo. The seriousness of the transgression is reflected in Kashiwagi's assessment of the situation. Genji, who in the past "had always sent for Kashiwagi when something interesting or important came up, but [from whom] in recent months there had been no summonses" (630), has summoned Kashiwagi to help arrange the festivities for an upcoming imperial visit. Kashiwagi does his best for Genji, but at their interview the strain proves too much for Kashiwagi: "There was nothing in Genji's manner to suggest innuendoes and hidden meanings. Kashiwagi was uncomfortable all the same, and afraid that his embarrassment might show" (632).

At the rehearsal for the emperor's visit, Kashiwagi becomes seriously ill. In the stream-of-consciousness soliloquy that opens Chapter 36, he reviews the various aspects of his situation and tries to decide what to do. It is worth quoting this soliloquy in full:

> The New Year came and Kashiwagi's condition had not improved. He knew how troubled his parents were and he knew that suicide was no solution, for he would be guilty of the grievous sin of having left them behind. He had no wish to live on. Since his very early years he had had high standards and ambitions and had striven in private matters and public to outdo his rivals by even a little. His wishes had once or twice been thwarted, however, and he had so lost confidence in himself that the world had come to seem unrelieved gloom. A longing to prepare himself for the next world had succeeded his ambitions, but the opposition of his parents had kept him from following the mendicant way through the mountains and over the moors. He had delayed, and time had gone by. Then had come events, and for them he had only himself to blame, which had made it impossible for him to show his face in public. He did not blame the gods. His own deeds were working themselves out. A man does not have the thousand years of the pine, and he wanted to go now, while

> there were still those who might mourn for him a little, and perhaps even a sigh from *her* would be the reward for his burning passion. To die now and perhaps win the forgiveness of the man who must feel so aggrieved would be far preferable to living on and bringing sorrow and dishonor upon the lady and upon himself. In his last moments everything must disappear. Perhaps, because he had no other sins to atone for, a part of the affection with which Genji had once honored him might return.
>
> The same thoughts, over and over, ran uselessly through his mind. And why, he asked himself in growing despair, had he so deprived himself of alternatives? His pillow threatened to float away on the river of his woes. (636-7)

Kashiwagi's soliloquy is remarkable for the subtleties and complexities of its assessment. His musings reflect the wide variety of ethical guidelines vying for control over Heian thought and behavior. The impression of the "unrelieved gloom" of the world, his belief in an afterlife and his yearning to prepare himself for it, his sensitivity to the passing of time, his recognition of the part his own deeds have played in creating his "fate," as well as the tropes of floating and the river, are all reflections of Buddhism—to which he makes, however, no explicit reference. Indeed, with the exception of the reference to the afterlife, they might almost be considered secular, so deeply has his culture been steeped in the Buddhist worldview.

Equally ambiguous are some of the references to Confucian values, especially his ambition and competitiveness, and his sense of shame, and his keen awareness of the impact of his actions on everyone with whom he is in relation. He weighs the effects and feelings of all parties, and considers both his feelings and his actions, both his responsibility in bringing about the tragedy and the effects of any seeming solution on each of the affected parties. More explicit are two subtly intertwined Confucian values: the recognition that his behavior (and his feelings as a result of his behavior) cannot be separated in fact from his parents' welfare, and second, the acknowledgment that filial piety prohibits suicide—the course to which his own feelings seem to prompt him. Yet it sounds as though he refrains from suicide less out of concern for the welfare of his parents than out of a Buddhist concern for his own soul, a desire to avoid acquiring bad karma. The Confucian work ethic, according to which one has a responsibility to do one's best and to excel as best one can for the sake of the family, which had encouraged his youthful ambitions, had long ago been overcome by the adversity he had met, as had the native propensity toward competition so evident in Heian culture (evidenced in poetry and painting competitions and celebrated in paintings of *The Tale of Genji's* competition among oxcarts). The result was he was discouraged and vulnerable to his emotions. Such a psychological state was easily exploited by Buddhist metaphysics, and spiritual ones succeeded his worldly ambitions. These, however, were held in check by Confucian obedience to his parents. (In Kashiwagi's case, this sounds more like obedience, following rules, than a more enlightened recognition of their need for him and his role in the family.) Now, having violated both Confucian and Buddhist proscriptions as well as the secular obligations of gratitude, he feels disgraced and is consumed by worry over losing face—again a primarily secular value (though with Confucian overtones). Toward the end of the soliloquy, the elaborate knot of his intertwining feelings seems to take over: desires to be mourned, to be remembered well by his lover, and to be forgiven, even loved again by Genji. This desire to rekindle the closeness he had formerly had with Genji may be taken as evidence of the core Japanese value called *amae*, the delight Japanese take in the reciprocity between an elder and her dependent, and in the giving and seeking of nurturance.[20] Kashiwagi believes, however, that these desires can be fulfilled only if he dies; his prompt demise would also have the positive result of avoiding further pain to his lover and shame to himself.

Ultimately Kashiwagi's feelings destroy him; he sickens and dies. His death, while hardly suicide *per se*, is clearly a result of his own psyche. He refuses to make himself a victim, and there is no suggestion of anyone else playing a role in his early death. Throughout it all he strives to maintain his own responsibility, refusing to blame others, the gods, or fate.

## The Gender Contrast: Kashiwagi and Kiritsubo

Kashiwagi is one of a number of Murasaki's characters who sicken and die under adversity. Some of these deaths are clearly identified as caused by evil spirits and/or the unconscious malice of others, others by the "victim's" internalization of others' envy and hatred. Ultimately each case is different. (This is what makes the work systematic.) Yet Kashiwagi's guilt-induced illness and death closely resembles that of Genji's mother Kiritsubo, whom we meet in the novel's opening sentence: "In a certain reign there was a lady not of the first rank whom the emperor loved more than any of the others" (Seidensticker, 3)—a sentence that signals Murasaki's awareness of the conflict between society and the individual, between social value and personal emotional value,[21] and that also suggests her awareness of limitations on the importance of intent, which Buddhism is often in danger of exaggerating.

Attracting such a deep love from the emperor, and without high-ranked protectors at court—and eventually giving birth to the beautiful baby Prince Genji—Kiritsubo draws the resentment of all the other court ladies, in spite of her goodness and good will: "Everything she did offended someone." She falls ill, and before long dies. Although in some later cases ghosts—or subconscious emotions—of (dead or living) envious female rivals seem to be attributed with actual power to harm living (female) human beings, in Kiritsubo's case it would seem death is due to her *knowledge* of the ill-will and the effects of this knowledge on her, rather than due to some magical effect of hatred itself: "Probably aware of what was happening, she fell seriously ill. . . ." Without meaning to, Kiritsubo has violated social harmony; unable to withstand the burden of knowledge of the resentment aimed at her, her own feelings overwhelm her. The parallel drawn both by Murasaki and by her fictional characters between Kiritsubo and the famous Chinese beauty Yang Kuei-fei underscores the ethical dimensions of this course of events. Yang Kuei-fei, too, was beloved by an emperor who was similarly considered to have lost all sense of proportion and self-control. The Chinese case had disastrous results: the emperor's weakness allowed rebels to take advantage of him, the court fell, he barely escaped with his life, and Yang Kuei-fei was killed. The story has gone down in Chinese cautionary literature and art, and enjoyed frequent allusions, retellings, and depictions in Japan as well. (There's a marvelous pair of six-panel screens of this story at the Freer Gallery in Washington, D.C.)

*The Tale of Genji* marks important differences between the male and female characters who sicken and die. (Here I will focus on Kiritsubo, but she is only one of a number of female examples; in fact the disparity of the numbers of men and women who follow this pattern is one of the most important differences.) While both Kashiwagi and Kiritsubo seem to die of an almost natural process, Kashiwagi is shown as an agent engineering the misfortune that results in his illness and death, while Kiritsubo is portrayed as passive, and indeed there is some question when she first falls ill as to whether she even knows the anger she has churned up ("*Probably* aware of what was happening, she fell seriously ill. . . .") (It is important to note that the Japanese language in general is far more sensitive than any Indo-European language to the limitations on certainty and to what we might call epistemological nuances and the varieties of epistemological positionings, so that it is far more prevalent, even necessary, in Japanese to indicate how one knows something ("I hear . . . ," "I see . . . ," "they say . . . ," etc.) as well as to give some sense of how likely it is to be true. We might speculate that it is this very trait within ordinary language that has made the development of philosophy as a discipline largely unnecessary in Japan, given that there is so much less naivete and error in everyday language to point out and analyze.)

Kashiwagi has done something wrong, and must pay—more, he himself *feels* he must pay; Kiritsubo has done nothing wrong, and is punished—or perhaps punishes herself—for her virtue and good fortune. Kashiwagi brings misfortune on himself by his actions; Kiritsubo is a purely passive recipient of undeserved ill-will. Kashiwagi wrestles with his conscience, examining in detail the effects of his transgression and the various courses of action open to him; Kiritsubo's anguish is caused by her ill-treatment by jealous rivals and she can envision no alternatives. By his death, Kashiwagi opens the way for Genji's acceptance of his son and eliminates several problems for his beloved (how to avoid him in the future, how to live with her loyalty divided between two men, both of whom have some claim on her, etc.). Thus his death has positive effects for others, and thus might even be said to incur good karma. Kiritsubo's death, on the other hand, benefits no one, either practically or karmically. It is an unrelieved tragedy for those who love her (Genji and his father) and to whom she is responsible—something we know she could never intend, and that must, therefore, be happening against her will. Ultimately, Kashiwagi's death is the result of his taking responsibility for his actions; while her death is the outcome of her internalization of other people's hatred and envy.

The differences between these two portrayals may be due less to the sex of the character than to Murasaki's own stage of life—her greater wisdom and maturity when she reached Kashiwagi's generation (a full two generations later than Kiritsubo) or, conversely her impatience to get on with the story when she was writing Genji's family history (whether that occurred at the beginning of the writing or later on, at the request of readers for more background—scholars are not sure of the relative dating of all sections). Certainly Kiritsubo's passivity in Chapter One is echoed in the fates of other ladies from the early chapters, most notably Yugao (aka "Evening Faces," Chapter Four) and Aoi (aka "Heartvine," Chapter Nine), who also die as a result of others' envy.

Women from the later sections of the book whose lives are overwhelmed by the actions and emotions of others tend not to die as a result, and some of them are quite creative in taking things into their own hands. Two things seem to have happened with these later female characters. First, the dangers the author sees for them shift from women's envy (in combination, it is true, with men's desire for and power over them) to men's actions. This is a complex shift in the cause assigned: from women to men, from the realm of the psychic to a more commonsensical or matter-of-fact level, and from emotions to actions in the world. It parallels a shift in awareness, from blaming the immediate oppressor to a recognition of the larger social forces at work, and thus signals a new sophistication and maturity on Murasaki's part, particularly since Murasaki had no theoretical analysis of power and oppression available to guide her. Second, in the latter part of the book, even those women who are most helpless at the hands of the men who desire them seem to have developed a repertoire for escaping and charting their own courses in life. Murasaki is not in denial about the power men have, but she no longer sees women as completely powerless to resist—and of course she no longer sees other women as a woman's primary enemy, but recognizes that it is the men who are benefiting directly from the system.

## Education

The relation between education and ethics is an intimate one in any society: the education of a child is not merely the transmission of the information necessary in order to survive and to contribute to one's society, but is also the process of making a good human being. Murasaki, like many philosophers (and novelists) pays a great deal of attention to the education of children, both male and female. Certainly she was one of the earliest Japanese thinkers to write extensively about education. Her portraits of the kind of education needed to produce good and warm and attractive human beings carry considerable conviction.

In Murasaki's view, children rarely need to be disciplined. Such waywardness as may be encountered—when, for example, they get less attention than they want—can be countered by gently withdrawing approval and attention. Like Aristotle, Murasaki knew that children learn by example and, even more importantly, by trying to earn the greater approval and attention of respectful adults. Given these premises, it goes without saying that physical punishment is virtually unimaginable. To what extent she was reporting what was already common practice and to what extent she was original in her prescriptions is hard to say, given the paucity of other documents on the subject. (The leniency of the parents of "The Lady Who Loved Insects,"[22] an earlier tale, suggests that the idiosyncrasies of young women sometimes met with great tolerance.) Regardless of originality, she was unquestionably influential; this depiction of successful child-raising has been so effective and so convincing that it remained in place until the modern era.[23]

On the other hand, Murasaki's emphasis on detachment as a virtue that would naturally be found in any admirable adult is consonant with long-standing Buddhist theory and practice—although there are few early Japanese secular texts that illustrate this quality to such a significant extent. Although she avoids its Buddhist name, detachment as virtue is illustrated again and again by what characters do, in keeping with her (novelist's) focus on character and action. And of course it can make a great difference just what it is that one is expected to detach *from.* In Buddhism generally, the most important object from which to detach is usually one's feelings. (Since reality in the Western sense has from a Buddhist point of view no reality, it is only one's reaction to phenomena from which one can detach.) Murasaki shows us this type of detachment in the (grown-up) Komurasaki, who, unlike Kiritsubo's despicable jealous rivals, is able to control her jealousy and insecurity when Genji behaves poorly toward her; her self-control, in fact, arouses his (and the reader's) admiration. In *The Tale of Genji*, however, this virtue of detachment from emotion vies with another, distinctly non-Buddhist value or virtue, *mono no aware.* This emotional indulgence is depicted in *The Tale of Genji* as most admirable and to be cultivated equally by men and women. *Mono no aware* has a Buddhist tinge in that it always conveys a sense that what one cherishes is the more precious precisely *because* of its transience (in the case, for example, of the cherry blossom) or because of the transience of life in general (in the case of a loved one), the transience of everything being a basic Buddhist metaphysical principle. Yet such sensitivity proves admirable in the novel only provided it causes no disruption of the social order. This provision suggests it may be shaped as much by Confucianism as by Buddhism.

*Mono no aware* has another Confucian dimension, for it depends for its expression upon an important Confucian virtue, self-cultivation. Although reputedly a spontaneous outburst of pure natural feeling grounded in primal, even primitive sensibility (it is often said to have arisen from the onomatopoetic expression "ahh"), and although it may also be expressed through physiological functions such as crying, or physical manifestations such as sleeves wet by tears, by Murasaki's time *mono no aware* required considerable cultivation of artistic sensibility.[24] This cultivation is dependent on the mastery of such arts as calligraphy, music, painting, dance, and poetry, the very means by which the Confucian self is self-transformed.[25] The arts had become means—literally "paths" or "ways"—(admittedly among others) to Enlightenment and to full responsible self-conscious personhood.

This points to crucial differences in the ways in which education is understood in East Asia and in the West. First, in East Asia, on the deepest levels there is no separation between ethics and aesthetics; they are intimately linked, both in their objectives and as a means to the cultivation of the responsible individual. Secondly, deep virtue and spiritual profundity are understood to ensue not only from intellectual training and psychological exercises but also—indeed often *primarily*—from physical cultivation of the type found in meditation, martial arts, and writing/calligraphy. This physical cultivation (thirdly) is a necessary part of artistic training.

In the *Lotus Sutra*, the creation of works of art based on the sutra and the copying out of the sutra are described both as inherently good acts and as bringing merit to the soul who performs them.[26] In addition, many Buddhist artworks from the Heian period are clearly designed to inspire confidence and faith and a desire for goodness in those who view them—and to have good effects on their viewers. At the same time, a copy of the sutra, say, would of course be written as beautifully as possible; this process requires years of training in calligraphy—training that is physical, but has both spiritual and intellectural dimensions, combining as it does breathing techniques and perfect control of one's muscles, as well as intellectual knowledge of written characters and styles of writing. Murasaki's society clearly extrapolated from these religious insights to a broader recognition—also very much in keeping with the Confucian understanding of calligraphy—that a person's character could be read in her or his calligraphy—and in the selection of papers, styles of writing, branches or flowers attached, etc. Similarly, the dances that the children perform in *The Tale of Genji*, and that the adults (and author and readers) find so endearing and entertaining, are not merely for the purposes of entertainment, display, or social bonding. They are a form of *gagaku/bigaku/gigaku*, a Court religious ritual dance that teaches the children ideals of physical comportment and control over their muscles, endows them with the basic rhythms of their culture, trains their memory for sequences of physical action (much as origami does today), and also orients them cosmologically (because the dance form is oriented toward the four cardinal directions and reiterates the fundamental values of the Chinese Confucian/yin-yang cosmology).

Murasaki's most original contribution to Japanese thought about education lies in her profound insight into the meaning of the arts and letters within her society, that in this context, the physical, the intellectual, the artistic, and the moral aspects of education interpenetrate. With each character, we see her insistence on the importance of a broad education for both sexes. Education for a boy must include not only reading, writing, and the Classics, but the arts, and emotional sensitivity.[27] Education for a woman must include reading, writing, and the Classics. While there is something of a chicken-and-egg problem here—clearly Murasaki would have been in no position to make such a case so powerfully had she not been well educated herself—I think we may take it that her successful depictions of such attractive characters, including both artistic and sensitive men and well-read and literary women, have provided powerful encouragement to the Japanese trend toward high literacy rates for women that was already in evidence and that continued to be so outstanding (compared, for example to Europe, India, or China) throughout subsequent history.

## Models of Heian "Self-Actualization"

Genji himself provides a model of full human development that, while informed by Buddhist, Shinto, and Confucian values, far exceeds the bounds of their usual concerns. As an ideal male, he combines typical male qualities (he is stalwart in adversity, persistent, responsible) with qualities often associated with femininity—he is easily moved to tears, he is deeply compassionate, and sensitive.

This male model is accompanied by a similarly complex, nuanced and compelling version of female development, primarily in the person of Genji's greatest love, Komurasaki. What is truly astonishing about this—and not just for the time, nor just for Japan—is the way the women in *The Tale of Genji* are shown not only for the qualities that appeal to men (although their appeal is important, given that the novel is comprised primarily of love stories), but in many other capacities, in their sometimes willful cultivation of characteristics that are not appealing to men, and in their own voices, from their own perspectives, and with their own concerns independent of men's wishes.

In a sense it is Heian Japan meets Henrik Ibsen or Kate Chopin—except that Murasaki *is* able to envision a number of possibilities for the woman who "leaves," rejecting the love of the man who considers himself the center of her world.

I don't want to oversimplify here, or remake Murasaki into a feminist dogmatist. She has many female characters who are hopelessly dependent, emotionally, socially, and otherwise, on Genji or other men. But what is more remarkable is the degree to which Genji criticism today focuses on female dependency, without recognizing the great range of female independence in the novel, and the degree of radical subversion provided by Murasaki's insistence on depicting the inner realities of women's points of view, whether dependent or independent (or, most commonly, some mixture of the two). As progressive and enlightened as we like to think of ourselves, this is something that many twentieth-century Americans still have difficulty doing: portraying women as strong protagonists, allowing female characters a variety of perspectives and individual points of view, and above all *identifying* with women, and especially women who are to some extent objectified by male Subjects, men who at least to some extent construct themselves as Subjects precisely by means of our objectification.

This is not to say that the book is a celebration of female independence. It is, however, a celebration of female subjectivity—women in the Subject position, women as they understand themselves to be. This subjectivity includes a wide variety of adaptations to the constraints put upon their lives by the several aspects of imported Chinese culture, including the imperial system.

The sheer variety of female types—in this case as seen by young boys seeking to assert their own privilege as males and take their position as Subjects by objectifying women—is thematized by the conversation among the teen-aged Genji and his friends in Chapter Two, in which they discuss varieties of female attractiveness and compare young women of their acquaintance, only to discover that there is no single female ideal that they can all agree to, and that a woman's intelligence, artistic talents, temperament, and character may be as important to men as physical appearance. This variety of female Subjects allows Murasaki to explore both the impact of the system of gendered power relations and varieties of human response as systematically as any modern philosopher.[28]

The format, meanwhile, fosters the examination of particular dilemmas from different points of view not merely in the sense of different personality types (or sexes or ages) having different "takes" on any given situation, but in the sense of the different ways a single situation can affect the several characters who are implicated in it.

## Murasaki's Contribution vis-a-vis the Concerns of Twentieth-Century Feminism

The ethical dilemmas raised by Murasaki include a number of situations that, because of disparities in power, affect women disproportionately: problems of extra-marital affairs and pregnancy, and how each party should behave afterwards; the problem of the betrayal of a young ward or adopted daughter by a guardian; the problem of rape (in a number of different forms). Murasaki has recently been criticized for her sometimes-laudatory portrayals of her culture's often-sexist males enjoying their privileges at the expense of their female companions. Her attention to gender-based power differentials, however, and her close attention to the varieties of female experiences of subjectivity and agency—as well as her model of male maturation, which requires *outgrowing* the treatment of women as objects, reveals this criticism to be very limited (as well as anachronistic).

These dilemmas are situated within a larger framework that highlights questions about power relations between men and women: What are the effects on women of the power men have over them? How can—and should—women respond? What social institutions are harmful to women? Do arranged marriages "work" as a social institution? Who benefits? Do they benefit men more than women? (There is a definite critique of arranged marriages in the novel, for instance; nearly all of them turn out badly, and are analyzed with great clarity: Genji's with Aoi, Kashiwagi's with the Second Princess, and so on.) How are men harmed in turn by the damage done to women?

Murasaki pays particular attention to the effects on a woman of seduction and rape. What factors, if any, might make a difference in how a woman experiences it? While Murasaki skirts the issue of incest *per se*[29]—I suspect because she is not interested in what she and her readers would consider wrong under any circumstances—she doesn't shy away from the related issue of the betrayal of trust that accompanies Genji's sexual overtures toward the young girl for whom he has been serving as guardian.

It is completely inappropriate, of course, to think of this in terms of modern-day feminism, which is grounded not only in Western values but as a response to patriarchy. Japanese society of Murasaki's day was considerably less patriarchal than we can imagine, Chinese institutions being strongly at odds with native matriarchal ones such as feminine inheritance, matrilocality, and so on.

## Development of an Ethics of Care

*The Tale of Genji* seems to bear out Carol Gilligan's theory, that women's ethics is primarily an ethics of caring.[30] In *Mapping the Moral Domain*, Carol Gilligan, Janie Victoria Ward and a dozen other psychologists trace out the implications of their study of women's ways of thinking about morality, which they have come to call the "ethic of care." They find women's ethical thinking to be at odds with ways of thinking, moral judgments, and self-descriptions characteristic of mainstream (and hegemonic) ethics, which have been based on men's reports:

> Two moral voices [in the reports they collected] signaled different ways of thinking about what constitutes a moral problem and how such problems can be addressed or solved. In addition, two voices draw attention to the fact that a story can be told from different angles and a situation seen in different lights. Like ambiguous figure perception where the same picture can be seen as a vase or as two faces, the basic elements of moral judgment—self, others, and the relationship between them—can be organized in different ways, depending on how "relationship" is imagined or construed. From the perspective of someone seeking or loving justice, relationships are organized in terms of equality, symbolized by the balancing of scales. Moral concerns focus on problems of oppression, prob-

> lems stemming from inequality, and the moral ideal is one of reciprocity or equal respect. From the perspective of someone seeking or valuing care, relationship connotes responsiveness or engagement, a resiliency of connection that is symbolized by a network or web. Moral concerns focus on problems of detachment, on disconnection or abandonment or indifference, and the moral ideal is one of attention and response.[31]

The two styles of moral reasoning are sharply correlated with the sex of the reasoner:

> Care focus, although not characteristic of all women, was almost exclusively a female phenomenon in three samples of educationally advantaged North Americans. If girls and women were eliminated from the study, care focus in moral reasoning would virtually disappear. (xix)

Following Gilligan's pioneering work, a number of psychologists have begun tracing the existing impact of North American women's voices on ethics. They have found it impossible to do this without challenging prevailing (male) conceptions of selfhood and relationship, going so far as to suggest that "[t]he contribution of women's thinking . . . is a different voice, a different way of speaking about relationships and about the experience of self. The inclusion of this voice changes the map of the moral domain."[32]

This ethic of care is clearly discernible in *The Tale of Genji*. As we have seen with Kashiwagi, however, it is not associated with women more than men; rather, it is characteristic of men and women who are ideal—mature, attractive to the reader, and to other characters. In Kashiwagi's soliloquy, concern for the well-being of those whom he loves and to whom he bears a debt of gratitude—primarily his parents and Genji—plays a major role:

> He knew how troubled his parents were and he knew that suicide was no solution, for he would be guilty of the grievous sin of having left them behind.

More fundamental than gender *per se*, for Gilligan, is the conception of self that is held by the individual. In America, conceptions of self differ depending upon gender, with women holding a more relational view. Gilligan concludes that women's preference for the ethic of care over the ethic of justice, which "may reflect an awareness on some level of the disjunction between women's lives and Western culture" (xi), derives from

> conceptions of self and morality that implied a different way of thinking about relationships, one that often had set women apart from the main-

stream of Western thought because of its central premise that self and others were connected and interdependent.[33]

In America, the hegemonic culture—white, male, educated—favors both the ethic of justice and the autonomous, objective, and independent self. In Japan, however, all three of the "axial-age" religions, Buddhism, Confucianism, and Taoism, maintain views of the self as connected, relational, and interdependent—in spite of the fact that they are associated with patriarchy and patriarchal institutions. The "overriding value . . . placed on separation, individuation, and autonomy" by Western psychologists, philosophers, and moralists is not only not shared in East Asia, it is barely intelligible. In this context, to see Murasaki's achievement as the perception, analysis, and/or championing of an ethic of care that is distinctively female would be a distortion. Rather, she gives an original and independent shape to ethical care and the relational self, bringing them out of the primarily religious domain comprised of prescription and moral imperatives, and into the secular realm of human feeling and daily life. She guaranteed their intelligibility and viability in terms of lived human relationships. And indeed this is one of the reasons it became so necessary to reinterpret her stories along more purely Buddhist lines during the middle ages (in Noh drama).

## Murasaki on Ethical Agency

In *The Tale of Genji*, Murasaki explores a wide variety of forms of ethical agency, developing new types of ethical agents. She also explores the interrelationships among different types of individual agents and the community. In some cases, the conflict between the individual and society is so clear-cut it seems almost liberal—that of Genji's mother Kiritsubo, for instance. Although Kiritsubo does not prove a very strong or resilient individual, there is a definite sense in her story that the individual and society are inevitably at odds—something quite different from what we have come to expect from Confucian thinking about the self and society. (Kiritsubo's story is somewhat murky from the point of view of Confucian morals, since by dying she does not serve her lord, and therefore can hardly be considered a role model. Moreover, if, as is sometimes asserted, the Japanese penchant for social harmony is to be understood as Confucian in origin or aspiration, this story confounds that, as well, for it is society itself that is blameworthy.)

Kashiwagi, too, finds his desires in conflict with his society. By this point in her novel-writing Murasaki is extremely interested in the ways individuals find to get their needs met and to assert themselves as the distinct personalities they are. Kashiwagi, who must search his soul, can only discover the solution to Kashiwagi's problem. It places the subject or agent firmly at the center of the decision, without offering him the "easy" route of rules to obey. Nor does it allow him to make the choice easier by excising his emotion; his solution must encompass both feeling and duty. Increasingly throughout the novel characters and their situations become more complex and their abilities to deal with their situations more nuanced.

Yet there are problems with female agency in *The Tale of Genji*. These must be understood on several levels, for agency is complex. First, agency is not to be confused with power over the events in one's life nor even with the power to act as one would wish. Second, we must distinguish between Murasaki's vision, her creation of an ideal world, and her utopianism, on the one hand, and her reportorial skill, her accuracy as an observer and her interest in describing precisely what happens to women, on the other. On both these levels, women's agency may be realized either as effectiveness in the world or as taking responsibility. (Of course, taking responsibility is not the same thing as being effective in alleviating or causing a problem.) Ethical leaders in every culture have recognized the importance of this difference: while every ethical agent ideally takes responsibility for what s/he does, no human being in fact has complete control over what happens to her. Socrates' responsibility for his actions cannot prevent others from preventing him from teaching: they can and do incarcerate him, can and do call for his death. His choices lie in when and where to accede to their demands, and finally in choosing how to die. In a somewhat different vein, Abraham's freedom lies in his willingness to obey God's command to act against his own deepest desires; Job's, to choose an attitude by which to surrender to what he cannot prevent.

Similarly, Murasaki's women cannot choose the freedoms the men enjoy. They can and do choose, increasingly as the book progresses, how they will deal with the situations in which they find themselves. (In a Buddhist worldview, of course, one's fate is not arbitrary, but the result of past deeds.) And of course Murasaki shows that the most interesting and desirable women are those who have been given the greatest intellectual, moral, and psychological freedom, through a good education and through being treated as full human beings.

## Murasaki's Contribution to the Notion of Responsibility

Perhaps most interesting of all, however, Murasaki in the novel develops a framework within which she carves out a new kind of responsibility. In spite of the well-known Buddhist and Confucian attacks on the notion of self, in fact both religions had long emphasized personal responsibility. Buddhism insisted on taking responsibility not only for one's actions, for following the precepts and the monastic code, but for one's intentions as well—for the attitudes and mental states that would lead to Enlightenment—and hence ultimately for one's very state of consciousness. Similarly Confucianism advocates not merely the following of rules that ensure moral acts but for becoming a certain kind of person—the Confucian "self-transformation" referred to earlier, which we saw Kashiwagi struggling so hard to achieve.

In addition, Murasaki gives perhaps the clearest evidence we have from the Heian period of some of the expanded dimensions of selfhood that we have become acutely aware of in the West since Freud and have since come to take for granted, most notably the subconscious, revealed in the novel in some of the dreams and in conflicts between repressed and acknowledged feelings. In a similar vein, she shows Genji's whole life to have been shaped by events of his early childhood—not so much in terms of practical matters, but psychologically: by the loss as a baby of his mother Kiritsubo. This early loss is what underlies his lifelong attraction to—and brief affair with—his father's subsequent concubine Fujitsubo; Murasaki makes explicitly clear that this is due to Fujitsubo's resemblance to Kiritsubo.

Such expansions of the boundaries of the self, into the subconscious and early childhood, bring us to the limits of our notions of self, of our sense of who we are, our sense of control over the events in our lives and control of our feelings about them—or our feelings prompting them. Genji, shaped by the loss of his mother, is a deeply flawed character whose well-being is threatened throughout his life by the possible discovery of his affair with his father's concubine. In Murasaki's view, however, this sequence of events and its terrible psychological toll are not matters of fate. They are not something external that has happened to Genji. Indeed, within the Buddhist karmic worldview there is no "fate" in the ancient Greek sense, there are no purely external or undeserved events. (The teaching of karma does not constitute determinism. One's deeds determine the *manner* of rebirth but not the *actions* of the reborn individual—karma provides the situation, not the response to the situation.) Everything that happens to Genji is already related to him in some way. Genji's task, as the ideal character that he is, is not to show no flaws, but to show ideal ways of dealing with his flaws and mistakes. Genji does this by utilising his own life's experience, his own illegitimate affair with Fujitsubo, when he must make the most difficult ethical decision of his life, namely, how to act when his wife conceives a child by another man.

## III: Ethical Innovation in *The Tale of Genji*

In showing Genji accepting his wife's child by Kashiwagi, Murasaki does two remarkable things. First, she shows how she believes their husbands should treat women who are seduced and how those husbands should treat the illegitimate child. For a woman to go on record with such a challenge to the patriarchal order is itself extremely rare until very recent times; for her to recognize so clearly the disparities of power between men and women, and the vulnerabilities of women's position in patriarchal systems such as an imperial court, is also rare.

Second, Murasaki invents a completely new kind of ethical decision-making, based neither on codes nor the over-all ideals or principles of the prevailing religions, but on generalization from one's own experience. This is one of the great conceptual breakthroughs in any culture's ethical history.

## The Situation

You will recall that Genji's wife Sannomiya has had an illicit affair with Kashiwagi, the eldest son of Genji's best friend, and gives birth to Kashiwagi's son Kaoru. We have seen how Kashiwagi handled the situation. The more interesting question is, what is Genji to do? What *should* he do? What options are open to him? What do people expect him to do?

There is no question that by the standards of the time, Genji is the injured party, and the injury is a serious one. Nothing in Heian-period ethics would excuse either the friend's or the wife's transgression in such a case, and Murasaki is well aware of the existing code. At the same time, she makes it clear that without the pregnancy, there would be little for any of them to worry about. At several junctures she alludes to the fact that such affairs are frequent, even occasionally with imperial consorts (a clear reference to Genji's affair with Fujitsubo); the important thing is to avoid getting caught and to be discreet. (This tolerance of female sexuality would seem to be a holdover from the earlier matriarchal culture, still very much alive during the Heian in such institutions as matrilocality and female inheritance.) It is the baby that makes the situation difficult.

Other than the pleasure of expressing his anger—were that an acceptable thing to do in Heian Japan (which it clearly is not, either for men or for women), Genji has little to gain, in purely worldly terms, from humiliating his wife openly. To do so would only reveal his humiliation to everyone at court. Genji has always been keenly aware of how he appears to others, and there are many who would revel in his humiliation. Genji is well aware of this: he fears that Sannomiya's attendants (those most likely to know of the affair, which has been kept secret) may be laughing at him, and his emotions run from anger through regret and coldness.

## Genji's Decision

Ultimately, in a move that proves to endear him to readers and artists alike, Genji decides to accept the child as his own.[34] That this was a difficult decision is evident from his behavior:

> Genji was determined that there be no flaw in the observances [for the infant's birth], but he was not happy. He did not go out of his way to make his noble guests feel welcome, and there was no music.

> . . . .Genji behaved with the strictest correctness and was determined to give no grounds for suspicion. Yet he somehow thought the babe repellent and was held by certain of the women to be rather chilly (640-641).

## Motivation and Rationale for Genji's Decision

Why does Genji do what he does? We are never directly told why Genji decides to accept the child, but we are shown his reasoning. And there are a number of possible motivations that can be eliminated.

Enlightened self-interest—a desire to avoid the public humiliation of revealing himself to have been cuckolded—may be dismissed for three reasons: first, it is unfitting a figure as ideal(ized) as Genji; he has never shown himself to be motivated solely or primarily by such factors previously, and he was in a powerful enough position that he could have found a way to dismiss his wife and the baby without revealing the secret, had he wanted to. (Sannomiya would certainly have agreed to almost anything, and indeed it is worth mentioning that Genji's decision takes place within a social and moral context in which both the offenders acknowledge their mistake and are deeply ashamed and willing to step aside. (Sannomiya, for example, "was ashamed and sorry. When she was alone she wept a great deal" (616); ultimately she becomes a nun, although continuing to care for the child.)

Buddhism, of course, provides a strong rationale for Genji's acceptance of the child, in its principle of compassion. What Genji did was in fact compassionate toward all three—baby, mother, and father. Yet there is no reference to compassion in Murasaki's presentation of the dilemma.

In fact, there is no reference to a principle of any kind. The baby is an innocent party, yet Murasaki does not mention this innocence—and its helpless dependence on Genji's generosity. No one makes an appeal to justice on the baby's behalf. Under the circumstances, there seems to be no need to take any responsibility. Genji, like many another man in a similar situation, would presumably have been exonerated by his peers if he cast out wife and baby. The baby is simply uninteresting to the author (at this juncture—he becomes a major character later on). At the same time, it cannot be coincidental that the two chapters in which this part of the story unfolds (*Wakana*, "New Herbs," and *Kashiwagi*, "The Oak Tree") also contain a number of references to fatherly love, including a lengthy description of the father of the Akashi Empress, who becomes a Buddhist monk but cannot break off his intense attachment to his daughter; his letter to her upon the birth of her son[35] in which he tells her of the joy with which he has followed her career is one of the most eloquent testimonies in all literature to the joys of fatherhood (and fatherhood of a girl, at that!).

Genji's bond with Kashiwagi and Kashiwagi's father To no Chujo was not one he would want to dissolve; indeed taking upon himself responsibility for the child would deepen the bond with the two men, and would strengthen his stature in his own eyes and in the reader's. Yet Murasaki says nothing explicitly about this, and while her style is allusive enough (even elusive enough) that we must be wary of reasoning based simply on what she says outright, the bond that Genji would strengthen by this adoption must surely be countered by the fact that he does nothing to keep Kashiwagi from dying. So the bond with Kashiwagi and his father cannot be the main motivation—in spite of the fact that it is precisely *because* of the resemblance to Kashiwagi that Genji eventually becomes fond of the baby.

Why, then, does Genji accept the child? For all her allusiveness and indirectness, Murasaki makes it clear that Genji's motivations stem from two things. First is the fact that he has never forgotten his own transgressions when young:

> But how very strange it all was! Retribution had no doubt come for the deed which had terrified him then and which he was sure would go on terrifying him to the end. Since it had come, all unexpectedly, in this world, perhaps the punishment would be lighter in the next (640).

Genji as a very young man had seduced Fujitsubo, his father's new concubine, whose great resemblance to Genji's mother Kiritsubo inspired the love both Genji and his father felt for her. It seems quite clear in the context of these two chapters that it is this central (quasi-Oedipal) drama that informs Genji's mature decision when his role in the love triangle is reversed, for the earlier affair has been alluded to here several times. Two of these references are ironic: in trying to persuade Sannomiya's maid to allow him to see her, Kashiwagi says, "Marriage is an uncertain arrangement. Are you saying that these things never under any circumstances happen to His Majesty's own ladies?" (616). Later, he considers such a case again:

> he was frightened. It was a terrible thing he had done. How could he face the world? He remained in seclusion. . . . It was a terrible thing for the Third Princess, of course, and for himself as well. Supposing he had seduced the emperor's own lady and the deed had come to light—could the punishment be worse? Even if he were to avoid specific punishment he did not know how he could face a reproachful Genji. (615-6)

Only the readers, of course, can appreciate the irony,, for Kashiwagi knows nothing of Genji's earlier affair. Genji had spent much of his life trying to get close to Fujitsubo (who did bear his child) and in terror of being found out, and himself makes the connection between his own behavior and his wife's and Kashiwagi's explicitly, as we have seen. At one point in his deliberations he even wonders whether his father had not known about the affair with Fujitsubo and simply understood and kept silent. He also considers whether his earlier seduction had not brought this one about: "It had been predestined, no doubt, that such a child be born, and there had been no escaping . . . " (660). The sprinkling of such comments throughout the chapters have the effect, regardless of who makes them, of keeping Genji's earlier affair as active in the reader's mind as we've been told it always was in Genji's.

The second important consideration for Genji is his awareness of his own role in bringing about the affair.

He realizes that, in his concern for Komurasaki during her nearly fatal illness, he has left Sannomiya alone far too much. Sannomiya, moreover, is not really his type, and her relative dullness, her childishness, and lack of cultivation prove a bit of a trial to him. She is not his favorite woman; he has been far closer to Komurasaki. Still, Genji has been married to Sannomiya for several years, and the bond between them is such that he is reluctant to hurt her more than he has to; so he recognizes that he himself contributed to the development of her affair with Kashiwagi, at the very least for not being more attentive to her and for failing to provide the closeness she longed for from her husband. (Yet even this must be shown to be not his fault, but the result of his good intentions and the lamentable custom of parents marrying off daughters with insufficient regard for temperamental suitability.)[36]

Indeed, Murasaki shows Sannomiya's behavior as understandable if not quite excusable, for it is this that allows her to raise the question of the husband's appropriate course of action given the disparity between men's and women's power; otherwise it would be all too easy to dismiss both wife and baby from further consideration. Murasaki therefore goes to great lengths to explain the reasons behind Sannomiya's weakness.

This seems to put the blame on Genji. Yet if he behaves too caddishly, is made to assume too great a burden, he ceases to be sympathetic, and he will be incapable of being the kind of man who develops a new way of understanding the situation and inventing a new behavior for such situations—and he loses his stature as an ideal man—a stature that is crucial to Murasaki's purpose of demonstrating ideal ways for men and women to behave. Genji's situation is also, therefore, elaborated with some care: his lack of concern for Sannomiya is shown to be the effect of his greater (and prior) love for Komurasaki (a love with which every reader already feels a deep sympathy by the time Sannomiya comes into the picture), and is exacerbated by Komurasaki's fatal illness, which draws Genji to her side and away from Sannomiya and everyone else. (Komurasaki, for her part, under ordinary circumstances would never have *demanded* Genji's time and taken her away from the Princess, but for the fact that she was on her deathbed and these were her and Genji's final days together.) No one is to blame, but the Princess is left feeling utterly forlorn, and has too much time on her hands. (Here we see the terrible consequences of insufficient education for a woman!) Into this dangerous gap comes young Kashiwagi, who had in fact always been somewhat in love with the Princess but who was of insufficient rank to be able to protect her interests at court, and who was, in any case, too diffident (perhaps too in awe of Genji?) to pursue her before she was married, when her father was so desperately searching for a husband for her. Now, however, finding her virtually abandoned emotionally by her husband (although well cared for in other respects), he finds a way to meet with her and seduces her.

## Significance of the Decision

Genji's decision to accept the child as his own and to continue relations with Sannomiya is important and innovative on two levels. First, it defies patriarchal mores about the importance of paternity and legitimacy, and assumptions regarding the cuckolded husband's right to punish the wife or abandon the child. Both the offenders feel deeply the gravity of their transgression, but they punish themselves, internalizing it completely (like Oedipus and Jocasta) and falling ill—dying in Kashiwagi's case, and becoming a nun in Sannomiya's.

Second, and more startlingly, Murasaki proposes here a new way of thinking about the moral life. At the time that she wrote, there were a number of ways set out for becoming a good person. From the point of view of Shinto, ritual observance and prayer were sufficient. From the point of view of Confucianism, carrying out one's duty in terms of one's social obligations (including those to the dead) were the primary responsibility. From the point of view of Buddhism, there were several paths: following the rules and guidelines of the Middle Way, the Eightfold Path, etc.; imitation of the Buddha as he was known through sutras or through images; and following the way of life through joining a Buddhist community.

Not one of these enjoined innovative ethical thinking or problem-solving. Not one of them was especially suitable for solving either new ethical problems or old problems in original ways.

In the Kashiwagi chapter, Murasaki proposes a new way of making ethical decisions: based on one's own experience, empathic understanding of the other person's feelings, and constructing analogies. Although there was surely nothing new about the situation, her perception of the situation as one which required innovative handling was new, and her proposal that one base one's actions on one's own experience was new.

This is an ethical breakthrough of enormous significance: nothing in Buddhism or Japanese Confucianism would have suggested that one should make ethical decisions based on one's own experience; at that point, the most advanced ethical thinking recommended either (a) following rules, (b) following the principles (such as detachment or compassion), or (c) acting in such a way that a value acknowledged by the group would be fulfilled. But in this version of the family drama, events have been set up that allow Genji to act as an individual and on the basis of his own experience.

## Conclusion

Scrutiny of Murasaki Shikibu as a philosopher is long overdue. My analysis suggests not only that she can take her place among the foremost ethicists not only of her time, or of Japan, but of all time. Her contributions to ethics, among them her careful working out of an ethics of care that transcends traditional Buddhism and Confucianism, her development of the principal of basing ethical reasoning on one's own experience, her visions of the ideal life, ideal education and ideal marriage for both men and women, her explorations of male and female subjectivity and agency, and her recognitions of the special demands that result from the situations women are placed in by patriarchal institutions, all command our respect and further study. I believe a number of them should even prove pertinent to the twenty-first century.

## Notes

1. I would like to thank Mark Ravina and Scott Robertson for reading an earlier version of this chapter.

2. Mara Miller, "Canons and the Challenge of Gender," *The Monist: An International Quarterly Journal of General Philosophical Inquiry*, Vol. 76, No. 4, October 1993, p 477-493.

3. Seemingly anomalous data from studies involving girls and women called attention to moral judgments that did not fit the definition of "moral" and to self-descriptions at odds with the concept [prevalent among psychologists and typical of men's self-reports] of "self." The data that initially appeared discrepant, thus, became the basis for a reformulation, grounds for thinking again about what "self" and "morality" mean. See Carol Gilligan, *In a Different Voice: Psychological Theory and Woman's Development* (Cambridge, Mass.: Harvard University Press, 1982).

4. I will use the term "Shinto" as a matter of convenience to refer to the congeries of native spiritual values and practices prevalent at the time.

5. A number of early works are arguably of equal or greater importance, but they are all compilations or anthologies, such as the *Manyoshu*, the *Kojiki* and the *Nihon Shoki*.

6. Translations of the complete *Tale of Genji* have been made by Arthur Waley and Edward G. Seidensticker (New York: Alfred A. Knopf, Inc., 1976). Quotations in this chapter are taken from the latter; page numbers follow within the text.

7. One young daughter of a provincial governor wrote of her love for the *The Tale of Genji*, her attempts to get hold of missing chapters, and its effect on her life in the Sarashina Diary, translated under the title *As I Crossed a Bridge of Dreams* by Ivan Morris (New York: The Dial Press, 1971). Murasaki's own copy was confiscated by Fujiwara Michinaga ((966-1027), grandfather of two emperors, the father of the Empress whom Murasaki attended, and the power-behind-the-throne) for his personal perusal, as we

know from her diary (*The Diary of Murasaki Shikibu*—a diary which was commissioned by Michinaga as a record of the events surrounding the birth of his new grandson.)

8. "Our nation's greatest treasure is the *Genji monogatari*. Nothing surpasses it," said Ichijo Kanera (Kaneyoshi) (1402-81), according to T.J. Harper's "Motoori Norinaga's criticism of the *Genji Monogatari*: a study of the background and critical content of his Genji Monogatari Tama no Ogushi," Ph. D. dissertation, University of Michigan; quoted by Richard Bowring in *Murasaki Shikibu: The Tale of Genji* (Cambridge, U.K.: Cambridge University Press, 1988), 81. Janet Goff, in *Noh Drama and The Tale of Genji* (Princeton, N.J.: Princeton University Press, 1991), 16, quotes poet and critic Fujiwara no Shunzei's (1114-1204) remark in a judgment for the *Roppyakuban utaawase* (Poetry Contest in Six Hundred Rounds) to the effect that "poets who have not read the *The Tale of Genji* are to be deplored" Goff and Haruo Shirane, in *The Bridge of Dreams: A Poetics of The Tale of Genji* (Stanford, Calif.: Stanford University Press, 1987) both give valuable surveys of medieval Genji criticism.

9. Of course, a hermeneutics of suspicion calls upon us to question the circumstances under which readings came to focus so exclusively on the purely aesthetic—however pleasurable we may find them. Indeed given the inordinate praise showered upon *The Tale of Genji* and Murasaki by subsequent generations of poets, particularly during the Kamakura period, a reader alert to issues of the "anxiety of influence" might expect to find hints that such an overwhelming work—especially if written by a woman—might demand to be contained and constrained by being consigned to a category like the "aesthetic"—marginalized and removed from the possibility of contaminating real-life categories of the political and the ethical.

10. Two camps were especially salient, the Buddhist and Confucianist moralists, and the Buddhist-inspired Noh playwrights/ actors. See Goff.

11. Miner, Earl, Hiroko Odagiri, and Robert E. Morrell, *The Princeton Companion to Classical Japanese Literature* (Princeton, N.J.: Princeton University Press, 1985), 95.

12. Miner, Odagiri and Morrell, 290.

13. The fact that the individual's discomfort at the occasion is irrelevant to whether it is *mono no aware* or not, that is, whether it is admirable or not—consider Genji's acute distress at being exiled to Suma—shows that Murasaki's championing of detachment is not a matter of what we might consider "enlightened self-interest."

14. Thomas Kasulis provides a philosophical analysis of this phenomenon of what is from a Euro-American point of view a confusion of source of and response to emotion in "Zen and Artistry," in *Self as Image in Asian Theory and Practice*, Roger T. Ames, Thomas Kasulis, and Wimal Dissanayake, eds. (Albany, N.Y.: State University of New York Press, 1998).

15. This use of "Komurasaki," meaning "Little Murasaki," follows the Japanese convention for distinguishing the author, whose actual given name is unknown to us, from the character. For a short study of the philosophical implications of Japanese naming customs for sense of selfhood and personal identity, see Mara Miller, "Views of Japanese Selfhood: Japanese and Western Perspectives," in *Culture and Self: Philosophical and Religious Perspectives, East and West*. Douglas Allen, ed. (Boulder, Colo.: Westview Press, 1997).

16. The literacy rate for Heian upper class Japanese women was already relatively high; Murasaki was one of over a hundred Japanese women in the Heian who were known as writers, and women were an important component of their audience. Yet she was unusually well educated for a woman and had had to struggle for the education she

received. At the same time, Murasaki not only explicitly advocated education for women in her writing, she also proved the value of women's voices and gave women cause and motivation to read, not only during her lifetime but throughout subsequent history—her novel was among the first of the classics to be printed, for instance, and it permeated the aesthetics and arts of the middle class during the Edo period.

17. Yiengpruksuwan, Mimi Hall, "The Phoenix Hall at Uji and the Symmetries of Replication," *The Art Bulletin*, Dec. 1995, vol. LXVXII, number 4, 467-472.

18. Chapter numbers for Waley's and Seidensticker's translations do not agree, owing to Waley's having dropped one chapter and added another which he wrote himself. For a table showing how the two sets correspond, see Bowring, viii-ix.

19. *The Tale of Genji* makes use of many different names, titles, and sobriquets to refer to any given character; for an explanation, see William J. Puette, *Guide to The Tale of Genji by Murasaki Shikibu* (Rutland, Vt. and Tokyo: Charles E. Tuttle Company, Inc., 1983), 154 ff. Since there are over four hundred characters, translators into English, for simplicity's sake generally choose one or two for a given person. This chapter follows Edward Seidensticker's translation, but for the convenience of readers more familiar with the other complete translation, Arthur Waley's will also be given, in parenthesis, at the first occurrence.

20. Takeo Doi, *The Anatomy of Dependence* (Tokyo: Kodansha International, 1971). See also Childs, Margaret H. "The Value of Vulnerability: Sexual Coercion and the Nature of Love in Japanese Court Literature." *The Journal of Asian Studies*. Vol. 58, number 4, November 1999.

21. This awareness foreshadows the conflict between "*giri*" or (Confucian) duty and "*ninjo*" or human feeling that becomes a burning preoccupation in the performing arts of the Edo period—although there the conflict is usually felt within one individual, rather than being projected, as here, onto different social entities. This awareness also puts her in unexpected sympathy with modern Euro-American thinkers, a feature that deserves more attention than it gets, although it cannot be taken too far—Murasaki is far from believing in the social contract, for instance.

22. Chapter III of *The Tsutsumi Chunagon Monogatari—11th-Century Short Stories of Japan*, translated by Umeyo Hirano (Tokyo: The Hokuseido Press, 1963), p 17-29.

23. As evidenced by the data in the Human Relations Area Files. See James W. Prescott, "Affectional Bonding for the Prevention of Violent Behaviors: Neurobiological, Psychological and Religious/Spiritual Determinants," *Violent Behavior, Vol. I: Assessment and Intervention*, L.J. Hertzberg, et al., editors (New York: PMA Publishing Corp., 1990), who summarizes the information based on research available from the Human Relations Area Files.

24. The term "indulgence" may be misleading if it connotes wild displays of any kind; feelings should rather be expressed artistically if possible. Yet tears are also an indication of *mono no aware,* as are sleeves wet with tears, which suggests that more primal biological and physical signs of *mono no aware* are highly valued, as well as symbolic expressions.

25. See, for example, Tu Wei-ming, *Centrality and Commonality: An Essay on Confucian Religiousness* (Albany, N.Y.: State University of New York Press, 1998) and *Confucian Thought: Selfhood as Transformation* (Albany, N.Y.: State University of New York Press, 1985), and James Cahill, "Confucian Elements in the Theory of Painting," in *The Confucian Persuasion*, Arthur F. Wright, ed., (Stanford, Calif.: Stanford University Press, 1960).

26. *Lotus Sutra*, chapter 2 Burton Watson, translator (New York: Columbia University Press, 1993).

27. Mathematics was considered part of the crafts and would have been out of the purview for a Confucian gentleman.

28. This use of literature for the purpose of systematic proving of varieties of ethical response is taken up also by the Nobel Prize-winning novelist Yasunari Kawabata—another author whose work is typically mistaken as purely aesthetic (and who was deeply influenced by Murasaki).

29. See Haruo Shirane, "Pseudo-Incest: The Tamakazura Sequence," chapter 7 of *The Bridge of Dreams: A Poetics of 'The Tale of Genji'* (Stanford, Calif.: Stanford University Press, 1987).

30. Carol Gilligan, *In a Different Voice: Psychological Theory and Woman's Development* (Cambridge, Mass.: Harvard University Press, 1982).

31. *Mapping the Moral Domain*, Carol Gilligan, Janie Victoria Ward, Jill McLean Taylor, with Betty Bardige, editors (Cambridge, Mass.: Center for the Study of Gender, Education and Human Development, Harvard University Graduate School of Education, 1988), xvii-xviii.

32. Carol Gilligan, Preface, *Mapping the Moral Domain*, v. Gilligan and others point out that in studies of contemporary Americans, the ethic of care is voiced by men as well as women, although it is less common among men. The ethic more characteristic of American men, referred to as the "ethic of justice," is also found among women—among whom it is, similarly, less common than the ethic of care. One of the contributors, Nona Plessner Lyons, concludes from her study that " . . . in real-life moral conflict, individuals in this sample call upon and think about both care and justice considerations but use predominantly one mode which is related to but not defined by or confined to gender. . . [t]he results reported here support the hypothesis that there are two different orientations to morality—an orientation towards rights and justice, and an orientation towards care and response to others in their own terms. Morality is not unitarily justice and rights, nor are these orientations mutually exclusive: individuals use both kinds of considerations in the construction, resolution, and evaluation of the resolution of real-life moral conflicts, but usually one mode predominantly. This finding of gender-related differences, however, is not absolute since individual men and women use both types of considerations." (39, 40)

33. Gilligan, *In a Different Voice*, x.

34. The scene becomes a favorite of artists: it is one of the most famous from the earliest surviving set of paintings associated with the story. I hesitate to use the word "illustration" in relation to these paintings, since, as the work of Akiyama Terukazu shows, the artists often develop a scene based, apparently, not on what is written but on what may be inferred from the text. In this case, the picture shows Genji taking the infant in his arms for the first time. No such event is recorded in the novel.

35. *Tale of Genji*, 572-74.

36. Of course, Sannomiya's father, the emperor, is also beyond reproach here, wanting only the best for his daughter under the most trying of circumstances: he himself had been forced to retire (retirement in the Heian period was not in the control of the individual emperor) and once he had left Court there would be no one who could protect her interests except a husband. Yet there was simply no one else prepared to marry her or as suitable as Genji.

## *Chapter Eight*

# Human Rights Law, Religion, and the Gendered Moral Order

**Lucinda Joy Peach**

## I. Introduction: Gender, Justice, and International Law

Is freedom of religion compatible with the recognition of human rights for women? International law, as embodied in treaties and other documents of the United Nations, prohibits discrimination based on religion[1] as well as sex.[2] These documents reflect an assumption that governments can protect both women's human rights and traditional religious and cultural practices. But how valid is this assumption that religion is compatible with other human rights, especially those of women? When we consider reproductive rights as a central feature of women's human rights, as United Nations documents clearly and repeatedly have done, and then consider how reproductive rights (which are fundamental to the protection of women's human rights) are denied by the manner in which others "manifest their religion or belief in "practice and teaching," this assumption can be seen to be in error.

In this chapter, I will argue that religious freedom frequently undermines or obstructs protection for women's human rights, and should be restricted where necessary to insure protection for other human rights, especially in cases where religious beliefs shape law and public policy. I will argue how international law as currently formulated embodies an unacknowledged tension between respect for religion and protection of reproductive rights that serves to weaken, if not completely undermine, the goals of establishing reproductive rights as human rights, and thus of women's rights as human rights. I will illustrate how this unacknowledged tension in international law has resulted in restricting women's human rights in a sampling of countries—Bangladesh, Israel, Ireland, Poland, Japan, and the United States—taking into consideration the significant role that religious institutions have had in restricting women's reproductive rights to abortion. This sample reflects a diversity of religious traditions and relations between religious institutions and governments. I will therefore conclude that the tension between women's human rights and religion is significant and irresolvable, and that a genuine commitment to the well being of women necessitates that in cases of tension or conflict between women's human rights and the religious freedoms of lawmakers, the former must be given priority. I will provide a rationale for resolving such conflicts based on principles of justice as fairness.

Some qualifications to this essay should be made: A comparison of the official positions of governmental and religious institutions regarding abortion in a limited sample cannot provide a complete understanding of either women's reproductive choices or a particular state's recognition of women's human rights. In addition to the dominant discourses of law and religion, there will inevitably be unofficial (perhaps subjugated) discourses operating as well which influence the extent to which women's reproductive rights are recognized and protected in any given locale. In addition, a complete analysis would need to consider a multiplicity of other factors, including, especially, women's own understandings of the relationship between their reproductive capacities and religion, the State, and their social status. Nonetheless, this selective investigation of the formal legal framework regulating the relationship between religion and women's rights can illuminate some dimensions of the larger problems of religious influences on women's human rights, and point to some steps that might be taken towards resolving the conflicts when they arise.

## II: Conflicts Between Religious Freedom and Women's Human Rights Over Reproductive Rights

The United Nations has prohibited discrimination based on religion and sex from its inception. One locus of conflict between the two sets of rights has revolved around issues of reproduction. The linkage of reproductive rights and women's human rights has been consistently endorsed in United Nations' sponsored reports, conferences, agreements, and conventions.[3] The dangers that pregnancy and childbirth present to women's right to life, the infringement of the rights to liberty and security of the person that government interference with women's reproductive choice represents, the right to privacy and family life, including women's right to plan, time, and space the births of children to maximize both their health and her own, the right to health care, and the view that protection of reproductive rights is a precondition for the enjoyment of other human rights have all increasingly been recognized under international law as supporting the indispensability of reproductive rights as human rights.[4]

Most recently, the *Platform for Action* ("Platform") drafted at the United Nations Fourth World Conference on Women held in Beijing China in 1995 (1995 Women's Conference) explicitly states: "The human rights of women include their right to have control over and decide freely and responsibly on matters related to their sexuality, including sexual and reproductive health, free of coercion, discrimination and violence" (United Nations 1995: para 96), that "the right of all women to control all aspects of their health, in particular their own fertility, is basic to their empowerment" (United Nations 1995: para. 92), and "forms an important basis for the enjoyment of other rights" (United Nations 1995: para 97).[5]

Despite these declarations of reproductive rights as human rights, as many as 300 million women throughout the world are denied the right to adequate family planning resources, including contraception and abortion. Statistics indicate that approximately one quarter of the world's population (one third of the developing world) lives in nations where abortion is either completely prohibited or allowed only to save the life of the mother.[6] Prohibiting or severely restricting legal contraception and abortion in effect coerces many women to become mothers against their will. Women often die as a result of such coercion; statistics indicate that at least a million women died in 1992 of reproductive causes, one-quarter of them attributable to unsafe abortion.[7] In addition, forcing women to bear unwanted children frequently results in denying them basic education and employment. It often relegates them to a life of poverty, without any realistic possibility of improving the life chances of either themselves or their offspring.

Religious influences contribute to the restriction or denial of women's reproductive rights, as the following discussion will amply illustrate. International law itself facilitates religious restrictions on women's reproductive rights around the world by failing to establish clear limitations on the extent to which religious laws and practices will be permitted to restrict women's reproductive rights. For example, the *Programme of Action* states:

> The implementation of the recommendations . . . is the sovereign right of each country . . . with full respect for the various religious and ethical values and cultural backgrounds of its people, and in conformity with universally recognized international human rights.[8]

This pronouncement is seemingly oblivious to the potential for conflict between protecting women's human rights and giving "full respect" to religious values when those values deny reproductive rights to women. The *Programme* further proclaims that

> men and women have a right "to be informed and to have access to safe, effective, affordable and acceptable methods of family planning of their choice, as well as other methods of their choice for regulation of fertility which are not against the law. [9]

The *Platform* document repeats this "legality" limitation on reproductive rights (United Nations 1995: paras. 94, 97). Such conditions upon member nations' adherence to the provisions contained in these treaties fails to acknowledge that certain methods of family planning, especially abortion, are often legally prohibited or restricted as a result of the influence, whether direct or indirect, of religious values and norms. By allowing domestic law and cultural values to override international protections for women's human rights, the U.N. in effect grants priority to religious freedoms over women's rights. Such qualifications on women's human rights also fly in the face of other language in these documents.[10]

However, the *Platform for Action* also states that

> While the significance of national and regional particularities and various historical, cultural and religious backgrounds must be borne in mind, it is the duty of States, regardless of their political, economic and cultural systems, to promote and protect all human rights and fundamental freedoms. The implementation of this *Platform*, including through national laws and the formulation of strategies, policies, programmes and development priorities, is the sovereign responsibility of each State, in conformity with all human rights and fundamental freedoms, and the significance of and full respect for various religious and ethical values, cultural backgrounds and philosophical convictions of individuals and their communities should contribute to the full enjoyment by women of their human rights in order to achieve equality, development and peace (United Nations 1995: para.9).

At first glance, this language suggests a shift from earlier treaties, which simply noted the member government's obligation to recognize and respect both religious and cultural values as well as prohibit sex discrimination. Here, governments are clearly required to give priority to protecting women's rights. In particular, the mandate that governments "ensure that gender equality and cultural, religious and other diversity are respected in educational institutions" (United Nations 1995: para. 81(p)), if implemented, would represent a major advance for the rights of women living in countries dominated, officially or unofficially, by a single religion. As we will see, in countries like Poland, Ireland, Israel, and the U.S., this would require limiting religious influences over public education, including education regarding reproductive health and family planning. Along the same lines, the requirement that governments "take action to ensure the conditions necessary for women to exercise their reproductive rights and eliminate coercive laws and practices" (United Nations 1995, para. 107(d)) would advance the status of women in many countries, especially those where religiously based or influenced laws have the intention or effect of denying women their reproductive rights.

Despite its advances over earlier international law documents, however, there are a number of problems with this language in the *Platform*. First, in obligating states to "promote and protect *all* human rights" (emphasis supplied), it continues to overlook potential conflicts between religious freedoms and women's human rights. Second, it ignores potential conflicts between full protections for women's human rights and existing laws regulating reproduction. Third, the *Platform* language fails to acknowledge that protecting some religious and ethical values, etc., will not only fail to contribute to women's enjoyment of their human rights, but will actively function to obstruct and prevent such enjoyment. This is especially likely at the level of individual versus community values. The *Platform's* language fails to take adequate account of religious and cultural diversity and the differential impacts that religious and cultural values may have within a single community depending on an individual's gender, race, sexual orientation, etc.

Further, when conflicts between religious values and women's rights are present, the *Platform* fails to indicate how the tension between them is to be resolved. Similarly, the *Declaration* specifies that protecting women's human rights also requires "the eradication of any conflicts which may arise between the rights of women and the harmful effects of certain traditional or customary practices, cultural prejudices, and *religious extremism*," yet it lacks any principles or procedures for determining how conflicts between women's rights and a state's "cultural practices" should be resolved.[11]

In fact, the tension between religious rights and women's rights has actually not been eliminated in the *Platform*, but, instead, simply has been sent underground. Among the internationally recognized human rights and fundamental freedoms it recognizes is that:

> The right to freedom of thought, conscience and religion is inalienable and must be universally enjoyed. This right includes the freedom to have or to adopt the religion or belief of their choice either individually or in community with others, in public or in private, and to manifest their religion or belief in worship, observance, practice and teaching (United Nations 1995: para. 24).

The protection provided for the right to practice and teach one's religious beliefs can be interpreted to include religious influences on lawmaking that serve to restrict or deny reproductive (and other) rights to women. The only explicit recognition of this potential is the statement acknowledging that "any form of extremism may have a negative impact on women and can lead to violence and discrimination" (United Nations 1995, para. 24)[12] and the recognition of the negative influences that religion may have on women's rights in the area of violence against women (United Nations 1995: paras. 118, 119, 224).[13]

Although the official teachings of many world religions support the principle of human rights generally, their official positions on women's human rights, especially reproductive rights, are frequently contrary to that of the United Nations. During the Cairo Conference, for example, members of the Vatican Delegation attempted to eliminate all references to abortion in all Conference documents.[14] During the Conference, Vatican representatives lobbied fundamentalist Muslim groups to join them in opposing a draft *Programme* on the basis that it could be interpreted to endorse abortion.[15] In addition, the Church and Islamic fundamentalists were allied in opposing family planning, contraception, sex education for adolescents, and homosexuality.[16]

The teachings of most world religions that women are divinely ordained to be child bearers and rearers help to perpetuate traditional essentialist ideologies that women *are* mothers, primarily if not exclusively, and thus not entitled to social, political, and economic equality. The influence of such religious teachings is enhanced when they are given official state sanction, backed by the coercive power of law to deny women access to the means to control their reproduction. Yet the U.N. endorses this result by according sovereignty to governments to determine how to implement the relevant U.N. treaties in accordance with their local cultural and religious traditions and norms. Such religious influences on government undermine religious freedoms for *all* citizens. The negative results for women's human rights in particular are evident in the following brief survey.

## III: "Authorized" Religious Restrictions on Women's Human Rights

As noted in the introduction, the following sample of countries was selected with a view to illustrating how women's reproductive rights are consistently restricted by religious influences on government, regardless of the religion in question or the official relationship between Church and State in a particular country. In Bangladesh, the Islamic religion provides the official basis for the civil law. In Israel, the Jewish religion has an official status in government and lawmaking. In both Ireland and Poland, the Catholic Church currently dominates abortion policy making, although in Ireland, the Church has had an unbroken influence on government, whereas in Poland, religious influence was suppressed by the communist government for most of the twentieth century, until 1989. Finally, in the religiously pluralistic nations of Japan and the United States, despite an official policy of separation of Church and State, in actuality religion has played an influential role in establishing current abortion policies. Finally, the influence of religion in restricting women's human rights is evident at the international level.

### Bangladesh

A country of over one hundred million, approximately eighty percent of the population of Bangladesh is Sunni Muslim. In general, Islam has had close ties to the state since Bangladesh was founded in the mid-twentieth century and, until recently, it has not maintained a division between public and private life.[17] The country officially became an Islamic state in 1977, when President Rahman inserted in the Constitution the Islamic declaration of God at the beginning of the *Qu'ran* and replaced the language declaring Bangladesh a secular state with a clause professing trust and faith in Allah.[18]

Given its institutionalized status, Islam has a significant influence on the government in Bangladesh. With regard to women's rights in particular, it has been a significant factor in the perpetuation of restrictive abortion laws in that country.[19] Traditional Muslim teachings state that abortion is a sin against God—Allah.[20] Although the *Qur'an*, the Islamic book of revelation, itself contains no express prohibition on abortion, several verses of the *Qur'an* refer to the sanctity of human life in general. These verses have been interpreted by some Islamic scholars as applying to fetal life as a form of human life constituted by the breath of Allah.

The general teachings of the *Qur'an* and the *Sunnah* (teachings and commentary of the Prophet Muhammad) are more often interpreted to prohibit abortion except for "valid cause or reason." Interpretations of what constitutes such a "valid" reason have varied widely. More literalist interpretations of Islamic law prohibit abortion except to save the life of the mother.[21] In cases of maternal-fetal conflict, even traditional Islamic teaching considers the mother's life to be more valuable, since she has established duties and responsibilities to others.[22] However, maternal deaths resulting from pregnancy out of wedlock are frequently viewed as "a well deserved act of God, a punishment commensurate with the enormity of the sin."[23]

As a former British colony, Bangladesh operated under the English Offenses Against the Person Act ("Offenses Act"), which made abortion illegal except where necessary to save the life of the mother. In 1972, this law was waived to permit abortions for women raped during the war of independence. Efforts by the National Population Policy to liberalize abortion laws beginning in the mid-1970s have been unsuccessful. The one exception is the government's 1979 exemption of "menstrual regulation" (MR) from the penal laws. This practice of vacuum aspiration permits a woman to undergo a relatively simple and inexpensive procedure for "establishing nonpregnancy" during the first 10 weeks following conception.[24] However, MR is often not provided to those women who need it the most, since government family planning clinics officially refuse the procedure to unmarried women and to women with a first pregnancy, and it is not available in all such clinics.[25]

Even beyond reproductive rights, women's social, political, and economic status is generally inferior to that of men in Bangladesh. Its interpretations of the *Qur'an* are so restrictive that the government of Bangladesh refused to become a signatory to the United Nations Women's Convention on the ground that its provisions would conflict with those of the Shari-ah (Islamic law).[26] In recent years, government leaders have espoused the further "Islamicization" of the state, which would entail confining women to the domestic sphere and restricting their mobility through the Islamic principle of *purdah* (seclusion).[27] The rise in religious fundamentalism in recent years has resulted in a backlash against the limited rights Bengali women have gained. *Shalish*, community arbitration councils, composed primarily of local religious leaders, have recently begun to impose harsh punishments on women for sexual transgressions, some of which are so severe that they have resulted in the woman's death.[28] Thus, women's human rights, including their reproductive rights, are significantly restricted by the influence of Islam on the government in Bangladesh.

Women's status is also frequently worse in Bangladesh than in other fundamentalist Islamic countries because of patriarchal cultural traditions in which, for example, marriage is viewed as the 'gift' of a virgin daughter by her father to a husband.[29] Large families are mandated by certain interpretations of the Prophet Muhammad's teachings, although attitudes appear to be changing.[30] Nonetheless, along with the intense social and economic pressure to bear male children, there have also been significant religious influences on government policy to keep the fertility rate high.[31]

Despite their general illegality, between one-half and one million illegal abortions take place in Bangladesh annually. Approximately one of every hundred such abortions ends in the pregnant woman's death, ten times that in the case of unmarried 15 to 19 year old women.[32] More than half the females marry by age 16, so unwed pregnancies are less common than in many countries, such as the U.S.[33] However, not all sexually active females are married by this age. The social stigma associated with pregnancy outside of marriage is so great that many young women end their own lives, and some parents poison their pregnant unwed daughters to death rather than suffer the stigma that exposure would cause to the family's reputation.[34]

## Israel

Although nominally a secular state, Israel cannot be understood without the Jewish religion, according to which "the people of Israel are a nation created by their covenant with God."[35] When the government was being formed in 1947, the governing body of the legislature and the two major religious parties agreed to a role for religion in public life, including giving religious courts continued jurisdiction over family matters like marriage and divorce. Today, several of the political parties in Israel that are integral to the coalition government are religious. These parties have consistently opposed any rights to abortion.[36]

The Jewish religion does not condemn all abortion *per se*. Rather, the morality of abortion in Judaism is determined in accordance with *Halakhah*, or Jewish law. This is comprised of detailed rules from biblical commands, the Talmud, and later rabbinic work.[37] Since *Halakhah* contains so many different strands, it has been subject to widely varying interpretations on abortion.

The biblical foundation of Halakhic interpretations of abortion is the book of Exodus (21: 22-25). Referring to miscarriage, these verses state:

> When men strive together, and hurt a woman with child, so that there is a miscarriage, and yet no harm follows, the one who hurt her shall be fined, according as the woman's husband shall lay upon him; and he shall pay as the judges determine. If any harm follows, then you shall give life for life,

> eye for eye, tooth for tooth, hand for hand, foot for foot, burn for burn, wound for wound, stripe for stripe (Exodus 21: 22-25).

Talmudic interpretations consider this passage to clearly establish that the woman is a living person (*nefesh*), whereas the fetus is not.[38] The Talmud is consequently generally interpreted as stating that the fetus is not a person until birth, but instead is considered to be part of its mother's body, lacking in legal rights.[39] Consequently, destroying the fetus through an abortion is not a capital crime. Rather, it is a crime of causing loss and destruction to the husband, more like a kind of property damage.[40]

Nevertheless, Jewish law considers all human life to be sacred because it is created in God's image. Consequently, abortion is not generally accepted. Orthodox Judaism generally limits the permissibility of abortion to life-saving situations.[41] Reformed Jewish teachings are usually more liberal, permitting abortion on health grounds, including severe emotional distress or trauma to the mother.[42]

Recent estimates of abortion rates in Israel suggest that approximately 20,000-24,000 (roughly 30 per 1,000) women of childbearing age have abortions annually.[43] Until 1977, Israel's abortion law was a vestige of British colonial rule, the same Offenses Act in force in Bangladesh and also in Ireland. In 1977, the Israeli law was liberalized to permit abortion for five different health grounds, upon certification by a committee composed of two physicians and a social worker. One of these grounds, "family or social conditions," was removed late in 1979 as a result of pressure from Agudat Israel, an orthodox religious party.[44]

Thus, even though Judaism generally has a more permissive stance towards abortion than does Islam, it has influenced governmental policy in ways which restrict women's reproductive rights. Legal restrictions on abortion access have created difficulties for women in Israel, especially for women emigrating from the former Soviet Union. These recent arrivals are familiar with life in a regime in which abortion was available on demand and generally funded by the state, but where adequate sex education and contraception were generally not available.[45] Israel's abortion restrictions thus present more severe hardships for recently immigrating Soviet women than for others. Judaism has also restricted the status of women in Israel in many other respects, in part through gender stereotypes that restrict women's normative roles to those of wives and mothers.

## Ireland

Although Church and State are officially separate in Ireland, the Catholic Church has maintained a strong hold on the reins of government since Irish independence from Britain in 1922. The Constitution ratified in 1937 contains a number of provisions that reflect Catholic social policy, including those that ban divorce, sex education, and contraception.[46] Irish abortion law is largely consistent with the centuries-old position of the Roman Catholic Church, which considers human life sacred from the point of conception, and limits the legitimate purposes of sex to procreation.

The official teachings of the Roman Catholic Church on abortion are well documented.[47] The Church opposes abortion on two basic grounds. The first, and most frequently made, is that human life is sacred and fully personal from the point of conception. The second is that abortion subverts natural law, in accordance with which the only legitimate purpose of sex is openness or intent to procreate within a married relationship.[48]

The Church's *Code of Canon Law*, first issued in 1919, prescribed excommunication for the sin of abortion for both the woman involved as well as any medical personnel who assisted. This has continued to be the Church's official position. In 1931, a Church law banning abortions under any circumstances was promulgated, although practice has permitted "indirect" abortions under the doctrine of double effect. According to this principle, where the intended effect of an operation is to save the life of the mother, but the fetus must be sacrificed as an indirect effect, abortion may be morally acceptable on the general ground that the intention is to save the life of the mother, not to harm the fetus. The doctrine of double effect only permits abortion in limited circumstances, however, primarily those involving ectopic pregnancies and cancer of the uterus.[49]

The Church's current position is contained in the encyclical *Humanae vitae*, issued by Pope Paul VI in 1968. *Humanae vitae* condemns abortion on the grounds of preserving life as well as the requirement that all sexual acts must be open to the life that may result: Because "human life is sacred," and "calls for the creative action of God" from the beginning, "the direct interruption of the generative processes already begun, and, above all, direct abortion, even for therapeutic reasons, are to be absolutely excluded as a lawful means of controlling the birth of children".[50]

A pronouncement published by the Vatican's Sacred Congregation for the Doctrine of the Faith with the consent of Pope John Paul II in 1987—the *Instruction on Respect for Human Life in Its Origin and on the Dignity of Procreation*—declares that every human being has a "right to life and physical integrity from the moment of conception until death" (Sacred 1987). Current pastoral guidelines prohibit Catholic hospitals from providing abortion services. Catholics willfully participating in such services are now subject to automatic excommunication.

Ireland has the highest proportion of Catholics in Western Europe—approximately 95 percent of the three-and-one-half million population—and, perhaps not coincidentally, the most restrictive abortion laws.[51] Ireland also has the highest birth rate in Europe.[52] Yet abortion has been illegal in Ireland, except when necessary to save the life of the mother, since the Offenses Act in 1861.[53] Not content with this law, pro-life forces organized and promoted by the Catholic Church pushed for a referendum in 1983, which resulted in a constitutional amendment instituting a right to life of the unborn, and prohibiting the legislature from enacting less restrictive abortion legislation without another referendum.[54]

The intolerable consequences of the abortion ban were brought to light in 1992 with the internationally-publicized "X Case," involving a 14 year old rape victim, whose parents attempted to take her to England to obtain an abortion. Pro-life groups were successful in obtaining an injunction preventing the girl from leaving the country, despite testimony that she was contemplating suicide if she could not obtain an abortion. The court that granted the injunction declared that the risk of the girl committing suicide was less than the risk to the life of the fetus if the girl were allowed to travel to England.[55] On appeal, the Irish Supreme Court ruled that the Constitution allowed abortion where there was a "real and substantial" risk to the life of the mother, and permitted the girl to travel to England for an abortion.[56] Pursuant to this precedent, over 100 Irish women began to leave the country legally each week (between 4,000 and 10,000 per year) to obtain abortions, mostly in England.[57]

Until recently, Irish women did not even have a right to information about abortion. In November 1993, a referendum on abortion rights resulted in public approval of the right to travel to obtain an abortion and the right to obtain information about abortion by a three-to-two margin.[58] However, an Irish Supreme Court ruling in July 1993 reversed the effect of the vote on the right to abortion information.[59] Thus, recent legal developments have done little to significantly expand abortion rights for women.

In addition to its views on abortion, Catholic teachings in Ireland inhibit women's rights in other respects suggesting that women have a moral duty to become mothers, and that their true liberation lies in the "vocational fulfillment of motherhood."[60] Such policies severely limit the ability of women to lead lives independent of male control and domination, especially since they are embodied in laws backed by the coercive power of the state, including significantly restricted access to the means for reproductive control.[61] In this situation of informal but substantial religious influence on government, women's human rights are adversely affected.

## Poland

Like Ireland, Poland is a predominantly Catholic country, but with a very different history. Although Poland has always been a Catholic country, religion was discouraged under the communist government. The Church did not directly involve itself in politics during the years preceding the end of Communism, but acted as an ally and supporter to the government opposition democracy movement Solidarity and functioned as a mediator between Solidarity and the government.[62] Although Catholicism is not officially the established Church in Poland, as Hanna Jankowska puts it, "[t]he Church has succeeded in filling the ideological vacuum left after the overthrow of the Communist regime."[63] Consequently, Church-State relations in Poland have undergone a great shift in the past several years. One commentator speculates that the Church is attempting to turn Poland into an official Catholic state, pointing to its success in introducing religious curriculum into the schools and making divorce more difficult to obtain.[64] This is especially true for the issues of abortion, birth control, and, most recently, restrictions on divorce, all issues that directly implicate women's ability to control their reproduction.

Religious influence has been decisive in restricting women's reproductive rights in post-Communist Poland.[65] The Catholic Church has lobbied against legalized abortion for decades, contending that "in no case is the interest of the woman recognised as superior to the life of the child in question."[66] In 1933, for example, the Church responded to arguments favoring liberalization of abortion laws by stating: "As painful and sad as the death of a woman may be, it is better to accept her death rather than accept the murder of a foetus. . . . One might add to this: where does the certainty that the mother's life, rather than the child's, represents a greater value for society come from?"[67] As the International Planned Parenthood Web Site on Poland describes the situation:

> Although services are available in hospitals, health centres and private clinics, the strong influence of the Roman Catholic Church and allied `pro life' organisations means that access to family planning and sex education is insecure and uneven. Contraceptives are available in pharmacies, but use of modern methods remains relatively low. The law enacted in 1997 to permit abortion in the case of difficult family and living conditions, was recently amended to remove the option of abortion for social reasons, following powerful lobbying by the Church which encouraged non-compliance with the law, and supported conscientious objection by health professionals (IPPF 1999).

The Church made several unsuccessful attempts to restrict abortion rights under communism. Polish Catholic teachings consider that "procreation is 'the supreme mission of woman,' even when it entails risks to her health or her life."[68] In 1989, the same year Communist rule officially ended, the Catholic Episcopate prepared a legislative bill to protect the rights of the "unborn child" by outlawing abortion and imposing mandatory three year jail terms for women and five year terms for doctors violating the law.[69] When the Pope visited Poland in 1991, he compared abortion to the Holocaust, and soon afterwards wrote to all Catholic bishops asking them to oppose laws authorizing abortion. Clergy, in turn, urged their parishioners to support political parties opposed to abortion.[70] As a result, legal abortion has been severely restricted in Poland since 1991.

Since March 1993, abortion has been illegal in Poland under a new law which provides exceptions only in cases of life endangerment or significant health problems of the mother or the fetus, or rape or incest when recognized as such by the police. The new law also bans fetal testing and certain contraceptives, including the IUD and the morning-after pill. It is unclear whether information about abortion is legal.[71] Although women who undergo abortions are not punished under the new law, doctors and others performing abortions for any reason other than to save the mother's life are liable to serve jail terms.[72] Nevertheless, abortion has been and remains a primary means of birth control in a country where sex education and contraception are frequently unavailable, largely due to the influence of the Catholic Church.[73]

Statistics on the number of abortions performed in Poland each year vary widely. Official statistics for 1993 state that 777 abortions were performed in hospitals in 1993, down from 11,640 in 1992 and about 31,000 in 1991, in stark contrast to the 150,000 abortions performed in 1971.[74] Although approximately 95 percent of the Polish population is Catholic, a majority of those polled object to the banning of abortion, and disagree with the official Church position on many other issues.[75]

The new law has made Poland, together with Ireland, the most abortion-restrictive states in Europe. Under communist rule, abortion was available for a number of reasons, including socio-economic grounds, during the first 12 weeks of pregnancy.[76] Since the new restrictions on abortion became effective, some women go to other countries for abortions, Germany if they can afford the safer procedures offered there, Russia if they cannot. Predictably, self-induced abortions have risen, often accompanied by medical complications, even death.[77] More than twice the number of babies were abandoned in maternity hospitals in 1993 as in 1992. In addition, the restrictive abortion laws contribute to domestic violence, as some men beat their wives for refusing to have sex with them from fear of pregnancy.[78] Although a new bill reintroducing "social grounds" for abortion was approved in both houses of Parliament, the President immediately vetoed it.

The Church's position on abortion is consistent with its view of women's dominant callings as those of "virginity, maternity, and faith."[79] Its view that women should be primarily wives and mothers legitimized firing women first during worker layoffs, and rehiring only men under privatization. The status of women in Poland has generally declined in the post-communist world, even though women's equality under communism was more official than actual.[80] Given the Church's influential role in bringing the current administration to power, it is difficult for the government to oppose Church policies, even if it holds contrary views.[81]

## Japan

The Japanese Constitution—drafted by the allied nations following the Second World War, and modeled on the U.S. and other Western constitutions—provides for the separation of church and state. This separation appears to be generally followed in practice.[82] Despite a diversity of active religious groups in Japan—including Buddhism, Shintoism, Christianity, and a plethora of alternative or "new" religions—there is little opposition to abortion by pro-life groups as compared to the U.S. and elsewhere,[83] since religious antipathy discourages alternative forms of birth control, unlike other countries, and since Buddhist priests have a vested interest in continuing to perform religious rituals for the "unborn" fetus," described below.

Although the Japanese generally view abortion as the taking of human life, the procedure tends to be viewed as a necessary or lesser evil. Buddhist cosmology may ease the moral difficulties associated with abortion, since the fetus is considered to be a "water baby," or "liquid life," a shadowy, only emergent and not fully formed person.[84] Buddhism indirectly accepts the practice of abortion by providing *mizuko kuyo*, rituals of mourning and consolation or ceremonial recognition of compassion following the loss of a fetus through abortion or miscarriage. Buddhist priests perform tens of thousands of *mizuko kuyo* ceremonies each year.[85] These ceremonies frequently involve prayers, recitation of scripture, and the installation on the temple grounds of a miniature statue of the Bodhisattva *Jizo* who is considered to be the protector of children, including fetuses, ensuring their safety even following abortion. The "parents" often return to visit as they would a gravestone of a departed relative at a cemetery, frequently leaving gifts or other mementos associated with their mourning for the dead "child."[86] Despite the general acceptance of abortion, Buddhism views abortion as contrary to the religious goal of overcoming one's ego.[87] Unscrupulous temples exploit the would-have-been parents by pressuring them into paying for rituals to ensure that the dead fetus will forgive them, and to facilitate its rebirth into a more favorable existence.[88]

Abortion has been legal in Japan since 1948, although prior to World War II it was restricted to cases where necessary to save the mother's life. An amendment in 1949 adding economic grounds to the list of acceptable reasons makes abortion effectively available to any woman who requests one.[89] Although *Seicho no le*, a religious organization founded in 1930, has waged anti-abortion campaigns on two occasions, once in the early 1970s and a second time in the 1980s, they were opposed by women's groups fighting to retain their abortion rights and were ultimately unsuccessful. Between one half and one-and-a-half million abortions are performed in Japan each year, a rate of approximately 14.9 per 1,000 live births, rivaling the rate of the United States in a country with half the population.[90] A significant factor contributing to such high abortion rates is the lack of adequate alternative birth control methods.[91] The lack of an established social system for adoption, the social disapproval of unwed motherhood, the profit motive of physicians and temple priests, and the desire for the better standard of living that is possible with fewer children also contribute to the higher abortion rate.[92]

The right and ability to terminate an unwanted pregnancy theoretically makes Japanese women better situated to improve their social, political, and economic status than women in most of the other countries examined here. However, their greater access is generally couched in language other than rights:

> Even today, the language of choice endorsed by Japanese feminists supports reproductive health, not rights. The Japanese government has viewed matters concerning reproduction as related to population control and motherhood. [93]

The widespread availability and inexpensiveness of abortion in Japan, coupled with the economic incentive of doctors and religious institutions to maintain the status quo, has meant that women frequently lack access to non-abortive methods of birth control. Although women have partial reproductive rights, they lack adequate access to safe and effective, convenient, economical forms of contraception that would make access to abortion unnecessary. Given the incentive of Buddhist temples to maintain abortion as the primary form of birth control, there is little reason to doubt that religion influences the reproductive rights of women in Japan.

## United States

In the United States, the separation of Church and State is guaranteed by the religion clauses of the First Amendment to the U.S. Constitution, which states that "Congress shall make no law respecting an establishment of religion, or prohibiting the free exercise thereof." In a religiously pluralistic society, such guarantees are essential to protecting the liberty of *all* citizens. However, lack of clarity about the extent to which the Constitution restricts religious influences on lawmaking has enabled religious groups to succeed in restricting access to reproductive rights for many women.

The right to an abortion was declared to be a constitutionally protected right of privacy by the Supreme Court in its landmark *Roe v. Wade* (410 U.S. 113 (1973) decision in 1973. The Court's opinion in *Roe* rejected religious views of when life begins as not relevant to its determination of women's constitutionally protected right to choose to terminate a pregnancy in the first trimester.[94] However, immediately following the Supreme Court's decision in *Roe*, several religiously-affiliated groups, many of them associated with the Roman Catholic Church, mobilized their ranks in a highly developed, well organized, and generously funded campaign to reverse the effect of the Court's decision.[95] Among the Catholic Church's pro-life strategies was the "Pastoral Plan for Pro-Life Activities" which specified that a "comprehensive pro-life legislative program must include passage of a constitutional amendment providing protection for the unborn child to the maximum degree possible,"[96] and "passage of federal and state laws and adoption of administrative policies that will restrict the practice of abortion as much as possible."[97] The Plan also called for a "pro-life action group" to be formed in each congressional district for the purpose of organizing people to persuade elected representatives to legally restrict abortion. The Catholic Church, often in conjunction with other pro-life groups, has been integral to many of the unsuccessful efforts to pass a Human Life Amendment to the Constitution that would reverse the effect of *Roe*.[98]

Another flurry of religiously-motivated activity to restrict state abortion laws followed the Supreme Court's 1989 decision in *Webster v. Reproductive Health Services* (492 U.S. 490 (1989) that states have an interest in protecting potential life *throughout* a woman's pregnancy, not only after the point of viability, as the Court in *Roe* had stated.[99] The Catholic Church was very influential in the passage of the restrictive Pennsylvania abortion statute upheld by the Supreme Court's 1992 decision in *Planned Parenthood v. Casey* (112 S. Ct. 2791 (1992)).[100] The Church has also been involved in legislative efforts in several other states, including New Jersey, Louisiana, Florida, Illinois, and New York.[101] Other religious groups have been influential in the passage of restrictive abortion laws in other states.[102]

Congress has passed a number of different restrictions on abortion since *Roe* that have been influenced by religious groups, including the Hyde Amendment prohibiting the use of public funds for abortion, and various "gag" rules—restrictions on the ability of doctors and other federally funded health care providers to counsel pregnant women about abortion.[103] These restrictions have disproportionately disadvantaged poor women, many of whom are of color, adolescent, and from rural areas. Pro-life groups have also made efforts since *Roe* to monitor the positions of elected officials on abortion, and to elect as many pro-life candidates as possible.[104] The religious right has also influenced the abortion rights of women living in developing countries by convincing Congress to pass the Helms Amendment to the Foreign Assistance Act, which prohibits the direct use of foreign aid funds for abortion services in recipient nations.

Thus, even though a separation of Church and State theoretically exists in the United States, religious influences have succeeded in significantly limiting women's access to abortion, especially for women lacking economic resources. Although many American women have relatively available access to other forms of reproductive control, the failure to protect abortion rights constitutes a failure to fully protect women's reproductive rights, and consequently, their human rights more generally. In fact, the United States has thus far refused to become a signatory to the *Woman's Convention*. Religious influences on reproductive rights in the U.S. represents one example of how American women continue to be treated as second class citizens, despite the legal recognition that women's rights to due process and equal protection of the laws are protected by the U.S. Constitution.

## International Law

The influence of religion in limiting women's human rights is evident at the international level as well. Chapter Five of the official UN *Platform* document contains the reservations and interpretive statements of a number of countries limiting their full adoption of the principles of reproductive rights enunciated in that document. Several of these, virtually all predominantly Catholic or Muslim countries or constituencies, reject abortion as part of the right to control one's sexuality or as part of reproductive rights.[105]

Other member nations expressly cite religion as the reason for restricting their adoption of the *Platform's* principles regarding reproductive rights. Several of these are officially or predominantly Islamic countries. For example, the Egyptian delegation states that Egypt's compliance with the *Platform's* recommendations are conditional upon "the rights of national sovereignty and various moral and religious values . . . and with the divine guidance of our true and tolerant religious law."[106] The Iraqi delegation issued reservations regarding paragraph 96 of the *Platform* which concerns reproductive rights, "because it is incompatible with our social and religious values."[107] Similarly, the Libyan delegation's adoption of the *Platform's* recommendations is limited, "in keeping with its religious beliefs, local laws and priorities for social and economic development," to "what is permitted by our beliefs and the laws and traditions which shape our behavior as a society."[108]

Several other of these countries are officially or predominantly Catholic. For example, Guatemala specifies that its implementation of the *Platform* will be "in full respect for the diverse religious, ethical and cultural values and philosophical beliefs of our multi-ethnic, multilingual and multicultural people."[109] Honduras rejects abortion as part of family planning on the basis that it is a signatory to the American Convention on Human Rights, which recognizes the right to life from conception, "on the basis of the moral, ethical, religious and cultural principles that should govern human behavior."[110] Although such reservations and limitations on women's reproductive rights are inconsistent with protection for the rights and ethical values of all persons, regardless of gender, the "loopholes" for religious and cultural values of individuals and communities in U.N. documents enables governments to avoid fulfilling their obligations to protect the human rights of all women. Thus, in many cases, governments on the basis of religion deny the full recognition of and protection for women's human rights. Religious influences on government which result in restricting women's reproductive rights frequently restrict women's lives in other respects as well, through traditional gender ideologies that subordinate women to men.

In sum, while international law recognizes that reproductive rights are especially integral to the fulfillment of women's rights as human rights, its simultaneous license to member nations to accord full recognition and respect to indigenous cultural and religious values undermines the actual protection accorded to women's human rights. In the following and final section, I will suggest a strategy for remedying this inconsistency in international law.

## IV: Recommendations and Conclusions

The preceding survey starkly illustrates the tension in international human rights law between upholding women's rights as human rights and according "full respect" for religious values. In many nations, religious influences on government have resulted in seriously restricting women's reproductive rights, contrary to the explicit protections for women's human rights in international law. Although too limited to be statistically valid, this survey also suggests that there is a correlation between the extent of a religion's influence on government and the status of women's human rights. The preceding survey indicates that the goal of recognizing and protecting women's rights as human rights cannot be fully realized without restricting the influence of religion on government policy in certain cases.

The current policy to uphold the sovereignty of local cultural traditions and practices must yield when those traditions and practices function to deny women their human rights. Several aspects of justice support the conclusion that women's rights should have priority in conflicts with religious freedoms. Since international law does not provide any explicit priority for one over the other, we must assume that they are entitled to equivalent weight. But in order for both sets of rights to actually receive equal consideration, it is necessary in certain cases to restrict religious freedoms. This is because certain actions taken under the rubric of religious freedom are antithetical to women's human rights, as amply documented above.

In addition, religious rights can be limited with less loss of individual freedom than can limits on women's human rights, since religious rights can be reinterpreted as individual rather than community rights. Such a reinterpretation accords the right to all to freely practice their religion, regardless of gender and regardless of whether or not it is supported by the state. Interpreting religious freedom as an individual right rather than a community one also better protects religious minorities against the overzealousness of the majority within particular communities. This interpretation helps protect against the problems we have seen with respect to establishments of religion, whether they be formal or informal.

Furthermore, even in cases of a direct conflict between an individual women's human right and an individual claim to religious freedom, protecting women's rights should take priority. In general, the denial of women's rights historically has been systematic and widespread across all religious traditions, whereas the denial of religious freedoms has been more limited and selected. Thus, according priority to women's rights is justified as a matter of compensatory justice. This is especially important where the women's rights at stake are those established by religious authorities acting without the participation or consent of women.

Since traditional religions, as we have seen, have accorded women secondary and inferior roles and generally limited (at least normatively) their status to those of wives and mothers, according priority to women's rights at this juncture in history serves to correct centuries of gender injustice and ensure that women can fully participate in all aspects of social and spiritual life. Religious beliefs and prescriptions relating to gender are frequently based on outdated patriarchal and sexist understandings of the appropriate roles between men and women in society. Most cultures have moved beyond such understandings, at least in formal law and at least in some respects. International law itself recognizes the importance of this progress. As a source of transcultural and religious norms, human rights law represents as close to a global consensus as is currently possible. All governments should recognize this progress by refusing to allow inconsistent religious values to be perpetuated in law and public policy. Given women's exclusion from the formulation and application of most religious prescriptions, it is unfair to allow such tenets to operate in ways that obstruct or deny women their human rights. As we have seen, the *Platform for Action* drafted in Beijing takes a step in this direction, but does not go far enough to mandate that governments ensure that their laws foster rather than restrict women's human rights.

Allowing religious rationales to restrict or deny women's human rights fails to examine the character of the "religion" in question. Are women themselves adherents of the particular faith involved in influencing reproductive rights? In many instances, it is evident that religious doctrines are enunciated and elite men who do not necessarily represent the sentiments of their entire community, never mind the women whose rights are being restricted thereby impose their dictates. The policies of the Holy See in relation to the Fourth World Conference on Women in Beijing and the World Health and Population Conference in Cairo discussed above provide ready examples of this problem. If the religious values and tenets that are the basis for the restriction of women's rights do not represent the beliefs of the women to whom they are being applied, it seems especially unfair to allow such values to "trump" women's rights where the two conflict.

Limiting religious freedoms to the level of the individual would go a long way toward this end. Since the human rights of women are especially vulnerable to being overridden by the institutionalization of religious values in law and social practice, this form of religious expression should be subject to limitation when it infringes on women's rights, especially since it is group instantiations of religious belief and practice that are most capable of restricting women's human rights, especially in the form of restrictive laws. In those cases where this restriction cannot resolve the conflicts, according priority to women's rights in this circumstance is in greater accordance with the consensus of the community than allowing religious tenets of particular faiths to dictate a government's laws and public policies.

Under the proposed strategy, the priority given to protecting women's human rights only would apply in a very narrow sphere—to religious influences on laws and public policies that operate with the effect or result of limiting or denying women's human rights. The intent of the proposed principle of priority is to insure that a government's laws and public policies do not undermine women's human rights; it is not to restrict or deny religious freedoms. Implementation of the proposal thus would leave unaffected the religious rights and freedoms of most citizens around the world. In some instances, as we have seen above, the only way to do the latter is through limiting religious freedom.

Some governments currently have established principles and procedures in place that make implementation of this proposal easier than in others. For example, in governments like those of Japan and the United States, constitutions guarantee the separation of church and state. But as these examples illustrate, even in such situations, religious influences on government may succeed in limiting women's rights, especially in the absence of a government's commitment to recognizing and enforcing women's rights. Implementation of the proposed priority principle is even more problematic in countries with governments that have established religions, either as a formal matter as in Bangladesh, or *de facto*, as in Ireland, Poland, and Israel.

Where the priority for religious rights (at least of the majority religion) is more entrenched, the evidence indicates that the denigration of women's rights is likely to be more in evidence. Nonetheless, implementation of the proposal even in these countries would not require fundamental restructuring of government, but only implementing of the priority principle in a limited number of instances as specified above. This could be accomplished by the application of international law norms as interpreted here at the domestic level. In other words, international law would be recognized as normative by judges and other legal personnel vested with jurisdiction to adjudicate cases of alleged human rights violations.

In conclusion, according women's rights a priority over religious rights when the two conflict serves to ensure that women's rights will genuinely be recognized and protected as human rights. Previous efforts to accord "equal time" to women's rights and religious rights in international law, as we have seen, have resulted in unjustly restricting women's human rights. If women truly are to be regarded as "human," their reproductive and other human rights must take priority when religious influences on government and lawmaking would operate to undermine or deny them.

## Notes

1. The principle of protecting human rights for all, "regardless of religion" is contained in almost all major human rights documents of the United Nations, including the *United Nations Charter* (United Nations, *Charter of the United Nations*, 1945), the *Universal Declaration of Human Rights* (United Nations, *Universal Declaration of Human Rights*, G.A. Res. 217, U.N. Doc. A/810, at 71, arts. 2, 16(1) (1948)), the *UN International Covenant on Civil and Political Rights* (United Nations, *International Covenant on Civil and Political Rights*, 999 U.N.T.S. 171, 173, 174, 179, (1966))(ICCPR), and several subsequent treaties and other documents. Article 18 of the *Universal Declaration*, for instance, states:

> Everyone has the right to freedom of thought, conscience and religion; this right includes freedom to change his religion or belief, and freedom, either alone or in community with others and in public or private, to manifest his religion or belief in teaching, practice, worship and observance (UN 1948: Art. 18).

The relevant language of the ICCPR is similar, and additionally states:

> 2. No one shall be subject to coercion which would impair his freedom to have or to adopt a religion or belief of his choice. 3. Freedom to manifest one's religion or beliefs may be subject only to such limitations as are prescribed by law and are necessary to protect public safety, order, health, or morals or the fundamental rights and freedoms of others (UN 1965: Art. 18).

2. Although framing women's rights as human rights is fairly recent, the U.N. has prohibited discrimination based on sex since the U.N. Charter was ratified (see U.N. *Charter of the United Nations* (1945): arts. 1(3), 13(1)(b), 55(c), and 76(c), and this prohibition has been repeated in the Universal Declaration of Human Rights (U.N. 1948), the International Covenant on Economic, Social, and Cultural Rights, arts. 2(2), 3 (U.N. 1966), and the International Covenant on Civil and Political Rights, arts. 2(1), 3, 23(4), 26 (U.N. 1966). The *Vienna Declaration and Programme of Action* adopted in June 1993 by the World Conference on Human Rights ("Vienna Declaration") specifies that "human rights of women and of the girl-child are an inalienable and indivisible part of universal human rights" (*Vienna Declaration and Programme of Action*, UN Doc. A/CONF. 157/23 (1993), reprinted in 32 ILM 1661 (1993) (UN 1993a)). United Nations Fourth World Conference on Women held in Beijing China in 1995 (Women's Conference) saw the fruition of years of campaigning by women's rights and human rights activists to identify women's rights as human rights. Similarly, the *Platform for Action* ("Platform") drafted at the Women's Conference frames women's rights "as indivisible, universal, and inalienable human rights" (United Nations, *Beijing Declaration and Draft Platform for Action*, U.N. Doc. A/CONF.177/20 (1995).

3. A series of resolutions sponsored by the United Nations in 1966 endorsed the concept of freedom of choice in family planning as a human right. In 1968, at the Teheran International Conference on Human Rights, member nations of the United Nations unanimously recognized as a human right the decision to choose the number and spacing of one's children (Jodi Jacobson, "Global Dimensions of Forced Motherhood," *USA Today*, 121, no. 2576 (May 1993): 34-35; Katarina Tomasevski, *Women and Human Rights* (London: Zed Books, 1993)). This right was amplified in the *World Population Plan of Action* (1974) ("Round Tables Address Critical Issues," *Newsletter of the International Conference on Population and Development*, Cairo, Egypt, 5-13 September 1994 (August 1993)). The explicit connection between reproductive rights and women's human rights was recognized in the U.N.'s *Report of the Special Rapporteur: Study on the Interrelationship of the Status of Women and Family Planning* as "the ability to regulate the timing and number of births [a]s one central means of freeing women to exercise the full range of human rights to which they are entitled" (*Report of the Special Rapporteur: Study on the Interrelationship of the Status of Women and Family Planning*, U.N. ESCOR, Comm. on the Status of Women, 25th Sess., Paragraph 31, U.N. Doc. E/CN.6/575/Rev. 1 (1973)). Article 16 of the *Convention on the Elimination of Discrimination Against Women* (*Convention on the Elimination of All Forms of Discrimination Against Women*, G.A. Res. 34/180, U.N. GAOR, 34th Sess., Supp. No. 46, at 193. U.N. Doc. A/34/46 (1979) (entry into force Sept. 3, 1981)) makes both rights over procreative decisions and the means to exercise such decisions a matter of "equality of men and women."

Establishing reproductive rights for women as basic to their human rights had become a goal of women's rights activists by the time of the United Nations Decade of Women Conference in Nairobi in 1985. The *Vienna Declaration* drafted at the United Nations Conference on Human Rights in 1993 states clearly that "the human rights of women throughout the life cycle are an inalienable, integral and indivisible part of universal human rights" (U.N. *Vienna Declaration and Programme of Action*, U.N. Doc. A/CONF. 157/23 (1993), reprinted in 32 ILM 1661 (1993)), and reaffirms women's right to accessible and adequate health care, including "the widest range of family planning services," as necessary to equality between men and women (see United Nations, "Round Tables Address Critical Issues," *Newsletter of the International Conference on Population and Development*, Cairo, Egypt, 5-13 September 1994 (August 1993)). The affirmation of reproductive rights as women's human rights made in the *Programme of Action of the United Nations International Conference on Population and Development*, held in Cairo, Egypt in September 1994 was endorsed almost unanimously by the conference delegates (see United Nations, *Beijing Declaration and Draft Platform for Action*, U.N. Doc. A/CONF.177/20 (1995): para. 216). While not explicitly endorsing contraception and abortion as basic to human rights, Principle 8 of the *Programme* affirms that

> States should take all appropriate measure to ensure, on a basis of equality of men and women, universal access to health-care services, including those related to reproductive health care, which includes family planning and sexual health. Reproductive health-care programmes should provide the widest range of services without any form of coercion. All couples and individuals have the basic right to decide freely and responsibly the number and spacing of their children and to have the information, education, and means to do so (UN 1994a: 8; see Fran Hosken, "Editorial: Women and the Population Conference—What Next?" *Women's International Network News* 20, no. 4 (Autumn 1994): 1).

This language is readily subject to a reading that abortion and contraception are included in the phrase "the widest range of services." However, the *Programme* explicitly states that abortion is not a means of population control, although it should be safe where legal, and should be an important health issue of government concern where "unsafe."

4. See, e.g. UN 1993: 5; Henry David and Anna Tikow, "Commentary: Abortion and Women's Rights in Poland, 1994," *Studies in Family Planning* 25, no. 4 (July/August 1994): 239-41; Joan Hoff, "Comparative Analysis of Abortion In Ireland, Poland, and the United States," *Women's Studies International Forum* 17, no. 6 (1994): 621-46; Donna Sullivan, "Women's Human Rights and the 1993 World Conference on Human Rights," *American Journal of International Law* 88 (1994): 152-67; Fran Hosken, "Vienna Declaration and Programme of Action," *Women's International Network News* 19, no. 3 (Summer 1993): 9; Fran Hosken, "Women's Declaration on Population Policies," *Women's International Network News* 19, no. 4 (Autumn 1993): 10; Katarina Tomasevski, *Women and Human Rights* (London: Zed Books, 1993), 18; Rebecca Cook, *Women's Health and Human Rights: The Promotion and Protection of Women's Health through International Human Rights Law* (Geneva: World Health Organization, 1994); Rebecca Cook, "International Protection of Women's Reproductive Rights," *New York University Journal of International Law and Politics* 24 (1991): 645-727; Sylvia Law, "Rethinking Sex and the Constitution, *University of Pennsylvania Law Review* 132 (1984): 955-1050.

5. The *Platform* further defines reproductive rights as "embracing certain human rights that are already recognized in national laws, international human rights documents and other consensus documents" (United Nations, *Beijing Declaration and Draft Platform for Action*, para. 95). The section of the *Platform* on "Human Rights of Women" claims that "The uni-

versal nature of these rights and freedoms is beyond question" (10, para. 211).

6. See Randy Frame, "Abortion Around the World," *Christianity Today* 34, no. 3 (Feb. 19, 1990): 32. Rather than showing an improvement in this situation in recent years, statistics indicate the contrary—that fewer women are able to obtain access to adequate family planning, especially to safe, legal abortions.

7. Jodi Jacobson, "Global Dimensions of Forced Motherhood," *USA Today* 121, no. 2576 (May 1993): 34; see United Nations, "Women, Population, and Development," *Newsletter of the International Conference on Population and Development, Cairo, Egypt, 5-13 September 1994* (March 1994): 5-6; Rebecca Cook, "International Protection of Women's Reproductive Rights," *New York University Journal of International Law and Politics* 24 (1991): 646; Ruth Dixon-Mueller, "Abortion Policy and Women's Health in Developing Countries," *International Journal of Health Services* 20, no. 2 (1990): 297-314.

8. United Nations, Programme *of Action of the United Nations International Conference on Population and Development* (U.N. ICDP Secretariat G-2 1994): 6; see Gordon Aeschliman, "Worldwide Abortion Rights Set Back in Population Debate," *Christianity Today* 38, no. 12 (October 24, 1994): 82-83.

9. United Nations, *Programme of Action*: 37, emphasis supplied.

10. For example, the *Vienna Declaration* specifies that the realization of human rights for women requires that states take measures "to counter intolerance and related violence based on religion or belief, including practices of discrimination against women. . . ." (U.N. 1993). The full import of this would appear to encompass all forms of religious discrimination, not merely that based on religious extremism. The *Declaration* also calls for the elimination of religious prejudices and the use of religion as a shield to evade responsibility for protecting women's fundamental human rights (see Donna Sullivan, "Women's Human Rights and the 1993 World Conference on Human Rights," *American Journal of International Law* 88 (1994): 152-67; Fran Hosken, "Vienna Declaration and Programme of Action," *Women's International Network News* 19, no. 3 (Summer 1993): 9, emphasis supplied). Similarly, the *Women's Declaration on Population Policies*, endorsed in preparation for the Population Conference in Cairo, states that "the fundamental sexual and reproductive rights of women cannot be subordinated against a woman's will, to the interests of . . . religious institutions" (Fran Hosken, "Women's Declaration on Population Policies," *Women's International Network News* 19, no. 4 (Autumn 1993): 10).

11. See Donna Sullivan, "Women's Human Rights and the 1993 World Conference on Human Rights," *American Journal of International Law* 88 (1994), 152-67.

12. A subsequent paragraph of the *Platform* specifying that the creation of an educational and social environment, in which women and men, girls and boys, are treated equally and encouraged to achieve their full potential, respecting their freedom of thought, conscience, religion, and belief, and where educational resources promote non-stereotyped images of women and men, would be effective in the elimination of the causes of discrimination against women and inequalities between women and men (United Nations, *Beijing Declaration and Draft Platform for Action*, para. 72) is also implicitly in tension with full protection for religious freedoms, since many religious traditions promote the very stereotyped images of women that are antithetical to their recognition as full human beings entitled to the full protection of human rights.

13. This echoes already quoted language from the *Vienna Declaration* to the same effect. Paragraph 118 of the *Platform* states:

> Violence against women throughout the life cycle derives essentially from cultural patterns, in particular the harmful effects of certain traditional or customary practices

> and all acts of extremism linked to race, sex, language or religion that perpetuate the lower status accorded to women in the family, the workplace, the community and society (United Nations, *Beijing Declaration and Draft Platform for Action*, para. 118).

Paragraph 124 requires that governments "condemn violence against women and refrain from invoking any custom, tradition or religious consideration to avoid their obligations with respect to its elimination as set out in the Declaration on the Elimination of Violence against Women" (para 124(a)). Again, in the context of violence against women, paragraph 224 states that

> religious and anti-religious extremism and terrorism are incompatible with the dignity and the worth of the human person and must be combated and eliminated. Any harmful aspect of certain traditional, customary or modern practices that violates the rights of women should be prohibited and eliminated (para. 224).

14. Even prior to the Conference, members of the American Catholic clergy stated publicly that the proposed *Programme for Action* was nothing more than a tool of the wealthy nations to control the Third World. The women who held a press conference in response to the Catholic announcement contradict this claim. These women "described their struggles against religious fundamentalism of various kinds and other obstacles to women's empowerment in reproductive matters" (United Nations, "NGO Women Speak Out for Reproductive Rights," *Newsletter of the International Conference on Population and Development, Cairo, Egypt, 5-13 September 1994* (April 1994), 6).

15. See Eugene Linden, "More Power to Women, Fewer Mouths to Feed," *Time* 144, no. 13 (September 26, 1994): 64-65; Jennie Ruby, "Commentary: Too Many People—Too Many Popes," *Off Our Backs* 24, no. 9 (October 1994): 2; Gayle Kirshenbaum, "Population Ploys and Promises At the Cairo Conference," *MS* 5, no. 3 (November-December 1994): 15; *Christian Century* Editorial Staff, "Islam Engages the World," *Christian Century* 111, no. 26 (September 21-28, 1994): 846-47; Edd Doerr, "Church and State: Cairo, Rome, and Beyond," *The Humanist* 54, no. 6 (1994): 35-36.

16. See Ruby, "Commentary: Too Many People," 2. Yet, at the closing plenary session, the Vatican delegation signed the *Programme* as a whole, expressing only minor reservations about the fuzziness of the term "sexual and reproductive health" (see David S. Toolin, "Hijacked in Cairo," *America* 171, no. 9 (October 1, 1994): 3-4).

17. Fazlur Rahman, *Health and Medicine in the Islamic Tradition: Change and Identity* (New York: Crossroad, 1987), 1-2.

18. See Naila Kabeer, "The Quest for National Identity: Women, Islam, and the State of Bangladesh," in *Women, Islam, and the State*, ed. Deniz Kandiyoti (Philadelphia: Temple University Press, 1991), 131. In 1987, the Constitution was amended to declare that "the state religion of the Republic is Islam, but other religions may be practised in peace and harmony in the Republic" (quoted in Kabeer, 131; Emajuddin Ahamed and D.R.J.A. Nazneen, "Islam in Bangladesh," *Asian Survey* 30, no. 8 (1990): 795-97).

19. See Kabeer "The Quest for National Identity," 115; Rahman, *Health and Medicine in the Islamic Tradition*, 114.

20. See Clarence Maloney, K.M. Ashraful Aziz, and Profulla Sarker, *Beliefs and Fertility in Bangladesh* (Dacca, Bangladesh: International Centre for Diarrhoael Disease Research, 1981), 212-14.

21. See Aziz & Maloney, *Beliefs and Fertility in Bangladesh*, 170.

22. The following rationale is representative:

> For the mother is the origin of the fetus; moreover, she is established in life,

with duties and responsibilities, and she is also a pillar of the family. It is not possible to sacrifice her life for the life of the fetus which has not yet acquired a personality and which has no responsibilities or obligations to fulfil (quoted in Abul Fadi Mohsin Ebrahim, *Abortion, Birth Control, and Surrogate Parenting: An Islamic Perspective* (Washington, D.C.: American Trust Publications, 1989), 93).

In recent years, more liberal interpretations of Islamic law permit abortion in the first 120 days after conception, in accordance with traditional Islamic principles of imposing punishment for harming a fetus in increasing severity corresponding to its stage of development. See Frame "Abortion Around the World," 32; Annalisa Pizzarello, *Abortion, Religion, and the State Legislator After Webster* (Chicago: The Park Ridge Center, 1990), 15; Rahman, *Health and Medicine in the Islamic Tradition*, 113; Halida Akhter, "Bangladesh," in *International Handbook on Abortion*, ed. Paul Sachdey (New York: Greenwood Press, 1988), 43 n. 1.

23. V. Fauveau and T. Blanchet, "Deaths From Injuries and Induced Abortion Among Rural Bangladesh Women," *Social Science Medicine* 29, no. 9 (1989): 1121-27.

24. See Dixon-Mueller "Abortion Policy and Women's Health in Developing Countries"; Akhter, "Bangladesh," 37. Menstrual regulation has been described as capable of being "performed without anesthesia or sedation by trained paraprofessionals on an outpatient basis in about five to ten minutes" (Dixon-Mueller, 302).

25. Fauveau and Blanchet, "Deaths From Injuries and Induced Abortion Among Rural Bangladesh Women," 1125.

26. However, views on this state of affairs are mixed. Another perspective is that the government has not aggressively implemented Islamic law (with its traditional regulation of women) because of modernist agendas of the leading political leaders, and that this has accrued to the benefit of women's rights (Kabeer, "The Quest for National Identity," 115, 121).

27. See Kabeer, "The Quest for National Identity," 135.

28. *Economist* Staff 1994, 42.

29. Ahmad, "Islam in Bangladesh," 40.

30. Whereas in 1975, 29 percent of Bengali women said family size was the will of Allah, in 1990, only 8 percent believed they cannot control their own destiny. See Malcolm Potts and Allan Rosenfield, "The Fifth Freedom Revisited: I, Background and Existing Programmes," *The Lancet* 336, no. 8725 (Nov. 17, 1990): 1227-31.

31. Rahman, *Health and Medicine in the Islamic Tradition*, 115.

32. See Dixon-Mueller, "Abortion Policy and Women's Health in Developing Countries," 298; Fauveau and Blanchet, "Deaths From Injuries and Induced Abortion Among Rural Bangladesh Women," 1122; Akhter, "Bangladesh," 41-42. Bangladesh has one of the highest population densities in the world, with 45 percent of its population under the age of 15.

33. See Akhter, "Bangladesh," 36.

34. See Fauveau and Blanchet, "Deaths From Injuries and Induced Abortion Among Rural Bangladesh Women," 1125-27; Aziz & Maloney, *Life Stages, Gender, and Fertility in Bangladesh*, 100-01.

35. Paul Morris, "Israel," in *Religion in Politics: A World Guide*, ed. Stuart Mews (Chicago, Ill: St. James Press, 1989).

36. Eitan Sabatello and Nurit Yaffe, "Israel," in *International Handbook on Abortion*, ed. Paul Sachdev (New York: Greenwood Press, 1988), 264.

37. The Talmud has two parts, the Mishnah, a codification of the law completed in the second century C.E., and the Gemara, a latter rabbinic commentary on the Mishnah. See

Rachel Biale, *Women and Jewish Law* (New York: Schocken Books, 1984); Adrienne Baker, *The Jewish Woman in Contemporary Society* (New York: New York University Press, 1993), 45; J. David Bleich, "Abortion and Jewish Law," in *New Perspectives on Human Abortion*, ed. Thomas Hilgers, Dennis Moran, and David Mall (Frederick, Md.: University Publications of America, 1981), 406. The Talmud is regarded as an authoritative commentary on the Hebrew Bible.

38. See Bleich, "Abortion and Jewish Law," 413.

39. See Dena Davis, "Abortion in Jewish Thought: A Study in Casuistry," *Journal of the American Academy of Religion 60*, no. 2 (1992): 313-24; David M. Feldman, *Birth Control in Jewish Law: Marital Relations, Contraception, and Abortion as Set Forth in the Classic Texts of Jewish Law* (New York: Schocken, 1974), 253-54.

40. See Biale, *Women and Jewish Law*, 220.

41. Some Orthodox teachings also permit abortion where there are severe fetal defects or where serious physical health problems would develop if pregnancy were carried to term (Pizzarello, *Abortion, Religion, and the State Legislator After Webster*, 15).

42. See Davis "Abortion in Jewish Thought," 317-18; Pizzarello, *Abortion, Religion, and the State Legislator After Webster*, 15; David M. Feldman, *Birth Control in Jewish Law: Marital Relations, Contraception, and Abortion as Set Forth in the Classic Texts of Jewish Law* (New York: Schocken, 1974), 287.

43. See Sabatello and Yaffe, "Israel," 268-69.

44. See Sabatello and Yaffe, "Israel," 264-65; Rebecca Cook and Bernard Dickens, "International Developments in Abortion Laws: 1977-88," *American Journal of Public Health* 78, no. 10 (1988): 1305-11. The four remaining valid grounds for abortion are (1) being under the age of 17 or over age 40; (2) pregnancy as the result of violence or coercion or an out-of-wedlock relationship; (3) fetal malformation; or (4) danger to the mother's health or life. See Eitan Sabatello, "Estimates of Demand for Abortion among Soviet Immigrants in Israel," *Studies in Family Planning* 23 (1992): 268-73.

45. Recent rates of abortion in Soviet countries are somewhere between 6 and 8 million annually, which correlates to one abortion case per 10 women of childbearing age, or a total abortion rate of close to 3 abortions per woman over a lifespan (Sabatello, "Estimates of Demand for Abortion among Soviet Immigrants in Israel," 268).

46. See Tom Garvin, "Ireland," in *Religion in Politics: A World Guide*, ed. Stuart Mews (Chicago, IL: St. James Press, 1989).

47. See, e.g Callahan, Daniel and Sidney Callahan, eds., *Abortion: Understanding Differences* (New York: Plenum Press, 1984); Charles Curran, "Abortion: Its Moral Aspects," in *Abortion: The Moral Issues*, ed. Edward Batchelor (New York: Pilgrim Press, 1982); John Noonan, "An Almost Absolute Value in History," in *The Morality of Abortion: Legal and Historical Perspectives*, ed. John T. Noonan, Jr. (Cambridge, Mass.: Harvard University Press, 1970). The Church's earliest statements against abortion are stated in the late first century document, the *Didache*, which proclaims: "You shall not kill the fetus by abortion or destroy the infant already born" (quoted in J. Gordon Melton, ed., *The Churches Speak on: Abortion* (Detroit, MI: Gale Research Inc., 1989), xcii). This early view did not consider the stage of fetal development in evaluating the culpability of abortion. In the fourth century, St. Augustine argued in the *Enchiridion* that the embryo does not become a human being until the time of "ensoulment," that is, when God infuses the soul with the spirit of life.

In the twelfth century, Ivo of Chartres and Gratian, prominent church theologians, held the view that abortion of the "unformed" fetus was not homicide. In the thirteenth century, St. Thomas Aquinas reiterated this view with the concept of *hylomorphism*, according to which the embryo does not become fully human until it takes on a human form. This position was the basis of church teaching and canon law for the next seven hundred years.

In 1869, Pope Pius IX issued a statement declaring that even though "the fetus is not ensouled, since it is directed to the forming of man, its ejection is anticipated homicide." In 1889, craniotomy (crushing the skull of the fetus to end a life-threatening labor) was prohibited; in 1902 surgery to remove an ectopic pregnancy was as well (see Kristin Luker, *Abortion and the Politics of Motherhood* (Berkeley: University of California Press, 1984), 59). In 1895, the ban on abortion was extended to include even those necessary to save the life of the pregnant woman. See Dallas Blanchard, *The Anti-Abortion Movement and the Rise of the Religious Right: From Polite to Fiery Protest* (New York: Twayne Publishers, 1994), 11. The Church has maintained this position as its official view ever since.

48. See Susan T. Nicholson, *Abortion and the Roman Catholic Church* (Knoxville, Tenn.: Religious, Inc., 1978).

49. See Blanchard, *The Anti-Abortion Movement*, 11.

50. Quoted in Elizabeth Adell Cook, Ted Jelen and Clyde Wilcox, *Between Two Absolutes: Public Opinion and the Politics of Abortion* (Boulder, Colo.: Westview Press, 1982), 95; Melton, *The Churches Speak on: Abortion*, xviii. The Catholic Church insists that abortion is a moral, not a religious, issue, and thus one that all women and men can agree is wrong, regardless of their personal religious faiths (see Timothy Byrnes, *Catholic Bishops in American Politics* (Princeton, N.J.: Princeton University Press, 1991), 55-56). This position is founded upon the Church's Natural Law doctrine, according to which certain moral principles are considered to be applicable to everyone, regardless of their faith, because they are understood to be based on reason, and not dependent on privileged insights or theological premises (see Timothy Byrnes and Mary Segers, eds., *The Catholic Church and the Politics of Abortion: A View From the States* (Boulder, Colo.: Westview Press, 1992), 3; Nicholson, *Abortion and the Roman Catholic Church*, 13-14). Since abortion subverts natural law principles that procreation and preservation of life are unconditionally good, the immorality of the practice is considered to be evident on the basis of reason and not depend upon theological premises.

51. Cook, Jelen, and Wilcox, *Between Two Absolutes*, 376. A study found that all of the countries in Western Europe with the least liberal abortion laws had the largest proportion of Catholics.

52. See WINS Editor 1992: 28.

53. Yael Yishai, "Public Ideas and Public Policy: Abortion Politics in Four Democracies," *Comparative Politics* 25, no. 2 (1993): 207-28.

54. See Joan Hoff, "Comparative Analysis of Abortion In Ireland, Poland, and the United States," *Women's Studies International Forum* 17, no. 6 (1994): 621-46; Rebecca Cook and Bernard Dickens, "International Developments in Abortion Laws: 1977-88," *American Journal of Public Health* 78, no. 10 (1988): 1305-11; Oliver Rafferty, "Abortion in Ireland," *America* 167 (October 24, 1992): 293-95. The Eighth Amendment states "the right to life of the unborn ... with due regard to the equal right of the mother. . . ."

55. See Rafferty, "Abortion in Ireland," 293. As one commentator points out, "The simultaneously tragic and ludicrous irony of the judgment was that legally X was a minor, a child. In Ireland, therefore, and according to the law, the 'right-to-life' of the *unborn* took precedence over the right to live of *born* children" (Ailbhe Smyth, ed., *The Abortion Papers: Ireland* (Dublin, Ireland: Attic Press, 1992), 165).

56. See Ailbhe Smyth, "The 'X' Case: Women and Abortion in the Republic of Ireland," *Feminist Legal Studies* 1, no. 2 (1993): 163-77; Rafferty, "Abortion in Ireland," 294.

57. See Smyth, "The 'X' Case," 174. In 1997, 5,336 women traveled to Britain for the purposes of obtaining an abortion. International Planned Parenthood Federation <http://www.ippf.org/regions/countries/irl/index.htm> (August 12,1999).

58. See Reed Boland, "Abortion Law in Europe in 1991-92," *Journal of Law, Medicine, and Ethics* 21, no. 1 (Spring 1993): 72-93.

59. See Hoff, "Comparative Analysis of Abortion," 642. The Irish Supreme Court upheld a ban on such information against students distributing addresses and phone numbers of abortion providers abroad. The European Court of Justice affirmed the judgment. See Smyth, "The 'X' Case," 169; Boland, "Abortion Law in Europe," 82. However, a suit against family planning clinics on the same grounds resulted in a final judgment by the European Court of Human Rights that the ban violated the clinics' rights to receive and impart information protected by the European Convention on Human Rights (see Boland , 82-86).

60. Yishai, "Public Ideas and Public Policy," 216.

61. There are some indications that the government's policies toward sexuality in general are becoming more liberal and tolerant. For example, condoms, once banned, are now available in vending machines. The law outlawing sodomy was recently invalidated, making Ireland the most liberal country on homosexuality in the United Kingdom. Sex education is being taught in schools, despite the opposition of religious groups. In addition, a scandal involving a Catholic Bishop's sexual improprieties with a male child has served to weaken the credibility of the Catholic Church in Ireland. See Dick Spicer, "Progress in Ireland," *Free Inquiry* 14, no. 1 (Winter 93/94): 20-21.

62. See Stuart Mews, ed., *Religion in Politics: A World Guide* (Chicago, Ill.: St. James Press, 1989), 220.

63. Hanna Jankowska, "Report: The Reproductive Rights Campaign in Poland," *Women's Studies International Forum* 16, no. 3 (1993): 291-96.

64. Boland, "Abortion Law in Europe," 75.

65. See Ann Snitow, "The Church Wins, Women Lose," *The Nation* 256, no. 16 (April 26, 1993): 556-59; Boland, "Abortion Law in Europe," 72-73.

66. Quoted Jacqueline Heinen, "Polish Democracy is a Masculine Democracy," *Women's Studies International Forum* 15, no. 1 (1992): 129-38.

67. Quoted in Heinen, "Polish Democracy is a Masculine Democracy," 131.

68. Matgorzata Fuszara, "Legal Regulation of Abortion in Poland," *Signs: Journal of Women in Culture and Society* 17, no. 1 (1991), 125.

69. The legislation failed to pass, but it prompted the Ministry of Health to promulgate new regulations restricting abortion, which deterred many doctors from performing abortions. See Snitow, "The Church Wins," 558; Jankowska, "Report," 293-94; Heinen , "Polish Democracy," 129; Hanna Jankowska, "Abortion, Church and Politics in Poland," *Feminist Review* 39 (1991): 174-81.

70. See Heinen, "Polish Democracy is a Masculine Democracy," 129; Boland , "Abortion Law in Europe," 72-73. Influenced by the Church, the medical association introduced a new code of medical ethics the following year. The new Code placed more restrictions on the ability of medical personnel to provide abortions, effectively deterring most doctors from providing any but lifesaving abortions. The Code was promulgated without consulting physicians generally or groups of doctors that specialized in gynecological and maternal health cases (see Snitow, "The Church Wins," 558; Boland, "Abortion Law in Europe," 72-74).

71. See Hoff, "Comparative Analysis of Abortion," 633.

72. See Snitow, "The Church Wins," 556.

73. See Heinen, "Polish Democracy is a Masculine Democracy," 135. In 1990, for example, Church pressure resulted in the only sex education textbook being withdrawn from the schools. Only approximately eleven percent of the population use modern contraceptive methods. Most rely on the rhythm method or withdrawal.

74. See Henry David and Anna Tikow, "Commentary: Abortion and Women's Rights in Poland, 1994," *Studies in Family Planning* 25, no. 4 (July/August 1994): 239-41; Boland, "Abortion Law in Europe," 74.

75. See David and Tikow, "Commentary," 241; Peggy Simpson, "International Trends: An Update of the Polish Election: What Did It Mean For Women?" *Journal of Women's History* 6, no. 1 (Spring 1994): 67-74; Boland, "Abortion Law in Europe," 75; Fuszara, "Legal Regulation," 127; Reed Boland, "Recent Developments in Abortion Law," *Law, Medicine, and Health Care* 19 (1991): 267-77.

76. See Boland, "Abortion Law in Europe," 72; Fuszara, "Legal Regulation," 117. Enactment of the abortion law under Communist rule in 1956 reduced greatly deaths caused by abortion, from 225 cases per year to 12 (see Fuszara, "Legal Regulation," 120). Estimates are that 97 percent of abortions performed prior to the end of Communist rule were for social reasons, and only 3 percent for medical reasons. See David and Tikow, "Commentary," 239.

77. See Boland, "Abortion Law in Europe," 74.

78. Ursala Nowakowska, Interview in "Poland: Feminists vs. the Church," *Off Our Backs* 24, no. 3 (March 1994): 10, 24.

79. Jankowska, "Report," 291.

80. See Jankowska, "Report"; Hanna Jankowska, "Abortion, Church and Politics in Poland," *Feminist Review* 39 (1991): 174-81. Despite the election of a female Prime Minister, and several other women in prominent public positions, the status of women generally in Poland is not very positive, and women's rights are on the decline rather than increasing.

81. See Nowakowska, "Interview," 11. The victories of three left-of-center parties during general elections in September of 1995 suggest that the Polish people have rejected the domination of politics by the Catholic Church, although the significance of this mood for women's rights is yet to be seen. Recent public opinion polls show that 60% of the population support the availability of abortion for social reasons (IPPF 1999). In general, however, the general populace, including women, seems to be fairly indifferent to the changes in abortion laws (see Boland, "Abortion Law in Europe," 75), and to their effect on women's other rights of citizenship.

82. This adherence is the more remarkable given the traditional view that the emperor was head of state as well as the "Prince of Heaven." Louis Allen, "Japan," in *Religion in Politics: A World Guide*, ed. Stuart Mews (Chicago, Ill.: St. James Press, 1989).

83. See Joyce Gelb, "Abortion and Reproductive Choice: Policy and Politics in Japan," in *Abortion Policy in Cross-Cultural Perspective*, ed. Marianne Githens and Dorothy McBride Stetson (New York: Routledge, 1995), 119-37; William R. LaFleur, "Ethical Discourse and Its Caretakers in Japan," *Philosophy East & West* 40, no. 4 (1990): 529-41.

84. Buddhist concepts of rebirth and karma are embodied in the view that water babies revert to a former state after abortion or miscarriage, and are reborn again later, either to the same or other parents. See William R. LaFleur, *Liquid Life: Abortion and Buddhism in Japan* (Princeton: Princeton University Press, 1992).

85. Scholars consider these ceremonies to provide a ritual form of mourning the loss of the aborted fetus, and alleviating the feelings of guilt, despair, etc., which often accompany the loss of the potential child (e.g. Bardwell Smith, "Buddhism and Abortion in Contemporary Japan: *Mizuko Kuyo* and the Confrontation with Death," *Japanese Journal of Religious*

*Studies* 5, no. 1 (1988): 3-34; June O'Connor, "Ritual Recognition of Abortion" (Paper delivered at American Academy of Religion Annual Meeting, November 22, 1993, Washington, D.C.)).

86. See Bardwell Smith, "Abortion in Japanese Buddhism," in *Buddhism, Sexuality, and Gender*, ed. Jose Cabezon (Albany: State University of New York Press, 1992): 65-90; O'Connor, "Ritual Recognition of Abortion"; LaFleur, *Liquid Life*, William R. LaFleur, "Ethical Discourse."

87. Gelb, "Abortion and Reproductive Choice," 131.

88. See Gelb, "Abortion and Reproductive Choice," 131-32 LaFleur, *Liquid Life*, William R. LaFleur, "Ethical Discourse," 535; Smith, "Buddhism and Abortion," 5.

89. See Minoru Muramatsu, "Japan," in *International Handbook on Abortion*, ed. Paul Sachdev (New York: Greenwood Press, 1988), 293-95.

90. See Gelb, "Abortion and Reproductive Choice," 123-25; William Nester, "Japanese Women: Still Three Steps Behind," *Women's Studies* 21 (1992): 457-78. The high rate of abortion is striking in a modern industrialized nation, especially since married women between ages 25-34 who have children obtain the majority of legal abortions. At 1.5 children per woman of childbearing age, Japanese women have the world's lowest child bearing record, lower than the 2.08 rate necessary to sustain a stable population. Alarmed by the low birth rate, in 1990, the government began to offer financial and childcare incentives to women to have children (Nester, "Japanese Women," 472-73). Yet this does not seem to have lowered the rate of abortion, at least not as of yet.

91. See Gelb, "Abortion and Reproductive Choice," 124-28; Guardian Staff, "A World of Conflict Over Abortion," *World Press Review* 39, no. 10 (1992): 22-24; O'Connor, "Ritual Recognition of Abortion." Besides abortion, the two main methods of birth control are the withdrawal method and the condom, both of which are unreliable, in part because they depend upon male responsibility (see Smith 1988: 6). The pill is banned, most recently on the rationale of the Minister of Health that its adoption would increase the spread of AIDS. Doctors do not encourage sterilization, IUD's or diaphragms.

92. See "Buddhism and Abortion," 6-7.

93. Gelb, "Abortion and Reproductive Choice," 135.

94. Justice Blackmun's majority opinion considered the relevance of theological opinion and canon law to the common law's lack of criminal penalties for abortions prior to "quickening" (the point in a pregnancy at which the fetus's movements are discernible). The opinion notes that "Christian theology and the canon law came to fix the point of animation at 40 days for a male and 80 days for a female, a view that persisted until the nineteenth century," and that St. Thomas Aquinas may have influenced the determination of quickening as the relevant point (410 U.S. at 134).

95. See Rosiland Petchesky, *Abortion and Woman's Choice: The State, Sexuality, and Reproductive Freedom*, rev. ed., (Boston: Northeastern University Press, 1990), 241-42.

96. See Timothy Byrnes, *Catholic Bishops in American Politics* (Princeton, N.J.: Princeton University Press, 1991) 58-59.

97. *McRae v. Califano*, 491 F. Supp. 630, 704, *rev'd sub nom Harris v. McRae*, 448 U.S. 297 (1980); see Byrnes, *Catholic Bishops in American Politics,* 58-59.

98. See Byrnes, *Catholic Bishops in American Politics,* 58-59.

99. The Court in *Webster* upheld Missouri's restrictive abortion statute, including its preamble, which contained "findings" of the legislature that "The life of each human being begins at conception" and that "unborn children have protectable interests in life, health, and well-being" (see, e.g., Timothy Byrnes and Mary Segers, eds., *The Catholic Church and the*

*Politics of Abortion: A View From the States* (Boulder, Colo.: Westview Press, 1992)), describing several state-level pro-life campaigns that the Catholic Church has been involved with since *Webster* to pass more restrictive abortion laws and David Smolin, "Abortion Legislation After *Webster v. Reproductive Health Services*: Model Statutes and Commentaries," *Cumberland Law Review* 20 (1989): 71-163, proposing a model for abortion restrictions based on a "comprehensive pro-life approach" that assumes that "pre-born" human life is fully equal in human dignity and value to "post-born" life, and which would make *self*-abortion and obtaining abortion felonies.

100. The Pennsylvania Catholic Conference was one of the strongest forces behind the legislation. Its representatives were involved in early consultations with the principal legislators behind the abortion bill. See Thomas O'Hara, "The Abortion Control Act of 1989: The Pennsylvania Catholics," in *The Catholic Church and the Politics of Abortion: A View From the States*, ed. Timothy Byrnes and Mary Segers (Boulder, Colo.: Westview Press, 1992), 87-104.

101. See Byrnes and Segers, *The Catholic Church.*

102. For instance, strong Mormon opposition to abortion was significant in the Idaho legislature's vote on an extremely restrictive law designed by the national Right-to-Life organization to test the limits of the constitutionality of restrictive abortion laws after *Webster.* The vote resulted in 41/46 Mormon senators voting for H625, along with 10/10 of the Catholics, and 21/38 of the Protestants. See Stephanie Witt and Gary Moncrief, "Religion and Roll-Call Voting in Idaho," in *Understanding the New Politics of Abortion*, ed. Malcolm Goggin (Newbury Park, Calif.: Sage Publications, Inc., 1993), 124-29.

103. A research study revealed that religion was the second most significant factor influencing the House members' votes on the Hyde Amendment, following political party membership (Raymond Tatalovich and David Schier, "The Persistence of Ideological Cleavage in Voting on Abortion Legislation in the House of Representatives, 1973-1988," in *Understanding the New Politics of Abortion*, ed. Malcolm Goggin (Newbury Park, Calif.: Sage Publications, Inc., 1993), 112). Several congresspersons made explicit reference to religion and religious themes in expressing their opposition to abortion. Many of these use explicit references to God (see *McRae v. Califano*, 491 F. Supp. at 630-740).

104. For instance, Catholic Bishops publicly and vehemently attacked the pro-choice positions of 1984 vice-presidential nominee Geraldine Ferraro and New York Governor Mario Cuomo for stating that they were publicly pro-choice, despite their personal pro-life convictions as Catholics. New York Bishop Vaughan warned Governor Cuomo that his views on abortion placed him in "serious risk of going to hell" (quoted in Byrnes, *Catholic Bishops,* 140).

105. See, e.g., United Nations, *Beijing Declaration and Draft Platform for Action*, Ch. V, para. 5 (Argentina); para. 7 (Dominican Republic); para. 11 (Holy See); para. 21 (Malta); para. 26 (Peru); para. 31 (Vanuatu); para 32 (Venezuela).

106. United Nations, *Beijing Declaration*, Ch. 5, para. 8.

107. United Nations, *Beijing Declaration*, Ch. V, para. 15.

108. United Nations, *Beijing Declaration*, Ch. V, para 19.

109. United Nations, *Beijing Declaration*, Ch. V, para. 10(a).

110. United Nations, *Beijing Declaration,* Ch. V, para. 12.

## *Chapter Nine*

# The Enlightenment Paradigm of *Native Right* and Forged Hybridity of Cultural Rights in British India[1]

## Purushottama Bilimoria

In part, this chapter is a critique of Locke, Rousseau and Mill in their respective silences or obfuscations on "cultural rights," and in part a response to Chandran Kukathas. The latter likewise, but for seemingly different reasons from the former liberal fathers, wants to either withhold all talk of cultural rights, or argue that minority claims against the violation of cultural interests by a majority community can be accommodated within the going liberal individualistic theory—namely, in terms of natural rights as the inalienable entitlement of each and every individual citizen regardless of their communal membership. Kymlicka will feature also in the discussion of Kukathas's argument. The flip side as it were of the chapter underscores a moral concern over the workings of colonial social engineering that have left us with an unresolved quiddity that seems to be one bizarre consequence of the liberal charter bequeathed by Enlightenment *philosophes*, and which in its post-colonial phase contributes to more injustice in liberal terms than might otherwise have been the case.

For my critique I draw somewhat from Kant's "cosmopolitan right" doctrine and Walter Benjamin's astute observations about the kind of impulse that motivated the development and wide dispersion of the "rule of law" as the overarching, universal, substantive system of canonical order and its meta-legal discourse inflected in those charters that also came to roost in the colonized world. This second part of the chapter—which will be very brief—takes me to the third longer part of the chapter where I examine certain interventionist processes that were set in place, through the ploddings of no lesser liberal progenitors than the Mills, James and John Stuart, through their involvement in the East India Company (John Mill wrote a damning utilitarian history of India for the company officials, and neither had visited subcontinent). I will illustrate the Indian case with three or four studies based on land and naming property title, handling of the question of sati (sutte), criminalization of petty acts, even involuntary behavior disorders such as "lunacy" or mental illness, and most significantly, the hybridized personal laws system. Postcolonial writers are still re-working this part of their history and much more scholarly groundwork remains to be done: my ruminations happen as it were on or from the side, and I am still trying to articulate what a decisive philosophical response would be like without usurping the several subaltern voices, women included, that are at the center of these continuing storms—or as the postmodernist would say, the sites of contestation.

## Part I

I take it as given and uncontroversial that a decent liberal theory advocates toleration, within certain limits, of a plurality of interests, even if it has no explicit program for promoting the same, being wary of conflicts that arise out of competing interests, and thus the menace of moral relativism. Above all, liberal theories uphold the *perspective* and well being of the individual, and this can be the only grounds on which interests claimed by groups, cultural communities, or other such collectives would matter.[2] Though at the end of the day, "liberal theories look at the problem of divining political rules from a standpoint which owes its allegiance to no particular interest—past, current, or prospective,"[3] I don't even mind liberalism viewing cultural communities "more like private associations or electoral majorities."[4] I concede that group allegiances can be astonishingly tyrannical especially where communities do not recognize the individual's right to dissent, to dissociate oneself from the community, or to refuse to be encumbered by that community's rigid adherence to pre-determined, non-personal goals (such as the Collective Dreaming, etc.), or where the social goods are not being distributed fairly and equitably. And I do believe the value of individual autonomy or meaningful choice is important, though not sufficient, to clinch the interests of cultural minorities. So I applaud liberal theorists such as Kymlicka in basing their defence of minority rights on principles of equality and choice for the individuals constituting a group; ditto for minority community rights against a dominant group or mainstream culture where there is palpable inequality in the same circumstances. Even more significantly, I understand it to be critical to liberal theory that "it does not sanction the forcible induction into or imprisoning of any individual in a cultural community. No one can be *required* to accept a particular way of life."[5] No one is obligated to be dominated: that freedom must be respected.

I wish to derive two implications with minor modifications to the liberal doctrine. My scenario initially at least is not really one of conflict between minority interests with majority dominance; in the context of the global reach of one community—read private, individual, corporate (think of Rupert Murdoch)—over other communities, read dispersed individuals—which begins in our era with colonialism—this fact cannot be overstressed, and so I want to cast communities *as individuals*, with the same kinds and degree of subjectivity, internal moral conflicts and agency as the *individualistic* individual is accorded in liberal political cosmology. The individual still matters, defensibly and absolutely, only that it wears a larger face than, say, the individual of classical liberals like Locke or Mill. For, in this larger picture, the situation is not that very different: the ground of conflict is not merely that between the differentiated individual interests (in one group) and the interests of individuals in another group, but precisely in respect of the paradigms or frameworks that attempt "forcible induction into" or imprisoning, that is, the dominance of an individual *qua community bound together by common personal goals* in or to another cultural entity, through imposed or imported rules. Putting it another way, individuals are first constructed and differentiated—in larger conglomerates of communal groups—and then told that they need an elaborate legal framework in order for their individual, indeed, cultural interests to be protected vis-a-vis one another, as the traditions or cultures to which they have hitherto been bound to do not provide the same resources or instruments for that efficacy. The alien institution, which is also an individual with his own set of albeit limited interests in the matter, promises to provide a system—an impartial rule-based or meta-legal framework—for the protection of interests and mediation of conflicts on the *presumption* that the extant traditions had nothing more than a limited retributive method—only the first leg of justice as Mill might put it— for dealing effectively with such matters. But in so doing the alien intervention severely disables and impairs one individual—whose interests it recognizes under liberal ethos—against another individual who, say, refuses to acknowledge the terms of reference of the attempted negotiation. Choice is recognized, and a compromise is reached which ensues in decreeing a set of watered-down hydridized and somewhat confused liberal interests ascribed to the by-now very perplexed and internecine individuals.[6]

The two individuals I speak of are the Hindu and the Muslim, and the rest of the chapter will develop this scenario with further implications. The alien individual is the British (both as settler-resident and later state-administrator of the subcontinent). Either the core individualistic values have failed to work, or Kymlicka is right (minority rights have been subverted); or there is the third alternative, which I choose to follow here: liberalism might be ultimately committed in its philosophical theorizing to the absolute worth of the individual; but its legal underside betrays this commitment as it slides toward communitarian excesses—the very evil grounds on which it anchors its major repudiation of cultural rights and through which it undermines those cultural rights and goods that even petit liberals and noisy libertarians happily endorse. So I want to focus on an antecedent framework that embeds the liberal project to the detriment of its own noble ideals. Secondly, one cannot help noticing that liberal theorists usually pick out isolated and articulated individual, including community, grievances within a wider social context that in most cases has already traveled two to three hundred years past the first point of colonial contact and interventions. But this wider context of changes and transformations is also used as a *justification* for locating with the view to moving the individual or community on, toward acquiescence or choice to complete its own personal projects and so on. However, *its* case for justification is precisely *the problematic* to other theorists—social theorists and postcolonials—among others, who express concern that rather than becoming ahistorically a factor in the negotiations or mediation, the grand shifts should be *seen* historically for what they are: the political enframing which not only impinges on but might itself have been responsible for introducing the legal—indeed, meta-legal framework on whose portals, as it were, the resistance is being waged, whether successfully or unsuccessfully. Why is the inevitability and essentiality of the present state of affairs so thoroughly binding to a problem that might have antecedent roots elsewhere? I call this the liberal blind spot.[7]

## Part II

In this Part, I wish to examine the Enlightenment paradigm of natural rights—rights inhering universally in humankind by virtue of natural law modeled on the idea of providence, and later on reason. My claim is that such rights as nature has endowed human beings with in equal measure and all over do, however, in their particularity peter out thinly as the canvass stretches out from the hub of the Enlightenment—or the Enlightenment *imaginary*—to the peripheries of the globe. Natural rights, in and of themselves, were deemed not to be sufficient to spell out all the variegated entitlements and relationships that would arise between individuals, and individuals and sovereigns, in their mutual commerce and transactions in accord with the social compact, for which derivative principles and rights at other levels come into play: notably, civil rights, positive rights, public rights, negative legal rights, moral rights, private rights, religious rights, even divine rights, parental rights, and such rights as we might nowadays class under the rubric of basic or human rights.

Now at least three specific kinds of problems emerged when the fathers of the Enlightenment found themselves confronted with subjects of other cultures who happened not to be of the European stock, or who were not recognized as falling within the parameters that govern the citizenry of the civil societies (in this class would belong slaves, merchants, visitors, and so on). These problems were:

(1) To ascertain the extent to which natural rights have matured sufficiently in these people for there to be derived the attendant rights of individuals and of their governing powers (such as kings and the aristocracy) commonly accepted in law (hence, common law) and so protected in civilized nations;

(2) To determine whether the regulative principles for such derivations are covert or whether they are overt in the minds of the representative lawmakers of these cultures;

(3) Either way, whether the native resources of law or, alternatively, an imposed "rule of law" would be adequate for securing their trans[re]formation and perpetuity.[8]

I now turn to some seminal *philosophes* who addressed the first of the problems and whose writings, it would seem, shaped the thinking of a generation or more of British administrators who had to work through the problems just outlined. The thinkers who stand out here are Kant, Rousseau, Hegel, Locke, and the Mills, Paine, and Burke (and there will be *in situ* Western advocates such as William Jones, Bentinck, Lord Macaulay and their trained Indian counterparts whom I will also refer to in the course of the narrative). Theories of justice, law, and rights are invariably based on the interests of the individual, *x*, and the need to need to protect these interests against the avarice, interference, or consequences of the acts or intentions of the other, another individual *y*, or the state, God, and so on. So if there is a force it comes preeminently and internally from the individual (the subjective intentions) and externally from the mediating politico-institution that enforces the order. There is however a school of thought beginning with Benjamin and developed more extensively in Levinas which argues that this conception is flawed in as much as it does not place equal weight on the other, *y* above, (except where *y* is the state, in which case the privilege tokens shift); in *Totality and Infinity* Levinas calls the "right of the other" the practically infinite rights—the heteronomic relations to others—which is part of his idea of justice as "sanctity."[9] One can take this simply as a plea to have the voice of the other counted in any theory that positions and therefore privileges the individual *x* as the right-bearer against the assumed evil or malicious intentions of *y*, the other. Benjamin's thesis alongside Kant's will be the subject of the second Part of the chapter. Parts three to five will turn to the narrative and examination of the Indian scenario of law and customary practices in the context of justice, moral particularity and hybridized legal codifications that have bedeviled the democratic process inexorably and almost irreparably in the subcontinent since its colonization under the French and British especially.

## Kant on Native Right vis-à-vis Cosmopolitan Rights

Kant defends his transcendental doctrine of right by insisting its maxims must be ethical, juridical, and publicly knowable: "The right of human beings must be held sacred, however great a sacrifice this may cost the ruling power. One cannot compromise here and devise something intermediate, a pragmatically conditioned right (a cross between right and expediency); instead all politics must bend its knee before right."[10] Like an axiom he then deploys this principle to illustrate instances of public right. To talk of the right of a nation would be empty unless a general will proceeds from some kind of compact that binds the various individuals, and which becomes a condition for continuing free association; likewise, *cosmopolitan right*, which bears analogy with the right of nations, extends its reach beyond the neighboring states to other, even more distant realms in the interest of greater unity of humankind—which for Kant is a universal imperative; there is a duty to realize the condition of public right, "even if only in approximation by unending progress" (351). Kant the moralist is confident that reason will facilitate moral development in the direction of greater respect and practical application for the concept of right even though there are detractors and countervailing forces of violence, malevolence and so on. But this latter confession is not trite, for Kant gives a detailed account of how treacherous politicians deal in despotic machinations and exploit human beings against the enlightened judgment; they choose instead the doctrine of prudence, from which three dishonorable maxims are derived: *fac et excusa*: appropriate at any cost; *si fecisti, nega,*: deny the guilt is yours, project it on to the subject; *divide et impera*: divide and rule, pit the stronger against the weaker. These false representatives speak not on behalf of right but of force (another instance of the transcendental illusion). Now the question arises: would Kant extend this restraint he advocates against the political moralist to the moral cosmopolitan as he meanders his way through uncharted territories in distant corners of the earth? Those who come to power, as a general rule, have a duty to exercise restraint, even as they seek out ways to improve the system of governance and bring it into conformity with natural right; and while violent means are undesirable, alteration may be necessary in order to approach the end. The task before a cosmopolitan moralist is no less onerous, except that there are conditions that underscore certain further duties toward the special class of subjects, let us call them, for want of a better term, *natives*.

Kant does not discuss the right of the native under a separate section as he does the other kinds of right (in *Perpetual Peace*, although he does in *The Metaphysics of Morals, MM*), but there are enough references from which a qualified thesis can, I believe, be extracted from his theory of *nature* (not as religion but as the state of nature within the limits of human reason). The first expression of nature is that people are able to live in all regions of the earth (332), but like animals, they previously—and in some parts of the earth continue to—dwell in the lawless freedom of hunting—a habit most opposed, Kant annotates, to a civilized constitution—and also fishing, or pastoral life, gradually driven to agricultural life, and trade, which for the first time brings them into a "peaceful relation" to each other and so into an understanding, that is community. From this "could" nature despotically willed as if by a concept of duty that they "should" live everywhere—but by a process of war and conflict and exile people related to each other have been driven apart to distant regions, but we know their unity through the common descent of their languages and so on.[11] In any case, they each, however imperfectly organized, by the mechanism of nature will approach in their external, public conduct, what the idea of right prescribes. The spirit of commerce carries out the inclinations of cosmopolitan right and sooner or later takes hold of every nation. Despite abuses nothing can annul the rights of citizens of the world *to try to* establish community with all and, to this end, to *visit* all regions of the earth [sounds like a blueprint for globalism and the Peace Corps].

But there are boundaries and limits on the relation with regard to rights to one's native land and to foreign countries. A native land is one to which a person has the right of citizenship by birth; a country of which he is not a citizen or native is a foreign country; a province is the larger realm of which a foreign country forms a part, but a province is not an integral part of the realm, it is only a secondary house, and it therefore must respect the land of the state that rules it as the *mother country*. (*MM* 478) Thus foreigners (colonists or visitors) settling in a province in a distant country (*termitarium*) have an obligation to respect the private ownership of the land of the native subjects, and they may be rightfully banished from the province.

And so a strong maxim stipulated: "Cosmopolitan right shall be limited to conditions of universal *hospitality*: Here . . . it is not a question of philanthropy but of *right*, so that *hospitality* (hospitableness) means the right of a foreigner not to be treated with hostility because he has arrived on the land of another." The other can turn him away, if this can be done without destroying him, but as long as he (the visitor) behaves peaceably where he is, he cannot be treated with hostility. Everyone can make use of the right to the earth's surface, which belongs to the human race in common, for possible commerce. Kant chides at the inhospitableness of inhabitants of seacoasts (Vikings) and of deserts (Arabians) "in regarding approach to nomadic tribes as a right to plunder them"; this is contrary to natural right. But there is a limit even to this right of anticipated hospitality: the authorization of a foreign newcomer does not extend beyond the search for commerce with the old inhabitants. In other words, while hospitality is a right of the foreigner and a duty of the inhabitant, it is also a duty of the cosmopolitan to respect the right of the inhabitant to the lawful possession of *his* goods and territory, for only through such commercial relations will all people be eventually drawn closer to a cosmopolitan constitution. The traders faced a dilemma: how to operate within the limits of "moral economy" while maintaining a political distance from the cultural values and configuration of the natives, but also develop social and cultural solidarity and even local identity which is a *sine qua non* of successful trade? The first horn of the dilemma underpins the Enlightenment obligation to native cultural right and reciprocated by hospitability; while the second trigger, echoes the motivations of an expansionist economy, what nowadays I suppose we call "pressures of global market economy," which the natives may choose rightfully to resist. Descartes even earlier than Kant had decreed that the foreigner adapt as much as possible to the ways and customs of the inhabitants. Empirical evidence available to Kant (some of which are verbatim from Rousseau), however, showed that while the native inhabitants kept their side of the pact, the "*inhospitable* behavior of civilized, especially commercial, states in our part of the world, the injustice they show in *visiting* foreign lands and peoples (which with them is tantamount to *conquering* them) goes to horrifying lengths. When America, the negro countries, the Spice Islands, the Cape, and so forth were discovered, they were, to them, countries belonging to *no one (like the waters of the sea), since they counted the inhabitants as nothing* [emphasis is mine]. To the East Indies (Hindustan), they brought in foreign soldiers under the pretext of merely proposing to set up trading posts, but with them oppression of the inhabitants, incitement of the various Indian states to widespread wars, famine, rebellions, treachery, and the whole litany of troubles that oppress the human race."[12] Likewise, Kant continues his observation:

> China and Japan (*Nipon*), which had given such guests a try, have therefore wisely [placed restrictions on them], the former allowing them access but not entry, the latter even allowing access to only a single community with the natives. The worst of this (or, considered from the point of view of a moral judge, the best) is that the commercial states do not even profit from this violence; that all these trading companies are on the verge of collapse; that the Sugar Islands, that place of the cruelest and most calculated slavery, yield no true profit but serve only a mediate and indeed not very laudable purpose, namely, training sailors for warships, and so, in turn, carrying on wars in Europe.

In the section on Cosmopolitan right developed further *in Metaphysic of Morals*, Kant pointedly raises the following question: in newly discovered lands, may a nation undertake to *settle (accolatus)* and take possession in the neighborhood of a people that has already settled in the region, even without its consent? His response is most interesting, it echoes the humanism of Rousseau, and it remains a great enigma that it was Locke's *tabula rasa* doctrine of foreign politics that impacted instead on settler-colonists. It is worth reflecting on this passage which I will re-cite in full:

> If the settlement is made so far from where that people resides that there is no encroachment on anyone's use of his land, the right to settle is not open to doubt. But if these people are shepherds or hunters (like the Hottentots, the Tungusi, or most of the American Indian nations) who depend for their sustenance on great open regions, this settlement may not take place by force but only by contract, and indeed by a contract that does not take advantage of the ignorance of those inhabitants with respect to ceding their lands. This is true despite the fact that sufficient specious reasons to justify the use of force are available: that it is to the world's advantage, partly because these crude peoples will become civilized (this is like the pretext by which even Busching tries to excuse the bloody introduction of Christianity into Germany), and partly because one's own country will be cleaned of corrupt men, and they or their descendants will, it is hoped, become better in another part of the world (such as New Holland). But all these supposedly good intentions cannot wash away the stain of injustice in the means used for them. Someone may reply that such scruples about using force in the beginning, in order to establish a lawful condition, might well mean that the whole earth would still be in a lawless condition; but this consideration can no more annul that condition of right than can the pretext of revolutionaries within a state, that when constitutions are bad it is up to the people to reshape them by force and to be unjust once and for all so that afterwards they can establish justice all the more securely and make it florish.[13]

The moral that Kant attempts to draw here is that a violation of right in *one* place of the earth is felt in *all*, such that cosmopolitan right has to be brought in line with public rights of human beings, and this entails, in one reading of Kant, a duty to respect native right.

Rousseau too was skeptical of the prospect for any kind of accommodation in relation to distant territories and peoples where it involved force and the violation of the dignity and natural rights of human beings. He admits that after several prolonged efforts neither has the European succeeded in converting the "savages" to his way of life, nor convincing him of the virtues of European life (sometimes missionaries have converted them into Christians but never civilized men!). "If one suggests," says Rousseau, "that savages have not enlightenment enough to judge their own condition or ours, I shall reply that the judgment of happiness is less an affair of reason than of feeling." There is a greater distance between our capacities of mind needed for us to understand the savages' taste for their way of life than between the capacities needed for them to understand ours.[14] However, the underside to this benign disposition on Rousseau's part is matched only by his estimate of the lack of the other non-physical capacities of the savage man, who is consigned by nature to instinct alone (which is a sort of compensation for the lack of other capacities which distinguish man from animals in the state of nature) until such time as new circumstances cause new developments within him, beginning with passions and moving toward sophisticated use of language, agreement to live under social compact, and making the most of his civil liberties, which in the present degraded state he has no recognition of. "To describe oneself as 'enlightened' meant that someone else had to be shown as 'savages' or 'vicious.' . . . Such alterity, what one might call the creation of doubleness." As Metcalf points out, "was an integral part of the Enlightenment project."[15] Still, Rousseau's noble savage is deserving of the respect that comes from the noble maxim of rational justice. " Do unto others as you would have them do unto you."[16] Rousseau had probably given Kant the question we saw him raise earlier. On the issue of "first occupancy" and its legality, he puts it in the form of an example, when Nunez Balboa, landing upon a strip of coast, claimed the Southern Sea and the whole of South America as the property of the crown of Castille, was he thereby justified in disposing of its former inhabitants, and in excluding from it all other princes of the earth? The conditions that Rousseau sets out are these: (1) there must be no one already living on the land in question; (2) a man must occupy only so much of it as necessary for his subsistence; (3) "he must take possession of it, not by empty ceremony, but by virtue of his intention to work and to cultivate it, for that, in the absence of legal title, alone constitutes a claim which will be respected by others." But immediately in the next paragraph, Rousseau wonders whether by invoking the imperative of work this right has not been stretched too far: Should not some limits be set to this right? Has a man only to set foot on land belonging to the community to justify his claim to be its master? "How can a man or a People take possession of vast territories, thereby excluding the rest of the world —presumably primarily the natives of the land—from their enjoyment, save by an act of criminal usurpation . . .?"[17]

It does not of course prevent explorers and settlers pronouncing a land uninhabited either visibly or on account of the agricultural fact that no labor seems to have been expanded to utilize the land for proper gains. This was the Lockean take, as it were, which made common law unwittingly and controversially an accomplice to wrongful appropriation of vast territories in the antipodes.

Locke has recently taken a bit of a beating for his role in the specific formulation that came to be known in the colonies as *terra nullius* (from his *Second Treatise of Government* where it is the investment of labor that maketh property, not mere ancestral claim or nomadic wanderings); the very idea of *terra nullius* has been linked with the most irreparable violence as in one judgment it tends to cast an entire people (race) into oblivion. But for all his sins, Locke does also talk about "native right" in the context of the right to shake off usurpation or tyranny brought upon native people by external rulers or conquest.[18]

> The inhabitants of any country, who are descended and derive a title to their estates from those who are subdued, and had a government forced upon them against their free consents, retain a right to the possession of their ancestors, though they consent not freely to the government, whose hard conditions were by force, imposed on the possessors of that country.

The conqueror might claim a right to the estates as well as powers over the persons won through a just war; but being persons free by native right and having properties at their own disposal, they can withhold consent and therefore reclaim the ancestral possessions: in other words, they have a right to repudiate contracts made under duress. But another kind of prejudice detracted from such sanguine concessions as might be afforded to the indigenous tribes in distant parts of the world. It was that they lacked individuality, which is necessary for social and intellectual improvement and even diversity in a community. Locke's view of *individuals as mobile particulars*, capable of making choices, mutually competing and taking actions, ascribes autonomy over his body and his labor, that in turn endows human nature with the quality of "property"— which is absent in the state of nature. In a pure "state of nature" there is no ownership, the land is given to waste and therefore tantamount to being "unoccupied" as the 1778 judgments of settlers in pre-colonial Australia indicated. John Stuart Mill reinforced this belief by invoking the image of static sameness in the Orient where custom is despotic and obeisance is demanded, and which is contrary to natural law. There is no freedom without individuality, and vice versa. This bourgeoisie ideology, which pervades the writings of British empiricists and social theorists of this period, served to legitimate the growing commercial and colonial interventions in distant lands as natural steps toward the evolution of market economy, proper government based on contractual formations, and civil society regulated by the "rule of law" (and) not some brute, savage force or by passions merely.

Hegel's writings on the concept of Right and its complete absence in machinations of the "Oriental despot" presents another interesting illustration of the Enlightenment view; he observed that "man had not been posited in India," meaning that the Concept, Thought, or Absolute Idea—the ultimate expression of Reason as Spirit—had only formed a glimmer of anticipation in the Indian soul and that only through a process of calculated de-brahmanization of the natives could Self-consciousness rise above the mystical imprisonment of the impersonal transcendence of Brahman. Likewise for the truly Oriental the Chinese, who lived mired under the shadow of Nature, that is the otherness and mere material manifestation of the Concept in the overgrown despotic Emperor. For their salvation Hegel commended imperial authorities not only open up trade communications and transactions with the region but to eventually move into the territories and transform them by instituting a system of government and education for the uplift of heathens. As J.L. Mehta puts it all rather succinctly, "It was Hegel who described India as 'the land of imaginative aspiration,' as 'a Fairy region, an enchanted world . . . as exhibiting the unearthly beauty of a woman in the days which immediately succeed child-birth.'"[19] Such an enslaved beauty of history and treasure of wealth should surrender herself to the masters of history, to whit, to the English Lords, "for it is a necessary fate of Asiatic Empires to be subjected to Europeans; and China will, someday or other, be obliged to submit to this fate."[20] In this way, Hegel cleared the house for imperialism and Western domination, politically, but also discursively and in meta-discourses. And they did in London heed the Prussian detractor's advice more than the sage of Konnisberg's.

So much then for arm-chair enlightenment equivocations on native right. I want now to demonstrate how the enlightenment attitude both facilitated a certain degree of restraint and self-reflection among the foreigners who arrived first as traders—only gradually to metamorphose into administrators, rulers, legislators, and jurists—but also fostered an equivocation exacerbating the already confusing realities facing them. I echo a moral concern over the workings of colonial social engineering that have—in the subcontinental location at least—left us with an unresolved quiddity that seems to be a bizarre consequence of the liberal charter bequeathed by Enlightenment *philosophes* , and which in its postcolonial phase contributes to more injustice in liberal terms than might otherwise have been the case.

On the margins of my critique I also draw from Walter Benjamin's astute observations about the kind of impulse that motivated the development and wide dispersion of the "rule of law" as the overarching, universal, substantive system of canonical order and its meta-legal discourse inflected in those charters that also came to roost in the colonized world. Here I examine certain interventionist processes that were set in place, through the ploddings of no lesser liberal progenitors than the Mills, James and J.S., through their involvement in the East India Company.[21] James Mill argued that the larger conglomerates of communal groups in India needed an elaborate legal framework in order for their differential cultural interests to be protected vis-à-vis one another, as the traditions or cultures to which they have hitherto been bound do not provide the same resources or instruments for that efficacy. The alien apparatus does better in providing a system—an impartial rule-based or meta-legal framework—for the protection of such interests, and mediation of conflicts, on the *presumption* that the extant traditions had nothing more than a limited *retributive* method—only the first leg of justice as Mill might put it— for dealing effectively with such matters. But in so doing the alien intervention severely disables and impairs one community—whose interests it recognizes under liberal ethos—against another community that, say, refuses to acknowledge the terms of reference of the attempted negotiation. Choice is recognized, and a compromise is reached which ensues in decreeing a set of watered-down hybridized and somewhat confused liberal interests ascribed to the by-now very perplexed and internecine communities. I will illustrate the Indian case with three or four studies based on land and naming property title, handling of the question of sati (sutte), and especially the hybridized personal laws—that is, the inscription of community-specific private rights. The only sane voice, though staged in maverick fashion, that argued against the British colonial zeal to underwrite the erstwhile native rights with Black Letter Law was Edmund Burke, as we'll see.

## Part III

The narrative that follows is written against the background of the kind of critique that has been articulated quite forcefully, I believe by Walter Benjamin. I will simply table this without arguing for its merit at this point. The Benjamin thesis briefly is that the founding of justice *(dike)* and law (Gewelt, *droit)* on the model of the Natural Law elevates it as a principle of the divine positioning of all ends. We all know how natural law theory comes out of the adaptations of Greek and Stoic views on justice and its adoption in Christianity, refined further by Enlightenment thinkers on the model of reason—as we saw in the first part of the chapter. In the austere reading of the uncharted discoveries of foreign lands and European settlement of provinces, natural law is continually and heteronomously imposed upon the larger human moral world; but in so extending its global reach, it sets aside the ancestral and even the earlier Socratic conventionalism, with the gradual absorption or rationalization of customs within the contours of *jusnaturalism* or ends that justify means, but increasingly as *means* justifying *ends* (think of *lathi* or batton charges, nowadays called "police shootings"). Benjamin claims that the very founding of the "rule of law" *(Gewalt, droit)* and its radicalization in Grecoid forms of authority, in so far as it privileges juridical or "legal contract" as though, or indeed on the model of divine convenant, betokens a force which is tantamount to conceptual violence (in parenthesis, recall the earlier remark on *terra nullius*). In time the presence of this "mystique" force passes into supplemental representation, obscured by the apparatus of institutionalized juridicism, legal bureaucracy, a hegemonic legalism, hierarchies, and the logic of the State (as the dispenser, conserver, and protector of justice and rights). Its totalizing representation manifests in a certain mythology of right, in Hegel's sense, the aesthetization of civil and political ideology, and in the fatal corruption of parliamentary and representative democracy through modern police-State structures. *It demands blood over life.* A powerful indictment indeed. It is here that Benjamin also makes the link between the founding violence of *driot* and *bastardierte* or the "eternal forms of pure divine violence" (*mit dem Recht)* It is this *abatardi* ("bastardy"), from the mythic or "mystique" to the secular-mundane or mediocrity, that creates *driot*, the "force of rule" that in its dual manifestation in "rule of law" or "Black Letter Law" and "statute-craft" "makes blood flow" and exacts payment in punishment or retributive justice.[22]

As I said I will draw merely on the suggestive observations about the Force of Law as it transmutes itself into rule-based ideals underpinning Common Law and especially Black Letter Law which the British took with them wherever they went. A "rule of law" is basically a legal system of rules within rules, that is constituent rules defining the manner in which the orderly rules of the system are to be identified, not unlike precepts of divine origin; it does not recognize conventional customs or normative cultures for setting up of the constituent rules in accordance with which laws are to be identified and decreed, although these may impact on the jurisprudential or hermeneutical rulings arrived at in the course of the application of the rules. And subsequently immense emphasis is placed on precedents or case law. This critique of the rule of law, I believe, provides a framework that is immensely helpful and extendable to experiences of non-Western peoples, especially in the context of the colonial experience and its ambiguous aftermath. It is now, for instance, generally agreed, but it was not recognized then (but through whispers in the hallways), that Hindu "law" (in the loose sense of a catalogue of mores, moral rules, and practices) has the most ancient pedigree of any known system of jurisprudence. Yet this fact was lost even on the legalistic Bentham and Mills, who were doubtless fascinated by the rival legal system but adjudged Hindu law to be simply another limited kind of traditional, religious normative culture, governing a small, albeit private area of life, which is consistent with their view on Oriental despotism. In some ways this characterization was true but the deductions were false: for, in Hindu law —as perhaps also for Cicero—immemorial custom has *proprio vigore* , the efficacy of law and is a constituent part of the law. Custom embodies prescribed rules and rituals (*acara, sadacara* etc.) that define a principle of reasonable conduct. Hindu legates looked upon the rule of law (common law and Bill of Rights in particular) as ways of enriching sacred law, but at the same time argued that their traditional model also enriches principled rules and general law—especially the principles of justice, equity, and good conscience. This was echoed two centuries later in Gandhi's briefing to the Indian Constitutional Assembly. But what interests us right now is the *inverse* intervention over the two centuries that almost jolted Hindu law, and for that matter the other dominant customary base, Muslim law, virtually out of existence.

## Part IV: Mills and the Historical Narrative–India in the Eighteenth Century

Circa 1700, Portuguese missionaries, French papal legates, Jesuits, and other European visitors—and visitors they were in Kant's sense to whom due hospitality was extended—were perplexed by the prodigious multitude of law and the absence of definitive rules on a par with civil and canon law in Europe. Before1751—when the British turned their interest to India also (on Hegel's commendation, and shortly thereafter sent fleets toward *terra australis*)— it would have been difficult to find in traditional India a conception of law that was comparable to the liberal Post-Magna Charta conception or the European canons of civil law, or even the idea of Common Law. Instead there were socially regulative and normative rules, *acara,* and punishments, *prayascitta* (generally lumped under the overarching category of *dharma)* that varied across different regions and peoples and caste ordering. Indeed, an autonomous concept of law was not yet distinguished from ethics and regulative norms, and its highly exegetical jurisprudence was one of its constituent parts, not aside or over it, and recognized issues of inequality, the disproportionate distribution of privileges and the denial of the rights of certain classes or groups of people. The bulk of the *dharmasastras* do not actually codify "law," although (with the Yajnavalkyasmriti and *nibandhas*) in the medieval period there begins an attempt at codifying social/religious codes of conduct based on earlier hermeneutical ("meta-legal") framework provided by *Purvamimamsa.*[23] But even then there is resistance to the predilection toward a monolithic legal framework, and Manu concedes that there may be different *dharmas* in different epochs, a principle known as *adhikara-bheda.*

In 1772 as the administrators of the East India Company established their base in India they too were bewildered by the diversity of customary rules, norms and practices, moral judgments and differential treatments of misdemeanors, as well as vastly different views on marriage, succession, contract, severance, property and inheritance rights, and so on. Each micro-community had its own complex system of village-based juridical hearing courts or *panchyats.* Administrators were astounded at the absence of an overarching central authority or even *ecclesia* that would systematically enact and enforce laws, rules of conduct and social imperatives, or monitor unequivocal adherence to common law of the land. The vastly different regional legal systems and configuration of group identity and community membership further befuddled them. The indigenous discretionary practice seemed to be uneven because of the flexible jurisprudential and interpretative schemas prevalent in different parts of the country (e.g. the Mitakshara would be different from the Deobargh in the East or Oudh elsewhere). Enlightenment sensibilities and expectations were utterly defied and even the strongest indigenous concepts seemed anathema to those derived from the Lockean reworking of Natural Law into Common Law, in which the administrators happened to be better versed. Before moving onto the enactments under the East India Company I want to discuss the role of the Mills in the formation of the East India Company.

I want to conclude by reflecting more specifically on the role of liberal philosophy and its more popular nineteenth century representation in the principle of utility though the writings and direct interventions of the Mills, who I mentioned earlier. James Mill served for seventeen years in the East India Company and John Stuart Mill joined his father and succeeded him to the premier post of examiner. James wrote the classic *History of British India* (published 1817) drawing on the Scottish Enlightenment historicist ideals of "scale of civilization," which following Bentham's criterion of Utility was a measure of social progress "exactly in proportion as Utility is the object of every pursuit." James's study of India showed that the Hindus were the most "enslaved portion of the human race."[24] The remedy proposed was a code of laws that would release individual energy by protecting the products of its efforts: "Light taxes and good laws" was the motto. This scheme promulgated the creation of individual property rights enforced by "scientific" codes of law. Once secure in their "property," the Indians could find in their own "industry" the means for their "elevation."

Now John Stuart Mill, who remained in the East India Company until its dissolution in 1858, modified James's rather more pessimistic view by elaborating on the rungs of the "ladder of civilization," the urgent calling was to liberate the Oriental races from their despotic condition. His prescription was that of individuality and mental liberty. The first ladder entailed radical transformations of the entire structure of the society through the introduction of institutions which defined Britain's civil society: the most ideal of which included, the idea of private property, the rule of law, the liberty of the individual, and education in Western learning. As Metcalf points out,

> Central to an understanding of both the contradictions and transforming power of British reform in India was the notion of the "rule of law." In nineteenth century England the legal order was meant above all to guarantee the rights of property, conceived of as vested in individuals and secure from arbitrary confiscation. In India too, from Cornwaliss's permanent settlement of 1793 onwards, private landed property was made the cornerstone of Britain's commitment to an India transformed.[25]

And here James Mill and his utilitarian disciples used utilitarian theory to divert property away from collective ownership so that greater unearned surplus is generated which the government could rightfully skim off, in the form of taxes, revenues, and so on. The intermediation of the zamindars became very important. Note that this reform did not entail extinguishment of native title, rather only its redistribution consistent with the rights of individuals as a way of ushering in a new liberal order.

Likewise, in the matter of judicial enactments and the framework for legal discourse, the transforming power of the "rule of law" ranked higher than all other ladders of reform. The East Indian Company in its various metamorphoses could not see itself imposing *ab initio* simple English law, but the British could bring its *spirit*, could use this as a model for transforming Indian law such as it was. So the intervention was more in terms of procedural codes than the substantive laws that were being introduced. The process of codification, and the separation of the codes of civil and criminal, marked an end to the archaic system of despotic law. Now the rules and regulations could be more predictable and reliably available to the courts in their judicial deliberations. Note however that these codes were also a veneer for incorporating the Benthamite, and utilitarian, desire for unity, precision, and simplicity in law, while at the same time clothing them in Sanskritic textual articles from Hindu law. The codes of procedure replace the indigenous moral resources and become the moralizing or civilizing force in its own right. This is the striking moral conquest of the rule of law; in this moralization of "law" the British colonial state staked its legitimacy. This moral conquest was elevated as being more important than the physical and military conquests even as late as 1875. But in terms of practical outcome, as I will show, indigenous moral codes and religious faith, which the utilitarians thought the subjects would overcome in time as they progressed up the ladder, never did clear off the desk. In the end, the administrators and courts on site, created a two-tiered vision for the structure of Indian legal order with an arbitrary demarcation of the "public and private," a remnant legacy of Victorian Puritanism, whereby the religious was relegated to the "private" and the codes of civil and criminal procedures to the public. The latter would presumably embody universal principles of justice that many men everywhere would eventually come to accept. However, given the stage or scale of civilization at which the Indians had become stuck, it seemed legitimate to retain parts of their substantive, hence, native moral order—or by now a recognized diversity within it—to govern certain restricted areas of their daily life, unless that order encroaches on the public space and of course the public purse. But the winds of time would blow these away.

By 1790 the East Indian Company had been dispersed and transformed from a trading arm of the government at a distance to the administrative and legal wing of the government *in situ*. A succession of Governor-generals, such as Warren Hastings, faced a challenge: how to dismantle the heterogeneous "law of culture" "from remotest antiquity" and secure the "Rule of Law," with the declared clarity, certainty, and finality of statutes, "Black Letter Law." Happily there was a transitional conduit to help facilitate the transformation from the chaotic moralism to the universality of Common Law aspired to by the colonialists. Echoing Descartes, Hastings would pontificate, "We have endeavored to adapt our Regulations to the Manners and Understandings of the People, and the Exigencies of the Country, adhering as closely as we are able to their ancient uses and Institutions."[26] The rhetorical sophistry aside, Hastings was charged by Burke for the rapacious excesses of the East Indian Company in preying upon the innocent natives and exercising "arbitrary power" in India, "shaking [its] ancient Establishments." India was a place of England's worse wrongdoings and hence a corruption of the royal British Constitution. But Burke's charges did not succeed and Hastings was never impeached. Meanwhile, the meta-legal framework set up by Hastings continued its work, the first task of which was to distinguish the publicly accountable obligations, and the retributions consequent upon their violation, from the private rights, such as those disposed to "usages" and "habits" of custom.

By separating out and codifying judicial punishments from other kinds of sanctions (especially religious, and what we nowadays call civil code or *Code Civil*), an artificial demarcation was drawn between public and private conduct, resulting in a series of uniform enactments for the good of public morality: notably, the Penal Code (1860) and the Code of Criminal Procedure (1861). This notwithstanding the cultural legitimacy that some of the practices codified might have previously enjoyed under certain circumstances or perceived personal necessities, or inexplicable psychological dispositions (e.g. the integral social acceptance of madness being a case in point, hereon certified as "lunacy" and classified as a crime and sentenced to institutional confinement). But even more significantly, the separation of the domain of culture into two spheres—the material and the spiritual, is analogous to the dichotomy of the outer and inner. Since the former, that is the material, was located in Western civilization its antithesis, the spiritual, for the purposes of a persuasive strategy of resistance, had to be located in the colonized people, who would learn from the West in organizing their material life to the optimum but would internalize, or "privatize" the spiritual life away from the public space.[27] The Penal Codes have continued to remain on Indian statute books and echo little else but eighteenth century ideas of Common Law, as embodying universal principles of justice, with its resistance to local/traditional variety to the homogenizing effect of the modern legal discourse.

However, in England too, common law was based on the supposed stability in legal culture and built up through a succession of precedents derived from individual cases reflective of the changing "usage and habits" of the English people.[28] So parallels were drawn between the antiquity of British law in its ancestral Greek and Roman formations.

Soon enough, however, the colonial agencies learned that India also boasted an equally hoary tradition of *textual* law, prescriptive authority, normative catalogues, precedents, legal opinions and jurisprudential literature that dated back centuries. This tradition suggested a legal reality closer to English Common Law.[29] This discovery at least undermined the thesis of "Oriental despotism," and here lay the promises of a solid bedrock for the much-needed Indian Common Law.

But these were encoded in obtuse texts, the *sastras*, barely accessible to the resident Englishmen. So they studied Sanskrit. Regardless of whether the *sastras* reflected grassroots practices beyond their codifications, or whether they were entirely an elite construct, it was the *sastras* that came to be prioritized as the pristine and authoritative sources of native law. This privileging of the *sastras* on the model of the "Black Letter Law" over (and against) prevailing practices retextualizes an epistemic construct that was to bedevil colonial legal thinking over the course of its career. The great Orientalist William Jones began to construct complete digests of the timeless tradition of Indian law which could be enforced in courts and over which British courts in India too would develop their own case law. But it began also to dawn on the legal administrators that an individual Indian is not a moral subject in his or her own right, rather that he or she is a moral subject by virtue of being a member of a moral community and, more significantly that, there is more than one moral community of which he/she may be a member. In other words, it was recognized that even the *sastras*, being the ethical texts of the Hindus, were not uniformly applicable across all the moral communities, especially the Muslims. (Without much discussion, Jains and Sikhs were included under Hindus.) The Muslims had their own scriptural sources, and so the same common-law approach is applied: if the *sastras* governed the Hindus then the equivalent texts for them represented their sources of law. *Sastras* or comparable law books then became the highest authoritative bodies of textual law, and orthodox Brahmanical learning became the flag-ship of Hindu law. So now the British courts developed distinctive "scientific" or rather positivists forms of Anglo-Hindu and "Anglo-Muhammadan law," which were to have profound effects not only on the working of the British Indian judicial system, but on the fundamental structures of the Raj itself.[30]

On the question of property, the Indians appeared to have a most elaborate system of land usage that did not depend as much on ascription or claim to ownership as to the differential tasks each group dwelling upon the lot were assigned to carry out. The link of caste to the various stages of productivity derived from the land was inexorably marked. The peasantry who tilled the soil had no right of ownership over the land, but was apportioned a share from the produce; likewise the lessee and sublessee, right up to the managing landholder or the zamindar. And it was recognized that property was always passed on through hereditary lines; even the monarch had no right to dispossess his subject's property at will. An illustration might be appropriate at this point. About the same time, settlers arriving in Australia also noted that there were clan demarcations and customary ownership observed among the indigenous people, but by 1821 propriety rights of the indigenous within common law had been rejected. In a cunning move, the British did not exactly reject propriety rights in the Indian context, but relocated these in the aristocratic landholder who "improved" the land, collected tax revenue and rent, distributed surplus to the array of workers, and was ultimately answerable only to a power higher than his own. This meant, in the transformed land tenure arrangement, to the Company as the official overlord. The zamindars became merely collector and intermediary agent for property management, a bit like the leasing pastoralists in the outback. But unlike in Australia, this system of landlording secured some claim to at least hereditary rights over the land. So the British took over the existing "feudal patriarchal system," and transformed it within the constraints of common law provisions, but became very concerned when women and widowed wives began to stake claims to inheritance and coparcenary shares under Hindu Mitakshara law or the dispersal of the same under customary laws and discretion under *sastric* law. The next move was to collude with Hindu pandits and find ways to restrict entitlements of women in this regard, and prevent, or where it suited them, abet alienation of joint family property. One might say these were creative, albeit disingenuous, responses of common law to local specificities. Curiously, the Privy Council which about at the same time heard cases from India and Australia, in good conscience could not ignore native Indian claims to proprietorship, while they were less disturbed by claims of colonial dispossession (again, but for faint whispers) in the indigenous Australian context.

The tension of negotiating and reconciling conflicts between customary practices, *sastric* or textual law, and the pressures of incoming British Common Law practices centered on impersonal principles of Justice, Equity, and Good Conscience remained endemic throughout the colonial period. An element of hybridization was unavoidable given the theoretical presuppositions of the textualization of Indian law. But it was soon recognized that the *sastras* formed only a part of the law and that in many matters Indians continued to be regulated by less formal bodies of customary law.[31] How could either in principle or in practice English law "supplant an already complex set of native rules?" Such questions were not far off the minds of the administrators. There was a presumption made that there must have been fixed bodies of prescriptive codification in India—one for Hindus and one for Muslims.[32] Pandits, "professors" of Sanskrit, and mullahs were enlisted and urgently consulted in the courts and by legal agencies to inform them of the patterns of Hindu and Muslim legal thinking, rules and ordinances, which would eventually achieve statutory codification or case law precedents, as well as extensive cataloguing. This led to the birth of the so-called Anglo-Hindu and Anglo-Muslim Law. It was mandatory for the courts to apply the law of the *sastra*: "The statutes did not require that what was to be applied to Hindus should be *deemed* to be derived from the *sastra;* but that it should be so derived."[33] Even after the help of the pandits was withdrawn from the courts after 1864, on William Jones' complaint the courts, benched by British legal administrators, were expected to have complete judicial knowledge of Hindu law, which was a pathetically tall order on merely eighty years of collective experience. And it was Brahmanical proclivity that was encoded in the legal manuals they would use for deriving Anglo-Hindu Law.

On the Muslim front, despite a slow revival of Islamic heritage and moral codes orchestrated by very skilful Muslim leaders, they became concerned and gradually blew the whistle on the corruption of Muslim *shariat* in the Anglo-Muslim codes. Curiously, however, it is this very codification under the hybrid Anglo-Muslim law, that came eventually to pass as the basis of Muslim Law in India after independence, and which Muslim orthodoxy set out to defend, as we shall show shortly. But the seeds of this confused morality, as I am at pains to demonstrate, were sown as far back as the mid-to-late nineteenth century in colonial tinkering with the diverse tapestry of Indian legal and moral customs.

So, Anglo-Hindu and Anglo-Muslim laws came to be the body of *Personal Laws* that, along with statutory codifications (Penal Codes, undertaken earlier by Lord Macaulay), became vehicles for administering justice among the major competing moral communities. Each community of course underscored claims to their respective distinct religious identities, indigenous traditions, ethical practices, and framework for authentication which each had developed, tested, and been served by over the past many centuries. The Privy Council in 1871 endorsed this strategy, in these words:

> While Brahmin, Buddhist, Christian, Mohamedan, Parsee, and Sikh are one nation, enjoying equal political rights and having perfect equality before the Tribunals, they co-exist as separate and very distinct communities, having distinct laws affecting every relation of life. The law of Husband and Wife, parent and child, the descent, devolution, and disposition of property are all different, depending, in each case, on the body to which the individual is deemed to belong; and the difference of religion pervades and governs all domestic usages and social relations. [34]

But how can equality of political rights be guaranteed across the board when religious allegiance through membership in the respective community governs the conduct of the individual? Liberal sentiments clearly have gotten mixed up with communitarian sensibilities. For this reason, the process has often been described as a disingenuous attempt on the part of the British to willfully transform and universalize Indian law so that it would more resemble British Common Law. In this way it would no longer be informed by the extant or traditional ethical practices and regulative imperatives of the disparate moral communities. Thus, the Anglo-Indian laws were, to use Derrett's compelling terms, products of a "bogus" enterprise, intellectual sediment of the imperial period, or as Gandhi would later adjudge, "egregious blunders" of the British in their interpretation of native law.[35] While intricate attention was afforded to questions of detail and *sastric* deliberations the re-working and distortions of Indian law cut deeply across both the textual and customary rules—not only of Hindus and Muslims but also Indian Christians, and other groups.

Let me give another example. *Sati* ("suttee," generally rendered as "burning of the widow") had been made illegal by 1829. When attempted suicide, which in most normal circumstances is a voluntary act, was made a criminal offense in 1860 (IPC S.309) (on the presumption that Indian attitudes against suicide are well-known), forms of voluntary *sati* were also included as "voluntary culpable homicide," and would therefore count as criminal acts. But Hindus had never thought of *sati* as a "voluntary" act, or for that matter as a crime, which therefore left open an area of ambiguity. How is it that a judgment of criminality or felony was thus attached to an act that, to enlightened Hindus, was simply the result of an undesirable superstition and culturally aberrant practice? Were one to show that a particular case of *sati* was not voluntary (as most were not, since the community's coercive expectations were already subtly coded in the martyrdom-like agency of the widowed), would the judgment be mitigated, that is, rendered offensive but not subject to criminal procedure? And if involuntary, who is to be the subject of the violation? Surely not the charred remains of the immolated widow! Could an entire community that bears apparently passive witness to this act be charged with an offense that remains basically undefined in substantive law? In a similar way, the debate shifted on the appropriateness of sanctioned sacred suicide—such as *jouhar*, voluntary mass-extermination, and fasting-to-death, a practice that Gandhi half-exploited in his *satyagraha* protests—precisely under the terms of this Penal Code. That is, under the rule of law there can be sanction for certain conduct which would otherwise be deemed criminal, and is therefore immune from punishment by the state—for example, killing another person in a war. Pandits who had earlier located classical texts that supported the British judgment of the inherent evil in the act, now rallied to show that there were indeed texts that also sanctioned the act under certain circumstances. Should this therefore not be a matter for jurisdiction under Anglo-Hindu or Personal Law? So, it was not so much that the debate silenced the victim of *sati* and foreclosed the question of agency as Lata Mani has argued[36]—or perhaps that too—but rather it elevated the degree of confusion and ambiguity that heretofore benighted the process of legal codification. Once codified, its attempted decoding will exploit the same referents, and perhaps more successfully than if the act had stayed being viewed as a cultural artifact or a "moral fall-out" of a bygone error and dealt with in these terms: for what is immoral does not always need a law, much less a criminal law, to regulate or proscribe it. The debate to this day has not recovered or gained firm grounds for a rational approach due to this epistemic blunder of historic (or histrionic?) proportions.

Let me touch on another example. The enactments of the Special Marriage Act of 1872, later revised under the Hindu Marriage Act, raised marriageable age to eighteen for males and 15 for females. But the rights of persons under this age to have marriage solemnized by customary rites was not taken away, even after the Child Marriage Restraint Act (1929) and its amendments (in 1938, 1949), in the Hindu Inheritance Act, the Muslim Marriage Act, and other codes governing dissolution of marriage, adoption rights, and inheritance, which extended to bigamy and polygamy. The Penal Codes of course had debarred bigamy, although Muslim men were later given exemption under Muslim Personal Law, and this exemption passed into Muslim Personal Law in the postcolonial era. Just recently the apex Court exhorted the government to review this provision under Muslim Personal Law as Hindu men had been converting to Islam, or taking on Muslim names, so as to be able to marry a second wife without properly dissolving the former marriage.[37] But even more worrying has been the question regarding the maintenance of the estranged wife, depending on whether she is Hindu, Muslim, or other. So, the nineteenth century witnessed a quasi-creative, even if patently false re-interpretation of indigenous law in as much as so-called "private areas of life" became enshrined under Personal Laws. Even with the enactment of the statutes, or one might argue perhaps by virtue of the enactment of the statutes, the restrictions in force that made the adaptation of Personal Law to Common Law difficult were not removed; in most instances they were honored.

## Part V: Post-Independence Epiphany

What happens in the twentieth century presents an even more ominous picture, to which I will now move.

With the advent of independence, Indian national leaders agonized over the status of Personal Laws. Many wanted to do away altogether with separate Personal Laws, Ambedkar being one of them. Hindu nationalist leaders opposed a separate Hindu Codes Bill introduced by Nehru in 1948. However, the violent communal clashes preceding independence and Gandhi's rapprochement gestures toward Muslims led to a deferral of the project. Some of this century's profoundest constitutional and transformative moral debates took place within the constitutional assembly, as India became a republic too. Nehru surmised that circumstances were not propitious or favorable in that moment to radically adopt common civil law. Nevertheless, the framers of the Constitution struggled to balance the diversity in the people's customs, religions, moral systems, and ethical mores, with the secular impetus imparted by the colonial administrators into the Indian legal mentality of both investing greater power in the State to control, intervene, and to reform these laws. The latter would entail, if not wholesale statutory legislation, then certainly a gradual move toward providing a uniform system of principles and rules overriding or annulling the practice of privileging a citizen qua individual over another, on the basis of religious identity or community membership or other parochial and local allegiances. However, this process has retarded judicial initiative as the State has often defaulted in its Constitutional responsibility, because the mandate was no more than a recommendation placed under the directive principles. The courts have been cunning: where a claim is brought under customary law, the reasoning is adduced from Common Law for equitable distribution of goods, for instance, which forms part of the charter or Bill of Rights.[38]

It is worth examining the relevant portions of this charter that forms Part III of the Constitution setting out the Fundamental Rights of the citizen. Under this section, which has echoes of the Fifth and Fourteenth Amendments of the U.S. Constitution, certain rights and principles are protected, significantly of equality, personal liberty, and non-interference except under procedure established by law (Articles 14, 21), along with freedom to practice, profess and protect religion if one so chooses, (Articles 25-28).[39] The Constitution also underscores equality of religions alongside freedom to practice one's faith, to establish and manage places of worship, as well as the rights of minorities to conserve their culture, language, and script, and to establish educational institutions of their choice (Articles 29-30). The Muslim leaders in particular took these provisions as a positive cue toward securing their own community interests and asked the Constitutional Assembly for protection of their Personal Law. In the ensuing debate Ambedkar opposed this move arguing that there would be anarchy and a common system of judicature impossible if each community's Personal Law were to be protected (as though these were on par with the fundamental rights of the citizens which the state was obliged to respect). So, the Personal Laws do not enjoy the protection of the Constitution, and any one of its provisions could be deemed *ultra vires* or in flagrant violation of one or the other fundamental right of the individual. In one or two instances the courts have resorted to provisions under the Criminal Procedures Code to set aside counter-claims brought against a grieved citizen under Personal Law

To the final example. The test case centrally involving Personal Law in respect of the legal rights of women and the power of orthodoxy closer to our time was borne out in the now famous, or infamous, Shah Bano case. This case also highlights many of the contradictions and dilemmas we have been exploring here. At the time of hearing, Shah Bano is a seventy-three-year-old Muslim woman, who is driven out of her home by her husband after forty years of marriage. Grieved, she brought a petition for maintenance from her husband under *Criminal Procedure Code (CPC) (Mohammed Ahmed Khan v Shah Bano Begum*, A.I. R. July 1985, Vol 72, S945). However, according to Muslim Personal Law she was entitled to maintenance only for the period of *Iddat*, that is, for three months following divorce. The lower court adjudicated in her favor. The husband moved a petition in the Supreme Court (the apex bench) against this award. While Shah Bano had the backing of the Muslim Women's Welfare, the husband argued that under Muslim Personal Law he had fulfilled his obligations. Why should this matter then be adjudged under the *CPC?* However, the Court dismissed the husband's appeal, and upheld the High Court's judgment that the *CPC* was applicable where Personal Law failed to make adequate provisions. Technically, the court was not suggesting that civil codes do not apply *simpliciter* to the case, as would be in order if, say, the case involved corporate theft or willful injury to another person. It was arguing that the applicable civil code, which in this case properly belongs to the principles of Personal Law governing the "dispositions" of the parties in dispute, have been deemed to have failed to provide the redress appropriate to the context being sought. And, one can only suppose that, in the absence of a governing common civil code for all citizens across the board, or the communal-caste divide, there was no other recourse but to prevail on statutory criminal codes (Penal or otherwise) to determine and obtain justice in the matter.

This caused a massive outcry, especially from the Muslim clergy, as the secular court had stepped on their toes. Shah Bano's attempt to assert that the traditions of her religion discriminated against her, and thus violated her gift of gender equality guaranteed by the Constitution, met with opposition within the community.[40] She backed down, and the then Prime Minister anxious not to lose the Muslim vote-bank, passed the so-called Muslim Women's Protection Act that overturned the Supreme Court's landmark ruling.

One upshot of this and such interventions by the State from the days of Hastings has been that in so far as Personal Law pertains to family, marriage, adoption, and inheritance, the subjects of these laws are mostly women and girls. In other words, a specific religious identity coupled with gender and community affiliation is what will ultimately determine and enforce the outcome. Religion, gender, and community define one's family interests and status. The common denominator is gender and there is no justice forthcoming in this matter: There is even a greater vulnerability for tribal people, especially tribal women whose rights to inheritance were eliminated by the Hindu Women's Inheritance Act (for it only recognized Hindu women and repealed an earlier Act that was better disposed toward tribal women). Kukathas might want to argue that, well she has the right guaranteed by the liberal Constitution to leave her community; but that would be an absurd proposition for anyone in that situation: she cannot, for religious affiliation determines which set of rules an individual's case or claim will be considered, and would she gain if she did exercise her choice to leave? That freedom of movement in and out of a community is not as easy to come by even in a modern nation-state that boasts in its Constitutional preamble to be a secular socialist republic whose citizens are guaranteed the right to liberty, fraternity, health, and other freedoms.

Thus, the judicial equivocation hermetically echoing that of the Constitution has in turn been exploited by the respective moral communities to secure their own ends as it has been perceived to serve them best, toward more orthodox rather than liberal reform inclinations. When this route has failed, they would move the Parliament or State to intervene on their behalf to safeguard their interests in terms of the Constitutional right of the individual's right to freedom of conscience, religious observances, and practice. But, as already noted, this specific right also clashes with the significant Articles of the Constitution that guarantee equality, including gender equality, to everyone, and prohibiting all forms of discrimination based on sex (or gender, in its more inclusive sense). Yet discriminatory practices continue, not least under existing Personal Laws, and the State is an accomplice in this matter either by dint of its own uneven treatment of women or its failure to institute wide-spread reforms in all areas of public and private life, moral and religious spaces, where such practices or repetitions continue to oppress women and other groups of individuals. And this inconsistent approach is also contrary to the spirit of the Constitution that, as we observed a little earlier, in its directive clauses urges the State to instigate such reforms. Either there is a uniform system of rights or there is no need to guarantee social and cultural rights for everyone. There is indeed a growing movement toward heralding in a uniform civil code. However, fuelled mostly by the Hindu Right it comes with certain strings: it will be predominantly based on Hindu norms, as defining the mainstream culture. Yet this is not only unacceptable to other communities, it will be utterly unworkable and unenforceable.

## Summation and Conclusion

Under British administration (East India Company) and sovereignty (British Charter for India), the Westminster and Common Law models were introduced. However, the erstwhile diversity of customs, culturally rooted practices of jurisprudence, the existence of vastly different regional legal dispensation systems and group identities, rendered the imported "Rule of Law" almost unworkable.

The British, in consultation with indigenous legates, devised the so-called Anglo-Hindu and Anglo-Muslim Laws, plus separate personal laws for Indian Christians and Parsees as well. Although these governed a narrower area of personal or "private" community conduct—pertaining to family law, marriage, inheritance, kinship, adoption, succession, collective property title, and so on—they nevertheless had specific implications for thinking on issues of citizenship, rights, and obligations (including the duty of the State toward its citizens within varying social and cultural contexts).

*Prima facie*, this made room for inequality and preferential treatment depending on which community membership a "subject of the state" identified her- or himself with and under which particular personal law process her or his case was to be tried or judged. Hindu patriarchy attempted to legitimate *Sati* ("Suttee"), or widow self-sacrifice, under traditional Hindu dharma or religious law, while Muslim men petitioned for recognition of polygamy under Islamic law.

So, especially under British sovereign rule and with growing communal divisions, the problematic of the role and rights of the "subject" became rather acute, which encouraged the discourse of citizenship and fundamental rights. But a consequence of the Rule of Law was the hybridization of customary habits with textual law. Nationalist struggle and the "Quit India" movement exacerbated communal tensions that created further wedges between the moral communities for whom "universal rights" and citizenship were being mapped out for the projected constitution and the broader purpose of establishing a "secular" democratic republic.

If we look upon each of the communities as individuals writ large, bearing the same sort of relationship with each other and with the State as any two individuals would in a given society, it is clear that the State has not been able to deal adequately with the respective interests of each in a rational manner. Further, where interests have clashed there has at best been an ambiguous and confused response (which continues to mar the relation between the two parties, leading often to riots and so on). The most vulnerable individual regardless of group membership is the female. There are resonances here for any "multicultural society" such as Australia and Canada on the broader issues of rights and citizenship.

In the context, then, of the history and politics of British India and a communally-riven modern India, and debates within the Commonwealth on the pros and cons of the autonomy of cultural rights, as also indigenous challenges to modernist models of Lockean-derived individualist claims over native property rights and other customary practices, the significance of this project cannot be more emphatically underscored. It provides one framework within which to reflect on the several issues facing a modern nation-state with a pluralist or multicultural face.

## Notes

1. I wish to express deep gratitude to Dr Renuka Sharma for her part in the research, formulation and completion of this chapter. But for her immense help and personal library I would have remained ignorant of the seriousness of this issue, beyond my academic interest.

2. Kukathas, in his 1992 article, "Are there any cultural rights?" *Political Theory* 20, no. 1 (February 1992): 105-139.

3. Kukathas, 112.

4. Kukathas, 115.

5. Cited in Will Kymlicka, *The Rights of Minority Cultures* (Oxford, U.K.: Oxford University Press, 1996), 126.

6. Cf. Bhikhu Parekh, "Decolonizing Liberalism" in *The End of 'isms'*, ed. A. Shtromas (Oxford, U.K.: Basil Blackwell, 1994) and "Liberalism and Colonialism: A Critique of Locke and Mill" in *The Decolonization of Imagination: Culture, Knowledge and Power*, ed. J.N. Peiterse and B. Parekh (London: Zed Books, 1995).

7. And to no small measure would attribute the failure of the big "L" liberal government to uphold the Wik judgment in Australia to be emblematic of what—in my view-is another kind of communitarian excess predicated on individualism. Cf. Joseph Raz, "Facing Diversity: The Case of Episteme Abstinence," *Philosophy and Public Affairs* 19 (1990): 3-46 and, Amelie O. Rorty, "The Hidden Politics of Cultural Identification," *Political Theory* 22 (1994): 152-6.

8. Of course, the confrontations need not be real, as they clearly were not for any of the major Enlightenment writers, who drew on accounts and tales from travelers, amateur anthropologists, and in a way preempted the trajectory of colonial encounters—certainly in the case of Kant and Hegel more so.

9. In Jacques Derrida "Force of Law: The 'Mystical Foundation of Authority',"*Cardozo Law Review* 11, no. 919 (1990): 921-1045 and Emmanuel Levinas, *Totalite and Infini* (The Hague, Netherlands: Martinus Nijhoff, 1961), 62.

10. In his essay "Toward Perpetual Peace," 347. Kant, Immanuel, "Toward Perpetual Peace," and "Public Right Section III. Cosmopolitan Right" in *Metaphysics of Morals*, reproduced in *Practical Philosophy, The Cambridge Edition of Kant,* Translation by Mary Gregor (Cambridge, U.K.: Cambridge University Press, 1996), Boyce Gibson Library copy.

11. Kant shows a remarkable knowledge of people, from Samoyeds on the Arctic ocean, the Eskimos in America, the Hawaiians of Polynesia, to Maoris of New Zealand, Sers of China and Mongolia, Lamas of Tibet and so. He is aware of their different scriptures also, mentions by name, Zendavesta (of Zoroastrians), the Vedas (of Brahmanism), the Koran of Muslims, reincarnation doctrine of Lamaism, and so forth.

12. Kant is writing this around 1795 by which time the British East India Company had collapsed and the Home Office had moved to bring India under British sovereign rule.

13. Kant, "Toward Perpetual Peace," 490.

14. Our academic anthropologists of course would dispute this contention of Rousseau's. See "A Discourse on Inequality," in *The Social Contract*, 168.

15. Rousseau, *The Social Contract*, 6.

16. Rousseau, 101.

17. Rousseau, 187.

18. Rousseau, 113 in "True End of Civil Government" where I first came across this exact term.

19. J.L. Mehta, *India and the West: The Problem of Understanding,* Studies in World Religions 4, Harvard University Center for the Study of World Religions (Chico, Calif.: Scholars Press,1985), 186.

20. Hegel, *Philosophy of Right,* Trans. By T.M. Knox (London: Oxford University Press, 1967),

21. John Mill wrote a damning utilitarian history of India for the company officials, and neither had visited the subcontinent.

22. Derrida 1990, 1037. The preceding and following pages are partly my own interpolation of Benjamin's radical thesis, which echoes some classical Indian and Jaina suspicions on 'law'.

23. Sheldon Pollock, "Ramayana and Political Imagination in India," *The Journal of Asian Studies* 52, no. 2 (May 1993): 261-297.

24. Thomas R. Metcalf, *Ideologies of the Raj, The New Cambridge History of India* (Cambridge, U.K.: Cambridge University Press, 1995), Special South Asia Edition, 30.

25. Metcalf, 1995, 35.

26. Bernard Cohn, "The Command of Language and the Language of Command," in *Subaltern Studies* IV. ed. Ranajit Guha (Delhi, India: Oxford University Press, 1985), 289; in Metcalf, 1995, 10 n.8; Descartes had preached something similar.

27. Chatterjee, Chatterjee, Partha, "The Nationalist Resolution of the Women's Question," in *Recasting Women Essays in Colonial History*, eds. Kumkum Sangari and Sudesh Vaid (Delhi, India: Kali for Women, 1989), 233-253.

28. Metcalf 1995, 3.

29. Metcalf 1995, 13.

30. Cohn in Metcalf 1995, 13, n12.

31. Marc Galanter, *Law and Society in Modern India* (Delhi, India: Oxford University Press, 1992), 21.

32. Metcalf 1995, 12.

33. Duncan J. Derrett, *Essays in Classical and Modern Hindu Law. Vol III, Anglo-Hindu Legal Problems* (Leiden, Netherlands: E.J. Brill, 1977), ix.

34. Quoted by Duncan J. Derrett *Religion, Law and the State in India* (New York: The Free Press, 1968), 39; also cited in Gerald James Larson, *India's Agony Over Religion* (Albany, N.Y.: State University of New York Press, 1995) with interesting discussion, 219.

35. Derrett, 1977, vii, ff.

36. Lata. Mani "Cultural Theory, Colonial Texts: Reading Eyewitness Accounts of Widow Burning," in *Cultural Studies* edited, and with an introduction, by Lawrence Groosberg, Cary Nelson, Paula A. Treicher et al. (New York/London: Routledge, 1992), 392-408.

37. "Hindu Men Converting to Islam for Marriage," *India West*, Foster City, California, 19 May 1995, 1, 13.

38. Derrett, 1977, III: pp. 154-156.

39. Though we say Common Law is embedded in the charter, Rau who had been sent to study the two major models, viz. the Westminster system and U.S. Constitution, recommended the U.S. model, which too had underpinnings of Common Law before it separated itself formally and in written form from the British system.

40. Ratna Kapur and Brenda Cossman, "Trespass, Impass, Collaboration: Doing Research on Women's Rights in India," in *The Other Revolution, NGOS and feminist perspectives from South and East Asia, Naari Studies in Gender, Culture and Society, No. 3,*

Renuka Sharma, ed (Delhi, India: Indian Books Centre, in association with Open Wisdom Publications, 1999), 57-82.

*Chapter Ten*

# Suicide, Assisted Suicide, and Euthanasia: A Buddhist Perspective

**Damien Keown**

## Introduction

The debate surrounding the so-called "right to die" has commanded increasing public attention over the last decade. Opinion polls in many Western democracies would appear to show increasing support for euthanasia and physician-assisted suicide, and a number of recent legal developments have further advanced the cause. As a result of court decisions since 1984, euthanasia has been legally permissible in the Netherlands; physician-assisted suicide was legalized in the State of Oregon in 1994 as a result of a ballot initiative, and in 1995 a voluntary euthanasia bill was passed in the Northern Territory, Australia. But, even more recently, the "right to die" campaign has suffered reverses. The implementation of the Oregon legislation has been halted by a Federal court pending a determination of its constitutionality; the Northern Territory legislation was overturned by the Australian federal parliament in 1997, and in July 1997 the United States Supreme Court, reversing the decisions of lower courts, declared that there is no constitutional right to physician-assisted suicide or euthanasia.

Although these questions have only relatively recently come into the public arena, often through headline-making legal cases such as those of Karen Quinlan and Nancy Cruzan in the United States, Sue Rodriguez in Canada, and Tony Bland and Nigel Cox in England, the issues involved are not fundamentally new. Whether it is right for doctors to use their power to kill rather than cure is a question that dates from antiquity.[1] It has, however, been given a contemporary urgency by modern developments in medical technology, which have too often led to the lives of patients being pointlessly prolonged, and also by an increasing emphasis on the value of personal autonomy among ethicists and in society at large.

A notable feature of the present debate is that it has been conducted almost entirely within the framework of the Western religious, cultural, and philosophical tradition. The views of other cultures—particularly those of the East—have been little heard. In the face of the sharp polarity that has opened up in the West between those who support and oppose the "right to die," perhaps it is now time to broaden legal horizons and take note of the arguments advanced within other religious traditions, including Buddhism.

In Buddhism, there has been little philosophical discussion of suicide. Nevertheless, in my view, an accurate understanding of basic Buddhist values does generate an authentic Buddhist ethic about end-of-life decisions. This chapter maintains that suicide, assisted suicide, and euthanasia are all contrary to Buddhist ethics. To offer loose definitions of these terms, by "suicide" I shall mean intentionally ending one's own life by one's own hand; by "assisted suicide" I shall mean providing the means by which another person may take his own life, and by "euthanasia" I shall mean the intentional killing of a human being in the context of medical care. While there are some definitional problems with these distinctions the underlying issue in each case, for Buddhism, is the intentional and deliberate choice of death as a means of avoiding pain, distress, or suffering. Although I will discuss these issues separately, they are linked by the common feature which renders them morally unacceptable in Buddhism, namely the intentional destruction of life.

Central to the assessment of any moral action in Buddhism is the intention (*cetanà*) which lies behind it. This much is clear from the way the Buddha defined karma in terms of intention.[2] In Buddhist jurisprudence the intention with which an act is performed is crucial to the assessment of the guilt or innocence of the perpetrator. For example, one is guilty of a breach of the precept against taking life when the killing act is done intentionally, but not if it is done unintentionally, just as is broadly the case in Western law and ethics. Thus, although Buddhist sources do not employ the rich technology of the contemporary Western debate, they are in keeping with Western legal and ethical principles that one is responsible only for what one intends. Following the precedents of the judgments recorded in the canon—judgments purportedly given by the Buddha—the first step in assessing the morality of any act is to ascertain the intention of the agent.

In Buddhism, intentionally to destroy (or harm or injure) life is to synthesize one's will with death. To seek death or to make death one's aim (even when the motive is compassionate, directed toward reducing suffering) is to negate in the most fundamental way the values and final goal of Buddhism by destroying what the traditional sources call the "precious human life" we have had the rare good fortune to obtain.[3] In doctrinal terms, to choose death over life is to affirm all that Buddhism regards as negative, identified as such in the First Noble Truth.[4] It is simultaneously to reject the goal of flourishing and fulfillment described in the Third Noble Truth (nirvana) and the due process by which it is to be attained, through the Path of self-cultivation by means of Morality, Meditation, and Wisdom outlined in the Fourth Noble Truth.

## I. Methodological Issues in Describing a Buddhist View on End-of-Life Decisions

Returning to what texts provide an authoritative source is itself a difficult task. What we know as "Buddhism"(a term coined by Westerners in the 1830s) is a phenomenon only loosely equivalent to the Western concept of a "religion," and in some ways quite different. Buddhism is made up of a collection of sects and schools embedded within distinct cultural traditions, many of which evolved during different historical periods. These sects and schools are often so different from one another that one is tempted to speak of "Buddhisms" (plural) rather than "Buddhism"(singular). The lack of cohesion among Buddhist groups means that little effort has been invested in formulating a "Buddhist view" on end-of-life issues. There is no Buddhist Vatican or other authoritative council competent to pronounce on these matters and I do not believe there exists anywhere a statement of policy that purports to represent the Buddhist position, nor, for that matter, even the views of a single school. What limited discussion of the issues has taken place has been instigated largely by Western Buddhists, and they have produced very little in the way of published scholarly material.[5]

### Methodology

Given the silence of contemporary teachers and practitioners, one must turn for guidance to scripture. Virtually all schools of Buddhism regard scripture—especially those canonical texts purporting to record the oral teachings of the Buddha—as authoritative and definitive on ethics and doctrine.[6]

But even with the limitation to scripture, another problem presents itself: which textual sources should be used? The major cultural traditions in Buddhism—those of India, Tibet, China, Japan, Korea—each have their own canons of scripture. Sometimes these overlap, but often they do not. Since my own background is in Indian Buddhism, I propose to concentrate on the collection of texts known as the Pali canon. Apart from the accidental fact of my own familiarity with these sources, there are good reasons for attaching particular importance to this body of material. The first is that historically it is the earliest surviving Buddhist literary corpus, and therefore the one likely to preserve most faithfully the Buddha's original teachings. This voluminous body of literature was preserved by oral communal recitation for several centuries from the time of the death of the Buddha around 400 B.C. until it was written down in Sri Lanka in about 75 B.C. A second reason for treating this collection with particular respect is that the language in which it is composed (Pali) appears to be closely related to the language the Buddha himself spoke. Clearly, when texts are translated into other languages there is greater scope for error. Moreover, the Pali canon is the basis of a largely unbroken living Buddhist tradition—it is the canon of the Theravàda school of Buddhism that is dominant in Southeast Asia in countries such as Sri Lanka, Burma, and Thailand. Although it reached these countries at different times and has evolved sometimes in haphazard ways, its teachings on ethics have informed the lives of countless adherents in this cultural region in the past and continue to do so today. Finally, while later schools have certainly evolved, they tend to develop new doctrine by adapting and incorporating material from the early sources rather than rejecting them.

Interrogating a body of ancient textual material from a culture which differs from our own is not without its problems, particularly when we are searching for answers to problems of a contemporary nature which may never have presented themselves to the ancients at all, or at least not in the form they do today. One problem that arises almost immediately is a linguistic one: there is no obvious term in Pali (or perhaps in any Buddhist canonical language) for English terms in use today such as the euphemism "euthanasia."[7] If one were to construct a term semantically equivalent to the Greek euthanasia, it would be *sumaraõa*, meaning "good death," but no such term is found in the canon. Needless to say, distinctions such as those between "active" and "passive" euthanasia, and its classification into various modes such as voluntary, non-voluntary and involuntary are not encountered either. To a lesser degree the same applies to the term "suicide," a neologism and comparative newcomer to the English language with no Greek, Latin, or Sanskrit ancestor.

A further methodological problem concerns the different historical and cultural evolution of East and West. Arguments in favour of the "right to die" often make reference to the principle of autonomy. A Buddhist discussion of the question is unlikely to use this terminology, unless those involved have deliberately decided to shift their conceptual ground in order to engage in the Western debate. The discourse of rights with its concept of autonomous rights-bearing agents is a post-Enlightenment Western phenomenon not found in Asian cultures. This is not to say that Buddhism is opposed or antagonistic to such notions, only that it traditionally approaches moral issues from the perspective of duties rather than rights. While it may be the case, as some suggest, that rights and duties dovetail, the different emphasis placed upon each cannot help but colour perception of difficult issues. Different social and family structures—such as the Western nuclear family or individual versus the Asian extended family—may also explain why euthanasia is more of a moral issue for the West than for the East.

A final problem is how to select an appropriate methodology for the cross-cultural study of ethics, for we cannot assume that Western ethical categories can be applied straightforwardly to an alien tradition like Buddhism. I have suggested elsewhere that the problems here are not as great as some have assumed, and that Buddhism can conveniently be categorised using Western ethical predicates.[8] Nevertheless, there is as yet no consensus on this matter among scholars.

In seeking a Buddhist response to the question of the morality of suicide and euthanasia, then, we face the three problems outlined above, namely: i) the sources do not use the terminology of the current debate; ii) the issues are not located within the same conceptual framework; and iii) there is as yet no agreed methodology for the cross-cultural study of ethics.

While not underestimating these problems, however, there is no need to feel paralysed by them. Although Buddhist sources may not use identical language, they certainly express a view on many of the questions that arise in discussion in the West. Questions such as the value of life, the meaning of human suffering, the role of compassion, and the treatment of the sick and dying come up in various contexts in the texts. East and West have evolved culturally along different paths, but share many points of contact and overlap. Despite their different theological foundations, similarities between Buddhism and Christianity have long been noted: and there is much agreement among these and the other world religions on fundamental moral issues such as human rights.[9] Finally, there seems no overwhelming objection to Buddhists joining a debate that transcends cultural frontiers. Disease is a cultural universal, and due to the global distribution of Western medical technology issues in medical ethics cross-cultural boundaries in a way that others do not. There thus seems sufficient common ground at least to begin a dialogue.[10]

## II. The Arguments Against Suicide: Texts and Principles[11]

In his 1983 paper "The 'Suicide' Problem in the Pàli Canon," Martin Wiltshire wrote, "The topic of suicide has been chosen not only for its intrinsic factual and historical interest but because it spotlights certain key issues in the field of Buddhist ethics and doctrine."[12] Wiltshire was right to identify suicide as an important issue in Buddhist ethics[13] as the simplest and most basic example of the class of life-negating action with which we are concerned. If Buddhism permits suicide then there is no *a priori* reason why it should not permit assisted suicide; and if it permits the latter, there is a strong supposition that it will also allow euthanasia. On the other hand, if Buddhism is seen to oppose suicide, there is a strong presumption that it will also oppose the other two.

Wiltshire identified an important problem in the title of his paper, namely that suicide seems to be regarded with ambivalence in the Pali canon. As Wiltshire wrote in his opening paragraph: "We should, perhaps, point out that suicide first presented itself to us as an intriguing subject of enquiry when we discovered that it appeared to be regarded equivocally within the Canon, that it was both censored and condoned."[14] The view that suicide is regarded equivocally in the canon goes back at least to the 1920s. In his 1922 entry on suicide in *The Encyclopaedia of Religion and Ethics*, de La Vallée Poussin wrote:

> We have therefore good reason to believe (1) that suicide is not an ascetic act leading to spiritual progress and to *nirvàõa*, and (2) that no saint or arhat—a spiritually perfect being—will kill himself. But we are confronted with a number of stories which prove beyond dispute that we are mistaken in these two important conclusions.[15]

In the same year F.L. Woodward expressed a similar opinion.

> There are, however, passages in the *Nikàyas* where the Buddha approves of the suicide of *bhikkhus*: but in these cases they were Arahants, and we are to suppose that such beings who have mastered self, can do what they please as regards the life and death of their carcass.[16]

Views of this kind have influenced Western scholarship over the past seventy years.[17] It should be noted that the scholarly consensus has been that suicide is permitted for the enlightened alone; there is no suggestion that suicide is condoned in the case of those who are not enlightened, and indeed the consensus is that it is prohibited for the unenlightened (in other words, virtually everybody). Various attempts (for the most part along similar lines) have been made to explain why suicide is prohibited for the unenlightened but permitted for the enlightened. In 1965 Lamotte wrote:

> The desperate person who takes his own life obviously aspires to annihilation: his suicide, instigated by desire, will not omit him from fruition, and he will have to partake of the fruit of his action. In the case of the ordinary man, suicide is a folly and does not achieve the intended aim.[18]

This situation is compared with the suicide of an enlightened person:

> In contrast, suicide is justified in the persons of the Noble Ones who have already cut off desire and by so doing neutralised their actions by making them incapable of producing further fruit. From the point of view of early Buddhism, suicide is a normal matter in the case of the Noble Ones who, having completed their work, sever their last link with the world and voluntarily pass into *Nirvàõa*, thus definitively escaping from the world of rebirths.[19]

The significant distinction for Lamotte, then, is that the Arhat acts without desire whereas the unenlightened person does not. Wiltshire shares this view, commenting that "suicide is salvifically fatal in most cases, but not for the arahant, since he cannot be motivated by *taõhà (S.I.121).*[20]

More recently, Becker—going well beyond the evidence of the texts—has spoken of the Buddha's "praise" of the suicides of the monks Vakkali and Channa[21] and claimed that there is a "consistent Buddhist position"[22] on suicide (a permissive one). Becker, too, sees the morality of suicide as turning entirely on motivation, although he highlights the role of the second of the three "roots of evil" (*akusalamåla*) rather than the first. "There is nothing intrinsically wrong with taking one's own life," he writes, "if not done in hate, anger or fear."[23]

Contrary to these views, it seems to me that Buddhism expresses the belief that there *is* something intrinsically wrong with taking one's own life (or indeed taking any life), regardless of one's enlightenment, and that motivation—although of great importance in the assessment of the moral status of actions—is not the sole criterion of rightness.[24] I am uneasy about allowing a determining role to motivation because it leads in the direction of an ethical theory contrary to Buddhist thought known as Subjectivism. For purposes of this argument, subjectivism holds that right and wrong are simply a function of the actor's mental states, and that moral standards are a matter of personal opinion or feelings. For the subjectivist, nothing is objectively morally good or morally bad, and actions in themselves do not possess significant moral features. The "roots of evil" approach to moral assessment Becker and others utilize is subjectivist to the extent that it claims that the same action (suicide) can be either right or wrong dependent solely on the state of mind of the person who commits suicide: the presence of desire (or fear) makes it wrong, and the absence of desire (or fear) makes it right.

If it were applied in other moral contexts, however, this reasoning would lead to unusual conclusions for a Buddhist. It would mean, for example, that the wrongness of murder lies solely in the perpetrator's desire to kill. But this is to take no account at all of the objective dimension of the crime, namely the wrongness of depriving an innocent person of his life. In murder, a grave injustice is done to someone, regardless of the murderer's state of mind. To locate the wrongness of murder solely in desire is to miss this crucial moral feature of the act. In suicide, of course, there is no victim in this sense; but the comparison illustrates that moral judgments typically pay attention to *what is done*, and not just the actor's state of mind. To say that suicide is wrong because it is motivated by desire, moreover, is really only to say that *desire* is wrong. It would follow from this that someone who murders without desire does nothing wrong.[25] The absurdity of this conclusion illustrates why a subjectivist approach to the morality of suicide is inadequate. Similarly, subjectivism leads to the conclusion that suicide (or murder) can be right for one person but wrong for another, or even right and wrong for the same person at different times, as his state of mind changes, and desires come and go.

The suggestion that suicide is right for Arhats but wrong for non-Arhats also seems strange in another respect. Arhats and Buddhas are held up by the tradition as moral paradigms: in all circumstances to imitate a Buddha or an Arhat is to do right. Suicide, however, according to the views of Lamotte and others, is an exception to this rule: in this one respect, the unenlightened should not emulate the enlightened. But why should suicide be the one anomalous moral issue; why should there be a common morality in everything else, and a two-tier morality in the case of suicide? There seems no obvious reason why suicide (and not murder, stealing, or lying) should constitute a "special case." The rejection of subjectivism calls into question the apparent consensus that Buddhism condones Arhat suicide and suggests that the grounds for this claim need to be reassessed.

In fact, only two cases in the canon give any reason at all for thinking that suicide may be condoned, those of the monks Channa and Vakkali;[26] in the third case often cited—that of Godhika—the Buddha voices no opinion at all on the monk's suicide. All three monks commit suicide by cutting their throats, two because they are suffering from a painful illness, and one (Godhika) as a way of seeking to attain nirvana. Godhika had some six or seven times achieved "liberation of the mind" (*cetovimutti*) in meditation only to fall away each time. He decides to commit suicide the next time he attains the state, and does so by cutting his throat. As noted, the Buddha makes no comment on his suicide. In the second case, Vakkali is described as gravely ill and in a deteriorating condition. Stating that he has no doubts or uncertainties about the doctrines of Buddhism, he kills himself. Shortly before this happens, the Buddha makes a prediction that Vakkali's death will not be "ill"(*apàpika*).[27] Although commonly taken to imply approval of suicide this statement could be interpreted in a variety of ways: it may be intended, for example, as a simple reassurance to Vakkali that he has nothing to fear from death, or it could be a prediction that he will gain enlightenment and die an Arhat.

Of the three it is only in the last case, that of Channa, that anything resembling exoneration is given after the event. Channa is described as "afflicted, suffering and gravely ill", and complains of intense pain in the head and stomach and throughout the body generally. He declares his intention to "use the knife" and cuts his throat. Just as he is about to die he gains enlightenment. On being asked about the fate of the deceased monk the Buddha makes a short statement that is translated by F.L. Woodward as follows:

> For whoso, Sàriputta, lays down one body and takes up another body, of him I say "He is to blame." But it is not so with the brother Channa. Without reproach was the knife used by the brother Channa.[28]

It would not be exaggerating greatly to say that the claim that suicide is permissible for Arhats rests to a large extent on the above passage. While I have suggested elsewhere reasons why the above translation may be doubtful,[29] even taking the passage at face value, we should exercise caution before interpreting it to mean that suicide by Arhats is permissible. First, the Buddha does not explicitly state, either here or anywhere else, that he condones suicide by Arhats. What the Buddha actually says in the first part of his statement is something slightly different: what he regards as blameworthy is grasping after a new body. This is merely an affirmation of standard Buddhist doctrine.[30] The Buddha could be seen here, as on numerous other occasions, as skilfully taking advantage of the context to make a point about the importance of remaining focused on the goal.[31] In other words, Channa's death becomes a poignant occasion for the Buddha to emphasize the urgency of putting an end to rebirth. It is trickier to explain the final part of the statement where the Buddha says "Without reproach was the knife used by the brother Channa." These words do imply, as Wiltshire and others have suggested, an exoneration with respect to suicide. Nevertheless, I do not think this leads to the conclusion that Buddhism *condones* suicide. In Buddhism, exoneration and condonation are two different things: exoneration is the removal of a burden (*onus*) of guilt, while condonation is the approval of what is done. These two terms reflect the distinction—also well established in Western ethics and law—between the wrongfulness of acts and the guilt incurred by those who commit them. Self-defence, provocation, duress, and insanity are all grounds which mitigate otherwise wrongful acts. Similarly, with respect to suicide, many traditions recognize that there may be psychological and other factors that may diminish responsibility,[32] which is one reason suicide has been decriminalized in many jurisdictions.[33]

If, like Woodward, we translate the Buddha's concluding statement to say that Channa used the knife "without reproach," it most likely means simply that the Buddha felt it would be improper to blame or reproach Channa (or someone in his situation). In other words it is an acknowledgement that the burden of guilt in many circumstances may be slight or non-existent.[34] Thus we might say in the present case the Buddha is exonerating Channa rather than condoning suicide. Wiltshire makes a similar point:

> Apart from representing putative cases of suicide, these stories share one further overriding theme—each of the protagonists is suffering from a serious degenerative illness . . . . So, when we try to understand why they are exonerated, it is initially necessary to appreciate that their act is not gratuitously performed, but constrained by force of circumstances.[35]

Thus, there is no reason to think that the exoneration of Channa establishes a normative position condoning suicide. Second, there are textual reasons for thinking that the Buddha's apparent exoneration may not be an exoneration after all or at least that it would not be safe to draw any firm conclusions.[36] Third, the textual evidence that suicide may be permissible in Christianity is much greater than in Buddhism in the sense that there are many examples of suicide in the Old Testament: this has not, however, prevented the Christian tradition from teaching consistently that suicide is gravely wrong. By comparison to these texts, Theravàda sources are a model of consistency in their refusal to countenance the intentional destruction of life. Fourth, the commentarial tradition on the Channa episode finds the idea that an Arhat would take his own life in the way Channa did completely unacceptable. Fifth, an obvious but previously overlooked problem is that if we accept the commentary and secondary literature assumption that Channa was not an Arhat prior to his suicide attempt, then to extrapolate a rule for Arhats from his case is fallacious. According to this commentary, Channa's suicide was in all significant respects the suicide of an *unenlightened* person. His motivation, deliberation, and intention down to the act of picking up the razor, thus, his suicide, cannot set a precedent for Arhats, for the simple reason that he was not one himself until *after* he had performed the suicidal act. Finally, and most importantly, suicide is repeatedly condemned in canonical and non-canonical sources and goes directly "against the stream" of Buddhist moral teachings.

Schopenhauer was not altogether wrong in his statement that the moral arguments against suicide "lie very deep and are not touched by ordinary ethics."[37] To state a single overriding objection to it by Buddhism is therefore not an easy matter. However, contrary to the unsatisfactory "roots of evil" critique of suicide—that suicide was wrong because of the presence of desire or aversion, it seems to me there may also be an underlying objection which concerns not the emotional state of the agent but an intrinsic feature of the suicidal act which renders it morally flawed. I believe, furthermore, that the "intrinsic feature" approach is not incompatible with a modified "roots of evil" explanation. On this modified account the wrongness of suicide is to be located in delusion (*moha*), the third of the three "roots of evil," rather than in the affective roots of desire and hatred. On this basis, suicide will be wrong primarily because it is an irrational act. By this I do not mean that it is performed while the mind is unbalanced or disturbed, but that it is incoherent in the context of Buddhist teachings and contrary to Buddhism's values on life over death. Buddhism sees death as an imperfection, a flaw in the human condition, something to be overcome rather than affirmed. Death is mentioned in the First Noble Truth as one of the most basic aspects of suffering (*dukkha-dukkha*) so a person who opts for death believing it to be a solution to suffering has fundamentally misunderstood the First Noble Truth which teaches that death is not the solution, but the problem. The fact that Buddhism believes in rebirth and thus that the person who commits suicide will be reborn and live again is not important. What is significant is that through the affirmation of death the suicide has, in his heart, embraced Màra, the personification of evil whose name literally means death. From a Buddhist perspective, such an embrace is clearly irrational, and thus the act of suicide may be regarded as morally wrong.

From this basic ground, many questions arise from how we define suicide *vis-à-vis* other forms of voluntary death, such as whether nirvana is a kind of suicide[38] (the Buddha was sometimes accused of nihilism), whether the Buddha's own death was suicide,[39] whether feeding one's body to a hungry tigress is suicide,[40] and whether the Japanese ritual of *seppuku* constitutes suicide.[41] These aspects of the question must await another opportunity for discussion.

## III. Assisted Suicide and Euthanasia: The Argument for Ahiüsà

Given these conclusions relating to suicide, there must be a strong presumption that Buddhism is unlikely to condone either assisted suicide or euthanasia. Chief among the aspects of Buddhist teaching which are most relevant to end-of-life decisions is the notion of *ahiüsà*, a pan-Indian idea shared by Buddhism, Hinduism, and Jainism. *Ahiüsà* may be translated literally as "non-harming," "non-violence" or "non-injury." In modern times, it was given prominence by Gandhi in his non-violent political protests against the British. *Ahiüsà* is fundamental to the system of ethico-religious belief and practice which in all three traditions goes by the name "Dharma." As is common with many Sanskrit terms, however, underlying the negative literal meaning is a more positive one. *Ahiüsà* means not just "non-harming" but includes a more positive attitude of the kind captured in English by phrases such as "respect for life" or "the sanctity of life," or what in the West some might term a "pro-life" moral perspective, or most effectively "inviolability of life."[42] The positive and negative aspects of the concept of *ahiüsà* are like the two sides of a coin: on the one side there is respect for life, and on the other the practical moral consequences of this attitude, which is to abstain from causing injury or death to living creatures. This dual aspect of *ahiüsà* can be seen in the description, found in many passages, of the person who observes the first of the Five Moral Precepts of Buddhism:

> He abstains from the taking of life. Laying aside the stick and the sword, he dwells compassionate and kind to all living creatures (D.i.4).

Someone who respects the First Precept "does not kill a living being, does not cause a living being to be killed, does not approve of the killing of a living being."[43] Abstention from causing harm or injury is seen as the natural expression of an affirmative attitude towards life. The concept of inviolability of life makes it clear that *ahiüsà* does not just require an attitude of benevolence but also embodies a clear moral imperative not to injure or destroy life, even when the consent of the person whose life is to be terminated is given, or the act is done at his or her request. What is to be respected is the *instantiation* of life in that person, regardless of the subjective valuation placed on their lives by individuals.

Buddhism's starting point for reflection on problems in medical ethics, then, is a belief in the inviolability of life as a moral absolute, a moral norm that has no exceptions. Those cases that in the West have been thought to be exceptional, such as self-defense and killing in the context of a just war, do not appear to be considered justifiable exceptions by Buddhism.

The textual material that is most relevant to these questions is found in a major division of the Pali canon known as the Monastic Rule (*Vinaya*). This is a corpus of material recounting the history of the Order and setting out the rules and regulations that govern monastic life. The Monastic Rule is an important and authoritative source for Buddhist ethics, and consists in large part of case law that evolved both during and after the lifetime of the Buddha. The penalty for breaking the precept is the most serious which can be imposed—lifelong expulsion from the monastic Order. Certain of these Monastic Rule cases have a direct bearing on euthanasia and the details recounted under the rubric of the precept against the destruction of human life are helpful in this respect.

The circumstances surrounding the promulgation of the monastic precept against taking human life (the Third *Pàràjika*) have a direct bearing on euthanasia. The Buddha introduced it after discovering that a number of monks had requested assistance in dying after developing disgust and loathing for their bodies, an attitude not unknown in ascetic traditions. The monks came to feel that their bodies were foul and impure and that they would be better off dead than associated with such a foul carcass. To liberate themselves, some committed suicide while others sought the aid of an assistant, who dispatched them with a knife. When the Buddha found out what had happened, he immediately took action to prevent any recurrence by introducing a precept into the Monastic Rule forbidding both the destruction of human life and also acting as what the text calls "knife-wielder" (*satthahàraka*)—that is to say, acting as executioner to someone seeking death. It is unlikely that the monastic prohibition was introduced because the monks were suffering from religious zeal and had not allowed time for sober consideration of their decision, a consideration based on autonomy, since the rule imposes not just a cooling off period before euthanasia is allowed but an absolute prohibition. This prohibition, moreover, is quite consistent with the general tenor of early Buddhist ethical teachings which, as noted, do not contemplate any exceptions or extenuating circumstances in which the destruction of life might be condoned.

Relating this episode to the present debate, it would seem that the monks sought voluntary active euthanasia on the basis of a quality of life judgement they had made. The fact that the monks were, as far as we can tell, competent autonomous agents seems to have had no great bearing on the matter. This implies that the principle of the inviolability of life cannot be overridden on grounds of autonomy. As mentioned earlier, autonomy is a Western concept that cannot be located easily within the Buddhist moral framework. Buddhism certainly recognizes that individuals have free choice and that they will suffer the consequences of their moral deeds for good or ill—this is the doctrine of karma. However, individuals are not conceived of as autonomous moral legislators but as nodes within a complex network of social and moral obligations within which every part is related to the whole, and the well-being of the whole is determined by the extent to which each part functions in accordance not with its own agenda but out of respect for the global principles of Dharma. While the importance of autonomy is recognized, it is not the ethical master-principle that it is often thought to be in the West. For Buddhism, autonomy is not a moral trump card, and it seems that more important than the right to choose is the obligation to choose what is right.

Apart from respect for autonomy, a second consideration sometimes advanced in support of euthanasia is compassion. Compassion is of great importance in Buddhism, and is embodied in the idea of the bodhisattva: someone who, inspired by compassion, takes a vow to seek rebirth over countless eons until all beings have been freed from suffering and led to nirvana. Some later sources reveal an increasing awareness of how a commitment to the alleviation of suffering can create a conflict with the principle of the inviolability of life. Compassion, for example, might lead one to take life in order to alleviate suffering. Such a conclusion, however, is generally resisted, as it is in the earlier sources described. Indeed, the very first case of life taking to be reported after the precept against killing was declared[44] involving a conflict between the principle of *ahiüsà* and the compassionate desire to alleviate suffering is described in favor of life:

> At that time a certain monk was ill. Out of compassion the other monks spoke favourably to him of death. The monk died.

The commentary expands on this rather terse account:

> "out of compassion" means that those monks, seeing the great pain the monk was in from the illness felt compassion and said to him: "You are a virtuous man and have performed good deeds, why should you be afraid of dying? Indeed, heaven is assured for a virtuous man at the very instant of death." Thus they made death their aim and . . . spoke in favour of death. That monk, as a result of them speaking favourably of death, ceased to take food and shortly after died. It was because of this they committed an offence (VA.ii.464).

Those found guilty did not go so far as to actually administer euthanasia, but only suggested to the dying monk that he would be "better off dead." The monk himself then ceased to take food and died, so technically their offence was incitement to suicide. Despite their benevolent motive, namely that a terminal patient should be spared unnecessary pain, the judgement was that those involved were guilty of a breach of the precept. According to the influential fifth-century A.D. commentator Buddhaghosa, the essence of their wrongdoing was that the guilty monks *made death their aim* (*maraõàtthika*). This suggests that to embark on any course with death as one's purpose, goal or outcome, whether accomplished through act or omission and regardless of how benevolent the motive, is immoral from a Buddhist perspective. In a modern context, this prohibition would seem to include anyone who aids or abets suicide, lends help in the context of assisted suicide or, of course, causes euthanasia directly.

Compassion, therefore, is not a moral principle that provides a blanket justification for actions. In the words of Edmund Pellegrino, writing in the context of Christianity:

> Compassion . . . is a laudable emotion and motivation, but, by itself, it is not a moral principle, a justification for whatever action appeals to a moral agent as compassionate. Compassion should accompany moral acts but it does not justify them. Compassion cannot justify intrinsically immoral acts. . . . Like other emotions, compassion must always be expressed within ethical constraint. . . . Compassion is a virtue only if its end is a good end.[45]

Among other cases and corresponding judgments reported in the *Vinaya*, which are in line with those considered so far, two concern the long-term care of patients with serious disabilities.[46] In one, the relatives of a man with amputated limbs express the opinion that it would be better if the man died. The motive is not reported: it may have been because they judged his quality of life to be so poor that he would be "better off dead," or perhaps they wished simply to be free of the burden of providing the care and attention he required. It may even have been a combination of these reasons. A monk tells the family to give the patient a certain drink, which proves fatal to him. We are not told if the patient agreed with his family's view that he should die, but the circumstances suggest this. It may be that the man's view about his death is not reported because it is not thought relevant, since intentional killing is judged wrong regardless of whether the victim consents or not. As in the previous case, the monk who gave the advice was expelled from the monastic Order. A similar verdict was pronounced in the case of a nun who recommended another concoction as a means of causing the death of another patient in the same condition.[47]

Although these cases are ancient, they cover the main grounds on which euthanasia is commonly thought justifiable, namely autonomy, compassion, and the patient's quality of life. Nonetheless, it is clear from the judgements that euthanasiast killing is not treated differently from killing in other contexts. The cases show a consistent pro-attitude toward life in circumstances where its value may be thought in doubt. Their common theme might be summed up as the principle that *death itself should never be directly willed either as a means or an end.*

The Buddhist attitude of respect for life is, of course, similar to the way Western law has regarded the matter, at least up to the present. It should be added as a rider that while in both cultures the act of euthanasiast killing would be judged wrong independently of the motive, the motive would certainly be important in assessing the degree of moral culpability, as in the Buddha's exoneration of Channa after his suicide.

## IV. Conclusion: The Middle Way

By way of conclusion, it might be helpful to try to locate the Buddhist position on the issues discussed above in the context of other philosophical approaches. Buddhism regards itself as taking the middle way in many contexts, and is itself sometimes referred to as the "Middle Way" (*majjhimà pañipadà*). The original sense of the term concerns the Buddha's rejection of the two extremes of sensual indulgence and harsh austerity, both of which he rejected in favor of a moderate and balanced way of life.[48] The idea is not dissimilar to Aristotle's doctrine of the mean as discussed in Book II of the *Nichomachean Ethics.*

From what has been said above, however, it may appear that the Buddhist position on the "right to die" question is not a moderate one. My earlier reference to moral absolutes, in particular, may make it seem uncompromising and even extreme. When understood correctly, however, I think it can be seen that Buddhism occupies the center ground between two philosophical extremes.

Much support for euthanasia arises from anxieties about the inappropriate use of medical science. There is understandable concern about patients being kept alive as "prisoners of technology" when many feel the appropriate thing is to allow nature to take its course. Would not the Buddhist principle of the inviolability of life force people in this condition to endure a living death hooked up to life support machines? Does it not oblige doctors to resort to one treatment after another to eke out a life which is spent, and subject terminal patients to the indignity of undergoing endless surgical and other procedures when what they yearn for is a peaceful and dignified death in the company of their loved ones?

The answer is no, for the principle of *ahiüsà* prohibits only intentional killing. It does not impose an obligation to preserve life at all costs. There is no obligation to resuscitate the dying or to resort to piecemeal treatments such as prescribing antibiotics for terminal patients. From a Buddhist perspective, there would be no objection to ceasing treatments that are futile or too burdensome in the light of the overall prognosis for recovery. Neither doctor nor patient is under any obligation to prolong life purely as an end in itself.

Indeed, in Buddhism, clinging to a life that has reached its natural end would be thought detrimental to spiritual progress. Buddhism attaches great importance to a calm and mindful death, seeing it as the springboard for the next rebirth. Its teachings include repeated reminders of the inevitability of death and the fragility of life. It encourages its followers to recognize that death is inevitable and to prepare themselves for it. To prepare for something, however, is not to seek it. In Buddhist teachings, to deny death and cling to life is wrong, but equally wrong is to deny life and seek death. The middle position is to live out one's allotted time (which many Buddhists believe is determined at conception) without resorting to extreme measures to shorten or prolong it.

Buddhist monks have practiced medicine and been involved in the care of the sick and dying for well over two thousand years. Rather than introduce assisted suicide or euthanasia as an option in terminal care, it seems likely that Buddhism would support the ideals of the hospice movement. In the West, the San Francisco Zen Center has offered facilities for the dying since 1971, and started a full-scale training program for hospice workers in 1987. In the U.K., the Buddhist Hospice Trust was formed in 1986 to explore Buddhist ideas related to death, bereavement, and dying, and develop a network of Buddhists willing to visit the dying and bereaved at their request.[49]

Buddhism may thus be thought of as adopting a middle way between two opposing positions. The first is the doctrine of vitalism, which holds that life is an absolute value to be preserved at all costs. At the other extreme is the quality of life view, or the belief that life has no intrinsic value and can be disposed of when its quality drops below an acceptable level. Buddhism occupies the middle ground, holding that the value of life is neither absolute nor does it fluctuate. While life must never be intentionally destroyed, there is no obligation to preserve it at all costs.

## Notes

1. On suicide and assisted suicide in antiquity see Anton J.L. van Hooff, *From Autoeuthanasia to Suicide: Self-Killing in Classical Antiquity* (New York and London: Routledge, 1990).

2. A.iii.451

3. Buddhism believes in reincarnation or rebirth. According to the quality of one's actions in this life, rebirth will be in one of five (sometimes six) realms, including the human world, the animal world, and various heavens and hells.

4. The First Noble Truth is as follows: "What, O Monks, is the Noble Truth of Suffering? Birth is suffering, sickness is suffering, old age is suffering, death is suffering. Pain, grief, sorrow despair and lamentation are suffering. Association with what is unpleasant is suffering, disassociation from what is pleasant is suffering. Not to get what one wants is suffering. In short, the five factors of individuality are suffering." This and

the other Noble Truths are discussed in Chapter Four of Damien Keown, *Buddhism: A Very Short Introduction* (Oxford, U.K.: Oxford University Press, 1996).

5. A noteworthy exception to this is Robert E. Florida, "Buddhist Approaches to Euthanasia," *Studies in Religion/Sciences Religieuses* 22, no. 1 (1993): 35-47.

6. Textual study and exegesis is central to most Buddhist traditions, and ethical and doctrinal views and opinions that are not in conformity with scripture and authoritative commentaries on it composed through the centuries, have little chance of gaining acceptance. I propose, therefore, to make frequent reference to primary sources in the following discussion.

7. According to Becker, the Japanese word for euthanasia is *anrakushi*. This is another name for the heaven or "Pure Land" of the Buddha Amida. See Carl B. Becker, "Buddhist Views of Suicide and Euthanasia," *Philosophy East and West* 40, no. 4 (1990): 543-550.

8. See Damien Keown, *The Nature of Buddhist Ethics* (London: Macmillan, 1992).

9. See Damien Keown, Charles Prebish, Wayne R. Husted, *Buddhism and Human Rights* (Honolulu: Curzon Press, 1998). On the relationship between Buddhism and Christianity, see Damien Keown, "Christian Ethics in the Light of Buddhist Ethics" *Expository Times* 106, no.132 (Feb 5, 1995).

10. For a discussion of issues in transcultural medical ethics, see Edmund Pellegrino in *Transcultural Dimensions in Medical Ethics*, Patricia Mazzarella and Pietro Corsi, eds, (Frederick, Md.: University Publishing Group, 1992).

11. This discussion on suicide has been adapted from my paper, Damien Keown, "Buddhism and Suicide: The Case of Channa," *Journal of Buddhist Ethics* 3 (1996), 8-31.

12. Martin G. Wiltshire, "The 'Suicide' Problem in the Pàli Canon," *Journal of the International Association of Buddhist Studies* 6 (1983), 124-40. A broader discussion of suicide may be found in a book on Buddhist ethics by Peter Harvey,published by Cambridge University Press, entitled *An Introduction to Buddhist Ethics: Foundations, Values and Issues*, and I am grateful to the author for sight of an advance copy of the relevant chapters.

13. The literature on suicide includes L. de La Vallée Poussin, "Suicide (Buddhist)" in James Hastings, ed, XII *The Encyclopaedia of Religion and Ethics* 24 (Edinburgh: T. and T. Clark, 1922); F. L. Woodward, "The Ethics of Suicide in Greek, Latin and Buddhist Literature," *Buddhist Annual of Ceylon* 4 (Colombo, Ceylon: W.E. Bastian and Co, 1922); Jaques Gernet, "Les suicides par le feu chez les bouddhiques chinoises de Ve au Xe siècle", in II *Mélange* publiés par l'Institut des Hautes Études Chinoises 527 (1960); Jean Filliozat, "La Morte Volontaire par le feu en la tradition bouddhique indienne" in *Journal Asiatique* 251 (1963), 21; Yün-hua Jan, "Buddhist Self-Immolation in Medieval China," *History of Religion* 4 (1964-5), 243; W. Rahula, "Self-Cremation in Mahàyàna Buddhism" in W. Rahula, *Zen and the Taming of the Bull* (London: Gordon Fraser, 1978); Louis H. Van Loon, "Some Buddhist Reflections on Suicide," *Religion in Southern Africa* 4 (1983), 3; E. Lamotte, "Religious Suicide in Early Buddhism," *Buddhist Studies Review* 4 (1987), 105 (first published in French in 1965); Peter Harvey, "A Note and Response to "The Buddhist Perspective on Respect for Persons," *Buddhist Studies Review* 4 (1987), 99; Carl B. Becker, "Buddhist Views of Suicide and Euthanasia," *Philosophy East and West* 40, no. 4 (1990), 543; Carl B. Becker, *Breaking the Circle: Death and the Afterlife in Buddhism* (Chicago, Ill.: Southern Illinois University Press, 1993); Stephen Batchelor, "Existence, Enlightenment and Suicide: The Dilemma of Nanavira

Thera in Tadeusz Skorupski," *The Buddhist Forum* 4 (1996), 9. Woodward refers to a discussion of the Channa episode in Edmunds, *Buddhist and Christian Gospels* ii 58, but I cannot locate this passage. For more general treatments see Upendra Thakur, *The History of Suicide in India* (Delhi, India: Munshiram Manoharlal, 1963); Norman L. Farberow, ed, *Suicide in Different Cultures* (Baltimore: Baltimore University Park Press, 1975); Katherine K. Young, "Euthanasia: Traditional Hindu Views and the Contemporary Debate," in *Hindu Ethics. Purity, Abortion, and Euthanasia*, Harold G. Coward and Julius J. Lipner, eds (Albany, N.Y.: State University of New York Press, 1989), McGill Studies in the History of Religions 71, esp. 103-07. There is additional literature on ritual suicide in Japan (*seppuku*), but I see this practice as bound up with the Japanese Samurai code and as owing little to Buddhism (Becker apparently disagrees).

14. Martin G. Wiltshire, "The 'Suicide' Problem in the Pàli Canon," *Journal of the International Association of Buddhist Studies* 6 (1983), 124.

15. L. de La Vallée Poussin, "Suicide (Buddhist)" in XII *The Encyclopaedia of Religion and Ethics* 24, James Hastings, ed. (Edinburgh: T. and T. Clark, 1922).

16. Clark 1922, 25. In a more recent encyclopedia entry Marilyn J. Harran writes: "Buddhism in its various forms affirms that, while suicide as self-sacrifice may be appropriate for the person who is an arhat, one who has attained enlightenment, it is still very much the exception to the rule." "Suicide (Buddhism and Confucianism," in *The Encylopedia of Religion,* Mircea Eliade, ed in chief, (New York: Macmillan, 1987), XIV, 129.

17. Views of this kind with certain variations are expressed by Poussin, "Suicide (Buddhist)"; Wiltshire, "The 'Suicide' Problem"; van Loon, "Some Buddhist Reflections on Suicide" (cited in note 13); Lamotte, "Religious Suicide in Early Buddhism" (cited in note 13); Shoyu Taniguchi, *A Study of Biomedical Ethics from a Buddhist Perspective* (unpublished MA Thesis, 1987), 86; Young, "Euthanasia: Traditional Hindu Views and the Contemporary Debate" (cited in note 13); Robert E. Florida, "Buddhist Approaches to Euthanasia," *Studies in Religion/Sciences* 22 (1993), 35-41.

18. E. Lamotte, "Religious Suicide in Early Buddhism," *Buddhist Studies Review* 4 (1987) (first published in French in 1965), 106.

19. Lamotte, 106f.

20. 1983:24.

21. Carl B. Becker, *Breaking the Circle,* 136.

22. Carl B. Becker, *Breaking the Circle,* 137.

23. Carl B. Becker, *Breaking the Circle*, 137.

24. On the criteria for moral evaluation in Buddhism, see Peter Harvey, "Criteria for Judging the Unwholesomeness of Actions in the Texts of Theravàda Buddhism," *Journal of Buddhist Ethics* 2 (1995), 140. See also Damien Keown, *Buddhism and Bioethics*, 37.

25. It may be objected that it is impossible to murder without desire or hatred. Regardless of whether this is psychologically true, the theoretical possibility of desireless murders that would thus be regarded as not immoral reveals the inadequacy of the subjectivist account. Another defect in the account is that the gravity of murders would be nothing more than a function of the amount of desire present. A "crime of passion," therefore, would be far more serious than a random "drive-by" shooting. The fact that courts often take an opposite view gives us reason to question this conclusion.

26. Other canonical suicides include those of the unnamed monks in the *Vinaya* whose deaths led to the promulgation of the third *pàràjika.* At M.ii.109F a husband kills his wife and then himself so they will not be separated. Cases of attempted suicide leading to enlightenment include those of the monk Sappadàsa in the *Theragàthà* (408), and

the nun Sãhà in the *Therãgàthà* (77) (both discussed by Sharma, 1987, 123f. Compare Rahula 1978, 22f). At Ud. 92 f. the aged Arhat Dabba rises in the air and disappears in a puff of smoke. There is a similar passage in Bakkula at M.iii.124-8.

27. *Mà bhàyi Vakkali . . . apàpakam te maraõam bhavissati apàpikà kàlakiriyà.*

28. I.B. Horner, *Kindred Sayings* IV (Oxford, U.K.: Pali Text Society, 1930), 33. In her introductory essay to the *Majjhima* translation, Horner seems to suggest that the compilers of the canon had actually "rigged" the text in order to exonerate Channa. Of the Buddha's exonerating statement she writes "they make him [the Buddha] sanction the unworthy act of the poor little sufferer" (xi).

29. Damien Keown, "Buddhism and Suicide: The Case of Channa," *Journal of Buddhist Ethics* 3 (1996): 8-31.

30. The use of the word "blameworthy," however, is unusual. The Buddha does not elsewhere describe those who are reborn as "blameworthy."

31. For example, when asked about worshipping the six directions in the *Sigàlovàda-sutta*, the Buddha deftly switches the context to social relationships.

32. This distinction is made clear in Catholic teachings. *The Declaration on Euthanasia* (Boston: Pauline Books and Media, 1980) prepared by the Sacred Congregation for the Doctrine of the Faith states at 7: "Intentionally causing one's own death, or suicide, is therefore equally as wrong as murder . . . although, as is generally recognized, at times there are psychological factors present that can diminish responsibility or even completely remove it."

33. The situation in four contemporary cultures influenced by Buddhism is summarized by Harvey in *An Introduction to Buddhist Ethics: Foundations, Values and Issues.* He reports that in Sri Lanka attempted suicide is punishable by up to a year in prison while aiding and abetting suicide is treated the same as murder. In Thailand, while it is illegal to encourage suicide, suicide itself is not illegal. In Taiwan, attempted suicide is not a crime. Japanese law does not criminalize suicide but it is an offence to assist or encourage it.

34. This is similar to Christ's reaction to the woman taken in adultery: in defending the woman with the words "Neither do I condemn thee," (*John* 8,11) Christ is not endorsing adultery by displaying compassion for the woman who has sinned.

35. 1983:132.

36. The textual problems are examined more fully in Damien Keown, "Buddhism and Suicide: The Case of Channa," 22-24. These turn upon the meaning of the term *anupavajja*, which is usually translated as "blameless". The commentary, however, plausibly in my view, understands it as meaning "not to be reborn" (apparently deriving it from the root *vraj*, meaning to go, walk, or proceed). The terms occurs again towards the end of the discourse in the context of certain families who are either "blameworthy" or "to be visited" (*upavajjakula*) depending on which interpretation is preferred.

37. A. Schopenhauer, *Foundation of Morals* quoted in Margaret Pabst Battin, *Ethical Issues in Suicide* (New York: Prentice Hall, 1982), 74.

38. This is suggested at *Miln* 195 and following.

39. As suggested, for example, by Robert E. Florida in "Buddhist Approaches to Euthanasia," 45. Compare Poussin, "In the case of øàkyamuni we have to deal with a voluntary death." We must bear in mind, however, that the Buddha had rejected Màra's overtures in this direction at the start of his teaching career (D.ii.102) and did so again three months before his death (D.ii.99).

40. The story of the hungry tigress is found in the *Jàtaka-màla* and the *Suvarnaprab-hàsottamasåtra*.

41. See Gavin J. Fairbairn, *Contemplating Suicide* (New York and London: Routledge, 1995), 144. Fairbairn suggests that *seppuku* is not suicide since the samurai does not seek to end his life, but only to perform his duty.

42. It is not easy to find a good English translation for *ahiüsà*. Terms such as "pro-life" and "the sanctity of life" have theological and other associations which may colour their use in a Buddhist context. The phrase "respect for life" is less loaded but not strong enough. More satisfactory, and the phrase I shall adopt to translate *ahiüsà*, is "the inviolability of life."

43. D.iii.48.

44. *Vin* ii.79.

45. Edmund D. Pellegrino, M.D., "Euthanasia and Assisted Suicide," in *Dignity and Dying, a Christian Appraisal*, John F. Kilner, Arlene B. Miller and Edmund D. Pellegrino, eds., (Carlisle, U.K.: Paternoster Press, 1996).

46. *Vin* ii.86.

47. *Vin*. iii.85.

48. S.v.420; *Vin*.1.10.

49. I am grateful to Peter Harvey for this information from his book mentioned above.

# *Chapter Eleven*

# In Extremis: Abortion and Assisted Suicide from a Buddhist Perspective

Michael Barnhart

## I

Bioethical issues know no international boundaries. As countries with traditionally large Buddhist populations such as Japan, Thailand, Sri Lanka, and others take their place in an increasingly technocratic world, biomedical issues long familiar in American and Western European societies become equally pressing for these industrializing countries. Problems concerning organ donation and transplantation, genetic testing and engineering, healthcare access, and the protocols governing medical experimentation with human subjects inevitably arise. How Buddhism understands these moral issues will be very important to people of conscience within such societies. However, we should not forget that Buddhism continues to develop in the modernized or "post-modern" West, especially in the United States. Not only does the flock of committed practitioners continue to grow, but many look to Buddhism as a kind of informal spiritual guide and a supplement to their settled religious commitments.[1] Therefore, it is not only in traditionally Buddhist countries that Buddhist opinion on such issues matters.

A complicating factor, however, is that the list of biomedical issues contemporary societies now confront remained undreamt of at the time of the Buddha. A great deal of extrapolation is required to develop a consistent Buddhist approach, even in regard to abortion and assisted suicide, which have been around far longer than modern scientific medicine. Yet, some textual evidence regarding Buddhist opinion on these issues survives, and so turning to these problems is obviously the place to begin a discussion on Buddhist bioethics. Furthermore, and perhaps more importantly, because abortion and suicide in general deal with life *in extremis*, at conception and destruction, they invariably invoke basic ideas regarding the nature of the self and the meaning and purpose of human life in general. How these views are applied will make a great deal of difference for what Buddhism can say regarding the list of other more contemporary problems.

It is quite clear from a variety of sources that abortion and suicide have been severely disapproved of in the Buddhist tradition. It is also equally clear that abortion has been tolerated in Buddhist Japan and both practices, the latter in the form of treatment refusal and physician-assisted suicide, have been accommodated under exceptional circumstances by some modern Buddhists in the U.S.[2] The often-cited sources that prohibit abortion are Theravada and ancient. By contrast, Japanese Buddhism as well as the traditions out of which a more lenient approach emerges are more recent and Mahayana. Superficially, the situation seems not unlike that of Roman Catholicism, where abortion in particular, though disapproved of in the strongest terms by Church authorities, drawing on the canonical tradition, is nonetheless practiced by a large number of devout Catholics and defended by at least a few, sometimes renegade, theologians and philosophers as acceptable in some circumstances. Therefore, if it makes sense to speak of a possible Catholic defense of abortion, then it makes equally good sense to speak of a Buddhist defense of abortion and some forms of suicide, a defense made in full knowledge that one is swimming against the tide of conventional interpretation but still within the tradition.

I will use the label "conservative" for the more traditional or orthodox view. By that I mean a disapproving view that sees the wishes of those individuals concerned to be subject to communal constraint. That is, the autonomy of the agent is not the primary moral concern governing the permissibility of these actions. By contrast, the more "liberal" or "permissive" position offered in this chapter is more disposed to respecting the decision of the affected individual or parties whatever that decision might be. However, autonomy alone will not be a reason for finding the actions or decisions of the individual morally justifiable. Indeed, insofar as Buddhism has any religious depth it must provide some sort of principled guide to conscientious decision-making. And that requires independent reasons for seeing the actual choice an individual makes as morally justifiable, besides the mere fact that it is the individual's own decision. Therefore, a defense of a "liberal" Buddhism may not itself be a piece of liberal ethical theory. In other words, I am not so much concerned to show that Buddhism has, does, or will support one's right to make such choices, as I am to show that they can be made in a manner consistent with Buddhist principles. Buddhism itself, therefore, speaks with more than one moral voice on these issues.

## II

Turning to the case of abortion first, let us consider the "conservative" interpretation of Buddhist principles. One of the strongest antiabortion cases from a Buddhist perspective emerges in Damien Keown's wonderfully thorough and insightful analysis of Buddhism's bioethical ramifications in the book *Buddhism and Bioethics.*[3] Keown argues that the preponderance of the Buddhist tradition is overwhelmingly antiabortion. In support, he develops two lines of argument. The first relies on the nearly uniform rejection of abortion especially in ancient Theravada texts, what Keown regards as the core of the tradition. Here, I believe he is on fairly firm ground although I am uncertain regarding his preference for what he calls "Buddhist fundamentalism" and his concomitant emphasis on "scriptural authority."[4] The second line of argument concerns his interpretation of these sources and their connection to the basic tenets of Buddhism regarding the nature of personal identity and the *skandhas*, karma and rebirth, life and death.

I find Keown's discussion of the sources that directly relate to the question of abortion fairly convincing. Especially in the *Vinaya* and the *Pitakas* or Buddhagosa's commentaries it seems quite clear that the practice of abortion is considered unacceptable. However, as Keown points out (92), the cases dealt with involve women seeking abortions for questionable, perhaps self-serving, reasons including "concealing extramarital affairs, preventing inheritances, and domestic rivalry between co-wives." In short, if these are the paradigm examples of abortion, then the case is heavily biased against the practice. Keown does comment in an endnote that Buddhism would surely have sided with a woman seeking an abortion in order to save her own life, a position he attributes to Hindu jurists of the time. Why Buddhism would make such an exception is unclear, especially given the case Keown builds against the practice. For if abortion is always in violation of the First Precept against taking life, especially such karmically advanced life as that of a developing human being, then why should the mother's imperiled condition make a difference? Why prefer one life to another?

One might, of course, argue that abortion in such circumstances was a form of self-defense. Indeed, Keown seems to feel that killing in self-defense is not itself an example of taking life (again indicated in an endnote). But pregnancy and its associated dangers present a wholly different kind of situation from that of self-defense. In the case of a fetus, if the mother's life is in jeopardy, it is not because the fetus is in some manner 'attacking' the mother as in most such cases. Rather, the mother's medical condition renders her unable to carry a fetus to term or give birth safely. Even if it is the fetus's medical condition that jeopardizes the mother, it is in no way analogous to a physical attack. The fetus is not responsible for its medical condition and in no way intends to harm its mother. Hence, the question why such special exceptions to a general prohibition on abortion are acceptable remains unanswered. Correlatively, if such exceptions can be made, why not make them in other, perhaps less threatening but still serious, circumstances?

Yet whether or not early Buddhism's condemnation of abortion is fully rationalized or not, the fact is that the scriptural evidence is against it. However, when it comes to connecting the apparent condemnation of abortion with the deeper inspirations of Buddhism the case is less compelling and perhaps affords a toehold in the Theravada tradition for a different evaluation of abortion. Keown argues that the First Precept and its prohibition against taking life is part of a much larger reverence for life, life being one of Buddhism's three basic goods—life, wisdom, and "friendship" (Keown's spin on *karuna* and other associated qualities). While respect for life is undeniable, the abortion issue usually hinges on whether the fetus is indeed a life in the relevant sense, and one could challenge either Buddhism or Keown on this point. That is, as Keown makes quite clear, though Buddhism values life, it does not value all life equally, and human life as a karmically advanced stage is particularly important. The fetus at any stage in its development is certainly in some measure living, but it is not obviously a recognizable human being at every stage. As a mere conceptus it lacks, of course, many of the attributes one might label distinctively human except its genotype therefore, unless one insists, reductionistically, that a certain genetic sequence just *is* the essence of our humanity, one cannot say that a fertilized egg is a karmically advanced human being just because it is a fertilized egg.

In other words, one needs a theory as to what constitutes a human being, a human life, and therefore a thing worthy of the greatest possible protection. This Keown attempts to provide through a discussion of the traditional *skandha* theory and its implications for the various embryonic stages of human development. With few exceptions, which I will return to, Keown argues that a fertilized egg is a fully human being because the ingredient most essential to such a life is already present—*vinnana* (in the Pali). *Vinnana*, usually translated as consciousness, is of course only one of five traditional components of a living being. The other four are: form (the body), feeling, thought, and character or disposition.[5] Keown's argument for treating *vinnana* as the most essential group is perhaps best stated in his discussion and rejection of sentience as the basic moral criterion for respect as a living being. He says,

> the most fundamental [category] is consciousness (*vinnana*), the fifth. To specify *vinnana* as the criterion of moral status is, however, simply to say that all living beings have moral status, since it is impossible to isolate *vinnana* from the psychosomatic totality of a living being. It is impossible to point to *vinnana* without in the same act pointing to a living creature, just as it is impossible to point to 'shape' without referencing a physical object.[6]

Although he does add, perhaps inconsistently,

> Overall, since neither *vinnana* not any other of the five categories by themselves can adequately encompass the nature of a living being, there is reason to be suspicious of any view which claims to locate in any one of them what is essential in human nature.[7]

Earlier he claims that "Although feeling and thought define the architecture of experience, it is . . . *vinnana* which constitutes it."

What I take Keown to be arguing here is that *vinnana* is the most important of the *skandhas* which, to my mind at least, seems most unBuddhistic. As he himself notes and the Pali canon repeats *ad nauseum*, it is the conjunction of all five of the groups that constitute a living being, at least by any meaning of constitute that I am aware of. So, why the emphasis on *vinnana*? The above-stated reasons are, to my mind, weak. It is no less true that without a body, without sensation, without disposition (in the sense of a karmic past), one would not be a living, at least human, being. That is, lacking form, a body, perhaps one could qualify as a hungry ghost, but the Pali texts are very clear that the "groups" form the basis of the human ego, or at least the illusion of an ego. "Accordingly, he [Buddha] laid down only five groups, because it is only these that can afford a basis for the figment of an ego or of anything related to an Ego".[8] Hence, no conjunction of the *skandhas*, no ego-delusion is possible; and furthermore no basis, consequently, for what Keown identifies as an ontological individual apart from its various phenomenal qualities. In short, it is impossible to isolate any of these groups from "the psychosomatic *totality* of a living being."

That said it is important to consider further what Keown means by the term *vinnana*. His chosen translation is not actually 'consciousness' but 'spirit' which I think raises if not antiBuddhist then at least unBuddhist associations and implications. Keown rejects the traditional "consciousness" translation of *vinnana* because "the experience of *vinnana* in this form [as consciousness] . . . is merely one of its many modes. It is better understood as functioning at a deeper level and underlying all the powers of an organism" (25). He goes on to remark that "*vinnana* resembles certain Aristotelian-derived notions of the soul in Christianity, namely as 'the spiritual principle in man which organizes, sustains, and activates his physical components.'" This then becomes the justification for the claim that 'spirit' is an appropriate translation of *vinnana*.

> There are times, however, when the refusal to use the obvious English term hinders rather than helps the process of understanding. The term in question is 'spirit', and I do not think it would be misleading to refer to *vinnana* in certain contexts as the *spirit* of an individual. *Vinnana* is the spiritual DNA which defines a person as the individual they are. (25)

Rather confusingly, he compares the role of *vinnana* with that of the electricity in a computer in order to clarify the kind of constituting spirituality he has in mind.

> An electrical current flows through the computer and is invisibly present in every functional part. When the power is on, many complex operations can take place; when the power is off the computer is a sophisticated but useless pile of junk. Like electricity, *vinnana* empowers an organism to perform its function. (27)

The reason I find this association confusing is that rather than being "invisibly present," electricity is all too visibly present. Electricity is a physical, not a spiritual, phenomenon. And if *vinnana* is to be understood on such a model, then not only is it no longer ghostly but no longer fulfills the functional purpose of accounting for the "spiritual principle in man which organizes, sustains, and activates his physical components." Electricity may, in a loose sense, animate a computer, but it doesn't in any way organize its physical components. Keown seems to be entertaining two rather different conceptions of *vinnana*. On the one hand, it is a quasi-Aristotelian soul-like entelechy that individuates and constitutes an ontological individual moving along the karmic ladder to eventual enlightenment. Ultimately, what I find unBuddhistic about such an interpretation is not the almost antithetical mixture of psychological and physical characteristics, but the purpose to which this hybrid is put and its association with the concept of a soul. That Keown intends to make such a connection is very clear, especially when he remarks that *vinnana* so understood acts "as the carrier-wave of a person's moral identity; in the stage of transition between one life and the next. . . . [I]t may be referred to as 'spirit'. An alternative designation for *vinnana* in the state of transition between lives is the *gandhabba*, which will be translated as the 'intermediate being'" ( 26). Thus, *vinnana* is meant to account for individual moral responsibility across the various stages of karmic life, including rebirth, to eventual nirvana.

However, such an account of human life still does not square with Buddhism's rejection of the Ego or *atman*. Indeed, Keown's version of *vinnana* rather resembles a Vedantic understanding of *atman*. Elsewhere he argues that the "moral identity" he mentions is not what Locke, for example, would identify as 'personhood'. Keown's notion is much broader, while Locke's concept with its attendant qualities of rationality and self-consciousness is inappropriate for a Buddhist anthropology. Such qualities or capacities flower at different times in the course of an individual's evolution, hence if all stages of individual existence are morally significant because they are karmically continuous, then a suitably broad understanding of the individual is required in order to valorize the entirety of a human life so understood. The strength of the *atman* concept lies in its transcendental vision of an individual life and support for a moral identity that holds across chains of rebirth. In short, the *atman* as it is traditionally understood accomplishes exactly these functions, preserving moral identity, while at the same time remaining irreducible to any particular human characteristic, including self-consciousness, as well as all human characteristics collectively. In other words, if Keown is looking for a translation of the term *vinnana* other than 'consciousness'. The term 'soul' seems better suited than 'spirit'.

However, it is exactly such a principle or entity which the Buddhist *skandha* theory would deny. An individual as such, the *Pitakas* argue, is like a chariot, not really there. If presented a chariot, a Buddhist would ask, "Where, exactly, is the chariot?"

> "Your majesty if you came in a chariot, declare to me the chariot . . . the word 'chariot' is but a way of counting, term, appellation, convenient designation, and name for pole, axle, wheels, chariot-body, and banner-staff."

Similarly,

> Nagasena is but a way of counting, term, appellation, convenient designation, mere name for the hair of my head . . . brain of the head, form, sensation, perception, the predispositions, and consciousness. But in the absolute sense there is no Ego here to be found.[9]

In other words, no *atman* whatsoever and, arguably, no ontological individual either. In fact, "strictly speaking, the duration of the life of a living being is exceedingly brief, lasting only while a thought lasts."[10] Buddhists, even early Theravada Buddhists, seem to feel they can get along quite well without anything which might subtend the processes of existence, of *samsara*, and provide "moral identity," ontological continuity, or the spiritual DNA explaining anyone's present predicament. The question really comes down to whether *vinnana* or any other quality need endure to explain personality or transmigrate in order to explain rebirth and karma. Keown seems to feel that logically something must and *vinnana* is the best candidate. However, the scriptural evidence is missing, and furthermore a non-substantialist and thoroughly non-Aristotelian explanation of rebirth can be given.

Supposing we understand rebirth, not as the rebirth of someone, but as a mere succession or process. In this view, all acts or events share some form of dependent connection (*paticcasamupanna*). Therefore, actions and events that take place now share intrinsic connections to actions and events in the past and in the future along any number of 'natural' dimensions. In the case of human beings, these dimensions correspond to the *skandhas*. Form, sensation, and so on all represent various sorts of dependency between phenomena. Because there is no self, soul, or ego we can look at this process in two different manners corresponding to the difference between enlightenment and delusion. On the one hand, we can look at the process as a mere empty process wherein nothing essentially happens, completely detached and hence freed from the bondage of desire or the expectations of life, and importantly, the anxieties of death. This represents an enlightened approach that is not an expectation of transmigration because there is nothing to be reborn.[11] So, the Buddha claims, this death is his last. Or, we can look at the process from the standpoint of belief in a thing that perdures. From this perspective, there is rebirth as transmigration, the expectation of future lives, the existence of past lives, and so on. One must, perforce, explain the process as the biography of someone, hence the fiction of an ego becomes necessary. It is this last which tempts us to rely on such quasi-Aristotelian notions as souls, spirits, or "spiritual DNA."

To be fair, Keown is aware of these issues and argues at several points that *vinnana* is not really a soul nor is it a "subject of experience" (26). He eloquently states:

> Buddhism does not ground its ethics in a metaphysical soul or self, and denies that any such thing exists. According to Buddhism, the five categories are what remain when the 'soul' is deconstructed. (28)

To which I would simply add why do we need to speak of "spiritual DNA" or "moral identity" in order to make sense of Buddhism? These categories themselves seem equally prone to fixation and quite contrary to the basic notion of *anatta*. In other words, I would argue that like all the other groups—form, sensation, and the like—*vinnana* also does not endure, either across or within lifetimes. None of the groups do, and this is the essential feature of the *anatta* doctrine. Hence, I would not equate *vinnana* in the state of transition with anything, much less the *gandhabba*, simply because it is not transitional.[12]

Keown makes much of the *gandhabba*'s essential role in the process of conception as portrayed in various Buddhist sources, interpreting the descent of the intermediate being when biological conditions at the time of conception are just right as offering what looks very much like an account of ensoulment. Such a strategy then justifies Keown's claim that for Buddhists "In the overwhelming majority of cases individual life is generated through sexual reproduction and begins at fertilization" (91).[13] Consequently, abortion is immoral because it deprives an individual of life and so violates the First Precept against the intentional taking of life.

In terms of a Buddhist defense of abortion, the main difficulty with Keown's analysis has to do with his understanding of the Buddhist view of life which subsumes abortion under the general heading of intentional killing. Given my understanding of *anatta*, I see no reason to subscribe to Keown's understanding of the Buddhist view of human life. For Keown, all biologically human life is normatively significant because it is animated by the descended *gandhabba* thus conferring the singularity necessary to view it as ontologically individual. However, given the distinction between the groups, I see no reason why a committed Buddhist can't hold that just because one has a body, form or *rupa*, one doesn't necessarily have a human life, especially one worthy of the strongest protection. A human life, in the moral sense starts unambiguously when *all* the *skandhas* are in place, and the Buddha as well as the early Buddhist scriptures leave room for a rather large number of interpretations as to exactly when such a condition occurs in the process of embryonic development. I suspect that much of Keown's enthusiasm for his interpretation stems from the ready parallels that may be drawn between the natural law tradition of Roman Catholicism and Buddhism if one's *vinnana* is identical to the soul-like *gandhabba* that pops into the development process.[14] However, as we have seen such an assumption provides Buddhism with a form of ensoulment that it goes to great lengths to avoid.

If *vinnana* does not in any way subtend the karmic process from individual to individual and may even be completely episodic within the context of an individual life, then (1) I see no reason to interpret *vinnana* as anything other than consciousness or some such equivalent, and (2) Buddhism need not take *vinnana* to be present at any particular point in the process of embryonic development. That is, *vinnana* or consciousness is present whenever one would customarily say it is and that could be just as well at viability as at conception. In fact, we would generally hold consciousness to be present only when, minimally, the cerebral cortex develops and perhaps later.[15] Thus, even though a Buddhist would hold that consciousness provides the platform for mind *and* body, making any conscious being a living being worthy of moral consideration, it is not clear exactly when such a point might first occur. Furthermore, even if scriptural sources would locate this point early on in the embryonic process, a Buddhist could still coherently question any such time designation as potentially arbitrary mainly because, as I have argued, Buddhism lacks any comprehensive theory of deep-level principle that *requires* the presence of consciousness or an intermediate being at any particular point in the biological process of human development.

In fact, Keown admits that a Buddhist could hold the above position as the Buddha laid down several conditions covering ontogeny, some strictly biological and mainly regarding coitus and the mingling of sperm and, mistakenly, "menstrual blood." That is, even on Keown's analysis, Buddhism traditionally separates the biological *basis* for life from the individual life itself. Thus, a fertilized ovum is arguably a necessary but not sufficient condition for a new life. Rather, one requires the presence of the full complement of groups including *vinnana* to complete the development of an individual life. However, this allows "the material basis for life to arise on its own" ( 81), which Keown admits seems to contradict the assumption that the biological and spiritual basis must always arise together. Keown replies that if an unanimated conceptus is possible, its long-term survival is not for it is not "a new individual," and therefore "from the standpoint of Buddhist doctrine it would seem impossible for it to develop very far."

The justification for this claim is the Buddha's statement "that if consciousness were 'extirpated' from one still young, then normal growth and development could not continue" ( 81). Incidentally, this claim also forms the basis for Keown's view that PVS patients (those in a "persistent vegetative state") are still individuals worthy of moral protection and should not be ruled as dead as some advocates of a higher-brain definition of death would allow. That is, their continued and stabilized biological existence (some can live on for decades) demonstrates the presence of *vinnana* and hence individual life.

However, a liberal Buddhist could claim that while the loss of *vinnana* might curtail growth and development, it's not clear that *vinnana*'s never having arisen need affect the biological development of the material basis of an individual's life. Indeed, one might argue that (1) because 'extirpation' of consciousness from one who already possesses it usually involves physical trauma, of course we would expect normal growth and development to stop; or (2) even though *vinnana* is essential to the life of an individual and its irretrievable loss signals the individual's demise, it doesn't follow that the mere biological platform and its growth and development signal the inevitable presence of *vinnana*.[16] That is, it doesn't follow that *vinnana*, however we interpret, it is essential to the life of the biological organism. Especially if, as Keown suggests, Buddhism allows the presence of the material basis of life without that of the *gandhabba*, then I don't see how Buddhism can rule out the possibility of simply a more extended existence of that material basis without *vinnana*. The biological basis of life may be organically integrated in the manner of a functional organism, but it is not itself the same thing as an individual life. I see no compelling rationale, based on Buddhist principles as articulated in the early scriptures, absolutely requiring the 'individual life begins at conception' point of view of radically 'prolife' antiabortionism.

I grant that the early Buddhist scriptures do seem to have a somewhat 'prolife' orientation. Yet, on closer inspection, I'm not sure the footing is there mostly because of the lack of a theory of ensoulment. Furthermore, had Buddhists of the time faced the bewildering medical possibilities of the late twentieth century, I'm not at all sure how doctrine would have evolved. For example, anencephaly, PVS, and various other comatose conditions where patients exist in only the most minimal sense and on life support, not to mention transplant surgery, the advances in human genetics, and so on surely pose a challenge to traditional ways of regarding the human body. Many of these cases are, to my mind, simply waved aside by Keown (or his version of Buddhism). To claim that the prolifism of Buddhism simply means that PVS patients are fully alive[17] is not to do justice to the complexities of the cases or of Buddhism, both of which suggest that 'life' is an extremely complex 'dependently arisen' phenomenon.[18]

## III

If one keeps to the traditional translation/interpretation of *vinnana* as consciousness, rejects any kind of soul, spirit, *atman*, or ego as a subsistent core of individual being either for the course of many karmic lives or a single individual karmic life, then I see no reason why, even a Theravada Buddhist could not adopt a socially liberal position on abortion as well as a variety of other biomedical issues. This is not to say abortion would be a trivial matter, but the idea that it necessarily demonstrated disrespect for present life would be undermined. Of course, since abortion does compromise future life, it is still a morally serious matter, but as such it does not of itself violate the First Precept. A prohibition on killing is not an injunction to 'be fruitful and multiply' by bringing into existence as much future life as is possible.[19] Rather, as long as consciousness is not yet deemed present, we face the material basis of a life, not the individual life itself.

In many ways, this version of the Buddhist view would echo what bioethicist Bonnie Steinbock has called the "interest view."

> On the interest view, embryos and preconscious fetuses lack moral status, despite that they are potentially people . . . the fact that a being has the capacity to develop into a person, does not mean that it has any interest in doing so, or any interests at all, for that matter. And without interest, a being can have no claim to our moral attention and concern.[20]

However, Steinbock does go on to argue that one's potential personhood *does* make a moral difference in regard to interested beings. So, in her view, a human infant rates more highly than even a fully developed chimpanzee on the grounds that chimpanzees are not moral persons in any relevant sense.[21]

The similarity to Buddhism rests on the role of consciousness or what is sometimes called "the developed capacity for consciousness."[22] As Keown tirelessly point out, the presence of *vinnana* is the key to individual status. If *vinnana* is consciousness and represents the platform on which mind and body are *conjoined*, then the presence of *vinnana* signals a karmically significant stage, that of an individual life for which either release or rebirth are the twin possibilities marking moral success or failure. Thus, on the Buddhist view, human life consists of a physical body and various sensori-motor capacities, conjoined with a mind or intellect all sporting a karmically conditioned past, that is always in context; individuals do not have any non-contextual existence. Consciousness is indeed the platform of mind and body. The body is not itself the mind, and there is no hint of physicalism or reductionism in this understanding of human nature. The mind, however, is always passing away; mind is identical to thoughts and these are fleeting. The stream of consciousness, one could say, is a Heraclitean river, never the same exact thing twice. Consciousness is the developed capacity for such a stream in a physical context. But this does not mean that consciousness, the mental stream of thoughts, the sensori-motor complex, or one's karmic context are themselves the subsistent individuals? Rather, to the degree such elements coarise we have an individual and the permanent absence of any of the groups is the loss of an individual. Surely, there is at least a prima facie plausibility in the claim that without your body you do not exist; without your consciousness you do not exist; without the mind you do not exist. But all of them together do not create some other thing we call the person that exists apart from these qualities, nor something that goes on after or existed before. Hence, each and every one of us is egoless strictly speaking, though we still retain "moral identity" and so can be held accountable for our actions. In short, when it comes to individual identity, Buddhism takes a similar position to philosophical nominalism.[23]

When it comes to marking the temporal boundaries of a human life, therefore, such Buddhist nominalism tolerates a fair degree of imprecision. The only way of working out a fairly acceptable answer to the question when does life begin and when does it end would probably be through the process of analogizing. We can say that each of us is a living, morally significant being. The question becomes how much like us are other beings? How similarly situated do we take them to be? My suspicion is that some of the variation one finds in Buddhist texts over whether to treat various life forms as deserving of compassion reflects differences in individual's abilities to imaginatively extend such analogies so as to creatively identify with the pleasures and pains of other beings, especially animals. Does a fetus constitute a morally significant being? The answer would depend on how like us any particular fetus is. Surely, a late term fetus is, not so certainly a fetus on the threshold of viability, and dubiously a conceptus.

Of course, such an approach does not help too much in the process of line drawing. But there are other Buddhist resources that may assist the line drawer. Any such act would be a matter of conscience, a morally significant act for the individual reflecting on such distinctions, as perhaps in the process of contemplating an abortion. What is important in situations of this nature is to negotiate the pitfalls of attachment and desire. Correct line drawing is not based in metaphysical distinctions regarding personhood, but in the moral fiber of the line drawer and the complex interweave of circumstance and motivation that color and inform practical judgments. Appropriate questions for reflection might be: What am I seeking to gain? Why am I having or not having this child? What sort of life is possible for this child? How do I feel towards this life, this new being? What kind of pain and suffering is involved in either life or abortion? In short, all those questions which people do typically seem to mull over when faced with unwanted pregnancies.

In short, though Buddhism encourages compassionate action, the question as to what is compassionate in the case of an unwanted pregnancy cannot be peremptorily answered by metaphysical proclamations as to when life begins. Thus, without leaving the province of a conservative Theravada Buddhism, a traditionalist Buddhism, one need not embrace the radical antiabortionism of Keown's Buddhist. Some confirmation of such a position can be found in testimony collected in William R. LaFleur's book *Liquid Life*. A Japanese woman and committed Buddhist reflects on the practice of *tatari* or propitiating the soul of a dead fetus in order to avert posthumous revenge.

> Buddhism has its origin in the rejection of any notion of souls . . . that souls cast spells. . . . Of course we who are Buddhists will hold to the end that a fetus is "life." No matter what kind of conditions make abortion necessary we cannot completely justify it. But to us it is not just fetuses; all forms of life deserve our respect. We may not turn them into our private possessions. Animals too. Even rice and wheat shares in life's sanctity. Nevertheless as long as we are alive it is necessary for us to go on "taking" the lives of various kinds of such beings. Even in the context of trying to rectify the contradictions and inequalities in our society, we sometimes remove from our bodies that which is the life potential of infants. We women need to bring this out as one of society's problems, but at the same time it needs to be said that the life of all humans is full of things that cannot be whitewashed over. Life is full of wounds and woundings. In Japan, however, there is always the danger of mindless religion. There are also lots of movements that are anti-modern and they are tangled up with the resurgence of concern about the souls of the dead.[24]

It is, of course, arguable that this way of looking at the issue is fundamentally incoherent. Either we are intentionally taking life or we are not, and if we are then we violate Buddhism's First Precept. The response a Buddhist may make, such as Ochiai Seiko's above, is in essence: "Yes, we should always avoid the ending of a life, no matter how insignificant it may seem. But 'life' is an ambiguous term, and the ending of one form of life in the service of others is not necessarily prohibited in Buddhism. And if one's intention is not so much to end a life as to rescue others, then we are not dealing with a simple case of 'intentionally killing'." In other words, compassionate action will always involve weighing up the full range of circumstances that bear on a situation or action. On this view, the point of the First Precept is to disqualify intentional killing where the clear purpose is to end an individual life. Such an action can never be compassionate in Buddhist eyes. However, questions as to the status and nature of the lives one weighs in such tricky situations where interests clash are obviously relevant. If we are talking about the lives and interest of mothers and fetuses, fetuses and families, or fetuses and communities (such as in times of famine), then we are directly faced with the issue of the relative moral standing of different sorts of 'life'. What I have argued here is that because Buddhism allows a distinction between the biological basis of life and its higher, cognitive as well as affective aspects, and insists that an individual human life requires the conjunction of all such aspects, no Buddhist need equate a presentient fetus with a sentient human. Thus, Ochiai's insistence that in dealing with the messiness of everyday living, abortion may qualify as a compassionate response need not contradict Buddhist principles. Especially if we are dealing with the material platform of an individual being before the point of cerebral development sufficient for the developed capacity for consciousness, then the moral seriousness of its claim to life may well be outweighed by other considerations.

## IV

The second biomedical issue which poses challenges to a Buddhist ethic is assisted suicide. Again, as in the previous case of abortion and the definition of death, the Pali Canon suggests the kind of conservative response Keown articulates on behalf of traditional Buddhism.

> In Buddhism, there has been little philosophical discussion of suicide. Nevertheless, in my view, an accurate understanding of basic Buddhist values does generate an authentic Buddhist ethic about end-of-life decisions . . . suicide, assisted suicide, and euthanasia are all contrary to Buddhist ethics.[25]

However, Keown is careful to distinguish what he calls vitalism from the rejection of assisted suicide and related practices. Invoking the traditional description of Buddhism as seeking a "middle way" on all issues, he argues,

> Buddhism may thus be thought of as adopting a middle way between two opposing positions. The first is the doctrine of vitalism, which holds that life is an absolute value to be preserved at all costs. At the other extreme is the quality of life view, or the belief that life has no intrinsic value and can be disposed of when its quality drops below an acceptable level. Buddhism occupies the middle ground, holding that the value of life is neither absolute nor does it fluctuate. While life must never be intentionally destroyed, there is no obligation to preserve it at all costs.[26]

He notes that many people support euthanasia because they believe that medical doctors are solely preoccupied with keeping patients alive at any cost, a form of vitalism. But, Keown argues, Buddhism need not share such a goal as "*ahimsa* [non-injury, compassion] prohibits only intentional killing. It does not impose an obligation to preserve life at all costs."[27]

Again, as in the cases of abortion and PVS patients, I agree with much of Keown's analysis of early Buddhist scripture. It seems clear that there is at least reticence, if not total disapproval, with regard to the subject of suicide in general. A more liberal interpretation must be based on more abstract ethical principles in Buddhism that may conflict with the teachings embodied in such ancient precedents. However, I do not see why such a reinterpretation of Buddhist orthodoxy is clearly inadmissable, especially since Buddhism has traditionally adopted a more free-wheeling attitude towards textual orthodoxy than is found in, for example, the Judeo-Christian tradition.[28] Thus, 'orthodoxy' in any matter is difficult to pin down. Furthermore, suicide is one thing and the various practices under discussion another. In fact, it is unclear that the cases Keown submits do prohibit assisted suicide, euthanasia, or even suicide itself as unequivocally as he thinks.

## The Cases

The case that Keown cites and seems to most unequivocally condemn suicide in general comes from the monastic literature and concerns Migalandika. In *Buddhism and Bioethics*, Keown relates how certain monks when instructed on "the theme of the impure"

> became over-zealous in their practice and developed disgust and loathing for their bodies. So intense did this become that many felt death would be preferable to such a repulsive existence. Accordingly, they proceeded to kill themselves, and lent assistance to one another in doing so. They found a willing assistant in the form of Migalandika, a 'sham recluse' (*samana-kuttaka*), who agreed to assist by killing the monks in return for their robes and bowls (169).

The Buddha's reaction was to condemn their actions and proclaim the following rule: "Whatever monk should intentionally deprive a human being of life, or should look about to be his knife-bringer, he is also one who is defeated and is no more in communion" (170). It is this prohibition of "knife-bringing" that constitutes the strongest textual evidence that Buddhism would indeed disapprove not only of suicide but also assistance in carrying out a suicide. And Keown goes on to link this prohibition with the broader precept against destroying life in general, as he does in the case of abortion.

However, there are significant differences between a case such as this one involving otherwise healthy monks, who subjectively loathe their own bodies as a result of misinterpreting the Buddha's teachings, and the cases of terminally ill patients suffering great pain and distress, barely able to function at a conscious level. The two sorts of cases are at least prima facie different. Of course, this is part of the problem in over-relying on ancient cases; they do not readily generalize to cover rather different situations. Clearly, the purpose behind the Migilandika case is to distinguish between advocating suicide and noting the imperfections and suffering of human existence. Of course, the case can indeed be read as voicing a general disapproval of suicide, but that is not clearly its purpose. It certainly doesn't advocate suicide. However, it is a false alternative to maintain that advocacy and disapproval are the only options for a principled stance. There is also judicious application of the practice.

Other cases further complicate the picture. Two cases in particular have led commentators to suppose a Buddhist toleration of suicide, those of Channa and Vakkali. In the case of Vakkali, as Keown describes it, the monk takes his life in the face of severe illness and the Buddha comments that Vakkali's death will not be "ill." The case of Channa is that of another ill monk, perhaps terminally so, who kills himself and attains enlightenment at the moment of death. The Buddha comments that, in this case, Channa's death was without reproach.
The passage, as cited from Horner by Keown, reads

> For whoso, Sàriputta, lays down one body and takes up another body, of him I say "He is to blame." But it is not so with the brother Channa. Without reproach was the knife used by the brother Channa.[29]

If anything, in other words, there may be exceptions to the requirement that one avoid "knife-bringing."

While expressing reservations regarding the exact translation of this passage as rendered, Keown's general philosophical objection is that one cannot read this as condoning suicide. Rather, what it amounts to is an exoneration of Channa specifically, thus as it were confirming the general prohibition on taking life and therefore suicide. In short, Channa's is the exception that proves the rule. "Thus we might say in the present case the Buddha is exonerating Channa rather than condoning suicide." And, "there is no reason to think that the exoneration of Channa establishes a normative position condoning suicide."[30]

Although I would agree that neither the Channa case nor the Vakkali case establish any sort of precedent for condoning suicide, this is beside the point in discussing cases of assisted suicide or euthanasia. For one thing, advocates for the legalization of such practices themselves distinguish between the issue of suicide in general and assisted suicide and euthanasia in particular. The point is that certain classes of individual, the terminally ill or the hopelessly suffering, are entitled to an exception to our general disapproval of suicide. They are also exceptions to the rule, and the important question concerns those criteria we justifiably apply in deciding who is entitled to such exceptions and why. In this regard, the cases of Channa and Vakkali may be relevant to understanding the basis for a specifically Buddhist approach to identifying such exceptional cases. So, while Buddhism does not condone suicide, as Keown notes, it does exonerate some suicides. Why? On what basis?

## The Moral Argument

The case of Channa not only suggests the Buddha's tendency to avoid absolute pronouncements of all sorts, but also also raises the entire issue of the significance of death in a Buddhist context. Without an understanding of the importance and meaning of death in Buddhism, the possibility of a more liberal or tolerant attitude on end-of-life issues may seem merely wishful thinking.

While I generally agree with Keown's overall view of Buddhist ethics as non-utilitarian[31] there is one significant respect in which Buddhism resembles utilitarianism. Because all other goals one may have are secondary and instrumental to the achievement of nirvana or enlightenment, nirvana stands to our religious practices as the general happiness stands to our actions. And to the degree that achievement of the general happiness confers value that would otherwise be lacking in our actions when considered in-themselves, so enlightenment confers value that would otherwise be lacking in a practice considered in-itself. This is, I think, one of the chief lessons to be found in the Buddha's tolerant attitude towards Channa. Channa's knife-wielding bore some instrumental relationship to his enlightenment.

This attitude is also on display in a wide variety of other, particularly Ch'an, enlightenment stories. To give an example, consider the story, as related by D.T. Suzuki, of Shen Kuang's achievement of *satori* under Bodhidharma:

> Finally, there came to him [Bodhidharma] a former Confucian scholar, named Shen Kuang, who, not being satisfied with the teaching of his native teacher, decided to follow the faith of Dharma. The latter, however, seemed to have altogether ignored this man, for he did not pay any attention to the earnest supplication of this seeker of truth. We are told that Shen Kuang in the face of this cold reception stood in the snow on the same spot throughout seven days and nights. At last he cut off one of his arms with the sword he was carrying in his girdle, and presenting this before the imperturbable Dharma, he said: "This is a token of my sincere desire to be instructed in your faith. I have been seeking peace of mind these many years, but to no purpose. Pray, your reverence, have my soul (*hsin*) pacified."
> Dharma then answered: "Where is your soul? Bring it out before me, and I shall have it pacified." Shen Kuang said: "The very reason of my

> trouble is that I am unable to find the soul." Whereupon Dharma exclaimed: "There! I have pacified your soul." And Shen Kuang all at once attained spiritual enlightenment, which removed all his doubts and put an end to all his struggles.[32]

I don't mean to suggest that dismemberment is a commendable or authentically Buddhist practice. But it does suggest that extremity can be important in provoking enlightenment, and indeed many Ch'an or Zen practices from the severity of the *sesshin* to the uncompromising rigors of *zazen* and koan study all aim to break our conventional ways of thinking through creating extremes of experience, so much so, that a kind of "personality death" appears absolutely essential to their success.

As an illustration, consider the Japanese philosopher Keiji Nishitani's description of what he calls the "Great Death." Quoting Takusai, he writes,

> The method to be practiced is as follows: you are to doubt regarding the subject. . . . Pay no attention to the various illusory thoughts and ideas that may occur to you. Only doubt more and more deeply, gathering together in yourself all the strength that is in you, without aiming at anything or expecting anything in advance, without intending to be enlightened and without even intending not to intend to be enlightened. . . . But however you go on doubting, you will find it impossible to locate the subject. . . . Doubt deeply in a state of singlemindedness, looking neither right nor left, becoming completely like a dead man, unaware even of the presence of your own person. When this method is practiced more and more deeply, you will arrive at a state of being completely self-oblivious and empty. But even then you must bring up the Great Doubt, "What is the subject . . ." and doubt still further, all the time being like a dead man. And after that, when you are no longer aware of your being completely like a dead man, and are no more conscious of the procedure of the Great Doubt but become yourself, through and through, a great mass of doubt, there will come a moment, all of a sudden, at which you emerge into a transcendence called the Great Enlightenment, as if you had awoken from a great dream, or as if, having been completely dead, you had suddenly revived.[33]

Nishitani's use of the phrase "Great Death," which is common in such enlightenment literature, is not simply hyperbolical either. He credits the effectiveness of the practice with its severity, a severity that, at least psychologically, kills. Now, it is not that the practice of meditation should be viewed as a form of suicide in the form of a personality death. It is rather that a death-like experience can be a legitimate occasion, in fact given human psychology is likely to be the most suitable occasion, for the religious breakthrough to enlightenment and nirvana. Of course, if any sort of death is a release into nirvana, it is not because the body or some psychological element or *skandha* "drops away." It is because one mindfully participates in the dropping away that the experience is an enlightened one. Otherwise, death is merely negative either as a deprivation of life or an occasion of psychological loss. That is, death, physical or psychological, is not valuable because it is death; it is valuable because it offers a unique opportunity to existentially confront the sheer contingency of the self, and thus come to understand the nature of suffering and its permanent relief.

That physical death can provide the same meditational opportunities as the principally psychological Great Death, or that physical death may be transformed into Great Death, is not only supported by the Channa episode and the Buddha's reaction to it, but also by the story of the Buddha's own death. It is traditional to relate that the Buddha attained or entered *nibbana* upon his death, that "he was no more of the World."[34] One way to interpret this claim is as the broadly Hindu view that an arhat is freed from samsara or rebirth; one will not return. Of course, the non-return of the Buddha marks the element that distinguishes traditional Theravada Buddhism from Mahayana with its emphasis on the transmissibility of Buddha nature across individuals by virtue of its universality. But whatever one's Buddhist persuasion, the Buddha's death and its finality are a matter of deep significance. The death itself is a confirmation of his enlightened state and as such, requires a clear understanding of what is going on, or at least some sort of alert participation.

Consequently, when Keown argues that Buddhism puts "[N]either doctor nor patient . . . under any obligation to prolong life purely as an end in itself" he is clearly right.[35] But life is not an end in itself because life, insofar as we can be and mostly are attached to it, has the potential for impeding enlightenment and reinforcing egocentrism. And to the extent that we must accept the flux of existence, change, so we must accept the inevitability of death. Yet, whatever we take death to be, it requires as much lucid participation, in the form of letting go, as we can muster.

When patients fear a lingering death, intubated, sedated to the very margins of consciousness, and physically incapacitated, what they fear and often label as undignified is fully understandable in light of Buddhist values. Such a death is more a lingering torture than it is an event in which mindful human participation is possible. It is difficult to see how enlightenment is possible in such circumstances, vegetative as they are. All Buddhisms have recognized that some form of structured activity is involved in the pursuit of nirvana, and some ways of dying, because of the kinds of associated incapacities, are not conducive to this end. Furthermore, it would be wrong to insist that good Buddhists must bear any torture in the pursuit of religious ends and so bear whatever affliction they face in complete resignation. Buddhism has always rejected the path of asceticism and enforced misery. When the means to alleviate unnecessary and utterly debilitating suffering are available, it seems perversely self-punishing not to take advantage of them. Suffering for the sake of suffering is not a Buddhist value, and suffering alone is not a path to enlightenment. However, right-mindedness is, and whatever else it may require, mindedness involves some degree of lucid awareness.

However, one could also argue that a good Buddhist should take whatever comes their way and not try, egocentrically, to manipulate fate, to accept, as Keown suggests, their allotted life span. "The middle position is to live out one's allotted time (which many Buddhists believe is determined at conception) without resorting to extreme measures to shorten or prolong it."[36] I suppose this would include the attitude that one not manipulate the dying process but simply accept growing incapacity allowing oneself to slip under whatever mental fog the disease process engenders. Perhaps we try too hard to control enlightenment and we must recognize many different ways of enacting it.

While there is ample justification for this view in Buddhist literature, I'm not sure that it offers a more "correct" approach to dying than does the desire to seek a more active, lucid, and voluntary role in the dying process. It isn't even clear that these approaches are inconsistent. Part of the problem hinges on the ambiguity of the word "allotted." Just as with the term "nature" we need to decide whether what is allotted includes or excludes human intervention. While it is certainly reasonable to say that what is allotted is the result of the natural lottery, since death is so contingent on human action, a clean line distinguishing what is one's allotted time as opposed to an extended or diminished time is not an easy one to draw. Furthermore, to accept any given time as the allotted time of one's death might involve subscribing to rather unBuddhistic values. That is, if accepting one's end involves any sort of fatalism or supposition of independence from the stream of becoming, of events, then we might as well question its Buddhist authenticity. If, on the other hand, what is allotted can be determined by the actions of oneself and others, then my allotted time might be up to me, and justifiably so if I make that determination in a manner consonant with core Buddhist values. In any case, it isn't clear that passive resignation is necessarily a more authentic Buddhist approach to death than is a more active involvement in the process.

So far, the moral argument from Buddhist principles may be summarized as:

[1] Death has a special significance as a potential source of supreme enlightenment.

[2] Supreme enlightenment requires some form of lucid participation.

[3] Some forms of dying, because of their associated incapacities, preclude enlightened participation.

[4] Therefore, some forms of dying are best avoided if one can do so in accordance with other Buddhist values.

## Killing, Allowing to Die, and the First Precept

In all fairness, Keown admits the force of pro-euthanasia arguments based upon the desirability of a mindful death.[37] However, he argues that the proviso mentioned in [4] above, points to a major loophole in the moral argument. To intentionally bring on death, no matter the purpose, is to violate Buddhism's First Precept. While this is a strong moral counterargument, there are two issues on which its interpretation of Buddhist values can be challenged. The first has to do with the weight given to life as a value and thus the moral weight of the prohibition on deliberately intending to kill. The second has to do with the role of precepts in Buddhist ethics, as opposed to other, perhaps more fundamental concepts.

With regard to the first issue, Keown wants to insist that while Buddhism rejects any form of euthanasia, it does not insist that patients be kept alive beyond the point of medical futility, that is, there are circumstances in which it is perfectly reasonable and humane to withdraw or withhold treatment. These are very complex issues hinging on important terminological distinctions. So first, some definitions. By treatment refusal [TR] I understand the refusal of necessary life-sustaining medical treatment on the part of the patient. By treatment withdrawal [TW] I understand the removal of life-sustaining medical treatment, by an attending physician in the usual case. By physician-assisted suicide [PAS] I understand the procuring of the means of suiciding for a patient by a doctor; this does not include the administration of such measures to the patient. By voluntary active euthanasia [VAE] I understand the administration of the means of death either by a physician or some other party besides the patient him or herself. VAE practiced on oneself is simply suicide. Some philosophers define PAS and VAE as "active" euthanasia and TR and TW as "passive" euthanasia. I will generally try to avoid these terms as I ultimately hope to show that the active/passive distinction is morally irrelevant, especially from a Buddhist standpoint.

The conventional moral arguments for either approving or prohibiting PAS and VAE both accept the permissibility of TR and TW. The major issue concerns whether or not the two types of "euthanasia" are sufficiently analogous to extend such permissibility from the latter to the former. Philosophers such as Dan Brock argue that the major reason for honoring TR is the patient's right to bodily self-determination, a reason that extends equally to cases of PAS and VAE. In both types of situations the patient conceives a wish to avoid further suffering and indignity and engages in or authorizes others to engage in actions that result in his or her death. The major moral consideration from this standpoint has to do with the voluntariness of the action. Of course, nonvoluntary forms of euthanasia are generally morally unacceptable, although there may be special exceptions.[38] By contrast, for philosophers such as Dan Callahan the two sorts of cases are clearly different. In TW we do not kill the patient but allow him or her to die. In PAS or VAE the doctor actively kills the patient either through direct administration of the means of death or indirectly through providing the means to death; either way, the doctor is morally culpable for the patient's death. In Callahan's view, oddly enough, to ignore the causal distinction between allowing the disease to kill the patient and actively killing the patient is to further encourage doctors in their already megalomaniacal view that they are solely responsible for the patient's health and consequently erode their commitment to allowing hopeless cases to die peacefully on the grounds that this is tantamount to 'killing' the patient.

A major weakness inherent in the latter position on PAS is its vulnerability to the objection that killing and allowing to die do not mark a moral difference in themselves. Philosopher James Rachels is well known for his "similar cases" arguments where one considers two cases, the only difference between them being that in one there is an act of killing and in the other an act of allowing to die. For example,

> In the first, Smith stands to gain a large inheritance if anything should happen to his six-year-old cousin. One evening while the child is taking his bath, Smith sneaks into the bathroom and drowns the child, and then arranges things so that it will look like an accident.
>
> In the second, Jones also stands to gain if anything should happen to his six-year-old cousin. Like Smith, Jones sneaks in planning to drown the child in his bath. However, just as he enters the bathroom Jones sees the child slip and hit his head, and fall face down in the water. Jones is delighted . . .[39]

The point here is that the causal issue, whether a case involves killing or allowing to die, does not affect the moral issue, as above, the equal unacceptability of both actions. In response, opponents of PAS have also argued that it invokes a different moral principle than TR or TW. Treatment withdrawal honors a patient's basic moral right to be free of unwanted invasive treatment while PAS and so on require a more far-reaching "right to hasten death" as the New York State Task Force puts it. That is, in honoring refusals of life-sustaining treatment we are not necessarily seeking the death of patients. We may simply seek to make their final period of life reflect their values and preferences, to provide a kind of psychological comfort. However, PAS and related forms of euthanasia aim to bring about the death of the patient.

While I agree that this is a morally serious point and that TR and TW need not aim at the patient's death, on the other hand, some cases do in fact reflect such a wish. And because we hold TR and TW morally permissible in allowing the patient to die, we must recognize that we are also not morally disqualifying the wish of someone to die. Furthermore, for the doctor to undertake such action as unplugging a machine, with the aim of bringing on the patient's death, remains equally permissible under this point of view. Granted, TW is generally regarded as an omission. But the important point remains that an omission that aims at death, whether the doctor, the patient, or both harbor that aim, remains morally acceptable. Drawing on Rachel's point that acts and omissions in such cases do not of themselves mark a moral distinction, we can ask the question: Why should it automatically be the case, therefore, that all *actions* that aim at the death of the patient be considered unacceptable?

In other words, we face the following dilemma: if we accept Rachel's general point that killing and allowing to die are not necessarily morally distinct, then either we accept some forms of "killing" as morally justified (because we accept most forms of allowing to die, barring Rachel's examples of course) or we reject some forms of conventional "allowing to die," namely those where death is the avowed purpose of the action. Obviously, we will have to come up with various grounds other than the killing versus allowing to die distinction for making these cuts. However contemporary philosophers may respond to this question, Keown's Buddhist position neatly grasps the one horn of this dilemma: not all forms of TR or TW are morally acceptable. Keown argues that in Buddhist jurisprudence and moral thought, the key distinction is not between acts and omissions but the actor's intentions. Furthermore, what makes killing wrong from a Buddhist standpoint is that it violates the First Precept which, again, prohibits the deliberate taking of life. Consequently, those acts or omissions that aim at the patient's death, whatever we might call these actions and whoever might harbor them, are morally unacceptable. On the surface, this suggests a more uncompromising position than, for example, Callahan's. While Callahan dismisses PAS and related practices as "killing" the patient, he does accept all forms of treatment refusal/withdrawal as morally acceptable "allowing to die." For Keown, to allow the patient to die may or may not be morally acceptable. If the purpose is to bring on death, then such instances of TR and TW are just as unacceptable as any other more active killing. As he says,

> . . . any course of action involving an intentional choice against life is deemed wrongful. Thus it is wrong to act as 'knife-bringer'; wrong to emphasise the positive aspects of death and the negative aspects of life; wrong to incite someone to kill another, and wrong to assist others in causing death . . . *death itself should never be directly willed either as a means or an end.*[40]

Consequently, the only morally relevant distinction is between those actions in which "the physician is typically endeavoring to . . . enhance through medical treatment the condition of the patient overall, in this case by freeing them from pain"[41] and those in which the physician deliberately intends to bring on death, whether actively or passively, or to "stubbornly prolong life" in the face of medical futility. Only the former are morally acceptable.

All of which raises the question: Exactly what is it to intend or deliberately intend to bring something about? In this regard, Keown cites the distinction between foreseeing and intending.

> To illustrate the point with a mundane example: a person may go out in the rain *foreseeing* that he will get wet but without *intending* to get wet. Likewise, in a legal context, murder is defined as intentional killing where death is the aim: it is not enough that death is merely foreseen, even foreseen as certain.[42]

In other words, any act or omission that aims at the death of the patient violates the First Precept and so erects an insuperable barrier towards the seeking of a "mindful death." Strong though this position is, it is not entirely impervious to criticism on a variety of grounds both Buddhist and pragmatic. To start with, it replaces the relatively bright line that Callahan proposes between killing and allowing to die with a much murkier one between acts performed under particular intentional circumstances. Whatever Keown is suggesting it is not the conventional killing versus allowing to die. But secondly, it ironically suggests a very strong rationale under which certainly PAS and perhaps some cases of VAE might be fully justifiable. And lastly, and this relates to the second issue with which we started, it may involve a view of rule-following that is characteristic of only some versions of Buddhism.

To explore the pragmatic angle a little more thoroughly, though Keown's move allows one to consistently oppose PAS and VAE and accept the moral immateriality of the active/passive distinction, it does so at the cost of a clear line between actions that are morally acceptable and those that are not. Whether or not one's actions are morally acceptable becomes entirely a matter of state of mind. What sort of test do we apply for this either in regard to others or even, for that matter, to ourselves? How do I know I'm not fooling myself when I suppose, as the doctor let's say, that I do not aim to bring about the death of the patient? What, in effect, really is the line between merely foreseeing that the patient will die and deliberately intending that death? Can we apply an objective test? Even in regard to Keown's example where I go out in the rain without the explicit intention of getting wet, to the degree that I foresee getting wet and know that this is an integral part of going out in the rain, one wonders if this isn't, for all practical purposes, a distinction without a difference.

All of which suggests an even more difficult problem. While it might be true that the doctor foresees yet doesn't intend the death of the patient in withdrawing treatment, how can this be said of the patient? How could a patient refuse life-sustaining treatment without in some manner intending to die? Yes, they may be intending to put an end to pain and suffering or to avoid treatment they do not prefer, but death is so integrally a part of any such outcome that it's hard to imagine how they merely foresee it without intending it. They certainly are not acting, as the doctor might be, on the principle of a patient's right to refuse physically invasive treatment. Though they may be availing themselves of this right, the right doesn't motivate their choices. It is not the end that they seek. However, if a patient cannot refuse such treatment without aiming to die, then from Keown's Buddhist vantage point, what the patient is doing is immoral insofar as he or she violates the First Precept against the intentional taking of life. Thus, the doctor is faced with the question: How can he or she morally assist the patient in committing an immoral act? In which case, many acts of treatment refusal would be immoral requests and no *right* to the refusal of life-sustaining treatment would exist. We would, in the words of the New York State Task Force, be faced with a "technological imperative" which would rule out the very exceptions that Keown himself favors.[43] Namely, those where we refrain from extraordinary measures to keep the patient alive in medically futile cases. As he says: *"it does not follow that there is a duty to go to extreme lengths to preserve life at all costs."*[44] I don't see how we can maintain the moral permissibility of some cases of allowing to die if we rule out all actions which have death as their aim.

If we do keep the intending/foreseeing distinction and claim the moral acceptability of some occasions of allowing to die, then we encounter another difficulty. There may be a strong case for some acts of PAS and VAE. Take for example, Dr. Timothy Quill's famous case of the patient Diane.[45] Diane was, by all accounts, an extremely lucid, reflective, and morally responsible leukemia patient, who after much thoughtful deliberation decided first, not to fight her disease in view of the uncertain benefits and tremendous suffering involved. Then, having considered the matter further and gone beyond the point where any treatment could have been effective, she requested assistance in ending her life before she and her family would be forced to endure the indignity and suffering of her death by leukemia. Quill, despite reluctance and protest, finally acceded to Diane's request and wrote her a prescription for the appropriate medication. In describing his thinking, Quill remarks that

> I wrote the prescription with an uneasy feeling about the boundaries I was exploring—spiritual, legal, professional, and personal. But I also felt strongly that I was setting her free to get the most out of the time she had left, and to maintain dignity and control on her own terms until her death.

At another point he remarks,

> it was also evident that the security of having enough barbiturates available to commit suicide when and if the time came would leave her secure enough to live fully and concentrate on the present.(252)

Whatever else we think of Quill's actions, it is clear that his deliberate aim here is not to end Diane's life. Indeed, while Quill could foresee the possibility that Diane would use the pills, it wasn't clear at the time that she would inevitably do so. And, in any case, he did not aim to bring about her use of the pills. His purpose was to restore a sense of dignity and control in Diane's life, that is to say, to enhance her present and remaining quality of life. In this sense, death is not "*willed either as a means or an end*" (173). Thus, for the same reasons that administering pain-killing yet life-shortening medication doesn't violate the First Precept, there is little reason to think that most cases of PAS would either (176). Both endeavor to "enhance through medical treatment the condition of the patient overall," in this case by writing a prescription.

What about cases of VAE? Could there be circumstances where such practices wouldn't, at least directly, violate the First Precept's prohibition on death intending action? Suppose an attending physician was to argue the following: In giving a life-ending injection, what I am doing is restoring some measure of control on the part of the patient. My overall aim is to bring peace, serenity, and a sense of autonomy in the midst of a dehumanizing condition. By complying with the patient's wishes I restore their sense of participation and control in their lives, and so enhance their remaining though admittedly brief period of existence. Of course, death results from such measures, but given the patient's overall condition and his or her values this is the only way to allow them to live to the fullest, to enhance their quality of remaining life. I can foresee their death as a result of my actions, but I aim for a very different end.

The only way to disqualify such an approach, I think, is to argue, as Dan Callahan has, against such a purpose as enhancing the life of the patient. Callahan argues that a doctor's job is to treat the patient's physical condition alone, not to "treat the patient's values." He remarks, "Medicine should try to relieve human suffering, but only that suffering which is brought on by illness and dying as biological phenomena, not that suffering which comes from anguish or despair at the human condition."[46] However well this may fit with traditional Western medicine and ethics, it does not represent a Buddhist approach. A sharp distinction between biology and phenomenology is not part of a Buddhist view, or, to put it differently Buddhism regards the body and the mind as experientially continuous, often speaking of the "body/mind" as one unit. Therefore, the idea that one can compartmentalize these issues would appear absurd. But equally, modern Western medicine has come to challenge such a view of the doctor's role. One does not have to be an advocate of "holistic medicine" to see the intimate connection between the patient's psychological and physical states.[47] To effectively treat a patient, one must also have the patient's confidence, and so one must always weigh treatment options in terms of the patient's sense of what is worthwhile. And once one considers such factors when weighing treatment options, one has started also "to treat the patient's values."

To conclude, even allowing for Keown's interpretation of the First Precept as prohibiting all actions that deliberately aim at death, given the way in which he interprets the word "intention," as well as his general rejection of what he calls "vitalism"—that is the attempt to keep the patient alive no matter what—I don't think he has made a strong case that all forms of PAS, VAE, and some forms of TR and TW are necessarily excluded as morally unacceptable. Those cases where one aims to compassionately enhance the patient's remaining quality of life by providing the means for meaningful participation in the act of dying do not represent a deliberate intention to kill. Death may be foreseen but not aimed at. In which case, such exceptional cases do not represent a violation of the First Precept and hence do not violate our former conclusion that "some forms of dying are best avoided if one can do so in accordance with other Buddhist values."

One final twist, even if PAS and VAE always violates the First Precept, they may yet provide a Buddhistically acceptable means to a mindful death. It is not clear that all forms of Buddhism are as committed to rule-following as Keown suggests. Suppose an act of VAE is the only means at one's disposal to a lucid and participatory death? Though the patient and the doctor directly aim at death, are their actions necessarily contradictory to the spirit of Buddhist law and ethics?

In order to fully answer this question, we must return to the basic principles and goods of Buddhism, and this is a large and complicated undertaking partly because such elements have never been formulated in any systematic or uniform fashion. The most basic goods found in all Buddhist texts typically number two: wisdom and compassion. Keown glosses these two goods as knowledge and friendship to which he adds a third, life. He bases this third good principally on the almost universal injunction of *ahimsa* or non-injury. And, of course, there is the First Precept which prohibits intentional killing. While I do not at this point want to engage in an analysis of early Buddhist sources in order to gauge the accuracy of Keown's claims, I do think it worth noting that non-injury, while supporting a general respect for life, does not make life an absolute value never subject to compromise, or death an absolute evil to be avoided at all costs. Keown, to be fair, recognizes this, arguing that a Buddhist respect for life is not equivalent to vitalism—life at all costs.[48] However, to claim, as he does, that non-injury means always refraining from killing is to beg the question in terms of the sorts of situations that we have been considering, namely those where the patient is undergoing great suffering and anguish. In fact, non-injury suggests that we must also consider the injury of requiring that such patients go on with their lives to the point of an incapacity that puts them on some form of life-support, and where they can be removed only if no one is directly "aiming at death" in so doing. To simply ignore the injury claims involved in such a course of action is to do something that seems equally non-Buddhist.

In any case, given the sorts of exceptions the Buddha was willing to make in the cases of Channa and Vakkali, one has to ask exactly what does the existence of a rule or precept suggest in Buddhist ethics. Certainly, when one turns to the Mahayana Buddhist tradition such as it is found in Japan or China, rule-following is at best morally problematic.[49] The problem is that rule-following substitutes obedience for moral judgment. To act mainly on the basis of judgment is always to act with an understanding of why one is doing or not doing whatever. And to understand requires that any rule or principle implied by one's behavior be simultaneously scrutinized for its provenance and suitability. Such deliberation gains its suasion from the depth of its reflective insights, not the steadfastness of the rules implicit therein.

Even from a more traditional Theravada perspective, however, it is not clear that rule-following is an absolute moral requirement. Again turning to Keown's analysis, he suggests that like all moral systems, early Buddhism recognizes a hierarchy of moral considerations, the bottom level of which is the body of rules and precepts that Buddhists are required to honor. Above these are the above-mentioned goods and values that are, in his view, largely unarticulated, at least in any systematic fashion. The fact that he locates the precepts at such a relatively low level of moral deliberation suggests that they are revisable in light of circumstances. Or, to put it differently, consideration of the meaning and significance of such higher order values as *ahimsa* with regard to such unusual cases as those of Channa and Vakkali, and perhaps terminally ill, suffering, and anguished patients, may require setting aside the generally serviceable First Precept.

## V

Thus, rule-following is not a slavish affair, and the status of the First Precept as an absolute moral command is certainly less than clear if one is talking of Buddhism as a whole. As a result, while Buddhism might always discourage abortion and assisted suicide, there is no blanket prohibition on each of these practices and perhaps even circumstances justifying them. All of which raises our original question: Is there any more substantive ethical insight which might establish what are allowable exceptions to rules such as the First Precept as well as point the way towards a principled response to the larger universe of biomedical problems looming on the horizon?

At most I can sketch the outlines of an answer. But we begin with what we have learned from the cases of abortion and assisted suicide. My reconstruction of a "liberal" Buddhist approach to these issues hinged on two elements: [1] Buddhism's understanding of the self, the doctrine of *anatta* in other words, and [2] Buddhism's emphasis on mindfulness in both life and death as well as the deep commitment to *ahimsa* or non-injury. With regard to abortion, [1] suggests that distinctively human life and the biological platform of life, whether purely genetic or embryonic, are different items. Human life is a composite of, yes, the body, but also consciousness, character, and so on—the five *skandhas*. Furthermore, there is no underlying identity or soul that binds these elements together or transmigrates through karma. The *skandhas* are an empty collection; that is, there is no underlying unity. Consequently, aborting a fetus before all the requisite elements are in place is not the ending of a human life because that life simply hasn't yet begun. With regard to suicide, assisted suicide, and voluntary active euthanasia, at least in some cases, [2] suggests that suicide may be necessary to a mindful death, again in very special circumstances, and to deny or impede such a course when it is in one's power may be to commit grave injury to such individuals. For a person whose continued illness and natural death may involve unimaginable suffering and indignity, actual participation and insight during the period of dying may be impossible. To insist on "living" in such conditions might suggest an inappropriate attachment to life if one is a committed Buddhist. To deny such individuals release would be to deny them expression of their religious views.

I have been calling such a position "liberal" because it suggests a tolerance of a similarly wide range of individual choices, and I have been reluctant to impose any *a priori* constraints on the range of acceptable choices consistent with Buddhist principles in the manner that Keown does. However, there is another sense in which such a position is liberal. Taking [1] and [2] above together, tends to suggest deference to the judgments of individuals in regard to their practice of Buddhist values. Correlatively, [1] and [2] also undermine the authority of rule-governed interpretive applications of Buddhist values and principles.

According to the Buddhist concept of the person, the individual is an association of features which is designated with a formal name for purposes of reference. However, Buddhism does not claim any underlying identity on which such an association hinges. As I argued earlier, I take this to be a more or less generic claim whatever tradition within the Buddhist umbrella one looks to, whether Theravada, Mahayana, or Vajrayana. To the further question, what brings these elements into association? the answer is that all elements dependently coarise, *pratitya samutpada*. In other words, the self, if one can call it that, is a composite entity like all others which is causally dependent on everything else. As a theory of action, this position suggests that whatever we do is ultimately attributable to the causal chains in which the elements that comprise us become associated in the specific ways that they do. To attribute our actions to a self or soul is, in fact, a mistake, if by that we mean some independently existing entity which, as it were, inhabits our bodies, habits and dispositions, feelings, thoughts, and so on. Of course, this doesn't mean we are not responsible for our actions. Our actions are attributable to us, to our character, feelings, unconscious dispositions, and so on. It is a theory of what individual responsibility means.[50] But this theory does tend to undermine a rule- or principle-oriented morality, what some have called an "ethic of justice."[51] What our responsibilities and obligations are will always be a highly situational matter dependent on those specific relationships that are constitutive of the composite self. Rules and principles will provide only very limited and incomplete guidance from a Buddhist perspective. Furthermore, without an independent self in which to vest moral authority or around which to construct a set of duties and obligations, a Buddhist normative perspective must emphasize the cultivation of character and judgment, a moral persona, as do most East and South Asian moral traditions I might add. Notably, character and judgment are by their very nature a kind of sensitivity to context rather than a consciousness of rules and principles. As Aristotle observed long ago, one can be conscious of a rule and lack the judgment and character to see it through in practice or to apply it properly.

This is not to say, however, that Buddhism lacks a conception of individual liberty or freedom. The individual as a composite, is not only morally responsible for action, but equally, responsible for the achievement of enlightenment and the relief of suffering. Ultimately Buddhism set these as its highest goals, and while I don't think this necessarily makes Buddhism a goal-oriented sort of utilitarianism, it does raise the same question one finds in utilitarian discussions: Who is best in a position to realize the exact or specific nature of these goals? Different versions of Buddhism give slightly different answers to these questions although certain general patterns emerge. In answer to the question of individual enlightenment, the answer is the individual in association with a teacher and religious community although, again, the importance of the individual's own recognition of nirvana is emphasized in all Buddhist meditational practices. In answer to the question regarding what constitutes the relief of suffering, for whom, and according to whom, the answer is again the individual albeit in a specific communal context. Furthermore, particularly in the case of enlightenment, its attainment is not a rule-governed or works-dependent affair, but something spontaneous and unique, specific and contextual, especially specific to the meditational practices of a particular individual.[52] In short, given the dependently co-arisen nature of things, such moments cannot be understood as predictable outcomes, but as highly specific individual events that entirely depend on a unique confluence of circumstances. Therefore, only the individual-in-context can enter enlightenment or accomplish the relief of suffering—good works. Which further suggests, only the individual can know or appreciate the nature of such goods. Hence, one can in the manner of Mill, argue for the necessity of a strong conception of individual liberty as the only ground on which the good can be realized for each and thus collectively. Freedom for the unique operation of our own constituting *skandhas*, in such a way that we do the good and attain nirvana, is the ultimate basis for the realization of Buddhist dharma, in other words.

Given such a moral theory, it is not surprising that rather than articulating moral principles and rules, much of Buddhist ethics speaks in terms of goods and virtues such as compassion and sincerity,[53] for it is these, rather than rules, that structure our individualized capacity for moral judgment. This is, of course, not to deny the existence of precepts and so on, but as Keown himself suggests, these are not the major preoccupation of Buddhist ethical discussions. This is especially so as one moves out of the Theravada tradition and into the later Mahayana, especially the Japanese forms of Zen and Pure Land. If morality is constituted within the space of unique circumstances bearing on individual judgment and discretion, then what matters most is the moral fiber and standpoint of the one doing the judging, not the rules on which judgment relies, which are, at best, only rules of thumb.

## Notes

1. See David Van Biema's article "The Americanization of Buddhism" in *Time Magazine* 150 (October 13, 1997). Thich Nat Han, the well-known Vietnamese Buddhist monk, has consistently maintained that Buddhism does not demand that one convert by renouncing one's previous religious convictions.

2. For example, Philip Kapleau or Robert Aiken as chronicled in Ken Jones, *The Social Face of Buddhism* (London: Wisdom Publications, 1989). For Japanese Buddhism's view of abortion see William R. LaFleur, *Liquid Life: Abortion and Buddhism and Japan* (Princeton, N.J.: Princeton University Press, 1992).

3. Damien Keown, *Buddhism and Bioethics* (London: Macmillan, 1995).

4. See Keown, xiv-xv where he gives a defense of his interpretive approach to Buddhism. While there is certainly nothing wrong with attempting to discover the scriptural basis of a religious tradition, it does tend to perhaps unduly weight the Theravada side of Buddhism which tends to be more textual and canonical than the Mahayana side where one finds, for example, the *Ch'an/Zen* tradition of antitextualism. As Mahayana Buddhism accounts for much of the tradition both ancient and modern, Keown's approach rather undermines his claim to speak authoritatively for Buddhists generally.

5. In the *Milindapanha* selection, "There is no Ego," as translated by Henry Clarke Warren in *Buddhism, In Translations* (New York: Atheneum, 1974; originally Harvard University Press, 1896), 133, we read: "When the Groups appear to view / We use the phrase, 'A living being'."

6. Of course, this doesn't exclude the possibility that there might be beings, perhaps not 'living' ones in the full sense, which lack *vinnana*. The substance of Keown's claim here is simply that if one has *vinnana*, then one is living; it doesn't tell you anything about the case where one lacks *vinnana*. Indeed, I argue further on that it is just such a possibility that makes abortion and perhaps some forms of euthanasia acceptable from a Buddhist standpoint.

7. Keown 1995, 36. All quotes in the following section are from this source and will be noted as page numbers in the text.

8. *Visuddhi-Magga*, chap. xiv, translated in Warren, 157.

9. *Milindapanha*, 25, translated in Warren 131-3.

10. *Milindapanha*, 71, translated in Warren 234-8. The question raised in this passage is how "rebirth takes place without anything transmigrating." The answer is essentially that nothing is continuous from one life to another, nonetheless lives may be causally linked so that "one is not freed from one's evil deeds." That is, just because you die, it doesn't mean that you cannot be held accountable for your actions and their future effects. Karma is real though one's personal existence is inherently limited. This is why I suggested before that early Buddhism does not have a 'theory of rebirth'; there is nothing to be reborn. But the doctrine of karma is even stiffer therefore: you are immediately responsible for the full effects of your actions no matter how far in the future they extend.

11. The tendency to substantialize the ego has been a persistent problem in Buddhism prompting much soul-searching critique (no pun intended) as for example on the part of the Madhyamika.

12. Compare with Dogen's discussion in the *Genjokoan* fascicle of the *Shobogenzo* where he states with regard to firewood, for example, "one should not take the view that it is ashes *afterward* and firewood *before*" (Norman Waddell and Masao Abe, "Shobogenzo Genjokoan," *The Eastern Buddhist* 5 (October 1972) 129-140). For Dogen this is the nature of all processes: none requires a subsistent and transforming element to tie the process together as a whole. Such a view contrasts sharply with Keown's portrayal of *vinnana* as "dynamically involved in all experience whether physical or intellectual" (Keown 26).

13. Although he does make room for cases where fertilization occurs but the intermediate being does not descend, in the case of twinning for example.

14. Keown announces early on in the book his intention to draw out and exploit such similarities arguing that Buddhism is itself a natural law approach to ethics. See xi-xii in the introduction.

15. Keown considers a somewhat analogous position advanced by Louis van Loon, see Keown 143-4. Van Loon supports a "higher-brain" definition of death thus equating an individual human life to that of the volitional self. Keown rejects this as not authentically Buddhist arguing that the capacity involved, *cetana*, is a higher mental function than the more basic *vinnana* and so possibly absent despite the presence of the latter. I too would tend to reject van Loon's position as volition and consciousness need not be the same thing, the latter being more basic than the former, so that someone could be conscious without will. Even better as a definitional criterion would be the "developed capacity for consciousness."

16. This parallels the attempt to define the beginning of life by reference to brain death. If cessation of a certain level of brain activity signals death, then doesn't its presence signal life? Hence, we have a nonarbitrary criterion for when life begins. The problem with this reasoning is that brain activity is, incontestably anyhow, only a necessary but not a sufficient condition for life. See Baruch Brody, *Abortion and the Sanctity of Life* (Cambridge, Mass.: The MIT Press, 1975) and Bonnie Steinbock's rebuttal in *Life Before Birth: The Moral and Legal Status of Embryos and Fetuses* (Oxford, U.K.: Oxford University Press, 1992) which also appears in a shortened version in John D. Arras and Bonnie Steinbock, *Ethical Issues in Modern Medicine*, 4 ed. (Mountain View, Calif.: Mayfield Publishing Company, 1995) 329-43.

17. Keown 158-68.

18. This may be the pitfall in going to *cases* rather than principles in the early scriptures to work out a Buddhist view.

19. See William R. LaFleur's discussion of what he calls "fecundism" in Japanese culture, particularly its military ramifications. LaFleur, 131-4, 206-10.

20. See Steinbock in Steinbock and Arras, *Life Before Birth*, (note 15), 337.

21. Keown himself echoes this point in his analysis of an implicit hierarchical ordering of life in Buddhism. Keown argues that the capacity to attain nirvana and enlightenment is the relevant criterion. Since humans are much further along the karmic path than animals in this respect, their lives are all that much more valuable. See Keown, "Karmic Life," 46-8.

22. By the "developed capacity for consciousness" I mean the capacity for consciousness that, of course, we possess even when asleep or otherwise temporarily unconscious.

23. That is, Buddhism denies the existence of a soul or other metaphysical and abstract entity on the grounds that it is a construction (*vikalpa*) out of phenomenal experience and a mere convenience. See *Milindapanha* 25 in Warren under the title "There is no Ego," 129-33.

24. See LaFleur 169-70. Although Japanese Buddhism is Mahayana, and Keown makes much of the differences between Japanese and other forms of Asian Buddhism, the sentiments expressed in this passage do not appeal to anything overtly Mahayana or Japanese. The principles expressed seem very generically Buddhist.

25. Damien Keown, "Suicide, Assisted Suicide, and Euthanasia: A Buddhist Perspective," *Journal of Law and Religion* 13, no. 2 (1998), 385-405; See Chapter Ten of this volume.

26. Keown 1998.

27. Keown 1998, 405.

28. Buddhists can claim no authoritative textual sources and Ch'an and Zen even reject the value of texts altogether preferring koan practice and zazen ("just sitting").

29. Keown, 1998, 17.

30. Keown 1998, 397.

31. See Keown's *The Nature of Buddhist Ethics* (London: Macmillan, 1992).

32. D.T. Suzuki, "The Zen Sect of Buddhism (1906)" in *Studies in Zen* edited with a forward by Christmas Humphreys (New York: Dell Publishing, 1955), 15.

33. Keiji Nishitani, *Religion and Nothingness*, translated with an Introduction by Jan Van Bragt (Berkeley: University of California Press, 1982), 20-21.

34. From the *Maha-Paranibbana-Sutta* (v and vi) of the *Digha-Nikaya* in Warren, *Op. Cit.*, 107.

35. Damien Keown, "Suicide, Assisted Suicide, and Euthanasia: A Buddhist Perspective" in chapter ten of this volume, 277.

36. Keown, 278.

37. Keown *Buddhism and Bioethics*, 179-180.

38. See Dan Brock, "Voluntary Active Euthanasia," *Hastings Center Report* (March-April 1992): 10-22.

39. James Rachels, "Active and Passive Euthanasia," *The New England Journal of Medicine* 292 (January 9, 1975): 78-80.

40. Keown, *Buddhism and Bioethics*, 173.

41. Keown, *Buddhism and Bioethics,* 176.

42. Keown, *Buddhism and Bioethics,* 175.

43. See The New York State Task Force on Life and the Law's report on PAS in Arras and Steinbock *Ethical Issues in Modern Medicine*, 266-273.

44. Keown, *Buddhism and Bioethics*, 167.

45. See Quill, Timothy E., "Death and Dignity: A Case of Individualized Decision Making." *The New England Journal of Medicine* 324 (1991): 691-694.

46. Daniel Callahan, "When Self-Determination Runs Amok," *Hastings Center Report* 22, no. 2 (March-April 1992): 52-5.

47. As even a cursory glance will reveal, a great deal of research is currently being devoted to the link between immune response and psychological well-being. For an entire website devoted to this topic see the American Institute of Stress <www.stress.org>.

48. Keown, *Buddhism and Bioethics*, 42 ff.

49. It is a very long and complicated story to establish the viability of such an interpretation of Mahayana ethics. However, superficially two sources readily suggest such an interpretation. On the one hand, the *dyana* elements of the tradition sport open hostility to rule-governed thinking. Take for example, the Zen claim that if one meets the Buddha one is to kill the Buddha. I take the sense to be that to meet the Buddha would require that Buddha-nature be conceived of as thing-like and determinate, rather than pure enlightenment. Hence, one cannot meet the Buddha or Truth in the largest sense. The other concerns the doctrine of *upaya* or skillful means. Above all, Buddhist instruction requires tailoring a message that fits the level of the listener rather than advancing pat formulas. For a discussion of this point see Christopher C. Ives, *Zen Awakening and Society* (Honolulu: University of Hawaii Press, 1992), especially Chapters 1 and 2 or Part III of Thomas P. Kasulis's book *Zen Action/Zen Person* (Honoulu: University of Hawaii Press, 1981).

50. The Buddhist position shares much in common with David Hume. See his essay in *An Enquiry Concerning Human Understanding* (Indianapolis: Hackett, 1977), "Of Liberty and Necessity" and Derek Parfit's version of reductionism in *Reasons and Persons* (Oxford, U.K.: Oxford University Press, 1984).

51. On this distinction, see for example Nel Noddings, *Caring: A Feminine Approach to Ethics and Moral Education* (Berkeley: University of California Press, 1984) or Joan Tronto, *Moral Boundaries: A Political Argument for an Ethic of Care* (New York: Routledge, 1993).

52. This is especially so in a Ch'an or Zen context where the koan or "just sitting" is the preferred method of enlightenment.

53. See Yoshifumi Ueda and Dennis Hirota, *Shinran: An Introduction to His Thought* (Kyoto: Hongwanji International Center, 1989).. Shinran, as well as much of the Buddhist tradition, argue that rules get in the way of enlightenment, and therefore the good I would argue. Shinran calls the application of rules, calculating, and warns strongly against relying on our powers of calculation in achieving nirvana. As nirvana is the highest of all values in Buddhism, the good itself is beyond calculation and dependent on highly individualized enlightenment. See especially Shinran's discussion in "Self Power, Other Power," 219-220.

*Chapter Twelve*

# Good Clinical Practice? Can East Asia Accommodate Western Standards?

**Carl B. Becker**

## Introduction

Over the past several years, a series of meetings in the United States, the European Union, and East Asia have worked towards the establishment of common standards for good clinical practice (often abbreviated GCP). The International Conference on Harmonization of Technical Requirements for the Registration of Pharmaceuticals for Human Use (hereafter ICH), based in Geneva, Switzerland, is the driving force behind this project. If successful, this project could expedite the study and sales of drugs from one country to another, reducing trade friction and obviating the duplication of research. However, there are a number of ethical and cultural problems lurking just under the surface of this project, particularly outside of the Euro-American context.

This chapter takes the latest available (1996) guidelines as one paradigm epitomizing the kinds of values that any ethical practitioner or researcher should be expected to follow.[1] The ICH GCP guidelines are not theories of armchair philosophers; they are the best efforts of some of the top legal minds in medicine and some of the most medically-minded government officials to hammer out a common ground of agreement for clinical trials and practices for many years to come. Because they are the basis of future policy, they are taken extremely seriously, and I do not mean to make light of them in any way. Rather, it is precisely because of their weight and importance that they serve to highlight some of the difficulties that their application to East Asia may face.

As a philosopher researching and teaching medical ethics and terminal care for many years in Japan, I am keenly aware of the kinds of difficulties we encounter in trying to relate Western European or American ideals with those of East Asia. I hope that my pointing up some of these cultural and ethical difficulties will lead to their resolution, and avoid larger problems that will lurk in the future if these issues are not recognized now. At the same time, I hope we can avoid a blanket imperialist imposition of Western standards and values on Asian cultures whose standards and values have enabled them to operate with great harmony and continuity for thousands of years.

This chapter has three parts. Part 1 sketches six broad ethical rules of East Asian society that should affect the application of ethical guidelines to the field of medicine in East Asia. Part 2 discusses the implications of these rules for the ICH-GCP Guidelines, and Part 3 picks up some concerns that are not yet directly addressed in the GCP Guidelines.

## Part 1: Ethical Rules of East Asian Societies

The Ethics of East Asia are not written in a single book like the Bible, but are taught and obeyed by their societies with at least as much rigor as any commandments in Islam. There is no time to footnote the thousands of examples of ethics in the history and literature of East Asia; I shall provide contemporary examples as they apply to our ICH project. For brevity and clarity, some generalization is inescapable; I shall use the word "we" to refer to the East Asian position. Young people and young companies may be exceptions, but the larger corporations, government and medical establishment, and larger drug consumers (elders) are likely to subscribe to the following ethical rules:

*Interdependence over Independence*

The idea that people could be "independent" is nonsense in crowded East Asia. The air I breathe is air you just breathed; the food I consume is food you cannot consume; no human can live without depending on a complex social network. Given a choice, we favor our families over strangers, countrymen over foreigners, colleagues over rivals, our own university graduates and members of our own professional organizations over other schools and organizations. We give business to the people we know, and we periodically exchange gifts in recognition of favors rendered. In the West, this has been misunderstood as "bribery" or "kickbacks;" but East Asians who fail to thank the people to whom they owe favors will not long be respected as adults.

*Hierarchy over Equality*

Equality is unthinkable. No two people have equal histories, abilities, or responses; even twins are elder and younger. The very structure of Korean and Japanese languages demands that we think that older is superior and newer is inferior, just as English demands identification of singulars and plurals. In the Korean and Japanese languages, the raising of questions is tantamount to challenging the authority of the listener. However, defiance of authority is unacceptable. In short, we should not question our superiors. That means that patients in hospitals should not question doctors, and employees in corporations should not question their bosses. Of course there are times when we do not believe our doctors or agree with our bosses, but since we cannot question them directly, we practice hidden disobedience (*mokusatsu*)

*Obligations over Rights*

The words as well as concepts of "rights" were introduced to East Asian languages in this century, but are not intuitively understood. Rather, our duties, to our families, to our superiors, to our groups, and so on are clear, as are the obligations of our juniors, students, and children, to us. We are very unclear about what is meant by "rights," how anyone could possibly prove that they "have" rights, or how they could be enforced even if they were imagined to exist. The idea of "rights" presupposes that people have invisible private "territories" whereas in East Asia, people's "territories" overlap. Nothing belongs to us privately except the thoughts which we never voice; words and deeds are all potentially public.

*Others over Self*

Decisions are never made in a vacuum. When a decision is to be made, we first consult precedent, and if there is a precedent, we follow it. If there is no precedent, we consult our seniors or colleagues, and follow their advice. At restaurants, we either order whatever our superiors order, or ask the cook to make us whatever he likes. Participation in decision-making is almost unknown, except in small committees, and even there, great pains are taken to ascertain what others will think before any opinions are expressed. Town meetings, faculty meetings, PTA meetings, and the like, are essentially places where decisions already made by authorities behind the scenes are announced and rubber-stamped by the silent majority who attend. Even in the rare cases where contrary opinions are voiced, decisions are never overturned at public meetings. We take pains not to offend others, and others take pains not to offend us. We flow with the trends rather than asserting personal preferences. Individuals who speak out are subject either to ostracism or to being laden with heavy workloads.

*Harmony over Confrontation; Resignation over Protest*

People in every society disagree sometimes. Some Western societies uphold the "right" to disagree, and value the clarification of differences in the search for "the truth." In our traditionally crowded East Asian societies, silence is golden; "not making waves," "not losing face," "not rocking the boat," "not sticking out" is critically important. It is far better to lie to avoid hurting someone than to tell the truth and risk hurting him or her. Protecting others is more important than truth-telling or full disclosure. When we have disagreements, we try to keep them to ourselves.

*Stability of Form over Change*
We like to know where we stand, and what assures us of our standing is tradition rather than law. Once precedents are established, they cannot be readily changed. Stability is preferred to experimentation in societies where the maximum supportable populations have already been reached and any crop failure could mean starvation for a whole village. When in doubt, inaction is preferable to action, as is seen in Confucius' golden rule: Don't do anything you might not want done to yourself. When new programs or policies are undertaken, they become precedents to be followed. This is one reason volunteerism is so difficult in East Asia; once we have volunteered, we must continue in that volunteer activity indefinitely. Our preference for formal stability also leads us to subvert or reinterpret laws rather than amending them, to follow prescribed forms rather than introducing creative deviations. Of course these are not the only rules of Asian ethics, nor can they be summarized in such few words. And some of these rules may apply to other societies to lesser degrees. In any case, if we ignore these rules, we cannot operate as adults in East Asian society.

## Part 2: Ethical Implications

Now let us apply the above ethical principles to some of the key points in the ICH-GCP Guidelines.

*Independent Monitoring*
Central to the effectiveness of the guidelines are conceptions like the "Independent Data Monitoring Committee" (1.25), "Impartial Witness" (1.26), "IRB/IEC" (Institutional Review Board / Independent Ethics Committee) (3), and "Third-party Monitoring and Auditing" (5.18, 5.19). However, "independence" is unacceptable to East Asian laboratories and hospitals. We should influence the selection of committee members so that we know them, and/or host and thank them in such ways that they would become morally bound to accept our procedures and reports. We shall oppose letting non-scientists onto scientific boards (cf. 2.6, 3.1.6), and even if they are allowed onto ethics boards, they will not have the power or authority to influence the majority of the scientists on any given board.

If *truly* independent third-party monitors are found, we shall tell them what they want to hear, report what they want to read, show them what they want to see, and carry on with our own work as we see fit. It takes hundreds if not thousands of casualties and over ten years before any authorities detect cases of mercury-pollution poisoning or the use of HIV-infected blood, so our profits from noncompliance may easily outweigh our risks of detection or prosecution. ICH guidelines (3.3.8) specify that ADRs (adverse drug reaction) which are serious and unexpected are to be reported, but this allows the doctor to judge either that an ADR was not serious or that it was in some sense expected, and thus to avoid reporting it. Even in the West, the effectiveness of IRBs is being questioned;[2] in the East, we should coopt or emasculate them before they can affect our activity.

*Informed Consent*

Informed Consent[3] is a second conception central to the testing of pharmaceuticals. But informed consent is problematic even in the West,[4] and undesirable if not impossible in the Far East.[5] Informed consent presupposes both the ability and desire to use information to make decisions about one's own health. Not only do we lack practice in such decision-making, but also it would be inconceivable for us to defy our doctor's intentions or seek an unrelated doctor's opinion. In fact, a research project at Waseda University is discovering that the more information Japanese patients are given, the more strongly they ask their doctors to decide for them and tell them what to do. ICH protocols try to protect "vulnerable subjects" (1.61), but in Asia, every patient is a member of hierarchies. The ICH definition itself recognizes that members of hierarchies are in vulnerable positions, but fails to recognize that this affects every East Asian patient. Protocol 2.3 suggests that the rights and well-being of trial subjects should prevail over the interests of society, but this runs directly counter to our ethical rule that the well-being of the group overrules individual well-being, and an individual almost never wins over a group or corporation when it comes to an Asian court of law.

*Doctor-Patient Communication*

Section 4.3.4 adds that investigators should try to find the reasons for subjects' withdrawal from projects. In our society, however, overt withdrawal from an agreement is virtually unthinkable. Although we may privately trash the medicines given to us or avoid taking them on schedule, we shall rarely admit this to any doctor or inspector. Thus, the doctor's best attempts to "check that each subject is following the instructions promptly" (4.6.6) will find only what the patients think the doctor wants to be told. Moreover, in our language and culture, giving the doctor or inspector the right to ask us why we refuse is tantamount to giving them the right to pressure us back into the experiment, at least superficially. If patients are fairly informed that the medicines they are about to take involve research, all but the most vulnerable subjects will refuse to use the medicines. On the other hand, the doctors' efforts to recruit test subjects may easily result in "undue influence."

*Documentation*

The fact that test protocols are "documented" (5.1.4 "Agreements in Writing") and "signed" by the participants has little meaning as written contracts are pro forma, and fewer people read or value them. When our boss or landlord asks us to initial a contract, we initial it without reading, out of trust in the boss or landlord; to read or question the contract would show a tactless lack of respect. Regardless of the wording on the contract, problems that arise will be settled by interpersonal negotiation thereafter, not by courts of law relying on the wording of the contract.

Much documentation in Japan follows forms without revealing content. This is obvious in the abstracts of articles presented in professional journals and conferences: they purport to show who did what, but fail to show the outcomes much less the implications or significance of the outcomes. So merely demanding written forms (4.11) will not in itself improve reliability.

*Enforcement*

The ICH guidelines specify that "Noncompliance leads to termination" (5.20), but the severer the consequences of discovery, the less likely anyone will reveal noncompliance, for whistleblowing is an offense punishable by ostracism from this society. In the entire 50 years of postwar Japanese legal history, there have been only a handful of events in which subordinates have testified against superiors in medical settings. In the 1968 heart transplant case against Wada of Sapporo Medical University, not a single subordinate could be found to remember the details of the homicide that Wada had unmistakably perpetrated. In 1977, the Juzenkai Medical Group sued its whistle-blowing employees for defamation, and the Kyoto Court ruled in favor of the Juzenkai: although the whistleblowers' claims were reasonable, they were not to protest their superiors' procedures. (1977.7.29) While the Osaka District Court reversed the decision (1977.9.26), and the Supreme Court ultimately supported the Osaka Court, the debatability of whistleblowing remains very high. In other cases of whistleblowing, theYamaguchi Court ruling on Chugoku Denryoku (1970. 12.3) and the Tokyo Court ruling on Teikoku Zohin Pharmaceuticals (1993.9.29) found essentially that companies could transfer whistleblowing employees anywhere, at any time, reaffirming the corporate authority over unwanted revelations from employees who did not tow the company line. Most recently, in the case of euthanasia admittedly committed by the director of Keihoku Hospital (Yamanaka), the whistleblowing nurses have been restricted to anonymous phone calls, face-covered and voice-distorted reporting, for if they are identified, they will find themselves unemployable in this society. In the context of ICH enforcement, only a very bold and foolish investigator would risk his future for the sake of publicly pointing out problems in the operation of a prestigious or expensive drug trial.

*Security of Information*

Security of Information (5.5.3) is rightfully a concern of the ICH, but in Asia, the notion of intellectual property is still far from well understood. Japanese law presently requires disclosure of details on foreign cosmetics and pharmaceuticals tantamount to a recipe for remaking the compounds within Japan. The copying of whole books and dubbing of rental CDs in Japan, and the pirating of computer programs in China may be beyond the power of governments to stop, particularly since the public tends to prefer pirated over legitimate copies.

By the same token, people with access to classified information are not only capable of modifying it (since virtually no Asian computer systems use sophisticated security measures), but more seriously, of clandestinely selling the information to interested buyers or competitors. Both drugs themselves and the information used in their manufacture may be channeled through dummy corporations or political fronts for monetary gain, as in the case of Kotaro Kanpo Seiyaku, where the Osaka Court (1970.10.22) determined that imports from the PRC (People's Republic of China) had been connected with the Japanese Communist Party.

*Quality Control*

While not precisely an area of ethics, quality control deserves careful consideration in the context of international pharmaceutical production, for if it is not maintained, the results may be disastrous for the consumer. It is well known that hygienic standards vary greatly from country to country in Asia (Kang-Yum). In many American states, for example, tap water is regulated for more than 30 chemicals; in Japan, for less than a third of that number, and to a weaker standard; in many parts of China, water is not regulated at all. Particulate air pollution is particularly high in China during the spring, when wind-borne soil is carried as far east as Japan, but China's laxer standards for air pollution also lead to higher quantities of particulates in manufacturing districts. Differences in education, cooking methods, and even toilet etiquette also affect each culture's notion of cleanliness. In turn, this may increase not only the percentage of contaminated products during manufacture, but also the risk of complications when a given drug is being tested on a local population.

Even in Europe, for example, one CFTR (Cystic Fibrosis Transmembrane Conductance Regulator) quality control study found only 62% of the 40 laboratories consulted could correctly identify 9 out of 9 samples, and only 2 out of 9 samples were correctly typed in all 40 labs.[6] Another study elicited responses from only 3 out of 16 Japanese corporations on in vivo cell mutation, and less than half of Japanese companies routinely repeated genotoxicity tests.[7] Of even greater suspicion is the fact that most Japanese companies respond "in strict accordance with JMWH guidelines,"[8] which may tell us more about the way Japanese companies reply to questionnaires than about their actual clinical practices. (As a civil servant, I am aware of countless instances where the documents submitted to higher authorities reflect what the higher authorities expect to see, rather than the actual status of the project in question.) So quality control involves issues not only of cost and education, but also of accurate information-gathering, which may again entail the problems noted in D and E above.

## Part 3: Additional Problems Not Directly Addressed in Guidelines

*Overprescription, Lack of Cross-Checks for Drug Interactions*

Japanese doctors receive an average of 40% of their income from drug sales and prescriptions. Most of their information about drug effectiveness comes from the advertisements of pharmaceutical manufacturers themselves. Even when they consult medical journals, most of their Japanese-language journals are not carefully peer-reviewed and lack critical comparisons.[9]

One problem is that the effectiveness and contraindications of the drugs themselves may not be adequately known. Another is that the drugs are prescribed in improper doses or for inappropriate symptoms. A third problem is that Asian doctors and pharmacists almost never investigate the interactions which inevitably occur among the variety of prescription drugs, over-the-counter remedies, and dietary habits of each patient.

In order to test the effectiveness of any new drug, however, we must have a clear understanding of what other drugs and even diet each patient already takes. Conversely, even a drug which appears safe in country A may show dangerous side-effects when mixed with foodstuffs or other medicines common in country B. Our international drug testing (including distribution and marketing) must be continually conscious of these cultural differences.

*Differences between Patients*

If we are going to use Chinese patients to test drugs going to a German market, or French patients for drugs coming to Japan, the differences of patient response to the drugs, and the differences of desired healthy "ideals" will play a significant role. Oriental patients show minor but possibly significant differences, both genetically, and in terms of diet and lifestyle, from their European or American peers. They have different consumption of salt and cholesterol, different tolerances for alcohol and lactose, and different intestinal length and flora. They exercise differently, using different muscle groups at different hours in their slightly different circadian rhythms. Moreover, the blood pressures, body temperatures, blood tests, and regularity of evacuation considered "ideal" for Japanese are all different from those considered "ideal" for a German or an American. So while a Japanese doctor might medicate his patient to move blood pressure in one direction, a German doctor might medicate the same patient to move it in the opposite direction. The schedule of a constipated American may be considered regular for a Japanese, who would treat American "regularity" as irritable bowel syndrome. All of these differences of life-style and cultural ideals need to be contemplated in our discussion of testing and application of international standards.

Another whole set of issues involves the autonomy, trust, and disobedience of patients. In America, my doctor would tell me my alternatives in treatment and ask me my choice; thereafter, I would not hesitate to tell my doctor that a drug disagreed with me and I had consulted another specialist. In Japan, my doctor rarely tells me even the most basic information about my condition unless I pry it out of him in a most un-Japanese fashion, and I dare not tell him that I stopped taking the medicine he prescribed, much less that I even contemplated going elsewhere for consultation.

Yet another factor is patient trust or distrust in the physician. NHK (Japan National TV) surveys have shown that doctors themselves have very low faith in their therapies and in each other.[10] This is reflected in a relatively high public skepticism of doctors in Japan. It would be interesting and valuable to obtain information about differences in placebo effects in East and West, for these will affect not only the testing of drugs (with lower results when the patients know the drug is still in testing stages), but also the efficacy of marketed drugs prescribed by doctors. Here again, we must be wary about blanket generalization from one culture to another.

*Differences in Government Structure and International Cooperation*
Most governments in Asia have not yet unified standards for the labeling of drugs, in terms of ingredients, dosages, warnings, purity, and expiration dates. To quote Masanori Fukushima of the Aichi Cancer Center in Nagoya,

> The ministry is hopelessly understaffed (only 20 qualified full time staff assessing clinical trials), academic standards among Japanese medical researchers are low, and there is a clear conflict of interest in the way drug companies sponsor the doctors who carry out their safety tests. . . . Unable to process the data itself, the ministry farms the job of testing new jobs to committees . . . some work for research foundations funded by the companies that wish to market the drugs they are testing.[11]

Government officials frequently retire to positions of authority in private firms, as in the HIV serum case now going to court, or accept the word of one university professor over another in reaching a decision, as in the case of the Minamata mercury poisoning. Government funding is rarely available for more than a year at a time, so there is undue pressure to design and conduct tests that can be completed within a year.

Furthermore, no intergovernmental mechanisms have yet been established for the exchange of information on pharmaceuticals between governments. In the case of narcotics abuse, for example, judicial assistance policies enable a government to use letters and commissions rogatories to subpoena foreign evidence. But there are governments present that do not cooperate fully with such procedures. Can procedures of information exchange be established and enforced in the case of pharmaceutical manufacture and testing?

Imagine, for example, that country A's tests proclaim a drug to be effective and safe against a certain disease, and that its industry exports the drug to country B for substantial profits. Then imagine that country B's patients suffer serious side effects. What kinds of information will country B be able to receive from country A's manufacturer or testing organization? And given the present political situation, what kind of compensation will country B's patients be able to receive from country A's manufacturer or testing organization? It is hardly conceivable that a developing country's manufacturer would pay the kinds of sums demanded by an American court settlement, or that Americans would pay large sums to a class action case decided in a Chinese court. In short, legal as well as economic arrangements for the limitation of compensations must be contemplated On the other hand, such limitations will encourage profit-minded corporations to market drugs without fear of substantial losses in the case of inadequate testing.

What shall be the legal requirement on each member state and/or corporation? What kinds of controls can be enforced for the contribution or "free-riding" of one country on another's development costs? What kinds of quality control can be enforced in both manufacture and transportation of pharmaceuticals? These are all questions that are not answered directly by the ethics of any single culture, but which demand response before the ICH's dream of harmonization of technical requirements can be practicable.

## Summary

For the sake of all countries involved, international standards on drug testing and manufacture are highly desirable. We have seen, however, that cultural and ethical barriers stand in the way of immediate implementation. Simply to impose the ICH guidelines on all the member countries will blind us to many of the problems lurking under the surface. On the other hand, blanket imposition of strict Western standards to overrule a set of cultural differences not only ignores the value of the ethics already functioning in any given culture, but fails to recognize their interdependence. It is a bit like killing one kind of "weed" with a specific poison, and failing to recognize the many ways other insects and animals may be affected by the loss of that single plant.

In short, any attempt to operate within a very different culture has to have a sensitivity, not only to the prevailing cultural practices and ethics already functioning in that culture, but to the multiple ramifications of its "new" policies for those who may try to adopt it. Even now, I run the risk of offending my Japanese colleagues just in writing this chapter. Then how much greater the risk for someone who attempted to criticize or inspect his countrymen's research. While hoping that viable standards can be not only discovered but embraced, I question the extent to which legal contracts and independent inspection can enable this to happen.

The above discussion should point out, not only that Western ethical standards may be difficult to apply to East Asian medical situations, but also that even within the Western position, the opportunities for abusing ethical standards by taking advantage of ethical "loopholes" in other cultures are legion. While consistency of philosophical principles is a goal most worthy of pursuit, we should not allow it to blind us to the fundamental differences in the value priorities of different cultures.

## Notes

1. ICH EWG E6: *Good Clinical Practice: Consolidated Guideline*, 1 May, 1996.
2. H. Edgar and D.J. Rothman, "The Institutional Review Board and Beyond," *Millbank Quarterly*. 73, no. 4 (1995): 489-506.
3. See ICH EWG, 1.28, 2.6, 4.8.
4. B.J. Culliton, "Illuminating Informed Consent," *Natural Medicine*. 1:11 (Nov. 1995), 1099 and S.B. Dowd and B. Wilson, "Informed Patient Consent," *Radiology Technology* 67, no. 2 (Nov.-Dec. 1995): 119-124.
5. H. Hattori et al. "The Patient's Right to Information in Japan," *Social Science and Medicine*. 32, no. 9 (1991), 1007-1016 and Kenji Nagayama, et al. "Informed Consent from Psychotic Patients with Cancer Regarding Surgical Operation," *Seishin Igaku / Clinical Psychiatry*. 36, no. 6 (June 1994): 625-632.
6. H. Cuppens, and J.J. Cassiman, "A Quality Control Study of CFTR Mutation Screening in 40 Different European Laboratories," *European Journal of Human Genetics* 3, no. 4 (1995): 235-245. CFTR is the a protein much researched in inherited cystic fibrosis of the pancreas. It is widely known and used in clinical studies, whence the surprise at its misidentification.
7. Delphine Purves, et al. "Genotoxicity Testing: Current Practices and Strategies," *Mutagenesis*. 10, no. 4 (July 1995): 297-312.
8. Purves, 304.
9. Robert Guest, "Japan Criticised for Unsafe Drug Licenses," *BMJ*. 311, no. 7019 (Dec. 9, 1995): 1521-1522.
10. cf. S. Fukuhara and A. Asai, "Attitudes of Japanese and Japanese-American Physicians Towards Life-Sustaining Treatment," *Lancet* 346, no. 8971 (Aug. 5, 1995): 327-328.
11. Guest, "Japan Criticised," 1521.

# Selected Bibliography


Almeder, Robert. *The Philosophy of Charles S. Peirce*. London: Basil Blackwell, 1980.

Ames, Roger and David Hall, *Thinking Through Confucius*. Albany: State University of New York Press, 1987.

Ames, Roger T. and J. Baird Callicott, eds. *Nature in Asian Traditions of Thought*. Albany: State University of New York Press, 1989.

Ames, Roger T., Thomas Kasulis, and Wimal Dissanayake, eds. *Self as Image in Asian Theory and Practice*. Albany: State University of New York Press, 1998.

Angle, Stephen C. *Human Rights and Chinese Thought: A Cross-Cultural Inquiry*. New York: Cambridge University Press, 2002.

Annas, Julia. *The Morality of Happiness*. Oxford, U.K.: Oxford University Press, 1995.

Barnhart, Michael. "Buddhist Ethics and Social Justice." Pp. 327-341 In *Justice and Democracy: Cross-Cultural Perspectives*, edited by Ron Bontekoe and Marietta Stepaniants. Honolulu: University of Hawaii Press, 1997.

———. "Nature, Nurture, and No-Self: Biotechnology and Buddhist Values." *Journal of Buddhist Ethics* 7 (2000).

———. "Getting Beyond Cross-Talk: Why Persisting Disagreements are Philosophically Nonfatal." Pp. 45-67 In *Negotiating Culture and Human Rights*, edited by Lynda S. Bell, Andrew J. Nathan, and Ilan Peleg. New York: Columbia University Press, 2001.

Bauer, Joanne R. and Daniel A. Bell, eds. *The East Asian Challenge for Human Rights*. Cambridge, U.K.: Cambridge University Press, 1999.

Becker Carl B., "Buddhist Views of Suicide and Euthanasia," *Philosophy East and West* 40, no. 4 (1990): 543-550.

———. *Breaking the Circle: Death and the Afterlife in Buddhism*. Chicago: Southern Illinois University Press, 1993.

Bell, Daniel A. *Communitarianism and its Critics*. Oxford, U.K.: Clarendon Press, 1993.

Bilimoria, Purshottama., "Rights and Duties: The (Modern) Indian Dilemma." Pp. 30-59 In *Ethical and Political Dilemmas of Modern India*, edited by Ninian Smart and Shivesh Thakur. London and New York: St Martin's Press, 1993a.

———. "Is *Adhikara* good enough for 'Rights'?" *Asian Philosophy* 3, no. 1 (1993b): 3-13.

———. "Legal Rulings on Suicide In India and Implications for the Right to Die."*Asian Philosophy* 5, no. 2 (October, 1995): 159-180.

———. "Kautilya's Political Philosophy." In *Routledge Encyclopedia of Philosophy.* London, U.K.: Routledge International, 1998.

Bloom, Alfred. *The Linguistic Shaping of Thought: A Study in the Impact of Language on Thinking in China and the West.* Hillsdale, N.J.: Lawrence Erlbaum Associates, 1981.

Bowring, Richard. *Murasaki Shikibu: The Tale of Genji.* Cambridge, U.K.: Cambridge University Press, 1988.

Brandom, Robert. *Making It Explicit: Reasoning, Representing, and Discursive Commitment.* Cambridge, Mass.: Harvard University Press, 1994.

Brody, Baruch. *Abortion and the Sanctity of Life.* Cambridge, Mass.: The MIT Press, 1975.

Brooks, E. Bruce and Taeko Brooks. *The Original Analects* New York: Columbia University Press, 1998.

Brubaker, Rogers. *The Limits of Rationality: An Essay on the Social and Moral Thought of Max Weber.* London: Routledge, 1991.

Butler, Judith. "Contingent Foundations: Feminism and the Question of Post-modernism" In *Feminists Theorize the Political,* edited by Judith Butler and Joan W. Scott. London and New York: Routledge, 1992.

Callahan, Daniel and Sidney Callahan, eds. *Abortion: Understanding Differences.* New York: Plenum Press, 1984.

Carse, James P. *Finite and Infinite Games.* New York: Free Press, 1986.

Chan, Wing-tsit. *Chu Hsi: Life and Thought.* Hong Kong: Hong Kong University Press, 1987.

———. *Chu Hsi: New Studies.* Honolulu: University of Hawaii Press, 1989.

———. ed., *Chu Hsi and NeoConfucianism.* Honolulu: University of Hawaii Press, 1986.

Chatterji, Probhat C. *Secular Values for Secular India.* Delhi, India: Manohar Publishers & Distributors, 1995.

Clarke, J.J. *Oriental Enlightenment: The Encounter between Asian and Western Thought.* London: Routledge, 1997.

Cook, Rebecca. *Women's Health and Human Rights: The Promotion and Protection of Women's Health through International Human Rights Law.* Geneva: World Health Organization, 1994.

Creel, H.G. *Shen Pu-hai: A Chinese Political Philosopher of the Fourth Century B.C.* Chicago: University of Chicago Press, 1974.

Danto, Arthur C. *Mysticism and Morality: Oriental Thought and Moral Philosophy.* New York: Basic Books, 1972.

Davidson, Donald. *Inquiries Into Truth and Interpretation.* Oxford, U.K.: Clarendon Press, 1984.

Derrett, Duncan J. *Essays in Classical and Modern Hindu Law,* (5 volumes). Leiden, Netherlands: E.J. Brill, 1975-1980.

Derrida, Jacques. "Force of Law: The 'Mystical Foundation of Authority'," *Cardozo Law Review* 11, no. 919 (1990): 921-1045.

Doi, Takeo. *The Anatomy of Dependence.* Tokyo: Kodansha International, 1971.

Donagan, Alan. *A Theory of Morality.* Oxford, U.K.: Oxford University Press, 1977.

Engineer, Ali Asghar. *Communalism in India.* New Delhi: Vikas Publishers Ltd., 1996.

Feldman, David M. *Birth Control in Jewish Law: Marital Relations, Contraception, and Abortion as Set Forth in the Classic Texts of Jewish Law.* New York: Schocken, 1974.

Fingarette, Herbert. *Confucius: The Secular as Sacred.* New York: Harper and Row, 1972.

Fleischacker, Samuel. *The Ethics of Culture*. Ithaca, N.Y.: Cornell University Press, 1994.

Florida, Robert E. "Buddhist Approaches to Euthanasia." *Studies in Religion/Sciences Religieuses* 22 (1993): 35-47.

Galanter, Marc. *Law and Society in Modern India*. Delhi, India: Oxford University Press, 1992.

Gardner, Daniel. *Chu Hsi and the Ta-hsüeh: Reflections on the Confucian Canon.* Cambridge, Mass.: Council of Asian Studies Harvard University, 1986.

Geertz, Clifford. *The Interpretation of Cultures*. New York: Basic Books, 1973.

———. *Local Knowledge*. New York: Basic Books, 1983.

Gibbard, Allan. *Wise Choices, Apt Feelings*. Cambridge, Mass.: Harvard University Press, 1990.

Gilligan, Carol. *In a Different Voice: Psychological Theory and Woman's Development.* Cambridge, Mass.: Harvard University Press, 1982.

Gilligan, Carol, Janie Victoria Ward, Jill McLean Taylor with Betty Bardige, editors. *Mapping the Moral Domain*. Cambridge, Mass.: Center for the Study of Gender, Education and Human Development, Harvard University Graduate School of Education, 1988.

Goff, Janet. *Noh Drama and The Tale of Genji*. Princeton N.J.: Princeton University Press, 1991.

Goff, Janet and Haruo Shirane. *The Bridge of Dreams: A Poetics of The Tale of Genji.* Stanford, Calif.: Stanford University Press, 1987.

Graham, A.C. *Disputers of the Tao: Philosophical Argument in Ancient China.* LaSalle, Illinois: Open Court Publishing Co., 1989.

Gutmann, Amy, ed. *Freedom of Association.* Princeton, N.J.: Princeton University Press, 1998

Hacking, Ian, "Language, Truth, and Reason." Pp. 48-66 In *Rationality and Relativism*, edited by Martin Hollis and Steven Lukes. Cambridge, Mass.: MIT Press, 1982.

Harvey, Peter. *An Introduction to Buddhist Ethics: Foundations, Values and Issues.* Cambridge, U.K.: Cambridge University Press, 2000.

Heidegger, Martin. "The Question Concerning Technology" In *The Question Concerning Technology and other Essays*, translated by William Lovitt. New York: Harper Colophon, 1977.

Henricks, Robert G., trans. *Lao-tzu Te-tao ching*. New York: Ballantine Books, 1989.

Herder, Johann Gottfried. *Reflections on the Philosophy of the History of Mankind*, abridged and introduced by Frank E. Manuel. Chicago: University of Chicago Press, 1968.

———. *Against Pure Reason: Writings on Religion, Language and History,* translated and edited by Marcia Bunge. Minneapolis: Fortress Press, 1993.

Hershock, Peter D. *Liberating Intimacy: Enlightenment and Social Virtuosity in Ch'an Buddhism*. Albany: State University of New York Press, 1996.

———. *Reinventing the Wheel: A Buddhist Response to the Information Age.* Albany: State University of New York Press, 1999.

Hirano, Umeyo, trans. *The Tsutsumi Chunagon Monogatari—11$^{th}$-Century Short Stories of Japan*. Tokyo: The Hokuseido Press, 1963.

Hoff, Joan. "Comparative Analysis of Abortion In Ireland, Poland, and the United States." *Women's Studies International Forum* 17, no. 6 (1994): 621-46.

Ivanhoe, Philip J. *Ethics in the Confucian Tradition.* Atlanta: Scholars Press, 1990.
———.*Confucian Moral Self Cultivation.* New York: Peter Lang, 1993.
Ives, Christopher. *Zen Awakening and Society.* Honolulu: University of Hawaii Press, 1992.
James, William. *Pragmatism*, edited by Bruce Kuklick. Indianapolis: Hackett Publishing Co., 1981.
Jones, Ken. *The Social Face of Buddhism.* London: Wisdom Publications, 1989.
Kant, Immanuel *Foundations of the Metaphysics of Morals*, translated by Lewis White Beck. New York: Macmillan, 1959.
Kasulis, Thomas P. *Zen Action/Zen Person.* Honoulu: University of Hawaii Press, 1981.
Kateb, George. *The Inner Ocean: Individualism and Democratic Culture.* Ithaca, N.Y.: Cornell University Press, 1992.
Keown, Damien. *The Nature of Buddhist Ethics.* London: Macmillan, 1992.
———. *Buddhism and Bioethics.* London: Macmillan, 1995.
———. *Buddhism: A Very Short Introduction.* Oxford, U.K.: Oxford University Press, 1996a.
———. "Buddhism and Suicide: The Case of Channa 3." *Journal of Buddhist Ethics* 8 (1996b): 8-31.
———. *Contemporary Buddhist Ethics.* London: Curzon Press, 2000.
Keown, Damien, Charles Prebish, and Wayne R. Husted, *Buddhism and Human Rights.* Honolulu: Curzon Press, 1998.
Kilner, John F., Arlene B. Miller, and Edmund D. Pellegrino, eds., *Dignity and Dying, a Christian Appraisal.* Carlisle, U.K.: Paternoster Press, 1996.
Kirkland, Russell. "The Roots of Altruism in the Taoist Tradition." *Journal of the American Academy of Religion* 54 (1986): 59-77.
———. "Taoism." Pp. 5: 2463-69 In *The Encyclopedia of Bioethics*, 2nd ed. New York: Macmillan, 1995.
———. "Taoism." Pp. 633-36 In *Philosophy of Education: An Encyclopedia*, edited by J.J. Chamblis. New York and London: Garland Publishing, 1996.
———. "Taoism." Pp. II: 959-64 and "Native American Religions." Pp. II: 707-11 In *Encyclopedia of Women and World Religion.* New York: Macmillan, 1999.
Kjellberg, Paul and Philip J. Ivanhoe, eds. *Essays on Skepticism, Relativism, and Ethics in the Zhuangzi.* Albany: State University of New York Press, 1996.
Kripke, Saul. *Naming and Necessity.* Cambridge, Mass.: Harvard University Press, 1980.
Kukathas, Chandran. "Are there any cultural rights?" *Political Theory* 20, no. 1 (February 1992): 105-139.
Kuper, Adam. *Culture: The Anthropologists Account.* Cambridge, Mass: Harvard Univ. Press, 1999.
Kymlicka, Will. *Liberalism, Community, and Culture.* Oxford, U.K.: Clarendon Press, 1989.
———. *Multicultural Citizenship.* Oxford, U.K.: Oxford University Press, 1995.
———. *The Rights of Minority Cultures.* Oxford, U.K.: Oxford University Press, 1996.
LaFargue, Michael. *The Tao of the Tao Te Ching.* Albany: State University of New York Press, 1992.
LaFleur, William R. "Ethical Discourse and Its Caretakers in Japan," *Philosophy East & West* 40, no. 4 (1990): 529-41.
———. *Liquid Life: Abortion and Buddhism and Japan.* Princeton, N.J.: Princeton University Press, 1992.

Larson, Gerald James. *India's Agony over Religion.* Albany: State University of New York Press, 1995.

Lau, D.C. *Confucius: The Analects*, 2nd ed. Hong Kong: The Chinese University Press, 1992.

Lopez, Donald S. Jr., ed., *Religions of China in Practice.* Princeton: Princeton University Press, 1996.

Loy, David R. *Nonduality: A Study in Comparative Philosophy.* New Haven: Yale University Press, 1988.

———. *Lack and Transcendence: Death and Life in Psychotherapy, Existentialism, and Buddhism.* Atlantic Highlands, N.J.: Humanities Press, 1996.

———. *A Buddhist History of the West: Studies in Lack.* Albany: State University of New York Press, 2002.

Luker, Kristin. *Abortion and the Politics of Motherhood.* Berkeley: University of California Press, 1984.

Lynn, Richard John. *The Classic of the Way and Virtue: A New Translation of the Tao-te ching of Laozi as Interpreted by Wang Bi.* New York: Columbia University Press, 1999.

Machle, Edward J. *Nature and Heaven in the Xunzi: A Study of the Tian Lun.* Albany: State University of New York Press, 1993.

MacIntyre, Alasdair. *Whose Justice? Which Rationality?* Notre Dame: University of Notre Dame Press, 1988.

———. "Relativism, Power, and Philosophy." Pp. 182-204 In *Relativism: Interpretation and Confrontation*, edited by Michael Krausz. Notre Dame: University of Notre Dame Press, 1989.

———. "Incommensurability, Truth, and the Conversation between Confucians and Aristotelians about the Virtues." In *Culture and Modernity*, edited by Eliot Deutsch. Honolulu: University of Hawaii Press, 1991.

Mair, Victor. *Wandering on the Way: Early Taoist Tales and Parables of Chuang Tzu.* New York: Bantam Books, 1994

Mani, Lata. "Cultural Theory, Colonial Texts: Reading Eyewitness Accounts of Widow Burning." Pp. 392-408 In *Cultural Studies* edited with an introduction, by Lawrence Groosberg, Cary Nelson, Paula A. Treicher et al. New York and London: Routledge, 1992.

Margolis, Joseph. *Pragmatism Without Foundations: Reconciling Realism and Relativism.* Oxford, U.K.: Basil Blackwell, 1986.

———. *Life Without Principles: Reconciling Theory and Practice.* Cambridge, Mass.: Blackwell Publishers, 1996.

Mazzarella, Patricia and Pietro Corsi, eds. *Transcultural Dimensions in Medical Ethics.* London: University Publishing Group, 1992.

Melton, J. Gordon, ed. *The Churches Speak on: Abortion.* Detroit, Mich.: Gale Research Inc., 1989.

Mews, Stuart, ed. *Religion in Politics: A World Guide.* Chicago, Ill.: St. James Press, 1989.

Mill, J.S. *Collected Works.* Toronto: Toronto University Press, 1969.

Miller, Mara. "Canons and the Challenge of Gender." *The Monist: An International Quarterly Journal of General Philosophical Inquiry* 76, no. 4 (October 1993a): 477-493.

———. *The Garden as an Art.* Albany: State University of New York Press, 1993b.

———. "Views of Japanese Selfhood: Japanese and Western Perspectives." In *Culture and Self: Philosophical and Religious Perspectives, East and West*, edited by Douglas Allen. Boulder, Col.: Westview Press, 1997.

Miner, Earl, Hiroko Odagiri, and Robert E. Morrell. *The Princeton Companion to Classical Japanese Literature*. Princeton, N.J.: Princeton University Press, 1985.

Moore, Cornelia N. and Lucy Lower, eds. *Translation East and West: A Cross-Cultural Approach*. Honolulu: University of Hawaii College of Languages, Linguistics and Literature and the East-West Center, 1992.

Moore, Edward. *American Pragmatism: Peirce, James, and Dewey*. New York: Columbia University Press, 1961.

Mu, Ch'ien. *Chu tzu hsüeh t'i-kang* (Overview of Chu Hsi's Learning). Taipei: Tung-ta, 1986.

Nandy, Ashis. *At the Edge of Psychology Essays in Politics and Culture*. Delhi, India: Oxford University Press, 1991.

Nicholson, Susan T. *Abortion and the Roman Catholic Church*. Knoxville, Tenn.: Religious, Inc., 1978.

Niranjana, Tejaswini, P. Sudhir, and Vivek Dhareshwar, eds. *Interrogating Modernity Culture and Colonialism in India*. Calcutta, India: Seagull, 1993.

Nishitani, Keiji. *Religion and Nothingness*. Translated with an Introduction by Jan Van Bragt. Berkeley: University of California Press, 1982.

Noonan, John. "An Almost Absolute Value in History," In *The Morality of Abortion: Legal and Historical Perspectives*, ed. John T. Noonan, Jr. Cambridge, Mass.: Harvard University Press, 1970.

Peach, Lucinda. *Legislating Morality: Pluralism and Religious Identity in Lawmaking*. Oxford, U.K.: Oxford University Press, 2002.

Peerenboom, Randall. *Law and Morality in Ancient China: The Silk Manuscripts of Huang-Lao*. Albany: State University of New York Press, 1993.

Petchesky, Rosiland. *Abortion and Woman's Choice: The State, Sexuality, and Reproductive Freedom*, rev. ed. Boston: Northeastern University Press, 1990.

Pincoffs, Edmund. *Quandaries and Virtues: Against Reduction in Ethics*. Lawrence: University Press of Kansas, 1986.

Puette, William J. *Guide to The Tale of Genji by Murasaki Shikibu*. Rutland, Vt. and Tokyo: Charles E. Tuttle Company, Inc., 1983.

Rachels, James. *The Elements of Moral Philosophy*. New York: Random House, 1986.

Rahman, Fazlur. *Health and Medicine in the Islamic Tradition: Change and Identity*. New York: Crossroad, 1987.

Rawls, John. *A Theory of Justice*. Cambridge, Mass.: Harvard University Press, 1971.

———. *Political Liberalism*. New York: Columbia University Press, 1993.

Raz, Joseph. *The Morality of Freedom*. Oxford, U.K.: Clarendon Press, 1986.

Rorty, Richard. *Contingency, Irony, and Solidarity*. Cambridge, U.K.: Cambridge University Press, 1989.

Roth, Harold D. "Evidence for Meditative Stages in Early Taoism," *Bulletin of the School of Oriental and African Studies* 60 (1997): 295-314.

Roth, John. *Freedom and the Moral Life*. Philadelphia: Westminster Press, 1969.

Rouner, Leroy S., ed. *Human Rights and The World's Religions*. Notre Dame: University of Notre Dame Press, 1988.

Sachdev, Paul, ed. *International Handbook on Abortion*. New York: Greenwood Press, 1988.

Sacred Congregation for the Doctrine of the Faith. *Instruction on Respect for Human Life*

*in Its Origin and on the Dignity of Procreation*. London: Catholic Truth Society, 1987.
Sandel, Michael J. *Liberalism and the Limits of Justice*. Cambridge, U.K.: University of Cambridge Press, 1982.
———. ed. *Liberalism and Its Critics*. New York: New York University Press, 1984.
Sangari, Kumkum and Sudesh Vaid, eds. *Recasting Women Essays in Colonial History*. Delhi, India: Kali for Women, 1989.
Scaff, Lawrence A. *Fleeing the Iron Cage: Culture, Politics, and Modernity in the thought of Max Weber*. Berkeley: University of California Press, 1989.
Schwartz, Benjamin I. *The World of Thought in Ancient China*. Cambridge, Mass.: Harvard University Press, 1985.
Shafer, Boyd. *Nationalism: Myth and Reality*. New York: Harcourt Brace and Company, 1955.
Sharma, Renuka, ed. *Representations of Gender, Democracy and Identity Politics in Relation to South Asia*. Delhi: Satguru Publications for Indian Books Centre, 1996.
Shirane, Haruo. "Pseudo-Incest: The Tamakazura Sequence," chapter 7 Of *The Bridge of Dreams: A Poetics of 'The Tale of Genji'*. Stanford, Calif.: Stanford University Press, 1987.
Simmel, Georg. *The Philosophy of Money*, David Frisby ed., Tom Bottomore and David Frisby trans., from the 2second ed. of 1907. London: Routledge and Kegan Paul, 1978.
Spivak, Gayatri Chakravorty. *In Other Worlds: Essays in Cultural Politics*. New York: Methuen, 1988.
Steinbock, Bonnie. *Life Before Birth: The Moral and Legal Status of Embryos and Fetuses*. Oxford, U.K.: Oxford University Press, 1992.
Taylor, Charles. *Philosophy and the Human Sciences*. Cambridge, U.K.: Cambridge University Press, 1985a.
———. *Human Agency and Language: Philosophical Papers I*. Cambridge, U.K.: Cambridge University Press, 1985b.
———. *Philosophical Arguments*. Cambridge, Mass.: Harvard University Press, 1995.
Taylor, Charles and Amy Gutmann. *Multiculturalism*. Princeton, N.J.: Princeton University Press, 1994.
Thakur, Shivesh C. *Religions and Social Justice* London and New York: St Martin's Press, 1996.
Thappar, Romila. *Cultural Transactions and Early India*. Delhi, India: Oxford University Press, 1987.
Tharu, Susie and Lalitha, K., eds. *Women Writing in India 600 BC to the Early 20th Century an Anthology with Introduction*. London: HarperCollins, 1993.
Thayer, H.S., ed. *Pragmatism: the Classic Writings*. Indianapolis: Hackett Publishing Co., 1982.
Thompson, Kirill O. "*Li* and *Yi* as Immanent: Chu Hsi's Thought in Practical Perspective." *Philosophy East and West* 38, no. 1 (January 1986): 30-46.
Tronto, Joan. *Moral Boundaries: A Political Argument for an Ethic of Care*. New York: Routledge, 1993.
Tu, Wei-ming. *Confucian Thought: Selfhood as Transformation*. Albany: State University of New York Press, 1985.
———. *Centrality and Commonality: An Essay on Confucian Religiousness*. Albany: State University of New York Press, 1998.
Ueda, Yoshifumi and Dennis Hirota. *Shinran: An Introduction to His Thought*. Kyoto:

Hongwanji International Center, 1989.

van Hooff, Anton J.L. *From Autoeuthanasia to Suicide: Self-Killing in Classical Antiquity*. New York and London: Routledge, 1990.

Waley, Arthur. *The Way and its Power*. London: George Allen & Unwin, 1934.

Waley, Arthur and Edward G. Seidensticker, translators. *Tale of Genji*. New York: Alfred A. Knopf, Inc., 1976.

Warren, Henry Clarke. *Buddhism, In Translations*. New York: Atheneum, 1974; originally Harvard University Press, 1896.

Watson, Burton. *The Complete Works of Chuang Tzu*. New York: Columbia University Press, 1968.

———, trans. *Lotus Sutra*. New York: Columbia University Press, 1993.

Wattles, Jeffrey. *The Golden Rule*. New York: Oxford University Press, 1996.

Weber, Max, *The Religion of China: Confucianism and Taoism*, translated by Hans H. Gerth. New York: The Free Press, 1951.

Williams, Bernard. *Ethics and the Limits of Philosophy*. Cambridge, Mass.: Harvard University Press, 1985.

Yearley, Lee H. *Mencius and Aquinas*. Albany: State University of New York Press, 1990.

# Index

# About the Contributors

Stephen C. Angle is Assistant Professor of Philosophy at Wesleyan University. He received his B.A. from Yale in East Asian Studies and his Ph.D. in Philosophy from the University of Michigan. He is the author of *Human Rights and Chinese Thought: A Cross-Cultural Inquiry* (Cambridge U.P., 2002) and the co-editor and co-translator of *The Chinese Human Rights Reader* (M.E. Sharpe, 2001). Angle studies Song- through Qing-dynasty Confucian ethics, politics, and philosophy of mind, and the interactions that develop between these traditions and both more recent Chinese thought and various Western philosophical discourses.

Michael Barnhart is Associate Professor of Philosophy at Kingsborough Community College of the City University of New York. He teaches courses in all areas of philosophy, but his research centers on issues in comparative philosophy and ethics about which he has written numerous articles.

Carl B. Becker is Professor of Comparative Religions and Ethics at Kyoto University in Japan, where he has researched death and dying for a quarter century. His English language publications include *Breaking the Circle: Death and Afterlife in Buddhism*, *Asian and Jungian Views of Ethics*, and a translation of Eiji Uehiro's *Practical Ethics for Our Time*. Becker is a consulting editor for *Mortality*, and for the *Journal of Near-Death Studies*.

Purushottama Bilimoria (Ph.D., La Trobe University) is presently Professor of Philosophy at Deakin University in Australia, since 1980, and senior fellow with the Department of Philosophy, The University of Melbourne. He has been a visiting professor at many prominent universities and participated in a number of grant-funded research projects dealing with law, culture, and ethics. Areas of specialist publication and teaching include Indian philosophy and ethics, philosophy of religion, and on cross-cultural issues in ethics, bioethics, social thought, and culture, with a major work on theories of testimony and scriptural hermeneutics. He also serves as editor of the international journal *Sophia* in cross- cultural philosophy of religion, a/theology, and ethics.

Samuel Fleischacker is Associate Professor of Philosophy at the University of Illinois in Chicago. He is the author of *Integrity and Moral Relativism* (E.J. Brill, 1992), *The Ethics of Culture*, (Cornell, 1994) and *A Third Concept of Liberty: Judgment and Freedom in Kant and Adam Smith,* (Princeton, 1999).

Alan Fox (Ph.D. Temple University, Religious Studies, 1988) is Associate Professor of Asian and Comparative Philosophy in the Philosophy Department at the University of Delaware. He has published articles and book reviews in journals, focusing on Daoism and Chinese Buddhism. He has also won several teaching awards. He spent 1986-87 in Taiwan on a Fulbright Fellowship.

Damien Keown is Reader in Buddhism at Goldsmiths College, University of London. His publications include *The Nature of Buddhist Ethics, Buddhism and Bioethics*, *Buddhism and Abortion*, *Contemporary Buddhist Ethics*, and *Buddhism: A Very Short Introduction*. He is the editor of the online *Journal of Buddhist Ethics*.

Russell Kirkland (Ph.D. Indiana, 1986) is a specialist on Taoism who has published a wide array of articles and reviews on the history and religions of China, Tibet, Korea, and Japan. He has taught at Oberlin College, Stanford University, and Macalester College, and is currently associate professor of religion at the University of Georgia. His recent publications include "Explaining Daoism: Realities, Cultural Constructs, and Emerging Perspectives," in Livia Kohn, ed. *Daoism Handbook* (Leiden: Brill, 2000), and he is presently completing the book, *Taoism: The Enduring Tradition*.

David R. Loy is Professor in the Faculty of International Studies at Bunkyo University, Chigasaki, Japan. His work is in comparative philosophy and religion, particularly comparing Buddhist with modern Western thought. His books include *Nonduality: A Study in Comparative* Philosophy (1988), *Lack and Transcendence: Death and Life in Psychotherapy, Existentialism and* Buddhism (1996), and *A Buddhist History of the West: Studies in* Lack (2002). He has practiced Zen Buddhism for many years.

Mara Miller is a philosopher who teaches and writes on ethics, aesthetics, feminism, and women's issues, and East Asia. Her book, *The Garden as an Art* was published by SUNY Press (1993). As a Mellon Post-Doctoral Fellow in East Asian Religion and Art History at Emory University, she taught a course on Lady Murasaki and *The Tale of Genji*.

Lucinda Joy Peach is an Associate Professor in the Department of Philosophy and Religion at American University. She holds a Ph.D. in ethics from the Department of Religious Studies at Indiana University, a J.D. degree from New York University School of Law, and a B.A. degree from the program in International Education at the University of Massachusetts, Amherst. She is the author of *Legislating Morality: Pluralism and Religious Identity in Lawmaking* (Oxford University Press, 2002), and the editor of *Women and World Religions* (Prentice Hall, 2002) and *Women in Culture: An Anthology* (Blackwell Publishers 1998) and articles on gender and violence, the ethics of war, and women's human rights, including the trafficking of women for the sex trade as a human rights violation.

Kirill O. Thompson, Ph.D. Hawaii, is a professor at National Taiwan University. He specializes in Chu His and Chinese Neo-Confucianism, but has published in other areas of Chinese philosophy, for example, classical Chinese Taoism and Logic.